THE
RAVEN'S
SHADOW

Also by Elspeth Cooper from Gollancz:

Songs of the Earth
Trinity Rising

THE
RAVEN'S
SHADOW

THE WILD HUNT
BOOK THREE

ELSPETH COOPER

GOLLANCZ
LONDON

The right of Elspeth Cooper to be identified as the author of this work
has been asserted by her in accordance with the
Copyright, Designs and Patents Act 1988.

First published in Great Britain in 2013 by Gollancz
An imprint of the Orion Publishing Group
Orion House, 5 Upper St Martin's Lane, London WC2H 9EA
An Hachette UK Company

A CIP catalogue record for this book is available
from the British Library

ISBN 978 0 575 13437 9 (Cased)
ISBN 978 0 575 13438 6 (Trade Paperback)

1 3 5 7 9 10 8 6 4 2

Typeset at the Spartan Press Ltd,
Lymington, Hants

Printed and bound in Great Britain by
Clays Ltd, St Ives plc

The Orion Publishing Group's policy is to use papers that
are natural, renewable and recyclable products and made
from wood grown in sustainable forests. The logging and
manufacturing processes are expected to conform to the
environmental regulations of the country of origin.

www.elspethcooper.com
www.orionbooks.co.uk
www.gollancz.co.uk

For Mags, the very best of friends

1

MORNING

ℯ✕✺

Masen walked through the whispering grass back towards camp from the river, carrying two buckets of water. He always liked early mornings, especially here in the north where the mighty peaks of the an-Archen bestriding the horizon made him feel as if he was standing at the edge of the world. He wasn't, of course. Beyond the mountains were the Nimrothi lands, tough, tussocky country jewelled with lakes and trimmed with a steep and jagged coastline. The Broken Land, they called it, after their broken people. A thousand years of exile later, there was still more to unite them with their Arennorian cousins than to divide them, but the mountains that stood between their lands remained a symbol of their differences, like a high fence that separated feuding neighbours.

Now the Veil was failing and a Hound was loose in the Broken Land. He couldn't help but see a connection there. The clan Speakers were no fools; they would have felt the weakness, too, and it didn't take much imagination to see them exploiting it. First a Hound, then the rest of the Hunt would surely follow.

Masen frowned. He hoped he was wrong, prayed that after the events of last year he was simply jumping at shadows, but there was a cold certainty hardening in his gut that said he was not. The same certainty had helped him convince Alderan to send such skilled *gaeden* as Barin and his brother Eavin to the mountain forts just in case – though the Guardian had been reluctant to weaken Chapterhouse's defences so soon after Savin's assault on them.

The two dozen or so Eldannar rangers with whom the four of them had shared camp had ridden on with the dawn, leaving only smoking embers in the ring of firestones and a few piles of dung from their horses. Beside the fire was a heap of blankets, approximately human-shaped, still snoring like a band-saw.

He set down one of the buckets and prodded the heap with the toe of his boot. 'Up you get, slugabed.'

The pile snorted something unintelligible, so he prodded it again. It groaned. 'Go *away*.'

'Come on. It's a beautiful day, the sun is shining and the birds are chirping.'

'Tell the birds to shut up. They're too damn loud.'

'If you have a headache, it serves you right for staying up drinking with the clansmen,' said Masen unsympathetically.

'But I was having so much fun!' Sleep-tousled dark hair emerged from one end of the blankets and a green eye regarded him blearily. 'You need to have more fun, Masen. Being sober all the time isn't good for a man.'

'Neither is being drunk, according to Saaron. Poisons the liver.' Another prod. 'Up you get, Sorchal. I've a bucket of water here – don't make me use it.'

Grumbling and squinting at the brightness of the pale plains sky, the young Elethrainian crawled out of his blankets. Wordlessly, Masen pointed to the bucket of cold river water and Sorchal winced.

'Do I have to?'

'I'm afraid so. I need you clear-headed today.' There was no time to be coddling the lad's tender skull.

With a sigh, Sorchal stripped off his shirt and knelt down by the bucket. 'You're sure?'

'I'm sure.'

'You're a cruel, cruel man.'

He dunked his head in the cold water and held it there for a count of ten, then sat up and shook himself like a dog, spraying water in all directions. Masen brushed a few stray drops off his jerkin.

'Feel better?'

'Yes. And no. Ow.' Scooping wet hair off his face, Sorchal peered around at the crushed grass of the campsite. 'Where'd everyone go?'

'The rangers rode out before first light, and Barin and Eavin went with them. I said we'd catch them up at the fort. You slept through it all.'

'I did? Oh. I was hoping to say goodbye.' Crestfallen, the lad looked around again, as if the Eldannar girl he'd been matching drinks with after supper might be hiding somewhere nearby. Masen guessed that Sorchal was more used to doing the leaving than being the one who was left.

'Ranger women never sit still for long, Sorchal,' he said, 'and they don't look back. Best you don't look back either.'

The young man rubbed his neck. 'Mmm. Pity – I would have liked to find out if those thighs were as strong as they looked.' He gave a rueful shrug. 'Another time, perhaps.'

Masen snorted. 'In your dreams, maybe!' Sorchal gave him a look but he laughed. 'I was your age once, lad – with twice the reputation, so I know what I'm talking about – and I never managed to woo the same one twice. Now get that fire stoked up and the kettle on whilst I see to the horses. We've still a ways to go to find that rent in the Veil.'

He took the animals their water and a bit of grain from the packs to fortify them for the hard miles ahead. His mare, Brea, greeted him by pushing her head into his chest so hard she almost knocked him over.

'Steady, girl, steady!' He chuckled and scratched her chin. 'Nice to know I haven't been forgotten.'

She snorted and shook her head as if to say she hadn't forgotten him but he wasn't yet forgiven for leaving her at livery in Fleet for half a year. He'd hardly forgiven himself, but there'd been no place for her on a barge down the Great River, so he'd had no other choice. At least the stablemen had kept her in good condition, exercised as well as fed, which in part explained the eye-watering bill he'd had to pay when they reached Fleet two days ago.

'I would have paid twice as much,' he said, patting her neck as she ate. 'And you know it.'

When he returned to the fire, Sorchal had set the kettle to boil and they broke their fast with home-cured sausage and the last of the fresh bread they'd brought from Fleet. As soon as they were done, Masen dug in his pocket for the horseshoe nail on a thread that he used as a compass to find Gates to the Hidden Kingdom.

'So,' he said, 'can you still feel it?'

Sorchal put down his cup. 'I think so.'

He scrubbed his palms on his trousers, then held one hand up in front of him and closed his eyes. At the same time, Masen felt the distinctive tug as the lad opened himself to the Song. Slowly Sorchal pushed his hand forwards as if pressing against a pane of glass. 'Yes. It's still there.'

Not for the first time, Masen wished he'd had an opportunity to find and close the rent last year, when the clansmen he'd met at Brindling Fall had first told him about it. If he had, though, he'd not have made it to Chapterhouse in time to help defend it against Savin's creatures. He sighed. Life was all about choices, and roads not taken. No matter how you might wish to, once the choice was made you couldn't go back and do differently.

4

Holding the nail up by the thread, he let it spin freely. 'Tell me what you feel.'

A frown of concentration creased Sorchal's brow. 'It's hard to describe.'

The nail slowed, wobbling back and forth, then began to spin in the opposite direction, untwisting the thread.

'Try.' *It'll feel like a wound, like a bruise on the world's skin. Something painful, and wrong, and your heart will ache to heal it.*

The Elethrainian shifted uncomfortably. 'I don't know, it's . . . something that should be whole but isn't whole any more.'

Masen touched the Song, letting himself sink into the sensation, feel the wrongness crawl over his skin. No wonder Sorchal was squirming; his entire reality would feel like it was stuffed with sow-thistles.

'Like a book with some of the pages ripped out,' the lad said at last. 'And I'm a librarian, or a bookbinder, and it's my job to fix it.'

Yes.

That was a good way to describe it. Not every *gaeden* felt the same thing, or with the same intensity; a Gatekeeper's gift manifested in much the same way as the ability to Heal, leaving some, like Alderan, barely able to draw a splinter, whilst Tanith could mend broken minds. Sorchal appeared to be one of those rare few who had not just the ability to tend the Veil, but also the compulsion.

The thread had finally stopped twisting around Masen's finger. The horseshoe nail's peculiar weight dragged at his hand; even without looking he could feel which way it was pointing. A little north of east, at the very edge of the Southmarch.

'Which way do we need to go?' he asked.

Sorchal's other hand came up and without hesitation pointed north of east. That removed the last of Masen's doubts. The lad had the makings of a good Gatekeeper – if he could keep his mind out of his underlinens.

'You can open your eyes now,' he said.

Sorchal did so and blinked at the shining nail pointing in the same direction as his hand. 'I got it right?'

'So it would appear.' Masen coiled up the thread and dropped the nail back into his coat pocket, where it pressed subtly but insistently against his hip. 'Not only can you sense Gates, you can feel rips in the Veil, too.'

'Huh.' Sorchal dropped his hands into his lap. 'Just when I was getting used to having no gift to speak of.'

'Now you've got the makings of a first-rate Gatekeeper.'

He pulled a face. 'I would have been happy just to be a first-rate fencer and seducer of women,' he said gloomily.

Masen showed his teeth. 'You can't always have what you want,' he said, and threw the dregs of his tea onto the fire as he stood. 'The trick is to learn to want what you have.'

'What I have is a hangover – I don't want that.'

'Serves you right for trying to outdrink a ranger.'

'I wasn't trying to outdrink her,' Sorchal protested. 'Just . . . you know. Lower her defences a little.'

This time Masen guffawed. 'Not quite the first-rate seducer you thought you were, eh? Face it, you were lucky she left you with only blue balls and a bad head.' Hefting his saddle onto his shoulder, he started towards the horses. 'Get your gear packed up. That hole in the Veil isn't going to mend itself.'

෨෬

'Fetch the Speaker!'

Drwyn's bellow carried clear across the camp despite the braying chatter of the fair. In her tent Ytha paused, soapy washcloth in one hand and water trickling down her thighs, wondering whether she had time to finish washing away the night's sweat before the messenger scratched at the tent flap.

'Aedon blast you, *now*!'

Sighing regretfully, she dropped the cloth back into the

steaming water and reached for her towel. Her bath with her rich lavender soap would have to wait.

By the time Drwyn's man arrived she was dried and dressed, and swept out of her tent in her snow-fox mantle without waiting for him to announce himself.

'Er, Speaker?'

'I heard,' she said. *The whole Scattering likely heard*, she added to herself, and set off in the direction of the chief's roar.

She found Drwyn outside his tent, fists on his hips and glaring at a travel-worn clansman standing next to a mud-spattered horse still laden with packs for a long journey. Through the open tent flap, half a dozen of the other chiefs could be seen lounging on cushions, all pointedly not watching the exchange between the man and his chief whilst no doubt straining to catch every word.

'My chief?' she said.

'Grave news, Ytha.' Drwyn shook his head. 'This could change everything. Our plans—'

Ytha held up her hand before he said too much – would the man *never* learn? – and glanced meaningfully towards the men in the tent, who all abruptly found their ale cups quite fascinating.

'Perhaps we should discuss this in private?'

'But—'

She thumped her whitewood staff on the turf between her feet to get his attention. 'In. Private. There is no need to trouble the other chiefs with this.'

He looked confused, then caught on. 'Oh. Yes, of course. Very wise.'

By the Eldest, the man hadn't the sense he was born with. Just as well she had wit enough for both of them. But instead of rolling her eyes she pasted on a polite smile and gestured that he should lead the way. 'My chief?'

Inside the tent she let Drwyn apologise to the other chiefs and arrange to reconvene their meeting later in the day after he had conferred with his Speaker on a matter that required his immediate attention. They looked from him to the woman in the snow-fox robe with barely concealed curiosity but none of them chose to press the issue, and in moments the tent was empty but for a litter of cups and a haze of pipe-smoke in the air. She seated herself on a cushion with her staff across her lap as the clansman came in, and nodded to the tent flap.

'Close it.' The clansman obliged with alacrity. When it was secure, she folded her hands in her lap and eyed the chief. 'Now, why don't you tell me what was so important you dragged me away from my bath?'

'News from the east.' Drwyn gestured impatiently at the clansman. 'Go on, tell the Speaker what you told me.'

The clansman cleared his throat. He looked exhausted, his face all sharp bones and hollows exaggerated by an unkempt beard, and not even the lingering scent of Ytha's lavender soap masked the smell of horse and long travelling.

'I've come from the eastern pass, Speaker,' he said. 'The four of us were supposed to relieve the scouts, but when we got close to the fort we found fresh tracks in the snow. Tracks from many horses.'

He stopped, looking anxiously at his chief, who was pacing back and forth.

'Go on.' Ytha kept her voice cool, but her thoughts raced. The forts were supposed to be empty!

'We moved up into the rocks, all stealthy like, and watched the fort for a day. There's men there, Speaker. Dozens of them – maybe hundreds.'

Ytha's stomach turned over. 'Iron men?' she asked, and the man shook his head.

'Didn't see none. The men are all in green.'

The Empire, then. Some consolation, but still a complication she could have done without. 'Are they scouting on this side of the mountains?'

'I reckon so. We saw small bands go in and out – looked like faithless bastards, by their gear. We drew lots for who should ride back; the others are still up there.'

'I see.' How in the Eldest's name did the Empire know to send men to the passes? The forts had been empty since before her greatmother's days, and she had been assured they would stay that way. 'And what of our scouts?'

'No sign, Speaker.'

Drwyn swung on his heel. 'This changes everything, Ytha,' he declared. 'The Empire knows we are coming.'

'Not necessarily,' she said, buying herself time to think.

'It's obvious! The men I had posted at the fort are gone – the Empire must have taken them, and now they know our plans.'

A twitch of power silenced him, then she gave the weary scout her full attention, bolstered with the merest lick of compulsion so that he wouldn't be tempted to look away from her and see his chief opening and shutting his mouth like a landed fish.

'Thank you . . .' She dredged her memory for the man's name. 'Gwil, isn't it?' The man nodded. 'You've done well, but I'd be obliged if you would keep this to yourself until the chief and I have had time to discuss it. Now go and get some rest – you've had a hard journey.'

When the man had let himself out, she turned back to Drwyn, who was turning red in the face as he strained to speak past the air she had stuffed into his mouth. Tempting as it was to leave him mute, she waved the magic away.

'Macha's ears, won't you ever learn to guard your tongue? Half the chiefs were in earshot of him telling you the news, and who knows what else they heard with you shouting like your fruits were on fire. How many times have I told you? You let them hear what we want them to hear, and not a word more!'

He gave her a truculent look, rubbing at his throat, but didn't argue.

'So what are we going to do?'

'Do? We do nothing, for now. Our plans have not changed.'

'You assured me those forts were empty, Ytha.'

'When I looked, they were.' And she had believed they would stay that way. She had trusted what she'd been told, that the iron men were gone and would not be coming back, but oh, there would be a reckoning for this, if she had any say in the matter! 'Situations change, and we must adapt to them.'

'How is doing nothing *adapting*?' He threw up his hands, prowling again. 'The Empire knows we are coming – we have lost the advantage of surprise!'

Patience wearing thin, Ytha hardened her voice. 'Stiffen your sinews, my chief, or you will be undone before you even draw your sword.'

'Aedon's balls, woman, we may be undone already!' He aimed a kick at one of the abandoned cups and sent it spinning across the tent in a spray of ale.

She raised an eyebrow. His mouth opened to say something and she arched her brow a little higher, daring him to challenge her authority. Dark eyes flashed but he stayed silent, though his fists clenched and unclenched at his sides.

Her thoughts raced, turning over the clansman's news whilst trying to keep her face calm, her voice cool. There had to be some way to . . . ah.

'Be easy, my chief – all is not lost. This news is unwelcome, true, but if we play it carefully, it may even work to our advantage.'

That pulled him up short. 'How?'

'As long as they remain unaware that we have discovered their presence in the mountains, perhaps we can manipulate them,' she said. 'I will need to scry to be sure, but if they can be induced to concentrate their defences on the low pass in the east, they may leave the others more lightly defended.'

He stared at her, and slowly his expression brightened as he realised where she was leading. 'Allowing us to strike where they least expect it.'

She allowed herself a thin, satisfied smile. 'Precisely.'

Drwyn began pacing again. 'We must call the chiefs together and put this new plan to them.' He rubbed his chin, whiskers rasping against his palm. 'The Scattering is almost over – we could ride out tomorrow.'

Ytha held up her hand. 'Patience, my chief,' she said. 'One step at a time. If we leap straight in, we may trigger a trap that the Empire is laying for us.'

Clearly frustrated, he growled, 'When, then?'

'A day or two after the Scattering ends. I still have to bind the other Speakers, and I must scry out the passes before we can move. Besides, the war band cannot be assembled in the space of a day.' He'd served his time as a war captain; he should not have needed to be reminded of that. By now thoroughly vexed, she pushed herself to her feet and leaned on her staff. 'I need to think this through. When the time is right, we will bring the chiefs together and let them believe that this new plan was our intention from the start, but until then,' she levelled a finger at him and dropped her voice to a hiss, 'don't breathe a word of this to anyone or so help me I will stop up your mouth so tightly you may never speak again.'

Drwyn bristled mutinously. 'I am the Chief of Chiefs, Ytha.'

She drew her mantle around her. 'Believe me, that fact attends me my every waking moment.'

He scowled, restless fists flexing down by his sides. 'I will not be mocked, woman!'

Ytha's hold on her temper snapped. She marched up to Drwyn and drove her finger into his chest. 'Then hear me, Chief of Chiefs. I did not spend years perfecting these plans to see them thrown into disarray by the first stone in the road. If you want to be the man your father could not, if you want your name to be sung down through the ages as the leader who brought the clans home again, you will hold your tongue *and stay the course.*'

She punctuated the words with sharp jabs of her finger, forcing him to back up a pace. He turned his ankle on a discarded ale cup and staggered, barely righting himself before he fell, then rounded on Ytha with his fists balled, fury and embarrassment battling for control of his expression. Her magic rose up, prickling over her skin, setting her fingertips tingling, but with a visible effort he reined in his passions. In a tightly controlled voice, he said, 'Speaker.'

She inclined her head curtly. 'My chief.'

They eyed each other a moment longer, then Ytha turned on her heel and left.

2

THE BINDING

୨୦

Savin jolted awake with his heart racing. For a second or two he was gripped by nameless dread, held down by the weight of the furs covering him, then his wits cleared and he remembered where he was. There were no circling foes, no dread fate looming over him, just grey daylight leaking around the drapes of his chamber in Renngald's castle and a faint musty odour on the air, like the smell of damp feathers.

Sitting up, he raked his tangled hair back from his face. He hadn't suffered night terrors since his childhood, not since he'd learned to block out his dreams and make sleep a blank and restful place. He'd forgotten what it was like to be jerked out of his rest with every muscle poised for flight. It was . . . almost refreshing.

His lips curved into a smile. The Leahn whelp who'd sent him that gout of throat-clenching panic was doubtless not enjoying it as much.

Savin could sense him at the back of his thoughts. Seen through the imperfect lens of the daemon's shadow the boy was a ball of emotion, feverishly hot and lit with desperation and sickly flashes of fear. He'd got himself into trouble, that much was plain, and was having some difficulty extracting himself from it. Interesting. As Savin watched, the emotions grew in intensity, whorled and splotched like paint on the canvas of some demented artist. The whelp still hadn't learned to mask his colours.

'Honestly, Alderan, is this the best your teachers can do?' Savin murmured, and reached out.

It was too far to touch the colours, of course, even for him: the gulf between minds was so deep at this distance that he couldn't even see the bright mess of the Leahn's talent in the void. Nonetheless he could feel it, a faint tugging at his own gift as subtle as the pull of a plant's leaves towards the light. Not much, but it was enough to discern a direction: south. Given the extreme northerly latitude of the White Sea, 'south' covered most of the known world, but still, it was a start.

Holding on to his awareness of Gair's location, Savin pushed back the covers and climbed out of bed. The perspiration on his skin chilled quickly in the cool air, but a thought restored the ward that insulated him from changes in temperature and with it his comfort. A further twitch of his will pushed back the heavy drapes at the windows. It did little to improve the light: outside, the day had barely begun and a dense sea mist of the kind the Nordmen called *haar* rubbed up against the bubbled, uneven glass like a large grey cat trying to cozen its way inside.

Savin clicked his tongue and flung a few ice-white glims into the air. By all the Kingdoms, he couldn't wait to be done with this place and its fogs and slithers, its unimaginative, superstitious people. It was all so dull, dull, dull – in every sense of the word.

From his neatly ordered shelves he took a map and unrolled it on the table, weighting the ends with a couple of books and the velvet-shrouded sight-glass. A proper map, not one of the Nordmen's charts annotated with currents and soundings in minute detail but with so little concerning the land's geography that anywhere more than about a league inland might as well be labelled 'Here be monsters'. He scanned southwards over the carefully drawn mountains and rivers of the Empire, past the Maling Islands in the Inner Sea, until his gaze came to rest at last on the Glass Hills and the city straddling the River Zhiman at their base.

El Maqqam?

Savin frowned. Alderan's apprentice blundering about in the desert was a complication he could have done without. There were pieces in play there key to the wider game, skirmishes whose significance could only be appreciated by one with the vision to see the entire board. His fingers drummed on the meticulous rendering of the Glass Hills. And what was the Leahn doing in Gimrael anyway? The last Savin had sensed of him he'd been on the Western Isles, still stewing in his misery. So why was he in the desert – and why now?

Alderan must have found something, learned something that would justify him sending a novice *gaeden* into the middle of a bloody uprising. Some reward that was worth the risk . . . the starseed? Savin quickly dismissed that idea; he'd spent long enough in Gimrael to be sure the stone wasn't there, so what could it be?

'What are you up to, you old fox?' he mused.

His gaze fell on the book weighting the edge of the map nearest his hand, a broken-spined thing whose fraying cover had once been blocked in gold. His drumming fingers slowed, then stopped. Little gold leaf remained, barely enough to pick out the shapes of the letters that spelled out the title – *Chronicles of the True Faith: A History of the Founding Wars.*

Was there a clue in St Saren's book, some hint he had missed? He sat down in his chair and pulled the battered volume towards him, letting the map roll itself up again. He didn't need it any more. Quickly he leafed through the worn pages to the section concerning the aftermath of Gwlach's defeat and the repercussions of Fellbane's confession. He'd read it so many times the pages were thickened with handling, and the merest glance at the words brought their meaning flowing up from his memory into the forefront of his mind, but he made himself read it again, searching for anything he might have overlooked.

The Lector laid plans in secret to take Corlainn's disciples into custody, so that the stain of magic could be forever removed from the Order's cloth. However, he was betrayed by those deepest in his counsel and the guilty, thus forewarned, fled the Holy City before arrests could be made. As word spread, more and more Knights hid themselves away in fear rather than face due justice, and the Order's wrath upon them was terrible to behold.

A soft chattering sound interrupted his train of thought and he looked up. Perched on the seat of the stool in her cage, long toes curled to grip the edge, the firebird watched him from the shadows with jet-bead eyes. The string securing her lacquered paper mask had rotted through days ago, and all that remained of her fine plumage now was a few bruise-coloured streaks of paint on her pale skin. As he returned her stare she cocked her head to one side as if awaiting the answer to a question.

'Later,' Savin said. She repeated the chatter, punctuating it with clacks of her curved bill. 'I said *later!*'

He returned his focus to the book on the table in front of him. At the edge of his attention, he heard the firebird hop down from her perch but paid her scant mind.

In every town heralds cried the news. Direst censure awaited the fugitives and all who harboured or abetted them, but their punishment on earth would be as nothing when set against the judgement of the Goddess, should they not repent and go to Her with their souls burned clean. And so inquisitors charged with the capture of the maleficents were dispatched to every corner of the land, east and west and south.

Interesting. Back then, the Holy City of Dremen had marked the northern edge of the nascent Empire. Apart from Milanthor, the wilds of the an-Archen foothills had barely been explored – Belistha was still the haunt of trappers and backwoodsmen and would not become a province in its own right for another hundred and seventy years. To the east was Leah, scene of some of the worst witch-hunts in the Empire's history, and in the west lay the Goddess-fearing heartlands where fugitive Knights in fear for their lives would have found little succour. Beyond them lay the fey kingdoms, Astolar and Bregorin, where there was little more. No wonder so few had survived the initial purges to make the voyage to the Western Isles.

Which left the deserts of Gimrael. In those early years of the Empire, as the southern Church struggled to establish itself in a cauldron of feuding, fractious tribes, Gimrael was a place in which men could disappear. After all, when the surface of the pond is already roiling, who notices a few more ripples? By the time the tribes had been forced to put aside their ancient enmities and stand united under a single banner – with Prince Yezerin's *qatan* resting lightly on their necks to make sure they respected it – there was more to worry about than a few refugees who'd long since found new identities and left their pasts behind.

Very interesting. Had those exiled Knights known what became of Corlainn's treasure after he surrendered it and taken that knowledge south with them? Had it survived to this day, written in some forgotten book – and had Alderan found it? Savin leaned on his elbows, fingers steepled, and stared thoughtfully into space. He might have to return to the desert sooner than he'd anticipated.

Metal scraped on metal, became a sharp clang. Irked, he glanced up to see the firebird squatting at the door to the cage with a pewter plate in one hand; when she caught his eye, she struck the plate hard against the bars.

He clicked his tongue at the interruption. She struck the bars again: twice, three times.

'Enough!' he barked, slamming the flat of his hand on the tabletop. The firebird thrust out her head and hissed, beak agape, then began hitting the bars repeatedly, as insistent as one of the Nordmen's brats beating its toy on the ground in a tantrum.

Irritation flared into anger. Apart from the novelty, Savin could hardly remember what had appealed so much about her in the first place. Once he'd taken her every way it was possible to do so, he should have simply disposed of her. Wrung her neck like a cage-bird that refused to sing and been done with her.

Power surged inside him, offering half a dozen ways to be rid of the *iniku* girl: slow ways, messy ways, or as quick and relatively pain-free as the way in which he'd dispensed with that housemaid in Mesarild. He was about to reach for one of them, anything to put an end to the relentless tinny clatter, when the noise stopped.

The firebird stared at him, utterly still. Only the rise and fall of her breasts betrayed the height of her passion, amber beads and gold rings gleaming in the glim-light. When she was sure she had his attention, she flung the plate across the cage and hopped onto the stool again with her back to him.

Defiance, now, was it? Temper boiling, he snatched for his power and heat engulfed him as if the door to a furnace had swung open. It filled his head with the roar of flames, scorched across his senses in a stink of burning meat, then the door slammed shut again and the heat was gone. At the back of his mind, his awareness of the Leahn went dark.

Hands hovering over the book, Savin waited, but nothing moved in the daemon's shadow. No colour, no sensation. Whatever the Leahn had experienced had been so intense it had overwhelmed him and snuffed him out like a candle in a draught. Hardly a surprise; for all the boy's raw strength he'd barely begun his training, and children tended to need to burn themselves in order to learn respect for the fire.

A smile tugged at his lips again. Whatever trouble the boy had blundered into in Gimrael had resolved itself neatly, and without any extra effort on his part. A most excellent solution all round. Now he could bend his attention to figuring out which gambit Alderan had afoot, and Saren's book was the place to start.

Dismissing the sulking *iniku* girl from his thoughts, he pulled the book towards him.

‰

The daub in the little wooden bowl glistened like fresh pitch. Kid's blood thickened with ash, with wolfsbane and seeing-eye and powdered firethorn bark. Other leaves, too, secret herbs that Ytha had gathered by this moon or that, with a copper sickle or a silver knife as each plant demanded, then dried and hoarded away until this day.

Now it was ready.

She withdrew the alder twig she'd used to stir the mixture and threw it into the fire. The flames leapt up to take it in gouts of green, reflecting in the eyes of the watching women. A little smoke escaped the draw of the vent in the roof and curled around the tent, drawing an earthy odour after it. She watched their pupils widen as it took them, then breathed the scent deep into her own lungs and closed her eyes.

When she opened them, the fire was alive. It danced and swayed, beckoning to her with golden fingers. Shadows cavorted around it, distorted into shapes that bore no resemblance to the figures that cast them. This was old magic, blood magic of the kind she had used to ensorcel the chief's spear. Magic of the mind, passed down from Speaker to apprentice from a time lost in the past, and which could be learned no other way for it did not depend on the Talent but on the will. Men knew a little of it – they made simple charms for successful hunting, or to hang from the tent pole for protection from ill will – but they could never touch its true power. That was the domain of women alone.

Cradling the bowl in her hands, she surveyed the circle of women. Each stood in her snow-fox robe with her staff at her side, the longest-serving to the newest, a trembling girl only a year or two into her staff for the Eagle Clan. As Speaker to the Chief of Chiefs, the honour was Ytha's to join them in a sisterhood that could be broken only by death.

She stood up. 'We begin.'

She dipped her fingers in the bowl and drew two lines across the first Speaker's left cheek.

'For common purpose.' Then two more, down from the hair-line to the jaw, through the right eye. 'For clear sight in the smoke of battle.' With her index finger, she drew a wavy line across the woman's brow from the downward pair to her opposite temple. 'For thought on the wings of the wind.'

The woman unfastened the front of her dress and held her shift open, baring her time-seamed chest.

Ytha dipped more daub and worked it inside her fist, then pressed her palm over the other Speaker's heart. 'For courage to the end.'

'To the end, my sister.'

The hand-print sealed it. It would sink into the woman's flesh and linger long after the daub itself had dried and flaked off her skin. The woman winced at the burning sensation of the firethorn. A little sweat broke on her top lip, but she took the bowl from Ytha with steady hands. She turned to the next Speaker in line and with the daub drew the first two lines on her face.

'For common purpose . . .'

Like a smith forging links into a chain, the binding grew. With each link the chain grew stronger; Ytha felt the throb of it in the air, in the sweat-sharp smoky reek that pressed in all around her like another skin, writhing and surging against her. She felt it in the weight of the stares fixed on her, not least that of Two Bears' Speaker, who came to stand in front of her with the bowl in her shaking hands, her entire body limp with terror but for her eyes, bright and glittery-hot, like lust and hunger and desperate avarice all rolled together.

'Speaker.'

The girl proffered the bowl. She'd chewed her lip bloody with anxiety; scarlet stained her teeth and dripped from her chin onto the dark hand-print just visible between her white breasts.

Ytha held still whilst the sigils were drawn on her face, then yanked open her dress, not caring when the fastenings tore. Next to the power waiting for her, all else was as insignificant as chaff on the wind.

'For courage to the end,' the girl whispered. Her hand, fever-hot and sticky with daub, pressed onto Ytha's chest.

Firethorn seared her skin and the force of the binding knocked all the breath from her lungs. She staggered, gasping as heat spread outwards from the hand-print, raced over her skin and lifted every hair on her scalp. It surged into her breasts, sank into her secret places. She was a woman seventeen times over and she *knew* it in every bone, every fibre, felt it the way the earth felt the quickening of spring.

Sweet Macha, it was *glorious*.

Head flung back, she reached for the power. It filled her in an instant; one of the other women gasped, but she didn't see who it was. Frankly, she didn't care. If they weren't strong enough to withstand the pull of the magic, they had no right to call themselves Speakers. They would stand or they would fall on their own merit; she would not carry them.

By the Eldest, this felt good. As good as the first time she'd ever wielded her power, against the fat herdmaster who'd wanted her to suck the juice from his root when she was ten, and laughed at her when she said she'd be a Speaker one day. As good as the day she'd taken the mantle from old Brynagh and, for the first time, saw a man kneel at her feet instead of the other way around. Better. With power like this, she would bow her head to no one.

Gradually, reluctantly, she let the power go. Some of the others were swaying, leaning on their staffs for support. Two Bears' Speaker was weeping, her daub-stained hand curled into a claw as if it pained her. She'd obviously never participated in a binding before, but when Ytha's eye fell on her she did her best to stand up straight and steady.

She had them, all seventeen clans. Conor Two Bears would not find it easy to break faith now. Through Drwyn she had the chiefs, and through herself he had the Speakers. There was a pleasing circularity to that. It put her in mind of two serpents, one black, one white, devouring each other's tails: a union of the masculine and feminine powers into a greater whole.

At that thought, a flicker of heat of another kind warmed her belly. She had neglected that hunger of late, in pursuit of other interests. Fired by the binding ritual, now it demanded to be sated. Liquid warmth pooled low down in her abdomen, loosening her muscles even as it tightened her nipples against the fabric of her shift.

No, that was not a pleasure to be savoured just yet. But later, oh yes.

'Now we are one, my sisters.' *Now you are mine.*

Ytha took the bowl from the girl and tossed it into the fire; after the herbs in the daub had permeated the wood it could never be used again. Fresh gouts of green flame leapt up to threaten the edges of the smoke-hole, and one by one the other Speakers bowed and took their leave to return to their clans. Their ways lay clearly before them; they did not need her to remind them, and the binding would hold them all true until long after the Scattering.

She stood awhile and watched the leaping fire, breathing in the potent smoke as the daub burned off. Her mind fixed on a warrior in Drwyn's personal escort. A young warrior, with quick green eyes and a full mouth she could so easily imagine fastened to her breast as she rode him.

Yes. A little *uisca* at the feasting tonight – but not too much, a subtle glamour to roll away the years, and he would be hers. It was past time she rewarded herself. A wave of arousal rolled through her and she shuddered, squeezing her thighs on the hungry ache between them. Well past time.

She purred at the thought, and with a twitch of her magic damped the fire. Inside her, the other flame only burned hotter.

3

AFTERMATH

Gair was on fire.

No matter how he writhed and struggled, he couldn't escape the heat. His skin split, juices ran; his flesh popped and hissed like a sausage in a skillet. Pain obliterated every thought, left him blind and deaf to everything but his agony. He opened his mouth to scream and choked on the stench of his own meat cooking.

His eyes flew open. For one endless second he was caught in the crushing grip of asphyxia, then his chest heaved in a breath. Another, and the clutching panic retreated, the pulse pounding in his ears began to slow. Weak with relief, he slumped on the pallet and sucked in lungful after lungful of the arid air as if it was as sweet and cold as Leahn spring-water.

Dear Goddess in heaven, he felt as if he'd been flung down a flight of stairs. His hip and thigh ached; so did the back of his head, and his right side was throbbing. He put a hand to it and found he was shirtless, his ribs snugly bandaged. Someone had taken care of him, but he had only the vaguest recollection of recent events. Flames, and falling, then nothing but bad dreams.

Propping himself carefully on his elbows, he looked around. The light was too dim to make out much more than vague, blocky shapes stacked waist high. There was a sense of space above him, a suggestion of beams in the shadows overhead, and a dusty, dry-wood scent to the air. From somewhere out of his line of sight he heard a susurrus that might have been voices, and soft scuffling sounds, like mice behind a wainscot.

Memory returned in broken pieces. Silver blades and yellow sashes. A flight of sparrows. The skirling, surging power of the Song turned to sawtoothed discord, and then flames.

There'd been flames inside his head, too, and they'd left his thoughts raw and tender as burns. He rubbed his eyes wearily. Even they ached.

'So you live,' said a woman's voice from above him.

He looked up. A young Gimraeli woman in a stained and soot-dappled *barouk* sat cross-legged on a pile of grain sacks next to his pallet, her *kaif* looped carelessly around her neck. Her name was Tierce, he remembered. She was eating a peach, levering pieces off the stone with the blade of her knife; between slices, she flicked the dripping knife through her fingers as if she was unable to sit entirely still.

'After a fashion,' Gair said, twisting around on the pallet so he could lean back against the wall, too tired and sore to hold himself up any more. 'What is this place?'

'We are not far from the Lion Gate. This warehouse belongs to a friend of ours. You can shelter here for a few hours, then travel on at dusk.' She bit into a piece of peach. Back and forth went the knife, sticky blade gleaming.

'Thank you.'

She shrugged. 'Consider it payment for all the Cultists you gave us to kill.' Holding out a tin plate of cheese and fruit, she added, 'The sisters say you must eat. When your wound opened it cost you some blood. You need red meat to make more, but this is all we have.'

He took the plate but had no appetite for the cheese, and contented himself with a handful of grapes. Their juice soothed his dry throat.

'Where are the others? Are they meeting us here?'

The desertwoman refused to meet his gaze, focusing instead on the peach in her hand. As she pried another slice off the stone, her *barouk* sleeve fell back, revealing a bandage on her forearm. A sudden unease prickled down Gair's spine.

'Tierce?'

'My brother sent me to fetch the rest of our cadre to help retrieve those books that your friend was so wedded to,' she said shortly. 'When we returned, the Daughterhouse was lost.'

For a heartbeat it didn't register in his smoke-fogged brain. 'Lost?'

'Lost!' Her voice rose in pitch. 'Taken! In flames! How many ways do you want me to say it?'

More memories. A column of smoke in a blue sky, and a woman's voice, low, afraid. *They may have escaped.* Tierce jabbed words at him like spears, and his mind flinched from them even as his imagination showed him the street door hacked to pieces, the burning lean-to that had fired the stables and the Cultist torches that had fired the rest. Roofs and floors, the carved vaulting in the chapel, all gone; only blackened stone remained. Of Alderan and her brother Canon there had been no sign.

Her hand began to tremble around the hilt of her knife. The jagged hurt in her eyes was too private to share and she looked away.

Gair covered his own face with his hands. Coming to Gimrael had been a mistake. A huge mistake, and he'd known it from the start. It had achieved precisely nothing. Now the books were destroyed, and Alderan was gone.

You and those books can go to hell.

Guilt stabbed at him. If he'd only kept his temper, maybe Alderan would still be alive. If only he'd managed to persuade him not to come to Gimrael at all . . . He raked his fingers through his hair.

Damn it, Alderan! Why wouldn't you listen to me?

25

'I'm sorry for your loss.' It was all he could find to say. 'Your brother was a good man. A man of honour.'

With a jerk of her arm, Tierce hurled the peach-pit at the wall and Gair had to duck as it rebounded off the plaster next to his head and rattled away across the floorboards.

'Do not speak of what you do not know, Empire!' Unshed tears shone in her furious, frozen glare. 'After Uril, my brother was the finest man I have ever known. He deserved a warrior's death, not to die for some *ammanai* books in a fight that was not even his.'

She hopped down from her perch and stalked away. If she'd been a cat, her tail would have been lashing.

'I meant no offence, Tierce,' Gair called after her, but she kept walking and gave no sign that she'd even heard him.

He let his hands fall into his lap. Even a shared grief only sharpened the woman's hostility.

Closing his eyes, he tried to make sense of it all. Inside his mind the fires had dimmed to embers, but the welts they'd left across his thoughts made it difficult to concentrate, especially when what felt like a hundred individual smaller wounds clamoured for his attention. Exhaustion didn't help; he'd apparently been unconscious for some hours, but he hadn't slept at all the night before and weariness dragged at his limbs like leaden chains.

'She won't hear you,' said the Superior from nearby. 'Not yet. Her grief is still too new, like yours.'

Gair squinted up at her. He hadn't heard her approach, had no idea how long she'd been standing by the grain sacks, Uril's *qatan* cradled in her arms. Long enough to have heard at least some of what had passed between him and Tierce, anyway. He let his head fall back against the wall again.

'You don't know anything about me, Superior,' he said and shut his eyes, hoping she'd leave him be. Saints, he needed to sleep.

'I know what I saw in your face just now,' she said. 'In the eyes are the gates of the soul.'

'Proverbs, chapter two, verse fifty-four. To find an honest man, look with the eyes of a liar.'

'Abjurations four, thirty-eight. You know your Book.'

'Ten years at the Motherhouse leaves its mark.' He rubbed his thumb over the scar on his palm. *In more ways than one.*

Her footsteps came closer. 'I brought this from the square – I thought you might have need of it.'

Gair opened his eyes again to see the nun holding the sword out to him. He took it and drew the blade a few inches. It had been cleaned and oiled by someone who knew how to care for a weapon. Tierce, perhaps? He slid it back into the scabbard and set it down beside the pallet.

'Thank you. I owe my friend N'ril enough as it is without losing his brother's sword into the bargain.'

He kneaded his brow, trying to think clearly. Trying not to think about Alderan. Part of him was tempted to reach out for the old man's colours, but remembering those rich hues turned muddy as an old tapestry, he pushed the power away again. The wound was painful enough without looking for reasons to pick at it. Still he was unable to silence the bitter hiss of vengeance at the back of his mind that said with the old man gone, there was nothing holding him here any more.

'Did you see what happened, Superior?'

'Some of it.'

She hitched herself onto the sacks where Tierce had sat, feet dangling several inches above the floor. With her round rosy cheeks and curly hair unconstrained by a wimple, she looked like a farm girl on a gate. Apart from the severe black habit, of course.

'I'd like to know what you saw,' Gair said. 'I don't remember much of it very clearly.'

She folded her hands in her lap, looking vaguely uncomfortable. 'When the Cultists appeared from the main street, you threw some kind of protection over the sisters. You drove the mob back with fire and with something else I could not see.'

'It's called the Song—' he began, but she held up her hand.

'It's called mortal sin, my son, and that is all I care to know about it.' Taking a deep breath, she collected herself. 'You fought until your foes became too many, then you surrounded yourself with flames. Something made you fall from your horse, because the fire went out and there you were on the cobbles in a dead faint. We thought you had been struck on the head by a stone, though later we could find no injury apart from the one in your side. Then the girl came, with warriors.' Shuddering, the Superior blessed herself. 'In the confusion of their attack, we slung you over your horse and fled, I'm afraid. She found us shortly after and led us all here.'

It was barely more than he already knew, but it was better than nothing.

'Who do I need to thank for taking care of this?' He touched the bandage around his ribs.

'Sister Resa. She appears to have taken you under her wing.'

'Please tell her I'm grateful.' He would tell her himself when he saw her, but for now he was too battered and weary to go looking for her. 'And to you, too, Superior.'

'We should thank *you*, Gair,' she said. 'You have put yourself in harm's way for us more than once in recent days and because of it, we all still have our lives. As a daughter of the Church I must deplore your methods, but as a fellow soul under the Goddess I can find little to criticise.' She rose to leave, brushing chaff from the skirts of her habit. A small smile softened her face. 'It appears even mortal sin can have practical applications.'

Then she walked away to rejoin the other nuns.

Leaning back, Gair let the wall support him. He needed sleep, lots of it, but he also needed to know why he had lost control of the Song again. No one had struck him. He'd taken no new hurts at all beyond a few bruises, most of which he must have collected from the cobbles in the fall. Nothing to explain why his grasp on his gift had slipped, why the Song had turned on him the way it hadn't since the iron room. Something inside him was broken.

Carefully, he probed the shield in his mind that scabbed over the worst of the reiving's scars. Like the dull ache of an old wound, he had become so accustomed to it that he barely gave it any thought, but as he tried to examine it, his focus kept slipping away. After a few attempts, he gave up and let the shield be. It wasn't as if he even knew what he was doing.

Alderan might have been able to explain some of it. Though he'd been no Healer, the old man had worked the Song for almost three times as long as Gair himself had drawn breath and his interests had been eclectic enough that he'd known a surprising amount about many, many things. Except Alderan wasn't there. Alderan was gone.

∽

Two days had passed without sign of Baer. Two days of bald, wind-scoured ridges where dead trees thrust skywards like fingers raised in admonition, and of precipitous, pine-choked valleys whose frost-hardened floors the sun never reached. Two days through mists and stumbles, with hunger gnawing at their bellies, through backtracks and deadfalls and stinging hail, and every evening the bitter shadow of Tir Malroth reached out and gathered them up. Two days had never felt so long.

A bright bead of blood glistened on the pad of Teia's thumb where she'd stuck herself with the needle. She couldn't sew with mittens on and without them the cold soon made her fingers next to useless. She sighed. It was almost worth leaving the rip in the knee of her trews unmended, were it not for the wind that found its way through the smallest gap in her clothing and pinched her hard enough to make her yelp. She sucked the blood away and tried once more to stitch the rent.

A dead tree had tripped her, sent her crashing down on hands and knees. Her mittens had saved her palms, but her trews had torn on the same sharp-edged rock that had gouged her flesh. Following her instructions, one of the other women had cleaned the wound and dressed it with some of Ana's salve, but the ragged fabric was proving more bothersome.

I should have thought to bring another pair. His sealskin ones, or even the elk-hide – something that would have stood up to rough treatment better than this wool. She puffed and grunted, straining past her belly to make the first stitch. *Or at least something else I could have put on to stay warm whilst I mend these! Macha, I'm so cold.* Another stitch and she fell back gasping. This would take for ever.

Neve appeared around the blanket that made the door to the women's shelter, carrying a steaming bowl. 'Tea, Banfaíth,' she said, setting it down next to Teia.

It was colourless, little more than hot water; the leaves had been reused too many times to have much left to give. She picked it up and sipped. Flavourless as well, but at least it was hot.

'Thank you, Neve.'

The other woman sat back on her heels. 'You'll burn your eyes, stitching in that poor light,' she said, taking the needle from Teia's numb fingers. 'Fetch it closer and I'll see to the mending.'

Wordless, grateful, Teia sent her little globe of light to hover over Neve's capable hands. She didn't even object as Baer's woman unpicked her clumsy stitches and started again. Banfaíth she might be to her little clan, but in the women's tent she was no more than a girl again. Neve saw to that.

Teia leaned back on her arms and tried to ignore the ache in her lower back. Moving into the women's tent had been her idea; it had felt wrong to her that the men should spend time constructing a separate shelter for her, just because she was the Banfaíth, before they could begin work on one for their families. It made more sense to have just two shelters, she had argued, one for men and one for women, which the warmth of their bodies could heat against the night's chill. She had expected an argument from the men, but without Baer, Isaak did not feel strong enough to stand up to her and the rest of the menfolk followed his lead.

'He's gone, isn't he?' asked Neve quietly, head bent over her sewing. 'Dead.'

'I don't know. I hope not.'

'Ought to have been back with us by now. It'd take more than a bit of snow to stop my man.' She twitched the rest of the rent closed and held it taut with one hand as the other dipped and drew, dipped and drew. 'Reckon dead makes most sense.' Her voice was brisk, dispassionate.

Reaching out, Teia touched Neve's arm. 'I haven't given up hope.'

'Aye, well.' Neve tied off the thread and snapped it around her fingers. She handed the needle back but didn't meet Teia's eye. 'Hope don't keep me warm at night, is all.'

'I can scry him out, if you like.'

The older woman hesitated. 'You can see where he is?'

'Not exactly, but maybe I can tell if he's—' She almost said *if he's alive*, then corrected herself at the last minute. 'If he's safe.' Surely she knew Baer well enough by now to seek him out.

Neve fussed with her shawl, folding and refolding her arms over it. Teia guessed she wanted to know but was afraid of what she might learn.

As gently as she could, she said, 'At least then you'd know, one way or the other.'

The older woman worked her hands deeper under her armpits and gave a crisp nod. 'True enough. I'll fetch some water, shall I?'

Teia held up her tea-bowl. 'This will do,' she said. 'It's near enough water as it is.'

The power came quickly, but all the tiny bowl showed was snowflakes the size of goose feathers swirling in the air. Teia squinted to see the landscape beyond them, but with no moonlight she couldn't make out more than ghostly grey shapes.

Show me Baer.

The viewing in the bowl turned to black and Neve recoiled. 'Macha's mercy!'

'It's all right,' Teia reassured her. 'I think he's under cover somewhere, and it's just too dark to see.'

Neve began to lean towards the bowl again then stopped, suddenly dubious. 'You're sure?'

'Sure as I can be,' Teia said, with more cheer than she actually felt. It was the absolute truth, but it tasted like the worst lie in the world. She was as sure as she could be on the basis of no more evidence than a feeling in her gut. 'If Baer was . . . well, if something had happened to him, I don't think the water would show me anything at all.'

Looking up, she met Neve's gaze. A little bewildered, a little haunted, but strangely resolute. Teia released her power and let the viewing fade. 'That didn't help much, did it? I'm sorry, Neve. Maybe if I try again in the morning, when it's light?'

'No.' The older woman sat back, rewrapping her shawl again. 'Thank you, Banfaíth, but I reckon I've seen enough for now.'

She pushed herself to her feet and Teia wished she hadn't made the offer to scry. It hadn't eased Neve's mind at all.

'Thank you for your help with this.' She gestured at her newly mended trews. 'And the tea.'

'It was no trouble. Banfaíth,' Neve added by way of excusing herself and left.

Teia watched the blanket fall closed after her, despair chilling her as much as the gust of cold air. *Oh, Neve, I'm so sorry.*

She should never have let Baer go. She was a fool to be so concerned about others when she had Lost Ones of her own to care for. They should be her first duty, always.

Teia swiped a hand across her eyes. The longer Tir Malroth's shadow lay over them, the more her strength dwindled, but they'd come too far to turn back now. The journey to the Broken Land would surely be longer than the distance that still lay ahead. It had to be. If she let herself believe otherwise . . .

No. She had to believe that the worst was behind them, not ahead. If she allowed herself even to think that was not so, she would lose what little hope she had left. She looked at the tea-bowl in her hand, still steaming faintly, and swallowed the drink down.

4

TO THE LION GATE

🙢

The sun was setting when the wide cargo doors at the far end of the warehouse were opened. The sudden noise startled most of the nuns onto their feet, and Gair had his hand ready on the hilt of the *qatan* even before he'd turned to see what was happening. Silhouetted against the orange light from outside was a *barouk*-clad figure; he shaded his eyes and squinted, trying to see who it was as he walked up to the door.

'Tierce?' he asked.

'It's time,' she said, signalling to someone behind her. A high-sided wagon drawn by a six-mule hitch clattered into the yard from the street. As soon as it was inside, the driver, a nondescript fellow in workman's clothes, leapt down from the seat and with a nod for Tierce disappeared back out through the arched entry, pulling the gates shut behind him.

Some of the nuns had drifted up to the door after Gair, the Superior amongst them. 'This is our way out of the city?' she asked.

'I assume so.' He fell silent as Tierce turned to face the group.

'The city is no longer safe for *ammanai*,' she said, without preamble. Her words were inflectionless and she kept her sand-veil firmly across her face, so only her eyes were visible. 'There is

34

water on the wagon and adequate provisions to see you as far as Zhiman-dar, although it will not be a comfortable journey. After that I suggest you leave Gimrael and never return.' She hesitated, then added stiffly, 'May your Goddess go with you.'

The nuns began whispering amongst themselves as Tierce strode over to Gair and the Superior. She eyed them without warmth.

'This is the best the *jihadi* can do at short notice. Do not ask for more.'

'I wasn't going to,' the Superior said mildly. 'On behalf of all our Order, I am grateful for everything you have done for us.' She reached out to take Tierce's hand between both of hers. 'I am sorry for your loss, my daughter. Your brother will be in all our prayers, as will you.'

Tierce snatched her hand back. 'I do not need your prayers!' she snapped. 'And my brother—' She stopped, looked away and collected herself with an effort. 'When you reach Zhiman-dar, go to the livery yard on the west side of Green Moon Square and ask for Tal. Tell him his Aunt Jamira is unwell and not expected to last the month. He will make sure the mules and wagon are returned to their rightful owner.'

She gave them brief directions to the square. The street names meant nothing to Gair, but the Superior nodded as if she knew the place well. Finally, the young woman glanced up at the evening moon, already halfway above the high walls around the yard and blushing pink with the setting sun.

'The Lion Gate will be closed in two hours,' she said. 'Don't waste time.'

She turned to leave, then stopped when Gair held out his hand.

'May your road speed you, Tierce,' he said, offering her the ritual farewell in Gimraeli. Suspicious black eyes flicked over his face, as if she couldn't be sure if he was sincere. Then she gave his hand a quick, dry shake and walked away.

'Prickly as a *guyyam* fruit, that one,' said the Superior with a sigh.

Gair watched Tierce making a show of observing the comings and goings on the street outside through a chink in the gate, but the tensely folded arms, the hunched shoulders betrayed her emotions.

'I think she has her reasons,' he said. 'Come on. We'd best get moving.'

It didn't take long to load the sisters and their few possessions into the wagon-bed, whilst Gair fetched Shahe from where she'd waited out the day in the stable adjacent to the warehouse. By the time he'd checked her over to be sure she was carrying no injury worse than a stone bruise and saddled her up, the nuns were settled as comfortably as they could be. With the Superior's help, he spread a canvas tarpaulin over the wagon and tied it down, then as the sun dipped behind the Governor's palace they set off for the Lion Gate.

Gair let the Superior lead, since she knew the way, and fell in behind the wagon as it rumbled along an alley lined with high, windowless buildings. More warehouses, perhaps, or bonded stores; they were somewhere in the underbelly of El Maqqam's mercantile district. He glanced behind him once as he rode away, but Tierce was busy closing the gates again and didn't acknowledge him. Maybe she was simply as glad to see the back of him and the nuns as he was to be finally leaving. He only wished the circumstances could have been different.

But however heavy his heart, he had no time for brooding. There was a hostile city to cross, and then a long ride to Zhimandar, which would in all likelihood be no friendlier. Grief and guilt were luxuries he could not afford. Settling his sand-veil high across his face and his *kaif* as low as he could and still see, he followed the nuns' wagon out of the alley onto a busy street.

The city teemed as raucously at the close of the day as it did at noon. Each street they traversed was thick with pedestrians, handcarts and ox- or mule-drawn wagons, both empty and full. Farmers returning home from market, merchants bound for the port at Zhiman-dar; in the dusty orange light of early evening, the Superior in her plain *barouk* resembled just another weary wagoneer plodding through the crush. Gair ambled Shahe along behind, keeping a watchful eye on the crowd around them as they passed out of the mercantile district and onto a wider street lined with shops still open for business. A steady stream of wagons occupied the middle of the street with foot traffic eddying along the margins and occasionally darting in between the slower, heavier vehicles to reach the other side, incurring curses and shaken fists on the way.

The street opened out to a square up ahead, but instead of the traffic speeding up it slowed to a crawl and finally stopped. Soon the crowd began to mutter and shrug, standing on tiptoe to peer ahead in search of the reason for the hold-up. Gair stood in his stirrups and shaded his eyes. The square was crowded with people listening to a man declaiming loudly in front of what looked like blackened trees. Occasionally the crowd cheered, and the man's shouts got louder. Yellow gleamed around his waist.

Burned trees. A flight of sparrows. Flames flared in Gair's memory and he recognised the square ahead. Instinctively, he glanced south and east, and saw a faint smear of smoke still staining the darkening sky.

Saints have mercy.

He shook out his *barouk* to cover the ornamented cantle of Shahe's saddle and sat down again. Black was not an uncommon colour for horses, but her silver-chased harness might be distinctive enough to mark her out if there was anyone in the crowd who'd been there that morning. He nudged her forward and the citizen throng obligingly shuffled sideways to let the horse through to the front of the wagon.

As soon as he leaned down to the Superior's ear, she whispered, 'I know.'

'Is there another way?'

'In this crowd? We'd never make it to the gate on time.' He saw her gaze flick around the exits from the square. 'Straight ahead's our best bet.'

Gair bit back a curse. Straight ahead would take them past the thickest part of the crowd, close by where the Cultist was holding court atop the well-cover.

'What is he saying?'

She listened awhile. 'The usual Cult rhetoric about godless oppressors— Wait, now he's denouncing someone. See him point-ing?' Across the square, several yellow-sashed men were shoving a stumbling figure to the front of the crowd. 'Hamesh the silk merchant has been trading with *ammanai*, profiting from his deal-ings with the oppressors . . . Now he's pulling off the merchant's rings – he calls them infidel gold, stained with the blood of the righteous—' She looked down at her hands on the reins. 'He's been sentenced to death.'

'Just for trying to make a living?'

'According to them he has strayed from the true path.' The Superior closed her eyes briefly, as if offering up a prayer. 'I used to love this city. Now I barely even recognise it.'

Her words echoed what Sister Avis had said when he had asked her about the sun-signs. The Cult was tightening its grip on El Maqqam, squeezing so hard the blood had begun to flow. *You mark my words, there'll be another desert war, and soon.* Alderan's pre-diction, from last year. The old man had known, had read the way the wind was blowing, and now the whole world was fraying apart.

'This is madness,' Gair muttered. 'We have to get out of here.'

'I'm open to suggestions,' said the Superior dryly. Shahe nodded as if in agreement, mouthing at her bit.

Ahead, someone began sobbing and pleading. Gair couldn't understand the words, but didn't need to. Hamesh the merchant was begging for his life. Gair shut his eyes. His instincts were screaming at him to draw steel and do something, but he was too far away, with too many Cultists and their supporters between him and the luckless merchant. So instead he had to listen to the gabbled pleas, the jeers of the crowd, with a dark, ugly fire inside and his hand clenching and unclenching around the whipped-leather hilt of the useless sword on his hip, and wait for it to end. It was one of the hardest things he'd ever done.

In the end, Cult justice was swift, if brutal. A harsh Gimraeli voice barked a command, steel *thunked* into flesh and a dripping object was hoisted into the air. The crowd bayed their approval and the Superior shuddered.

'Did they . . . ?'

'Yes.' Gair forced himself to release the sword-hilt as, amazingly, the press of bodies and vehicles ahead began to stir. Faintly, he heard the distinctive ringing of hammers on nails and guessed what was happening to the merchant's corpse. 'When we pass the well, I suggest you don't look up.'

One by one, wagons lumbered into motion. The crowd was still hooting and chanting, but as it thinned around the edges space opened up for the carts to pass by. The pace was hideously slow. Every yard of the way, Gair expected a shout to ring out and a horde of yellow-sashed swordsmen to appear around the nuns' wagon. The back of his neck itched with imagined scrutiny, but no one spoke up and the mules plodded on across the square.

As they passed the well, he couldn't prevent himself glancing across at the scorched shapes of the trees. What he saw made his gorge rise. Poor Hamesh's body was propped in a sitting position against the largest tree, his colourful robes defiled by gory stains. Flies swarmed around the bloody stump of his neck and the slack-jawed head that sat above it, pinned to the tree's trunk with long black nails through the eyes.

Stomach surging, Gair dragged his gaze forwards again before he gave himself away. The act was horrific enough, but what truly sickened him was the Cult warrior standing to one side of the corpse, grinning triumphantly, brandishing the bloody sword above his head as if he was proud of what he'd done.

Gair's pulse pounded so hard it made his head swim. Dear Goddess, was there no depth to which the Cult would not stoop? He caught a worried glance from the Superior and realised he had a white-knuckled grip on the *qatan* again, and his jaw ached from grinding his teeth. It took a half-minute or more to make himself let go. It took another half a mile of crowded street before his heartbeat slowed to something close to normal.

Close to the Lion Gate, the wagon's progress became erratic and then stopped altogether. The larger vehicles could only pass through in single file, and the city watchmen in charge of the gates also had to contend with travellers outside wanting to come within the walls before nightfall. It made for a frustrating wait, everyone packed into the foregate square like so many salt fish in a barrel. Sulky teams stamped and shook their heads at the flies and their drivers grumped to each other like wagoneers everywhere. Gair pitied the poor sisters sweltering in the wagon-bed under the heavy canvas; the heat wasn't a great deal less outside, but at least there was fresh air to be had.

He watched the gate guards over the heads of the crowd in the square. They didn't appear to be overly vigilant; with luck they'd be as bored and lazy as the guards had been in Dremen when he'd fled the motherhouse, at their post more for the look of it than any real effort at security, but given the tension and violence in the city – never mind what he'd just witnessed – that might be too much to hope for.

Bending low in the saddle so only the Superior could hear him, he asked, 'Will the watch want to see a manifest, or inspect the cargo?'

'I don't know,' she whispered back. 'It's been more than twenty years since I came through here on a supply wagon.' Lines of strain pinched the corners of her eyes as she hunted back and forth from the watchmen at the gate to the carts in front of her. Most were waved through, but some drivers were being quizzed. 'I am loath to ask this, but as they say, when a nail needs driving . . . Is there anything you can do to help us remain unseen?'

With less of a crowd around them and more time to prepare, he might have been able to spin an illusion to disguise both her and the wagon. He had a sound grasp of the principles, but he had never attempted to mask a moving object before, and on the evidence of the last few days, he was afraid it would go badly wrong – assuming he could hold on to the Song long enough even to attempt it.

'Nothing I'd be happy trusting your lives to,' he replied.

'But what you did for the sisters this morning—'

He shook his head. 'That was crude stuff. Illusion on this scale requires more finesse than strength.'

'Then we must put our faith in the Goddess.' She snapped the reins to start the mules forward again.

In fits and starts they crossed the square, trundling forwards a few yards, waiting again as carts and pack-trains came through the gates the other way. Each delay wound Gair's nerves a little tighter; responding to his increased anxiety, Shahe grew restless and began to fidget. By the time they reached the gate, the sun had sunk halfway behind the city wall and shadows were pooling on the cobbles. The gate guards were clearly as fed up as everyone else in the square and waved the nuns' wagon through with only a few terse words. Gair and Shahe received a hard look, but he gathered the mare up and trotted her past with as much head-high inner-desert haughtiness as he could manufacture, and they let him be.

Once clear of the walls, the Superior sighed with relief. 'Goddess be praised!'

'We're not out of the woods yet,' Gair said, fighting the urge to glance back over his shoulder.

She gathered up the reins to snap them over the mules' backs. 'Then let's get out of here.'

With a sharp pang, Gair remembered what Alderan had said as

they left the Holy City. *When you look as if you have every right to be there, everyone else will assume that you do.* 'Keep them at a walk,' he said. 'Don't hurry.'

She shot him a quizzical look.

'The last thing we want is for one of those watchmen to wonder why a six-mule hitch is pelting away from the city.' He saw her gaze slide sideways. 'And don't look back, either.'

Above her sand-veil, her eyes narrowed. 'In addition to your other gifts, you appear to be an accomplished sneak.'

'Not really.' He paused to let a smaller, faster cart overtake them and vanish into the billow of dust raised by the other traffic on the road ahead. 'But I had a good teacher.'

They rode on in silence as the evening purpled softly towards night. At a hundred yards out from the city with no sound of pursuit, Gair began to relax; at three hundred or so, he heard the Lion Gate thud closed and finally let the tension ease out of his shoulders. If the Cult wanted to come after them now, they'd have to persuade the city's officials to order the gates opened. Even if they had the Governor in their pocket, that would take time, and every minute he and the nuns spent travelling took them further out of the Cult's reach – at least for now. Zhimandar would be another story, but he'd worry about that when they got there.

5

WOODSONG

ॐ

Between one step and the next, the stillness of the wildwood became the damp chill of an autumn field. A tingle of something passed over Tanith's skin, as if she'd walked through a draught, then cold air hit her lungs, smelling of turned earth and burned stubble. Rags of mist straggled over the turf, and on the horizon a copse huddled black against the pale sky.

'Spirits, where are we?' she asked.

The forestal looked around alertly, like a hound scenting the air. 'We must hurry. There is not much time.'

Then he broke into a run, uphill towards the trees, and she had to follow him or be dragged by the rope tied around her wrist. Wet grass squeaked under her boots as she skidded and stumbled to keep up.

Halfway to the copse, two figures lay sprawled on the dewy turf, their clothes already beaded by the mist. One of them was Ailric, who lay face up, staring unblinking at the sky. The other was the warrior she'd seen through the stones, his rough woollen shirt black with blood around the arrow in his back.

Owyn dropped to his knees beside Ailric. 'Give me the token.'

She fumbled out the acorn she'd found in Ailric's coat and

pressed it into the forestal's outstretched hand. 'What happened to him? Will he be all right?'

'He crossed without a token, so the way back was barred to him. It is too complex to explain now.' He gripped the acorn tight, his lips moving, then stuffed it into Ailric's trouser pocket and heaved the Astolan up onto his shoulder. 'Come. We must leave.'

Beside them, the warrior moaned, struggling to lever himself onto his arms. Kneeling, Tanith pressed him gently back down.

'Stay still,' she said. 'I'm a physician.'

Frightened blue eyes peered up at her, showing no sign of understanding, but when she drew her knife to slit open his shirt he redoubled his efforts to escape. Tanith calmed him as best she could, and quickly cut through the wool. The fabric was glued to his skin with blood; as she peeled it away, crimson welled up around the white-fletched arrow that pierced his back next to his shoulder-blade. He coughed, the arrow twitching, and a little blood appeared on his lips.

It had reached his lung. Unless she acted fast, he'd drown.

Owyn shook his head, teeth gritted under Ailric's weight across his shoulders. 'Leave him. We cannot linger here, lady.'

'I'm a Healer,' she snapped back. 'I won't leave a wounded man if I can help him.'

From somewhere beyond the trees, trumpets rang out. The warrior plucked at Tanith's hand, slurring words she didn't understand. She disengaged him and took a firm grip on her knife. It was no scalpel, but it was sharp.

'I'm sorry. This will hurt.'

She made a swift, deep cut, down alongside the arrow-shaft. The man screamed. Trumpets sounded again from the copse, followed by drumming hooves. She probed the wound with her finger, searching for the arrow-head.

Quickly, quickly, or the welling blood would kill him faster than the arrow would have. Her finger slithered over a hard shape – the arrow-head. Not barbed, thank the spirits. Gritting her teeth, she dug the point of her knife behind the head and with her other hand drew the shaft free. The warrior's scream became a wet bubbling moan as he vomited blood onto the grass.

Throwing the arrow aside, Tanith pressed her hand over the wound, thrusting out and down with the Song. There was no time to be gentle; this was battlefield Healing, swift and graceless. His body thrashed, eyes starting from his head, his mouth working soundlessly.

A sharp yank on the rope pulled her hand away. 'Lady, leave him! He is already dead!'

The turf trembled under her and she looked up. Over by the copse, a dark shape was moving in the mist, accompanied by a low rumbling. White banners with a blue device appeared from behind the trees, then the dark shape resolved into a phalanx of cavalry thundering over the ridge towards her at a flat gallop.

Bloody spears swept down to the couch. She saw bared teeth and flying manes, then Owyn tugged the rope once again, hauling to her feet.

'Hurry!' he shouted, lumbering up to a run with Ailric still slung across his shoulders like a hunter's kill. For an instant she agonised over the fate of her patient, then pelted after him.

Never had two hundred yards felt so much like two hundred miles. The sloping field looked endless, the green of the forest drawing further away with every stride instead of closer, whilst the cavalry surged down the ridge behind her. The thudding hooves, the creak and jingle of harness grew so loud that she imagined at any second she would feel the horses' breath or a spear in her back.

Through the clearing mist, she saw the two stone pillars beneath the trees at the forest's edge, the symbols carved into them still white from the mason's chisel. Twenty yards away. She dared a glance back over her shoulder. The wounded warrior was on his feet, sword held aloft in salute. She slowed, raising her own hand in acknowledgement, and saw the line of charging horsemen rise behind him like a breaking wave.

Even as she drew breath to shout a warning, a spear-point burst from the man's chest. A flicker of stunned incomprehension crossed his face, then he was gone, ridden down without a cry.

'No!'

The pillars loomed either side of her and the world flashed silver to black. Disoriented, dragged forwards by the rope around her wrist, she fell to her hands and knees in the leaf litter of the clearing. When she looked over her shoulder again, the battlefield had vanished and all she could see through the stones was the far side of the glade.

Panting for breath, she let her head fall. Despite her best efforts, her patient was dead.

Every Healer knew that sometimes a patient would not survive, that sometimes fate or time or sheer blind chance meant there was nothing a physician could do except ease their passing. She had experienced it before, more than once. It was the curse that came with the gift, the shadow cast by the light of the Healer's power. But she had never saved a life only to see it wrenched away again by violence so quickly. It was a wrong so vast she could scarcely wrap her mind around it.

Then she saw her dagger in the dirt, its blade bright and clean. No blood. There was none on her hands either, yet she'd felt the man's raw flesh, the heat of his life slicking her fingers as she cut out the arrow-head. Disbelief chilled her.

'Did it really happen?' she asked, rocking back on her heels.

Owyn had heaved Ailric down onto his bedroll and was spreading a blanket over him. 'Yes,' he said. 'And no.'

Tanith frowned. 'I don't understand. Either it did or it didn't.'

He tucked the blanket around the Astolan's legs.

'How do we ever know that something has happened? We know because once it is done, the world as it was is no more. The event has changed it. For that warrior, nothing changed.'

'But I saw him. I touched him.' *I felt his pain smelled the fear-sweat on his skin oh spirits I Healed him why couldn't I save him?*

46

'Then for you, it was real.' The forestal straightened up, sliding the noose off his wrist. His face was grave. 'You should have left him, lady.'

Tears threatened and Tanith tilted her chin defiantly, determined they would not fall. 'I will not betray my Healer's oath. I will render aid wherever I can.'

'Even when it is hopeless?'

'Even then.' *Damn it, no! I will not cry!* 'At least this way he died quickly instead of drowning in his own blood.' *At least I know I made a difference, however small.*

He cocked his head on one side. 'But he is still dead.'

To that, she had no answer. The helplessness, the sheer unfairness of it, yawned like an abyss, and she stood on the very edge. Owyn watched her for a long moment, until she had to look away or she really would cry, no matter what she did.

Back on this side of the stones, dawn had given way to a dull and cheerless day, and despite the warmth of the air she began to shiver. The shock, she realised, combined with the run, the change in temperature. Oh, spirits, she couldn't stop shaking.

Hunkering down at her side, Owyn draped her blanket around her shoulders. She thanked him and he reached into his jerkin and took out a small silver and leather flask.

'Here,' he said, offering it to her. 'This will help warm you.'

When she unscrewed the cap, the smell of some kind of spirits made her head spin. Gingerly she took a sip and gasped as the stuff seared down her throat.

'What *is* that?' she asked when she could see straight again. The shuddering had stopped and her stomach was aglow.

'*Kavit.* We make it from birch leaves.' Owyn took a sip himself, then sealed the flask and stowed it away. 'Better?' he asked.

'Better.' She was, in a way; the jolt of strong spirit had anchored her in the immediate, in the now, and given her something to hold on to whilst the strangeness washed over her. But she would never forget that warrior's blue eyes.

Tanith looked over at Ailric. His golden skin had a pallid cast and a little frown creased his perfect brows, as if he was vaguely disappointed in something, but that apart he appeared none the worse for his passage through the stones. She was glad for that. Any tender feelings she held for him had long since burned out, but she had loved him once and wished him no harm.

'Will he be all right?' she asked as Owyn slipped the noose from her wrist. He followed her gaze.

'I think he took no lasting harm, but his head will hurt when he wakes.' He snorted and jerked the tail of the noose to untie it. 'Perhaps it will teach him to take better heed in future.' Mouth set in a hard line, he coiled the rope around his palm and elbow, snapping out the kinks with quick, angry movements.

Tanith glanced at Ailric again. Passing through the portal without his token had evidently put him in considerable danger. Owyn had said that without it the way back from there was barred to him, but only now did it occur to her that he hadn't said exactly where *there* was.

She dug her own acorn from her pocket and studied it from sharp tip to nubby green cup. Apart from its weight, so out of proportion to its size, nothing distinguished it from any other windfall that might be found on the forest floor. Turning it over in her palm, she thought again about the tingling sensation she'd felt when she first took it.

'Where was that place, beyond the stones?' she asked. 'It wasn't part of this forest, was it?'

'No.' He did not look at her, busy stowing the coil of rope in his pack.

There was more to it than that, she was sure of it. 'Where was it? *When* was it?'

He exhaled sharply. 'There is knowledge I cannot share with you,' he said, buckling down the flap on his pack. 'Even if I could, you would need half a lifetime to see it clearly.'

She frowned, nettled. 'My people are as old as yours. We are wise to this world.'

Owyn jerked his head in Ailric's direction. 'As wise as yon lover? I warned him to keep the token close!'

So the forestal *had* overheard them – enough to come to the conclusion that they were intimate.

'He's not my lover. Not any more.' Tanith kept her voice low in case it woke the sleeping Astolan. 'Please, Owyn. Whatever mistake Ailric made, those stones took us somewhere *else*, and I want to understand what happened.'

He stared at her, then turned his head aside, a muscle in his jaw working as he mastered his temper.

'Then I must ask your forgiveness,' he said. 'When I say you will need half a lifetime to understand, I do not mean to insult you. It is more that I cannot explain it adequately. Amongst my people, I am not renowned as a teacher.'

'I'll struggle along,' said Tanith, and he gave her the merest quirk of a smile. Pushing his pack aside, he sat down cross-legged in the leaf litter.

'Once this world was all forest, from the mountains to the sea. Every wood, every forest that has ever been was once part of that first forest, and in the heart of the wildwood, the trees remember. All those forests exist there, endlessly reflected upon one another. If you have the skill, or a guide, it is possible to move between them, and so cover great distances with ease.'

'So what we saw beyond the stones—'

'Was a memory. Of a battle already lost, and of a warrior already slain.'

'I couldn't have saved him, no matter what I did?'

'No,' the forestal said gently. 'I tried to tell you. He had to die because he was already dead.'

She remembered the weight of time she'd sensed at the cloven oak. 'What happens when a tree dies? Are the memories lost?'

'The memory is in the forest. A tree dies when its time is done,

49

for such is the order of things, but its fruit gives rise to a new tree in its place. The individual may pass but the forest remains, and so memory endures.'

That made sense, of a sort – as long as she accepted the idea of trees possessing memory. She studied the acorn in her hand again, still looking for something remarkable about it, and found nothing.

'The fruit of the oak. You said it will protect us.' She held it up by the bit of twig attached to the cup. 'Protect us from what?'

'Lady, would you have me tell all my secrets?' said the forestal with a laugh. 'Oaks are the gatekeepers of the forest. There is a reason why I found you at an oak tree, and why all the paths returned you there, just as there is a reason why oaks surround this glade.'

He gestured at the black shapes of the trees around them, whose branches spread so wide they overlapped each other and wove their twigs together like children linking their hands in a ring.

Like one of Masen's Gates in the Veil. 'It's a doorway. A portal to another place.'

'In a manner of speaking.' Owyn leaned his elbows on his knees and laced his fingers together. 'Bregorin is . . . a many-folded land. The ways of the wildwood are deceptive, and it is possible even for we who dwell here to become lost. The oak token ensures safe passage, shall we say. It is important that you keep it with you at all times.'

'I will.' Tucking the acorn back into her pocket, Tanith asked, 'If you go deep enough into the wildwood, can you travel into the past and change the outcome of events?'

'No,' he said, shaking his head. 'That only happens in stories. In the Grove there are trees so ancient they were seeded long before the settlers came out of the east, even before the free peoples ever gave this land a name, so the forest's memory is long, and the wildwood runs deep, but what is past is past. It is not possible to make a change, only to witness it.' He unfolded himself and stood. 'It is still very early. Sleep some more, lady, if you can. We will leave in an hour, and you must be rested before we move on. The next stage of the journey may be perilous.'

More perilous than the memories of the trees?

Tanith lay down under her blanket and gazed up at the roof of the ancient forest, the chinks of pale cloud visible through the branches. Though she tried not to dwell on it, she could not help but wonder whether trees that dreamed could also have night-mares.

6

DECEPTIONS AND DESIRES

ᘒᘔ

As the first light touched the mountains, Ytha left the green-eyed warrior snoring in a tangle of sweaty blankets and walked back through the camp to her own bed. Nothing stirred in the cold blue shadows between the tents but a few twists of smoke from the fires, so there was no one to see her as she let the glamour dissolve. The rolling-hipped, red-headed girl she used to be blurred into the air, but the memories remained, and she strode towards her tent with a smile of lazy contentment on her face.

Gods, but there was little to compare with a young man at his peak. Strong as a Stone Crow stallion and more than willing to be ridden hard – hard enough to satisfy even her long hunger. Once the Scattering was over she would no longer be able to pretend to be some wilful daughter of a distant clan, but until then there was plenty of *uisca* and darkness to give them both what they wanted. And they'd wanted plenty. She shook back her hair, remembering, and the memories made her purr.

As she neared her tent, she noticed her wolf's-head standard slumped askew, its bone charms clacking together in the breeze. Ytha frowned. Some drunkard must have blundered into it during the night and the men on guard hadn't bothered to straighten it. A fine impression that made in front of the other chiefs and their

Speakers. The men would catch the rough side of her tongue for that; dung-picking for a week might make them remember their duties in future. She rounded the flank of the tent, gathering breath to berate the guards, and stopped when she saw that there were no men on watch at the entrance, and no sign of them anywhere nearby.

Wandered off after drink, most likely, the useless dolts. Ytha growled, imagining worse punishments than dung-picking. By the time she was done with them, they'd wish they'd stayed sober. She wrenched the pole upright and drove its bronze spike further into the ground with a twist of power to keep it there. Let them try to pull that up when the time came to break camp!

Smacking aside the door-curtain, she stalked into her tent. After the brightness of the morning the darkness temporarily blinded her, so she conjured an orb to light her way amongst the chests and cushions. The last thing she needed now was barked shins.

The globe's pale light revealed the pair of Hounds sitting with their backs to her, ears pricked intently, and her hand went straight to her knife. When she saw what – or, rather, who – they were watching, she drew it.

'You!' she snapped. 'You have no right to be here!'

The dark-haired man reclining on her cushions looked up and smiled. 'Is that any way to greet a friend?'

'We are not friends.' She flexed her fingers around the hilt of the knife. 'Now go, before somebody sees you.'

He bridled. 'Not friends? You wound me, Ytha. Besides, nobody will see. I sent your guards away, and no one walks into the Speaker's tent uninvited.' The smile became salacious, his near-black eyes twinkling. 'Especially not when she is . . . entertaining.'

The man was certainly dressed for pleasure. His hair spilled loose about his shoulders and his deep red robe draped open almost to the sash at his waist, revealing a considerable amount of pale, firmly muscled chest. The shining fabric clung to his form in a way that left no place to conceal a weapon, nor much of anything else.

'And what if they talk?'

He gave an airy wave. 'They saw nothing untoward, I assure you. No one will learn of our arrangement.'

Unconvinced, Ytha scowled. However he'd managed to deceive the guards, she'd have their hides for ground-skins later.

Levelling the knife at him, she snarled, 'You have a nerve, showing your face here after you lied to me. All this time, I have been the one to bear all the risk, and you've given me nothing but empty words!'

'Nothing?' He flicked a languid hand at the hangings around the walls of the tent, worked with animals unknown in these lands, in colours richer than anything a Nimrothi dyer could create. 'Hardly nothing, my dear.'

Ytha glowered. They were costly gifts, right enough, but that didn't mean he owned her.

'I am not a whore to be bought!' she snarled. 'We made a bargain, you and I, and you promised me the forts in the passes would remain empty.'

He examined his fingernails and drawled, 'As I recall, I promised the forts would remain empty of Church Knights – the ones you call the iron men.'

'They are swarming with the Empire's soldiers!'

Dark eyes fixed levelly on hers. 'But no Knights, so I think you will find that I have kept my word. Have you kept yours?'

He doubted her? Aedon's balls, she ought to open his belly right now, and never mind the ruined carpets. She glared down her nose at him. 'Of course.'

'You have the war band?'

'I do.'

'All the chiefs?'

'All seventeen.' Pride bloomed in her chest, reminding her of the deep burn of the firethorn that bound the other Speakers to her in an unbreakable chain, and she stood up straight, chin tilted haughtily. 'All the Speakers, too. You should not have doubted me, southman.'

'That is most excellent news.' He folded his arms and sighed. 'Put the knife away, Speaker. I'm not going to hurt you and you can't hurt me, so spare us both the posturing, please.'

Ytha glowered at him, reluctantly sliding the knife back into its sheath. 'I don't trust you.'

'Oh, but you should.' He gestured to the two Hounds, who shuffled their paws and licked their chops as if they knew he had a choice morsel for them. 'I see you received my little gift.'

His gift? 'These are Maegern's Hounds.'

'True, but She did not release them.'

Impossible. 'I spoke with Her. She promised us the Hounds as a token of Her favour!'

The man laughed indulgently. 'My dear Speaker, your faith in your goddess is commendable, but consider this: faith does not require that things are true, only that you believe them to be so.'

Macha, the man twisted words like a Speaker avoiding an untruth. 'Speak plainly.'

'Is it not obvious?' He spread his hands. 'If your goddess had the power to reach into the daylight world, She would have freed Herself centuries ago. She might have commanded the Hounds to come to you, but She needed help to release them.'

Before she could stop herself, the knife was halfway from its sheath again. 'Lies!'

Amused, he cocked an eyebrow at her. 'It hadn't occurred to you? I *am* surprised.'

The notion had never even crossed her mind. Maegern was a goddess of the Elder realm – She raised Her hand and Her will was done. Ytha had never had reason to doubt it, and yet . . . after the Breaking, mortal men had sealed the goddess and Her Hunt away. Powerful men, with a powerful weapon, but mortals nonetheless. That realisation shook Ytha badly, even worse than finding out yesterday that the forts were not empty, but she stiffened her knees and snicked the knife back into its sheath. No pale-skinned southerner would see the Speaker of the Crainnh at a loss, no matter what he said.

'So it was you who loosed them? If you are so mighty, why not free Maegern yourself? Why make a game of it with us?'

His shoulders lifted in a shrug. 'Because the Eldest are not my gods. What happens to them is of no concern to me; my only interest is in seeing the Empire brought to its knees – which your war band will do very handily, I think.'

'So what are you doing here?'

'I came to check on your progress. I must say, I am impressed. You have done better than I ever anticipated.'

He had assumed she would fail. How *dare* he?

'I have fulfilled my side of the bargain,' she said coolly. 'I have the clans at my back, and now the Hounds are with us. We are ready to retake our lands and grind the Emperor's face in the dust.'

The southman gave her a gracious nod. 'And I have fulfilled mine. The iron men will not challenge you. You will have your lands again, if your warriors will fight for them.'

'They will fight, have no fear.' Ytha allowed herself a thin smile. 'Nimrothi men do not give up their spears when the battle goes hard.'

'I'm glad to hear it.' He got to his feet in a swirl of glossy fabric. Pink tongues lolling, the Hounds jumped up, too, and milled around his legs, plumy tails waving over their backs. He scratched their ears absently and they licked at his hands. Strange; she'd never seen them fawn like that over anyone. 'Have they shown you the way?'

Ytha eyed him warily, wondering how much to reveal. She'd been telling the truth when she said she didn't trust him – and not just because his drawling accent made her fear he was mocking her, or the odd way he twisted words around until she suspected he hadn't meant what she'd heard.

'They have,' she said. 'Our course is clear.'

He didn't press her for more, just straightened up and dusted yellow-grey fur from his fingers. 'Then I think our business is concluded. I will observe your advance most carefully.' He made his obeisance in his own strange fashion, leaning forward a little at the waist. 'Speaker.'

'Southman.'

She gave him a nod and he left the tent. A breath of some heady scent followed him, rich and musky – perfume of some kind? On a man? Ytha shook her head and eyed the two Hounds who were staring as if bereft after her departed guest. Truly, these southerners were strange, soft creatures! All scented airs and lustrous fabrics – they had never ridden the long plains after the herds, never stared the wind down and spat in winter's eye. How they had ever secured an Empire was beyond her. Was it just that there were so many of them? Perhaps their fat lands and easy lives made them fecund, the way good pasture quickened the beasts.

A sudden, tight grin bared her teeth. Maybe when those fat lands were hers it would be amusing to watch the southerners attempt to scratch a living from the hard earth of Nimroth. Aye, and then she'd sit in a scented bath right up to her neck and watch them, and by the Eldest she would *laugh*.

❧

The marquetry box on the mantel was almost empty. Only a dozen or so leaf-wrapped twists of resin remained next to his pipe, filling the air with their burned-honey scent. Savin snapped the lid shut before it woke his hunger and locked the box securely. There'd been so much to do, so many wheels to start turning, that there hadn't been time to return to Sardauk to replenish his supplies, and now they were almost exhausted.

That was . . . vexing. The only Gate he knew of there was several days' ride from the Sardauki capital Marsalis, and even further from the *kalabal* groves in the mountains where the purest resin could be obtained. Worse, it opened into empty desert, so he would have to go prepared for travel, which was impossible from his cramped quarters here amongst the Nords. Even going to the Sardauki interior via Gimrael would take two weeks or more, and that was time he did not have to spare.

No, he would just have to be frugal with it to make sure the *mezzin* lasted. Not for the first time, he cursed the necessity of stranding himself in the north with only limited access to the trappings of a civilised society, then tucked the little brass key back into his pocket.

The air in the tower room pressed down on him, heavy as the moment before thunder cracked the sky. His contact in the Hidden Kingdom was waiting. Irritated, he frowned. More admonitions, no doubt; more querulous demands for reassurance. Did they think he had no idea what he was doing? By all the Seven Kingdoms— His expression settled towards a scowl, but he arrested it, smoothed it out into something neutral before he turned to face the velvet-shrouded sight-glass amidst the books and papers on the table. The sooner these meddlesome creatures were dealt with, the sooner he could get back to work.

He lifted the cloth, lips framing a greeting he didn't get time to deliver.

We are waiting.

The chilly tones of the Hidden Kingdom's representative held more than the usual amount of displeasure. Savin swallowed down his irritation.

'Soon, my friends. All is proceeding according to plan.'

You promised us results.

'And you shall have them, I assure you.'

Your assurances are worthless. We demand proof.

Proof? Savin ground his teeth. There was no proof on earth that would satisfy them unless he was holding the starseed in his hand, and when that happened, of course, he wouldn't need to prove himself to them ever again. He clasped his hands behind him to keep them from clenching into fists and smiled benignly at the teeming blackness within the glass.

'It is all a matter of timing,' he said. 'The trinity moon is approaching—'

The movement of celestial bodies is of no importance to us.

'Nor to me, but these people are primitive, shackled to their superstitions. The triple conjunction is significant to them, therefore everything must occur in accordance with their prophecies. If it does not, we risk losing their credulity and by extension their usefulness.' It was so tiresome having to explain things that should have been obvious; he barely managed to keep the bite from his words.

Around the silver frame, fanged creatures yawned and stretched. Nothing reflected in the glass itself, of course; its blackness remained absolute, a bottomless void that pulled at his gaze as if it would suck his eyes clean out of their sockets. Deliberately he shifted his focus to the top edge of the frame. Dealing with the Hidden was wearing enough without giving himself a headache into the bargain.

He waited for them to conclude their deliberations. It was never clear to him precisely how many creatures he was addressing through the glass; only a single voice spoke, but it used plural pronouns and occasionally, like now, there would be a pause in which the sense of presence faded, as if his interlocutor's attention was elsewhere. Quelling dissent, conferring with others, Savin had no way to tell, but it was yet another annoyance in dealing with the wretched creatures.

At last, he felt the weight of their attention press on the air again.

Continue.

Finally. 'As I said, the trinity moon is approaching and their army is poised to push through the mountains. Now that the Hounds are free, they will lead the clanspeople to your treasure.'

And the Empire?

'Preoccupied with matters in the desert. There has been no unrest in the north to trouble them since Milanthor fell.' A thin smile curved Savin's lips. 'The Hounds will not be opposed.'

This is pleasing to us. The writhing figures that made up the sight-glass frame all turned their faces towards Savin and bared their shining, needle-sharp teeth. *What of the Guardian's new apprentice?*

At that, Savin's smile widened. 'He has ceased to be of concern to me.'

Laughter boomed through the air, resonant as the creaks and groans of a calving glacier. *Then all is in place.*

'As I assured you it was.' Savin gave a little bow for the benefit of the creatures on the other side of the glass. It was dangerous to mock them openly, but he was weary of playing subservient to them when power was almost within his grasp. 'All that remains is for you to fulfil your part.'

Silver shapes flowed together, became the gaping jaws of a serpent. Fangs as long as his hand curved in front of the glass, tapering to points so fine they glistened as if dripping with venom.

We are not yours to command, human.

Not yet, at any rate, whispered a gleeful voice in the back of Savin's mind. He kept his face carefully impassive.

'Indeed not, but if the Eldest wish to be freed from their prison, they have a role to play, too. Since they will not deign to speak with me . . .'

He left the rest hanging. The Hidden were old, and proud, and long out of practice at dealing with mortals; it amused him to remind them that a human held the key to the freedom that had eluded them for so long. In the silence that followed his words, the serpent's fangs strained up and out, shining bloody with the reflection of his scarlet silk robe.

We will be ready. The darkness in the glass seethed. *We will all be ready.*

7

ON

꘠

Teia reined Finn to a halt amongst the last straggle of trees and studied the sloping ridge before them. Bald as an egg, its untracked snow polished dazzlingly smooth by the mountains' perpetual wind, it undulated up to a saddle between two blunt peaks that represented the highest and most exposed point on their journey so far.

Shading her eyes against the glare from the cloudless sky, she scanned the way ahead. From the rightmost peak, as she looked at it, ran a sharp ridge of sawtoothed crests like the spine of a fish, bounding up to end in a forked tail flicked impudently across the face of the sun: the Haunted Mountain, Tir Malroth. On the left, the ridge dived into the tumbling white-capped waves of pine forest surging over the feet of the mountains as they marched into the distance. There was no other way to go but across the vast snowfield of the saddle ahead.

But that unbroken snow intimidated her. It dared her to violate its perfection, then when she hesitated, it mocked her for weakness. If there'd been an animal print, or the lacy trail of bird tracks, anything to put a blemish on the snow's white face, she would have had no hesitation in urging Finn on. But there wasn't. There was only her and the mountain and the blank stare of the snowfield in between.

Teia nibbled at the chapped skin of her lip. For six days now, she'd led the Lost Ones south because she didn't know what else to do. They'd climbed too high to linger here, with no game to be had, and by the Eldest she wasn't prepared to go back down to the plains and become Drwyn's plaything again, so onwards it had to be. Why was she faltering now?

A sense of being watched prickled over her mind and she shivered, squinting up and to the right at Tir Malroth's glittering peak. The glare made her head throb, especially around the scar.

Take one more step and everything changes, it seemed to say. *Take one more step and you can never go back.*

Footsteps crunched through the snow behind her and Isaak appeared, walking up to stand at Finn's head. The gelding nodded to him and was rewarded with a scratch under the chin.

'Do you feel anything here, Isaak?' she asked him.

'I feel cold,' he said, with a show of teeth at his weak joke. Then he squinted out over the snows, leaning on his spear. 'Yon mountain's staring at me, if that's what you mean. Makes the back of my neck itch.' He hunched his shoulders inside his patched coat as if to escape the stare, then peered up at her from beneath his curly hair. 'But we had to come this way, right?'

'It's the only way that's safe.'

Lenna's man dug the heel of his spear into the snow. 'Begging your pardon, but I can't say as it looks like a very safe way to me.'

Teia studied him, his big man's hands on the spear-haft, the awkward knobby wrists jutting at the cuffs of his coat that said he was still a boy who hadn't quite finished growing. 'Do you fear the dead, Isaak? They can't hurt you.'

He shrugged, darted a glance from beneath his brows and went back to prodding the snow. 'I've heard stories about folk who've gone this way and not come back. They say the spirits here can drive a man mad.'

She'd heard the same tales herself. The stories were in her blood, told and retold so many times by generations of her ancestors that they were a part of her. When a person died there were rituals to observe, chants to be sung by his sons and brothers, her sisters and daughters, so that the soul found its way to the afterworld. Those with none to mourn them came here. She looked up at the cloven peak of Tir Malroth again. Was that why she felt so daunted? Because she was stepping into a realm where the living had no place?

'You'll see us safely through, won't you, Banfaíth?'

Teia didn't answer straight away, her eyes still fixed on the mountain's great forked crown, gleaming silver as a salmon's tail and all spangled around with blown snow. The thin, ice-clear air made it look close enough to touch. Beyond it, across the wide white saddle and down through the rumpled peaks and ridges on the far side, lay her destination: the Empire. Ancient enemy, even more ancient kin.

She closed her eyes. *Lord Aedon, shelter us all.*

So far still to go. Would they all survive to see it? Isaak and the other bowmen had brought down two more deer before they left the river valley, but without a way to cure the meat they'd had no choice but to gut the carcasses, pack them with snow and hope it would last. At least it was too cold for blowflies. Other provisions were desperately short now; little flour, few beans, some preserved fruit. With snow to melt for water they wouldn't thirst, but people soon sickened on a diet of naught but meat. And there was no end to their journey in sight.

'Banfaíth?' asked Isaak anxiously.

Teia opened her eyes again. 'Sorry, Isaak,' she said. 'I think yon mountain was staring at me, too.'

Afraid or not, she had no choice but to go on, Haunted Mountain be damned.

'You go first. Use your spear to find out how deep the snow is and we'll follow your trail.' After her fall into the river, she trusted his judgement in these conditions more than her own. She forced a smile despite her headache, chapped lips cracking. 'We are relying on you to keep us safe.'

He bobbed his head. 'I'll not let you down, Banfaíth.'

'I know you won't.'

Slowly, yard by yard, the band moved out across the snowfield. Isaak and his spear led the way, probing the thigh-deep snow carefully before he took a step; three of the strongest men followed him to break trail for the rest and take their own turns in the lead. As the day advanced, so the chill hand of Tir Malroth's shadow reached out of the west towards them, drawing the night after it.

The cold bit deep. Snow, so soft and feathery when it fell, became a monstrous weight on the ground, resisting every stride and making the next one harder. Limbs grew heavy and muscles burned as the thin air stabbed at lungs accustomed to lower altitudes. Even with Finn and the deer-laden pony to widen the trail in Isaak's wake, their progress was defined in yards, sometimes less, as the sun settled and the shadows lengthened. With every slow-passing hour, winter sank its talons a little deeper into flesh and bone.

Teia's head ached as if icy hands were clamped around her temples and squeezing her skull. Up on Finn's back she was more exposed to the wind; no matter how she huddled into her coat, it numbed her cheeks and chin and pinched her ears until they burned. And still she sensed the patient bulk of the Haunted Mountain at her side, waiting for her to fall.

She twitched her fur collar higher around her neck, hands clumsy in her thick mittens, but the sensation persisted, almost exactly as if she was being stared at. *Stare all you want – I will not die here!*

The sun touched the shoulder of the western mountains before they were two-thirds of the way across the snowfield. Isaak, back in the lead after being spelled for a time by one of the other men, whistled for a halt and looked back.

'Banfaíth!' he called hoarsely, leaning on his spear-haft. 'We're losing the light.'

Teia shook her head, the ache behind her eyes making her wince. 'We can't stop here. We must push on.'

'It'll be too dark to see in an hour.' Already blue shadows swarmed over the snowfield, with only the far eastern rim and Tir Malroth's peak still gilded by the dying day.

'We go on, Isaak. I can provide more light when we need it.' *I won't die here.*

A commotion behind her made her twist in the saddle. Some-one had fallen and was being helped up by two other figures, near invisible in the gathering dusk. Stiffly, she swung down from Finn's back. Her numbed feet almost pitched her onto her back-side in the snow, and she had to hang on to the stirrup to stay upright.

'Come here,' she called, waving the figure forwards. 'Ride for a bit. You, too, Lenna.'

'But Banfaíth—' Lenna protested, lips cracking in the cold and her heavy skirts crusted with white.

'You've walked enough,' Teia said. 'Let someone else have a turn, eh?'

Amazingly, several smiles flashed in the dimness. Good. If they could still find the strength for mirth, they were not beaten yet.

Lenna mounted Finn first, then the woman who had fallen was bundled up behind her by Varn. Dead-eyed and scrawny as a starveling kitten, she had to be instructed to hold on to Lenna's coat. Teia watched her anxiously; the woman struggled to form a fist in the thick furs and, despite the frigid air, her breath barely steamed. At last she managed a clumsy grasp and Lenna set Finn walking again to catch up with the rest of the band, now some yards ahead.

Teia followed in her horse's tracks for the easiest going, though it could hardly be described as easy. With the approach of night the snow froze as fast as Finn's hooves broke it up; it crunched like river pebbles under her boots as she slipped and slithered after him through the gathering dusk.

As the day faded, so the wind strengthened. It poked cruel fingers into her clothing, seeking skin to pinch. It whipped the dry snow of the surrounding field into twisting columns that danced like wraiths in the distance, and close to spat stinging needles of ice into eyes and faces. She had to keep one hand raised to shield against it, but even then her vision of the Lost Ones shambling ahead of her came and went as if through flapping veils.

Before the sun was out of sight, the evening moon rose. Only a quarter full and fading, it added little light. When the second moon crested the peaks an hour later its brighter, whiter illumination, combined with the strange pink glow that followed the sunset as if the mountains blushed, prolonged the dusk for a few more precious minutes.

Teia slogged through the broken snow, legs trembling with the effort. Each step sapped more and more of her strength. Soon she was gasping; every breath sent silver splinters of pain lancing into her lungs. The raw air made her cough until her head spun and strange lights dappled her vision.

Dear Macha, what on earth had possessed her to think she could cross Tir Malroth so early in the year? She should have stayed safe in the caves and waited for the spring. She should not have brought these people here, to certain doom. Now the mountain would have its due.

Yard after yard, doubts whispered to her. She pushed them away and they returned twice as loud. She heard recrimination in the wind that shoved at her, saw pale, reproachful faces in the whirling snow. No matter how many times she told herself that she had done what was needful with the fate of her people balanced in the scales, her words were flung back to her laden with spite.

What of the people she had left behind? How selfish to abandon them – was her responsibility not to stay, to stand between them and Ytha's insane ambition and somehow temper it? That would be bravery, in truth; what she was attempting now was folly, cowardice dressed as self-sacrifice, and the Lost Ones would pay the price.

Her steps faltered. She saw Baer's face in front of her, gaunt and grey, and her eyes stung with sudden tears.

I'm sorry, Baer! I've failed you – you put your trust in me and I've let you down. I'm so sorry!

She held out her hand, imploring, but he turned away, fading into the ice-wraiths that crowded about her.

Please! Baer! Don't leave me here!

Stumbling after him, she missed her footing. Dragged down by the weight of her belly, she sprawled into deep snow and all her breath whooshed out. The tears came then, tears of shame and despair and exhaustion, and all she could do was lie there in the snow and sob until they were done. Then she rolled onto her back, staring up at the darkening sky and the stars wheeling slowly overhead, and waited.

Strangely, she wasn't cold any more, only tired. It would be good to rest there for a while, lie down. Lie in the downy snow, so soft, so comfortable. Lie down and close her eyes, just for a little while.

Yes. Her weariness sang seductively in her ears. Her eyelids drooped. *Time to sleep, little Teisha.*

She shook her head. No, that was wrong. No one called her Teisha but her parents, and they were far away. She'd left them behind, hadn't she? Frowning, she tried to look around for them but she was lying in a hole and couldn't see anything but grey shadows and the vault of heaven above her, with Macha's white face smiling down . . .

Except that wasn't Macha, it was the moon. Confusion. She'd have to get up to see properly. She rolled onto her knees, crusted

67

snow flaking off her coat. Why was she lying in the snow? The murmuring voice of exhaustion encouraged her to lie down again and rest, but she shook her head angrily, trying to shake some sense into her thoughts.

Cold crept into her knees, numbing them. Not good. She lurched to her feet and the moonlit snows and sweeping shadows around her swayed, then settled into focus. Deep snow. Mountains. Dark shapes strewn about like a child's scattered toys and a crowd of pale figures marching silently past her, dozens of them. Hundreds. An army, their hair streaming in a wind that blew contrary to the one she felt on her cheek.

Her heart lurched. The unsung dead, walking into eternity, never to be granted rest. Scrubbing blown snow from her face, she looked back the way the Lost Ones had come. She had fallen behind the group, and down the trail of trampled snow there were only more ghostly figures. They were everywhere. Gaunt and grim, they streamed across the snowfield as far as she could see in each direction: men mostly, but women and children, too, looking neither right nor left as if they had a purpose from which they could not be shifted. She swung to face southwards again and saw another of the shambling Lost Ones ahead of her totter and fall.

No. The dead would not have her, nor any of those who had followed her into the mountains. Not today.

Darkness had fallen, sudden and swift as only a mountain night could descend. Scant light from the two aging moons, and that as pale and brittle as the ice underfoot. Step by painful step, Teia resumed walking. Her cold-stiffened muscles burned so severely that tears sprang to her eyes again, but she dragged a foot forward, leaned her weight on it, swung her other leg around.

'I will not die here,' she mumbled. 'I will not die here.'

Stride followed stride mechanically, like a shuttle across a loom. Five yards covered, then ten. The nearest of the sprawled dark shapes was closer now; she put her head down and concentrated on making each step, one after another, trying to ignore the pain in her legs, the stabs into her chest with every breath. She would rest when she reached him, and not before.

The figure was Varn, face down in the snow. Panting, she heaved him onto his side.

'Varn.' Her voice came out as a croak. 'Varn! Wake up!'

He groaned. She shook his shoulder and his eyes fluttered. Had the dead done this, or exhaustion? Mountain-sickness, after a life on the plains? No time to wonder; she had to get him up and moving or it would be too late. Teia shook him again, fruitlessly, then stripped off a mitten and slapped his face hard.

The report of skin on skin was shockingly loud. Varn's eyes flew open and he sucked in a breath of cold air that set him coughing.

'Get up,' she said. 'Come on, I need your help.'

He nodded vaguely. Looked past her and frowned, his expression lost and somewhat troubled, as if he had turned to do something but could not remember what it was. Teia grabbed his arm.

'Varn, look at me.' A twist of her power spun a light above her shoulder. *'Look at me.'*

The light caught his attention and he squinted, raising his hand to shield his eyes from the brightness. 'Banfaíth? What's happening?'

No time to explain. 'Help me with the others, quickly, before the night takes them.'

Another nod, and he heaved himself to his feet. Supporting each other, they stumbled to the next fallen one: Gerna, on her knees in the snow.

'It's the dead,' she moaned when Varn shook her shoulder. 'They've come for us.'

Varn shoved a hand under her arm and hauled her up. 'On your feet, woman.'

Teia left him to it and made her way unsteadily to the next man, then the next. With words of encouragement – and slaps where words failed – she coaxed them to their feet and sent them to help the others who had succumbed to whatever subtle power was at work here that made men forget and falter. She sent other lights skywards; with the glow of her power she pushed back the dark, and the silent figures of the dead retreated with it. Whether it was her magic that dispelled them or just the power of light, she had no way to tell, but when something cold touched her cheek, like a farewell caress from icy fingers, she shuddered.

They had to keep moving. It was far from safe to linger. She watched the fur-wrapped people emerging from the dark to gather around her, their cold-drained faces anxious, uncertain. They were waiting for her, she realised. They were waiting for her to tell them what to do.

She almost laughed. As if she knew. *I could use a little help now, Baer.*

Some light, first – proper light. *Let the dog see the rabbit*, as her father used to say. At least that wouldn't require much physical strength. Reaching down inside her, Teia found the place where her magic waited and the music surged up. With a gesture, she flung a globe of light into the air above their heads, brighter than the two moons together, and let her smaller lights dissolve. It flooded the snowfield with pale yellow light and illuminated the figures of Isaak and his men some distance ahead, waving their arms in the air. Finn was with them, and behind them the snow sloped down to a line of scrubby trees, black against the night. They had made it to shelter at last.

Relief engulfed her so suddenly she almost fell to her knees.

'Go on.' When her voice did not carry, she simply waved her arm. *On, on.* 'Everyone, get up to the others. We'll go into the trees and make camp.'

The last hundred yards or so passed in a fog of weariness. Teia was barely aware that someone put their arm under hers to support her; she needed all her strength and concentration to set one foot in front of the other without falling. She fixed her eyes on Finn's broad backside and willed herself to keep going.

She was stumbling when she finally reached him, almost fell against Finn's rump when the person who'd been supporting her – Varn, she realised – eased out from under her arm. The horse snorted, twitching away, but she managed a pat for him.

'Good lad,' she murmured. 'Good lad.'

For a minute she leaned on him, pressing her face into his hide to share his warmth. Slowly her dizziness passed and she was able to breathe more easily. Macha, her belly was heavy. She curled an arm around it and wished she could sit awhile, but she didn't dare. Not there.

'Who were they, Banfaíth?' Lenna asked. 'We saw people in the snow, and then the wind started swirling . . . Isaak wouldn't let us go back.'

Even speaking required a great effort. 'Isaak did well,' Teia said. 'Let's get into the trees; I'll explain later.'

With her hand on Finn's rump, she followed the big gelding and his burden of two women down the snowy slope. The trees remained tantalisingly out of reach for what felt like an hour or more, but the snow grew perceptibly shallower, the going easier now they had an end in sight, until at last she stumbled into the pine-scented gloom. An equally exhausted Isaak caught her and steered her to a fallen tree where she could sit as the last of the Lost Ones trooped in after her.

Behind them, glowing under her light, the snowfield stretched up to a black horizon beyond which she could see nothing but the moons. The line of peaks, of which Tir Malroth was the highest, spanned the skyline, a palisade between her and her homeland. A sudden pang of loss cut into her, hollowing her out like a knife.

Macha keep you, Mama. Lord Aedon watch over you, Dada, and shelter you both from the storm. I miss you.

Carefully, she hoisted herself to her feet and grunted at the sudden contraction in her womb. She rubbed her belly gently and the spasm eased. Not long now. Another moon's turning, plus a few days. Right under her hand, the baby kicked strongly. At least her daughter was unaffected by the privations of their long journey. For the moment, anyway.

Turning her back on the north, she walked into the forest just in time to see the woman who had shared Finn with Lenna fall lifeless from his back.

ᏭᎦ

Next day, the men built a cairn over the woman's body. It was mostly packed snow, with the few stones they'd unearthed laid on top; they wouldn't deter scavengers much, but this high in the an-Archen Teia doubted there would be many beasts to trouble a grave.

'I didn't know her name,' she said as Isaak and the others laid the last few stones. 'She never told me.'

'Wasn't much of a talker, that one.' Neve tugged her shawl more tightly over her breasts and refolded her arms. 'Pale little thing, creeping around the camp like a mouse. Never let on how she ended up with us, just appeared one day with a bundle of things in her arms. Now she's gone the same way, all quiet like.'

Their first death. In all the band's time together, all the leagues they'd travelled over snow and rock, they'd lost no one. Even the clash with the other Maenardh down in the foothills had left them with only a few cuts.

Reaching out, Teia laid her hand on the topmost stone, the one Isaak had scratched with the sign of protection, and said a prayer for the dead woman so her soul would find its way to Macha. As she did so she felt Neve's eyes on her. The weight of the questions in the older woman's gaze was palpable as a hand on the back of Teia's neck. Would there be anyone to build a cairn for her man Baer? Would anyone mark his passing with a stone?

Seven days now without any sign. Neve didn't say anything, though sometimes her restless hands betrayed her anxiety and her gaze would linger on the Banfaíth a little longer than it should. Seven days. He ought to have caught up with them by now. The others had only been a day behind them at most, he'd said. No wonder Neve was feeling the strain.

On the morning of the third day after Baer left Teia had scried again, as she'd offered. Once more she'd seen nothing but snow: thick as fleece on the ground, mounded over trees and rocks so that it was difficult to tell one from the other, and still more falling.

She thought she'd seen a figure moving, the faint lines of tracks through the drifts, but without a clear skyline to pick out a familiar landmark she had no clue where she was looking. Knowing she'd seen something, but not knowing what it was, turned out to be twice as frustrating as knowing nothing at all, for her and for Neve, and she'd flung the water out of the bowl in a fit of temper. Gerna, tending the fire that day, had been caught unawares by it and all but swallowed her tongue with fright.

Teia hadn't looked into the waters for Baer since.

She stared back the way they'd come, at the vast expanse they'd crossed yesterday and the louring clouds with their burden of snow rolling slowly along the spine of the mountains. It didn't take much wit to guess that they were the source of the blizzards that had so clouded her attempts to scry.

Aedon shelter you, Baer, wherever you are.

Carefully she swung herself up onto Finn's back and extended her arm for Neve to mount behind her. Banfaíth she might be, but that didn't mean she couldn't share her mount with another of the women. She'd ordered their dwindling supplies redistributed amongst the men so Lenna could ride the pony; the girl's time was fast approaching and she couldn't keep pace with the others on foot, not even amongst the trees where the snow was not so deep.

'All ready, Isaak?' she called. The young man looked up from kicking snow over the remains of their fire and nodded. 'Then let's get on, and make the most of the light.'

She chirruped Finn into a steady walk and guided him down through the snowy trees and the slanting bars of sunlight towards the distant rumble of another river. Shortly, Isaak jogged past her into the lead, flanked by a pair of bowmen in case they should start any game.

Provisions were a constant worry now. The last of the venison would feed them for another day, if they were frugal with it, and the bones could be boiled for broth with their remaining beans to give it some substance, but after that . . .

Teia nibbled at her chapped lip. After that they would depend solely on the accuracy of the men's bows. Deer if they could bring one down. Birds. Maybe snow-hares. She tasted blood and muttered a curse at herself, dabbing her stinging lip with the back of her mitten. And after that, without bread or vegetables they would all eventually sicken.

How much further, to find a way out of those cursed mountains? She did not have to look up to know Tir Malroth still glowered down at them. Even though they had braved the dead and passed over the ridge onto the mountain's southern side, she could still feel it, dragging at her like a stone in her pocket.

Are you with them, Baer? Did you die somewhere in the snows, unsung? I should never have sent you back. I don't know how to lead these people – I don't even know where we're going!

Cold fingers of panic plucked at her stomach. She'd have to look into the waters again, try to somehow probe that bottomless darkness they always showed her now and find out what lay on the other side. *If there is anything to find at all.*

8

A HOLE IN THE WORLD

୧୦

After parting from the other *gaeden*, Masen and Sorchal spent two more days tracking eastwards across the plains, harried by spring showers. He let the younger man lead, consulting his horseshoe nail compass every few hours to be sure they were on the right course, but he needn't have bothered: Sorchal's Gatekeeper's senses proved to be just as accurate, and a good deal more nuanced. On the morning of the second day he felt the faint tug of something that so bothered him he wouldn't ride on until Masen produced the nail and convinced him it wasn't a Gate.

'See? Not a twitch.' Masen had said, holding up the nail on its thread. It pointed unerringly in their direction of travel, away from whatever Sorchal could sense.

'But I can feel something over there!' Sorchal pointed northwest.

Masen looked around, fixing the geography of river bend and broken-backed ridge in his mind, then dug through his saddlebags for his maps. The one of Arennor had been folded and refolded so many times it was scattered with star-shaped holes, but he spread it out carefully over Brea's neck and peered at the faded symbols. And blinked. Double-checked the location against the landscape and then barked a laugh.

'Well, I'll be damned!'

'What is it?' Sorchal leaned over from his saddle and Masen pointed at the map.

'There *is* something there – look. That red square with a cross in it.'

'Is it a Gate?'

'It used to be, a long time ago. It's been sealed, lintel-stone pulled up, the lot.' He eyed his apprentice. 'And it wasn't done in my lifetime, either. That's why I didn't recognise where we are straight away.'

'When?'

Masen rubbed his chin thoughtfully. ''Bout three centuries ago, I think, but I'd have to check the ledgers to be sure.'

Sorchal gaped. 'Three hundred *years*?'

'We Gatekeepers didn't come down with the last shower of rain, you know.'

The Elethrainian scanned the symbols inked onto the map. Most were faded with age, apart from one, a neat square on the far western edge of the map, high on the flank of the Brindling Mountains. Masen saw the lad looking at it.

'That's the one I found last year,' he said. 'Awkwardly placed bugger, too – right over a waterfall. The empty square means it's still open. A cross would mean it's been sealed.'

'And the red ink on this one?' Sorchal pointed.

'Means the Gate had partially collapsed, or was dangerous in some way.' Masen started refolding the map carefully along its most recent creases. 'When we get back to Chapterhouse I'll help you make your own set of maps, and explain the other symbols as we go.'

Sitting back in his saddle, Sorchal gazed ruminatively in the direction of the sealed Gate. 'So what I'm sensing . . . is where a Gate used to be?'

Masen stowed his map and buckled his saddlebag.

'You're probably feeling the scar – looks like the neck of a drawstring bag. I'd take you up there and show you, but we've still got that rent to find.' He grinned. 'Nothing like some practical experience, eh? Beats book-learning every time.'

A few hours later, the skies cleared and late sun set the wet grass shimmering like the ocean. Sorchal reined up on the crest of a rise and cast about like a hound questing for a scent.

'It's here.'

A yard or two behind him, Masen stopped and pulled the horseshoe nail from his pocket. It snapped straight out to the length of its thread. He hardly needed the confirmation; this close he could sense the wrongness of the tear, so different from his awareness of a Gate.

'Right again, lad.' With some difficulty, given the tension in the thread and the risk of it disappearing back to the Hidden Kingdom if he let go, he retrieved the nail and stowed it away again. He dismounted, giving Brea an absent pat. 'You see to the horses and I'll make a start while the light lasts.'

The Song rose up the instant he thought of it. His senses sharpened, letting him smell every wild flower, see every stem of grass as it swayed in the breeze, almost count the seeds in each feathery plume. The plains were singing, and he felt it in his blood and his breath and his bones.

Carefully he reached out his hand, fingers spread. They tingled with the Song he held, acutely sensitive to the wind rushing between them. He moved his hand as slowly as he could until he encountered resistance and then stopped. The Veil's slippery fabric billowed against his palm like a sheet on a laundry line. Spangles of pale light fluttered around his fingers, the threads glistening.

Masen followed them in the direction the nail had pulled at him. Here and there he found snags and frayed strands, the sort of minor damage that would be good for Sorchal to practise on but not severe enough to be attended to immediately. For the moment, the rent commanded all his attention.

There. Under his hand, the gentle hum of the Veil's interwoven threads abruptly ceased. Beyond it was . . . emptiness. A hole in the world, with only darkness beyond. Looked at with the Song he could see it, black against the daylight world like ink splashed across a painting. He reached up as high as he could, trying to feel the limit of it, then traced the edge downwards. About the height of a tall man.

Masen frowned. *No. Surely not.* 'Sorchal? Get over here.'

His apprentice came to stand next to him. 'You've found it?'

He gave a terse nod. 'See if you can feel the edge.'

Sorchal's Song rose up, tingling over Masen's skin at such close range. The boy had no great strength in his gift, but what he did have was subtlety: he could twist and flick the power as deftly as the forty inches of Sardauki steel he wore on his hip. Masen watched him gently testing the air with the flat of his hand, then the lad's brows shot up.

'It's there, and then it's gone,' he said. 'Like it's been cut off.'

'Exactly,' Masen said heavily. *Like a sharp knife through a sheet of paper.*

'Can you mend it?'

'If the edges haven't withered, yes, but it'll leave an ugly scar.' Stitching up the Veil wasn't that dissimilar to suturing a cut: the quicker you could do it, the better it healed. This wound had been left far too long. It would result in a thick, twisted rope of a seam, like a scar down the face of a pretty girl, if it could even be closed at all.

'But if the Veil's been cut, doesn't that mean someone let the Hound out?'

Even though the same thought had already occurred to him, hearing Sorchal voice it still made Masen's blood run cold.

'It rather looks that way.' The Veil thrummed and rippled in response to the power they held, the slash across it visible now. Its edges glinted, but between them was a darkness blacker than the void between stars.

78

'Because it was weakening, I assumed it had simply frayed apart and allowed a Hound to escape. But this,' he touched a finger to the edge, 'this means it was deliberate.'

Sorchal's green eyes widened. 'Who has the power to do that? The Nimrothi Speakers?'

'I'm pretty sure they could, if they worked together – although I have no idea how they'd reach all the way here to do it.'

Chewing at his lip, Sorchal ran his hands carefully down the edges of the gap in the half-seen fabric. 'Could it have been cut by something from the other side?' he asked. 'Something from the Hidden Kingdom?'

It shouldn't be possible. In all the years Masen had been Gate-keeper, all the books and lore he'd absorbed during that time, he'd never seen or heard such a thing described. He remembered the hunter he'd seen last year when this sorry story had begun, and the icy knife that lodged in the boundary between worlds when it should have bounced back at the thrower's feet.

'Maybe,' he said. 'Unlikely, but maybe, if they were strong enough and found a weak spot.' Even as he said it, though, Masen knew it wasn't what had happened. His mind raced. This changed everything, made their journey into Arennor even more urgent. If the Speakers had the ability to pierce the Veil, who knew what they could unleash? 'We must warn the others. How far can you hail?'

'I don't know – I've never really needed to reach further than the other side of Penglas.'

Masen clapped him on the shoulder. 'Time to start trying. Barin and Eavin need to know what might be coming at them up there.'

He heard Sorchal move away, felt him gather the Song, then put him out of his mind. There was enough to concentrate on with the task at hand. Letting his own Song fill him, he studied the slash in the Veil.

Like any living thing, when it was cut, the Veil would eventu-ally form a scab over the wound, and then, in time, a scar. Scar tissue was thick, and tough, and no matter how carefully he stitched it together, scarred edges would never seal. Sometimes there was no option but to cut out the damage – make the wound bigger in order to help it heal.

'Goddess, I hate doing this,' he muttered, and shaped his will into a scalpel.

✑

Night had well and truly fallen by the time Masen coaxed the last fibres of the Veil into position and wove them together with strands of the Song finer than spider-silk. The darkness was hidden once more behind a rippling, shimmering wall of colour, already beginning to restore itself. He caressed it with his fingertips and it thrummed.

There you are, my beauty, he whispered and let the power go.

Exhaustion hit him like a slaughterman's mallet and he dropped inelegantly onto his rump on the ground. Oh, ye saints, he'd forgotten how much a working of that size and complexity would take out of him. He propped his head on his hands and his elbows on his knees and groaned.

Sorchal hunkered down next to him and proffered a steaming mug. 'That looked like hard work. Tea?'

'I could do with something stronger,' Masen admitted, and the Elethrainian grinned.

'I found that flask of brandy you keep in your pack and poured about two fingers' worth into the tea. Get it down your throat and I'll fetch you some supper.'

'Bless you, boy,' said Masen gratefully and cradled the cup to his lips.

It appeared Sorchal had not been idle whilst he was working. There was a fire lit, with a potful of something savoury simmering over it, and the horses and pack pony had been unsaddled and were dozing nearby. Beyond the circle of firelight, the plains were wrapped in velvety darkness, in which Miriel hung quarter full and

yellow like a lamp in night's window. The sun went down quickly
and early this far north, but the evening moon so high meant it
was pretty late.

His apprentice returned after a minute or two with a bowl and
some trail bread for Masen and sat down beside him.

'It's only bacon and beans, but it's hot.'

'Aren't you eating?'

'I had mine about three hours ago,' Sorchal said, and Masen's
spoon stopped halfway to his mouth.

'How long was I busy?'

'It's gone midnight now, so about six hours.' Sorchal sipped at
his own tea. 'I watched what you were doing. I've never seen
anything like that before. There were so many threads!'

'I'm sorry I wasn't able to give you a lesson with it. A job that
size, I needed all my concentration.'

'I think I got the gist of it.' He pulled a face. 'Although I think I
should have paid closer attention when my sisters were stitching
those tapestries they like so much.'

Masen shook his head, sopping a piece of trail bread in his
beans. 'You'll do fine. Carry on the way you're going and you'll be
a better Gatekeeper than me! Did you manage to hail Barin?'

Sorchal nodded. 'He didn't believe me at first when I said the
Veil had been cut, but I told him you'd seen it, too, and he said
they'd be careful. They're still with the rangers, so he's passing the
word.' He stopped talking, but to Masen, watching whilst he ate,
he appeared to have more to say, turning his empty mug round
and round in his hands as if he didn't know where to begin.

Masen finished his supper and put down his bowl. 'Something
on your mind, Sorchal?'

The lad shrugged. 'It's probably nothing. Just a feeling.'

'After what you've done this last couple of days, I have a
healthy respect for your feelings.'

'It was while you were busy. After that sealed Gate this morning, I thought I should try to see what else I could sense, and . . .'

He peered into his mug and frowned. 'And I think I found another cut in the Veil.'

Masen felt chilled. 'Where?'

'To the west. A good distance away.'

A conversation with some clansmen on a bitter night last year, at Brindling Fall. They'd told him about butchered kine in the Southmarch, and in the west . . .

Oh no. Not two of them.

'You're sure?' he asked, not wanting to be right.

'It feels the same, just very, very faint.' Sorchal looked up. 'I mean, it might be nothing, right? I'm still new at this.'

New you may be, but you've got the best instincts for Gatekeeping I've ever seen. Masen drained his tea, needing the jolt of the brandy in it. 'I say we swing westerly tomorrow, on our way up to the mountains, see what we see. You might make more sense of things if we get a bit closer.'

Later, when Sorchal was rolled in his blankets by the fire, Masen took a short walk up to the crest of the rise. He was still desperately weary, but even with brandy in his belly he knew he wouldn't be able to sleep for a good while yet. At the top he sat down with his back to the wind and fished the horseshoe nail out of his pocket. Holding it up in the lee of his body, he watched the flashing sliver spin and settle, then oh so slowly drift around to point more or less due west.

Two rents in the Veil. Two Hounds. That explained the two attacks the clansmen had described, such a distance apart. He hadn't realised it was significant at the time – the legends said the Hounds were tireless, so it hadn't been much of a leap to assume they were also swift. Blessed Eador, no one but that seeker, Kael, had even *seen* a Hound in about a thousand years, so why would it occur to anyone to question the assumption that there was only one of them?

He stowed the nail away and stared out into the night, watching the moon edging down from its zenith. Two Hounds loosed.

A trinity moon rising. If those weren't signs and wonders like in the campfire stories his grandfather used to tell, he didn't know what were.

'I have a bad, bad feeling about this,' he murmured, and wondered if there was enough brandy left in his flask to drown it.

9

THE STUFF OF SAINTS
AND HEROES

☙

Moving by wagon was slow and uncomfortable for the sisters, even travelling at night to avoid the worst of the heat. Nonetheless they bore it stoically, taking turns to drive the mules, and at the end of each night's travel divided the chores of making camp and tending the beasts. Gair lent his strength and reach wherever they were useful, whether that was excavating a latrine pit in the bone-hard earth or rigging the tarpaulin between the wagon and a tree to provide shade.

When they travelled across the moon-silvered plain, he kept a close eye on their back-trail for signs of pursuit. Any plume of dust that appeared too large for a slow-moving mule-train or laden wagon sent the sisters off the road and into whatever cover could be found amongst the dry gullies and stands of scrub, until they could be sure it was not a party of soldiers or Cultist swords looking to finish what they'd begun at the Daughterhouse.

In between, when the road was clear and the night quiet but for insect-chirr on the wind, he rode alongside the wagon and kept Shahe reined in to the ambling pace of the mules. She tolerated this only for short periods, dancing and tossing her head in frustration. She wanted to run, and with nothing more urgent to occupy them his thoughts raced with hers: why he should never have come to Gimrael; whether he should have done more at the Daughter-house when the Cultists attacked. Even though he knew that accompanying the nuns out of the city had been the right thing to do and it served no purpose to wallow in what-ifs, he couldn't escape the sly stabs of guilt that told him he had let down an old friend.

But mostly his thoughts were fixed on the north. Every mile that passed under Shahe's hooves, every paling dawn that found him further from El Maqqam, brought him closer to Savin. The renegade *gaeden* haunted his dreams, the fractured halls of memory in which he loved Aysha and watched her die again and again, with Savin's handsome face reflected in every glistening tear, every drop of spilled blood. Laughing at him. And when he woke, and lay sweating in the shade of wherever he'd managed to rig an awning, surrounded by the whine of flies and Sister Avis's genteel snoring, he tasted something sour in his throat that no amount of water would wash away.

When they reached Zhiman-dar, tired and gritty-eyed from five nights on the road, he left the sisters to refresh themselves in the shady garden of a teahouse and, following the Superior's careful directions, took the wagon and team to the livery yard on Green Moon Square. Tal, the *jihad*'s contact, spoke good common and gave Gair directions to the souq, which would lead him down to the docks. Shahe didn't care for the hawkers and the crowds at the stalls, but Gair made faster progress through the press of people with her bulk to clear the way than he would have done on foot – although it did mean having to duck the awnings strung at random heights across the alleys if he wanted to avoid throttling himself.

The souq was as brawling and raucous as he remembered. Harsh sun striking off pale stone, thick heat scented with spices and perfumes – he even thought he saw the chicken-shooing woman in her gaudy veil. There were a few more deep desertmen, too, each with a *qatan* on his hip, but he saw no yellow sashes. If the Cult had increased its presence in Zhiman-dar, they were not advertising themselves. Good news, of a sort, but he still felt a chill down his spine when any of them stared at him a little too hard or too long.

It was a relief to finally emerge from the soupy heat of the souq onto the street that led down to the docks. The morning sun was eye-searingly bright, but his *kaif* did a surprisingly good job of shielding him from the worst of it, and a suggestion of a breeze took the edge off the temperature. The wharves thronged with ships both large and small, landing cargo and taking on new stores. Bulging nets swayed from cranes, stacks of crates and barrels appeared and disappeared at the hands of bronze-backed stevedore teams that communicated in whistles and gestures with barely a word of spoken language, whilst gulls cackled and shrieked overhead.

The instant Shahe's hooves hit the cobbles she was swarmed by gap-toothed, grinning wharf-boys in ragged trousers and not much else. They were hard-handed and wiry, like the souq-rats they resembled; he guessed they eked out a living holding horses and running errands along the waterfront for coppers.

'*Ishi sulqa, sayyar!*' they cried, running alongside the horse. '*Ishi!*'

Gair shook his head at their pleas, and one by one they dropped back as he rode further up the quay, scanning the moored ships for any under a recognisable flag.

A blue and white painted hull at the next dock caught his eye. Something about her looked familiar. Her lazily flapping ensign showed an imperial crest and her home port's blazon in the opposite quarter, and he was grateful he'd paid attention all those summers ago when Uncle Merion had taught him how to interpret a ship's ensign. Cockle shells on a scarlet chevron meant the vessel's home port was the White Havens in Syfria. Perfect.

He turned Shahe towards the next dock, intending to speak to the vessel's master. A small shape darted across his path and he pulled up. The last remaining wharf-rat stood at the mare's shoulder, a solemn-faced specimen of nine or maybe ten years. He didn't beg or chatter, just held out his hand and let Shahe snuffle it, then stroked her neck, all without the mare even attempting to nip him.

Gair took that as a good sign and nodded his agreement. The boy nodded back and trotted along next to the horse as Gair walked her to where the blue and white ship was moored.

Teams of seamen were busy unloading what looked like pig iron and stacking the ingots onto a waiting wagon, leaving little room for foot traffic. He left the boy holding his mount and picked his way amongst the ropes and bollards to the foot of the gangway where stood a burly mate with his arms folded and a belaying-pin through his belt. The man cast a jaundiced eye over Gair's desert garb, lingering pointedly on the hilt of the *qatan* protruding from his *barouk*, then shifted his weight as if settling himself for a possible exchange of blows.

So the ship's master was nervous about the reception he'd receive in Zhiman-dar. Gair wondered what had happened here in the last few days, and if the news had filtered up from El Maqqam. Gimrael was no longer a safe place to be, even for Gimraelis.

He dropped his sand-veil to show his face, but before he could say anything to the mate a voice hailed him from the stern deck.

'Gair?'

He looked up. The shirtsleeved man leaning over the railing was Captain Dail, which meant the blue and white painted ship was the *Kittiwake*. No wonder she had looked familiar.

'Blow me down, lad, come aboard, come aboard!'

'Expecting trouble?' Gair asked as he climbed the creaking gangway to the deck.

'A precaution, is all,' Dail rumbled. He glanced along the wharf, then lowered his voice. 'I spoke to some other captains in the harbour master's office, and they told me the northern merchants

87

are finding it difficult trading here just now. A few too many yellow signs on doors, if you know what I mean.'

Gair knew all too well. 'It's only going to get worse, judging from what I saw in the capital,' he said.

The captain eyed Gair's desert clothing. 'And I'm guessing that's why you're rigged like a native o' these parts.' He scratched his beard ruminatively. 'I think this might be my last run south for a while. It grieves me to make it with an empty hold, but I can't seem to take the desert heat as well as I could when I was younger. Cooler waters might suit me better for a spell.'

'If you're heading north again, I've a cargo for you.'

Blue eyes sharpened. 'Oh aye?'

'Me, one horse, and thirty-four Syfrian nuns.'

Dail's brows shot up. 'Blessings be! Is this a mission of mercy?'

'Something like that. The Cult burned down the Daughter-house in El Maqqam and they have nowhere to go but back to their cloister. I can't pay much, but I'll give you what I can.'

He dug in his pocket for his purse but the captain waved it away.

'No need. Ask their Superior to make out a warrant and the Church can pay me when we get to Syfria. Is Alderan not coming with you?'

Dail knew Alderan from years back. Gair had to tell him, but saints, the words lodged in his throat like fish hooks. Spitting them out was painful.

'I'm afraid not. He was trying to save some books from the flames, and . . .' He couldn't finish, but didn't need to. Dail's eyes clouded and he looked off through the forest of masts in the harbour towards the open sea.

'She comes for us all, eventually,' he murmured. He was quiet for a moment, then brought his attention back to the present with a visible effort. 'If you can be here and ready to board before the end of the first dog watch, we'll be away on the evening tide.' His beard twitched as his lips pursed. 'And if you've a mind, mebbe then we'll share a tot for the old rogue.'

'We'll be here – and I'd like that tot very much.'

Dail gave him a brisk nod and strode off, booming for the bosun. Gair made his own way back to the dock and retrieved Shahe from the urchin he'd paid to hold her. He had one more errand to run in the city, then he'd be able to leave Gimrael for good.

Navigating carefully back through the noise and bustle of the souq, he found his way to N'ril's house with only one wrong turn, but when he knocked on the blistered door and asked the house-boy who answered for N'ril, the name was met with a shake of the head. From the houseboy's mixture of simple Gimraeli words and mime, Gair learned that his friend was not there.

He slid Uril's *qatan* from his sash and held it out.

'Tell N'ril seven,' he said. The count was most likely higher, but of seven he was certain. 'And my thanks.' He wished he could say more, explain that the sword and N'ril's teaching had probably saved his life, but he was already stretching his meagre vocabulary of the desert tongue to its limit.

The boy took the weapon with a solemn bow, then scampered away. In less than a minute he was back with Gair's longsword, wrapped in a cloth.

After the whisper-thin blade of a *qatan*, the longsword felt clumsy and crude. Nonetheless the worn leather grip was familiar, and his hand closed around it as instinctively as a baby's around a proffered finger. He was reluctant to let it go again.

ᄋᐢᄋ

True to his promise, Gair brought the sisters to the dock before the dog watch rang out, and the *Kittiwake* sailed with the tide some two hours later. Once she was clear of the harbour, he stood at the stern-rail to watch Zhiman-dar fall into the sea behind her, its blocky buildings pinpricked with bright lamps to welcome the advancing night.

El Maqqam was too far inland for him to see any smoke, but in his mind's eye it smeared across the southern horizon like a greasy thumbprint, the way he had seen it as he shepherded thirty-three frightened nuns and their acerbic Superior through the sleeping city and left Alderan behind.

He'd had a week now to adjust to Alderan's absence, but the world still felt slightly off balance. The old man had given him so much, not least the first tools to begin to master the Song. Deciding to go with him to the Western Isles had so shaped the course of Gair's life that the sudden loss of him left a hole into which, every day, a little of the sun's warmth drained away.

He looked down at his hands on the rail. He'd relived the scene in the plaza more than once in the last few days – sometimes consciously, trying to puzzle out where and why his control of the Song had gone awry, and sometimes in dreams, further spoiling his sleep. Each time, when he woke, he held up his hands and was surprised to see whole skin: the pain, the flames, had been so real that he'd felt death's hand on his shoulder before the darkness claimed him.

Soft footsteps sounded on the deck behind him, and the whisk of long skirts; he turned to see the Superior approaching.

'Good evening,' she said, coming to stand beside him.

He inclined his head. 'Superior. Are you well?'

'I am, thank you. The sea air is so refreshing after all the heat and the dust. I think it agrees with me.' She rested her hands on the rail and watched a pair of porpoises arcing through the ship's wake, her eyes narrowed against the setting sun. 'And how are you feeling, my son?'

'I'm still a little sore, but the wound is mending.'

She hadn't been asking about the cut along his rib, and the twitch of her lips said she recognised his evasion for what it was but graciously let it slide.

'Captain Dail tells me we should make landfall in four days if this wind holds. It will be good to see the green fields of Syfria again.'

'Have you been away for long?'

'I was born there, but I've spent most of my adult life in Gimrael. I've not been back to the convent in Syfria since our previous Superior died and I was appointed in her place – more than ten years ago now.' She gave a short, disbelieving laugh and shook her head. 'How time flies.'

'Once we land, I would be honoured to accompany you back to your cloister,' Gair said.

'Oh, we'll be quite safe, don't worry. Sofi and Avis can see the sisters to the convent.'

He raised his eyebrows, curious. 'You're not going with them?'

'No,' she said. Her face grew very still, made more stern yet by the severe white wimple that framed it once again. 'The Lector needs to hear of this outrage, Gair, and first-hand, not by messenger. I intend to take word to Dremen myself.'

From the White Havens to Dremen overland would take weeks. 'That's no small journey.'

'I'm not afraid of the saddle.'

'There's trouble with thieves along the highways. You should take an escort – surely the Governor would provide some men-at-arms for you? I'd go with you myself, if I could.' The Superior knew he was an excommunicate; there was no need to explain to her what would happen if some Church official got wind of what he was. He'd be dragged off to the stake, and she'd likely find herself in a whole world of trouble to boot.

'I understand. Besides, I think there is somewhere else you need to be, eh?' Her shrewd gaze flicked up, caught his. 'Something's driving you, Gair. I can see it.'

The acuity of her regard was so unsettling he had to look away. 'It's personal.'

For a moment he felt her watching him, taking the measure of him somehow, and it made him increasingly uncomfortable. Then she murmured, 'So I see,' and turned back to watch the sunset.

In the ship's wake, the porpoises gave a last leap, sleek bodies shining, and disappeared into the darkening water with barely a splash.

'You remind me of someone I used to know,' she said, after a while.

Her comment caught him off guard. 'I do? In what way?'

She flashed him a brief smile. 'A good one, don't worry! Like you, he was stone-stubborn with a strong sense of honour. Rather more than was healthy for him, if I'm honest about it. The stuff of saints and heroes,' she said whimsically, and then sobered again. 'He was a Knight, too.'

Something in her tone hinted at loss. Gair wondered whether the man she'd known had gone to the Goddess in the desert war, but before he could say anything the Superior dug something from a pocket in her habit and held it out to him.

'Sofi brought this out of the chapel with the pyx. I think you should have it.'

From her fingers dangled a small silver medallion on a fine chain. Gair didn't have to look closely to recognise the face stamped into it.

'I can't accept that – I'm not a Knight.'

'And I don't have the authority to make you one, but you have acquitted yourself in the best traditions of the Suvaeon Order and that deserves recognition.' The St Agostin medallion swung back and forth in the breeze, winking.

'Superior—' he began, and then stopped when he realised he had no idea how to say what he wanted without sounding rude or ungrateful. He tried again. 'I only did what was right – it doesn't make me anything special. If I wore that I'd feel like a fraud, pretending to be something I'm not. Besides, if anyone from the Church caught me with it . . .'

Her lips pursed as if she was about to argue with him, then she

92

gave a crisp nod. 'Understood.' The medallion and chain vanished back into her pocket and she turned to leave. 'I'm sorry about your friend, Gair, truly. He is in my prayers, as are you.'

After she'd gone, Gair remained at the stern-rail, staring southwards and remembering. Friends gained and friends lost, and the tiny, sharp-edged reminders of Aysha he had found, which cut into him like slivers of glass. Only when the lights of Zhiman-dar had finally disappeared into the dark line of the horizon did he turn his back on the desert. He had to focus on what lay ahead of him now. Finding Masen, delivering his burden of news. The Order's agents in the Havens and Mesarild had been lost last year, along with the Yelda safe house, so Fleet was the most likely place to start looking if he couldn't snag the Gatekeeper's colours directly.

Overhead, the hard-bellied sails shone pink as seashells in the fading light. The wind blew his hair around his face, tugged insistently at his shirt and urged him on his way. His journey south had come at too high a cost, with nothing to show for it. Now it was time to strike back.

His fists bunched, tight enough to drive his fingernails into his palms. *And see Savin dead.*

10

THE WHITE HUNTER

ଚ୶

Hushed voices dragged Tanith from a fitful doze.

'You should not have left the clearing.'

'How was I to know the stones would take me somewhere else? An arrow struck—'

'You cannot leave the path, no matter what you see or hear.' Owyn's anger was only barely contained, his words a viper's hiss. 'There is danger here and we have scarce entered the wildwood. When you are with me the woodsong protects you, but if I have to leave you, then wherever you are you must not move, must not draw attention to yourself in any way. Memories are awakening in the depths of the forest which are best not brought into the light.'

'And you knowingly led her into this?'

'Events can outpace us all, Astolan. When I agreed to guide her, I did not know what awaited us here. Even with the forest stirring I can protect her, but two to watch over is more than twice the trouble – especially when they do not heed me!'

Ailric did not respond to the rebuke. Tanith was about to sit up when his next words held her still.

'She must go back. Return to her home. Her life is too precious to risk on concerns that are not hers.'

'She spoke to me of the Veil and of a reiver who means to tear it down,' Owyn said tersely. 'It seems to me that should concern us all.'

'Humans!' Ailric spat. 'This so-called reiver is a human – let the humans deal with him, if they can. This is no business of Astolar, and none of its future Queen.'

Shock hit her like a blow to the breastbone, robbing her of breath. *He's as bad as Emelia and the rest. Worse: he should know me better.* Then she understood. Ailric believed he knew her better than she knew herself.

Owyn was speaking again; she dragged her attention back to his deep voice. '—not think she will be easily swayed from her course. She has spirit, that one.'

'You can tell her it is too dangerous, that she must take the long road if she is bent on making this journey. Give me time to persuade her.'

'I will not lie, not for you or any man. Not for any reason.' The coldness of Owyn's tone bordered on contempt, implying that he considered Ailric's motives to be less than worthy.

'Her people need her! She should be with them, in a role that befits her station, not running through the woods putting herself into danger for humans.'

'That may be so, but she has made her decision, Astolan. As I have made mine. Do not press this.'

Owyn was too soft-footed for her to hear him walk away, but from the nickering and the chiming of buckles, he had set about unhobbling the horses ready to move on.

But Ailric she sensed like a fire at her back, burning with frustration and with something darker, fiercer. She heard him mutter a curse and the crudity of the words appalled her.

When had he become this man? His disdain for humans had hardened even more than she realised; it was blinding him the way it blinded the Ten, who saw only what happened within Astolar's borders as being of import and wilfully ignored a threat greater than anything they'd faced since the Founding. She shut her eyes. Or had he always been like this, and *she* was the one who had changed? A hand touched her shoulder.

'Time to go, my love,' Ailric said, smiling down at her. His face betrayed nothing of the heated words so recently exchanged with Owyn.

'How are you feeling?' she asked, sitting up. 'I was worried about you.'

'I am well enough. A headache and some strange dreams is all.' He helped her to her feet. 'Owyn has scouted the way ahead and says it is clear. We should move on.'

Clear of what? Tanith wanted to ask, but kept it behind her teeth.

With no sun to see and too much cloud for shadows, she had no way to guess the time. Noon, perhaps, or close to it. She tied her bedroll behind her saddle and mounted up, taking station between Ailric and the forestal.

The glade remained as silent as when they had first found it, but once beyond the encircling oaks the woods breathed again. Small, quick things scampered amongst the leaf-litter and birds flitted through the canopy overhead, their flight punctuated with brief torrents of song.

As the forest changed around them, Owyn's flute played a subtly different melody. Fewer beeches and oaks grew here, more ash, elm and dark-toothed yew. The trees themselves were more widely spaced, admitting more light, but instead of ferns and shrubby undergrowth, the forest floor sprouted only brambles amidst lichen-scarred limestone slabs that mimicked walls and stairs, as if the wood had swallowed the ruins of some great city. Yet through it all the forestal picked a way that gave the horses sure footing and did not require him to pause his eerie, mournful song.

Time and again Tanith smelled the same dark, dank odour she had detected in the portal clearing. A hint of standing water, or old earth newly turned. A stale sort of scent: a little unpleasant, but not in itself perturbing. If Owyn felt any threat he gave no indication of it, walking tirelessly ahead with Tanith's reins looped over his arm. He followed no obvious path, the kind deer or badgers might have made, but he made turn after turn without pause or uncertainty and his music always danced around them.

She watched the bright strands turning in the air. They appeared thicker, slower, more like honey than the fluid, rippling light of the day before. When she touched one it clung to her fingers for a few seconds before drifting away behind her. Carefully, she called the Song and held it, looking around at the wood.

Now she saw the glowing threads were only part of the pattern in the air. The music surrounded her in shifting, swirling, near-invisible lines. Where they touched tree or briar they coiled it into their embrace; where they touched stone they stretched out in a veil. Individual strands wove together and then parted, gyred like smoke from a dying fire, then passed out of sight entirely. So enthralled was she that she did not notice Owyn had stopped walking until tension on the reins tugged her horse to a halt.

Still playing, he shook his head.

'I should let go of the Song?'

A tilt of the head. Yes.

Taking one last look at the intricate, ethereal patterns around her and wishing she could have studied them, Tanith released her power. They faded into the air, leaving only the lambent trails from Owyn's flute as they continued their journey.

Without sight of the sun, judging the passage of time in the wood was almost impossible. The music had a somnolent quality, too, rather like a lullaby; Tanith found it all too easy to lose herself in it, let it wrap her up in a drowsy inattention reminiscent of lazy afternoons on a riverbank with nothing to do and nowhere to go, when even thinking required too much effort . . .

The chattering alarm-call of a bird jolted her out of her doze, heart racing. A blackbird swooped across the trail ahead, chattered again and vanished.

Just a bird, she told herself. Spirits, it had given her a fright – the horses must have startled—

With a sudden rush of wings every bird in the leafy canopy fled.

Owyn lowered his flute, the final note wavering into the air and finally into silence. Slowly turning in place, he scanned the gloomy trees. As his gaze passed over Tanith she saw his wariness, the caution of a wild thing caught on unfamiliar ground.

'Owyn?' she ventured. He held up his hand, his meaning plain.

Ailric urged his horse forward. 'The lady asked you a question.'

This time the forestal slashed the air with his hand, his teeth bared in a snarl. Lips thinning, Ailric turned his head away, clearly irritated at being silenced in such a peremptory fashion.

Before Owyn could complete his circle, drumming hooves sounded off to the left of the trail. Branches snapped and whipped, and a dozen or so hinds flashed across the trail and off into the trees on the other side. Behind them came a glossy-coated stag with a full rack of antlers, smooth and sharp as if he'd run straight from full summer. Breath rasping, he pounded after his herd and was gone, leaving only shivering leaves behind.

A chill of foreboding settled over Tanith's skin. Those deer hadn't been startled; they'd been terrified. But no predator emerged from the deep woods in pursuit. In fact, nothing stirred at all: not an insect, not a squirrel. Even Owyn was still, moving only his head as he searched the surrounding forest for signs of danger.

Then she smelled that odour again. Stronger now, ranker, and she knew what it was. The smell of fear.

Slender figures flitted amongst the trees, swarming over the rocks with darting, supple movements. They had pinched faces crowned by shaggy, moss-like hair, and such clothing as they wore consisted of scraps of leather and fur cobbled together with thongs. Where their pale skin showed through, it was whorled with tattoos.

'Flee!' cried one of the creatures, voice shrill as a weasel's shriek. 'He comes!'

The cry was taken up by the others. 'He comes!'

'The Hunter comes!'

'The White Hunter!'

'Flee! Flee!'

Chattering like sparrows, the creatures scattered into the gloomy yew and hemlock underwood.

'Owyn?' said Tanith, dread dragging at her heart. 'What were those creatures? Who is the Hunter?'

'Woodlings,' he said. 'They are shy and easily startled, but I have not seen them this frightened in my lifetime.' He paused, listening intently, but though she strained her ears she could not hear anything but her own accelerating heartbeat. 'Something stirs.'

Another party of woodlings chased after the first. Silent, this time; the only sound was the pattering of their hands and feet as they leapt from branch to rock to earth, the brief swish of leaves marking their passage. They were gone as quickly as they'd appeared, every ounce of their energy spent on putting distance between them and whatever lay behind.

Other creatures followed. Squirrels, snuffling badgers, a vixen and her cubs, yellow-eyed and anxious.

Something stirs.

Abruptly Owyn swung around and slung the reins back over her mare's head. 'We must go. Now.'

He put his flute to his lips and began to play. Rich and plangent, the woodsong spread out over the group like a warm winter cloak, and Tanith immediately felt comforted. Chirruping to her mare, she urged her after Owyn who had set a smart pace into the trees ahead.

The route he took led between banks of bramble scarcely far enough apart for a horse and rider to pass. Low branches forced her to duck; arching briar-stems plucked at her coat. Yet Owyn never faltered, his feet carrying him over and around obstructions without the loss of a single note.

Where his music spread, leaf and twig were gilded as if by sunlight. Colours shone more brightly and the air smelled of summer rain and growing things. Beyond it, though, the under-wood grew dim as the dark days of winter. Shadows clustered thickly beneath the trees. A twisted hemlock bole became a leering face; the branches of a shaggy yew leaning over the track became arms reaching out to snatch Tanith from her horse.

She blinked and the trees were trees again. When she looked directly at them, she saw them for what they were, but as soon as she glanced away the corners of her vision were peopled with half-seen eldritch figures, flitting from trunk to trunk as they kept pace with the horses.

There's nothing there, she told herself, fixing her eyes on the back of Owyn's coat. Just shapes in the shadows – except shapes in the shadows had given her the terrors as a child, and she couldn't shake the itching, crawling sensation on the back of her neck that said someone was watching her. Off at the edge of hearing, almost lost in the flute's song, someone laughed.

Her head snapped around to follow the sound. 'Did you hear that?' she asked Ailric.

'The bird?'

'No,' she said, eyes searching the shadowy underwood. 'It sounded like laughter, out there.'

'That was your imagination,' he scoffed. 'It was only a bird.'

She frowned, irked by his tone. 'I know what I heard.'

But whatever her ears had told her, her eyes showed her nothing but rocks and trees and folds in the ground, made gloomy and foreboding by the bright ribbon of Owyn's music floating through the air above her. Perhaps her imagination *was* playing tricks on her: the wood was so close and airless, almost holding its breath in anticipation, that combined with the shadows it was more than enough to set anyone's spine prickling.

A broken branch dangled from an elm tree beside the trail, the damaged limb suspended over the path by a hinge of bark. She ducked under it, then gasped at a rush of air across her head that felt as if something had swiped for her neck and missed.

Behind her, Ailric swore and she looked back to see him fending off the swinging branch with his arm. Glowering, he wrenched the broken piece from the bough and threw it into the undergrowth.

'That almost took off my head.'

'I didn't touch it!' she protested.

He dusted bits of bark off his palm on his leathers. 'You must have. Branches do not move of their own accord.'

'I didn't, I swear!' His face said he didn't believe her. 'I am *not* imagining things, Ailric.'

Something *had* set the branch to swinging without her touching it; she *had* heard laughter amongst the trees. She was sure of it, and instead of making her doubt herself his scepticism only hardened her conviction that they were not alone in the wood.

A flicker of movement at the corner of her eye snagged her attention, but when she looked ahead, all she saw was Owyn beneath his ever-changing canopy of music. Tanith frowned, peering intently into the trees.

'What is amiss now?' Ailric grumbled.

'I'm not sure.'

Searching for those sprite-like figures was fruitless, so instead she fixed her gaze on the forestal's shabby coat again and waited. Either they were growing bolder, or she was getting better at seeing them: within a few seconds, the insubstantial shapes had reappeared at the very periphery of her vision.

There.

A twitch on the reins brought her mare to a halt, Ailric close behind on the narrow trail. The darting forms faded, then a gaunt face peeked out from behind a tree to her left, sharp-eyed and cruel. Others clustered around it, wispy as ghosts.

'There,' she breathed. Her eyes watered with the effort of not looking directly at the face. 'Do you see them?'

'I see nothing. What should I be looking for?'

'Creatures in the trees.' Her breath curled around her face on the air. The sudden chill pinched her cheeks, tweaked painfully at her ears. 'Watching us.'

'It is your imagination, nothing more.'

The pale, pointed face bared its yellowed teeth at her. Above its head the last twisting gleams of Owyn's woodsong winked out and the misty breath of winter wove through the trees. Where it passed frost bloomed on every rock, furred the edge of every leaf. Tanith began to shiver.

'You can't see them when you look straight at them, only out of the corner of your eye,' she whispered. There was a crowd of them now, peering through the trunks of a clump of alders. Thin as reeds, white as bones, watching her with ice-bright eyes and hating that she was warm.

'Where?' Irritation edged Ailric's voice. 'Show me!'

'By the alders to the left of the track.' Leather creaked as he shifted in his saddle behind her. 'Don't turn too far or you'll not see them.'

Now the closest face was leering at her, eyes glittering like mica flecks. Too-long fingers gripped the alder trunks as the creature squeezed its crooked body between them, and frost spread out-wards from its touch.

'I see nothing but trees.'

'But it's . . . right . . . *there!*'

Cold gripped Tanith's bones. Her facial muscles were so stiff she could scarcely move her jaw to form the words. Tears formed and froze on her lashes. *Oh spirits it's so cold colder than winter colder than death.* Her breath sparkled into crystals before her face. *Colder than the space between stars.* 'Don't you see it?'

He gave an impatient sigh. 'Tanith, there is nothing to see.'

The nearest creature tipped its head on one side and its grin widened. A bony arm unfolded towards her. One knobby finger extended, the yellowed-ivory talon reaching out as if to lift her chin. Tanith tried to jerk away from it but her muscles were paralysed by the cold. She couldn't even move her jaw to shout out. The creature's smile grew predatory.

Dear spirits are you blind it's right in front of me why can't you see it the others are coming closer they dart tree to tree like birds head cocked they're listening for something moving faster now I have to get away but I can't move oh dear spirits I'm so cold I can't move it's closer reaching out help me Ailric I can't move—

A bump against her leg. Something big. So white around her, so cold. Man's face, breath curling around his mouth. Pretty, like feathers in the air. Cold.

'Tanith?'

Me. Yes. Cold. Shaking her arm. Crackle as flakes of ice fell away. Sleepy now.

'Tanith.'

Sleep.

'We have fallen behind, love.' More pretty white feathers. 'Owyn is waiting.'

Owyn? No. Not me. Leave me alone. Want to sleep.

'We must go.'

Sharp crack. Whinny. The world lurched, jolting Tanith into motion.

No. Stop. Jab in her belly. Brown shape by her face. Her thoughts stirred again. She struggled to sit up, but she was jouncing, bouncing. Jab in the belly again – saddle horn? Yes. She was on a horse, a brown horse *oh spirits so cold*. Her limbs were stiff as baulks of wood, her hands knotted into lumps on the reins, but she had to get away from this white, white place.

'We will freeze to death here,' Ailric shouted and smacked the mare's rump again. She lurched into a canter, throwing Tanith back into the saddle. With aching, burning muscles, she fought to keep her seat.

In only a few strides woodsong was winding around her, wrapping her up like a thick down comforter after playing in the snow. As the preternatural chill fell away, with it went the creeping forms at the edge of her vision. Her blood began to warm and stir again. She gasped and sucked in a lungful of moist forest air.

Warmth. Blessed spirits, she hurt. Her limbs throbbed as circulation returned to them; she wanted to curl into a ball and sob.

'So cold,' she mumbled.

'We will soon have you warm again.' Ailric draped his jacket about her shoulders and she pulled it close, soaking up the heat that lingered from his body. 'What happened?'

'Why didn't you see them?' she asked. Huddled inside his coat, she looked up, but Ailric's question hadn't been for her. He was staring at the forestal, his face hard.

'Tell me, Bregorinnen!' he demanded. 'What danger do we face here?'

Owyn, pacing back and forth in front of their horses, kept playing his flute. Warm golden notes floated above him like little pieces of summer. Where they drifted into the forest the frost melted away, but not far. Winter lurked in the gloom of the underwood to either side of the trail, only held in abeyance by the strength of his song.

For a long, long moment he held Ailric's gaze, then shifted it to Tanith.

'I'm all right,' she said, trying and failing to find a smile. 'Cold, but all right.'

He dipped his head, but his eyes held a warning. Then he loped ahead again, leading them on into the wildwood. Tanith urged her mare to follow him.

Ailric brought his black alongside again, matching the horse's pace to hers. 'Are you sure you can ride?'

'I'm fine,' she said, one hand holding his coat around her, the other gathering the reins. Her fingers tingled as her warming blood reached them. 'Let's not fall behind again.'

Fussing with his reins, he cast a sharp glance up the trail at the forestal. 'Can we trust this man? He has done nothing but lead us into danger.'

That wasn't entirely true, but Tanith was too weary to argue. 'I trust him.'

'I would have been happier if you had not chosen to make this journey,' Ailric said. 'You should not be risking yourself like this.'

'It was my choice.' Tanith flexed her fingers to help restore her circulation. Though the chill was gone, it had bitten deep. She dreaded to think what would have happened if the creature had touched her. 'Thank you, Ailric. If you hadn't got me out of that cold, it might have gone badly.'

His face softened and he smiled. It lit up his flame-coloured eyes, and he gave her a graceful little bow from the waist. 'I am at your service, love. Always.'

Ailric took her expression of gratitude as licence to stay by her side for the next hour, even on stretches of the trail that were barely wide enough for one horse, much less two. It took several reassurances that she was quite all right – and a whippy branch or two across his face – to persuade him to resume his position behind her.

When the long forest dusk finally dipped towards night, Owyn called a halt at an ancient oak, its bole so thick that even if the three of them joined hands they would not have been able to encircle it. Beneath a dense blanket of leaves, its mighty roots ridged the forest floor like the legs of a sleeping giant. Nothing grew in its shade, not even ivy.

As Tanith and Ailric tended their horses and prepared a cold supper, Owyn walked the perimeter of the oak's reach and played his flute. The woodsong rose into the air to cluster amongst the young green leaves overhead, each note glowing like a fire-fly, each phrase a constellation twinkling in the canopy. Done at last, he sat down with his back against the trunk and let out a long sigh.

Tanith brought him a cup of water and a plate of food. He

looked tired. Deep lines that she did not remember seeing before scored from his nose to either corner of his mouth and shadows hollowed his eyes.

'Thank you.' He sipped the water but set down the plate untouched.

'You should eat,' she said. 'You need food and rest.'

'I know.' He closed his eyes, laid his head back on the furrowed bark.

She sat down on the dry leaves at his feet.

'Owyn, what did I see? When the air became so cold?' He didn't answer, but opened his eyes and focused on the glimmering canopy overhead. 'Ailric says I was imagining things, but he felt the cold, too. I know he did.'

'All that means is that he did not see anything. It does not mean there was nothing to see.' The forestal sat up, rubbing his hands over his face. 'Long ago, there was a great winter. Snows came from the north and there was no spring, no summer to send them back again. Winter blanketed the land, cold to crack your bones and freeze your blood. The animals fled or perished. Even the Grove was marked by it and so the forest remembers.'

'That's what the woodlings were referring to.' *Winter as a hunter, clothed in white. Subtle, silent and killing everything in its path.* She shivered, remembering the crushing grip of the cold she had felt on the trail.

'The woodsong protected you from it, until you strayed out of its reach.' Owyn sampled the cheese on his plate and appeared to find it to his liking, as he broke off another, larger piece and popped it into his mouth.

'So what were those creatures I saw, watching us?'

'Elementals, most likely. Winter spirits. They ride on the Hunter's coat-tails like crows after a storm.'

'I see.'

The forestal, slicing an apple in half, shook his head. 'No, my lady, you do not.'

She stared at him.

'In the heart of the wildwood, the trees remember. All that is past, everything, and sometimes they dream. You saw one of those dreams for yourself, beyond the runestones.'

The wounded warrior. His blue eyes, not understanding, then widening in shock as the lance-head burst from his chest. *I'm sorry!*

How much Owyn saw in her face she did not know. She looked down at her hands, twirling a dried oak leaf between finger and thumb.

'We are not beyond the runestones now. The dream of the White Hunter has broken free and is roaming the forest.' He bit into the apple and chewed. 'Have you ever had a nightmare, lady, from which you could not wake?'

'Yes.' *Ever since Chapterhouse.*

He swallowed, dipped his head. 'Then now you see,' he said.

Carefully, she asked, 'Are we in danger, Owyn?'

'Not here.' He patted the thigh-thick root beside him. 'Oak for protection and woodsong for shelter. We will sleep safely tonight. Tomorrow you will be in the city and the White Hunter will be far behind you.'

'And you? Will you be safe, returning to your people?'

Dark eyes twinkled. 'As safe as you will be in a city, I think. In the wildwood, one treads more lightly than three.'

She smiled and left him to his supper. Her own was waiting, next to Ailric, but she felt too restless to settle and paced awhile under the spreading boughs of the oak, watching the flicker and glow of the woodsong on its leaves.

Mesarild tomorrow. With luck, an audience with the Emperor. Glancing down at her well-worn leathers, she made a wry moue. Perhaps this was not the best first impression to make, but her message would be the same, whatever she wore. Spirits willing, the weight of her warning would be enough.

11

HOPE

꤀

The blizzards had moved on across the Broken Land, leaving the landscape blinding white and so unfamiliar in its mantle of snow that Teia hardly recognised it. Even the figures riding away from her were rendered anonymous by their thick furs, hoods pulled well forward against the driving east wind and its burden of stinging ice crystals.

She let her viewing swoop closer, arrowing in on one particular figure. Ana's leather-brown face was creased with concentration, dark eyes narrowed beneath a fur-mittened hand as she squinted at the horizon. No mountains marched across the sky, only the gentle folds of the plain, confirming the clan's direction of travel: north.

A fierce pang of loss drove into Teia's chest. All she wanted to do was fling her arms around her mother and hug her tight, but the gulf between them was too great now, in more ways than simple physical distance.

Macha keep you, Mama. I will come back, I promise.

The sentiment sounded hollow. Even if she could cover the leagues between them, a fear lurked in the corners of her mind that there might not be anything left to come back to. Maegern would not easily be stopped.

Blinking away tears, Teia watched her mother ride on until she was no more than a speck in the waters. Only then, as the clan drew away, did she realise how few of them there were. The same number of horse-sleds followed each family, with elders who could no longer ride tucked amongst the baggage and tent skins. The same herds of livestock were chivvied along by boys on nimble ponies with dogs bustling at their heels, but there were fewer goats and sheep to flick their quirts over, and only a handful of spare horses.

Her heart sank. The clan was moving north but the warriors were gone. Though their thick clothing made it next to impossible to discern their gender, she knew that almost every one of the figures she watched was female. Every man who could lift a spear, from the grizzled veterans to the youths bristling at any suggestion that they were still boys, had stayed with the chief.

And her da would be with them. He'd not been a war captain since before she was born, when he'd almost died in the desperate battle that finally ended the Stony River rebellion and secured the clan torc for Drw, but however scarred he was, he remained a fine horseman and scout. Drwyn would no doubt find a use for him.

Curse you, Ytha! You and your by-the-Eldest ambition – if you hadn't begun this, my father would be safe! We would all be safe, and I would still be with my family!

Her viewing wavered in the heat of her rising anger. She kept it locked on Ana's distant figure, ignoring the tug towards the Speaker. With practice she'd learned how to avoid being distracted by random thoughts, but there was still too much she didn't understand to risk straying too close to Ytha.

A commotion at the entrance to the shelter finally broke her concentration. She looked up from her scrying bowl; the brightness of the snows in her viewing had deepened the gloom around her, and all she could make out were vague shadows swaying like spirits across the blanket that served as a curtain. Urgent whispers hissed back and forth between them. One of the voices sounded like Isaak's.

Letting her power go, she lowered the bowl to the floor. 'What is it, Isaak?'

The young warrior ducked inside the curtain, his bow in his hands. His face was leaner now, as all of theirs were, and pinched with anxiety beneath his shaggy curls.

'Banfaíth,' he began then hesitated, fiddling with the elk-horn nock on his bow as if unsure how to proceed. 'Varn says there's someone ahead of us.'

Her first thought was that it might be Baer, but she quickly realised that he could not have overtaken them from so far behind, not without leaving tracks. This was the only route through the mountains below Tir Malroth; they'd taken enough wrong turns into blind canyons to be sure of that.

'How many?'

'Three, maybe four men on horseback.' Isaak scratched the back of his neck. 'Not seen them myself, but Varn's got a good eye. He says he saw them coming down from the next ridge, before they disappeared into the forest.'

'They're heading towards us? Northbound?'

He nodded. 'More or less.'

Men from the Empire? It was possible but unlikely, with the stone forts standing empty. More Lost Ones, then, living in the high meadows? Even more unlikely, unless they had feet the size of a shrew's: they'd seen no bigger tracks in three days.

'There's no other way for them to go than through this valley?' She inflected it as a question to give herself time to think, though she was sure what the answer would be.

'It all funnels down to the river hereabouts – and too steep for horses to go any other way.'

So she had to assume these strangers were hostile – most likely Drwyn's men, scouting out the pass that she had been so sure they'd leave alone for fear of the Haunted Mountain. She quailed. *Oh, Baer, I could use you now!*

But there was only one thing she could do. No other choice remained, if she was to protect her people.

She twisted onto her knees and grasped Isaak's arm to haul herself to her feet. 'We must prepare a welcome for them.'

'Banfaíth?'

Teia forced her voice level, tried to sound how she imagined Ytha would in such circumstances: calm, assured, in perfect control. 'Ready your best bowmen. If we must meet these men in the valley, let it be on our terms.'

℘∞

Young Isaak might be, but he had learned well from Baer. He sited their ambush at the narrowest point of the valley, he and his three archers placed in good cover on the far side of the river, where it ran close to the trees, with a pair of spearmen concealed on the near bank to close the trap. They'd hidden their tracks by moving into position through the dense pine forest; to a traveller coming towards them from the ridge, the snow stretched unbroken to the river bend. If Lord Aedon favoured them, their guests would suspect nothing until it was far too late.

'What can you see?' whispered Lenna, and was quickly shushed by Neve.

Teia let their words sluice over her and disappear, like leaves in a stream. She held her focus on Isaak, hidden in the trees with the other bowmen. He had a good vantage point there, with lines of sight both up the valley and down to the place where the trap would be sprung without having to move and give himself away. All that remained now was the waiting.

She was no warrior; she couldn't second-guess his plan, or argue the placement of the fighters at his disposal, so it was fruitless to fret over it. What would be, would be. Only the Eldest knew how it would play out.

The image in her little basin skewed abruptly to the left as something caught Isaak's attention. Hidden as she was with the rest of the band in a gully well above the ambush site, she was too far away to hear anything but the chatter of the river; she could only wait until whatever Isaak had seen revealed itself.

Lenna and Neve leaned closer, their breath clammy on Teia's face as they attempted to share her viewing.

There. Shapes moved at the edge of the trees on the south side of the valley. Three horses, maybe four; she couldn't be sure. The tree-shadows stretching over the snow were too dense and the basin of water that held the viewing too small to make out more than an impression of the riders. She waited, trying not to let her shivers disturb the image.

Faintly, she heard a voice. Crunching snow, a horse snorting. The images sharpened as the riders emerged from the trees: three men, each wrapped in thick plaid. One of them led a well-laden pack pony. The breath of men and beasts floated after them like smoke on the still air.

So they were Drwyn's scouts after all. But they were coming away from the pass? That didn't make sense. Teia frowned, her viewing blurring as she lost focus. Unless they'd done what they came to do and were returning as instructed.

'What's happening? Is it Isaak?' Lenna's voice, then Neve's, sharp with admonition.

'Hush, child! Let her work.'

Heading away from the pass into the Broken Land, carrying supplies for a long journey. Foretelling fluttered at the back of Teia's mind, a bird trapped in the cave of her skull. The dusty smell of its feathers tickled her nose, then great wings swept her up and with powerful beats carried her into battle.

Arrows sang. Horses whinnied and men shouted, in triumph, in despair. Death came, spreading her black cloak over the battlefield as a thousand ravens settled upon the dead and began to feed.

Cold water soaked Teia's legs, wrenching her back to the

present. Neve was shaking her shoulder with one hand as the other attempted to pry the half-empty bowl from her numbed, cramped fingers. Lenna had tears in her eyes; beyond her, the rest of the camp stared fearfully, huddled amongst the trees.

Teia swallowed, then wished she hadn't. Her mouth tasted of blood and something worse. She turned her head to spit into the snow but couldn't muster any saliva.

'Water,' she croaked. 'Please.'

Neve filled a cup from a water-skin and gave it to her. Teia rinsed out her mouth first then drank the rest.

'Slowly, girl. Sip it,' Neve said, stroking her hair back from her face. 'You went awful pale.'

Lenna was near frantic. 'What happened? What did you see?'

'Foretelling,' Teia said. How could she be so cold, yet feel so hot? It made her dizzy. She held the cool cup to her forehead and closed her eyes.

'An ugly one, too, I think. There now, it's over.'

The gentle touch of Neve's fingers reminded Teia of her mother, when she was sick as a little girl.

I miss you, Mama.

Abruptly exhausted, weary down to her bones, she leaned towards the older woman and let herself be folded into an embrace.

'I'm sorry,' she whispered against Neve's prickly woollen shawl. 'About Baer. About everything. I'm so sorry.'

'Hush you now. Don't fret.' A hand rubbed her back. 'There's naught to be sorry for.'

But there was. If she'd not argued with Baer, he would not have gone back down the trail to prove her wrong – or right. If she'd not been so insistent, he would still be alive. A sick headache began to pound her brain.

The snap of bowstrings carried over the rush of the river. Shouts followed, a horse whinnying. Teia sat up, peering downhill through the trees. All around her the other Lost Ones did likewise, some of them springing to their feet to see better. Then a man screamed.

She flinched, and Neve's arm tightened around her. *Please let Isaak and the others be safe. I couldn't bear their deaths on my conscience!*

More shouts. Someone running through the trees towards them. Faces froze into expressions of dread, women and men poised to fight or flee. A few minutes later, Varn scrambled into view, his bow on his shoulder.

'It's over!' he shouted. 'We've got their horses, supplies, everything!'

With Neve's help, Teia got to her feet. 'Are the others all right?'

He winked at Lenna. 'Not a scratch.' The girl sagged with relief.

Macha, Teia's head hurt. She couldn't seem to spin her thoughts into words – could barely manage a nod of acknowledgement. She ought to go down and see what the men had found, but even the thought of it left her daunted.

Come on, girl. You're leading these people now.

Moving slowly under the physical weight of her belly and the mental burden of the foretelling, Teia struggled onto Finn's back and guided him carefully along the gully to the junction with the main valley.

Down by the water, two men were dragging arrow-struck corpses into a ragged line. Between them, two others held the reins of the riderless horses and the pony, whilst Isaak poked through its packs. He looked up when Varn hailed him and came forward to greet Teia.

'Banfaíth,' he said, with a dip of his head. He tried to look unruffled, but a boyish grin kept sneaking onto his face.

'So what do we have, Isaak?'

With the toe of his boot, he turned the head of the nearest dead warrior towards her. Even without the snarling wolf's-head tattoo on his cheek she would have recognised him from the war band, though his name escaped her.

'Crainnh,' she said. 'All three?'

'All three.' He turned the other heads to show her. She recognised them too and flinched at the last, with one eye put out by an arrow. Ulloch would never again play knucklebones with her father for coppers.

All Crainnh. Chilly fingers stroked Teia's spine, turning the sweat there to ice-rime. *If word got back to Drwyn now . . .* 'None got away?'

Isaak shook his head. 'There was only the three and we brought 'em down neat as you like. They didn't have time to do much more'n yell.'

No one would be riding back to Drwyn from the Haunted Mountain after all.

Teia's head went light and the valley slewed and darkened. Macha's ears, she was going to throw up. Clutching the saddle horn, she shut her eyes tight, waiting for the feeling to pass.

'Banfaíth? Are you sick?'

'I'm fine, Isaak.'

Except her stomach wouldn't settle, rolling like a pot on the boil. Acid burned at the back of her throat. She swallowed it down and straightened up, cautiously opening her eyes. Sunlight on the snow was still too bright, water over rock too loud, but she had to overcome the nausea. Put herself beyond the pain and be the Banfaíth the rest of them expected to see, however she felt inside.

It was easier to say than do.

Isaak was hovering at Finn's head, an anxious frown creasing his brows. She dredged up a smile for him, hoping it looked less sickly than it felt.

'You've done well,' she said. 'Those provisions will make a great difference. I suggest we camp here and make the most of them. A hot meal and a few hours' rest will do us good.'

Thinking about food made her unruly stomach surge again. She pressed a hand to her breastbone and wished she had some bidewell root left amongst her simples. Will-power wasn't quite as effective – even if it did taste better.

'Have those bodies stripped before they stiffen, and get Neve to see to it that the clothes and any blankets they had are distributed to those who need them most.'

Isaak bobbed his head. 'As you wish, Banfaíth.'

He strode away, shouting orders to the Lost Ones emerging from the trees.

Teia turned her horse to follow him. The riverbank was exposed and the wind was finding its way through her clothes again. Her belly had grown so large now that even oversized men's garments didn't fit, and gaps were forever opening up as the wretched things came untucked.

Letting Finn's reins lie on his neck, she held her mittens in her teeth and worked both her hands under her coat to retrieve her shirt. A squeeze or two of her calves kept the horse walking whilst she struggled to right her clothing. So many layers, and they all had to be loosened and straightened and buttoned up again; if it wasn't for the need to void she had half a mind to get Neve to sew her into them. At least then she'd stay snug.

Finn stopped, and Teia looked up. Ahead of her the snowy pines spilled down to the water's edge in a tangle of rocks and deadfall, piled up all silver-white like the bones of a monstrous beast. Strange; she didn't remember seeing that before. It took a second or two's casting around to recognise the place. They'd climbed this little ridge from the other side, further up through the trees, precisely because of that rockslide. She clicked her tongue in annoyance at herself. Stupid girl. In her distraction she'd ridden straight past the spot where Isaak and the others were making camp.

Teia pushed her cold hands into her mittens and gathered up the reins again.

'Come on, my lad,' she muttered. 'Back we go.'

As she swung the big dun around, she heard dry wood snap in the trees above her.

Her bow was with her baggage, with Neve and the others, but she wasn't defenceless. Her magic was already rising, a sweet, fierce music singing into her muscles.

'Who's there?' she called, scanning the trees upslope. Her heart pounded; she cocked her right arm up and back as if she was about to hurl a weapon. 'Show yourself!'

Nothing moved amongst the dark trunks. The light was dim in there, the snow thickly slatted with shadows from the bright sun above, putting Teia at a disadvantage. She didn't dare move, though, for fear of what she might be blundering into. Curse her inattention!

Slowly, she scanned the trees again, from left to right. Someone was watching her, she knew it – she *felt* it, deep inside. The magic hummed, and all around her the quiet intensified. Not the quiet of nothing there, but the quiet of someone trying not to make the slightest sound.

A glint of sun on metal caught her eye, but she deliberately looked past it and used her peripheral vision to make out a sliver of shadow too irregularly shaped to be a tree-trunk but perfectly matching the silhouette of a shoulder and arm holding a bow at full draw.

Let him think I haven't seen him. If he'd wanted, I'd be dead already. Another of her father's lessons.

Pulse accelerating, she shaped her magic into a long stick, and with a flick of her fingers smacked it into the snow-heavy treetops immediately above the bowman's hiding place.

Snow whumped down. Arms flailed and someone let out a very girlish shriek as a winter's-worth of cold landed on her head. Teia urged Finn up into the trees towards the sound. She had another fist of air ready to smack her stalker silly when she got there, but she didn't need it. The figure spluttering and floundering in the snow was ragged and coltish, all legs and elbows. No breasts or hips to speak of, straight black hair cut short like a boy's, and frost-pinched, bony features. A mulish set to her cracked and scabby lips warred with black eyes just this side of bursting into tears. She was all of fourteen years old; not that much younger than Teia herself.

'Who are you?' Teia demanded.

The girl didn't answer, busy scuffing snow from her hair and shaking it out of her clothes.

'There's more snow where that came from, you know.'

'Go ahead – can't make me any colder.' A sullen glance, face hot with embarrassment, then the girl began kicking through the drift, looking for her bow.

Releasing her magic, Teia almost felt sorry for her. Her shabby clothes were far from adequate for the cold, her hands so pale and thin they resembled a bundle of chicken bones. 'What's your name?'

'Aelfen.'

'Why were you pointing an arrow at me?'

The girl's foot unearthed one end of her weapon. Dropping onto her knees, she scrabbled it free of the snow, turned it over and exclaimed the wet string. Teia sighed. The conversation was distinctly one-sided.

'Aelfen. Why were you—'

'I wasn't sure who you were, all right?' She sniffled and dragged her cuff across her nose, dark eyes shining and angry and desperately hurt. 'I wasn't sure if it was true. That you were a Speaker, like Ulf said.'

Teia frowned, puzzled. 'Ulf?'

'Our chief – or he was. Told us lots of things were true as true and they turned out not to be.' The girl's shoulders slumped and her head dropped. Her fingers plucked restlessly at the damp bowstring. The littlest finger on her left hand stuck out oddly, swollen and black with bruising to halfway up the edge of her hand.

An idea began to form in Teia's mind.

'You're hurt,' she said gently. 'I have some medicines that will help, if you like.'

Aelfen glanced at her finger. 'It's broken,' she said.

And I've a feeling I know who broke it, too. 'I can make knitbone tea, and set it properly. It'll never mend straight if you leave it like that.' She waited for a response and didn't get one. 'It's up to you.'

One shoulder lifted, an almost-shrug that meant nothing but said far too much. 'Hafta find my arrow. Ain't got so many I can afford to lose one.'

Without another word, she hunkered down and resumed digging through the snow where she'd found her bow. Teia watched her. She had no pack or supplies, and those clothes would never keep her alive overnight up here. Even a girl – a child – could be a scout for a larger party.

Carefully, she drew her magic in again in case there were other, better-concealed bowmen in the trees. 'How far behind are the others, Aelfen?'

'Not far. An hour, maybe.' The girl paused to blow on her hands to warm them, then suddenly scrubbed her fingers over her scalp, leaving her hair sticking up in all directions. 'Damn lice.'

Teia blinked. The girl had sensed the power. 'They're a problem, aren't they?'

'Sometimes. Must be hungry with the cold – they're biting something fierce.' Aelfen went back to digging in the snow. A few seconds later she pulled out her arrow with a triumphant, 'Ha!'

No. Aelfen couldn't have the gift, could she?

'Will you close your eyes for a moment?' Teia asked.

Busy plucking the bedraggled fletching straight, Aelfen frowned. 'What for?'

'Just do it, and tell me what you feel.'

With a theatrical sigh, she did as requested.

Teia waited to be sure she wasn't peeking, then crooked her finger and summoned a tiny light, no bigger than a blushberry. At once the girl rubbed her hands briskly up and down her arms.

'Cold?'

'Damn lice again,' she grumbled. 'Brought their friends this time. Can I open my eyes now?'

The girl did have the Talent. Macha's mercy, what were the odds of finding a gift in the middle of the mountains?

'Yes, of course.'

Aelfen did so, and immediately blinked at the pale yellow globe hovering at Teia's shoulder. 'So you *are* a Speaker.'

'I am Banfaíth to the people camped further downriver.'

Aelfen beamed, wide enough to wrinkle her nose like a hound pup's. 'Then you're who I came to find.'

ര⁊

The daylight was fading by the time the first folk came creeping through the trees. Teia enlarged her light and sent it higher to show them the way, and in twos and threes they made their way down the slope towards her, and the other Lost Ones who'd come up from the camp to stand with her, after she'd told Isaak what was happening.

They were in a poor state – if anything, worse off than her own little band. Ragged men and women, clutching bundles and peering uncertainly around them, shepherding a few big-eyed, silent children. As Neve and the others came forward to welcome them, some of the women started weeping out of sheer exhaustion, their wet faces shining in the light of Teia's magic.

Leading a pony in the middle of the group was a limping, unshaven fellow in hard-worn clothes. A newly grown iron-coloured beard matched the long braid over his shoulder and half-hid the elk-head tattoo on his cheek.

'You're back.' It was all Teia could think of to say. Seeing his familiar face was almost like seeing her father again.

Baer nodded. 'Aye.'

He folded his arms and grinned at her, and she was torn

between kissing his hoary cheek with relief and slapping the impudence out of him.

'And about time, too!' exclaimed Neve, pushing past to fling her arms around him. Teia turned away, too pained by her own losses to watch the joy of their reunion.

In the deepening twilight, Isaak led the way back along the shore to the camp. Baer followed, with Neve at his side. A tightness around his jaw said whatever his injury was, he was making less of it for her benefit – just as her eyes said she wasn't the least bit fooled. Like an old wedded couple, Teia thought, chirruping Finn after them, still playing the game long after they'd each learned the other's moves.

She counted heads as she rode along and her heart sank. Her little band had roughly doubled in number. How on earth had she imagined they would feed everyone? The newcomers had precious little to share, and only a couple of the men looked fit enough to hunt. But they had bows, which would be useful. More eyes to keep watch. She squashed down the yammering voice in her head that said they were more mouths to feed, that the thick meat pottage she saw simmering over the fire up ahead would have fed her own band of Lost Ones for two days. They were cold, hungry, frightened people who'd made a long and arduous journey to find her. She would not leave them on the mountain to die.

Later, she sat near the fire with Baer, enjoying the first bowl of tea made with nearly fresh leaves that she'd had in weeks, thanks to the Crainnh warriors' supplies. The pony's packs yielded a goodly amount of provisions, but shared out amongst fifty-two mouths, there would be barely enough for another day or two. Maybe four, if the men could start some game to eke it out. But for now there was enough to give everyone a hot meal, with a few dried berries each for after. Once the cooking was done, the men had fed the fire in the communal pit to a mighty blaze, as much for the light and comfort it would bring to the new arrivals as for the heat, and Teia was almost able to call herself comfortable.

Across the fire, Aelfen sat hunched over her bowl, bony arms folded in around it as if she expected someone to try to take it from her. She ate fast, and without really looking at her spoon, her eyes constantly darting, searching for threats in the shadows.

Pain, Teia thought. *Pain and hunger and never feeling safe.*

'There's a story there,' she murmured.

'Who, Aelfen?' Baer followed the direction of Teia's gaze. 'I'd say so.'

'Did she tell you anything?'

'No.' He scraped his spoon around his bowl after the last bit of pottage. 'She's all spines and thistles, that girl, but I saw which way the wind was blowing.'

'He abused her, this Ulf?'

'Reckon so.' Squinting into the flames, Baer sighed. 'Reckon he'd helped himself to all the women old enough to—' He stopped, corrected himself. 'All the ones old enough.' The spoon clattered into the bowl and he stretched his legs out towards the fire. 'That's better. Bit of hot food makes all the difference.'

'It's good to have you back,' Teia said. 'I felt sure we'd never see you again once we crossed the mountain.'

'Aye, well, you nearly didn't.' Face turned away, he prodded at the end of a branch protruding from the fire with his boot. 'I lost four in the high pass because they didn't trust me enough.'

Memories chilled Teia in a place hot tea couldn't reach. 'I'm sorry to hear that.'

Baer made a non-committal sound. 'They were frightened from the start. When they saw the dead walking, it was too much for them.' Another kick shifted the branch and sent a column of sparks into the night. 'You know, for a bit of a girl, you've a good arm on you.'

She blinked, thrown by the subject shift. 'What?'

'They're the same Lost Ones we fought, like you guessed. That fellow you skewered was Ulf.'

There was something about the way he said *was* that alarmed her. 'I killed him?'

'No, but the wound had gone foul for lack of care,' he said, rubbing at a knot in his thigh. 'When I found them, the poor bastard was half-mad with the pain and the stench. Raving about coming after us and having his revenge – not even his own warriors could get sense out of him.' Shaking his head, he sipped at his tea. 'That's no way for a man to die.'

Hardly daring to ask, not sure she even wanted to know the answer, Teia said, 'What happened?'

'I sent him on his way.'

Baer didn't elaborate. From what he had already said, it was a mercy – and if their suspicions were correct, a sort of justice for Aelfen and the other women. Yet the silence between them asked for something, an acknowledgement, perhaps. A word to say she approved, or at least understood.

She looked down at her tea-bowl, cradled between her hands, then made herself look at him. 'I see.'

'Some of his men left the next morning, but the rest of the band came with me. Seems they'd heard how we had a Speaker. Thought it was a good omen.'

'So you brought them here.'

'Couldn't leave 'em behind, now, could I?'

Her own words, back at her. No malice, though; no bitterness. He might not have agreed with her decision but he respected it. Easing his thigh again, he winced.

'Thank you, Baer,' she said. 'Now what happened to you? You'd best tell the truth, before Neve bursts.'

He chuckled. 'Fell on my arse, didn't I? Turned it black and blue as a stormy sky.' Further around the fire, Neve snorted. 'It'll mend,' he added, with a wink for his woman that, to Teia's surprise, made her blush like a maiden.

Later, when the shelter was quiet and all the women were rolled in their blankets and the warm fug of unwashed bodies, Teia sat at the entrance by the embers of the fire, wrapped in her own blankets. For all she was as exhausted as the rest of the Maenardh, she couldn't sleep. Her child was kicking, and her supper sat so sourly in her stomach that if she lay down she felt as if her gullet was afire. So she sat listening to the women snore, now and then poking the embers with a stick just to watch sparks shoot up like glow-flies, and tried to pick apart her last foretelling.

Weeks had passed since she'd seen a vision unbidden like that. All her dreams had been of darkness and foreboding, but no images had come to her in the daylight. Was her future clearing? Had the balance of her fates finally shifted? The only way to know would be to scry again, but her body was too weary to carry her outside into the cold night and there was no privacy in the women's shelter. Or was there? She looked around the shelter behind her. All were asleep, pretending to be, or had their backs turned to her. As long as she did not wake them with a shout, she was as good as alone.

Quickly, before her courage deserted her, she dug her bowl from her pouch and filled it from the nearby water bucket. Settling herself as comfortably as she could with backache and indigestion, she drew in her will and focused it on the water.

Darkness at first, as always, impenetrable and forbidding as death. She reached further.

Show me.

The music tingled over her skin, raising every hair until her clothes prickled against her as if they'd been washed in itchweed. Sparks crawled across the surface of the water and dripped to the ground from her hands, where they vanished. The darkness quivered. Closing her eyes, she summoned still more power.

Show me what I seek!

Magic rose up inside her, gyring higher and higher. Down her arms, out of her hands into the bowl, into her vision of what was to be. She opened her eyes again and the darkness blew into fragments.

The women's tent was gone. Instead Teia sat on flat slabs of stone, almost lost on a plain of silver-tufted grass dotted with yellow and white flowers waving in the wind. The air was soft with spring and the sun smiled down. She looked back over her shoulder and saw her shadow stretched out over the cracked and weedy stones towards the fishtailed peak behind her, no longer so ominous with the sun on its face.

Behind her.

Teia began to laugh. She was facing south, with the mountains at her back. Ahead of her lay the Empire, and it looked exactly like home.

12

NORTH

ഏ

Yelda was not a beautiful city. Upriver, its architecture tended towards the four-square, with russet tile roofs and pale stucco walls, its streets and squares laid out in a direct if rather staid grid pattern. Downriver, by the docks, the smelteries squatted toad-like beneath a permanent pall of smoke and noise. From his vantage point on the crest of a hill overlooking the wide river valley, it put Gair in mind of a red-headed labourer who'd donned a clean shirt to receive company but forgotten to wipe the muck off his boots.

Stretching his legs in the shade of a towering oak at the side of the road, he sipped water from his canteen and watched the barges plying the broad expanse of the Great River. There was little sign here of the previous winter's devastating floods: the river was busy as a highway, the land around it exuberantly, almost fervently lush with leaf and blossom. Further south had been a different matter. Many of the shops and residences in the Havens still wore their scars in the high-water marks on their crumbling render, but it was the smaller towns and rural communities that had suffered the most. Fields that should have been rippling with barley or wheat lay bare and blackened, empty farmhouses bleaching like skulls in the sunlight. Nothing good could grow in that rancid, salt-spoiled silt. Even the birds had fled, leaving the skies silent.

Gair took a last mouthful of water and contemplated emptying the remainder of the bottle over his head in an effort to cool down. He'd been glad to leave the floods' devastation behind, but the further inland he'd ridden the worse the heat had become. Sweat was gathering uncomfortably around his waist, despite having his shirt open to the last button; for a northman like him, Syfria's humidity made even a spring day harder to bear than the open furnace of Gimrael.

Shahe, grazing the verge next to him, had no such difficulties. After sulking for the first day to register her displeasure at the sea voyage – and the indignity of being winched into and out of *Kittiwake*'s hold in a sling – she had adapted to the climate magnificently. Even the change of diet hadn't unsettled her, though he was careful to ensure she didn't gorge herself on too much new grass.

He patted her shoulder. 'At least one of us is comfortable, eh?'

She flicked an ear, but otherwise ignored him.

He stoppered the canteen and hung it back on the saddle. It was time to get moving again. His arse was finally accustomed to the seat of a Gimraeli saddle, which was just as well with so much ground to cover.

Dipping into the Song, he sought Masen's colours. Alderan had not given him much clue where he might find the Gatekeeper beyond the far north, nor how current a location that was, so all he could do was keep searching as widely as he was able while he travelled. A vivid flare over on the far side of the river caught his attention, but on closer inspection it resolved into several individuals, none of whom he recognised.

At a guess that was the new Yelda safe house, replacement for the one Masen had reported lost last year. If he called on them, they would provide shelter for him and Shahe, maybe even a bath. He'd had a swim the day before yesterday, but a pond was no substitute for hot water and soap. The *gaeden* there might even have a few more specifics about the Gatekeeper's whereabouts.

For a moment he was tempted, but then decided against it. Making camp in the open was no real hardship and a bit of dirt wouldn't kill him. Better to ride late and be away early, without disturbing anyone. It would only lead to questions – about himself, about Alderan – that he had no stomach to answer.

His search found no sign of Masen. He reached further, skimming over the outlying villages, the small towns that were strung like beads along the river and roads. Amidst the muddy smear of humanity in general a few untrained talents appeared as brighter points, but nowhere did he see the spruce-forest blues and earthen reds of the Gatekeeper's colours.

Gair drew in his will and a sour note quivered through the Song he held. Not much, not yet, but it was enough to put him on his guard. Like the twinge in his side whenever he took a deep breath that said the sword-score along his rib was not yet healed, that faint harmonic was a warning, the shifting coils of an adder before it struck. With Resa in the Daughterhouse chapel he hadn't known what it was; he thought he'd done something wrong when he tried to Heal her. After the events in the plaza during the nuns' flight from El Maqqam, he'd realised that something more was amiss. Something worse.

His thoughts drifted back to the scarred sister. Was it familiarity after the journey together that had made the scars' cruel sneer look softer, her smile easier, when she bade him farewell on the Haven-port dockside? Or had he really helped her with his impulsive attempt at Healing? He'd probably never know. She was gone now, returned to the cloister with the other sisters, and their paths were unlikely to cross again.

Another warning tugged his attention back to the task at hand. Quickly, he concluded his wider search but it was as fruitless as the others. No Masen. He let the Song drain away and pulled a pair of deerskin riding gloves from his belt. Time to hide his own scar, regardless of the heat of the day. Yelda was the crossroads of the Empire, its third most populous city, and it was no place to take chances.

Gloves on, he gathered Shahe's reins and mounted. North of the city, dust drifted over the head of the valley. Only thousands of feet could have raised such a plume, or many, many horses. That meant soldiers. Garrison rotation, perhaps, or maybe more trouble in the Arennorian marches. Either way the roads would be choked with that soft red dust all the way to Mesarild unless he could get ahead of the source.

With a squeeze of his calves he urged the mare into a walk, then a rolling, mile-eating canter. The most direct route north should be the high road through the city. Smaller roads through the outlying villages would have less traffic, but having only ever come through Syfria by riverboat he wasn't sure of his way. The city it would have to be.

By the time he reached the south gate, though, he had to rein Shahe back again. Wagon after wagon blocked the road, their mules complaining noisily, their drivers swinging up and down from each other's seats to talk and laugh. By the side of the road, a group of army officers, buttoned-up in imperial green and mirror-polished boots, waited with their horses in the shade of a stand of moss-hung trees, looking hot and bored as they passed water canteens amongst themselves.

Gair rode up the verge to the head of the queue. The gate was completely blocked, even to foot traffic: one of the wagons had cast a wheel right at the gatehouse. It was surrounded by curious onlookers, some of whom offered helpful – and not so helpful – suggestions to the detachment of sweating soldiers heaving meal-sacks off the wagon-bed to lighten it in readiness for the wheelwright. He eyed the long line of stalled carts. This queue could be set for the rest of the day or gone in an hour; there was no way to tell.

Swearing in frustration, he turned Shahe around and headed back up the road towards the trees. He might as well follow the officers' example and get out of the sun for a while. He found some shade on the far side of the oaks and dismounted, looping Shahe's reins over a broken branch. When he'd watered her and slackened off her girths to make her more comfortable, he turned to find one of the officers leaning against the tree trunk, watching him.

In age somewhere north of thirty, the officer's mahogany skin and black eyes said he was desert-born but he wore no *zirin*; instead his raven hair was cropped short in the military fashion, neatly combed and oiled to a high shine. Though his uniform was the same imperial green worsted as that of the soldiers unloading the wagon, it had been cut and fitted to flatter the man's trim physique, and the double row of buttons had the soft gleam of real silver. A dandy, then; the kind who could afford expensive tailored uniforms and didn't care that he might be called upon to ruin them.

'She is beautiful, *sayyar*,' he said in impeccable common, with only a trace of an accent. 'May I ask, what is her breeding?'

Gair hung the canteen back on his saddle. A dandy he might be, but the man had an eye for a horse.

'She's by Lord Kierim's warhorse, out of one of Uril al-Feqqin's mares. I'm afraid I don't know any more of her pedigree than that.'

'Do I need to know more? That is an impressive bloodline.' The officer levered himself away from the tree and paced round Shahe to admire her from every angle, then made to pat her neck.

'Careful,' Gair said quickly. 'She bites.'

For emphasis, Shahe curled her lip and flattened her ears, and the officer backed up a step.

'So I see. Would you entertain an offer for her?'

'She's not for sale.' Gair held out his own hand and the *sulqa* pushed her velvety muzzle into his palm. Realising he'd sounded ungracious, he added, 'Sorry, I'm rather fond of her. She reminds me of someone I used to know.'

'Then I envy you. You clearly had a fine acquaintance.' A smile and a nod hid the man's disappointment. 'If ever you decide to breed her, I would be interested in one of her foals. Top price.' He offered his hand. 'Ysen al-B'kaa.'

'The sun smiles on our meeting, Ysen.' Gair returned the clasp. 'My name is Gair.'

The desertman's expression brightened. 'I see you have travelled the sands.'

'A little.'

'You have visited recently? I have been away too long, and I am eager for news from my homeland.'

Gair hesitated, trying to gauge how much he should say. The desertman was courteous and friendly, but there was no knowing if that immaculately tailored tunic concealed a tattoo in the shape of a many-rayed sun.

'El Maqqam is restless,' he said. 'The city governor has sealed the northern merchants' enclave and imposed a curfew on them.'

Ysen clicked his tongue. 'Cultists making a nuisance of themselves, yes?'

'Rumour says it might be so.'

A tight smile creased the desertman's face. 'Speak freely, *sayyar*,' he said. 'The Cult is not welcome in B'kaa lands.'

Gair relaxed a little. 'Then you should know that all is not well. I saw sun-signs over half the houses and shops in El Maqqam, trade is suffering and the place is rank with fear. Their bully-boys wear their allegiance openly and challenge anyone whom they think does not belong.' He gave Ysen a brief account of what had happened to the Tamasian nuns. The desertman shook his head as he listened.

'Bad business,' he said. 'They have not been so bold in many years. El Maqqam was always vulnerable, but not towns so far north. Zhiman-dar has always been the least conservative of our cities – *khalanjir al sho'meht*, they call her, because she opens her arms to anyone with money.'

One of the syllables was familiar, but Gair couldn't place it. 'The what?'

'Ah. Forgive me, it is not a polite phrase. *Khalanjir al sho'meht* translates as,' Ysen coughed delicately, 'the Whore of the North.'

N'ril's language had been gentler, but the meaning was not so different. 'I see.'

'I will dispatch a courier to the Warlord with this information at once, though I cannot think he will be pleased to hear it.'

The desertman looked away southwards and muttered under his breath. Restless black eyes searched the horizon. 'I should be there, not here.' He sighed, then flashed a wry glance back at Gair. 'But such is fate, eh? She makes hostages of us all. I took Theodegrance's shilling and he will release me only when it is spent.'

A ragged cheer from up by the gate said the wheelwright had arrived. The spectators began to drift away, the wagoneers returning to their charges. The queue would start to clear soon.

'Where are you bound?' Gair asked, adjusting Shahe's girths and preparing to move on.

'You have not heard?'

'I've been travelling since Saint Saren's. I'm a little out of touch.'

'The Warlord has ordered the Archen border forts to be regarrisoned, in defiance of the Emperor and Council both. He has taken the Sixth Legion north into the mountains, and the Ninth,' Ysen nodded in the general direction of the distant dust-haze, 'is bound for Fleet to replace them.'

The news jolted Gair upright. 'What's happened?'

'I have only hearsay to share,' said Ysen. 'You will hear as much and worse in the city, but it appears the Nimrothi clans are stirring again.'

With the Veil weakened? 'This is not good news.'

Ysen rocked his hand in a *perhaps, perhaps not* gesture. 'We shall see what awaits us. Too much peace is not good for soldiers, my friend.'

Another cheer signalled the wheelwright's work was done. 'Neither is too much war,' said Gair, swinging up into the saddle, and the desertman laughed.

'A hazard of our occupation, I fear.' He straightened his tunic, the gold rank insignia on his collar winking in the sunshine. 'May your road speed you, Gair.'

'And yours, too.' Impulsively, for even on short acquaintance he'd come to like the man, he added, 'I wish you good fortune.'

'Whatever God wills, I am content.' With a wave and a smile, Ysen walked back to where the other officers waited.

Gair urged Shahe up the road towards the south gate of Yelda and steered her into the first space between two wagons that opened up for him. After hearing Ysen's news it was now more imperative than ever that he find Masen, and quickly. It didn't hurt that that meant travelling further north, because in the north he had an appointment to keep.

Some seven miles out of Yelda, he overtook the column of marching soldiers. The long supply train winding through the city had held him up far longer than either he or Shahe was comfortable with; once clear of the gates he gave the black mare her head to run off her fidgets, then walked her through the cooling evening to find a place to rest. After a fitful night broke into a damp and misty dawn that promised another warm day to come, he was on his way again before the sun was more than a fingernail above the horizon.

North. It drummed in his head in time with Shahe's hooves on the road, held his attention as unerringly as it held a compass needle. When he woke in the night from another helpless, hopeless dream, he heard it in the pounding of his heart. *North.*

For two days it drove him onwards, the weather gradually cooling as he rode. On the morning of the third a sudden spring storm broke over the valley, turning the road into a sucking stew through which Shahe had to slog for twelve miles until they finally came to a wayhouse that still had rooms available. After seeing the mare dried and fed in a well-littered stall, he carried her sodden gear upstairs with his belongings to dry in his room, then lavished another silver sixpence on the use of one of the deep hip-baths in the inn's bathhouse.

A freckle-faced boy brought bucket after bucket of hot water to fill the tub, darting glances at Gair as he stood shirtless in front of the looking-glass on the wall over the washstands and attempted to pick out the stitches in his side with the tip of his knife. Sister Resa had made a fine job, but she'd used a sturdier thread than Alderan's boiled silk. A razor would have made short work of it, but lacked the narrow point required to lift the loop away from his skin. His belt-knife had the point but not the keen edge, for which Gair was profoundly grateful when it slipped.

'Damn it, I need three hands!'

He scowled at his image in the glass. Rainwater seeped from his sodden hair and trickled down his face like tears of frustration. Leaning his left elbow high on the glass, he tried again. In the reflection, the bucket-boy watched him.

'Yes?' Gair growled.

'Yon cut. Is't from a sword?' the lad asked.

'Yes.'

'Hurt some, I bet.'

'Some.'

Gair eased the dagger's tip under the first stitch and held his breath. A quick tug, a sharp sting in his skin and the loop slipped off the blade. Again. He bit down on a curse.

'Did ya kill 'im?'

Pretty sure I did. 'I didn't stop to find out.'

The boy swung his empty buckets back and forth as if contemplating some great thought. 'My ma's got scissors. Could fetch 'er for you.'

Gair lowered his arm and tried to be gracious. 'That would be a great help.'

'For a ha'penny.'

Despite being soaked to his bones and in an ill temper, he smiled.

'Be quick and I'll make it a penny,' he said, and the boy was off like a hare. A penny was a small price to pay to spare himself three flights of stairs to fetch his whetstone from his saddlebags, to say nothing of the potential for sliced fingers afterwards.

A minute or so later there was a knock at the door and a woman's voice asked if he was decent. When he answered in the affirmative, the door opened to admit a round-faced, round-hipped woman in a cook's apron, with a pair of embroidery scissors in her hand.

'My boy said you've some stitches need snippin'?'

'Yes, thank you.' Left side turned towards her, Gair raised his arm again. 'Forgive me, I've not bathed in a while.'

The woman's ample cheeks creased in a smile.

'Bless you, sir, I ain't feared of a bit o' sweat on a man.' She winked. 'Good beef needs a little salt in the gravy.' Deftly she snipped the stitches, then dropped the scissors into her apron pocket and picked out the threads. 'There now, good as new.'

Whether it was the saucy wink from a woman old enough to be his mother that made him careless or just plain weariness, Gair didn't know, but he was slow to keep his left palm out of sight. He didn't see her look directly at it, but her smile vanished and a tightness replaced the lines of mirth around her eyes. A hasty departure followed, the door closing after her with a disapproving thud.

He sighed. Would he never learn?

He had time to bathe and dress but not shave before the door opened again, without a knock this time. The man who stepped into the bathhouse wasn't as tall as Gair, but he filled the doorframe from side to side and carried a blackthorn stave through his wide leather belt. His scowl matched his beard for blackness.

'I'll thank you to show me your hands,' he growled.

Gair finished combing his damp hair and snapped the *zirin* in place. Without a word he held up his hands, palms out.

'Aye, that's what Cook said. Get your things. We don't want no trouble here.'

'What makes you think I'm going to cause trouble?'

The man rested his hand meaningfully on the thick knot in the end of the stave. 'We're Goddess-fearin' folk here, and there's children to think on. So be on your way, hidderling.'

There was no point saying anything. There was nothing he could say that wouldn't, in all likelihood, just make things worse. Gair picked up his wet clothes and walked out of the bathhouse, feet squishing unpleasantly in his still-soggy boots.

After he'd fetched the rest of his belongings from the room he'd paid for – whose bed he hadn't even had a chance to sample – and loaded Shahe up, he returned to the wayhouse common room. The burly fellow was standing behind the counter, his blackthorn stick prominently within reach. As Gair walked to the bar, conversation amongst the patrons at the battered tables dwindled to an expectant silence. Stares crawled over the back of his neck and all but struck sparks off the well-worn longsword on its baldric over his shoulder.

He dug a penny from his pocket and pressed it down on the polished counter with a snap. 'This is for the boy,' he said. 'I keep my promises.'

Mutters followed him to the door as he left. A few braver souls even shouted after him.

'Aye, get yourself gone!'

'Don't want no witch-kind here.'

Stools scraped back and feet scuffled on the wooden floor. Footsteps sounded behind him, becoming hollow on the veranda that ringed the building, no doubt to be sure that he left. Gair ignored them, though his temper twitched at his sword-hand every span of the short walk down the steps and into the yard. They were simple folk with simple fears. He should have expected no less in rural Syfria – nor anywhere else in the Empire, come to that – but the experience had left a hole in his purse and naught to show for it save the bath.

No one trailed him to the stables, but he felt them watching, imagined them peering around the corner of the wayhouse like children, half-curious, half-afraid. For one insane second he considered pushing the air around to detonate a thunderclap over their heads, then thought better of it. Amusing as it might be to make them jump, and an outlet for his poor temper, it would only provoke them. Someone would run for the nearest lector, and he'd have the Church on his heels again all the way north.

That was too great a risk to take just because he was out of sorts. He fetched Shahe from her stall, closed the stable door quietly and saddled her up, hoping all the while that the gawpers would get bored and leave him be. No such luck; they were still there when he rode back, glowering and blessing themselves as he passed.

Irked at being saddled again with a damp blanket, Shahe tossed her head restively as he urged her out onto a road still thick with mud, if beginning to steam under the suddenly blue sky, and turned north. He kept checking behind him, but no one followed.

Maybe it would be better if he avoided other folk altogether, no matter what the weather did. It only led to questions, suspicion. Loss, if they got too close to him, like Darin and Alderan. *Like Aysha*. A bitter pang twisted in his heart. *Like everyone I have ever cared about, even a little*. Maybe it was better to be alone.

As soon as the ground dried out enough, he left the highway for open country. Where northern Syfria rolled into southern Elethrain the towns were small, little more than a cluster of dwellings grown up around a wayhouse or coaching inn. The weather had turned dull and breezy but stayed mostly dry, so apart from purchasing provisions and grain for Shahe he had little to do with the inhabitants, and as often as not the only creatures to watch him ride through were stray dogs or a handful of geese on the green.

Five days after the unpleasantness at the wayhouse, the dense woodland either side of the highway forced him back onto the road as it climbed towards the hills south of Mesarild. It was a lonely stretch of the north road, the land surrounding it too steep for ploughing or too well wooded for sheep. The isolation suited his mood. On the odd occasion when he spotted a tell-tale plume of dust on the road ahead he made sure he stayed well out of sight; even with his deerskin gloves on he shied away from contact with strangers, just to be sure, and every few miles searched again for the Gatekeeper without success.

The nearest village was several miles behind him when Shahe pulled up lame in her off foreleg. Gair dismounted, soothing her with a pat before pulling up her foot to examine it. Her shoe was sound but she'd picked up a stone, wedged between the hoof wall and the frog. As he pried it out he heard, somewhere behind him, the distinctive creak of a bow under stress.

He lowered Shahe's foot and straightened up slowly, the sharp stone still in his hand.

'That's it, nice an' easy,' said a man with a rolling Syfrian accent. 'Lose the blade, friend.'

Gair unslung the baldric and hung it on his saddle horn. He'd only heard one voice, but he doubted the speaker was alone; like street dogs, brigands and their ilk usually ran in packs. From the speed with which they'd closed in, they must have targeted him some distance away, and Shahe's lameness had simply saved them the trouble of an ambush.

'I have nothing of value,' he said, turning to see an unpleasant yellow smirk at the hilt end of a levelled sword. *No bow. The archer must be in the trees.*

'Nothing of value, he says.' The fellow laughed. 'Yon horse should be worth a pretty penny, eh, lads?'

Out of the corner of his eye Gair saw two other men, both with shortbows drawn, creeping forward at the edge of the trees. Like the swordsman they were unshaven and dressed in clothes that had seen the hard side of several winters.

He reached inside for the Song. Time to dance. 'She's not for sale.'

The smirk widened. 'Not yet, anyways.'

'Not ever.'

With his right hand he hurled the stone at the swordsman, cutting him above the eye; his left hand swept a shimmering shield between himself and the bowmen. Bowstrings twanged and two arrows blew into fragments against the shield. Shahe whinnied, dancing back.

Cursing, the swordsman dashed blood from his eyes with the back of his hand, leaving his face streaked with scarlet, and raised his blade. Clumsy. Gair pivoted on one foot and drove the other into the fellow's midriff even as two more arrows shattered around him. The swordsman folded onto his knees, his weapon in the dust.

Before he could rise, Gair had his own longsword at the man's throat, the point pricking the soft hollow between the fellow's collarbones.

'Do it and die,' he growled.

The man stopped groping for his own blade, but his brown eyes remained surly as they glowered up at Gair along the sword. Behind him the other two brigands charged down the brackeny slope from the trees with knives in hand and ran into a wall of solid air that tumbled them onto their backsides.

The Song hummed uneasily. Gair's shield flickered then steadied again, but something *wrong* sawed across the music in his head like a rusty knife.

'I'm riding north,' he said, peripherally aware of the bowmen picking themselves up. 'You and your friends are going to ride south or east or any other direction you like, as long as it's away from me. I don't want to meet you again.'

The man swallowed, eyes flicking to the steel kissing his windpipe and back again. He nodded carefully.

'Then we understand each other.' Gair stepped away and sheathed his sword.

The three brigands collected their weapons and dusted themselves down, all the while shooting poisonous looks in his direction. Dabbing his bloody brow with his wrist, their leader glowered. Cowed, for now, but not broken.

'Any direction but north.' Gair kept his voice even. He walked to where Shahe waited, her ears flicking anxiously, and gathered up her reins in preparation to mount. 'I suggest you start moving.'

'Shadowkin bastard,' one of them muttered, and spat on the road.

As Gair swung himself into the saddle, something bounced off the shield at his back. He wheeled Shahe, saw a dagger winking in the dirt and thrust out his arm with the Song already raging. Fire blossomed up from the road and lit the brigands like torches.

13

NEWS

Tanith and Ailric were in the saddle again soon after dawn. The woods Owyn led them through now were not the tangled, gloomy caverns in which the White Hunter had so nearly trapped them, but wide halls of stately beeches, solemn oaks in glades barred with morning sunlight. The music from his flute was likewise lighter, more playful, borrowing refrains from the many birds that sang in the canopy above and trilling along so brightly that Tanith half-expected the thrushes and robins to join in.

From time to time she glimpsed traces of man's shaping hand as they travelled: a coppiced area through the trees with a smoking charcoal kiln at its centre, another nearby half-built; a crudely railed enclosure in which a couple of sows rooted through last year's beech-mast. The forestal flinched away from these places, seeking less well-travelled routes, but before mid-morning he halted beneath an oak tree dripping with spring rain and lowered his flute. Lines of strain deepened the creases at the corners of his eyes and his breathing came raggedly, as if playing their way had demanded more of him than air.

'Is something wrong, Owyn?' Tanith asked, reining up.

'I can go no further,' he said. 'These woods – it is difficult for me to find a way here.'

Ailric urged his horse forward and glared down at the forestal. 'You said you would take us to the edge of the forest,' he said curtly.

Tanith winced at his tone. He had never warmed to the Bregorinnen; in fact, since Owyn had rebuked him for disregarding his instructions and becoming trapped beyond the runestones, he'd been openly hostile. Now he was trying to use the height advantage of being on horseback to intimidate the man on foot.

'Ailric,' she chided, but the forestal was unmoved, meeting the stare calmly.

'All is well, lady,' he said. 'You will come to no harm this close to the road. Keep the sun to your right hand and ride straight, and you will reach it in less than an hour.'

'This was not our agreement.' Ailric scowled.

The look Owyn fired at him was laden with scorn. 'I made agreement with the lady, Astolan. You would do well to heed her.' He turned to face Tanith. 'I will carry word of what you told me to the Grove. I cannot say what the King will choose to do with the news, but at least his choice will be an informed one.'

'Thank you, Owyn. For everything.' Tanith dug in her pocket for the acorn token and offered it back to him, but he shook his head.

'Please, keep it. If you have need of me again, call for me at an oak tree. I will find you.' He gave a small bow, which in no way included Ailric, and lifted his flute back to his lips. As he began to play, a chattering blackbird burst from the oak's branches and she instinctively turned her head to follow its flight into the trees. When she looked back to say goodbye to Owyn, the forestal had vanished.

Tanith peered after him, straining her ears for the sound of woodsong, but heard nothing except the wind in the canopy and the patter of rain on leaves. 'He's gone,' she said. Not just hidden in the trees but completely absent, back within the wildwood that abutted this world, twined with it, but was no more a part of it than dreams were a part of the waking day.

'Surly wretch,' Ailric fumed. 'How dare he speak that way to me?'

'You haven't exactly been gracious to him,' she pointed out, urging her horse into motion.

The Astolan drew himself up in the saddle. 'I did not care for the dangers he led us into.'

'We brought most of those dangers on ourselves – you can't blame Owyn for them. It's thanks to him that we are here in one piece.'

'Yes, well.' Ailric fiddled with his reins. 'If you had travelled as befits your station, on the high road, I doubt you would have faced any danger at all.'

'Dear spirits – I'm a grown woman, not a piece of Isles crystal that has to go everywhere packed in lambswool lest it chips!'

'No, you are something far more precious,' he fired back. 'You are a Daughter of the White Court, a future Queen of Astolar! You cannot afford to be reckless with your safety.'

Tanith rolled her eyes. The same threadbare old arguments, and oh, how they wearied her. 'If I'd travelled the high road, with a company of men-at-arms like my father wanted, this journey would have taken five times as long – maybe ten times. Instead I'm within a day's ride of Mesarild less than a week after leaving home.' She looked over at him, wondering why she was having to explain this to him again when it appeared so obvious to her. 'I had to come through the wildwood, Ailric. This is far too import-ant to waste time over. The Empire needs to be warned.'

Exasperated, he flung out a hand. 'And why is it your task to warn them? You could have simply sent word to the legate and stayed safe in Astolar. Why come all this way yourself?'

'Because I had to,' she snapped. 'Because I was *there* when the Veil was torn, and I saw what Savin is capable of. Even if Emelia would have let me use the Court couriers to send a message, my voice will carry more weight in person than a few dry words on a piece of paper.'

Her voice hadn't carried much weight with the rest of the Ten, but she believed – she *had* to believe – that humans would perceive the threat for what it was. Surely they would remember the last rending of the Veil and understand. If they did not, and she found herself once more crying into the wind, more people than she could count were going to die.

Angrily, Tanith kicked her mare on. The sooner she got to Mesarild, the sooner she could be rid of him – though she would have to endure more of his sneering first, and there would be much for him to sneer about in the city, she had no doubt, from the architecture of the palaces to the stink of the middens. Of course, he would dress it as concern for her comfort and well-being: she should be travelling in a curtained palanquin to spare her the dust of the streets – and his eyes the sight of so many humans. An escort of soldiers would speed her way through the city – and keep the filthy creatures at a goodly distance, as if humanity was some kind of contagion.

Tears of frustration pricked at her eyes and she shook her head. Blessed spirits, what had she ever seen in him?

Another charcoal-burner's camp appeared ahead, two soot-stained men raking out their kiln, and before long the forest began to thin. Tanith glimpsed green hills ahead and a bright spring sky. Mature trees gave way to saplings and scrub, then she emerged into sunshine on a tussocky slope sparkling with the recent rain. Below them lay the wide ribbon of the North Road, with Mesarild's great redstone promontory dominating the southern horizon like a wedge of some enormous layered cake.

The imperial capital was considerably larger than she'd imagined. Truly told, it was vast. For a moment all she could do was sit her horse and stare, and wonder how the blessed spirits she was going to find the Astolan Court legate's official residence in such a huge city.

Reining up beside her, Ailric cast a jaundiced eye over the city's aggressive breadth, its buttressed walls and the towers that punched up towards the sky, and grunted. 'It looks like an anthill,' he said. 'Where lies the legate's palace?'

Tanith ground her teeth but tried to stay civil. 'It's on the Queen's Round, up by the Citadel. Father gave me the address, but we can get directions at the gate.'

Dismay quickly became distaste as he eyed the road below them. Farm carts and merchants' wagon-trains were churning its surface to mud, and he sighed. 'Very well. The sooner we can get there and into civilised company, the better.'

By civilised company, of course, Ailric meant other Astolans: the legate's staff, other nobles from the White Court or scholars and artists with interests in the capital who might be lodging there. Not humans, though. Her lips tightened. No mere human, however nobly born, could ever be considered Ailric's social equal.

'Be very careful what you say next, Ailric,' she warned him, her voice low. 'Whatever you may think of them as individuals, humankind is our sworn ally, not our enemy.' Taking a deep breath, she tried to steady herself. Nothing good would come of lashing him with her frustration and her fears for the future, but the effort of reining them in made her voice tremble.

'I know you don't think Savin is anything Astolar should be concerned about, but I believe he's the greatest threat this world has faced in a thousand years, and we will need all our allies, all our friends, to stand against it. If you truly care for me, support me in this, because you will not change my mind.'

There, it was said. She'd made a mistake allowing him to accompany her into the wildwood. Her intentions had been good: ensuring her father's peace of mind, securing a potential ally amongst the Ten, but spirits, there had been a cost. Ailric had antagonised Owyn, proved an irritation to her and jeopardised the safety of all of them at the runestones. True enough, he'd saved her from the White Hunter's icy embrace, but she wasn't sure she could tolerate another moment of his arrogance, his wilful blindness to the dangers facing them.

To her surprise, he smiled. It lit up his eyes, warm and golden as candle flames. 'But of course, love,' he said. 'You have only to ask.'

The sudden capitulation left her off balance, as if she'd swung her fist in a punch that was never going to land.

'Oh.' Recovering her composure, she added, 'Thank you.'

'I am yours to command.' He gave her a half-bow, gesturing ahead. 'Shall we continue? The sooner we reach the legate, the sooner you will have your audience with the Emperor.'

With a shake of the reins, he started his horse down the slope towards the road. Tanith urged her mount after him, trying to make sense of his shift in attitude. In the years she'd known him he had never given much thought to the world beyond Astolar's borders, save to exercise his contempt. She'd not been much different herself, once, before she'd travelled to the Western Isles to study Healing and opened her eyes to a different way of seeing. But where her regard for humankind had grown over time, Ailric's attitudes had only hardened.

She stole a glance at him. So what had changed so suddenly? Was it because she had appealed to his emotions instead of trying to persuade him with reason? She wasn't sure – wasn't even sure whether he was acceding to her only to win her gratitude, so he could manipulate it for his own ends.

Oh, it was too tangled to puzzle out. She had his support, and that was all that mattered for now. She'd worry about the rest later.

Tanith caught up to Ailric as he joined the road behind a cartload of caged fowl. 'Once we reach the palace you'll be able to return to Astolar,' she said. 'I'm sure Owyn would guide you back through the wildwood.'

'I would not dream of leaving you alone in this city, love.' He looked faintly hurt that she'd even suggested it. 'I promised your father that I would see to your safety, and I will not consider that duty discharged until I have delivered you back to him.'

Did he actually mean to wait with her? Dismayed, she exclaimed, 'But what about your responsibilities in Astolar? Your family's estates?'

'I have a very competent steward.' He smiled, almost like a parent indulging a child, and reached to squeeze her arm. 'For now, you are my only concern. You are my future Queen,' he lowered his voice and his fiery gaze grew more heated, 'and the queen of my heart.'

Tanith pulled her arm from his grasp. 'Don't, Ailric, please – that's hardly appropriate now.'

Disappointment flickered in his eyes, and he hid it with a deep inclination of his head. 'Forgive me, I overstepped myself.' *Though it was the plain truth, my love.*

Before she could remonstrate with him for invading her thoughts, the traffic plodding towards the city ahead of them slowed to a halt. Hooves thudded on the road and a flapping green banner appeared over the heads of the carters.

'Yield the road!' a voice yelled faintly. 'Make way! Make way!'

Tanith stood in her stirrups to peer ahead. One by one the carts and wagons were shuffling onto the verge to leave the greater part of the road clear. Now she could see the rider cantering towards her as he called for the road: a clansman, by the looks of his leather clothing and feather-trimmed hair. The banner billowed, revealing a white-bull blazon.

'Some jumped-up oaf demanding the road, I suppose,' Ailric muttered irritably, reining his horse onto the grass. Tanith sat down. He might support her on her mission to alert the human Empire to the danger facing it, but she feared he would never feel them worthy of the warning.

'No,' she said. 'That's the Warlord's bannerman, and he's in a hurry.'

A rumbling as of many running horses reached her ears. She looked ahead again and saw a larger party of mounted men behind the bannerman, buckskin-clad and riding hard.

Why cool her heels in the legate's palace, waiting on the Emperor's indulgence, when the commander of the Emperor's armed forces was right in front of her?

Urging her mare back onto the road, she raised her arm and hailed him in the common tongue. 'Ho, bannerman!'

He slowed his horse to a trot. 'I must ask you to yield the road,' he shouted back. 'The Lord of the Plains has urgent business in the north.'

'And I have urgent news for him.' Tanith sat her own mount squarely in the middle of the road, forcing the clansman to haul on his reins to avoid riding her down. 'I am come directly from the White Court to speak with the Warlord.'

Several nearby carters swivelled around on their wagon-seats to watch. The bannerman circled his restive mount, frustrated at being balked.

'My lady,' he began. The drumming hooves behind him were louder now, and he darted a glance over his shoulder then back to her. 'This is not the place.'

'This news will not wait,' she said firmly.

The approaching horsemen were slowing – all except two, a tall clansman on a powerful bay horse and a slight, rather bookish fellow in imperial green on a much smaller dun. Despite the army uniform, she doubted he was the Warlord.

'Slaine's stones, Colm! What's the hold-up?' the tall man barked as he reached them. He had a deep, resonant voice, his expression darkened by a thunderous glower. The bannerman backed his horse out of the way, indicating Tanith with a nod.

'Someone wishes speech with you, my chief.'

Fierce, cat-green eyes lit on her. With his soft buckskin clothing and the traditional beaded saddle-charms decorating his mount's harness, the Warlord looked every inch the plains ranger. Only the lack of braids in his thick brown hair and a heavy gold signet on his left hand betrayed that he was more than he appeared.

Exasperated, he exhaled sharply. 'Speak. My time is short.'

The remaining two dozen or so clansmen caught up with him and encircled the little group in the middle of the road, all without a word of command.

Ailric came forward. 'My lord Aradhrim, may I present to you the Lady Tanith, High Seat of House Elindorien, Daughter of the White Court and Second Ascendant to the throne of Astolar.'

Awed murmurs rolled through the watching carters. Tanith felt their eyes on her as they tried to relate the string of titles to the young woman on the mud-spattered horse in front of them, and just for a second wished for a liveried attendant or two to make her feel less like a vagrant in front of the Warlord. Then she tilted her chin up and straightened her back. Flunkeys be damned; it was the message that mattered, not the messenger.

One heavy brow twitched, but otherwise he gave no reaction to her rank.

'Forgive my language,' he said, a tad abruptly. 'I was not expecting to meet with a lady under such circumstances.'

'Nor I you, but I have news you must hear.'

He clicked his tongue. 'I am fighting time, my lady, and have more to do than I have hands to do it. Would you not be better served by going into the city and seeking an audience with the Council through your legate?'

'Frankly, no,' she said. 'This is a matter of grave importance. I travelled the wildwood to get here as quickly as I could – I'd rather not waste the time I saved kicking my heels in some antechamber.' She shot a look at the watching carters, some of them now standing on their footboards in an effort to see over the ring of clansmen. Aradhrim followed her glance.

'Then tell me as we ride. I mean to be twenty miles from here before the sun sets.'

They took the first mile at a canter, with Colm the bannerman in the van to secure the road. Once clear of the worst of the city-bound traffic, they eased back to a walk to rest the horses and Tanith found herself riding at the Warlord's side.

'So what brings you east in such haste, my lady?' he asked.

She had no idea how much Aradhrim might already know. Masen had shared with the senior Masters what he'd been told by the clansmen he met at Brindling Fall, but how far the word had spread was anyone's guess.

'May I speak freely?'

'Please do.' Lips twisted sourly, he added, 'I have had a gutful of politicking lately.'

She flashed him a rueful smile. 'Me too. That's why I've come here – of all the members of the Emperor's Council, I think you are best placed to comprehend the nature of the danger.'

Aradhrim held up his hand. 'If you are referring to the weakness in the Veil that the Gatekeeper found, my kinsman brought me word at Firstmoon.'

'There's more to it than that, I'm afraid.' She took a deep breath. 'There is a renegade *gaeden* at large who is hunting the starseed Corlainn Fellbane used to end the Founding Wars. If he finds it, he could rip the Veil to shreds.'

That made the Warlord blink. 'A renegade Guardian?'

Tanith gave a resigned shrug. 'Every family has its black sheep. It happened before I went to the Western Isles and the Order doesn't like to talk about it much, so all I know is that Savin is extraordinarily gifted, and extraordinarily cruel. The Order exiled him, at some cost, and earlier this year he returned to attack Chapterhouse, looking for the starseed.'

Aradhrim's eyes narrowed intently. 'Did he find it?'

'It was never there,' Tanith said. 'But Savin believed it was because so many of the Knights fled to the Western Isles to escape the Inquisition's purges. He thought they'd taken it with them, but the truth is it's lost, and has been for centuries.'

He swore under his breath and pinched his brows as if his head ached. Disquiet settled into the pit of Tanith's stomach.

'My lord?'

'This . . . . complicates matters.' He let his hand fall back into his lap and sighed, looking off beyond his bannerman and outriders to the green hills of Elethrain that separated him from his homeland. 'I am riding north to prepare my chiefs for a possible assault on Arennor by the Nimrothi clans.'

'What?' She could only stare. 'You're sure?'

'I am very sure. They have named a Chief of Chiefs and declared their intent to retake the lands they lost in the Founding, with the Wild Hunt at their head. They already have two of Maegern's Hounds to aid them.'

Freeing the Hunt meant breaching the Veil – and with the Nimrothi Speakers united under a Chief of Chiefs, they posed a threat that made Savin's ambitions seem almost petty. The disquiet in her stomach curdled into a sick dread and she shut her eyes.

'Then they have the starseed,' she said.

Spirits, she had never imagined this. Her efforts to persuade the Ten, her journey through the wildwood, it had been a waste of time. She'd bent her every thought on Savin, and all the while the greatest danger was coming from a completely different direction.

'Do not despair, my lady,' the Warlord said. 'I think if the Nimrothi had the stone we would know about it, and so far my scouts have seen no sign of the Hunt beyond those two Hounds. We have a little time yet.'

His words did not reassure Tanith much. Even without the starseed the Nimrothi Speakers would be a potent force, one that none alive knew how to fight. 'Then how do the Speakers mean to free the Raven if they don't have the stone?'

'That I do not know,' Aradhrim admitted. 'I mean to take

counsel from my own Speaker, Maera of the Tears, on the way north, and then we shall see. But if the Nimrothi come into Arennor looking for a war, by Slaine they will find one.' His eyes narrowed thoughtfully. 'Do you think this renegade is in league with the broken clans?'

'It's possible,' she said. 'We know he's in the north somewhere – the Nordmen have been sheltering him – but whether he's allied himself with the Nimrothi as well . . . From what I've learned of him, Savin is more full of tricks than a conjuror's pockets.'

The Warlord's teeth gleamed in a tight grin. 'Dangerous, too, I wager.'

'Very much so.' In brief sentences, she related the siege of Chapterhouse, how Darin had been duped with a glamoured gem into breaching the defences and the terrible losses suffered before the shield could be restored. Emotion seeped through her words like blood through a bandage; it was impossible to refer to the slaughter of children and remain dispassionate. She spared Arad-hrim the details of what had happened to Gair, beyond saying that a *gaeden* had almost died bringing news of Savin's intentions to the Order. Discussing his scars behind his back, as if he was a stranger, felt somehow disloyal.

By the time she was done, she sensed Ailric staring at her from behind, where he was riding next to Aradhrim's adjutant. She wondered how much he'd heard, and whether he'd use it to castigate her once more for endangering herself in a human cause.

Then the Warlord sighed and looked off to the north again.

'I am grateful for your warning, Lady Elindorien, though it piles troubles upon troubles for me,' he said, with weary resignation. 'The most pressing concern, though, is securing the northern border against incursion. That is where I must direct my attention for now. If Arennor falls, the whole Empire is vulnerable, so I must ensure it does not fall.'

'I understand.' And she did, but she could not help but feel a twinge of disappointment – although realistically, what was she expecting him to do? Even as she thought that, an idea formed. 'If I may, I'd like to ride with you to meet your Speaker. She may have some knowledge about the whereabouts of the starseed that would be helpful to the Order of the Veil.'

He looked dubious. 'It will be hard riding, and we will have few comforts to offer a lady of your standing.'

'I'm not afraid of sleeping on the ground,' she assured him, indicating her riding leathers, and he smiled.

'So it would appear. If the road does not daunt you, then you will be right welcome. A patrol from the Fleet garrison is deployed in the Marches, where I expect to receive word from Maera – you will have a chance of some privacy when we reach their camp. Now if you will excuse me for the moment, I need to discuss matters with my captain.'

Another nod and he heeled his bay up to a trot to catch the clansmen riding ahead. His adjutant followed, and Ailric immediately took the officer's place at her side.

'I gather we will not be taking our ease at the legate's palace tonight,' he said, in Astolan. Tanith detected the faintest reproof in his tone.

'I'm afraid not.'

'Have you not done enough, love? You have delivered your message – is it not time to return to Astolar?'

He had a point. She had completed the task she'd sworn herself to; she could leave it at that and go home again, to begin repairing the political fences she had kicked down with her hotheadedness in the council chamber. Part of her even whispered that that was what she *should* do – except fulfilling only the letter of her intent and not the spirit of it was a half-measure she could not stomach.

'Not yet,' she said. 'Savin is still searching for the starseed. The Warlord's not *gaeden*; he can't be expected to tackle him without *gaeden* support. If his Speaker can help us track the stone down, that helps both of us.'

'But surely—'

'No, Ailric!' Rounding on him, she twisted so sharply in the saddle that her horse jinked a step. 'I can make a difference here. I can't just walk away and expect to sleep easy at night, knowing I could have done more but chose not to. I just can't.'

He huffed out an exasperated sigh. 'This is not your responsibility, Tanith.'

'No one else was taking it, so I made it mine. I *will* see this through, whatever it requires, because who knows what will happen if I don't?' She moderated her tone. 'You said you would support me. If you find you can't do that, I suggest you go back to my father right now.'

'And leave you alone and unprotected with these ruffians?' Ailric gestured up the road at the buckskin-clad clansmen.

She rolled her eyes again. 'I am sure I will be quite safe with the Warlord, Ailric. These men are his personal guard – his honour is in their hands.'

'Forgive me if I am not so trusting,' he growled back. 'I swore to your father that I would keep you safe, and that is what I mean to do.'

'Then you'll have to accompany me north.'

For a moment she thought he would argue with her. His mouth opened to speak, then he closed it again, looked away. When he looked back, the angry fire in his eyes had dimmed to a smoulder. 'As you wish, love.'

A sharp whistle from the clansmen ahead caught their attention. One man raised his fist and circled it in the air above his head. At the signal, every man clapped heels to hide to urge their horses into a canter, and there was no more time for arguing. It was time to ride or be left behind.

14

LIFE AND DEATH

ॐ

Sweat beaded Lenna's bare skin, though the rough women's shelter was barely warm despite having a good fire. Teia wrung out a cloth in a basin of water and wiped the labouring girl's face and chest.

'Make it stop,' Lenna whimpered. 'Make it stop!'

'There's a little while to go yet, sweetling,' said Neve, sitting on a stool behind her. Lenna squatted between Neve's knees, the older woman's hands on her belly and feeling for the shape of the child beneath the milk-pale skin, the spidering veins. Another contraction made Lenna sob, her hands gripping Neve's knees. 'Breathe with it, girl. Don't fight it.'

'I can't!'

'You can, Lenna. Every woman can. Macha made us in Her image, to be mothers like Her. You can do this.'

Neve's voice was soothing as she rocked the girl gently from side to side. It had never cracked, never wavered, in all the long hours since Lenna's labour had begun. The girl shook her head and wailed.

Teia, washing her hands, wondered if her own labour would be like this. It would not be long now. She had felt the baby moving in her womb, the shape of her belly changing as her daughter began her slow descent towards the world.

Kneeling at Lenna's feet, she slipped her first two fingers between the glistening lips of the girl's sex. Almost at once she touched the slick dome of the baby's scalp. 'I feel it,' she said and smiled up at Lenna's tired face. 'Your baby's coming, Lenna.'

'Perhaps not so long after all.' Neve pressed a kiss to the girl's head and flicked a glance at Teia. 'Good practice for you, eh?'

Lenna yelped at another contraction. At its height a dark prominence surged towards the air then retreated, still just visible within its mother's enfolding flesh.

Teia stood up, wiping her hands on a rag. 'I have an idea.'

As soon as she stepped outside the small shelter where she had spent most of the last day and a half, the attention of everyone in the camp was on her. She swallowed uneasily. Her small store of medicines, the basic skills her mother had taught her, had earned her a reputation as a healer of sorts within her little clan. No wonder they looked to her to care for Lenna at the birth, even though it was Neve who had the practical experience.

Isaak strode towards her, his face anxious. 'Banfaíth?'

'Not yet, Isaak,' she said, breathing deeply of the cold, clean air. So refreshing after the smoke and the sweat and the oddly meaty smells of childbirth. 'But soon. Very soon.'

He darted a pained look towards the shelter. 'I hear her crying. Can't I go to her?'

Remembering what Ytha had said to Tevira's husband when her sister had been labouring with his firstborn, Teia laid a hand on his arm. 'This is woman's work,' she said. 'Your task comes later, to build a home for your family and teach your son what it means to be a man.'

His face lit up. 'It's a boy?'

How had she known? She had no idea, but it sounded so right inside her, like the striking of a sweet clear bell, that she nodded.

Isaak clutched at her hands. 'I have a son? I have a son!'

Men poured out of their shelter to surround him, clapping his shoulders and shouting their blessings. For the first time, real laughter swept up her little band of Lost Ones in its arms and hugged them.

Teia extricated herself and went to the women's shelter to fetch the looking-glass from her saddlebags. When she returned to Neve and Lenna, the baby's crown was more prominent, dripping bloody fluid into the basin placed between the girl's feet.

Neve looked up as Teia knelt to angle the glass. She smiled. 'Look, Lenna.'

The girl's eyes opened. They were bleary, unfocused, her whole face sagging with weariness. It took a few seconds before she saw the bright reflection of her own womanhood pouting around the emerging dark oval.

'Your son,' said Teia. 'Listen. The men are already celebrating.'

'My son?' Lenna mumbled. She reached down to touch him, stroking the wet black hair. 'He has hair.'

'Yes, he does. Soon you'll be able to hold him, Lenna,' said Neve. The girl gripped her knees with the next contraction. 'Teia?'

She put the glass aside and washed her hands again. Lenna moaned, her body strained and with a wet sound the baby's head popped clear in a rush of fluid. Under Neve's instruction, Teia wiped the slippery membrane from the child's face.

'Next time,' the older woman said.

After that it was surprisingly sudden. A further push from Lenna and, with a little cautious help from Teia's fingers, a tangle of arms and legs and purplish life-cord arrived in her hands. His face was crumpled in a ferocious frown, wet and angry and streaked with white birth paste, but as she wiped him clean with a damp cloth he drew in a breath and howled. Outside, the men cheered their answer.

Turbulent emotion surged in Teia's chest and her hands trembled as she laid the newborn in Lenna's arms. The girl was already crying, with joy and relief, and tears spilled down Teia's own cheeks. There was more work still to do, afterbirth to deliver and cord to cut, but for this moment the three women could rest and wonder at what had just arrived: a new life in the world. Outside, the men roared until the night sky shook, and for a few minutes the Maenardh could forget everything that they had lost.

ᕔ

Cold water dripped onto Gair's neck. He huddled further into his cloak to escape it but the wool was already damp; the rain would soon find its way through. With only one good arm he hadn't been able to make much of a shelter against the weather before night fell, but even if it hadn't been raining he doubted he would have got much sleep.

Held against his chest, his left forearm and hand radiated an unnatural heat. The skin felt stretched tight, as if sunburned, and the slightest movement stung like a cut. He couldn't bear anything to touch it, but he had to keep the cloak over it to protect it from the rain when a single drop bursting on his skin made him howl. Yet there was nothing to see to explain such pain. His arm was whole, intact, but it burned from the inside with an unholy fire.

He'd killed them. Saints and angels, he'd burned those three men alive. The more he'd tried to stop it, the higher the fires had blazed. Every time he closed his eyes he saw them again, the aimless staggering as they were consumed, and heard their shrieks clawing at his ears. Even Shahe had been terrified, rearing and tugging at the reins to escape the noise, the stench. Then the screaming had stopped and only the roar of the flames remained.

The hiss and spatter of broiling meat. Not men any more, but meat.

Bile soured his throat. As his stomach heaved he rocked onto his knees away from his gear, but he was empty of anything to vomit. Nonetheless his belly continued to cramp, the muscles already aching from repeated spasms. He spat some sour saliva away into the dark and dropped back onto his heels. He was beyond the meagre cover offered by his shelter, but he didn't care. He was already wet and cold and damned for all eternity – what harm could a little rain do?

Foetal huddles. Greasy cinders.

Oh, Goddess. Eyes screwed closed, Gair threw back his head. Rain pattered across his face and he wished it could wash him clean. *I am a monster.*

He'd killed before, perhaps more than his share in El Maqqam, but never like this. Not with fire, with the Song. With steel it was simple; more honest. Facing a man squarely, knowing his intent and him knowing yours. He'd trained for it for most of his life, and a sword in his hand felt as natural and comfortable as a breath in his lungs. But this . . . He'd reached for the illusion of fire to give those brigands pause; instead it had burned them alive, and he'd been powerless to stop it.

'My, you have had a busy day, haven't you?'

The smooth, sardonic voice was familiar. Gair opened his eyes and squinted into the forest night. A man in a pale silk shirt leaned against the trunk of the nearest tree with his arms folded across his chest. Glossy dark hair spilled about his shoulders in an artfully casual fashion. He cocked an amused eyebrow, his black eyes shining.

'Well? Aren't you going to say hello?'

Savin.

Fury. Sudden, unthinking. Gair threw off his cloak, snatched up his sword and charged. How dare that man appear here, now, and taunt him – and how typical. Too incensed to feel the pain in his arm, he hacked at Savin with all his strength and the rain-spangled blade swept through the renegade's midriff without even ruffling his shirt.

The lack of impact threw Gair off balance. Recovering, he struck again, two-handed, down through the collarbone with its great artery underneath and deep into the chest: a killing blow, with his full weight behind it. The blade thudded into the forest floor and he pitched forward, losing his footing in the wet leaves. He landed on one knee, breathing hard.

Savin clicked his tongue. 'I thought you would have worked it out after your first try,' he said. 'I'm not really here. This is a sending, an illusion. You know how silk marks in the rain.' Idly, he adjusted the perfect set of his cuffs.

'Just as well, or you'd be coughing out your last.' Gair tugged his sword from the soft earth and propped it beside him. His left arm was throbbing from the sudden movement. 'What do you want?'

'I was going to ask you the same question. You've been thinking about me for weeks.' Savin treated him to a disarming smile. 'Have you missed me?'

Gair bared his teeth. 'Only just now. Next time I'll make it tell.'

'Ooh. Scary.' Savin feigned a shudder, his ivory shirt shimmering. 'Tell me, did you snarl at your woman like that when you took her? Did you overpower her with those rippling muscles?'

The mockery drove into Gair like knives. He thrust himself to his feet, sword drawn back to his shoulder, ready to strike. 'Shut up.'

'Or what – you'll kill me?'

'I said shut up!' The rage was white-hot, blinding. It roiled in Gair's belly until he thought he would spew again.

'Look at you,' Savin sneered. 'You're nothing but a barbarian. You think a sword solves everything when a scalpel is so much more effective. You lack precision, Leahn, and it trumps brute strength nine times out of ten. You would be wise to remember that.' He snorted in contempt. 'Not that wisdom was ever your strongest suit – not when you had Alderan around to do your thinking for you. Where is the old man, anyway? I'm surprised he's left you running around loose – especially the state you're in.'

Gair's hand flexed restlessly on the sword's hilt. He burned to hack that pretty shirt to a bloody ruin but Savin's shape was an illusion, and a better one than he had ever seen – he couldn't even feel the shape of the weaving. A projection of bended light and will had no substance, no flesh to cleave nor blood to spill, but oh, the temptation.

Slowly, he lowered the weapon to his side and almost staggered at the wave of pain that rolled up his arm and set his head to spinning. It took him a moment to catch his breath.

'Alderan had business in El Maqqam. I left him behind.'

Dark brows arched. 'So you *did* go to Gimrael. I thought as much. Ghastly place, isn't it? Shame you wasted your time there, although you did do a marvellous job of stirring things up.'

'Did I waste my time?' Gair made it offhand, but Savin's eyes glittered.

'Don't be coy – you know very well what I mean.'

The man knew something. 'Humour me.'

'That starseed you're looking for – the one Corlainn had. I know where it is.'

Gair's heart sank. They'd been too late. Probably too late from the start, making Alderan's death even more of a waste. He tried to keep the hurt from showing on his face. 'What makes you think that's what I was looking for?'

'My dear fellow.' Glee sparkled through the words. 'What else could you have been looking for? Alderan thinks it's the key to preserving the Veil.'

Pieces of memory flashed, sharp-edged and painful. Snow and grey skies, an iron-coloured sea. And Savin's voice inside Gair's head. *Where is the key? You cannot hide it from me, boy!* Unable to help it, he flinched.

'I see you remember.' Savin smiled, and Gair scowled back at him. The bastard was enjoying himself!

'Enough games,' he rasped. Rainwater trickled into his eyes and he blinked it away. 'I have no interest in talking to you.'

'Are you sure about that?' said Savin silkily, cocking his head on one side. 'For someone who wants nothing to do with me, you've been thinking about me awfully hard recently. I'd have to be deaf not to have heard you.'

It had never occurred to Gair before, but it made perfect sense. No one could have ventured so far into his mind and not left some trace of their passing, like the prints of muddy boots on the stairs. 'You can read my thoughts.'

Chuckling, Savin pushed himself away from the tree. His shirt gleamed like polished bone, catching the light of a moon from another sky.

'Of course. You didn't realise? I know you, Leahn. I can read everything about you. Every thought. Every dream. Every desire.' Dark eyes glittered. 'I must say how much I enjoyed your memories. Tasted sweet, didn't she? Like strawberries.'

'You have no right to speak of her,' Gair snarled.

The chuckle became a laugh. 'And I suppose with your face buried between her thighs you could forget she was a cripple, eh?'

Fury blinded him. It consumed the pain in his arm, devoured it and hungered for more.

'*Bastard!*'

Steel arced towards Savin's belly and bit into the trunk of a young beech tree. Gair wrenched the sword free and swung again, roaring in pain and anger. Higher thought clamoured unheard; his hindbrain was driving his muscles now, and his hindbrain wanted blood.

'*You have no right!*'

Bone-white chips spat from the tree trunk. The impacts buzzed through his wrists, numbing his fingers. He hauled the blade back again and his boots skidded on the rain-slick litter of last year's leaves. Unbalanced by the weight, he hit the ground on his knees, the old sword tumbling from his hands.

The nerves in his left arm shrieked as if the skin had shredded, and every bead of rain was vinegar on an open wound. He sobbed and hugged it close, trying to shield it with his body.

'I told you that was pointless,' Savin chided. His sending was very close now; even without lifting his head Gair could see the glossy black boots, their shine unmarred by damp or dirt. Dear Goddess, his arm *hurt*.

'I will find you,' he panted. He hauled one foot under him,

heaved himself upright and went down again when a pain-induced whirling light-headedness sent his senses askew. His stomach churned. 'I will make you pay for what your creatures did to her.'

Savin snorted his contempt. 'You can try. But honestly, if you are Alderan's great hope for the Order of the Veil . . .' He shook his head. 'For all his moralising, his high ambition, he has achieved precisely nothing – except perpetuating some archaic notion of *service* that's as outdated as your precious Knights!' He laughed. 'Hadn't you realised? There is no Goddess, no higher purpose. There is only power, and those who have it will rule.'

Stepping back, the sending began to fade. 'Goodbye, Gair. Don't bother getting up. You're suited to being on your knees.'

Gair's right hand balled into a fist. 'Enough of your games!' he snarled, scrambling to his feet. 'Face me fairly, damn you!'

Without another word, the illusion vanished into the rainy night.

'*Face me!*'

Not a sound but the patter of rain on leaves, the slow drip of it onto the earth. Even his own voice had been swallowed up, deadened by the wet wood. Savin was gone. Untouched, untouchable.

And he knew where the starseed was.

15

TOUCHSTONES

The skinny young librarian entered Ansel's study with his hands folded in his sleeves and waited for the liveried sentry to close the door behind him. Dust streaked the cuffs of his brown robe and he blinked uneasily in the evening sunlight streaming through the windows, like a mole caught outside at noon.

As the door snicked into its frame, Ansel set down his pen. 'Well, Alquist?' he asked, although the librarian's mournful expression had already told him the news was not good.

'I'm sorry, my lord, I couldn't find anything.'

'You checked everywhere?'

'All the shelves I have access to. I suppose it might be in the locked vaults, but only Keeper Vorgis has keys to those.' He produced a brass key from his pocket and laid it carefully on the Preceptor's desk, then folded his hands again. 'I am so sorry.'

So Malthus's journal remained unfinished, the truth it held untold.

Ansel scowled unseeing at the papers on his desk. Without the journal he had no proof of his suspicions. No contemporaneous histories remained that the Church had not redacted; every account of the Founding he had unearthed in the great libraries of the Empire had differed only slightly in the details of those last desperate battles. It was a small miracle that the first volumes of the Preceptor's journals had escaped the Inquisition's bonfires and instead been left to moulder amongst the Apocryphae. Perhaps it was too much to ask that they all be there.

Damn it, he was running out of time. The first phase of his plan had unfolded. He had seen the doors of the Order opened to allow women to offer their fealty and service to their Goddess, if they so chose. He could not afford to lose momentum now. The winter had almost done for him; he would not see another spring. This was the time to move.

'Or all will come to nothing,' he murmured.

'My lord?'

'Hmm?' The letter he had been about to sign had crumpled beneath his splayed fingers. He smoothed it out carefully. 'You have done well, Alquist. I am enormously grateful for all your efforts. We must—'

A discreet, almost apologetic knock sounded on the door. *Now what?*

'Yes?' he called.

The sentry opened the door a few inches and peered inside. 'Forgive my disturbing you, my lord, but Elder Goran is demanding an audience.'

Today of all days. Ansel glanced at the windows, the ruddy flush of the sky outside. Almost sunset. He had little enough time without wasting it on that overfed deviant. 'Tell him to make an appointment with my secretary in the morning, the way everyone else has to.'

'I tried to explain, but he is most insistent,' the sentry said, then the door was thrust inwards out of his hands and Goran's portly shape filled the frame from side to side with Curial scarlet. The sentry and an equally discomfited marshal were barely visible beyond him.

It appears I no longer have a choice.

Sitting back in his chair, Ansel laced his hands across his belly and dismissed the hovering sentry with a nod.

'Elder,' he said coolly. 'How nice to see you again.'

Eleven weeks of confinement to the Motherhouse in his comfortable chambers, with nothing to do but divide his time between his library and holy service, had not had much of an effect upon the Elder. If Ansel had his way, the man would have been clapped in irons, but until his culpability could be determined to the satisfaction of the Lord Advocate, Curial privilege obtained. As a result, Goran's face was as meaty and flushed as ever, testament to the fine wines and choice foods his personal servants prepared for him. He stalked into the room as haughtily as his bulk allowed and slammed the door behind him with a flourish.

Ansel's brows twitched towards a frown. *Perhaps I should have insisted on a penitent's diet of bread and boiled fish, as well as depriving the man of liberty. It would have considerably improved the hang of his robes.*

'You and I need to talk, Ansel,' Goran barked, advancing into the room. Alquist squeaked and pressed himself back against the bookshelves, out of the way.

'Do we? After I ordered the Lord Provost to take you out of my sight, I didn't think we had anything left to say to each other.'

Bristling at the man's lack of courtesy, Ansel picked up his pen, dipped it in the silver inkwell and signed the topmost letter. As he put it aside for his secretary, he glanced up and feigned surprise. 'Still here?'

Goran reached the desk and leaned on his fists on the edge. 'You may feel comfortable ignoring me, but you won't be able to ignore what I have to tell you.'

'Really. And what is that?'

'Witches,' the Elder declared, with an unwholesome degree of glee. 'Magic users. A whole nest of them, discovered on the Western Isles.'

Despite the sudden twitch of anxiety across the back of his neck,

Ansel maintained a bored tone, leafing through the papers on his desk. 'I see. How did you come by this information while under confinement, may I ask?'

'That traitorous wretch you let go last summer. I had him followed.' Goran's smile was singularly unpleasant. 'He led my man straight to them. Hundreds of them, all in one place. They call it Chapterhouse, in some vile parody of our own Order.'

From his sleeve he produced a piece of near-translucent paper, folded several times and tightly curled from being rolled into a pigeon's message capsule. He unfolded it and laid it triumphantly on the desk.

Reading it would at least buy Ansel some time to think. He pulled it towards him and scanned the crabbed writing. Not the work of a man well used to a pen but legible enough, and it read like a military report: strength of numbers, defences, supply routes and civilian support.

'Interesting,' he said. 'Your man makes detailed observations. Has he had some military experience, this fellow? Your witch-finder?' Looking up sharply, he caught the guilty flicker in Goran's eyes. Ansel's lip curled. Even now the man continued to proclaim his piety whilst consorting with occult powers. The hypocrisy was breathtaking. He laid the paper down again. 'Thank you for bringing this to my attention, Elder. I will deal with it in due course.'

'In due course?' Goran reared back, his colour heightening. 'This nest of vipers must be crushed immediately, before their corruption spreads.'

'That decision will be mine to take.'

'It is your sworn duty, Ansel, the duty of every Suvaeon Knight!'

Hips twinging, Ansel levered himself out of his chair, its feet squealing backwards on the polished floor. He too leaned on his desk, his face so close to Goran's that he could smell the goldwine oozing from the man's pores.

'And I will give the order when I am good and ready and not before,' he ground out. Goran blinked. 'You appear to have forgotten, Elder, that your coup was unsuccessful. I am Preceptor here, and when I am satisfied that this report represents a true and accurate assessment of the situation, I will determine the appropriate response.'

The Elder slid a glance in the direction of Alquist. Ansel could almost see the man's mind working as he weighed his next words with the care of an apothecary.

'Forgive me for speaking in haste, Preceptor. I should have realised that this discovery would not be news to you.' Straightening up, he folded his hands in his sleeves. 'I must congratulate you on your cunning, my lord. The Curia will be most impressed.'

Ansel said nothing, easing himself back into his seat, determined not give the fat man the satisfaction of seeing him wince. He should have expected a counter-move; Goran had been too quiet for too long. In his youth, the Elder had been accounted a fine chess-player. The only reason he would disclose information now would be to bait a trap, offering his queen as a lure whilst his knights waited to pounce. Confining him had only given him time and space in which to plan his next moves.

Goddess, my wits are deserting me as fast as my strength.

'When they learn that you let the Leahn boy go as a ruse, to lead you to these heretics so that the Knights can destroy them, they will realise that the hero of Samarak remains a worthy choice to lead our Order. We need have no fear that he will lead us astray.' The Elder gave the merest suggestion of a bow.

Ansel ground his teeth. Goran had no need to spell out the alternative, damn him. Not with his attempted coup still fresh in the Motherhouse's memory – and with a witness in the shape of the pop-eyed young librarian it was better left unsaid, for both their sakes.

'Very kind of you to say so,' he replied, deliberately cool. 'You will understand why I was not at liberty to make this public earlier. I could not risk this information falling into the wrong hands.' He fixed the portly Elder with a stern eye. 'I still cannot.'

'But of course.' Goran was equally cool, but a smile crept furtively about his mouth like a small boy up to no good.

'I confess I am a little surprised that you second-guessed my intentions and sent your own agent on the same mission.'

'Our thoughts are clearly aligned on this matter, Preceptor. We both have the best interests of the Order at heart.'

Ansel fingered the flimsy message paper. He could have done without this, especially today. Time to give a little to get a little.

'I trust I can rely on your discretion in this matter?' he said. 'Until my own agent reports to me and the intelligence has been properly evaluated?'

Another bow, this one a little deeper. 'Naturally.' The merest pause, whilst the Elder's features moulded themselves into an expression of casual inquiry. 'I trust by then the Lord Provost's investigations will have concluded that these allegations against me are without foundation, and I can resume my seat in the Rede? It chafes at me to sit idle when there is work to be done, but I do understand that the proper procedures must be seen to be observed.'

The manufactured sincerity was so cloying it almost turned Ansel's stomach.

'When Lord Bredon delivers his report, you can be assured that I will be sharing the contents with you.' He dipped his pen and reached for the next letter, weary of fencing with the man. 'Good evening, Elder Goran.'

'And good evening to you also, my lord.' Goran bowed himself out.

Ansel held his temper until the chagrined sentry had closed the door after the Elder, then slammed his fist down on the desk hard enough to rattle the silver-chased inkwell on its stand.

Threats now, was it? Goddess rot him! Were there still no

bounds to his ambition? He scowled into the fire opposite. *Think, man, think.*

What exactly did Goran know? That the Guardians existed, in number, and where to find them. Nothing more. Nothing immediately dangerous. But if Ansel failed to act as his office demanded, Goran would appeal to the Rede – or rather Ceinan would, on Goran's information – claiming the Suvaeon needed a new Preceptor, and it would take more than finagling a quorum to defeat that motion. Yet he could buy the Elder's silence by dropping the charges against him and letting torture and perversion go unpunished.

Not whilst I have breath in my body, by the Goddess!

There had to be some way he could stall for time. Bredon had held off from instructing the Lord Advocate to prepare a prosecution until the Leahn lad could be located, but there were some weeks yet to go before he would know whether his marshals had been successful. Time, as ever, was in short supply. Time to think, time to act. So much of his plan depended on it. He'd always thought he would have enough.

Shuffling feet reminded him Alquist was still there. He glanced up and saw the boy sidling towards the door. The lad looked terrified. 'Um, if that will be all, Preceptor?' he quavered.

'Yes, Alquist, thank you. If I have need of you again I will send for you. Get to your supper.'

The boy bobbed a bow and all but fled the room. No doubt he hadn't understood the real meaning underneath the words he had heard, but that was no bad thing. If he didn't understand, he could not betray a confidence.

Ansel looked through the window, at the burnished copper clouds above the spires of the Sacristy, the first stars already pricking the darkening sky beyond. In a moment the bells would sound, ringing out the old day. He had promised himself that he would be there when they did. Too late now, thanks to Goran, but the living would understand and the dead, who had already waited so long, would wait a little longer.

ᘒᘓ

If the Sacristy was the crown of Eadorian ecclesiastical architecture, then the Knight's Chapel was the perfect pearl that topped it. Not that it was ornamented; far from it. It was as simple and austere as a Knight's vows, but there was beauty in simplicity, in clean lines, in craftsmanship.

Pale marble columns rose to pointed arches, the spandrels between worked into reliefs of oak leaves and acorns. At the rear of the apse stood a simple altar covered by a white cloth embroidered with the Oak in gold thread. Behind that, facing out towards the high altar at the head of the nave, knelt the statue of the Knight.

Head bowed and eyes closed in prayer, he held his sword point-down before him, his other hand resting on his shield. Since the founding of the Suvaeon Order he had shared vigil with every novice, prayed with every Knight on the eve of battle. Mourned every broken body laid in honour at his feet beneath a white and gold banner. And no one knew his name.

Some said he had been sculpted after Endirion, though he lacked the stocky build and short beard of the Order's founder. Others claimed it was Agostin, the only Knight in the Suvaeon's history to have been raised to sainthood, whose lead-lined reliquary rested beneath the altar. The stories about the statue of the unknown Knight were as many and as varied as the wild flowers that grew on Templemount and none of them were correct.

Or rather, they all were, in a certain way: the statue represented the ideal of Knighthood to which every novice aspired. The courage to speak and to act for what he knew to be right, even though it might mean his death. Strength for the weak, defence for the defenceless, true to his vows and his word.

For the Oak and the Goddess, to his last breath. Ansel smiled, watching the light of the altar candles flicker over the Knight's serene features. *I rather suspect that if he'd actually lived, he'd have been insufferable.*

Then he remembered and sighed. He'd served with a few who were better Knights in every way than he could ever have hoped to be. Fought alongside them, raised ale with them – often several ales, to rinse the dust of battle from their throats, sometimes with the bloodstains on their surcoats not yet dried. Laughed at jokes that weren't funny simply because they were so glad to have survived one more day that laughter bubbled out of them wherever it could find the smallest chink.

So many faces, gone now to memories. So many hands he'd held through the last agonies, before riding back into battle with their names on his lips as he took lives to pay for the ones his brothers had lost. Their faces billowed through his mind like pyre-smoke, brought a sting to his eyes then blew on.

So many absent friends.

He touched the breviary on the rail before him and breathed a prayer for them, his brother Knights gone on to the Goddess whilst he was left to linger. The walk from the Motherhouse had left him weeping in his pew from the pain in his joints, but as long as he could still walk he would continue to come here every year, on this day, the anniversary of the victory at Samarak, to remember the dead.

Then when I can't walk they can wheel me here in a chair, like poor Tercel. They can carry me in on a litter if they have to, but I will honour you, my brothers in arms.

Normally he would have gone up to the altar and lit a candle for them at the very feet of the unknown Knight and to hell with the protocols, but not this time. On this night, the chapel apse was sealed. A white cord stretched across the entrance, its ends secured in the centre with lead ribbon crimped into the shape of the Great Seal by the Master of Novices as his last act for the youth entering into contemplation. In the morning, it would be Ansel's duty to break that seal and release a new Knight to receive his spurs.

From his position in the right-hand pew he could see the white-robed vigilant kneeling in prayer with upright sword, almost a mirror to the statue above the altar. More memories clamoured for Ansel's attention. Recollections of his own vigil, of the moment he had felt himself touched by the Goddess's grace like sunlight through a window on his face. Other recollections, equally moving, made his hand press down on the worn leather binding of his breviary and the much-folded paper tucked inside.

Just as well he knew every word of Jenara's letter by heart; the paper had been handled too many times and had long ago begun to fray apart along the creases. But he kept it, hidden in the binding of his prayer book so that he would never be without his two touchstones. One for his faith, and one for his heart.

There is no place for me now, out in the world, she had written. *I have lived and loved, I have sinned and been blessed; now it is time for me to offer something back for all the gifts I have been given in this life. The most precious gift, Ansel, I place in your keeping. Please treasure her, for she carries my heart.*

He blinked away a sudden prickle in his eyes and looked into the chapel again, noting the upright spine, the squared shoulders. Even though the wound sustained in the tourney must still be paining her, Selsen had insisted she was fit to stand her vigil. Not even Hengfors had dared argue with her, though the physician had cautioned her to keep her arm strapped up across her chest, however much it limited her ability to balance herself as she held her sword. The asymmetry in her silhouette said she had kept her word.

And in the morning, against all the odds and three hung Redes before they had finally given their assent, she would achieve her dream.

I WILL NOT FAIL.

Ansel smiled. Twisted fingers traced the faint outline of the letter that time had worn into the breviary's leather cover.

Ah, Jenara. She will be the Knight I could not be, I think. She will make you proud, wherever you are. He patted the book gently. *She will make us both proud.*

16

RECKONING

~

Ytha lifted her hands from the rim of the bronze basin on the carpet before her. In the water, an image of rock and snow and trees faded to nothing more than a reflection of the oil-lamps hanging from the tent poles above her head.

Drwyn, pacing back and forth across her carpets in his slushy boots, swung to face her. 'Well?'

'Nothing,' she said. She reached for her tea and grimaced when she felt the bowl was cold. A sign of how long she had been sitting there, scanning the endless snows through her scrying basin. So far, the mountains were as white and empty as weathered bones, but Drwyn remained dissatisfied.

'We will be at the pass soon,' he muttered. 'Eight or nine days more. Ulloch and the others should have been on their way back to us by now.' He fretted at his bottom lip with his teeth. 'You're certain there's no sign of them?'

She treated him to a frosty look with all her years as Speaker of the Crainnh behind it. 'Yes, my chief. I am certain.'

'You heard what Gwil said, and now this message from Eirdubh's Speaker that his scouts have taken some prisoners, on top of the two Arennorian riders they'd already killed before we even entered the foothills. How many of them are there? What if Ulloch and his men have been taken, too?'

'There are other possibilities.'

Drwyn grunted and kept pacing, swigging from the cup in his fist.

Ytha watched him, noting how his preoccupation had increased as they rode from the Scattering eastwards across the plains. 'The mountains are dangerous – your men may have been delayed by poor weather or a snow-slide. They are not uncommon in the high Archen as the thaw begins.'

He shook his head. 'No. They have been taken, I know it.' Back and forth, grinding the slush into her carpets in a long, dirty line. 'Now we do not know what awaits us there – except trouble, curse them.'

By the Eldest, the man was as skittish as an unblooded warrior before his first battle, shoring up his courage with *uisca* and seeing foes behind every tree. Where was the Chief of Chiefs who had taken the other clans' pledges at the Scattering, so assured and regal? Was he losing his nerve? Worse: was she losing his trust?

It took some effort to maintain her neutral tone. 'You should not assume the worst without any evidence. In all my searching I have seen few tracks and little to indicate that the Empire's scouts have ventured far from their stone forts, or in any great numbers.'

'A heavy fall of snow and any tracks would be covered.' Drwyn emptied the cup and tossed it from hand to hand. 'Those forts were supposed to be empty, Ytha.'

'And as I told you when your man Gwil brought us the news, situations change,' she said coolly.

'Situations change,' he mimicked, in a childish, sing-song voice. 'You talk of working this to our advantage, but I can't see it myself! Aedon knows how they are so well prepared.'

Ytha ground her teeth, willing her temper not to rise. 'Perhaps your first scouts gave themselves away – those five who did not return before Firstmoon.'

He snorted. 'We could be riding our war band into the maw of their whole army! I promised the chiefs I would not squander their men. I am not Gwlach, I said, and here we are, facing a disaster. They'll have my head for this!'

Calm, Ytha, calm. 'I have scried the forts. I have seen no army.'

'Can you be sure?' he demanded. 'Do you know how many men they have?'

'No,' she said icily. 'I have seen them cutting timber for new gates and other repairs, but they work turn and turn about. I cannot guess at their numbers. More than a hundred, that is all I can say.'

'More than a hundred,' Drwyn echoed. 'Isn't there some way you can be more precise?'

'Maegern's teeth, Drwyn,' she snapped. 'I cannot be watching the Empire's soldiers every minute of the day – not with all else I have to do before we reach the pass! We hold to our plan, and that's the end of it.'

The two Hounds nosed open the tent flap, their muzzles bloody. They had evidently fed well. Ytha smiled at them, spreading her arms in welcome. 'Ah, my pets.'

Without a glance at Drwyn, they padded over and flopped onto the carpet to either side of her. She dug her fingers into their dense yellow fur and scratched them under the ears. Tongues lolling, they panted happily at her.

When she looked up, Drwyn was scowling, tugging at the thick torc around his neck. The wolf's-heads' emerald eyes glittered.

'I don't like it,' he growled. 'I was counting on those forts being empty.'

'Surely you did not think we would ride into the Empire unopposed?'

'I am not a fool, Ytha.' Impatience gave his words an edge. 'I had simply hoped to add surprise to our strike.'

She laughed. 'Oh, they will be surprised, have no fear of that!' Fondling the necks of the Hounds beside her, she imagined them charging across the plains at her command. Tearing into green uniforms and buckskins alike, rending flesh.

She could hardly wait.

'What have you seen of the girl?'

The question surprised her. She thought he'd let go of the notion that Teia bore an heir for him, but no, the old wound was itching again. He must have reckoned up roughly when her time would come due. Such initiative was . . . unwelcome.

Still stroking the Hounds, she said, 'If she spoke truly, she was carrying a daughter.'

Drwyn grunted, gave the torc a last tug and let it drop. 'If she spoke truly.'

'I have no reason to think she lied.'

'She lied to you about everything else,' he shot back. 'She lied about her gift. Years she kept it from you, and from her family, in defiance of clan law. How difficult would it be for her to keep this from you, too? You said you couldn't delve the child.'

Ytha pursed her lips. The memory of that failure stung worse than a wound – some power had been at work there, she was sure of it. Some power that she did not comprehend. How else to explain it? Now this. By the Eldest, even presumed dead that girl was a trial!

And the worst of it? Drwyn knew that she was not all-powerful. He had seen her bested by a mere chit, and now he asked her questions for which she had no answers.

Curse the bitch! Curse him, too, for finding the stones to stand up to his Speaker!

'Concealing the truth is not the same as lying,' she said tightly. 'I never caught her in an outright untruth.'

'You split hairs,' he scoffed. 'However finely you care to slice it, Ytha, she played you for a fool.'

'She played us both for fools! Don't think for a moment I've forgotten that!'

She glared at him but he did not meet her eye, merely snorted and resumed dirtying her carpets, striding from one side of the tent to the other.

'I want what she carries,' he growled. 'I want my son.'

'You've bedded half the girls in the clan. Surely one of them will bear you a boy eventually.' *Unless* . . . Her eyes narrowed suspiciously. 'What makes her so precious to you, Drwyn?'

He didn't answer. Ytha turned possibilities over in her mind. The most obvious was that he was fond of the girl after all, though in the past he had shown no inclination to treat his women as more than receptacles for his lust. It wouldn't be the first time she'd seen a man struck witless by love when he least expected it. There was, however, another possibility, and it was far more troubling: he saw Teia as a potential shield or even a weapon against *her* in the days to come, and that could not be tolerated.

No matter how young, no matter how untrained the girl might be, Ytha would suffer no rival.

'Do you want her more than you want to lead your people to victory and see your forebears avenged?' she asked.

He rounded on her, black eyes snapping. 'That child is my blood. My heir. I will have him.'

'Then you've blinded yourself to what we can achieve.'

Drwyn stared at her, sullen as a thunderhead. Ytha pushed herself to her feet. She had shown him the whip; now it was time for the sweetleaf. 'You stand on the brink of greatness, Drwyn. You have a chance to ensure your name will outshine any other in the histories when you lead our people home again. Do not let that slip through your fingers. You can always father another son.'

His hunger for renown had always been his weakness, that desire to stand taller than his father ever had. She saw her words smooth his tangled brows, calm the muscle that bunched and twitched in his jaw. Even his hands unclenched from fists and hung open at his sides once more.

Good. Good that he remembered who had brought him this far, this fast. Half a year after Drw passed on and he stood as Chief of Chiefs, as she had promised he would, with the war bands of seventeen clans waiting on his will. Teia could never have gifted him that kind of power.

'Keep your eye on the quarry, my chief,' she said softly. 'If the fates decree it, you will have your son, but for now there is greater game afoot.'

There was silence, then he raked his hands back through his thick hair. 'You are wise, as always, my Speaker. We hold to our plan.'

'Are your captains prepared?'

'They are. What of these new prisoners Eirdubh has taken?'

Ytha smiled thinly. 'I will tell his Speaker that he should keep them, for now. Find out what they know, and then when we are close, send the Empire a message.'

A wolfish grin split Drwyn's beard. 'So the reckoning begins.'

On their carpet, Maegern's Hounds licked their gory chops and grinned.

ℰℋℐ

Lenna smiled down at her newborn son sucking lustily at her breast in a nest of furs and blankets. The men had helped Isaak make a sled for them from young pine trees that one of the horses could pull and he walked at the animal's shoulder all the while, just to be near. A smile was never far from his lips, either, especially when he thought no one was looking.

Teia, riding Finn alongside the sled, watched the mother and child. Lenna's pretty, scarred face was drawn and it would be a while yet before she was fit to ride or even walk very far, but the rapt way she gazed at her nursing baby, as if nothing else in the world mattered to her, not the snow nor the jolting of the sled, was a good sign.

'Have you chosen a name for him?' she asked.

'Not yet.' Lenna touched the infant's shock of dark hair tenderly.

'It's only been two days. You've time yet.'

Leaning down, she squeezed Lenna's shoulder, then urged Finn up to the head of the column, where Baer led the way with Neve at his side. He had a tall walking staff in his hand, though his limp was much improved, and she was carrying a bundle of furs.

'Banfaíth,' he greeted her. 'A fine day, eh?'

It was a fine day. Blue skies without a trace of cloud, and now that the sun was well up there was an undeniable softness in the air. Here and there trees showed green again as they shrugged off winter's white, and in quiet moments the mountain stillness was punctuated by the slow drip of meltwater. Even the going was easier. Though the snow remained knee-deep, they travelled through a wide, shallow valley scattered with trees over ground that sloped more downhill than up, and the peaks ahead were markedly lower than the ones at their backs.

'We've passed the worst now, don't you fear,' Baer said, as usual reading the way her thoughts were tending. Just another of the many ways in which he reminded her of Teir. The anguish of leaving her parents behind had solidified into a dull ache below her breastbone. It still pressed on her heart but it no longer cut at her, as if distance had blunted the edges.

Did they ever think of her? Did they wonder where she was now, or did they mourn their youngest daughter's death, the way most parents did who lost a child to exile? With a start she caught herself wondering whether Drwyn missed her, since the child in her belly was of his get, and shook her head at her foolishness. Drwyn already had a daughter by his first wife and scarcely acknowledged her since abandoning her to her greatparents after he set her mother aside when she was unable to give him a son. Why would he care about another one?

That fate would not befall *her* daughter – whoever her father might be, and whatever the manner of her conception. *She is mine.*

'Banfaíth?' Neve's voice brought her out of her thoughts.

'Yes?' Teia reined up, then steered Finn to one side of their route to let the others pass. Baer and his woman stopped with her.

'You're the closest to a Speaker we've got,' Neve said. She was breathing hard from trying to speak clearly whilst labouring through the snow. 'So me and the women, we thought you should have this.'

She held out the bundle she had been carrying. Teia took it and unfolded a thick fur cloak. Not white snow-fox, but wolfskins carefully pieced together to put the silveriest pelts at the top, around the shoulders.

A peculiar thrill squirming through her stomach, she ran her fingers over the fur. 'You made this? For me?'

Neve smiled shyly. 'We put together what we had, all the women. Those Crainnh had fur vests and such and they don't need them no more. It's only right.'

'Neve, it's beautiful. Thank you.' Steadying Finn with her knees, she swept the cloak around her shoulders.

'Fair look the part now,' said Neve.

Baer cleared his throat. 'Missing something, though,' he said gruffly, and held out his walking staff. 'This should do it, I reckon.'

The staff was taller than Teia herself, fashioned from a single length of weather-bleached wood, carved into a fanciful flame-like shape at the top, following the grain. A Speaker's staff and robe. It didn't quite match her vision of all those months ago, but it came close enough. She looked over at the line of trudging figures, faces resolutely turned to the south. Isaak, beside the sled, stopped and stared. After a second he shouted for Varn, and then someone pointed. More pointing, tugging at sleeves, Lenna twisting around on the sled so she could see, the whole line shambling to a halt. One by one they turned to face Teia.

Macha's ears. She swallowed, her mouth suddenly dry.

And then Isaak dropped to one knee. The others followed suit, a mixture of nervous bobs from the newcomers and deeper reverence from the ones who'd known her longest. All of them, from Gerna to Aelfen.

These are my people. I have led them here, to this new life. The responsibility abruptly felt heavier than a mountain and as light as scudding clouds. *I am their Speaker, their Banfaíth, and this is my clan.*

There was only one thing she could do. As gracefully as she could, she bowed back to them.

17

PATTERNS

❧

Masen detected the first sign that all was not well two days into the Westermarch, when Brea baulked on a low rise and refused to go any further. He clicked his tongue and urged her on but she stood fast, tossing her head and snorting as if she could smell something unpleasant.

'Come on, girl, now's not the time for games.' The second rent in the Veil was very close; the horseshoe nail in his pocket was digging into his thigh like a thorn. He squeezed the mare's ribs to no avail, then gave her his heels. She shied and whinnied, but advanced not one yard.

He exhaled sharply. The mare clearly knew something he did not. 'All right, I understand.'

Reining in his impatience, he patted her neck and murmured soothing words. For all this part of the plains looked no different from any other, he'd ridden too many miles on Brea to mistrust her instincts.

He looked around at the rippling grass, the scrubby trees along the stream-banks. There were no elk or horses about that might have attracted predators, and no smoke on the wind, though it was still too early in the year for wildfires. Nonetheless the mare was as on edge as if she'd caught the scent of a mountain lion –

crag-cats, as they were called up here – but they preferred the foothills and rarely ventured onto the open plains. So what was she afraid of?

Even touching the Song told him nothing more than his other senses already had: there was nothing ahead but rolling dirt and running water. Whatever Brea sensed, it was nothing physical.

Hooves sounded behind him, punctuated with some choice oaths. 'What the hell's ahead of us, Masen?' Sorchal shouted. 'The horses are all spooked.'

'I'm not sure, but I don't think it's anything good,' Masen called back, eyes shaded to peer at the sky. No scavenger birds such as ravens or grass vultures. Not even a hawk, and they were as common as pigeons in a landscape as rich in small squeaky things as the great plains of Arennor.

With much puffing and muttering, Sorchal drew up beside him. His chestnut pranced uneasily and the pack pony, fidgeting behind, was pulling back against the leading rein, head and neck outstretched and eyes rolling.

'Blood and stones, that was hard work,' the Elethrainian grumbled. He frowned at the land ahead. 'I can't see or sense anything that would upset them this much.'

'The horses obviously can, though.' Masen scanned the grass again, slowly this time. Beside him he felt Sorchal drawing power in, reaching out with it.

'It's not the rent in the Veil.'

He grunted. He could have told Sorchal that even without the nail trying to burrow through the meat of his leg. Off to the right where the grassy waves broke irregularly as the wind pushed through them, a flash of something pale caught his eye. Another gust showed him more of the pale object, and he realised where they were standing. This wasn't the place where the second Hound had come through the Veil, but it was the first place it had stopped after it did.

'Come on,' he said, dismounting. 'Leave the horses here. No point distressing them any more than we have to.'

Once the animals were lightly hobbled, he led the way through the grass towards the uneven patch, certain now of what they were going to find.

'Imagine you've just been released from prison,' he said over his shoulder as they walked. 'What's the first thing you'd want to do?'

'Visit Madame Eliza in Threepenny Yard?' Sorchal offered, and Masen glared at him.

'Be serious, boy!' He kept walking, catching further glimpses of white ahead as wind and grass played peek-a-boo with the bones. 'Imprisoned for a thousand years, in the dark, cold space between two worlds. What would you do when you were freed?'

'I'd want to get as far away from walls as I could.' Sorchal rested a hand on the dagger he wore on the opposite hip to his rapier. 'Then I think I'd like to kill the person responsible for putting me there.'

A few more yards and they were close enough. Masen stopped and gestured ahead. 'Personally, I fancy you'd just kill the first living thing you came across.'

The grass was littered with bones. Some two dozen horses had died there: adults, yearlings, spring foals, all lying where they'd fallen, their skulls and long bones half-hidden by thick, rank grass out of which their ribs arched like the bleached beams of abandoned buildings. Scraps of hide and hair still clung to them, and as far as Masen could tell the skeletons were intact, undisturbed by scavengers. Whatever fear prevented the saddle horses from approaching had kept them away, too. Wild creatures apparently sensed something of what the Arennorian seeker Kael had felt when the beast was near.

Sorchal gaped at the bones in disbelief. 'What happened here – a battle?'

'This is where that other Hound made its first kills, I reckon,' said Masen. *Don't ask me to describe what we saw in that place.* 'One night's work, according to the clansmen who told me about it.'

'Goddess above.'

In the presence of such wanton cruelty, a prayer was about the only rational response. The Hound hadn't fed, hadn't done anything but vent its spite in the only way it knew how: slaughter. That was its nature, after all. That was why, of all the creatures from the Hidden Kingdom that could have found a tear in the Veil, a Hound was one of the worst.

Dread settled in the pit of Masen's stomach. Knowing the Hounds were loose was one thing; seeing the skulls staring up at him made it real in a way that words alone could not. The wind whipped the grasses back and forth, hissing over the bones, pattering against his boots. It sounded almost like laughter.

'How many Hounds are there?' Sorchal asked at last, all trace of levity gone.

'As many as the feathers on a raven's back, according to the legends.' Masen sighed. 'More than you'll ever want to meet, at any rate.'

'That's for sure,' said Sorchal, with feeling. 'Have you ever seen one?'

'No. No one had, not since the Founding, until this.' Masen gestured at the grim display in front of them. 'They were all safely locked away behind the Veil.'

Hands shoved in his pockets, Sorchal gave the bones one last look. 'Now someone's letting them out. I suppose we'd better repair that rip before anything worse comes through.'

The only thing worse than Maegern's Hounds was the whole Hunt riding free, and if the Veil was now so fragile it could be cut this easily, that was surely only a matter of time. He was watching the first shifting pebbles that presaged a landslide, had seen the first cracks in a dam before the flood. And the worst of it was that the Veil might even be irreparable – Goddess, Masen had darned enough socks over the years to know that it was never the mend that tore next time.

'There's someone else we need to warn,' he said. 'Maera of the Tears.'

Sorchal looked puzzled. 'Who?'

'She's Speaker to the Lord of the Plains.'

The Elethrainian spread his hands in a shrug. 'Still none the wiser.'

'Good Goddess, did you pay *any* attention to your lessons when you were a child?' Masen rolled his eyes. 'The Lord of the Plains is Aradhrim – you know, the Warlord? Second most powerful man in the Empire? Maera's been his clan Speaker since his father's time, and if she didn't already have a calling I think Alderan would have wanted her for a *gaeden*.'

'She's powerful?'

'In her own way, incredibly so. Not like your friend Gair – Maera's gift isn't raw strength, it's knowing. Seeing connections, chains of consequence. Making sense of things that to you and I look like absolutely nothing of significance.'

Arms folded, Sorchal shook his head. 'I have no idea what you just said.'

'I've no clue how it works either, and I've known her for years.'

'So where will we find her?'

Masen scratched his ear. 'That's the thing with Maera, you don't exactly find her, she . . . arranges to find you. I'll have to hail her and hope she's listening.'

They started walking back to the horses.

'Why's she called Maera of the Tears, anyway?' Sorchal asked.

'Long story – and a sad one, too. Next time we meet some clansmen, ask them to sing it for you. I guarantee you'll weep.'

The Elethrainian scoffed. 'Sure I will.'

Masen remembered the first time he'd heard the Lay of Maera, and smiled sadly to himself. Sorchal noticed and laughed disbelievingly.

'What – you're telling me you cried?'

'Like a broken-hearted girl,' Masen said, patting Brea's neck. 'Still makes me tear-up now, if the bard's any good.'

'Every time?' Incredulous, Sorchal stared at him.

'Every bloody time.'

∽∽

The second rent proved to be less than half a mile away, black as pitch under the Song and ending in a jagged tear where the restless tugging of the Veil had begun to fray its delicate fabric apart.

Under other circumstances, Masen would have used the tear as a lesson to teach Sorchal the first principles of repair, but the lad would never be able to weave the strands together with a great rent flapping about above it, so he'd have to fix that first. Another excision, unfortunately, but as a rule amputations proceeded more swiftly with someone to hold the patient still.

'You remember what I said the other day about practical experience?' he called to Sorchal.

'I remember.'

'You're about to get some.'

Eyeing the gashed Veil one last time, he let the Song go and went to help with the horses.

∽∽

Later, when the bloody work was done and the gaping wound had been stitched closed – perhaps not as neatly as Masen would have liked, but soundly – and his apprentice had collapsed onto his blankets, he took himself a short distance away to seek out Maera's colours on the wind.

After all the years he had known her, he remembered them well: hoof-brown and hide-golden, blue and clear as the high plains sky, pale as the grass at summer's end. Picturing the pattern in his mind, he reached out for them.

189

Speaker.

She didn't answer immediately so he waited awhile, listening to the restless breeze and the chirp of crickets, then sent out another hail.

Speaker.

Maera's presence filled his thoughts. *Gatekeeper. It has been some time since last you rode the plains to see me.*

She spoke the common tongue, but even in his mind she kept her rolling accent that always reminded him of the shape of the land itself.

I'm just passing through this time or I'd have come to see you in person. I have some news I thought I should share with you.

The Hounds? I felt them running. A deep pang of loss shaded her colours and moved on, like cloud-shadows. *I felt them killing, too.*

The Veil was cut to free them.

Silence.

I saw where it was done. The first rent was on the edge of the Southmarch, and the second is here, in the west. I've sealed them, but the Veil is fragile here, and tears easily.

Again nothing but the breeze, the buzzing of insects.

Speaker? Do you know who might have rent the Veil?

No, but both Hounds have gone north into the Broken Land.

That confirmed the very worst of Masen's suspicions. *So it was the Nimrothi?*

Perhaps. There is a pattern here, but I cannot see it clearly yet.

Can you tell where they are?

I feel their presence on this world the way you feel the horseshoe nail in your pocket, but I can discern no more than that they are here, where they do not belong. Another pause. *You are not the only* gaeden *here, Gatekeeper.*

The Guardian sent us to the passes in case the Nimrothi—

I am not speaking of the lords of water and air, nor of you, nor the others in the west. Someone comes from the south. A Leahn.

A Leahn *gaeden*? There was only one person that could be, but here? The last Masen had heard, he was in Gimrael with Alderan. *Gair is in Arennor?*

Ah. She said it as if the Leahn's name was significant to her. *After all this time. I felt him searching, and was curious. Now I see.*

Perplexed by the Speaker's interest in Gair, Masen frowned. *You know him?*

Not exactly. What can you tell me of him?

Not much, Masen sent. *Alderan brought him out to the Isles from the Holy City. I only met him briefly when the reiver came against Chapter-house. Gair helped turn the battle but before it was done a couple of close friends of his were killed, and I heard he took it hard.*

Patterns within patterns, the Speaker mused. *He is a Knight, you say?*

As far as I know.

And now he is gaeden, *too.* A hint of a smile lifted her voice. *So the pattern turns once more.*

Masen laughed. *He's no Corlainn Fellbane come again, I can assure you of that! Alderan has hopes for the lad but I don't believe in heroes out of storybooks. I remember what happened the last time we tried to raise the perfect* gaeden.

You do not have confidence in his abilities?

Oh, he's strong in his gift – stronger than he knows what to do with, in fact – but he's just a man. Empties his bladder every morning, same as the rest of us.

But a man in whom several patterns intersect, she sent back, somewhat tartly. *This makes him interesting to me. Perhaps you should attempt to understand before you mock, Masen.*

Maera so rarely allowed the mask of formality to slip, even with him and despite what they had once shared, that Masen couldn't help but smile. He wouldn't understand the patterns she saw in the smallest things, not if he had six lifetimes in which to try, and she knew it, too. This was an old argument between them, with all the rancour long since boiled out of it. Even though she couldn't see him, he held up his hands to concede her point.

As you say, Speaker. As you say.

She gave a delicate snort. *So you are bound for the forts?*

Saardost Keep, yes, he said. *Barin and Eavin are going to King's Gate, and another Master and two of the best adepts from the mainland should already be at Brindling Fall, though we don't expect the Nimrothi to chance their army in Whistler's Pass. Their Speakers have long memories.*

As do Arennor's. Has the starseed been found?

Not to my knowledge.

And so we must wait. She sighed. *My chief sent word by fast rider that he is coming north to join the soldiers at Saardost. I will tell him of your plans.* The Speaker paused, concern shading her colours a touch darker. *The Guardians mean to act openly again? After all these years?*

We don't have a choice. If the Nimrothi come down through the passes and send their Speakers into battle against ordinary soldiers, it'll take more than stout hearts and straight arrows to stop them.

Alderan hadn't been happy about it, after so many years working in the shadows, but Masen had pointed out that at least it was in Arennor and not the heartlands – and besides, it was better than sitting on their hands in seclusion whilst the world went to hell around them. On that at least the Guardian hadn't needed convincing.

Have a care, said Maera, perhaps guessing the way his thoughts were tending. *Wars are hard on our friends.*

Are we still friends? he asked lightly, not wanting to end the exchange on a dour note. *It has been a long time since we, uh, renewed our acquaintance.*

She burst into laughter and sounded like a girl again. *Lickerish as ever, you old goat.*

He chuckled. *I try not to disappoint.*

I remember. Maera touched his colours fondly. *Be well, Gatekeeper.*

And you, Speaker.

Then the sense of her presence was gone, leaving only a fading warmth in his thoughts. Masen waited until the last trace of it vanished, then heaved his tired body back onto his feet and walked down to where Sorchal sprawled on his blanket, limbs everywhere like an exhausted puppy. He'd let the lad sleep for now. From tomorrow they would need early starts and long days if they were going to reach Saardost in time.

18

THE MARCHES

෨෮

Glancing around the army commander's tent, Tanith noted the clutter of saddlebags and map-chests which had been pushed to the far end to accommodate a second folding cot, both of them made up with army-issue blankets. A storm lantern flickered on a collapsible table between the two narrow beds and the air smelled of crushed grass and hot lamp-oil. After a week on the road in the company of Aradhrim's clansmen, each night sleeping on the ground with only a star-strewn sky for a roof, the simply appointed officer's tent felt as luxurious as the legate's palace.

'I trust you will be comfortable enough here,' said the Warlord, standing somewhat round-shouldered by the entrance. He was tall for one of his people; he could only stand upright directly under the ridgeline of the tent, and even then his mane of hair brushed the canvas above him.

'Shouldn't these be your quarters?'

'The patrol captain gave up this tent for me, yes, but a Daughter of the White Court cannot be expected to bed down beside the fire in the middle of an army camp.'

She smiled. 'Yet the Warlord can?'

'Here in Arennor, I am Clansman of the Durannadh first, Lord of the Plains second and the Warlord very much last. If I did not bed down around the fire with them, my countrymen would accuse me of putting on airs. Besides,' he added, with a shrug, 'I prefer being out under the stars. We may have to wait here for a day or two before Maera's apprentice arrives to lead us to the Singing Stones where I will meet the chiefs, so I suggest you enjoy some privacy while you can.'

'I seem to remember spending five or six nights on the road without any. Don't you trust your men?'

'My clansmen, with my life – but a hundred unwashed legionaries from the Marches patrol?' He shook his head. 'I will sleep better knowing you are safely guarded. So if you have everything you need?'

'Yes, thank you. You must have much to attend to. I'll see you in the morning.'

With a smile and a nod that was almost a bow, Aradhrim departed.

Alone and suddenly weary, Tanith gave one of the camp cots a cautious prod. Finding it sturdier than she'd expected, she sat down. It creaked but held firm, although she wondered how the Warlord folded his long legs into it. He probably couldn't, which might be another reason why he preferred sleeping outside.

She eyed the second cot across the tent as she heeled off her boots. What had Ailric said to ensure he shared these quarters? Or had the Warlord's adjutant simply made an assumption about two Astolans travelling together? She should probably have said something as soon as she entered the tent; explained the misunderstanding and put up with Ailric's outraged bluster afterwards. Sighing, she kneaded her eyes. Whatever. It was too late now. At least she knew Ailric wouldn't snore – unlike some of the Arennorians who, she'd discovered, grunted and squealed in their sleep like rutting hogs.

She stifled a yawn with her hand and lay down to rest her weary limbs. Spirits, she'd never ridden so hard and for so long in her life. The clansmen treated it as no more arduous than a stroll through a meadow, having the breath to talk and catcall amongst themselves when at first she was hard-pressed just to stay in the saddle. Her strength and endurance were improving, but had come at some cost: she was so tired at the end of each day's travel that she could hardly keep her eyes open.

A week in the saddle had brought them from Mesarild into the Arennorian Marches. The fertile, hilly country along the northern border of Elethrain was well farmed and sported a number of thriving market towns, but for every prosperous manor they passed she saw another two that were crumbling shells robbed for building stone, or mouldering into overgrown gardens and parkland choked with bramble and scrub.

The number of estates fallen into ruin had surprised her, until Aradhrim explained that many of the powerful Marcher Lords, who owed their considerable wealth and lands to the favour of a long-dead Emperor in the early years after the Founding, had little interest in maintaining them beyond collecting the rents. Some only used their seats for summer hunting; several families had died out, or intermarried and been absorbed, leaving crumbling manors and vast tracts of untenanted farmland. Banditry was a constant threat, and the task of quashing it fell to him twice over: once as Warlord, enforcing Theodegrance's writ, and again as Lord of the Plains when the cattle raids extended north into his own country. His tone of voice as he'd spoken had told her of his distaste for the task.

A scratch at the tent flap roused her from a doze. Ailric stepped inside, carrying a flask and two cups.

'Soldiers' rations are not much of a meal and I found no wine worth the name, but the Warlord gave me this.' He held up the flask. 'Perhaps it will help improve the taste of our supper.'

'What is it?'

'*Uisca*. The clansmen drink it as if it is water, but I understand it is quite palatable.' He tilted the flask in her direction, eyebrows raised enquiringly.

'Just a little,' she said, propping herself on one arm. 'Thank you.'

He poured two measures and handed one of the cups to her. The loamy scent of the spirit was softer than Owyn's *kavit* but even a small sip left a fiery trail down her gullet. She hid a smile as Ailric swallowed a larger mouthful and struggled not to cough.

'Potent,' he managed, when he'd finally choked it down. 'But yes, quite palatable.'

He sat down beside her. When the cot protested at the additional weight he leapt up again and took a seat on the ground instead. 'I fear that contraption will fold up and swallow us both.'

'I'm sure it's quite safe.' Tanith sipped at the *uisca*. Once she got past the smoky taste the spirit warmed her from the inside out and wrapped her tired body in a cosy blanket ready for sleep. 'Although I'm so tired, if it eats me in the night I'm not sure I'll care. The pace the clansmen set – their backsides must be made of leather.'

Laughing, Ailric topped up their cups. 'They are born saddle-shaped, I think.'

Tanith smothered another yawn and leaned back on her elbow. The cot was more comfortable than it looked, or else the week's hard cross-country riding had taken such a toll on her that anything felt comfortable after the back of a horse – even her dear brown mare. Absently she sipped at her drink. The golden spirit tasted better with each mouthful.

'It has been quite a journey.' Again the flask travelled from cup to cup. 'A toast,' Ailric said, holding up his drink. 'To journey's end.'

'It's not over yet,' she said. 'There's still a way to go.'

'But once you meet this Speaker, you can go home. Back to Astolar, where you belong.'

Where you belong. That rankled, but she was too weary to argue with him over it. For the most part he'd held true to his word and refrained from openly disparaging humans or her choice to help them, but his real feelings were never far from the surface. He would not be best pleased when he learned that her journey was far from over, depending on what Maera of the Tears was able to tell her about the starseed. She kept that to herself, too.

'Back to the Court.' Tanith drank a deeper swig to drown the memories of her confrontation with the Ten. Her gullet burned. 'The Queen will not be happy with me. I offended the whole Ten – including your grandmother.'

He smiled. 'Leave Morwenna to me. And besides, Emelia will not remain angry with you for long. As one of her heirs, you are too important.'

'Mmm.' Tanith wasn't convinced. 'She has a long memory.'

Somehow her cup was empty. Ailric refilled it for her.

'Then we will face her together. You and I.' He propped his elbow on the edge of the cot. 'Come back with me, Tanith.'

Not this again. 'Ailric—' she began wearily.

'This journey – the reiver, everything – they are human problems, not ours. Nothing holds you here now the Warlord knows there is a threat.'

'I still need to speak to Maera,' Tanith protested. 'The starseed—'

'Has been lost for a thousand years,' Ailric finished for her. 'The Warlord knows all that you know now; let one of his men ride halfway across the world to find it. There is work for you to do at home, and Astolar needs you. *I* need you.' Eyes the colour of flame searched her face as his knuckles rubbed back and forth along her thigh. 'You have held my heart since I was a boy, love. All I have ever wanted in this life is you.'

His face was very close. He really was handsome. High-cheekboned, full-lipped – and those eyes, looking into her, firing her soul the way they had since the very first glance her way.

'You are so beautiful,' he whispered. 'What daughters you will bear, with your copper curls, your tawny eyes. What sons.' One finger traced the line of her jaw. 'Come back with me. Please.'

He was close enough that every word stirred the fine down on her skin, started a shiver that travelled all the way to her toes. His cedar-wood scent was mingled now with leather and clean sweat into something earthy, masculine. She breathed it in, deep into her lungs as kisses danced down her cheek. They felt so good. Dreamily Tanith turned her face in to his neck to savour his scent. Warm lips found her mouth, and stole her breath.

Oh!

ᘒᘓ

Even after five days the pain in Gair's left arm had not lessened, though there was not a mark on his skin to prove that it was real. Washing and dressing were difficult enough that he hadn't attempted to shave; the effort of saddling Shahe each morning almost drove him to tears. Sleep was impossible for more than an hour or two at a time, when the least movement of body or blanket jolted him awake gasping in pain, and he met each day scratchy-eyed and increasingly weary.

On the sixth day, he woke to a knife at his throat.

He lay completely still. The blade was as long as his forearm and gleamed wickedly in the dawn light. Behind it was a leather-faced woman in worn buckskin clothing, her dark hair gathered into a topknot decorated with raven feathers. Several long, thin braids threaded with coloured glass beads dangled over her shoulder and she had a star-shaped scar on one cheek.

Her soft leather garb and high, wide cheekbones identified her as an Arennorian clanswoman. Their women were as warlike as their men, so he'd heard, and this one surely looked as if she knew what she was doing with a blade. She had an air of easy competence that said if he gave her cause, she'd slit his throat as casually as if he was a hare for the pot.

Very carefully, he said, 'Good morning.'

'Good morning.' She replied in the common tongue, revealing

a couple of broken teeth to go with the scar. 'Who are you and what business do you have in the Marches?'

Two more clansmen ghosted out of the morning mist and stood over him with shortbows in their fists. Seasoned rangers, like the woman, all lean muscle and wary eyes.

'He's alone,' said one of them, and whistled sharply through his teeth. Hoofbeats sounded in the distance.

The clanswoman gave Gair's cheek a gentle slap.

'I'm waiting, northman,' she said, her pleasant tone at odds with the long blade in her other hand.

'My name is Gair. I'm just passing through.' Wincing, he spread his hands to show they were empty, but kept them palm down just in case.

'Where are you bound?'

'North. I'm looking for a friend who's travelling this way.'

'Palgrim?' she asked over her shoulder. The way she gave the order said she was a commander or captain of some kind. The man who had whistled disappeared from view and a moment later, Shahe whickered.

'Desert horse, supplies for travelling and he carries a long-sword,' Palgrim reported. Gair heard the sound of a blade half-drawn and scabbarded again. 'Old but well kept.'

A flicker of interest crossed the woman's face.

'Not a Marcher brigand, so what manner of beast are you?' She sat back on her haunches, knife still ready in her hand. 'Up you get.'

He kicked off his blanket and stood carefully, moving his left arm as little as possible. The clanswoman rose with him. She was taller than he'd expected, long-boned and rangy.

'This friend of yours,' she said. 'What is your purpose in meeting him?'

'I have a message to deliver. A mutual acquaintance has passed on.'

'And your friend's name?'

'Masen.'

She raised her eyebrows. 'The Gatekeeper?'

'The same.' Gair rubbed his face. His head was aching from too little sleep and his arm burned. Being woken with a knife to his throat had done nothing to improve his temper. 'Look, Captain, I've been on the road for weeks, so unless I've done something wrong—'

She cut him off. 'That remains to be seen. These are tense times, and I have my orders.'

'Which apparently include harassing innocent travellers.'

'Innocent?' Tossing the knife from one hand to the other and back again, the clanswoman smiled, as thin and hard as the blade. 'That is for my chief to decide.'

Another clansman came riding out of the mist, leading two mounts that presumably belonged to her and Palgrim.

'Colm, take his weapons,' she said, 'then pack up his gear. He's hurt.' The captain sheathed her knife, watching him. 'I can see your arm pains you. Give me your word that you'll behave as we ride and I won't bind your hands.'

'Given, but where exactly are you taking me?'

'To the chief,' she said crisply. 'I think he will want to speak with you.'

Gair marshalled his temper with an effort. 'Then tell Colm to be careful of my horse. She bites.' He gave a short bow, hand over his heart. It was a little late to start being polite, but it did no harm.

'Ha!' She grinned. 'Amusing, northman. We shall see if the chief is similarly amused!'

೧൦

Daylight seeped into the tent with the sounds of restive horses and shouting men. Pain stabbed through Tanith's skull and she winced. Too much *uisca*. Clearly, clansmen's backsides weren't the only parts of them made of leather if they drank the stuff like water. Spirits, her head hurt.

Cautiously, she sat up, pushing her tousled hair back from her face. She hadn't had a wine-head this bad since her first year on the Isles – but oh, she'd slept. Deeply, floating through a web of delicious dreams. Perhaps that kind of rest was worth a little pain.

Stretching her arms above her head, she yawned. The blanket slipped, baring her breasts to the cool morning air.

Bare?

She snatched the rough wool back up to her chin, her headache abruptly the least of her worries. Her gaze darted around the tent, but she was alone. Both camp cots had been stripped of pillows and blankets to make the warm nest on the floor in which she sat. Her clothes lay across one bed; the other was empty. Realisation sank into her as inexorably as a slow knife.

Oh, spirits keep me.

There was no denying it. She smelled it on the air, felt it in the tender flesh between her thighs. Those delicious dreams had been real. A lover's hands on her, stirring her. A hard body pressing, piercing—

No. Oh no, no, no.

The memories crawled over her like lice. Tanith flung the blanket away and scrambled to her feet, dizzy and sick to her stomach with more than just the drink. She stumbled to the folding washstand and flung the Song at the water jug until it steamed.

The *uisca*. It had breached her defences, allowed him too close. She washed her face first to clear her wits, then scrubbed the rest of herself with lots of soap and the water as hot as she could bear it. Her breasts, her neck, between her legs; anywhere his hands had touched or his lips had kissed. Mortified tears scalded her cheeks.

No! Not him, not Ailric.

When the water was cold and too spent with soap to lather any more, she dried her reddened skin and dressed herself. Braided her hair in a neat plait, even rolled the unused pallets from the cots, ready in case the men came to break down the tent. Anything to keep herself busy, to keep from focusing on the truth that throbbed in her skull in time with her headache.

She heard the tent flap lift and fall behind her as someone came in. She knew who it had to be and did not turn around to acknowledge him. Only one man would enter this private space unannounced, without permission. Her fingers trembled on the blanket she was folding.

'Good morning.' He stepped up behind her and slid his arms around her waist. 'Did you sleep well?'

She twisted out of his embrace. 'No.'

'Tanith?'

'Don't speak to me, Ailric.' With quick, angry movements she set down the blanket with the others, then snatched up her saddlebags and began stuffing her discarded clothes inside. 'Don't even come near me.'

'Is something wrong, love?'

Flinging the bags down, she rounded on him. 'And don't call me that! *You* don't get to call me that.'

He spread his hands, brows furrowed, not understanding. 'Tanith, please—'

'*No!*' Tears started; she was helpless to prevent them. 'You let me drink too much and then you took advantage of it.'

'I took nothing that was not freely given.'

He moved a step towards her, reaching out to cup her cheek in his hand, and she swatted his arm away.

'Don't touch me.'

'After what we have shared?' Ailric took hold of her, wrapped her in his arms too firmly to break away. He pressed his face into her neck, inhaling deeply. 'I made your body sing, my love. How can you refuse me now?'

She struggled to free herself, no longer caring if she offended him. 'Let me go, Ailric. Now, or I'll—'

He laughed, his breath tickling her ear.

'Or what?' he whispered. 'You will send for the guards? They will not intervene between a man and his betrothed, I think. But as you wish. Your words are my command.'

In an instant of horrifying clarity, she realised that the two cots in the tent had been Ailric's doing. Either by careful implication or the telling of an out-and-out untruth he'd arranged to share these quarters, no doubt intending this very outcome. The sheer duplicity stunned her.

'You *bastard*!'

Ignoring her sudden profanity, he placed a lingering kiss on her cheek and stepped back. 'The Warlord expects to meet with us both in the command tent in a quarter of an hour. Until then, my love,' he said and walked out.

19

WARLORD

 လည

A brisk ride through the hilly March-country brought Gair and his captors to the rim of a shallow valley in which stood a small army camp, a neat square of tents under a green imperial standard with stands of spears and horses tethered in rows. Just beyond it was the clansmen's more casual encampment, also under a green banner, this one bearing the white-bull blazon of Clan Durannadh. As it flapped and snapped in the wind, he saw a golden torc worked around the bull's neck and recognised the significance of it from his years at the Motherhouse.

'Aradhrim's standard,' he said. 'The Warlord's here?'

The clanswoman nodded. 'And he is my chief. I am the ride-captain of his escort.'

That explained why she was so wary of strangers, at least. Meeting the Warlord hadn't figured in Gair's plans and he could have done without the additional delay, but it might prove useful: Aradhrim would understand about a threat to the Veil, why he had to find the Gatekeeper. Of all the peoples of the Empire, the plainsfolk had the best understanding of the danger – and the longest memories. Then he could be on his way and see his task through.

The captain jerked her head at Colm and Palgrim and they

peeled off towards their own encampment whilst she guided her mount towards the largest of the tents, a squarish pavilion in the middle of the army camp. A hitching-rope had been strung outside at which several horses were tethered, picking at hay-nets close by. With stern instructions to Gair to stay put, she unhooked his weapons from her saddle and strode inside.

Careful of his arm, he dismounted and looked around. Closer to, the tents were patched and grubby and the few soldiers he saw looked either weary or bored. After a winter living under canvas, far from the comparative comfort of a city barracks, he was not surprised.

'Gair?'

The voice sounded like Tanith's, but that couldn't be possible – she'd gone home to her people even before he'd left the Isles. He turned and for a second didn't recognise the young woman in riding leathers hurrying towards him from the command tent, slender as a sylph but with a knife on her hip. Then he registered her golden skin and the coppery hair pulled back into a braid, and stared in disbelief.

'Tanith? Holy saints, you're the last person I expected to find here!' He pulled her into a one-armed embrace. 'I thought you'd gone home to Astolar.'

'And I thought you were still on the Isles! When Magda said your name I couldn't believe it.' Her arms tightened around his waist. 'It's so good to see you,' she whispered.

'And you.'

It *was* good, but the pleasure of seeing Tanith again only made the news he carried even harder to share. She had known Alderan much longer than he had. He rested his cheek on her wild-flower-scented hair, and just for a second wished he could stay like that and not spoil the moment.

'I need to tell you something,' he said, releasing her.

She stepped back, her delight fading. 'What is it? Has something happened?'

206

Saints, it was doubly difficult now. 'I'm afraid I have bad news about Alderan. We were in the desert, looking for some books at the Daughterhouse in El Maqqam. There was trouble with the Cult, and the Daughterhouse burned down while he was inside.'

Her mouth fell open in a helpless O. 'He's dead?'

Gair nodded miserably. 'I wasn't there when it happened. I'd left to see some nuns safely out of the city. When we saw the smoke I hailed him, but he told me to go, and then . . .' He broke off, remembering the sudden silence, the stinging lash of guilt. *Goddess go with you, Alderan.*

Tears welling, she reached out blindly. Her hand found his left arm and pain lanced through it. He gritted his teeth against a yelp and immediately she let go.

'Oh, spirits, are you hurt? Let me see—'

'It's all right.'

She frowned. 'Gair—'

'Honestly, it's fine. I'll tell you about it later.' He held his arm awkwardly across his body, waiting for the hot tide to ebb. 'I'm so sorry, Tanith.'

In a shaky voice, she asked, 'Does the Council of Masters know?'

'Not yet. Do you have any idea where Masen is? I know he's in the north somewhere – or at least he was. I've been trying to find him since I reached the Havens.'

'No. He was still on the Isles when I left. He'll be devastated when he hears. And the Council . . .' She collected herself with a deep breath and wiped her eyes. 'We have so much to catch up on.'

A white-blond Astolan man emerged from the command tent and came towards them. He had finely carved features and the assured manner of one born to high station, his pale good looks a striking foil to Tanith's autumnal colouring. Stopping beside her, he slipped his arm around her waist and curled his hand on her hip in a proprietorial manner.

'We are keeping the Warlord waiting, love.'

Hurt flashed in her eyes, jagged as broken glass. She stepped away from him immediately but gracefully turned the movement into a gesture of introduction. 'Ailric, this is Gair. We were at Chapterhouse together.' Nonetheless Gair heard the faintest tremor in her voice; taken with the intimacy of the man's touch, it implied a lovers' quarrel, and abruptly he realised how little he knew of Tanith's life outside of Chapterhouse.

He dropped Shahe's reins and extended his hand. 'I am honoured, sir.'

Fire-bronze eyes flicked over him, from his darned shirt to his well-worn boots.

'Well met.' The Astolan's tone was indifferent, only a hair short of bored. He turned to Tanith. 'Shall we go?'

So much for courtesy. Jaw tight with anger, Gair lowered his unshaken hand and busied himself tethering Shahe to the hitching rope and seeing to her comfort. He heard Tanith say she'd follow in a moment, but didn't look up until he heard Ailric walking away.

'I'm sorry,' she said in a low voice. 'There was no call for him to be so rude.'

Gair made sure there was a hay-net and a water bucket within reach for the mare. 'You have nothing to apologise for. Tell me, does he dislike all humans, or just commoners?'

Tanith flushed. At once Gair was ashamed of himself: someone else's lack of manners was no excuse for his.

'Now *I'm* being rude,' he said. 'I'm sorry, it's been a difficult few days.'

'I understand.' She touched his good arm and managed a smile, though there remained a hint of something wounded about her. 'I'm glad you're safe – more or less, anyway.'

She led the way to the command tent. The interior was dominated by a table strewn with papers and charts, camp stools and map-chests pushed back against the tent walls to leave space around it.

Judging by the dirt that smeared the canvas groundsheet, it had seen a lot of pacing.

At one end of the table was a rangy clansman in buckskins, presumably the Warlord, brooding over a folded paper in his hands. Next to him stood Magda, the feather-topped ride-captain, with Gair's sword and knife in her arms. At the opposite end of the table was Ailric, eyes flat as flames behind glass as his gaze swept from Tanith to Gair and back again.

At the sound of new arrivals Aradhrim looked up, refolding the letter and tossing it onto the table. With his fierce, heavy brows and shaggy mane of hair he resembled a hunting cat – moved like one, too, all loose-limbed lazy confidence as he came around the table to greet them.

'Magda's mysterious traveller,' he said. A resonant voice matched his demeanour, and he studied Gair intently. 'Perhaps you can explain how a Leahn on a very fine Gimraeli horse comes to be in the middle of Arennor.'

Behind him, a neatly pressed adjutant attempted to tidy up the clutter of papers on the table. The chart underneath appeared to be a detailed map of the Archen Mountains, annotated with figures and symbols.

'As I told your captain, my lord, I'm just passing through,' Gair said. 'I'm no sell-sword, and I'm not looking to start any trouble here.'

The Warlord grunted, unconvinced.

'I can vouch for Gair,' Tanith put in. 'He's *gaeden*, like me.'

'Is that so?' Green eyes raked over him, and Gair bowed.

'My lord.'

'That explains why you are searching for the Gatekeeper, at any rate.' Aradhrim nodded to Magda, who returned Gair's weapons to him. 'My apologies for the welcome. The Marches are unsettled just now, on top of everything else. We cannot be too careful about armed strangers in our midst.'

'I understand.' Gair slipped the knife back into its sheath on his belt but left his sword on a chest by the tent wall. The baldric pulled his shirt uncomfortably against his left arm.

'You are welcome to rest and reprovision here before you go on your way,' Aradhrim added, 'but I confess, I am curious why there are so many *gaeden* traipsing about my fair country.'

The words were spoken mildly, casually, but there was nothing casual about the Warlord's gaze: it remained fixed on Gair the way a cat's fixed on a mouse. He blinked. 'I'm sorry?'

'Is it connected to the renegade *gaeden* Lady Elindorien told me about?'

The question caught Gair off guard. From what Alderan had told him, the Order of the Veil wanted as little to do with the Empire as the Empire did with it; it didn't seem possible that word of the attack on Chapterhouse could have spread so far and so fast. He glanced at Tanith, who nodded.

'The Empire needed to be warned about Savin,' she said quietly. 'If he brings down the Veil, nowhere will be safe.'

Turning back to the Warlord, Gair chose his words with care. There was no need to trouble Tanith with the real reason he was in the north. 'Savin's activities are of great concern to the Order,' he said, 'but my first duty here is to find Masen and pass on what I know.'

Arms folded, the Warlord leaned back against the edge of the table. 'Three *gaeden* on the plains. A renegade somewhere hunting the clans' missing starseed. The clans themselves rattling their spears and threatening to loose their war band again.' He paused. 'Forgive me if I find all that difficult to choke down as a coincidence.'

Savin's voice echoed in Gair's head. *I know where it is.* 'So it's true? The Nimrothi mean to come down through the passes?'

'And in numbers, it appears.' Cat-green eyes narrowed. 'What do you know of this?'

'Only what one of your officers told me, which wasn't much.'

The Warlord's head came up as if he'd scented prey. 'So you are the same Gair that Commander Ysen mentioned in his last dispatch?'

Gair nodded. 'I met him outside Yelda on my way north.'

Levering himself back onto his feet, Aradhrim gestured to his aide, who produced a leather document case and from it another piece of paper, still curled from being rolled into a courier's message tube. '"Today I met with a man named Gair",' the clansman read, ' "recently returned from El Maqqam, who brings with him disturbing news of Cultist activity, attacks against mercantile interests who trade with the Empire, and violence and intimidation of all kinds".' Is that about the size of it, would you say?'

'Pretty much.' Images filled Gair's mind, of Resa's scars, the silk merchant's severed head. 'Mostly worse.'

'Then we will discuss it further when you have a moment. I hear much the same from my agents, but first-hand intelligence is worth five written reports.' Aradhrim flicked the document in his hand towards the table, where it was deftly fielded by the adjutant and returned to his case.

'At the turn of the year a Nimrothi scout was captured at Saardost Keep,' he went on. 'Under questioning he revealed that the clans had raised a Chief of Chiefs who means to retake the lands lost in the Founding. As soon as I heard, I sent scouts of my own to King's Gate and Brindling Fall –' he picked up a pencil and indicated the fortresses' locations on the map '– and brought the Sixth Legion up from Fleet to form initial garrisons. The Ninth is marching from Yelda to replace them. I had hoped to use the Ninth to reinforce our positions in the mountains, but the Emperor places a different value on the strength of the intelligence and I suspect I will be overruled.'

Pacing back and forth on the far side of the table, Magda snorted. Her opinion of the Emperor's decision was abundantly clear.

Gair pictured a map of the Empire in his mind's eye. Rolling

Marcher country was all that lay between Arennor and the rest of the Empire. Little to stop a well-armed, agile force wreaking ruin all the way to the Great River, and if they crossed the river . . .

'This Chief of Chiefs,' he said. 'Does he have the men to press this?'

The Warlord rubbed his chin. 'We don't know precise numbers, but there will be enough for Drwyn to give the Empire a bloody nose, especially with the desert situation drawing Theodegrance's eye. But however many spears he can raise will be immaterial if his Speakers summon the Hunt again.'

Ailric stirred. 'The Wild Hunt?' he said. 'The Speakers do not have the strength to pierce the Veil – they lost their talisman centuries ago.'

'I have it on good authority that two of Maegern's Hounds are already free,' said Aradhrim. 'My kinsman Duncan has a seeker in his ride, and he tracked the beasts through the mountains.'

'And this seeker, he is certain?'

'One of the Hounds took his horse out from under him,' Aradhrim said dryly. 'He's certain. They tore through several herds here on the plains, then vanished. When Kael lost their trail, the Hounds were both bound more or less due north.'

'Into clan lands,' Tanith said quietly, her face pale. 'The Veil has already been pierced.'

'Surely they do not have that power?' Ailric made no attempt to hide his disbelief.

'If the clans are united, I imagine their Speakers are, too,' Tanith said. 'Who knows what they could achieve acting in concert – even without the starseed.'

Blood and stones. It hardly mattered whether Savin found it first or the clans did, the outcome would be the same. The Veil rent, the Hidden Kingdom exposed and the Wild Hunt free to rampage across the daylight world with nothing but a few *gaeden* to stop it.

Dear Goddess above.

Gair raked his hand back through his hair. He looked across at Tanith, knowing she would understand.

'The starseed is not lost,' he said. 'Alderan and I went to Gimrael to search for clues to where it was taken after Corlainn surrendered it. Before we found anything useful Alderan was killed, and the archive we were searching burned to the ground, but on my way here I saw Savin, or at least an illusion of him – what he called a sending.' His voice thickened in his throat. 'He told me we'd wasted our time because he already knew where the starseed is.'

Grim-faced, the Warlord looked from Gair to Tanith and back again. 'I think you'd better tell me everything you know.'

20

TANITH

〆め

Explanations took the better part of the morning. Gair described his dangerous and ultimately fruitless journey into Gimrael, his speech growing more and more terse until the tale was told, whereupon he excused himself and strode from the tent with a face as bleak as Tanith had ever seen it.

It had fallen then to her to answer the Warlord's questions, as best she could. Did she know where Savin was? Somewhere in the far north, she thought, amongst the Nordmen. Had he allied himself with the Nimrothi clans, with their Chief of Chiefs? She couldn't say. And what of the starseed? On and on it went.

As she spoke, Ailric came to stand beside her and slipped his arm around her waist. She stiffened. Even through her leathers his touch made her cringe – with regret for what had happened between them, with mortification that her treacherous body had responded to it and even now part of her revelled in his nearness. Every nerve was alive to him, like a sound she could still hear no matter how hard she pressed her hands over her ears. Deliberately, she took a half-step out of his reach.

At noon, Aradhrim sent for refreshments, but her stomach was too clenched for food and even the smell of the soldiers' rough red wine made her already sore head spin. Not long after, his attention was called away when a patrol rode in with two men wounded and three dead laid over their saddles. She offered her assistance as a Healer but he declined; the men's injuries were not so serious that the field surgeon could not tend them, and the dead were past anyone's help.

So she left the command tent to Aradhrim and the patrol's returning captain and walked away from the bustle of the camp, as horses were saddled for the next patrol and greasy smells began to billow from the cook-fires. Out beyond the last row of tents the air was clean, the breeze scented with a northern summer: fresh grass and water and tiny, heady flowers. Turning her face into the wind, she closed her eyes and let it blow away some of the strain.

Oh, spirits, what a tangle her life had become. Headache and heartache, her body tired from travelling, her mind torn by conflicting responsibilities and unable to rest. She'd made a fool of herself with Ailric – it was hard to know whether she was more angry with him for taking advantage of her, or with herself for letting him. He should have respected her repeated refusals to rekindle their relationship. Equally, she should have had the self-control to resist him, *uisca* or no *uisca*.

What a mess.

She opened herself to the Song and let the music fill her. She felt the turf beneath her boots, crammed with sparks of life, and let herself soar with the insects and birds on the vast gentle breath of the uplands. There was an order in nature, a pattern, subtle yet all-embracing; finding her place in it again would soothe her. Not as much as meditation, but it would help until she could find some time and space to be truly alone.

In the middle distance, beyond a cluster of scrubby willows beside the river that bisected the shallow valley, she saw Gair's familiar colours of emerald and amber. Loss scored the vibrant pattern a little more deeply than before, deep lines of silver-black distorting it the way a badly healed scar distorted skin.

So much grief. His lover lost to violence, his friend Darin, and now Alderan had been taken from him, too. Thinking of the Guardian gave her a pang of her own, sharp enough to set her eyes stinging. Dear Alderan, with his fierce good humour and fondness for pithy aphorisms. If ever she returned to the Isles, Chapterhouse would be colourless without him.

'You should not stray far from the camp if there are bandits about,' said Ailric from behind her, in Astolan.

Spirits, was there no escaping his presence? Letting the Song go, Tanith opened her eyes but did not look at him. 'Leave me alone.'

'My only concern is for your safety. I promised your father that I would keep you from harm.'

Cool fingers curled around her hand. She snatched her arm away and rounded on him, glaring. 'Touch me again without my permission and it will be the last thing you ever do with that hand!'

His lips twitched, hiding a smile. 'You gave me permission last night,' he murmured, deliberately looking past her, across the valley. 'You rode to ecstasy on my touch, as I recall.'

Her ears burned to hear it. 'I was drunk!'

'Drunk enough to salve your conscience, perhaps.' Now Ailric faced her. 'We are made for each other, love. We both know it. I will be a good husband to you; I will not stray, and I will help you, work alongside you. If you would only give me the chance, we could rule Astolar together, side by side.'

'Stop it.'

'Admit that you still want me, Tanith. Your words refuse me, but your body—'

The crack of her open palm across his cheek silenced him. Eyes blazing, he touched his tongue to the corner of his mouth as if she had actually hurt him.

'I did not deserve that.'

'Get out of my sight.' Tanith's voice, the very air in her lungs, quivered with rage.

Ailric sneered. 'So you can go to your human pet?'

'He's my friend, and we've both lost someone dear to us. That's all.' He laughed, shaking his head, and she sharpened her tone. 'My friends are none of your business, Ailric, and neither is my bed. Find somewhere else to sleep from now on.'

'As you wish.' Lutenist's fingers traced the reddened handprint on his cheek. 'Tell yourself whatever lies you need to hear. But you will come to me, my lady Elindorien, when you admit what you truly crave.'

'Never!' Angry tears threatened and she blinked them away, then turned her back on him so she would not have to watch him walk towards the tents, long-legged and supple in his leathers. Damn him for his arrogance! But in part, at least, he was correct. His touch still had the power to make her body hum like a plucked string and he *knew* it.

Face flaming, head pounding, she kicked out at a loose rock and scattered the rabbits grazing amongst the gorse. It was childish but strangely satisfying, like cursing at the top of her voice, except that thanks to her upbringing, the foulest language she knew wasn't very foul at all. She needed soldiers' curses, something truly vile, for the way she felt now.

What a tangled, torrid mess.

Slowly she walked along the river. More rabbits scampered from her path, white scuts bobbing. Soon the camp was out of earshot and all she could hear was water chattering over stones and the willows on the banks rubbing their dry fingers together in the wind.

Ahead of her, Gair sat on a boulder above the water, his legs drawn up and long hair blowing loose. He'd changed since she'd last seen him, on the Isles. Even allowing for a week's worth of beard he looked older, harder somehow, as if Gimrael had peeled away the last soft pith of youth and only heartwood remained.

She wondered if there had been other changes, too, ones that she couldn't see. What was hiding from the light under that shield in his mind? Tender new flesh, or a festering chancre? She already knew that Savin's touch was deadly as poison – that parasite he'd left in Gair's mind! Even now the memory of it made her shudder. If only she could be sure she'd cleansed it all and not left any fragment behind that would cause more problems later, like the head of a tick left embedded in a bite.

As if he'd heard her speak, Gair turned his head towards her.

Shading her eyes against the bright sky, she peered up at him. 'Am I intruding?'

'Not at all. They say misery loves company.'

He gave her his hand to help her scramble up onto the rocks where he sat, and she settled herself beside him, arms wrapped around her knees.

'Your eyes look a little pink,' he said. 'Is everything all right?'

'Too much *uisca* last night.' She made a rueful face. 'What about you? When you left so abruptly, I was worried.'

'I just needed some space. Talking about it all . . . it's hard.'

He looked down at the *zirin* in his hand, turning it slowly to read the inscription. Aysha's gift to him; perhaps all he had left of her. Tanith knew a few words of Gimraeli, mostly medical terms, but nowhere near enough to read the flowing script for herself. A guilty pang pricked her for even wanting to know what it said. That message, lover to beloved, was for no one else's eyes.

'I'm so sorry about Alderan,' she said gently.

'I should have stayed with him. Helped him save the books, or tried harder to persuade him to get out before it was too late.' Gair squinted away over the river. 'We parted on bad terms.'

Oh, Gair. 'If you had stayed, you both might have been lost.'

'Maybe. Or maybe Alderan would still be here.' Emotions chased across his face before he hid them away. 'That trouble with the Cult? It was my fault. They threatened some of the nuns in the street and I stood up to them, so they burned down the Daughter-house. I got the nuns out of the city and back to Syfria, but . . .' His voice trailed off helplessly. 'I couldn't leave them, Tanith. Not for some books that might not mean anything at all. I just couldn't.'

There was more to be told, she was sure of it, but he'd said enough for her to understand. She laid a hand on his good arm.

'You did the right thing. I know you did.'

'Funny how that doesn't help me sleep at night.' He looked out to the eastern horizon and the tiny silhouettes of mounted pickets along the valley's rim. 'You and Ailric look well together.'

'We always have; that's half the problem.' It certainly made it difficult to explain to her father why she and Ailric were so incompatible, when they made such a striking pair.

'I'm sorry, I assumed—'

'Most people do.' She only just stopped herself from adding *and that's the way Ailric likes it*. 'I'm sorry you had to see him display his prejudices like that.'

Gair pursed his lips. 'He seems very protective of you.'

'He wants to marry me,' she admitted. 'Politically, it would be a good match – his grandmother is First Ascendant to the throne and she dotes on him, but . . .' Now it was her turn to shrug.

'You don't love him.'

Love shouldn't matter to someone in her situation. Considering what was at stake, it couldn't be *allowed* to matter, but it did, in every way that made marriage meaningful to her.

She sighed. 'I did once, years ago. He thinks we can have that again.'

'But you don't?'

'No, although it would solve a lot of problems if I did.' Resting her chin on her folded arms, she studied the toes of her boots. 'In Astolar, our names descend through the female line. If I don't marry and have daughters of my own, House Elindorien will end with me.'

It sounded so simple, said like that, so matter-of-fact, when there were a thousand generations of Astolar's history bound up in it. Her father's hopes and expectations. Her duty as High Seat to ensure the survival of her House. And a tiny girl in ribbons, running through the sunlit corridors of the palace with a carved wooden horse in one pudgy fist, looking for her mother. Tanith dashed a finger across her eyes and told herself it was only the wind making them water.

'I barely know what it's like to have a family, much less one of any station,' Gair said at last. 'Much as I wish I could, I can't offer you any advice.'

'I wasn't looking for any. Just a friendly ear.' She grimaced. 'I can't exactly talk to Ailric about it. I've tried to tell him a dozen times but he acts as if he didn't hear me – as if he knows better than me what I really want.'

He gave her a ghost of a smile. 'Do you have to decide straight away?'

'I suppose not, but Ailric's offer is a good one and as my father likes to remind me, I'm not getting any younger.' This time he smiled properly, freely, knowing they weren't far apart in age. 'Oh, I don't know what to do. I didn't ask for all this, the White Court, the politics, the responsibility that comes with it – I've tried to avoid it for years. All I ever wanted to be was a physician.'

Gair's eyes were on the swirling waters of the river below the rocks but his expression said his attention was very much further away. 'I was raised always to do what was right,' he said. 'But then someone told me that we are what we make of ourselves, and we shouldn't let anyone force us into being what we are not.' He looked up again. 'You have one life – live it as you see fit.'

'I'm trying to,' she said, and sighed. *If only my life were that simple.* 'So what happened to your arm?'

Glancing at it, he dismissed her concern. 'It's nothing.'

'Gair, when I touched it you almost leapt out of your skin. That's not nothing. Let me take a look.'

'There's nothing to see. It just hurts as if there should be,' he said, but twisted around to face her and held out his left arm.

She sensed the heat as soon as she touched his shirt-cuff to unfasten it. Though he tried not to show it, he tensed at the slightest brush of fabric against skin as she eased his sleeve up past his elbow. As he'd said, his forearm was unmarked. Well muscled by weapons-work, browned by the sun, but with no bruises or abrasions, no obvious swelling. Only the way he held his fingers curled into a loose fist as if he couldn't straighten them said there was anything at all amiss.

Gathering the Song, she held her palm a scant inch above his forearm. Savage heat struck up from his skin and she hissed.

'How long ago did this happen?'

'About a week or so. I lost control of a fire-weaving and the heat turned back on me.'

Spirits, his arm was shrieking as if he'd thrust it into boiling water. Every nerve was jangling, his entire arm and hand a twanging tangle of pain. When the breeze pebbled his skin into gooseflesh he swallowed hard.

'That hurts?' she asked, glancing up.

He nodded, the strain showing around his eyes. 'Like every hair was a hornet sting.'

It was a wonder he hadn't come half-unhinged with the pain. She soothed the nerves as best she could, but with no damage to skin or muscle, there was no physical recovery process she could harness with the Song as she would for a burn or scald. There was only pain, and heat trapped in his flesh, with nothing obvious to cause it. After seeing his reaction to the breeze she couldn't use air to cool him; water she suspected would be even worse, and ice would only add the risk of frostbite. Nothing she could think of to counteract the searing heat wouldn't cause more damage or inflict pain in the process.

Her thoughts raced. All the techniques she knew for the treatment of burns were predicated on the prior existence of a burn to treat, and Gair was not burned. If she could just take away the heat . . .

Of course. The riddle – she remembered it from when she was a child: what would you take out of a burning house? And the answer: take out the fire.

'Can you put your hand flat on the rock?' Gair did so, a grimace twisting his face. 'I'm afraid this might hurt.'

Earth-Song wasn't the strongest aspect of her gift. Nonetheless she summoned what she could and wrapped it carefully around the heat, pushing it down into the boulder on which they sat. Warmth bloomed in the stone and Gair's eyes flew wide. Sweat broke on his brow, in the hollow of his throat, and he swore.

Maybe I should ask him for some better curse-words.

'It's gone – the pain, all of it.' Wonderingly, he flexed his hand. 'That's amazing, thank you. What did you do?'

'I took the heat from you and pushed it into the stone. It's unconventional, but then I've never seen anything like this before.' She fixed him with a look, though she kept her tone gentle. The pain she'd shared, however briefly, had been agonising. 'What happened, Gair?'

'My own fault – I was careless.' He ducked his head to avoid her eye, concentrating on pulling his sleeve down again and fastening the cuff. 'I promise I'll be more careful next time.'

Not the truth – or at least, not all of it. In the time she had known him, Tanith had never seen Gair make a mistake with the Song. During the attack on Chapterhouse he had drawn vast flows of power, controlled a dozen weavings simultaneously. Mishandling a single fire conjure so badly that he hurt himself struck her as unlikely, to say the least.

'I'm worried about you,' she said. 'I think you still need Healing, after what Savin did.'

He looked away when she said the name, a muscle working in his jaw as if he was struggling to master his temper. 'I'm all right.'

But he wasn't; she *knew* he wasn't. That Healer's instinct she'd learned to trust over the years was telling her what looked whole and healthy on the surface was far from it underneath. She bit her lip, then ventured, 'If it's the reiving—'

'Then you've already told me there's nothing you can do.'

Standing up, he tucked the *zirin* into his pocket. 'We should be getting back.'

He hopped down from the rocks and turned to offer her his hands. 'Be careful, it's further than it looks.'

Tanith watched him for a moment, wondering what he hadn't told her and why. Then she got to her feet, took his hands and jumped down to the turf. He was right: it was further than it looked. She landed awkwardly, stumbling on the rough ground, and would have fallen if Gair hadn't caught her in his arms.

Her next breath was filled with him. Leather. Horse. Sweat and steel that prickled her nose, but mostly the male musk of his skin, and it sliced to the core of her so sharply it made her dizzy. Dear spirits. How did humans not understand the potency of their natural scent? They drowned it in exotic perfumes, tried to wash it away with soap – she'd spent her first few days on the Isles with all the symptoms of a head-cold until she became accustomed to the assault on her nostrils. Held against Gair like that, so close she could hear his heartbeat under her cheek . . . Dear *spirits*.

He looked down at her, concerned. 'Are you all right?'

'What?' Her thoughts were in disarray. 'Oh, yes, I'm fine – just jarred my ankle.' She made a show of flexing her foot around in circles to buy time in which to collect her wits, then compelled herself to take a step back, out of his embrace.

'Are you sure?' He offered his arm. 'It's a good walk back to the camp.'

'I'm sure, thanks.' She folded her own arms tightly across her chest to keep herself from linking them with his just so she could drink him in some more. It only made it worse when she had to let go. He was not for her, and that was that.

He gave her a touch of a smile and started walking. She follow-ed, keeping a little distance between them and her eyes firmly fixed on the pale rectangles of the army tents ahead instead of on Gair. Not that it made much difference – she could have pictured him with her eyes closed, from hawk-sharp cheekbones to battered old boots.

The reason his scent had set her reeling had nothing to do with her keen Astolan senses, and everything to do with her emotions. She'd thought going home would give her the distance she needed to master those wayward feelings, but she'd been deluding herself. A couple of months had not been long enough, her homeland not far enough away, and it never could be.

Abruptly she realised she'd fallen behind and Gair was looking back over his shoulder for her. Mustering a bright smile, she hurried to catch him up again, but every stride of the walk back to the camp, the truth drummed in her head.

She was a Daughter of the White Court, the last Elindorien, and she was deeply, irredeemably in love with a human man.

21

GUILT

〇⊙

Gair waited for Tanith to catch up to him then resumed walking back to the camp, stride shortened to match hers in deference to her jarred ankle. She looked distracted, head down and arms folded tightly across her chest as if to keep something inside. Brooding on Ailric's suit for her hand, no doubt. That sudden sparkle of tears he'd glimpsed before she dashed them away said she was far from delighted with the notion.

He slid a glance in her direction. It had never occurred to him that she might be affianced. Given her station it was hardly unexpected: the sons and daughters of noble houses were more often matched for political advantage than for love. He'd seen it happen, back in Leah, although at the time he'd been of an age where he was more interested in all the feasting and hawking that was going on than in the reason why there were so many guests to be entertained. Astolan society was matrilineal, names and Houses descending through the female line, but he imagined the manoeuvring was much the same. He glanced across again, but her gaze was fixed firmly on the grass in front of her boots. The lack of affection certainly appeared to be.

The breeze tugged at his shirt as he walked. The absence of pain in his left arm was so marked it felt almost numb; he had to make a fist and squeeze it in his other hand to convince himself that the agony truly was gone. Unfortunately the guilt remained. That couldn't be pushed into a rock and left behind.

On the far side of the camp, well away from the river, four men in plain shirts and green uniform trousers were digging. Shovels glinted and black soil flew, the spoil heap already knee high. Burial detail, Gair realised, seeing the pale canvas-wrapped shapes on the ground. His footsteps slowed. Men he didn't know, being returned to the earth.

I am a monster.

Something sickly squirmed in his belly and he drifted to a halt.

Tanith stopped with him and followed his gaze across the camp. 'May they find some rest,' she murmured, then added, 'If you don't mind, I'd like to go and check on the wounded who rode in with them.'

He tried to summon up a smile. 'A Healer's work is never done?'

'Something like that. Aradhrim said the army orderly could manage, but . . .' Her shoulders lifted. 'Whenever I see sick or injured people I feel obliged to help them.'

Gair walked her to the surgeon's tent, then looked over at the gravediggers again. Two of the men were leaning on their pick handles, passing a water-skin between them, whilst the other two shovelled spoil from the deepening grave. His feet began carrying him towards them almost before he'd decided to move.

The two pick-men looked up as he approached and exchanged glances. The older and surlier-looking of the two hefted the water-skin.

'Work don't go no faster with somebody staring at it,' he said, and aimed a jet of water into his mouth. He swirled it around, spat into the grass, and added, 'Begging your pardon.'

'I didn't come to stare,' Gair said. 'I came to help, if you'll have me.'

Another glance passed between the two of them, and this time the spade-men stopped and looked up, too, sweating faces squinting against the sun.

'Why?' one of them asked.

He couldn't tell them, so instead he said, 'Why not?' and peeled off his shirt.

୭୦

The pick bit deep into the black, stony earth, breaking it up so the soldiers taking turns with shovels could clear the spoil. Hard work and slow progress; the land had never known a plough, so as often as not the pick jarred on a rock or snagged old gorse roots, but Gair relished the exertion. Swing, thud, pull and swing again. Simple, repetitive labour in which he could lose himself until his breath rasped and the sweat ran.

The four soldiers on burial detail hadn't taken much persuading to let him spell them for a time. They'd seen it as their personal duty to make a resting place for their comrades in this foreign soil, but once he'd explained that he'd spent ten years with the Suvaeon they'd also seen a fellow soldier, and his broad shoulders and hard hands had been welcome to share the burden. None of them had asked him any further questions, and for their silence he was grateful.

Swing and pull, over and over. Steady, like a heartbeat thudding in the earth. He'd shucked off his shirt for freedom of movement and his hair clung to his sweaty back. Swing and pull, deeper now, exposing the bones of the land. More rocks, stubborn in their sucking clay beds, spoiling his rhythm as he worked them loose and heaved them up over the side of the pit with his bare hands. In those pauses, memory returned.

I am a monster.

Three bodies waited off to one side, the washed and canvas-wrapped remains of some soldiers killed on yesterday's patrol. He felt no silent reproach from them, no empty eyes staring at him, but he swung and pulled, swung and pulled, to do honour for them in expiation of his guilt for the men he hadn't given a grave to. The ones that had been rolled into the ditch at the side of the road, unmarked and unmourned, like the meat they had become.

But not unwept.

When the grave was deep and wide enough to accommodate the three corpses and the sunset had begun burning up the sky, Gair swapped pick for shovel and levelled the bottom as best he could before he scrambled out.

One of the soldiers gave him a companionable nod and the skin of water. 'We'll finish it,' he said.

Gair drank deeply and handed the skin back. 'Thank you.'

That was all that needed to be said. They had exchanged few words during the afternoon's labour beyond what was needed for the job at hand; there were no farewells as he scooped up his shirt and walked away to let them grieve for their brothers in peace.

ᴄᴏ

When the dawn trumpet blew to rouse the soldiers, Tanith was already up and washing by glim-light. She'd lain awake for much of the night with her thoughts chasing in circles, then when she'd finally fallen asleep she jerked awake less than an hour later with the Song tingling in her fingertips and her ears straining for the sound of someone entering the tent. Fortunately, Ailric chose to make his bed elsewhere and did not test her repertoire of defensive weavings, but nonetheless her rest was ruined and she greeted the new day tense and weary.

Not long after she finished dressing, Aradhrim's adjutant arrived and announced with a diffident cough that the messenger from Maera had arrived, and the chief and his retinue would be riding out within the hour.

Relieved, Tanith thanked him and packed up her things. Once the Warlord's party left the army camp behind, she might sleep better – hard ground and snoring clansmen notwithstanding. Ailric would not attempt to press his attentions on her again without a tent between him and watching eyes.

She broke her fast with the ride-captain, Magda, leaning on their saddles in the grass in the clan style. Ailric greeted her politely from a distance, but didn't approach; after he left, she busied herself with her bread and fruit and tried not to notice the curious look that Magda flicked from her to the Astolan man and back again. For all Tanith liked Magda and admired her spirit, their acquaintance was too new yet for the sharing of confidences. Afterwards, she hefted her saddle onto her shoulder and went to ready her mare.

The messenger from Maera of the Tears was waiting near the command tent. She was a clan girl no more than fourteen or fifteen years of age, sitting her horse astride with her skirt kilted up and brown legs bare. A single eagle feather decorated her dark hair. Soldiers assembling for patrol milled around her and made no secret of their curiosity, but she endured their stares with great composure, not even blushing when one of the men made a ribald comment.

'This . . . *child* is who we have been waiting for?' asked Ailric.

Tanith started, her heart lurching, and looked up from buckling her mare's girths to find him at the next hitching rope with his gear at his feet. In all the bustle she'd not heard him approach. Nearby, Magda scowled at him over her own horse's back.

'Show some respect, Astolan!'

He spread his hands in conciliatory fashion, but the ride-captain gave him a flat eye as she stalked away with her mount to rejoin her men. His lips parted to say something, then he clamped them shut and heaved his saddle onto his horse's back.

'The gift is rare amongst their people, Ailric,' Tanith said, lowering her stirrup. 'They treasure those who have it, even children.'

'Superstitious fools.' Ailric slung his bags behind the saddle and began buckling them on. 'They treat the Song as if it were magic, yet it is all around them, if they would only open their minds to it.'

Wincing, Tanith stole a glance in the direction of Maera's messenger, but the girl's expression remained unreadable. If she'd overheard Ailric's rudeness, she wasn't letting it show.

'The clans are as open to the Song as any,' she hissed. 'Probably more than most. They simply don't take it for granted.'

He snorted, slapping the last strap through its keeper. 'I cannot see why you are so enamoured of these humans. They are peasants, wedded to the earth. You do not belong here.'

'Where I am is where I choose to be,' she exclaimed, 'and I choose to be where I can do most good!'

Shaking his head, Ailric untied his horse's reins from the hitching rope. 'You deserve so much more than this, love,' he said. 'When will you come to see that?'

Then he led his black away and she was left with outrage boiling in her chest and no outlet for it.

Footsteps sounded behind her. 'Good morning,' said Gair's voice.

'It was, anyway,' she muttered, then sighed and turned to face him. 'Good morning.'

'Is something wrong?'

'Not really. Just Ailric, trying my patience again.' Quickly, she manufactured a smile.

Hitching the saddle on his shoulder, he flicked a glance in the direction the blond Astolan had gone. 'If he truly loves you, he shows it in the strangest of ways.'

'It's all right, Gair. This is my problem, I can deal with it.'

He searched her face, clearly not convinced. 'If you say so, I will leave it to you.'

'I do say so.' Impulsively she touched his arm. 'That was a good thing you did for the soldiers yesterday. Helping them dig, honouring the dead.'

His gaze slipped away from hers again, as if the compliment had made him uncomfortable. He propped the saddle on his boot to free his hands and spread the blanket across his horse's back.

'They have no chaplain here. After the cairn was built, the Warlord asked if I would read a few words for them, since I was raised in the Church. I don't think the men know that I'm an excommunicate.'

'Does it matter to the Goddess who prays, as long as the prayer is said?' Tanith asked softly.

'You would think not, but . . .' He shrugged and lifted the saddle into place, then bent to pass the girths under the mare's belly.

'So where are you bound now? Are you riding with us?'

'For a while – at least until we're out of the Marches and there's no more risk of bandits.' He straightened up and leaned on the ornamented saddle. 'Aradhrim's idea, since I'm heading the same way.'

Her heart leapt at the prospect of a few more days of his company, even as she dreaded the inevitable parting. 'And then?'

'Further north. I have to find Masen, let him know about Alderan, then figure out how to bring all this to an end.' He rubbed his freshly shaved chin. Not looking at her, but unable to settle his troubled gaze on anything else, like that day at the harbour in Pencruik when she'd left for Astolar.

'Do you really think Savin knows where the starseed is?'

'Honestly?' he said. 'I don't know. It felt like the truth, but it wouldn't surprise me if it wasn't, and he only said he knew where it was because it would wind me up like a mantel-clock. He's been inside my head – he knows exactly how to goad me.' His face tightened, free hand flexing restlessly down by his side. 'He said things, Tanith. About Aysha, about the two of us.'

Tanith caught his hand between hers and held it. The scar across his palm felt like spilled candle-wax.

'Don't let it eat into you, Gair,' she said. 'Don't let him use your grief against you.'

'I'm not sure I can help it.'

He squeezed her fingers and let go as the Warlord emerged

from the command tent, firing last-minute orders over his shoulder to his patrol captain. In no time the tall clansman was mounted up, flanked by his bannerman and the Speaker's messenger, with his fussy little adjutant following on behind.

Without any obvious orders being passed, Magda's ride arranged themselves into scouts and escort, and somewhere in the chaos of departure Tanith and Gair were swept up and swept apart. She found herself riding beside Ailric in the middle of the band, with Gair further ahead, near the Warlord.

She watched him, tall in the saddle with his familiar longsword across his back once more, and saw how he dipped his head respectfully as he passed the stone cairn over the soldiers' grave.

'Did he know them, those soldiers?' Ailric asked.

'I don't think so,' she said, not looking at him.

'Then why honour them so? Why grub in the earth for them?'

'Because he thought it was the right thing to do.' She twisted in the saddle, angry now. 'Why are you still here?'

'I promised your father I would keep you safe.' He smiled, flame-coloured gaze lingering deliberately at the neck of her shirt before sliding over her hips and thighs in her leathers. She stifled a shudder. 'I want to be close by in case you need me.'

'I will never come to you,' she spat.

'Are you so sure?'

His self-assurance made her want to slap him again. 'Never!'

'I will wait. I am a patient man, my love.'

Growling, she set her heels to her mare and cantered away from him. Shame burned hot and sour inside. She'd cursed herself six ways to sundown so many times for ever letting him lay hands on her, sworn she'd never let him touch her again, but she had. Never mind the *uisca*, she'd let those fiery eyes burn up her inhibitions and fill her head with smoke.

She urged the mare faster, into a flat gallop, following the river. The horse's lashing mane stung her face. Never again. Never, ever again.

Two riders appeared from the rumpled hills to either side of her on converging courses. Clansmen, matching their speed to hers, hands reaching out for her reins. She recognised the nearest as Magda and realised what she was doing. The Marches were no place to be charging off alone.

Reining back her mount, she raised her hand in acknowledgement of her error. 'I'm sorry,' she said as they brought their blowing horses to a halt beside her. 'I lost my temper.'

'It is not safe to be away from the others, my lady,' the ride-captain admonished, fierce-eyed. 'There are still raiders here-abouts.'

'I know. It was foolish of me.' Tanith scooped her wind-tousled hair back from her face. Maybe because Magda was a woman, she added, 'Men make fools of us all, sooner or later.'

The clanswoman laughed, displaying her broken teeth.

'Isn't that the truth? I've buried two husbands and so should know better, but I still get my head turned around from time to time and wake up with a boy I should have sent home to his mother.'

That struck too close to the heart. Tanith looked away, hoping the breeze would cool the flush in her cheeks. Damn Ailric, and damn his refusal to just go home and leave her alone.

'Go on back to patrol, Colm,' she heard Magda say. 'I will escort the lady.' When the hoofbeats of Colm's horse had faded, she added, 'The one you fought with. He's pretty.'

'Too pretty for his own good,' Tanith said, with feeling.

Magda concealed a smile. 'So that's why he was pacing like a shut-out hound this morning – wants what he can't have?'

'Something like that, yes.' Tanith urged her mare into a walk and wheeled her back the way she had come, with the Arennorian woman falling in at her side.

'You should find yourself a strong young clansman to warm your blankets,' the ride-captain advised. 'That'll set him straight in the saddle.'

Spirits, if only it was that easy! 'It'd only spur him to try harder to win me back, and I'm afraid my heart's already been stolen.'

It was difficult, so difficult, not to look past Magda's scarred face and seek Gair out amongst the approaching riders. If she did, surely the captain would notice the direction of her glance and realise a certain northman was the one in her thoughts, and she didn't want to share that knowledge yet.

22

THE HAUNTED
MOUNTAIN

ফুওঁ

Several sets of hoofprints were clearly visible in the snow, despite
the advancing thaw that had softened the edges. Looking down
from Finn's back, Teia's mouth dried. Someone was moving in
the pass ahead of them.

'How many?' she asked, despair thick in her throat. *We're so
close! We've come so far – not this, not now.*

Hunkered down at the side of the trail to examine the prints,
Baer grunted. 'Not sure. They've been back and forth more than
once, see?' He pointed at the overlapping tracks.

'Could it have been the three Crainnh, the ones Isaak brought
down?'

'Maybe.' Straightening up, Baer rubbed his chin, palm rasping
over his newly grown beard. He lowered his voice, for her ears
alone. 'Truly told, Banfaíth, I don't know. I can track game well
enough, but men? Like this? Best I can tell, it was four or more
horses, travelling some time after the last big snow.'

'And there's no way to tell who they are?'

'Not from this spoor alone.'

Drwyn had sent scouts through the passes. She knew that; she'd
overheard him talk about it. But how many? Had the three men

Isaak ambushed been the only ones, or were they members of a larger party? Were her Lost Ones about to walk into an ambush of their own?

So many questions – too many of which she had no answer for, but she was too close to her goal to allow them to stop her. She could not yield to fear now.

'Then we must proceed cautiously,' she said. 'You'll send scouts on ahead?'

'Two good men. But I'm thinking it might be best to make camp here until we know what's waiting for us.'

Teia glanced at the set of the sun. They still had a good half of the day left before the light failed, but Baer was right to be dubious about pushing on. 'Just in case?' she said lightly.

He nodded. 'Aye. Just in case.'

She kept her voice low. 'Then just in case, don't send Isaak this time, eh?'

Baer's eyes hardly flickered, but she knew he'd looked past her to where the young father knelt next to Lenna's sled. The girl had insisted on walking part of the way now that the going was easier. Though she could walk a little she couldn't ride and she tired easily, worn out by childbirth and too long on short rations. She needed Isaak's strength more than ever now. Her and her five-day-old son, who still lacked a name.

'Understood,' Baer said and loped off to issue his orders.

Teia swung Finn around and urged him through the last straggle of trees to the lip of the wide, bowl-shaped valley. The tracks were still faintly visible as they crossed the snowfield, though reduced to mere dimples by the restless, fretting wind. Meltwater streams sparkled under the new sun and even the air smelled green.

So close now. The thaw was upon them – down on the plain, summer would have begun, and the Empire was almost close enough to touch. Finally they would be able to rest and she could be delivered of her awful burden of news. *And delivered of my daughter.*

She laid her hand on her belly, so hard and prominent now, and shifted in the saddle for the thousandth time that day. The ache in her back had returned and nothing she did seemed to ease it. Not a folded blanket between her rump and the saddle, nor any way she could find to sit Finn differently. Neve had tried warming a stone in the fire to put behind her at night, which was soothing, but she still couldn't sleep more than an hour at a time without waking to a sour stomach or a complaining bladder as the unborn child pressed on one or the other.

If she'd reckoned up rightly, she was due in three weeks, or thereabouts. By the time the wandering moon waned again, she'd be a mother. There'd be a use for her milk-heavy, blue-veined breasts and for the tiny clothes she'd almost left behind in the caves, then at the last minute forced into her already overloaded saddlebags instead of another pound of meal. At last there'd be an end to the waiting.

Her backache twinged more sharply and she reached behind to knead her spine. All these hours on a horse were not good for her. She should get down and walk more often, give her muscles something different to do, except once she was astride it was such an effort to dismount and remounting was even more taxing. She had barely the strength for either, even after a night's rest, to say nothing of how sore her bottom had become between pregnancy and an all-meat diet.

Taking a last look at the snowfield, she nudged Finn back the way they had come. Her little clan were already hard at work making camp. Baer's two best warriors were checking their quivers and receiving final instructions from the grizzled chief-who-was-not-a-chief. She waited until he was done, then called his name.

He looked around. 'Banfaíth?'

'Whatever they find, we should move on tomorrow. We can't hide in the mountains for ever.'

'If that is your wish.' Doubt sat heavy on his voice, but half the camp was within earshot and he kept his misgivings to himself.

'It is. Unless there's a whole clan war band waiting out there, we move on in the morning.'

I must see this done, and soon. My time is running out.

ᥱᥲ

The Haunted Mountain stood pale against the night sky above Teia's head, jagged as a broken tooth. Black trees and white snow surrounded her, in a silence unbroken except for the thin hiss of the wind. No sounds of horses or sleeping men, no crackle of a fire. Though she knew they were there somewhere, they were outside of this place. Elsewhere. In the foretelling, she was always alone.

Up she rose, towards the peak. Higher, borne on the night's cold wings, above the treeline to where Tir Malroth spread her snowy skirts around her feet and the smaller peaks that surrounded her nestled into them as if for shelter. Then higher still, into the burning cold beyond even an eagle's reach, before swooping down again across the far flank of the mountain and into the pass.

And then Teia was not alone any more.

Half-seen forms drifted in her peripheral vision, pale and filmy as milk dripped into water. Swirling, changing, vanishing only to reappear on her other side. Too many to follow with her eyes, and if she tried they frayed apart on the wind. But in the corners of her vision the dead clustered like shadows.

These were not the shades of those lost to Gwlach's folly, doomed for ever to haunt the pass in the far western mountains where they had met their end. These were the unsung dead, trapped in the trailing hem of the daylight world without a lament to speed them on to the next. They reached out to her, their eyes imploring.

Release us . . .

Many voices, but none of them louder than a breath. Illusory hands touched her face, her hair.

Let us go . . .

Face after face emerged from the dark. A crowd of them, rippling and distorted like reflections on water. She couldn't make them out, though they had a teasing familiarity that plucked at her with insubstantial fingers.

I don't understand what you want from me, she said.

We want peace . . .

She wasn't sure that was in her power to grant, but she could try. *Who are you?*

Ghostly laughter, a chorus of whispers hissing: *Do you not recognise us?*

No, but I want to help you. She searched the shifting moon-shadow faces forming and re-forming in front of her. *Please, tell me your names, that I may release you!*

You know our names. You brought us here. The faces rushed towards her. *We are your people.*

Baer. Lenna. Varn and Isaak and Aelfen and Neve and the others, their eyes corpse-clouded, dead mouths open in silent accusation.

No! She recoiled, stumbling backwards. *I'm trying to save you – all of you. I'm doing the best that I know how!*

A cold presence behind her arrested her flight as surely as a stone wall. An icy voice caressed her ear and its breath left frost-crystals in her hair. *And now they are mine.*

Teia jolted awake clutching at a sudden pain in her ear, a piercing, penetrating cold as if an icicle had been driven into her skull. She cried out, pressing her hands to her head as if she could somehow squeeze the pain down to manageable proportions, but still it left her gasping.

Soft sounds of women stirring in their blankets. A sense of

someone moving in the dark, then a shape passed in front of the thin moonlight seeping around the blanket rigged up at the door.

'Banfaíth?' Lenna's voice. Silver moon-glow picked out the line of her cheek and shone on the scar.

As the pain began to fade, Teia took her hands from her head and sat up, supporting her distended belly with one arm. 'It's all right,' she said. 'Go back to sleep.'

'I heard you speaking, but I couldn't wake you.' The girl sounded anxious. 'Was it a foretelling?'

Kneading her lower back, Teia nodded.

'What did you see?'

'Lenna, please. Just go back to sleep.' She had no desire to talk about what she had seen. She could still feel the mountain looming, its dark and heavy hand pressing down on her thoughts. Macha's mercy, were they all going to die here?

This was not how I wanted it to end.

ॐ

Morning came to the mountains slowly, almost reluctantly. Teia watched the sky lightening from the edge of the trees, wrapped in her wolfskins against the bitter chill. It was too cold and she was far too tired to be standing there, but after her dream of the dead there was little chance of any more sleep. So she'd slipped out of the fug of the women's shelter before dawn was more than a gleam on the shoulder of the mountains and come out here to the edge of the camp to be alone with her thoughts.

They made for poor company.

Baer's scouts sent out the day before had not come back. Only one set of tracks crossed the sloping snows towards the forest on the far side of the valley, where it kinked around a steep ridge and vanished into the gloom beneath the distant trees. None returned. No shouts had been heard, no clash of weapons; the forest had simply swallowed the men up and not even spat out their bones.

Two more lives lost. How many of them would live to see the

plains of their ancestors, or would the mountain take them all, in the end? The fateful words from her dream sounded again in her mind and she shuddered.

Her foretellings had never been incorrect. Sometimes they had misled her, unfolding in ways she hadn't expected, or were different in some small detail, but they had never been flat-out wrong. All those premonitions that had come to pass had been true.

Had she brought all those people through the mountains just to die here? She couldn't believe that – wouldn't believe it, no matter the chilly certainty in the pit of her stomach, the dreadful sick lurch inside that said she'd made a terrible mistake. They'd followed her of their own free will; it was no responsibility of hers that they'd come this far. Yet she couldn't help but feel responsible.

These are my people.

A breeze slid over the bone-white snows, thin and sharp as a paring knife. She burrowed her shoulders deeper inside her furs, then stiffened as the wind brought her the sound of trudging feet. Someone in the camp stirring, perhaps; it was almost light enough to move on. She'd have to tell them the men hadn't come back, and thanked the Eldest again that she'd persuaded Baer for once not to send Isaak. For Lenna to gain a son and lose a husband in the space of a sennight would have been too cruel.

At her left side, she sensed the looming presence of Tir Malroth. For days now they'd been deep amongst the peak's skirts, unable to escape them. Its great forked crown blocked out half the sky and cut off much of their daylight, left them grubbing through shadow and gloom like ground-squirrels but for a scant hour or two either side of noon. Even the land around them had the touch of the harrow-bird on it: the woods empty, the rivers barren. None of Aedon's creatures walked this earth save her few Lost Ones, and she couldn't help but wonder what the birds and the beasts knew that she did not.

Looking up, she eyed the massive peak, black as the Raven's shadow against the bright morning sky.

Did you take those men? she wondered. *Are you keeping us wandering here so you can snuff us out one by one? That would please you, wouldn't it – more ghosts for you?*

Impassive, implacable, the Haunted Mountain gave no answer.

Talking to a mountain. Shaking her head, she turned away. Macha keep her, the place had addled her wits.

The sound of someone scrunching through the snow had grown louder. It was coming from the west, to her right; she strained her eyes into the gloom beneath the snow-laden trees and made out a thickly wrapped figure, shoulders hunched, breath steaming above its head on the still air. A few yards more and she spotted the tail of a braid swinging after him: Baer.

As if he'd felt her eyes on him he looked up, and changed direction to come towards her instead of returning to the camp. 'Banfaíth,' he greeted her gravely, a little out of breath. His cheeks were reddened by the cold. 'I guess you couldn't sleep either.'

'I was awake half the night worrying about Hagen and Col.'

He gestured towards the far end of the valley. 'I've been down as far as the bend in the river to see if I could pick up a trail.' A quick, grim shake of his head. 'No sign.'

So the mountain would have its due after all. 'Then we go on.'

Baer followed her gaze across the snows to where the first sun was spilling over the mountains and gilding the tops of the trees. 'It's still early,' he mused. 'Could search the east side, give them a bit longer, mebbe.'

Teia straightened up and tried not to nibble at her chapped lips. 'No. We must go on.' *Or the mountain will surely take all of us.*

His expression hardened. 'And what if they've stumbled into danger? Will you leave them there, or march the rest of us into it, too?'

'I have no choice!' Honed by anxiety, the words came out more sharply than she had intended. 'What else would you have me do

242

– throw more men away? I have to think of the good of the many, not the few. If we stay here, we die.'

He snorted. 'Is that the foretelling talking?'

For an instant she wanted to tell him what she'd seen, but what good would it do? Forcing herself to keep her tone level, she said, 'It's practicality. We're almost out of food and we've not seen any game in two days – not since we came into this valley. We have to move on.'

Baer gave her a long, considering look – it would have done a Speaker proud – then dipped his head curtly. 'As you wish.'

He turned on his heel and strode off through the trees towards the others. Teia watched him go, noting the stiff back, the barked instructions to break camp. He did not approve. She shut her eyes a moment, then opened them again, fixed them on the tracks that led through the snow to the far side of the valley. She hated arguing with Baer – hated even more that she was right: if they stayed, they'd die. In ones and twos, in their sleep, in the cold, that cursed mountain would have them all.

She sensed its presence at her back as if she'd called it by name. It rose so high, spread its arms so wide that no matter which way she faced it was there, leaning into her peripheral vision. Fighting the urge to look, she concentrated instead on the forested far slope of the valley until her eyes watered, and still the mountain's vast unquiet sucked at her attention like a silence waiting to be filled.

The sooner her little band could make it out of that fold in the mountain's skirts, the better. Baer had recalled the hunters when he sent out the scouts, reasoning that if there was danger at hand, it was best to keep the people together – on that at least she and he agreed – but it meant their food stores had dwindled fast. Without game to hunt, they'd soon have nothing but snow to fill their bellies.

Her back twinged and she winced, rubbing at it through her furs. Macha's mercy, could she possibly grow any bigger? She felt as heavy and shapeless as a bag of curds hung up to drain. Even

Neve's deft needle couldn't find any more give in Drwyn's old trews; she'd already gusseted them twice with a bit of blanket to accommodate Teia's belly, and the fabric would fall apart if required to bear much more stitching – or wear, come to that. The trews were so filthy the first touch of laundry-soap would probably dissolve them and leave only the buttons.

'Banfaíth?'

She turned around, glad of the chance to stir her cold-stiff muscles. Lenna stood a little behind her, cradling a steaming bowl in her hands.

'You should be resting,' Teia said to her.

'The baby's still asleep, so I thought I'd stretch my legs a little.' The girl held out the bowl. 'Break your fast, Banfaíth. You need to be strong, too.'

'You have it, Lenna. You're feeding the little one now.'

'Oh, I've already had mine.'

Teia smiled. 'You can't lie to me. I'm the Banfaíth, I can read you too well. That's the end of the broth, unless I'm mistaken.' Made from the bones of the last scrawny deer, it was grease and hot water for the most part, with a few grey shreds of meat lurking at the bottom of the bowl. Scant nourishment, but hot. 'Go on, Lenna. I am well.'

The girl bit her lip. She looked pale in the early light, the scar on her cheek taut and angry. 'If you're sure?'

'I'm sure. Go back to your son. Choose a name for him before the sun sets on his first week. It's bad luck else.'

Lenna cradled the broth to her lips and sipped. 'We thought Aren, since we are in Arennor. For his ancestors.'

It meant free. Free-born, the way the ancient peoples of the plains had been. Teia gave an approving nod.

'A good choice.'

A smile lit up the girl's face. 'You think so?'

'I do.'

Sunlight touched Teia's cheek and she looked south across the snowfield again, shading her eyes against the strengthening light. The pre-dawn shadows were retreating from the ridges ahead, the mountains' snowy heads glittering. Between the peaks, misty in the distance, she saw a bluish haze that might be the open plains.

At last.

'Look, Lenna!' she exclaimed, pointing. Hope lifted her voice. 'There – do you see?'

Only a few days away. Across the snows, down through the trees, south as the thaw raced northwards, onto the sunlit side of the Archen Mountains, as she had seen in her scrying-bowl.

Behind her, Lenna gasped. Teia looked around just in time to see the bowl of broth tumble from the girl's fingers. A cloaked figure behind her held her still with an arm across her throat and a knife next to her face. Shadows under his hood hid his clan tattoo.

'Shh,' he warned.

Teia opened her mouth and a bow creaked by her ear. She turned her head a fraction, far enough to see another cloaked and hooded man with a shortbow trained on her. They must have come around the side of the valley through the forest to leave no tracks across the snowfield. More figures moved stealthily amongst the trees towards the camp, every one of them armed, and she couldn't even shout a warning.

Her heart fell. Her journey was over with her destination in sight.

23

THEN WE ARE
ALL DEAD

ᘒᘛ

Walking back to the Lost Ones' camp, Teia felt the bowman's presence behind her like an itch between her shoulder-blades. Each time she stumbled in the snow or had to reach out to steady herself on a tree, the itch intensified until she found herself anticipating the snap of the string. The impact of an arrow at such close range would drive her to her knees.

Who was he? She didn't dare stop to look and a stolen glance over her shoulder revealed little: he wore thick winter clothes and a cloak with a deep hood that hid his face. Was he one of Drwyn's men? No, he couldn't be from the Crainnh war band; he'd shown no sign of recognising her. One of the other clans, then: Amhain, maybe. She darted another glimpse behind her. No bow-charms, but that didn't mean anything. Macha, her thoughts were scurrying around like startled chickens.

Renewed sobbing made Teia look across at Lenna. The girl had tried to run, and hadn't made it very far. Now she stumbled along with one arm twisted up behind her back by her captor, who held his long knife ready in his free hand. Hopeless tears shone on her cheeks.

This was not how it should have ended, Teia thought. After all those miles, all she had endured, surely she had earned a better end than this, caught like fowl in a net on the very borders of the Empire. She had paid enough to get this far, but apparently the Eldest enjoyed a good joke as much as man.

She stumbled again, and only a frantic stab at the ground with her staff prevented her from falling. She clung to the pale wood until she was sure of her feet, then straightened up. Lenna and her captor were a few yards ahead now; flanking them were other figures, ghosting through the trees with the sure-footedness of hunters. Her people were already taken.

So much for the Banfáith's visions, she thought bitterly, shutting her eyes. They hadn't foretold this.

She sensed the bowman an instant before his hand grasped her elbow. Her eyes flew open again and she snatched her arm away. Magic sang inside her.

'I can walk!' she snapped.

Leaning on her staff, she set off again, faster than she was really comfortable with but by the Eldest she would not be marched in front of her own people like a prisoner. Her fist tightened on the smooth shaft of her staff. She'd come far too far for that.

Ahead, the trees opened up into the clearing where the Maenardh had made camp. Men and women huddled together in the melting snow under the watchful gaze of a dozen or more cloaked clansmen, each with a shortbow drawn and an arrow nocked. Some of the women were weeping, and Aelfen sat with her arms wrapped around her knees and her face buried in them. Off to one side were the men who'd been standing sentry and the two missing scouts, kneeling in a circle with their hands laced across the backs of their necks, guarded by yet more cloaked warriors.

Baer looked up at the sound of footsteps in the snow. Defiant eyes and a bloody lip said he'd not submitted without a fight. She would have expected no less from him. Next to him, Isaak leapt to his feet when he saw Lenna.

'Lenna!' A hideously scarred clansman grabbed his shoulder, but he shrugged the man off. 'Please, don't hurt her!'

A kick to the back of the knee dropped Isaak into the snow. Before he could get back up, the scar-faced man had one hand knotted in his shaggy hair and a knife under his chin.

'Stop!'

Sharp and clear, the word startled Teia. It startled her even more when she realised she had said it. Everyone in the clearing turned to look at her: hooded clansmen and pale Maenardh faces with frightened, pleading eyes. Even Aelfen lifted her head, peering out from under her hair.

This is not how it was supposed to be!

The man holding Isaak's hair scowled at her. 'Who are you to give me orders?'

The sonorous roll of his accent rendered his speech awkward to follow. Some of the outer clans spoke like that, but she couldn't make out his tattoo for his lank hair and the scar that distorted his cheek.

Teia planted her white staff firmly between her feet. 'Leave him be. He is only concerned for his family.'

The fellow's stare didn't falter and the wickedly sharp blade stayed snug beneath Isaak's jaw. 'Or what?'

Her confidence wavered. No one in the Crainnh would have dared to defy a white staff, but she was beginning to wonder if that was more down to the sheer presence of the woman who wielded it.

A tall man on the far side of the captives turned to face her. Like the others he was cloaked and carried a bow, but his was up on his shoulder and all his arrows were quivered.

'You lead here, then?' he asked. He had the same rolling accent as the scar-faced fellow.

'No.' She pointed towards the grizzled chief-who-was-not-a-chief. 'Baer there is our leader, but the people are under my protection.'

She expected him or his men to laugh, or to at least smirk at the idea that a mere girl could protect more than fifty folk from armed warriors, but they didn't. Not one of them – though they didn't relax, either.

The tall man put back his hood, revealing a mane of wavy brown hair framing an easy, open countenance, made harder by several days' worth of beard. She thought his eyes might be blue, like hers.

'Is this everyone?'

'If you count fifty-three, you have us all.'

He pursed his lips, his gaze moving from her tall white staff to her wolfskin mantle and much-darned clothes, before settling on her heavy belly. Without turning, he asked, 'Kael?'

'Fifty-three,' the scarred fellow answered, 'counting the babe.'

'Don't touch my son!' Isaak gasped. Again he struggled to rise, and the scarred man hauled back on his shaggy curls until he was still again.

'Isaak . . .' Lenna whimpered, fat tears rolling onto her cheeks. Her knees sagged; only her captor's grip on her wrist made her struggle upright again.

Reaching out a hand, Teia touched the girl's arm. 'Easy, Lenna. I won't let him be hurt.'

The blue-eyed man raised his eyebrows. 'I am interested to learn how you think you can do that,' he said, tapping his bow meaningfully on his shoulder, 'when we appear to hold the advantage here.'

Power tingled in Teia's fingertips again. There were too many armed warriors around the clearing, she knew that, but she wasn't going to allow them to bully her, not when she'd brought the Lost Ones this far. If this was the endgame, then so be it, but by the Eldest she would not let anyone haul them back to Drwyn.

The power rose up, heightening her senses. Colours became more vibrant: the wintry blue of the tall man's gaze, the redness of the wound that had pulled Kael's lip into a sneer. The air rang with sounds that would otherwise have been too small to hear; her nostrils filled with the scents of cold and wet pine and fear. All she had to do was shape her will—

The scarred man flashed her a hard look.

'Have a care, Duncan,' he said. 'She's got the gift.'

All around the clearing bows creaked under increased tension. Amongst the huddled women, Aren whimpered in Neve's arms as if he too sensed the danger.

The tall man – Duncan? – made no move to ready his bow. He didn't need to. He simply tilted his head a little to one side and in a perfectly reasonable tone said, 'Let the power go, or Kael slits the lad's throat.'

Magic humming, Teia hesitated. Isaak struggled to say something but with his head held painfully back by the hand in his hair, all he could do was pant, his eyes hunting desperately from her to his woman and back again.

Kael's black eyes glittered. Teia had no doubt that he'd slit a man's throat. And how had he sensed the magic in her? She'd never heard of a man with the gift; it always followed the female line. She stared at him, and something empty stared back.

Lenna broke. 'Banfaíth, please!'

It had been a foolish hope at best. There were too many arrows pointing from too many angles – not least of them the one aimed at Teia's own back. Quick as the magic was, she'd never stop them all. Carefully, she willed the power into quiescence.

Only when it was completely still did Kael give a short nod. 'It's gone.'

'Thank you,' said Duncan. 'Now we can be polite. What is your business here?'

'We are travelling,' Teia answered warily. 'We mean you no harm, clansman.'

'I'm relieved to hear it.'

She blinked, thinking she'd misheard. Humour? Or was he

mocking her? Then he gave her a gracious nod and she realised he wasn't.

'Speaker.'

Teia nodded back, not inclined to correct his assumption just yet. 'Captain.'

'You're a long way from your lands.'

'We have no lands. We were only looking for somewhere safe to spend the rest of the winter.'

'I see.' Duncan considered, then turned to his men. 'Stand down. You too, Kael.'

Kael frowned. 'What if they tell someone they've seen us?'

'Who are they going to tell?' Duncan spread his hands. 'Look at them, Kael – they're Lost Ones, two days short of starving and with barely enough weapons to defend themselves.'

The scar-faced man made a disgusted sound but he complied, as did Lenna's captor. At once Isaak ran to the girl and snatched her into his arms. Sobbing, she buried her face in his chest whilst her man glared over her shoulder at the fellow who had held her prisoner until he stepped clear.

Around the clearing bowstrings were eased and hoods were flipped from heads. Teia was surprised to see that several of Duncan's warriors were in fact women, as lean and sun-toughened as the men, many with feathers braided into their hair.

Lip curled, Kael thrust his long blade into its sheath and stalked away into the trees.

Never mind what rent his face, Teia wondered, watching him go. *What rent his heart?*

Duncan was walking towards her. As he drew closer she realised he was only a few years older than she was, in the early half of his twenties, and already a captain of men. His eyes were indeed blue, intensely so, like vallain flowers, and his generous mouth had an upward kink at one corner, as if smiles came easily to him. A face more suited to mirth than murder, she thought, wondering if he would really have given the order to Kael. Probably not; it had been a ruse, and she'd fallen for it.

Then she noticed something else. High on Duncan's cheek, almost hidden by his hair, was a tattoo in the shape of a stylised horse, its head and neck outstretched, forelegs reaching for the next stride. A clan symbol, yes, but not one she had ever seen before.

As she stared at the mark, her heart turned over its toes. 'Arennor,' she whispered.

Macha's mercy, men of the Empire – here, in the mountains, where she had least expected to find them. She might not have to ride into the heart of their lands after all. The sudden relief was dizzying.

'Why are you here?' she gasped.

Duncan looked amused. 'These are my lands, Speaker – the question is surely why are *you* here? I'd be well within my rights to have your whole band charged with vagabondage and hauled before my brother's justice.'

'I have information that must be brought to your battle chief,' she said. 'Can you take me to him?'

'I can send a fast rider with a message—'

'You don't understand,' Teia interrupted. 'I must speak with him myself – he will want to question me.'

He frowned. 'It's a long ride and your people are exhausted. Are you sure—'

By the Eldest, would he just listen *for a moment?* 'Captain, there is no time! The clans are sending their war bands against you and your battle chief must be warned.'

'He knows.'

Teia blinked, struck momentarily mute.

'That's why we're here – we're watching for the war band coming south. When we found you, well . . .' He lifted his shoulders. 'Some of my ride are understandably a little jumpy.'

The Empire knew. 'W-what? How? I thought—'

She looked around her, at the bewildered Maenardh picking themselves up off the ground, at Isaak and Lenna wrapped so tightly in each other's arms that it was hard to discern where one ended and the other began, and could hardly make sense of the thoughts tumbling in her head. Two months. Countless hungry leagues, and the Empire already knew, had already anticipated Drwyn's plan.

Like a flight of startled birds, scenes of horror and death filled her head. Oh, Macha, the slaughter that would come. Her knees buckled and she would have fallen had Duncan not slipped his arm around her waist.

'Steady there,' he said. 'When did you last eat?'

She let him steer her a few steps to where a knuckle of rock protruded through the snow. 'I-I don't remember.' Tumbling, still tumbling; she couldn't think clearly.

He swept the rock clear of snow and guided her to sit, hunkering down next to her. 'Are you all right?'

'I think so.' She wasn't all right; she was either going to faint or throw up – possibly both – but she had to know. 'How?' she asked. 'I've been riding south to bring word of Drwyn's plans. I thought I was the only one who knew – and now this.' A twitch of her hand took in Duncan's warriors. 'How?'

'We tracked two of Maegern's Hounds,' he said. 'We lost one of them north of Whistler's Pass and were halfway home when Kael picked up the trail of another one east of here, where we caught an Amhain scout. He told us the rest.'

The Hounds had come this way? 'You know about the Hunt?'

He nodded. 'All of it.'

Aedon preserve us. Instead of filling her with relief the news deflated her, left her abruptly exhausted, too tired even to shiver at the cold. She leaned her head against the smooth wood of her staff and shut her eyes. 'Oh, Ytha, you've damned them all.'

Duncan bent closer to catch her words. 'Speaker?'

So much death. She shuddered. 'There's something I need to

tell you,' she said in a low voice. 'I'm only a Speaker's apprentice, but I have the gift of foretelling. I have seen the outcome of Ytha's plan, and it spells ruin for the plains. I *must* meet with your battle chief.'

'The girl spoke truly, when she named you Banfaíth?'

Still leaning on her staff, Teia nodded.

'It's eight days' ride and more to Saardost Keep. So near your time . . .' Duncan looked dubious. 'I would be happier if you stayed safe at King's Gate and let me send a messenger.'

The names meant nothing to her. 'I can't. I must speak with your chief immediately. Once the Hunt is loosed, only the iron men can stand against it.'

His blue eyes clouded. 'Iron men?'

Had the Empire forgotten its history? 'The men who built the stone forts, who slew Gwlach and drove us north. The iron men!'

'The Knights?' Duncan's expression cleared. 'But Banfaíth, there are no Knights in Arennor. They have not ridden out to war in more than twenty years.'

The black maw of prescience yawned at the back of Teia's mind. Yellow-fanged Hounds poured out of the darkness, filled her ears with sounds of rending flesh and her nose with the stink of the charnel house. Scarlet sprayed the silvery grasses. Ravens blackened the sky and laughter rang out, the dark hunter's laughter, booming over the plains like thunder. She closed her eyes but could not escape the vision.

'Then we are all dead,' she whispered.

ᏽ

Duncan frowned. He didn't know who this Ytha was, nor fully understand everything that the Nimrothi girl had said, but there was no mistaking the horrified tremor in her voice. When she opened her eyes again and turned that bleak, blasted stare on him, it chilled him to the bone. Whatever she saw it wasn't him, or the

clearing in the mountains in which she sat, but a vision so terrify-
ing it defied articulation.

The Wild Hunt would be freed; the girl was sure of it. If the
Warlord needed confirmation that what the Amhain scout had
told them at Saardost was true, he would have it as soon as this
extraordinary young woman – this seer – was brought before him.
Arennor was riding to war.

He touched the girl's arm and she blinked, put a hand to the
savage scar that ran up her brow into her hair. How had that
happened – and how had a Speaker's apprentice, with a child on
the way, come to be riding with the Lost Ones?

'I'm sorry, I . . .' Violet-blue eyes cleared slowly as she came
back to the now, but remained troubled by shadows. Even with
her staff to lean on the girl was barely able to hold herself upright,
so pale and hollowed-out with exhaustion that Duncan imagined
her bones might break through her skin at any moment.

'You're in no state to be travelling, Banfaíth,' he said.

'Please, Captain. Your battle chief must hear what I have to
say.' Her speech had the cadence of his own tongue but her
phrasing was archaic; he had to concentrate, translating her
words in his head and picking his own carefully in reply to be
sure they were understood. Strange how she seemed so familiar
and at the same time so very different.

'I understand and I agree, but you should eat and rest awhile
before we move on.' He pushed himself to his feet. 'I'm afraid I
must keep your men's weapons, but you will come to no harm
with us.' She made to protest. 'You have my word, Banfaíth.'

Walking back towards the Lost Ones' little fire, he gathered up
Cara and a few others with a nod.

'Get that fire built up and a kettle or two boiling. We haven't
much time but I want these people to have some hot tea at least,
and something to eat.' As two warriors loped off to do his bidding,
he turned to Cara. 'Pack up their weapons, then let them move
freely. I don't think there's any threat here, but be careful, eh?'

She nodded her understanding, but hesitated. 'They're coming with us back to King's Gate?'

'No. I'll leave three four-man patrols here, then the rest of us will escort the Lost Ones to Saardost.' Her eyebrows rose. 'She's determined to speak to the Warlord, Cara. If she truly is Banfaíth, and I think she is, then he needs to know what she knows, and I've a feeling she won't leave a single one of her people behind.'

Cara shot a dubious look over Duncan's shoulder at the young Nimrothi, then tilted her head in an *if you say so* gesture. 'I'll pick out the patrols,' she said, voice carefully neutral.

He grinned. 'Very diplomatic of you. You're in command; I'll take Kael with me. I don't want him trying to stop the war band single-handedly.'

'He won't like it.' Cara shook her head.

'And I like leaving him to his own devices even less, so it's settled. Get together what supplies you need and be ready to move by noon.'

⚬

When the tea was brewed, he took a bowl and some rations from his own pack to where the young Banfaíth still sat on the rock, leaning on her staff with her other arm curled around her belly. She looked up as she heard him approach.

'Here,' he said, handing her the bowl. 'This should warm you up.'

Letting her staff rest against her shoulder, she took the bowl in both hands and cradled it to her lips, savouring the warmth. 'Thank you.'

'I brought some food, too. It's just trail bread and dried meat, but it'll keep your stomach from eating itself.'

'Trail bread?' she repeated uncertainly.

He held out the hard oval bread and strips of meat and her face lit with recognition – and hunger. Apparently he'd guessed right about the state of the Lost Ones' supplies.

As the young Banfaíth started to eat, Duncan swept away another patch of snow from the rock so he could sit down. She watched him with half an eye, and in between bites flicked glances across the clearing at the rest of her people, who were receiving their own scratch meal with expressions that veered between bewilderment and deep distrust. In the trees beyond them, by the horses, Cara's patrols were readying for the off.

'Can you tell me what happened?' he said after a while. 'What you saw?'

'I saw the plains burn.' She dabbed crumbs from her chapped lips, but didn't look at him. 'I saw ash and death and slaughter, and I heard the Raven laugh.'

Thin fingers tore off a shred of elk-meat but didn't lift it to her lips, as if her appetite had abruptly deserted her.

'And this Ytha is . . . ?' Duncan prompted her gently.

'She's the Speaker of the Crainnh – Speaker to the Chief of Chiefs, now. It was her idea to make a pact with Maegern.' Her hands began to shake. 'I tried to warn her, but she wouldn't hear me. So I left – my clan, my family, everything – to find the iron men, and now the iron men are gone.' Sudden tears spilled over her lashes, made sparkling trails down her pale cheeks. 'It's all been for nothing.'

'The iron men are not gone,' Duncan said. 'They're just not here.'

'Then how will they stop the Hunt?' The girl's shoulders lifted and she spread her hands helplessly. 'How, Duncan? They are the only ones who can stand against the storm. If the Hunt is freed, my people and your people and all the Empire will suffer.'

Slaine's stones, she'd taken the troubles of an entire nation onto her shoulders, and the weight was crushing her, an ounce at a time.

'Aradhrim will know what must be done,' he assured her. 'He is my chief but he's also the Warlord, battle chief to the Emperor. He has tens of thousands of soldiers at his disposal.' When they'd met in Mesarild, his cousin hadn't been hopeful of more than two legions, but the situation might have improved since then. Duncan hadn't been back to Saardost in over a month to find out.

'Without the iron men, he will fail.'

'Banfaíth—' he protested, but the girl was adamant. As suddenly as they'd started her tears had dried, and she drew herself up with all the shabby dignity she had.

'I have seen it,' she said simply. 'Only iron can cage the Raven. All else is dust on the wind.'

24

ARENNOR

ꝏ

The rolling Marcher country gave way to open plains of silver-beige grass threaded with bright streams. Scrub willow and alder provided what little tree cover there was, but mostly nothing stood between the Warlord's ride and the ragged blue line of the Archen Mountains except the occasional herd.

Despite all his searching, Gair had found no trace of Masen's colours. Had the Gatekeeper returned south, or moved further away than Gair could reach? He had no idea of the limits of his range, or if there was a more efficient way to search, which gave him some cause to regret not paying better attention during his lessons at Chapterhouse. With each day that passed, anxiety gnawed at his nerves a little more.

After five days spent riding hard from dawn until close to dusk, Aradhrim called a brief halt at a river that marked, he said, the southeastern edge of his clan's range.

'Beyond this is my birthland.' The rangy clansman had a light in his eye that said he was pleased to be back, like a horse that knew the road home.

'It's beautiful,' Gair said. Arennor was indeed a wild and lovely place. The rippling grasses around them sparkled with overnight rain and a fresh breeze blew down from the distant mountains, giving the air a washed-clean scent, as if the day had been rinsed off and hung up to dry.

A memory of the maps in the command tent prodded at him. 'Is that the River Riannen?'

'It is.' Aradhrim pointed northwest where a ridge of sharp hills could be seen arching down into the plains from the an-Archen, like a rib from the spine of the world. 'The Cut lies yonder. Had we more time, we could ride up there and you could see it for yourself, the spot where the Knights broke Gwlach's advance for good.'

Gair pictured the map in his mind, the winding course of the Riannen from its source in the high Brindling eastwards into the plains before it curled onto a more southerly course to join the Great River above Fleet. Caer Ducain, the easternmost city of the fallen kingdom of Milanthor, must be somewhere west and south of his current position, its ruins slowly being reclaimed by the grasslands.

'So River Run was fought northwest of here?' he asked.

'More west than north, but aye. About fifteen leagues away.' The Warlord leaned on his saddle horn and smiled. 'You stand on the pages of history.'

Bronze tokens appeared on the map in Gair's mind, representing units of foot and squadrons of horse, and were nudged across the parchment with a yardstick as Elder Prentiss described the Suvaeon's most celebrated campaign in a drone that robbed it of all colour and drama until it was as faded as the dusty banners drooping from the lecture hall's rafters. How much more vividly Gair could picture it now, seeing the landscape spread out before him, with its rushing rivers and dense grass that would have tugged at the infantrymen's boots and made each furlong feel like a mile. How much more of an achievement that forced march now appeared.

He rubbed his thumb across the scar hidden under his glove and remembered what Alderan had said about him being born at the wrong time. Some of those long-dead Knights he would have been proud to call his brothers.

'So how much further do we have to go to meet with your Speaker?'

'Not far,' Aradhrim said. 'We will reach the Stones tonight, where I will meet with the chiefs, then, gods willing, see Maera. Finna?' He looked to the girl beside him for confirmation and she nodded.

'You will see her tomorrow.'

They were the first words she had spoken since her arrival at the army camp a week previously. Her voice was clear and measured, far older than her years, as if a mature woman spoke through the child's lips.

Once, as a boy, Gair had ridden his pony further than usual, over the high fells past the Giant's Table. He'd come to a tarn, steely-cold amongst the crimson heather, and stopped to water his mount. On the far side of the pool had stood a woman with a wide silver basin in her hands. Though there was no grey in her long brown hair, no young woman could have had a face so still and knowing. Only one who saw the warp and weft of time itself. A Soothseer. Knowing he should be respectful, he had bowed and she had given him a grave nod in return before pouring water from her basin back into the pool. The bright silver dish caught the noon sun and dazzled him; when he looked again, the Sooth-seer was gone. If he'd heard her speak, he thought she would have sounded exactly like Maera's messenger.

Finna turned and looked directly at him. Dark eyes held his; cool colours touched his mind with astonishing delicacy for one so young. With a hint of a smile, she dipped her head.

Welcome to Arennor, Gair of Leah.

Startled at being addressed directly, it took him a moment to respond. *How do you know me?*

Come to me at the Singing Stones and you will see.

Gair blinked and the contact was broken. The girl faced ahead again, though he had not seen her turn away.

'She spoke to me,' he murmured.

'Who?' Aradhrim asked.

'Maera, I think. In my head. She wants to meet me.'

The Warlord's eyebrows rose. 'A rare honour. Few outsiders are summoned to an audience with Maera of the Tears.' He gathered up his reins. 'We should not keep her waiting.'

☙❧

The land grew more populous as the miles unrolled beneath the horses' hooves. They passed herds of long-horned cattle, tended by youths with switches and ropes. Herds of horses, too, heavily pregnant mares and watchful new mothers, and tented villages where children ran to point at the Warlord's banner. Greetings were called back and forth and every man-at-arms raised his spear in salute as they passed.

At noon, when the party slowed to rest their mounts, Gair searched for Masen's colours again, as he had every day. Still he found no trace of them. The further north he travelled with no indication of the Gatekeeper's whereabouts, the more his nagging unease had begun to grow into outright worry. Alderan had said Masen was in the north, but so much time had passed since then the Gatekeeper could have travelled halfway across the Empire, leaving Gair searching in entirely the wrong place.

Sooner or later he'd have to make a choice: keep looking, or pursue his own course. Time was a-wasting, but he'd promised Alderan, and guilt made a sharp spur to keep his word.

The sun was dipping towards dusk when one of the forward scouts whistled to say she'd seen something ahead and the whole ride reined up whilst she went to investigate. Moments later a mounted figure appeared on the crest of the next rise, spear held high and glinting in the afternoon light. Palgrim, sitting his horse next to Gair, let out a whoop.

'The chiefs are assembling – we will sup well tonight!' He grinned. 'If one of the chiefs has brought his bard, many tales will be sung. You may even hear the story of how Maera got her name, and that's a tale to make grown men weep!'

Another clansman laughed. 'Aye, it will melt even your cold northman's heart!'

Gair forced a smile. 'I look forward to hearing it,' he said, trying not to be offended.

Talking animatedly in their own tongue, the Arennorians urged their horses ahead with the others to greet their fellow countrymen. Tanith, who'd been riding on Gair's other side, steered her horse closer to let the rest of the Warlord's men stream past up the hill.

'I don't think they meant anything by that, you know,' she said. The ride's women appeared to have adopted her as one of their own: she wore a bluehawk's tail feather in her braid now and a string of coloured glass beads on her wrist.

He grunted. 'Cold? Really?'

'I don't think so, no.' She smiled kindly. 'They can see you're not at peace with yourself, that's all.'

Not at peace? That was an understatement. *You don't talk, you don't laugh. You only want to kill.*

Tanith tried again. 'If they knew what had happened—'

'I doubt it would make any difference.' He focused on his hands, gloved to hide the witchmark, but he could still see what they'd been capable of on the road north of Yelda. *I am a monster.*

She laid a hand on his arm. 'It will get better, Gair, I promise.'

The touch caught him off guard and he looked up again. There was no way she could possibly be sure of that – she didn't know what he'd done, and he hoped she never learned of it – but her expression was so earnest that just for a second he almost believed her. Then the yawning gulf inside him sucked him down again like a dinghy into a maelstrom.

'I wish it could,' he said.

263

Hoofbeats pounded towards them and Ailric pulled up aggressively, making his black toss its head and mouth at the bit. Foam speckled the animal's chest. 'Is everything all right?'

'Everything's fine.' Tanith straightened up, withdrawing her hand. Ailric saw where it had been resting and his gaze flicked to Gair's face, glittering hard and bright as topaz.

'We should keep up with the others,' he snapped. 'There is safety in numbers in these lands.'

'We're in the middle of Arennor, Ailric – and I'm hardly alone,' Tanith said, with more than a touch of asperity.

Ailric's horse danced and he jerked at the reins to wheel it in a tight circle, barging it between Gair's mount and Tanith's like a stockman cutting out a beast from his herd. Tanith's mare skittered away but Shahe flattened her ears and lunged to snap.

Gair patted her to calm her, keeping his head down to hide his distaste. The Astolan was showing off how tall and powerful the black was, and by implication how tall and powerful the man who was able to master it. He had little time for men who would use animals so.

'You'll bruise his mouth if you keep doing that,' he said mildly.

The Astolan glared at him. 'I know how to handle my own horse, Leahn!'

'All the more reason not to abuse him, then.'

Out of the corner of his eye, Gair saw a thin-lipped Tanith circling her own mount to bring it back under control. Then Ailric blocked his view by pushing in front of him, all fiery eyes and bared teeth like a hound deprived of its bone.

'When I want your advice, human, I will ask for it,' he snarled. 'Until I do, I suggest you stay out of what does not concern you.'

Gair drew himself up and leaned into the Astolan's stare. 'Then have a care for how you treat her,' he nodded at Tanith, 'or it *will* concern me.'

He wheeled Shahe away with his pulse thumping in his ears. He'd said too much – knew he had, even as he said it, and still hadn't been able to stop himself. Saints, the man got under his skin! No wonder Tanith was uneasy with the idea of marrying him.

Sensing his irritation, Shahe broke into a bouncing trot, her ears flicking back and forth. Gair ground his teeth and willed his temper under control. He had given his word to Tanith not to interfere between her and Ailric; baiting the fellow would not help the situation. Nonetheless his hand itched for the hilt of the longsword across his back.

On the far side of the ridge, the clansmen were gathering in a bowl-shaped depression sheltered by a stand of alders. Several dozen men were already encamped there, a handful of clan banners scattered around cook-fires, and shouts and catcalls rang out as Aradhrim's men descended the slope.

After he'd seen to Shahe, Gair looked around for Tanith, but she was deep in conversation with Magda and a couple of other lean, sun-browned Arennorian women. She appeared to have formed a particular friendship with the scarred captain over recent days, spending time with her whenever Magda's duties to her chief allowed.

As he watched, one of the women made a comment and illustrated it with an explicit gesture. Magda followed it with another that was downright obscene, and Tanith clapped a hand to her mouth before all four of them exploded into laughter.

Gair walked away, reluctant to intrude on their merriment. Tanith was in good company, and he had a feeling that Ailric wouldn't risk the women's long knives to harass her. He wove through the camp until he found Palgrim and a few others he recognised from the ride, who hailed him to join them. No sooner had his backside hit the turf than Palgrim thrust a cup at him, followed by a bowl piled with roasted fowl, some kind of baked root vegetable and dense, doughy bread still warm from the coals.

'Eat – there's plenty,' he said, then explained that those clan representatives who arrived first at a moot with another chief or chiefs had the honour of hosts and provided for the rest. He produced a *uisca* flask from inside his coat and waggled it. 'And after, something to wash it down, yes?' Chuckling, he set to with his own meal.

The aroma from the dish was enough to set Gair's stomach growling, and a freshly prepared meal made a welcome change from the hard biscuit and leathery dried meat that comprised the clansmen's trail rations. As he ate, he listened with half an ear to the conversations around him. Most were conducted in the Arennorians' own tongue, so he was unable to follow the thread, but took his cue from the others when to smile at their jokes. In between he sipped at a cup of *uisca* that became less harsh and fiery the more of it he drank – and there certainly was plenty of it to drink: the clansmen passed around flasks that never appeared to run dry and, as far as Gair could tell, gossiped worse than women on washday.

By nightfall all twelve Arennorian chiefs were present, and withdrew to sit with the Lord of the Plains around a separate fire, far enough away not to be overheard. Around the main fire the banter grew steadily more raucous and some of the young bucks tried their hands at flirting – including with Tanith's new-found friends, to which Magda provided enthusiastic commentary.

Ailric watched stony-faced from across the fire. He sat on his own between two knots of Arennorians, close enough to the fire to appreciate its light and warmth as the evening closed in, but carefully far enough away from his neighbours to avoid being drawn into their conversation. And all the time his eyes never left Tanith, intent as a heron on a riverbank.

When the new-moon sliver of Miriel sat high on the shoulder of the night and Lumiel's rise was near, Maera's apprentice came and led the chiefs away to their meeting with the Speaker. After what she'd said when she greeted him, Gair half-expected to be summoned as well, but it came as no real surprise when he wasn't. He had told Aradhrim all he knew of Savin's intentions and the mystery surrounding the starseed's whereabouts and had nothing more to offer. Now it was up to the chiefs to decide what they would do with that information.

Nonetheless he remained curious what Maera had in store for him. He couldn't fathom how she even knew his name, unless it was through his tenuous connection to the starseed, but all he really wanted to do was find Masen and move on with his own journey.

On the far side of the fire, one of the clansmen produced a fat-bodied stringed instrument similar to a lute. He played a lively, jigging tune to which two other men danced, shirtless and shining in the firelight. A few feet away, Tanith and Magda had their heads together again, the older woman nodding at one of the dancers and sketching suggestive shapes in the air. The ride-captain clearly had more than a streak of sauce.

A laughing clansman appeared in front of Gair, proffering the lute. 'Will you favour us with a song, Leahn?' he asked.

Gair shook his head. 'I'd be happy to, except I can't carry a tune with both hands and a bucket,' he said, and the listening Arennorians roared with laughter.

Undeterred, the fellow moved on around the fire to where Ailric sat. 'How about you, friend?'

The Astolan considered. 'I will give you a tune,' he said, and took the proffered instrument. Cradling its round belly in his lap, he strummed it a few times, then adjusted the tuning as the clansman returned to his seat. Once the strings were set to his liking, he began to play.

The melody soared like birds in flight over a complex tapestry of counterpoint, the Astolan's fingers dancing on the fret-board. At once Gair knew he was in the presence of a master lutenist. Then Ailric opened his mouth to sing and his lilting tenor voice added a dimension to the music that could only be described as magical. The entire camp fell silent to listen. Though the language was alien, it painted an unmistakable picture of longing that deepened and sharpened with every verse.

When the last plangent note faded into the air, there was a heartbeat's stillness, then the clansmen roared. They leapt to their feet, cheering and whistling, but Gair saw Tanith sitting as if frozen. Tears glittered on her lashes, her skin colourless as bone. Magda touched her shoulder and she turned, mouth open to speak but unable to articulate a single word. Every line of her face screamed with pain.

Only one other person in the hollow was sure to understand a song in Astolan, and what she had heard had devastated her. Across the fire, Ailric merely smiled and acknowledged his applause.

You utter snake.

Gair threw down his cup and thrust himself to his feet. Whatever Ailric and Tanith had been to each other and however it might have ended, he had no right to publicly humiliate her.

'Something troubles you, Gair?' Palgrim asked. Holding out his flask, he shook it. 'A little *uisca* will help you forget.'

With an effort, Gair reined in his temper. 'No thanks. I think I've already had too much.' He sketched a bow. 'Please excuse me.'

As he stalked away he looked for Tanith, but she'd vanished into the dark. He reached for her colours, then thought better of it. The mood he was in, if he saw how upset she was he might forget he'd given his word to stay out of her troubles with Ailric.

Saints, she deserved better than him. Gair pushed his way through the alder thicket towards the crest of the hill, slapping branches out of his path. *Uisca* boiled in his belly, fuelling his anger. What kind of a man professed love then dealt out hurt like that? She deserved *so* much better!

Emerging from the thicket, he turned to face the mountains, their snowy heads gleaming in the dark. A chill breeze blew down from the heights, rippling the plains grasses like moon-silvered water. It cooled some of the heat in him, but not enough; fired by the clansmen's smoky spirit, his instincts still snarled at him to go back and take the song's price out of Ailric's self-assured hide. It was no less than the bastard deserved – and he would be lying if he said the idea didn't hold some appeal.

Except he couldn't. He'd given Tanith his word. A flare of guilt reminded him that he'd given his word to Alderan, too, and hadn't had much compunction about breaking it when push came to shove, but when he weighed the lives of the nuns against saving those books, he knew which choice lay easiest on his conscience.

But Tanith . . . Tanith he owed his life to. Her good opinion mattered to him, and reaching for violence now would do nothing to enhance it. If she learned what bloody thoughts surged in his brain he would never be able to face her again. He could only hope she never discovered the blood already on his hands.

ᘓᕽᘔ

Tanith walked blindly through the dark. She had no idea where she was going; she simply had to get away. Away from the fire, away from Ailric, away from anyone who would see the scorching lines of tears on her cheeks and realise how bitterly she had been betrayed.

So much for his promise to support her on her mission to alert the human lands to the dangers facing them. It had all been a ruse, an excuse to stay by her side, barking and growling at anyone who came too close so that if he couldn't have her, then no one else could. How had she not seen it? Dear spirits, was she really so naïve?

And then he had played that song, knowing everyone would be entranced by the melody but only she would understand the lyric. She folded her arms tightly beneath her breasts, over the hollow ache where her heart had once been, as if holding the hurt inside would somehow enable her to master it. That song was one of longing, of heart-stopping, breathless desire; the most beautiful thing Ailric had ever given her. Once it had been a prelude to lovemaking, but he used it now to wound. Though he'd altered not a word, she'd heard its true meaning and it mocked her for her weakness, revelled in the physical passion he saw as his power over her.

'Damn you, Ailric!' She dashed the back of her hand across her eyes. 'Why can't you just leave me alone?'

In her heart, she knew the answer. She'd suspected it since she turned eighteen and he made his first suit for her hand when she returned from the Isles for a visit. Once, all Ailric had wanted was his music – and her to play it to. Now he wanted to rule.

Be my bride and we can rule Astolar together.

Under Astolan law he could not ascend the throne himself, but she was the youngest surviving Daughter of the Ten, and next in line after his grandmother Morwenna. She had no doubt that if they were to wed, Ailric intended to keep her so busy with a garden of beautiful daughters and handsome blond sons that she would have no time for the administrative chores of rule, and little by little he would loosen her grasp on the reins of her power. First as High Seat of her House, then as Queen, until her role was as empty as the head on her shoulders.

Never. That was something she simply could not allow. For years she had fought the confines of her station, the pageantry and politics of the White Court, but only because it was hers to kick against. She would not permit anyone, no matter how he professed to love her, to take that away.

A tussock in the tall grass caught her boot and she stumbled to a halt. The ground was rising here, the wind fresher as it tugged at her hair and pattered the grass-stems against her legs. She looked around, suddenly realising how far she'd walked. The campfire's light was well behind her now; she could barely make out the shapes of horses and men around it. Ahead, silvery as the sea in the moonlight, the grassland rolled up to the crest of a low ridge.

Tanith started walking once more, uphill. It was as good a

destination as any. The ridge was open enough to sit for a while and let the night wind clear her head, and high enough that she could see the camp in order to find her way back. She wasn't yet ready to be amongst people again.

If only Ailric would return to Astolar and his family's ample estates and leave her in peace. Then she could think, decide what to do next. She had warned the Empire, as she had set out to do, but she couldn't just walk away. There were still things she could do. Speak to Maera, if she was willing; perhaps learn what the Speakers knew about the starseed. If there was still a chance to stop Savin, they had to take it, and that stone was at the centre of everything. Whoever found it first controlled the game.

Her thighs began to burn with the slow climb. At the crest of the ridge she paused to catch her breath and look around, let the breeze blow her tears dry. Ahead of her lay a hollow in the silvery plain, similar to the one in which the clansmen were camped. In it lay a circular pool of water at the foot of a lichen-scarred dolmen. Figures were seated around the water's edge in the moonlight, short spears across their knees. Just one was recognisable at this distance and then only by his height: the Warlord, at the base of the stones. The others must be his clan chiefs. Opposite Aradhrim, the figure robed in snow-fox fur with a braid that reached her ankles could only be Maera, with her apprentice, the girl Magda had called Finna, at her side.

Maera spread her arms and the subtle web of a vast weaving prickled over Tanith's senses. Water-Song filled her mind, speaking of sunless rivers in the belly of the earth, of the restless yearning of all water for the sea. Wherever water was, she was there, from a raging torrent in the mountains to a dewdrop on a leaf. All water was as one. But there was something more, something older. In water there was memory.

The first images appeared in the pool. Random scenes, landscapes Tanith did not recognise, always with water in them somewhere. Finally it settled on an image of the little hollow in which they sat, but it was empty. A fiery sunset sky burned overhead. Slowly the point of focus moved, climbing to the rim of the hollow to look down onto the plains. What coloured the sky in Maera's vision was not sunset, but fire. Arennor was in flames.

Terrified horses and cattle thundered southwards, pounding over tinder-dry grassland. They were followed by wagons and overladen carts, jouncing and clattering. Men and women on foot hurried after, clutching meagre bundles and tossing fearful glances over their shoulders. Mounted warriors, bloody and dispirited, brought up the rear, harried by packs of yellow wolves. They rallied once to make a stand but were soon broken and forced to flee, leaving corpses strewn in their wake like fallen fruit. And behind them all came a moving wall of flame, consuming anything in its path.

Every living thing that walked or crawled or flew fled before it. Panicked deer, running for their lives. Birds faltering and falling in the ash-choked, heavy air. Furred, helpless things struggled to escape the ravening flames, fell and expired with tiny cries as their flesh crisped on their bones.

Tanith's knees hit the turf. Fresh tears spilled over her lashes, this time not for herself. At Maera's side, Finna moaned in horror, her face leached white in the stark light of Lumiel, the moon gleaming like a shilling nailed to the sky. Then the image changed. Gone were the flames, the rolling grassland of Arennor reduced to smoking ash. To the north, inky clouds crowned the Archen Mountains and lightnings stalked amongst the peaks. Deep in the murk, something stirred.

A horseman, taller than a house, broader than fortress gates, mounted on a sin-black horse. Human scalps made tassels for its harness, decorated with amulets fashioned from disturbingly small bones. Topping the rider's knobbed and spiked armour was a snarling helm plumed with crow feathers. In one hand he held a monstrous war-axe; on the other arm was strapped a round shield painted with a glaring red eye.

Gasps rose from the assembled chiefs. Whispered prayers, blessings for self and soul. Swaying, Finna reached out a hand to Maera's shoulder, her eyes black holes in her face. In the waters, the awful horseman hefted his axe, then with a swinging overarm movement hurled it at the ground. The blade bit into the charred earth in a puff of soot and the haft quivered with the force of the blow. As if the axe had plunged into her own flesh, Tanith cried out. Head thrown back, the horseman laughed. It was unmistakably a woman's voice.

Finna fainted, collapsing into the grass. The vision wavered and abruptly darkened, the reflected moon surfacing in the water as if through smoke. Tanith sagged sideways onto her arm.

Spirits forfend. The Wild Hunt, free, south of the mountains. Led by the one they called the Raven: Maegern, the clansmen's goddess of battle and death. It was true. It was all true.

'Mother have mercy,' exclaimed one of the chiefs. 'Is this a foretelling? Will the Hunt ride free?'

'This is what I have seen,' Maera said, her voice frayed by the ceaseless wind.

'Then we should leave now.' Another of the chiefs had stood up, gesturing with his spear. 'Take our clans and ride west, into the empty lands.'

'There are too many ghosts in the west, man!' A third voice, from further round the circle.

'Ghosts cannot hurt us. The Hunt can. I say we ride west!'

'And I say we stand.' Aradhrim was on his feet, spear cradled across his chest like a sceptre. 'I will not slink away into the night like a stray dog. If the Nimrothi come, I will fight them. If that fight costs my life, then so be it. I will not surrender one furlong of my birthland to an enemy without they pay dearly for it!'

A ragged cheer greeted his words. Several of the assembled chiefs leapt to their feet and thrust their spears above their heads, swearing to follow the Lord of the Plains to whatever end. In a matter of moments they had drowned out the one dissenter and the hollow rang with war cries.

Their instinctive, unhesitating courage should have cheered her. Arennor would not be defeated easily. But all Tanith could picture was the league upon league of open country between Fleet and the rest of the Empire and shudder with foreboding.

If Savin truly knew the whereabouts of the lost starseed, or had somehow allied himself with the restless Nimrothi clans, even Arennor's courage would not be enough to stop him.

25

THE SINGING STONES

In the morning, Gair woke early to low mist and a paling sky. Apart from a couple of men on watch the camp still slept, and the fires had dwindled to smoking cinders. He sat up slowly, kneading his temples in an attempt to chase away the dull ache of too much *uisca*. He'd slept, but not got much rest from it – there'd been too many dreams of vengeance, raw and red, against a faceless, laughing foe. The kind of dreams that woke him with his heart racing and his hand groping for his sword. He rubbed his eyes wearily. The kind of dreams he didn't want to be having with other people around.

When he opened his eyes again, Maera's apprentice was sitting cross-legged at the foot of his blankets. He hadn't heard her approach; she might as well have dropped out of the air like a bird, green dress, eagle feather and all.

Trying not to let his surprise show, he greeted her with a polite, 'Good morning.'

She smiled. 'New day's blessings to you.' Her voice sounded like a girl's this time. A composed and self-aware one, but a girl nonetheless. 'I am to take you to the Speaker.'

'Now?' Saints, he hadn't even had a chance to wash.

'When you are ready. I will wait for you over there.' She

nodded across the hollow to a path he hadn't noticed in the dark the evening before. When he looked back, the Speaker's apprentice was gone.

Gair got to his feet but there was no sign of a girl in a green dress anywhere in the camp. All he saw were grazing horses and sleeping clansmen. Perplexed, he cast around the hollow again; had she actually been there at all? The turf near him was too trampled to tell. A simulacrum, then; an illusion, like Savin's sending. After he'd left the camp last night to cool his temper he'd sensed a weaving nearby and assumed it was Maera's work. If the Speaker had the ability to craft illusions that skilful, she had a considerable gift indeed.

And what did she want with him? *Come to me at the Singing Stones and you will see.*

No doubt he would find out soon enough. Rooting through his saddlebags, he hunted for a fresh shirt.

☙❧

Ten minutes later, after as thorough a wash as he could manage in a bucket of river water and wearing his least-stale shirt – in the absence of one that even approximated to clean, after so long on the road – he crossed the hollow towards the spot where Maera's apprentice had told him she would wait.

By then the watch had changed and the clansmen were stirring; Palgrim hailed him from beside the fire with an offer of breakfast, but he shook his head and kept walking. After the *uisca* of the night before, his stomach was too sour for food.

Gair half-expected the girl not to be there, but she was waiting as she'd promised. She sat cross-legged in the long grass, busily plaiting together some sprays of pink and white flowers. As he approached, she tied the braid off and fastened it around her wrist, then without a word started up the path out of the hollow.

Behind the hill the path wound on, little more than a game trail through the gently undulating grasslands. As the day warmed, the mist evaporated and, after what could only have been a quarter of an hour but felt four times as long, Gair asked where they were going.

Smiling back over her shoulder, the girl gestured ahead. 'We are here.'

Set against the gentle slope of the next hillock were two rough stone pillars, capped by a long slab that ran back into the hill itself. Lichens splotched and whorled the limestone and beneath the dolmen the shadows clung so thickly Gair could see nothing of what might await him.

At the foot of the stones was a small pool, perfectly circular, perfectly reflecting the robin's-egg blue of the sky overhead. Aligned with the dolmen, but set in the grass on the near side of the pool, was another stone, roughly squared off.

'Please wait here,' said the girl.

Gair thanked her and looked around to see where the Speaker might come from. They had walked a good way from the camp and he could hear no sounds but the unfamiliar songbirds overhead and the ceaseless whisper of the grass. When he turned back to speak to the girl, he was alone again. She had departed as noiselessly as she had arrived at the foot of his blankets.

Nothing to do but wait, then, and hope his headache faded. He sat down on the squared-off stone, glad of his sheepskin jerkin against the morning chill, though the rising sun on his face was warm. Nothing moved in the hollow. No birds, no rabbits. Nothing to see but the gently sloping hillsides dotted with harebells, mossflowers and yellow jack-o'-the-ways. The wind whined around the dolmen and he wondered whether they were the Singing Stones.

You will find out soon enough.

Maera's voice spoke clearly in his mind, though he had felt not a whisper of her presence.

My lady?

He looked across the hollow. Now the shadows under the

weathered stones had a shape, as if someone was waiting beneath them.

He crossed to the foot of the stones and bowed. 'Speaker.'

Standing before him was a slightly built woman in a russet dress with glass beads worked around the neck in a design of twining flowers. Her brown hair was swept back into a neat braid, crowned with a fan of owl feathers. Her handsome, tranquil features were younger than he'd expected, cheeks firm and brow unlined, but twin flashes of silver hair at her temples said that like the Soothseer from his childhood, she carried more years than she showed. Both eyes were milky pale and unmistakably blind.

'I have been waiting for you,' she said. Her voice was the one he had heard through the girl yesterday.

He straightened up from his bow. The crown of the Speaker's head barely reached his chest. 'No one knew I was bound this way.'

'I saw your face in the waters long ago,' she told him. 'I knew that one day you would find your way here. I felt your feet set upon this path the moment you crossed the border of Arennor.'

It was the same mysterious nonsense he'd heard from fortune-tellers at the fair, all portentous delivery and no real substance. The heavy pounding of his head left him little patience for games. 'Speaker, I don't mean to be rude, but why am I here? Why did you want to see me?'

She indicated the deeper shadows beneath the dolmen. 'Will you walk with me into the earth and glimpse your future in the Stones?'

'I already know what I have to do.'

The faintest smile curled the corners of her mouth and he realised that however blind her eyes, she saw him more than clearly. 'What you know and what you think you know are not always the same, Gair of Leah. Even though you believe it almost ended, your story has barely begun.'

She spoke in riddles. 'I don't understand.'

'Come with me and you will see.'

Turning away, she walked into the shadows. Bewildered and more than a little annoyed, Gair hesitated, reluctant to follow but unable to think of a reason not to other than sheer contrariness. A memory tugged at him. *I think there is work for you to do yet, but it's not here and not now.* Alderan had said that, on the day he bade his last farewell to Aysha. Was that what the Speaker meant?

What does she know about me?

The only way to find out was to follow her. He growled in frustration, then stepped into the dark.

After the brightness of the morning outside, his eyes needed time to adjust to the gloom as Maera led the way down a narrow, sloping tunnel. The walls and floor were unfinished; trailing roots brushed against Gair's head and the air had a warm, loamy scent that made him think of summertime.

Here and there niches had been cut to hold clay oil-lamps, their yellow light enough to see where he was putting his feet but no further ahead, as if the lamps beyond Maera had not yet been lit. When he looked back over his shoulder, those behind had been extinguished. Strange. If there was some working of the Song there, it was too subtle for him to detect.

Judging the passage of time was difficult in the featureless tunnel. If he tried to reckon it by the steps he took he lost his count. Nor could he keep track of seconds or minutes. His muscles told him he'd been walking for some distance and that was the only measure of it he had.

No sooner had he given up trying to work out how far they had come than the tunnel opened into a round, stone-vaulted chamber, perhaps three times as tall at the centre as he was. Oil-lamps hung on slender chains from the ceiling, made of polished brass, with glass chimneys to steady the flames. They shed a clearer light than the lamps in the passage, illuminating the whole chamber and the extraordinary stone formation at its centre.

A huge, many-faceted crystal rose out of the unfinished earth floor, a jumble of pillars and lances and rounded nubbins, all of different heights and thicknesses. Each aspect was a different colour, too: blue-green or milky white, pale rose, golden amber, or clear as water. No two of them were the same and yet it appeared to be all of one piece, like a frozen star half-buried in the earth.

Maera stepped to one side, allowing him to make a circuit of the chamber, admiring the crystal from all angles. He had never seen anything to compare with it. Its colours, its form, took his breath away.

'These are the Singing Stones?' he asked.

A reverberation followed his words. Not an echo – the chamber was too small to throw his voice back at him – but there was a resonance in the air after he spoke, similar to the way a plucked harp-string continued to hum until it was muted by the harpist's palm.

Reaching out, he touched the tip of the nearest crystal lance. A jolt of light crossed his vision, as abrupt as a lightning-strike. He snatched his fingers back, the hairs on his arm prickling against his shirt.

'Incredible,' he breathed. Even speaking softly caused the Stones to thrum.

When he returned to Maera's side, he realised he had not seen the entrance to the passageway by which they had come in. The walls between the stone pillars that supported the roof were solid earth. She appeared to sense his startlement.

'No one may enter this place uninvited,' she said, and her voice brought music to the edge of hearing. 'I am the keeper of the Stones. Unless I will it, the way to them is closed.'

Blind eyes watched him. He studied her face, able to see it clearly for the first time. Sun-browned, like all the plainspeople, and webbed with fine lines that the dolmen's shadow had hidden.

Now he could see the grief that had given her the name Maera of the Tears. She bore it like a long-healed scar: familiar, accustomed, her features worn to the shape of it like old shoes to feet.

'The Gatekeeper named you *gaeden*,' she said abruptly. 'And a Knight, as the Guardians were of old.'

Gair blinked. 'Masen was here? When? I have urgent news for him.'

The Speaker held up a hand. 'In time,' she said. 'First I must know: did the Gatekeeper name you truly?'

'The *gaeden* part is true enough, but I was expelled from the Suvaeon Knights before I could try for my spurs. I am not welcome in the Church any more. Speaker, please, when was Masen here?'

'I spoke with him nine days ago,' she said. 'He was in the west then, but bound for the Northmarch and Saardost Keep.'

The Northmarch was the most northerly region of Arennor, stretching from the borders of Belistha in the east to Caer Ducain and what had once been Milanthor in the west. According to Aradhrim's campaign maps the grassy plains grew tangled there, heaped and tumbled like blankets over a restless sleeper as the Archen Mountains heaved skywards from the folds. Difficult terrain to track a man across, but assuming Gair could use the Song to follow Masen, nine days was not so far ahead. Riding hard, he could be within hailing distance in two, maybe catch the Gatekeeper by the end of the week, then he could move on. Head for the reckoning he burned to make.

I will see Savin broken.

He reined in his animosity. After what Savin had said about being aware of his thoughts, it was probably dangerous to brood too long.

'If you confront your enemy now, it will be the end of you.'

Her voice, the subtle music of the Stones, jolted him out of his thoughts. 'My lady?'

'I know what you seek, Gair. You reach for it like a lover denied a last embrace.' She faced him, blind eyes pale and hard as pearls. 'If you pursue your vengeance it will destroy you.'

Sudden rage boiled inside him. 'You don't understand!'

'I think I understand more than you realise.' She tilted her head to one side, like a bird. 'Do you think you are the only one who has ever lost? Do you think you are the only one who has ever wept?'

Sick with it, he burst out, 'I *loved* her!'

'Then be comforted that you warmed yourself at love's fires once, however briefly, instead of living forever in the cold.'

'No!'

How could she even say that? She couldn't comprehend the pain that swelled inside him like rot in a wound. It never lessened, never relaxed the iron hand it clenched around his heart. Talking about it only reminded him how much it hurt.

The Speaker was unmoved. 'If you had never known it, it could not hurt you now.'

'If I'd never known her, I'd count my life the poorer,' he fired back. 'I mean to call Savin to account, Speaker. I mean to make him pay in full for all he took that day.' *He will pay for what his creatures did for making me watch her bleed oh Aysha forgive me I was too late.* He flinched from the memories, screwed his eyes shut to blot them out. It didn't work – it never did, and he'd never be free of them.

Taking a deep breath, he tried to regain control of his temper. His temples throbbed; anger and *uisca* were an ugly combination. Another deep breath. 'Please forgive my rudeness.'

'And I should ask your forgiveness, too. I did not mean to open up your hurts, only to show you the choice that now lies before you.'

'What choice?' She still didn't seem to comprehend. 'I don't have any choice. I *will* see this done.'

'Then you would waste the gift of life your mother gave you.'

He swung to face the edge in the Speaker's voice, but as quickly as it had hardened she softened it again, became gentle. 'You have the look of her.'

That knocked the wind out of him. 'You knew my mother?'

'I saw her in the pool, before you were born.' A brief smile. 'Leah's Soothseers are not so different from Speakers, and the strongest of us converse from time to time, when there is need for counsel.'

Impossible – incredible. Twenty-odd years and countless miles from the place of his birth, he'd encountered someone who had known his mother. All thoughts of revenge were thrown clean out of his head by a sudden need to learn more about her.

'What was she like?' The Speaker frowned but he rushed on. 'My lady, please! I never knew her – I don't even remember her face. She gave me up to charity when I was only a few days old.'

'That story is not yours to hear,' said Maera. Behind her the Stones chimed, briefly discordant. 'I can say that she gave you her grey eyes, and the red in your beard is from her hair. All else comes from your father.'

'Who was he? Did he love her?'

'Your life was sparked in love,' she said. 'Beyond that lie only questions I cannot answer. Please, do not ask them.'

'But—'

'Do not ask, Gair. Not because I do not know the answers, but because her story is not yours. I have told you all I may.' She laid a hand on his arm, as unerring as someone fully sighted, and fixed her pale eyes on his face. 'This is the blessing and the curse of Speakers. We may speak the story of one life, the one who asks, but must guard the secrets of all others. It can be no other way.'

She squeezed his arm and let him go.

Gair raked his hands back through his hair. Somehow knowing a little, even just that his mother had been red-haired, stung worse than knowing nothing at all. It tied a thread to her and knowing how slender, how fragile that connection was, was more painful than being cut adrift.

'I understand.'

He didn't, not really, but he fought down all his questions, blinking away the threat of tears. *Life sparked in love.* So she wasn't forced, at least; only forced to give him up. He took another deep breath, exhaled right to the bottom of his lungs.

'Why did you bring me here, Speaker? How did you even know I would come to Arennor?'

'I have always known,' she said. 'Before I knew your name, even before I saw your face clearly, I knew you would come. Your mother showed you to me. The Gatekeeper gave me your connection to the reiver, and your connection to all the other *gaeden* who have ever lived, back to the First Knight who made a choice that has shaped the course of your life to this day.'

'Are you saying this is some kind of prophecy?'

'No.' She smiled, a little dreamy, a little sad. 'As a Speaker I would give my teeth for the certainty of prophecy, but there can be no such thing because the future is not absolute. It cannot be known. What I am speaking of is merely a probability, but one that grows stronger with each new connection you make to the greater pattern.'

More riddles, and sweet saints, he'd drunk too much last night to make sense of them. Corlainn, Savin – he could see how they were connected by the starseed, and he grasped how that connection extended to him, but what was the greater pattern? What was his place in that?

He spread his hands helplessly. 'You've lost me.'

The Speaker smiled again. 'Perhaps.' She trailed her fingertips over the nearest Stone and it chimed softly, like an Isles crystal goblet struck with a spoon. 'Or perhaps you are simply finding a different path to understanding.'

'Speaker?'

'It is a gift of mine to see patterns,' she said. 'I can fathom the shape of a bowl from its broken shards, see a tapestry in its ravelled threads. The more shards and threads, the more clearly I see. Your mother was the first thread I found, as I said. When the Gatekeeper brought me another, a pattern was revealed.' Her blind gaze swung back to his face, utterly compelling. 'You stand at a fork in the road, Gair of Leah. Two ways lie before you: one of life, one of death. You must choose which path you will follow.'

The Speaker's talk of threads and patterns had left Gair hopelessly confused. 'I don't understand what you're asking me. What two ways? How do I know which is which?'

'You already know. What you must decide is whether you care.' She folded her hands at her waist. 'Touch the Stones and choose.'

'Now?'

'What better time could there be?'

The Stones winked in the lamplight. One that had been blue had turned rosy as a dawn sky; an amber lance was now glacial, shimmering white. He reached out a hand and hesitated, his fingers only an inch from the gleaming stone. The air hummed with possibility.

What will I see? 'What if I'm not ready?'

Her hand covered his.

'No man is ready when his path is revealed to him,' she murmured, and closed his fingers around the slender spike.

A searing flash, then absolute dark enshrouded his mind. Gair opened his mouth to say there was nothing to see, but as he did so the darkness lifted and his voice died in his throat. Blood on white stone. A fire-eagle shining under the sun – a female fire-eagle, flying away from him. Without thinking he reached out for her, but he was too late to catch more than a glimpse. Other images came then, too fast, too fragmented to hold, and each one tore into him like a demon's talons.

Aysha. Candles burning at the corners of her bier, the only lights in the midnight chapel aside from the sanctuary lamp. Cold stone under his knees, hot tears coursing down his face. Lighting her pyre. *Aysha!*

More images, more broken pieces of memory. They slammed into him like blows, driving the breath from his lungs. His fingers spasmed but could not release the stone. It thrummed under his grip like a thing alive and struck a note from the Song inside him. The note rose and grew, splintering into great chords, shattering again and again, and every shard was sharp as a dagger.

'Enough,' he gasped. 'I've seen enough.' *Mercy, please. Enough!*

From the pyre's flames came a roar unlike anything he had ever heard before. Rawer than his grief, more brutal than his rage; his ears shuddered with it. Deep in the fire, a beast's eyes burned.

Pain exploded within Gair's skull and drove him to his knees. As soon as his hand broke contact with the crystal the visions were snuffed out and he was left leaning on his hands fighting for breath, with every hair on his body standing away from his skin.

Saints and angels. *I truly am a monster.*

Slowly he sat back on his heels. Overhead, the lamps swayed drunkenly, smearing their light across the earthen walls of the chamber.

The Speaker's touch on his shoulder was gentle. 'Do you see your path clearly?'

Still panting, he pushed himself to his feet.

'I saw what I've already become.' He looked around the chamber for a way out. 'Let me go, Speaker. You can't show me anything of the future that will change what I have to do.'

She regarded him gravely for a moment, then dipped her head. 'Very well.'

The shadows on the far wall lifted, became the golden glow of oil-lamps at the entrance to a tunnel. 'This path will return you to the camp. Should you wish to look again, find my apprentice Finna and she will bring you here.'

'I won't,' Gair said. Dear Goddess, he couldn't wait to get as far away from the Singing Stones as possible.

'Then may your Goddess go with you,' she said.

'Lady, She abandoned me a long time ago.' He started to walk towards the passageway. 'I've no more use for prayers.'

26

DESPAIR

෨൪

Gair strode up the sloping passage away from the Stones. His long legs ate up the ground faster than the lamps lit ahead of him and left him striding constantly into shadow. It suited his mood.

Maera had spoken of a choice to make, of caring whether he lived or died. He had seen no choice, only a beast, the monster inside him. A creature of fire and destruction. How could he choose not to be what he already was?

All he could hope to do was keep the beast leashed tight within him for long enough to do what had to be done. To make Savin pay in full for Chapterhouse, whatever it cost. Then when the tether finally frayed and his temper snapped it, it wouldn't matter any more. Until then, he had to isolate himself. Stay far away from other people, so he would not have to watch anyone else burn.

Seeing sunlight ahead, Gair quickened his pace. Air. Space. Freedom from the earth. Inside him the Song surged like a flood tide, dragging at his defences. As he approached the tunnel mouth, he reached into the storm of music and found his escape.

Golden wings beat, whirling dust from the tunnel floor. Then he arced into the morning sky with the sun on his back and the crisp air buoying him up to shriek his vengeance at the horizon.

In the Durannadh camp, faces lifted and arms pointed at the

unfamiliar bird. One of the faces was framed with copper hair. She didn't point, just shaded her eyes and watched him fly. Colours brushed over him, all the watercolour shades of a spring dawn.

Gair?

I have to get away for a while. I need to think—

Dissonance. The soaring melody of flight abruptly became a deafening clangour, tumbling him through the air like wind shear off a mountainside. He beat his wings hard to steady his descent but the complex flight muscles were only barely under his control. Still thrashing at the air, he began to fall.

The silvery grassland spiralled closer. His wings offered no lift, the feathers fraying as his grip on the eagle-shape slipped. He flung himself into the Song for another form, one he could hold long enough to land safely, but even a peregrine's wings couldn't arrest his fall. In desperation he stretched for other shapes, spotted owl, briar-finch, but they all fluttered through his fingers and were gone.

The wind tugged at him, tumbling him over and roaring in his ears. He struggled to right himself but the ground rushed towards him, dizzyingly fast. Another shape; there must be others he could try. Grey goose wings slowed him a little but not enough before they too unravelled. As bird after bird failed panic clawed up his throat.

Dear Goddess, no time!

Then a different shape reached for him. Its song was one of terrible, roaring power, rising up inside him and turning every fibre of his being to liquid fire.

The earth slammed the breath from Gair's body. Over and over he spun, grass lashing his face, rocks bruising his body. Something struck his forehead, leaving a hot sting above one eye. And then there was stillness, silence but for the buzz of insects, the rasp of his own breathing.

He was still alive. He opened his eyes and dizzy clouds stuttered their way across the heavens, so he shut them again and waited for his wits to stop tumbling inside his head. Saints, he hurt. His forehead throbbed; a wet tickling sensation said it was bleeding, but his limbs moved when he willed them to and nothing hurt enough to be broken. Incredible. Somehow he'd fallen from the sky and had nothing worse to show for it than bruises.

Slowly, he attempted to sit up. His muscles hung on his bones like someone else's clothes, ill-fitting and unfamiliar. After so many failed shapes, even his own felt wrong. Nausea surged and he rolled onto his side, coughing and spitting bile into the crushed grass, then he fell back, panting. With every beat of his heart, fireworks of pain burst behind his eyes.

Blood and stones, that creature! A thing from the dark places in human memory, fanged and clawed; it had reached through the Song for him, instead of the other way around. He had never experienced that before, not in all the shape-shifts he had made since the day in the Long Glen when he had watched a fire-eagle soar and envied it its wings. Since the first time he'd shifted, he had never felt that the power to change shapes was not his to command. Not until now.

Was he losing his gift? He hauled himself onto his hands and knees and slowly sat back on his heels. Had he escaped the stake only to see his life end in fire regardless?

'Gair!' Tanith's voice, edged with fear. She was perhaps fifty yards away, casting about for him in the tall grass. Still too dizzy to stand, his head hurting too much to even think about a hail, he raised his arm and heard her running through the grass towards him.

Face frozen with anxiety, she dropped to her knees at his side. 'What happened? Are you hurt?'

'I'm all right.' He dabbed cautiously at the cut on his forehead and his fingers came away smeared with scarlet. 'Just bumps and bruises, I think.'

'Spirits, you scared me! When I saw you fall, I thought—' She broke off, peering at his face. 'Gair, what happened?'

He looked down at his grazed and bloodstained hands in his lap, wondering if they were trembling. *What if I can't fly?* The idea so shook him that the truth spilled out.

'I couldn't hold the shape,' he said. 'The reiving – I can't always control the Song these days.' *Saints and angels, what if it means I can't fly?*

'That's how you hurt your arm, isn't it?' she asked. 'When the weaving got away from you, you tried to pull the fire back and took it into yourself. Gair, that's so dangerous.'

'I had to try something, and I didn't know what else to do.' Remembering the men's screams, he flinched. 'It was too late, anyway.'

Once he'd lit fire in them, nothing could have saved those men. No matter what he'd tried, only death had brought them any release.

Goddess have mercy.

He covered his face with his hands. He should never have let her Heal him. Six days' suffering was not penance enough for what he had done. Nowhere near enough.

A tingling along his nerves said Tanith had gathered the Song. As she reached for him, he shied away.

'Don't.'

'I'm a physician, Gair—'

He held up his hand to fend her off. 'It's the reiving. You can't Heal it.'

'I was only going to delve you for internal injuries. You've had quite a fall.'

'You think I don't know that?' he snapped. 'I'm fine, Tanith. Just leave me alone.'

Slowly, her hands fell into her lap. Wide, wounded eyes stared back at him, and only then did he notice they were reddened and puffy with lack of sleep. He hadn't even thought to ask her if she was all right after last night. Ashamed of himself, he ducked his head.

'I'm sorry. That was . . . beneath me.'

'Yes, it was,' she said quietly. 'I'm only trying to help you, you know.'

'I know.' He couldn't face her, busying himself brushing the dirt from his hands. 'I'm fine, really.'

She sighed, more wistful than exasperated.

'You're a very long way from being fine, Gair,' she said. 'Look at what's happened to you these last few months. The reiving, Chapterhouse. Now Gimrael.' She spread her hands, let them fall. 'You've lost too much to be *fine*. You need time to rest, time to heal.'

As if he needed reminding of what he'd lost. As if he didn't feel it every day, punching his chest with its leaden fists. His friend Darin, then Aysha, and lastly Alderan. All gone, like the mother he'd never known.

He began dusting off the bits of grass that peppered his clothes. 'I haven't got time to rest, not right now. There's too much to do – finding Masen for starters.'

'And after you find him, what then? You'll go after Savin?'

So it was too late to worry about her learning the real reason he'd come north. She'd apparently already worked it out. 'He's dangerous, Tanith. You saw what he did at Chapterhouse.'

'And I saw what he did to you.' Even though her voice was gentle, he flinched. 'I was there with you, remember?'

His fists clenched, a muscle jumping in his cheek that he couldn't stop. 'This isn't about Aysha.'

Except it was; it was *all* about her. The pain that drove him on, the gnawing, nagging hunger that kept him awake when every muscle in his body cried out for sleep, was all about making Savin pay for tearing her away from him.

'It wasn't your fault, Gair,' Tanith said, but all he heard was another woman's voice, husky, warm with Gimraeli spice. *You gave it your best, out at the Five Sisters.* His eyes prickled and he shut them tight.

Tanith's hand on his arm startled him. 'Would she really want this? Another death? It won't bring her back to you.'

She was watching him, searching his face with such compassion that he couldn't hold her gaze for long.

'No, but it might make me feel better about it.' He swiped irritably at the blood trickling into his eyebrow. 'Alderan thought he had a way to cut Savin's nets by finding the starseed first, and it came to nothing. This is all there is left to do.'

'There are always choices, Gair.' Before he was even aware that she'd called on the Song, her hand touched his brow and the hot-cold flush of a simple Healing washed through him. In moments the throbbing pain in his skull had dulled and even his bruises felt easier.

'There,' she said. 'That'll be gone by tomorrow.'

Wrongfooted by her grace, he could only stare. 'Don't you ever get tired of patching me up?'

She smiled brightly. 'Well, it's a burden, but someone has to do it.'

'I'm glad it's you.'

He didn't know where the words came from; they were simply there on his tongue and flown before he could think twice. Her smile softened, and she squeezed his arm.

'So am I – though it would be less of a burden if you'd be a little kinder to yourself.' She tilted her head to one side, searching his face. 'Please? If not for your physician, then for a friend?'

He started to protest, then relented. He'd hurt her feelings enough for one day. 'I'll try – but I can't make any promises, mind.'

'That's good enough for me.'

Abruptly she looked hunted and stood up, taking a step away from him. A second or two later, Gair heard hoofbeats on the turf. Over the waving grass that surrounded him he saw Ailric's pale hair, his horse tossing its head. A volley of lilting Astolan reached his ears and he stole a glance at Tanith. Forehead creased in irritation, she said something curt that made Ailric scowl.

Gair got to his feet. The bruises blooming over his back and legs protested at the movement, and the bright sun in his eyes combined with the lingering effects of the knock on the head made him dizzy again. Ailric looked him over with barely disguised contempt then thrust out his arm towards Tanith.

'Come, I will take you to your horse. We are leaving.'

She shook her head. 'Thank you, but I'll walk.'

'It is a long way, love.'

'I'm sure it is, but Gair is hurt.' She folded her arms. 'And don't call me that.'

Ailric's gaze swept over the grass stains and burrs on Gair's clothes, the drying blood on his face.

'Then Heal him and be done with it. We have wasted enough time here.' He wheeled his horse around, gave her a bow from the saddle. 'My love.'

Then he heeled the black away at a gallop.

Tanith hissed something after him in her own language and kicked at the grass in front of her.

'Are you all right?'

'That man!' she muttered. 'He doesn't listen to a word I say.'

'Then he doesn't deserve you.'

She folded her arms, but didn't meet Gair's eye. 'House Vairene is well connected at Court,' she said colourlessly. 'As a future consort he's an excellent choice, and my father has already given his blessing.'

'But it is still *your* choice?' he asked, and she nodded. 'You're not marrying just his House or his political skills, Tanith. You're also marrying the man, and *that* man,' Gair pointed after the disappearing Astolan, 'is not worthy of your hand.'

She gave him a look he couldn't read. 'Imagine how you'll feel once you *really* get to know him,' she said, and started walking.

Her bitterness surprised him. He'd never heard Tanith say an unkind word about anyone; to hear her speak like that was disconcerting to say the least. It made him think that the situation between her and Ailric went much deeper than an unwelcome suit. In a couple of long strides he caught up to her.

'Tanith, I'm worried about you now. Has he threatened you in some way?'

'No, nothing like that.' She hesitated, choosing her words. 'He tries to hold the past over me, that's all. Like that song, last night. Did you hear it?'

'I heard.'

'Ailric wrote it for me, years ago. He used to sing it to me when we were alone. I suppose you could say he seduced me with music.'

'I thought it was beautiful, until I saw your reaction to it.'

Tanith sighed. 'It *is* beautiful, and he still plays as well as he ever did, but it doesn't mean the same thing any more.' Even though the day was warm, she shivered and hugged herself.

Gair wondered what other message had been in Ailric's words to make her so uneasy now. 'Was that what he was trying to do last night? Seduce you again?'

'I think he was trying to remind me of something, of how things used to be.' A flush coloured her cheeks and the tips of her ears and she looked down at her boots. 'He won't believe me when I tell him there's nothing between us any more. I wish he would just go home, but he's decided he won't leave until I do.'

So the man was possessive as well as arrogant. 'You know if there's anything I can do—'

'There isn't, not really. But thank you.' She leaned her head briefly on his arm as she walked beside him. 'Did you find out what the Speaker wanted with you?'

Gair could only shrug. 'I didn't understand half of what she said, to be honest, but that might have been last night's *uisca* to blame.'

He hadn't had time to process any of what he'd been told and winnow the sense from it; crashing from the sky had seen to that.

Carefully he explored the cut on his forehead, but thanks to Tanith's Healing it had already scabbed over and the swelling was much reduced. He scratched at some dried blood in his eyebrow.

'She told me a little about my mother, and that she'd spoken to Masen.'

'Do you know where to find him?'

'According to Maera, he's on his way to Saardost so it looks like I'll be riding with the Warlord a while longer.'

They were nearing the camp now, which was bustling with clansmen and horses. From the number of banners on display, the other chiefs were on the move, too, no doubt back to their clans to ready them for war should the Suvaeon fortresses fail to keep the Nimrothi penned behind the an-Archen. Gair watched Tanith searching the crowd anxiously, presumably so she could avoid Ailric, but there were too many men and animals moving about to pick out familiar faces.

He touched her elbow. 'If you want me to walk with you, I will,' he said, but she shook her head.

'I'm supposed to be Second Ascendant to the throne of Astolar. If I can't deal with an uppity nobleman, I don't deserve a Seat at Court.' She sounded braver than she looked, and her smile was bright enough to almost convince him. Almost.

'Ho, Leahn!' Palgrim's roar carried across the bustle of the camp. The clansman was coming to meet them, waving his fist in the air. 'That she-devil you call a horse just bit me!'

'She probably thought you deserved it!' he shouted back, then turned to Tanith. 'Sorry, I really should go and pack up my gear, and speak to the Warlord.'

'I'd better go, too,' she said. 'Don't worry about me, I'll ride with Magda today. Give Masen my best when you hail him.' Then she was gone, weaving through the crowd and quickly lost from view.

Gair watched her go and mulled over his misgivings about

Ailric. Life would be a great deal simpler for her if the Astolan man would just take no for an answer and leave her be, but it looked as if she was not destined to be that lucky.

After retrieving Shahe from Palgrim, who insisted on showing off a black and red bruise on his forearm where the *sulqa*'s teeth had made contact, Gair went looking for the Warlord. He was deep in conversation with his ride-captain, the ever-present adjutant hovering nearby with a pair of spectacles perched daintily on the bridge of his nose as he shuffled papers in his leather document case.

When Magda strode off, barking orders to her ride, Aradhrim caught sight of Gair and beckoned him over. His eyebrows rose when he noticed the blood.

'Are you hurt?' he asked.

'Nothing serious, my lord. Tanith has already Healed it.' Gair hooked a thumb in the direction of the general bustle around the camp. 'I take it you're moving on today?'

'We are. It's five days' ride to Saardost from here and I am anxious to find out what has been happening in my absence. I receive regular dispatches, but by the time the information reaches me it is already out of date.' He indicated his adjutant's papers, then eyed Shahe's packs, the longsword hanging from the saddle. 'Leaving us already?'

'Actually, I was hoping to ride on with you, if I may. The Speaker told me the Gatekeeper was bound for Saardost, so it makes sense for me to meet him there.'

The Warlord gave him a nod. 'But of course. From what Lady Tanith has told me, your presence at the fortress would be most welcome if battle is joined – both as *gaeden* and Suvaeon.'

That made him wonder just how much the Warlord had been told. 'You should know I was only a novice when I was expelled from the Order,' he said. 'I was never raised to Knight.'

'Would you have been raised if you had stayed in the Holy City?'

'I'd like to think so,' Gair hedged. The Master of Arms had rarely expressed displeasure with his performance on the field, anyway. Keeping the Song in check until the next Grand Tourney, though, would have been a different question.

'Then surely what matters is how you spent your time there, not how you performed in some contest at the end.' Aradhrim clapped him on the shoulder. 'Ride-captains are not made in one day, my friend.'

ல

Tanith found her way through the crowds to where she'd left her mare and began saddling her, but her mind was only half on the task at hand. Ailric's words kept echoing in her head.

So he calls, and you go running, he'd spat at her, with such venom that she'd only just remembered to reply in Astolan to avoid Gair being offended. And then he'd dressed it up in tenderness, calling her *my love* as if that somehow excused him! She heaved on the girths, drawing a grunt from her mare. The arrogance, the presumption, the sheer *rudeness* of the man!

She snatched up her bedroll, still fuming. Someone seized her by the arm and swung her about, the bedroll tumbling to the ground. Heart leaping in her chest, Tanith gasped. Ailric's perfect features were white with rage.

'So that is how a lady of the Court comports herself,' he hissed, his grip on her arm painfully tight. 'Frolicking in the grass like a beast!'

'Let go of me.' She jerked her arm. 'Let go, Ailric!'

For once he did what she asked, and she rubbed her pinched flesh.

'Do you have no respect for your station?' he demanded. 'A human!'

'A *patient*,' she retorted. 'And we were hardly *frolicking* – didn't you see the state of him? Gair lost control of a shape-shift and fell. He was lucky not to be more seriously hurt.'

298

He laughed scornfully. 'So he can't even control his gift? Your precious Guardians do not seem particularly impressive, I have to say.'

Tanith ground her teeth. 'Accidents happen, Ailric.'

The laugh became a snarl. 'It is surely no *accident* that I find you always at *his* side when you should be at mine.'

Despite all that had happened between them and everything she had said, he still believed she was his. That the foolish pledge two children had exchanged years ago on the lakeshore, with rings woven from grass, still bound their hearts. Dear spirits, what did she have to do to make him see that she was not that child any more?

'Where I go and who I choose to spend my time with are *my* business.' She scooped up the fallen bedroll. 'Now leave me alone.'

Flame-coloured eyes smouldered. 'Be quick. We are leaving here.'

Her temper flared. 'Yes, we *are* leaving. For Saardost Keep, with the Warlord and his men.' The decision had made itself in the time it took to frame the words, yet it sounded right. He'd never follow her further into human lands, not after this. 'If you don't like it, you can go home with my blessing.'

He was silent. Bedding rolled up, she fastened it behind the saddle of her patient brown mare then turned to face him. 'Well, Ailric? No more smart comments to make about my station?'

'I thought you wished to speak with this seer of theirs, Maera.'

'I've changed my mind. I can do more good as a Healer for now.'

'And the White Court?'

'Emelia is as healthy as a horse and your grandmother stands in line before me. The White Court can wait.'

'I see.' His expression turned closed, guarded. 'And I suppose your *pet* will be riding with us?'

'Must you always disparage him so?' If Gair ever learned how

Ailric referred to him, blood would run; Tanith was certain of it. 'Once Gair's spoken to the Gatekeeper I don't know what he plans to do.'

Ailric considered this. 'Very well,' he said at last. 'I would be derelict in my duty to your father if I did not accompany you.'

Tanith felt sick. She'd been sure he'd see this next leg of her journey as a step too far for his comfort, that it would make him finally leave her alone. Quickly she smoothed her expression to hide her dismay.

'Go home, Ailric,' she said.

He gave her a thin, cold smile. 'You know I cannot, my love. I gave Lord Elindorien my word that I would protect his only heir, and I will do so even if it means I must protect her from herself.'

With a crisp little nod, he excused himself and went to fetch his own horse. Left staring after him, Tanith wanted to weep with despair. Merciful spirits, would she never be free of him?

One thing was certain: she would not stand around meekly waiting for his return. Mounted up, she searched for Gair over the heads of the crowd and found him talking to the Warlord. At least if Ailric followed her over there, the presence of the Lord of the Plains might compel him to remain civil.

Both men turned towards her at the sound of hooves approaching. 'Gentlemen,' she greeted them, trying to appear composed.

'Gair was telling me that the Gatekeeper is likely already at Saardost Keep, or on his way there,' Aradhrim said. 'It appears our roads lie together for a few more leagues.'

'And mine, too,' she said.

Gair looked concerned. 'You're coming with us? It could be dangerous, if the clans come against us.'

'All the more reason to have a good Healer on hand, then,' she said lightly, flashing a smile at the Warlord. 'With your permission, of course, my lord.'

'Permission granted, and right gladly. As Gair said, we might have need of your skills in days to come.'

Colours of emerald and amber brushed her mind. *I can't imagine Ailric being too pleased about this.*

He's not. I hoped by going north I could make him leave, but it didn't work.

Then the Warlord was speaking again, and she had to concentrate on what he was saying in order to avoid appearing rude, her mind too unsettled to carry two conversations at once. She felt Gair's grey eyes on her from time to time, gently anxious, but the only eyes she could see were ones the colour of flame, burning bright, and they made her just a little afraid.

27

GHOSTS

Ansel eyed the pile of papers on his desk. Not even Ninth, and already he was up to his neck in documents. There was always more paper, and if it wasn't paper it was people, clamouring for his attention, his advice, his judgement. It never stopped. Broke, maybe, for meals and sleep and holy worship, but never stopped, relentless as the tide.

The outer door to his study opened to admit his reedy secretary with yet another stack of administrative mundanities. Letters written up in Euan's fine crisp hand, minutes, requisitions, grants. Ansel scowled. Sometimes, and most especially on days like this, he feared the Suvaeon Order would not meet its end on the battlefield, nor fade gently into irrelevance through lack of numbers, but would instead choke to death on its own paperwork.

Sighing, he dipped his pen to make his signature on the first sheet Euan placed in front of him. Then, whilst the door was still ajar, he heard a woman's voice rising clearly above the dull mutter of the petitioners waiting their turn to see the Preceptor.

'Why, Danilar,' she said, with real warmth in her tone. 'How lovely to see you again after all these years.'

The burly Chaplain's reply was cut off by the door swinging

closed. Ansel's pen stopped moving. Surely not. He was hearing things. *Here?*

In a cloistered military order, where servants' duties were performed by the novices to teach them humility, a woman's voice was a rare thing to hear. A mother, perhaps, bravely hiding her tears as she surrendered her son into the care of the Suvaeon, or received back his spurs on a white and gold cushion with her grief running unabashed down her cheeks. But in the anteroom of the Preceptor's study? And *that* voice in particular?

Black ink gathered under the pen's nib, shivering with the trembling of his hand like a teardrop about to fall onto the smooth white page. The letters of his half-formed signature blurred.

Not her. Not here.

Blinking to clear his vision, he completed his name with care to avoid blotting it, then added the letter to the pile of correspondence stacked on his desk, its contents already forgotten. He was imagining things. The monotony of the administrative minutiae that occupied so much of his day had allowed his mind to wander, that was all, and he had to call it to heel like a wayward hound. He *must* be imagining things. But even as he thought it, he knew he was not.

'Just leave the rest for now, Euan. I can hear my appointments getting restless out there.'

'My lord,' his secretary murmured. He set down his papers, collected the signed pages from the desk and bowed himself out. Again the opening and closing of the door brought Ansel a few snatched words.

'—such a long time. You are looking well—'

The mantel clock chimed the hour, but he barely heard it. His head was too full of memories to have any space for music. Carefully, he wiped the nib of his pen and returned it to its stand. His hands twitched over the papers on his desk, wanting to tidy them, to hide the teacup and plate that signalled working through his breakfast. Knowing it was pointless to attempt to hide the truth from someone who knew him so well.

Danilar slipped into the room, lighter on his feet than a man of his size had any right to be. A troubled look sat uneasily on his leonine face. 'Ansel—' he began.

'I know. I heard.'

'But—'

'I can't refuse to see her, Danilar.' A hand clenched round Ansel's heart at the thought.

'It's been sixteen years since you saw her last.'

'I know!'

Silence but for the faint ticking of the clock, the twitter of a bird in the cloister garden below the window. She'd made an appointment with his secretary, like any other petitioner. She was there at the top of the neatly printed schedule of audiences that the redoubtable Euan gave him every morning, but listed by her title, which had meant nothing to him. Now he knew, and the knowing cut through him like a blade.

Danilar pursed his lips. 'I could see her in your stead, if you want.'

'That's a kind offer, old friend, but no. A man must face his ghosts eventually.' Ansel sat up straight in his chair and forced his crooked fingers not to grip the carved arms too tightly. 'Please ask Euan to send her in.'

Turning towards the door, the Chaplain paused with his hand on the latch. 'Are you sure this is wise?'

'She has asked to see me. I'm sure she has her reasons.'

The face Danilar made said he had a mouthful of words and wasn't sure whether or not to spill them, before he finally settled for swallowing them unsaid. 'Very well.'

The door closed behind him and Ansel blew out a long breath. His heart was drumming so loud in his ears he could scarcely think; it was worse than waiting for the trumpets to sound the charge – worse than waiting for the dawn the day the Knights had made their stand at Samarak. Not even that had frightened him as much as the thought of seeing her again.

Tick, tick, tick as the clock measured out the seconds, each one longer than the one before, then the polished oak door swung open again and Euan bowed two women in. One was robed and cowled in the brown of a Tamasian sister, the other in Superior's black, a starched white wimple framing her round-cheeked face. Years of sun and wind had given her complexion the patina of fine kid-skin, no longer young but handsome yet, and her eyes were still as pale and bright as flax-flowers.

'Superior, Sister, welcome.' He greeted them warmly, making the effort to hoist himself onto his feet. Pain flared in his hips, then vanished when the Superior smiled.

'Preceptor Ansel,' she said. 'I'm sorry we have to meet again under these circumstances.'

'So am I, Superior.' *Oh, Goddess, so am I!* He gestured to the chairs on the far side of his desk. 'Please, be seated. What brings you all this way from Gimrael?'

The young Tamasian sister sat, but the Superior shook her head. 'Thank you, but no. After almost a month in the saddle up from the Havens I've all but forgotten why the Goddess gave me feet.'

She folded her hands at her waist and all trace of a smile vanished from her face. 'The Daughterhouse in El Maqqam is lost. It was burned to the ground by Cultist thugs. I would have sent word, but I preferred to bring you the news in person.'

The simmering pot had finally boiled over – and in El Maqqam, too, where the last war had started, twenty-four years ago. How history came about full circle, in so many ways.

'I have heard reports of renewed Cultist activity,' Ansel said, 'and I know Kierim and the Emperor have, too. What was the governor's response?'

Her lips thinned. 'Next to nothing. He's too corrupt or too afraid to challenge them, and I don't know which is worse. Half the doors in the city have sun-signs. The Empire's merchant quarter has been walled off and placed under curfew by the city guard, whilst the imperial garrison is away at the Sardauki border. Now the Cult is attacking Church property and there is no one in the city with the will to stand against them. They almost killed Sister Resa.'

The younger nun put back her cowl, baring her face. Livid scars scored across her cheeks from the corners of her mouth and pulled her top lip slightly askew.

'Blessed Mother!' Ansel exclaimed.

'I will take this to the Lector himself, Preceptor, but I thought it only fair to warn the Suvaeon first.'

'You mean to press him to declare a crisis of the faith?'

'I don't think I will have to press him hard. This atrocity demands a response and, like most bullies, I fear the Cult will only take note of force.'

And the white and gold will fly over the bloody sands again. Ansel closed his eyes and offered up a brief prayer. *Only I won't be there to see it this time. One war like that in a lifetime is enough for any man.*

'We stand ready, Superior.' *Ready to send more young men to their deaths, Goddess help us.*

There was a pause, and then she added, 'There is one other reason why I came here first. We only escaped with our lives thanks to the actions of a former novice of yours. A young man called Gair.' The Superior watched his face for a reaction. 'I see you remember him.'

'I do,' said Ansel. *The Leahn is in Gimrael? I had Bredon send his marshals sixteen hundred miles west!* 'He was accused of witchcraft last year and expelled from our Order.'

Blue eyes regarded him guilelessly. 'One of my flock was told he was innocent of the charge.'

'I'm afraid not, Superior.' Ansel spread his hands on his desk, bracing himself. He knew her expressions too well not to suspect

306

something was coming. 'He made a free and full confession of guilt. I had no choice but to sentence him accordingly.'

The Superior's eyebrow twitched. 'Really.'

Now he was intrigued. 'He denied it?'

'No, actually, he did not – it was his companion. I don't think Gair himself spoke a word of untruth to any of us. Without his quick sword and his . . . gift, his magic, however you want to call it, the thirty-four of us would not have survived that night.'

'Song,' said Sister Resa. The word was slurred and indistinct, but recognisable. Laying a hand on the girl's shoulder, the Superior smiled warmly.

'Thank you, Daughter, yes. The Song, he called it. Using it, I think he gave Resa back her voice after the Cult cut out her tongue.'

Ansel sat down hard. The jolt of pain up his spine burst out as a curse that made the Superior wince.

'I see your language hasn't improved with age,' she murmured. 'Resa, would you wait in the anteroom for me, please? I would like to speak to the Preceptor alone.'

Cowled once more, as befitted a nun, the girl slipped out. When the door closed after her, the Superior finally took a seat, folded her hands and returned his incredulous stare as calmly as if she'd simply commented on the weather.

The Leahn had restored the girl's voice? Nothing under heaven could do that, surely.

Taking slow, deep breaths, Ansel waited for the pain in his back and hips to diminish to its familiar dull throb. 'How?' he asked.

'I don't know, exactly. Resa says he put his hand on her face and told her she would feel something strange, then she saw the most beautiful colours in the air around her. The way she describes it, she was touched by the Goddess's grace. Since then the scarring has diminished a little more every day. Halfway here she attempted her first words since she was injured.'

'When was that? When was she hurt?'

'Less than five months ago.'

'But those scars look years old!'

'Remarkable, isn't it?' The Superior smiled. 'Most of her tongue is gone and can never grow back, but whatever Gair did eased the pain and has given her enough flexibility that she can shape simple words with what remains.' One hand touched the Oak on her breast, as if for reassurance. 'If the boy was more pious I'd agree with Resa – that we have witnessed a miracle.'

A miracle. Oh, something miraculous was happening, without a doubt. A trinity moon about to rise, the whole world turned about and upside down, but in the midst of suffering of all kinds something marvellous, something beyond his wildest hopes had occurred.

He looked up, tears burning at the back of his eyes. 'Blood and stones, I've missed you, Jenara.'

ᘒ

It might not have been a consideration to the fortress's builders, but Masen thought the view from the upper watchtowers of Saardost Keep was possibly one of the finest in the Empire.

He leaned against one of the lichen-scabbed merlons along the wall with a fresh cup of tea and admired the blade-sharp peaks rearing out of rumpled pine-choked valleys, green again now that the thaw was well advanced. Higher in the pass, where the keep spanned the old north road, the snow still lingered in streaks and smears, but down in the valley below the walls there were bright flowers amongst the rocks and the river had become a milky torrent of meltwater, throwing spray up over the bridge parapet as it passed like handfuls of diamonds.

So pretty. Too bad it was likely to become a battlefield in the not too distant future.

The hail came ringing through the air as bright and clear as church bells on a winter morning. Masen recognised the colours at once; after his conversation with Maera he'd been half-expecting a hail for almost a week, but the sudden clarity of it was still enough to make him spill his tea.

Do you have to shout? he grumbled, swiping at the splashes on his jerkin. *I may not be able to hail as far as you, but it doesn't mean I'm deaf.*

There was a startled pause, then Gair said, *My apologies. Good morning. Speaker Maera told me I'd find you up there.*

I thought you were still in Gimrael with Alderan. What happened – did the archive come up empty?

Not exactly. The Leahn's vibrant colours dimmed. *There was trouble with the Cult in El Maqqam – they burned down the Daughter-house and all the books with it.*

The mug stopped halfway to Masen's mouth. Steam twisted away on the cold mountain breeze, the tea forgotten. He had a sudden, gut-clenching feeling of dread. *Go on.*

Alderan was trying to retrieve the books we hadn't looked at. He was trapped inside.

But you escaped? The words came out with more rancour than he'd intended.

I wasn't there. I'd already left to escort the nuns out of the city.

Masen stared unseeing into the crystalline air. His old friend was gone. After all the years, all the miles, all the bad jokes and near misses, gone. And that left Masen with a responsibility he didn't want, and couldn't shift.

'Damn it,' he said, and hurled the mug out into the void. He watched it fall, spilling out its contents over the river, the smashing of its pottery lost in the roar of the water. *You'd better tell me.*

We had problems with the Cult from the minute we arrived in Zhiman-dar. They ambushed me in the souq, and when we left we just barely escaped a mob burning prayer books. In the capital it was worse. They harassed the nuns—

What Gair had said before finally registered. *Wait a minute. Nuns?*

The Daughterhouse in El Maqqam belongs to the Tamasians now.

The Cult has been making their lives difficult for months – one of the sisters had her tongue cut out for daring to teach some children a nonsense rhyme.

Good Goddess.

The desert wars had begun in a similar way. Hostility at first, long stares and short tempers developing into harassment, out-right intimidation, then violence. The Knights launched reprisals, the Cult retaliated and the whole bloody mess boiled over. Masen shook his head, only half-listening as the Leahn described accompanying the sisters out into the city to do their good works and the ugliness that had followed.

You killed them.

Some of them. A flare of defiance lit up the boy's colours again. *I won't stand idle whilst women are assaulted in the street, not when there's something I can do about it.*

No, I don't suppose you would. Masen sighed. *Not after a decade in the Motherhouse, anyway. And now we have Knights in the desert killing Cultists again, twenty-odd years after the last round.* He could imagine how well Alderan would react to that news. Belatedly, he realised what he'd said and corrected himself. Would have reacted. Past tense. *Holy Mother bless you, old friend.*

I did what I thought was right, Gair said stiffly.

I'm sure you did, lad. And the books?

We found nothing of use.

So it had all been for naught. He shook his head. Alderan was so sure there'd be something helpful in those old books, the ones the fleeing *gaeden* had carried out of Dremen. He'd argued that it was the one avenue the Order of the Veil hadn't pursued. Short of scouring the Apocryphae in the Motherhouse library, it was their best chance of finding contemporaneous records from the time of the purges. Now they were all gone to ashes.

With a sigh, he tried to push his grief aside. There'd be time for it later. *Where are you?*

A day and a half southwest of you. We're travelling up from the Singing Stones with the Warlord and his ride.

We?

Tanith's here. It's a long story.

Masen blinked. Tanith was in Arennor too? She should have been at home in Astolar, not traipsing across the wilds.

You can tell me all about it when you get here. We've got plenty on our plates at the minute with the Hounds and the war band breathing down our necks.

They've reached the pass? Gair sounded alarmed.

Not yet, but they're not far off. The patrols have observed some scouting parties, but we still don't know exactly where the war band is. There's a lot of broken country up here where an army could be hiding.

We'll get there as soon as we can.

There's one more thing, and you might want to pass this along to Aradhrim, Masen added. *When the Speakers come against us, those Hounds might not be all we have to face.*

You've seen something?

I saw where the Veil was cut to let them out.

A shocked pause. *You're joking.*

Where the Veil's concerned, I don't joke, he said shortly. *Two separate locations, two clean cuts, by someone who knew what they were about. I've stitched them up, but if the Speakers have that kind of ability, I don't believe for a minute that they'll stop at a couple of hellhounds.*

Gair was silent for a while. *Do you think they can free the Hunt?* he asked at last, colours heavy with dread.

I don't know, and that's the truth of it. The Nimrothi have kept to themselves for generations; no one has any idea what kind of power they possess. For all I know, they might already have Corlainn's starseed – it would certainly explain what gives them the brass balls to march against the Empire after all these years.

I've some thoughts of my own on that subject, said Gair in a dark tone. *I'll explain when I see you.*

Then get here quickly. I've a feeling we haven't got a lot of time.

28

SECRETS

The first time Gair laid eyes on Saardost Keep, squatting at the neck of the valley, it put him in mind of a monstrous grey toad at the bottom of a bucket. Thick towers planted firmly on the rocky floor of the pass, its upper reaches warted with bartizans, it scowled pugnaciously over its walls at all who approached, from north or south, and dared them to draw arms.

A curtain wall spanned the pass from Saardost itself to a daughter keep on the eastern side, not much more than a fortified tower jutting from the mountain's flank. The arch at the wall's centre was filled by massive timber gates, well tarred against the weather, closing the north road that was now so overgrown with brush and tough, tussocky grass that its ancient cobbles were all but invisible. The gates to the keep itself stood open to allow the passage of working parties and wagons laden with fresh lumber from the valley slopes, bald but for pale stumps like the skin of a freshly plucked fowl.

The sight of the Warlord's banner brought a flurry of bugle-notes back and forth, and before long his ride were clattering into the bailey to an enthusiastic welcome from a smaller number of their kinsmen. Waiting on the steps to the keep was a thickset, bull-necked fellow in imperial green, whose shoulders and sleeves glittered with enough rank insignia to suggest he was the Sixth Legion's commander, Brandt. He quickly vanished back inside with Aradhrim and Magda at his heels.

'Do you see Masen anywhere?' Gair asked Tanith as they dismounted. She shook her head, studiously ignoring Ailric when he proffered his arm to help her down.

'He's inside somewhere, by his colours,' she said.

A piercing whistle split the air and all three of them looked up. A swarthy young man was leaning between two of the merlons atop the gatehouse.

'Good morning,' he shouted.

Gair shaded his eyes against the bright sky to see him better. 'Sorchal?'

'One and the same.' The Elethrainian gave one of his florid bows. 'My lady Tanith, such a delight to see you again.'

Gair winced, imagining how Ailric would react to that, but fortunately the Astolan kept his feelings to himself. Sorchal disappeared from view, emerging from the gatehouse guardroom a minute or so later to greet them all. Ailric remained stiffly formal in the face of Sorchal's charm, and the Elethrainian must have read something in his posture or manner because he made no further attempt to flirt with Tanith.

'So how did you end up here?' Gair asked when the introductions were over. 'I thought you'd still be at Chapterhouse.'

'So did I, but I'm the Gatekeeper's new apprentice.' Sorchal grinned at Gair's incredulous expression. 'Let me assure you, no one is more surprised than me. There I was, resigned to a life of feckless debauchery, and it turns out I actually have something of a talent after all.' He made a face. 'Woe is me, and so forth. Come on, I'll help you get settled and then we can catch up.'

Once the horses had been handed into the care of the legion's stable-boys, Sorchal showed Gair and the others to their sleeping quarters so they could relieve themselves of their gear. Brandt's quartermaster had allocated them accommodations on the floor above the barracks, along from the senior officers, he said, leading them to a stone-flagged corridor with a row of roughly finished doors along one side.

'Little more than cells, I'm afraid, but they're out of the weather.'

He opened the nearest door, revealing a space that was just about big enough to lay out a bed for one and still have room to get washed and dressed.

'This will do perfectly,' said Tanith, stepping in front of him.

'But your room is—'

'This one's fine,' she said, with a bright smile. 'Now I'd like to freshen up before I go down to see the infirmary, so if you'll excuse me, gentlemen?'

The door was closed gently but firmly in their faces, leaving Sorchal mid-sentence and Ailric, who'd been about to follow Tanith inside, snubbed and fuming.

'Ah.' Sorchal shot Gair a quizzical glance behind the Astolan's back, and he responded with the merest shake of his head. Recovering magnificently, the Elethrainian became every inch the courteous host, murmuring his apologies for the confusion as he steered the stony-faced Ailric to the next door along. There he swiftly retrieved his own belongings, bowed the other man inside and beat a hasty retreat towards the far end of the corridor with Gair close behind.

'I hope you don't mind sharing,' Sorchal said as he let them into the last room and dumped his gear on the floor.

'Not at all.' Gair would have preferred not to have an audience if the dreams came, but liked the idea of having to explain why he'd prefer to sleep on his own even less.

'Good,' said Sorchal with a sigh, 'because that was awkward. I usually arrange to be somewhere else when lovers argue.'

Gair set down his own things and conjured a glim to illuminate the room. Apart from an additional window slit it was no better appointed than the one Tanith had taken, but it was roughly twice the size. Large enough for two, in other words.

'They're not together. Not any more.'

'From the look on his face, he seems to think they are.'

'It's long over, according to Tanith, but Ailric's still hearing yes when she says no. He's been following her around like a second shadow all the way through Arennor.' Recalling his own brushes with the fire-eyed Astolan, Gair added, 'And he doesn't make a secret of how he feels about humans, either.'

'So showering Tanith with sweet words would be a bad idea?'

'Spectacularly so.'

'Huh.' Sorchal fondled the elegant swept hilt of his rapier, green eyes sparkling. 'On the other hand, I'm getting bored. Is he any good with a blade?'

Gair snorted. The man was incorrigible. 'I haven't a clue, but from what I've sensed he has more than enough of a gift to smack you silly before you got within reach. I could use some sparring practice, though, if you like.'

'How about now? It's a couple of hours until supper.'

It had been too long since he'd worked the forms to clear his head, but there was something else he had to do first. 'I'm afraid I must see Masen immediately. He needs to know everything that happened in El Maqqam. Tomorrow?'

'Tomorrow – but please can we meet at a civilised hour for once?'

☙❧

Gair found the Gatekeeper where Sorchal told him to look: atop the keep's highest watchtower. Up there the wind blew sharp and cold despite the bright sunshine, and the vast spread of the valley below set the fire-eagle's Song tugging at him. On the north side of the tower, a couple of the Sixth's legionaries were on watch; Masen leaned against the wall on the far side, gazing southwards into the Empire as if he was searching for something he'd lost. He glanced over his shoulder as Gair approached, but was soon staring south again.

'So you made it up from Gimrael in one piece,' he said tonelessly.

Even though there was nothing in either the words or the inflection to suggest a rebuke, Gair couldn't help but feel the sting of one.

'More or less. I'm sorry about Alderan.'

Masen grunted. 'It had to happen eventually. Could have wished for it not to be so soon, though.'

'How long had you known him?'

'Over thirty years. I met him when I was about your age – all spit-in-your-eye temper and no clue where to put it.' Masen looked down at his hands, hanging loose over the edge of the wall, and shook his head slowly. A faint smile tweaked at the corner of his mouth, as if he was remembering something that amused him. 'Alderan saw beyond that, and we were friends from then on.'

'We didn't part on the best of terms, but I still miss him.'

'As do I, lad. As do I.' The Gatekeeper gave one last wistful look out over the mountains, then turned to face him. He looked tired, Gair thought, his features pouchy and sagging, as if he hadn't slept much lately, though with his weather-beaten face it was difficult to be sure. 'So what did you fight about? The books?'

'I thought we were wasting our time with them – we'd found nothing, after days of searching, then when the Daughterhouse was attacked, he wanted to save them and leave the nuns to make their own way out of the city.'

'And you disagreed.'

'I did.' Gair folded his arms, set his feet. 'Thirty-four women in a city full of zealots who'd already assaulted them? I couldn't—'

A somewhat pained gesture cut him off.

'What's done is done.' Masen clamped his mouth shut in a way that told Gair there was much more he wanted to say.

And I probably don't want to hear it, Gair thought. A mortified flush burning up his neck, he dropped his gaze to his boots. The Gatekeeper hadn't called him to account for Alderan's death, so there was no need to justify his actions. He'd had a few seconds in which to make a decision, and he still believed he'd made the right one, but having to look a man in the eye and own to robbing him of his best friend . . . that was hard. It made him feel sick and cold inside, and brought the guilt storming back.

'I'm not making excuses,' he said quietly. 'I just wanted you to understand.'

'Aye, well, I do understand, and that's half the damn problem,' Masen muttered.

An uncomfortable silence fell, in which the clatter of the banner's toggles against the flagstaff and the thin whine of the wind sounded very loud. When Gair couldn't stand it any longer, he asked, 'So what happens now? Alderan told me I should try to find you, that we might be able to help each other.'

The Gatekeeper sighed gustily. 'What happens is that with Alderan gone, I'm Guardian of the Veil, Goddess love me.'

Startled, Gair looked up. 'I had no idea.'

'I'm not the strongest *gaeden*, nor the best administrator, but I am the one who's known Alderan and his plans the longest, so a few years ago the Council decided that I should be his second. I never stayed on the Isles long enough to argue them out of it, and . . .' He shrugged. 'Here we are. Now I have to figure out a way to stop this war band and all their Speakers when we don't even know how many they are, never mind where they're going to strike.'

'The scouts still haven't found anything?'

'They've seen some outriders, but that's all. Clansman Sor reckons the main Nimrothi force is staying well out on the plains to hide their intentions, damn their eyes.' Masen scratched his chin ruminatively. 'I was hoping you might have brought some better news out of Gimrael, to be honest.'

You and me both, Gatekeeper.

'There is one thing I can tell you. Savin claims to know the whereabouts of the starseed.'

Masen's head came up and he stared at Gair incredulously. 'How the hell—'

'I was in Syfria, and he decided to pay me a visit. Not in person – it was a sending, an illusion of himself.' Gair's left arm burned with the memory and he rubbed it without thinking. 'Actually, I think he was just taunting me, but I thought you should know.'

Masen frowned. 'Taunting you? Why?'

'Because he can?' It was difficult to keep the bitterness out of his voice. 'Because he thought I was valuable to Alderan in some way, and it amused him to play games with me just to spite the old man? Whatever his reasons, he surely had fun doing it.'

I must say how much I enjoyed your memories. Tasted sweet, didn't she? Like strawberries. Quickly Gair slammed closed the door on that remembrance, breathed deep and slow to keep it shut tight. There was no knowing who might be listening.

'Well, that sounds like Savin right enough,' Masen growled. 'Did he say where the starseed was?'

Gair shook his head. 'He was too busy laughing and telling me I'd wasted my time in Gimrael.'

'You're saying it *isn't* in the desert?'

'It could be, I suppose, but I don't think Alderan ever thought it was. From what he told me, we were looking for clues to where the starseed might have been taken, not its actual location.'

'Leaving us no further forward than we were.' With a gusty sigh, Masen shoved himself away from the wall and began prowling back and forth. 'And even if our mutual friend really does know where it is, it's immaterial. There's nothing we can do about it from here.'

'Is it possible the Speakers have the starseed?'

Still pacing, Masen shook his head. 'If they did, the Veil would be in shreds by now. I'm not even sure they're the ones who cut it to free the Hounds.'

'That doesn't make sense,' Gair said. 'Maegern's a clan goddess, and the Hounds are Her minions. Who else would have had reason to release them?' A possibility occurred to him. 'Surely you're not suggesting an *Arennorian* Speaker could have been responsible?'

'Of course not!' Masen shot him a disgusted look. 'Maera would kill me for even bringing up the idea. But if it had been the Nimrothi, they'd have simply turned the Hounds loose north of the mountains. Why come so deep into the plains?'

There had to be a reason, but for the life of him, Gair couldn't see it. 'A ruse? Something to draw our eye, or keep us guessing?'

'Maybe.' Masen scrubbed a hand across his face. 'Damn it, my brains are all but scrambled with thinking about this.' He muttered something under his breath that Gair didn't quite catch, something about nimbler minds, and planted his fists on his hips. 'All we can do now is wait, I reckon. Hunker down, and when the clans come knocking we throw them back on their arses.'

'And the starseed?'

'Without knowing where it is?' Masen clicked his tongue against his teeth. 'We'll just have to hope Savin was tweaking your tail. There's precious few other cards to play.'

He looked down at the stones under his feet, mouth working on the words he wanted to say, lining them up behind his teeth. Gair waited, expecting the worst.

'You were right, you know. Alderan did consider you valuable to the Order.'

'As a weapon against Savin? He didn't think I could beat him.' A flash of temper soured the words.

Masen shot him a look. 'Put your hackles down, lad, that wasn't what I meant.' Then he sighed. 'Alderan never intended you to go up against anyone. He wanted you to be everything Savin was not.'

'I don't understand.'

'Back then, children born to *gaeden* parents were rare. When Aileann gave birth, the Order looked on her child as this precious gift that had to be nurtured, like a hothouse orchid. We tried to make him into one of us, and everything we gave him he threw back in our faces. It nearly destroyed the Order.'

'So what were Alderan's plans for me?'

'Absolutely nothing,' Masen said simply. 'When he got that letter from his brother and went to the Holy City, he was only thinking about keeping you from the stake. After he discovered the extent of your gift, he knew he had to let you choose what to do with it, or we'd just repeat our mistakes.'

A gift not given freely is no gift at all. Alderan had said that after the testing, back before Gair had known anything about reivers or starseed – before he'd even known the truth about Corlainn Fellbane. He turned the words over in his mind, seeing new significance in the emphasis the old man had put on choice. Perhaps that was the real reason why it had rankled so much the one time Alderan had taken choice away from him, and he'd been too caught up in his own selfish pain to see it. Strange how it didn't seem to matter quite so much now that the old man was gone.

'I didn't know Alderan had a brother,' he said at last.

'Yes, a couple of years older than him. He and Danilar were estranged for a good while, but—'

'Wait a minute. *Danilar?*'

Masen blinked. 'You didn't know who sent the letter that saved you?'

'Holy saints, Masen – of course I didn't know!' Gair levered himself away from the wall, spread his arms. 'Danilar is the Chaplain of the Suvaeon Order!'

෧෨

'I haven't heard my given name spoken in a very long time.' Jenara laid down her fork and dabbed her lips with her napkin. 'It's good to hear it again, instead of "yes, Superior, of course, Superior, right away, Superior".'

Across the table, with its starched napery and gleaming silver, Ansel could only stare at her. Picking up her wine glass, she darted him a look over the rim. 'Stop that.'

'I can't help it,' he said. 'You haven't changed at all.'

'I've about thirty pounds around my middle that would beg to differ.' She drank, then returned to her fish. 'I hear you've been unwell.'

He grunted. 'News carries fast in the Church.'

'The Superior at Caer Amon keeps me informed.'

'He was supposed to keep his mouth shut!'

Her eyes twinkled. 'Don't be too hard on him. When you've held a bottle for a man who's too badly wounded to walk to the latrine, there's not many secrets he can hide from you.'

Ansel shook his head and tried not to laugh. Jenara had ever been resourceful; it had enabled her to run a hospital in a hostile country on a budget a sparrow's kiss away from nothing and still save more lives than the Order's field surgeons. Nothing she achieved should surprise him any more.

'I ought to offer you a job – you'd make a far better spymaster than Elder Cristen.'

'Thank you, but no – pigeons make me sneeze,' she said, daintily dabbing butter on a piece of bread. 'Superior Beldene said he thought you might be dying.'

'Last winter was . . . bad,' he admitted. 'That's why I sent for Selsen. I didn't dare leave it any longer. I thought it was already too late, if I'm honest, but I had to try to finish what I'd started. When she wrote with the date to expect her arrival, it felt like a sign.' Jenara's brow creased uncertainly, and he added, 'Saint Saren's.'

Her expression cleared, and she smiled thinly. 'The patron saint of lost causes. Maybe it was a sign at that.' For a time there was no sound but the gentle chink of silverware on china as she portioned her food into neat bites, ate, swallowed. 'I would have come, Ansel, if I'd known.'

The words held no reproof, but still they stung. 'I didn't know where you were. Besides, after that time in Syfria, we agreed . . . It was for the best, you said.'

He'd argued, she'd insisted. He'd pleaded, they'd both cried, and that had been that. He'd heard nothing more, until the letter came entrusting him with her greatest gift.

'I remember,' she said. 'So who else knows?'

'That you're here, and taking supper with the Preceptor in his private apartments?' Ansel shrugged. 'About two dozen people.'

'That's not what I meant.'

He swirled his wine around the glass and inhaled the bouquet. Fresh, like green apples, but he suddenly had no taste for it, nor the baked trout, either, and put the wine down untouched.

'Only Danilar, and only about you. He took my confession, after Samarak, when I . . . fell into doubt.'

He fidgeted with the stem of his glass, turning it in circles. Refracted candlelight danced across the tablecloth. Rainbows, all around him, every one a fragment of memory.

'Those were hard days.' Jenara's fork, with its burden of succulent pink trout-flesh, paused halfway to her mouth. 'You need to forgive yourself, Ansel.'

'I can't.' He picked up his own utensils and stabbed at vegetables on his plate as if they were mortal enemies. 'Believe me, I've tried.'

She ate, swallowed. 'What's done is done. We cannot change it, however we might wish differently. We must learn to accept it.'

'Please, Jenara, I'm not one of your novices. Don't preach to me.'

'I'm not trying to.'

Nothing seemed to ruffle her. He threw down his fork. Silver clattered on china and herb butter spots bloomed on the pristine damask tablecloth.

'I broke my vows! How can I hold myself as an exemplar for the Suvaeon? How can I sit in judgement on the sins of others when I am a sinner?'

'Our sins are what make us human, Ansel.' Blue eyes watched him, soft and forgiving. 'I'd rather be judged by a sinner who truly understood the sin than by a passionless marble saint whose eyes are so fixed on heaven he cannot see the earth under his feet.'

A candlewick fizzed and the flame fluttered. Wax shimmered and ran. Ansel picked up his glass and downed the wine in quick swallows.

'Why didn't you tell me about her?' he asked hoarsely. 'Why did I have to find out by accident four years later? I could have helped you.'

'You didn't need me,' she said, placing her cutlery neatly at the side of her plate. 'You were the hero of Samarak. You didn't need a woman trailing around the place after you, embarrassing you. Raising questions.'

Though she spoke gently, every word stabbed him like a blade.

'We could have made it work.'

'No, we couldn't.' The Superior folded her napkin onto the table. 'Would it have been worth all the lies, the deception? What we had would have been demeaned by it, and turned into something tawdry. I couldn't have borne that.'

He leaned back in his chair, all strength gone, and let the carved wood hold him upright. As usual, she had the right of it. What had burned so brightly under the desert skies, when neither of them had known how many days remained and every minute together was a gift, would never have survived in another time and place. Better to remember it as it was, brave and true, than watch the fire crushed slowly out of it by the lives they each had to live.

'I begin to see how you were advanced to Superior so quickly,' he said at last. 'I envy you your wisdom.'

Jenara smiled. 'Becoming a mother shifts one's perspective quite a bit. Such clarity comes when your first priority is no longer yourself.' She eased back her chair and stood. Ansel struggled to get to his feet but she held up her hand. 'Please, don't. I know how much it pains you.'

He slumped back into his cushions. 'You know all my secrets, Jenara.'

'And I hold them all in my heart,' she said tenderly. Folding her hands at her waist, she drew herself up, every inch the serene Superior. 'Resa and I have an appointment with the Lector of Dremen tomorrow afternoon, then we must return to Syfria. I'd like to see my daughter before I go.'

'Of course. My private garden is at your disposal. The wild roses are in bloom, I believe.' Just for an instant, her eyes clouded, and he was ashamed of himself. 'That was cruel. Forgive me.'

'No, it's all right.' She sighed. 'I think you were owed that. I should have told you. You shouldn't have had to find out the way you did.'

Bright sunshine bouncing off the walls of that little courtyard garden behind the Tamasians' guest hall. Hearing footsteps on the stone flags, rising from the bench as the little girl who'd made him a daisy-chain leapt up and flung herself against the skirts of a brown habit. Seeing Jenara's expression flash from pleasure to shock as she realised who was waiting for the hospitaller beneath the rose-covered arch. No, he shouldn't have had to find out in that way that he had a daughter, but as she'd said, those had been hard days.

'I should never have let you go.' His shoulders lifted helplessly. 'I loved you, Jenara. I still do.'

'More than you loved the Goddess?'

Ansel winced. 'Don't. Please.' *Don't ask me questions I cannot answer. Don't force me to make comparisons no man should ever have to make.*

She walked around the table and, sheltering the flames with her hand, blew out the slender candles one by one. With only the sunset to see by, she stopped at his side. 'Hard days,' she murmured. 'Hard choices. I missed you, too, Ansel.'

Slowly her arm slid across his shoulders and pulled him to her. He wrapped his own arms around her waist and let her cradle his head against the breast of her habit.

So many memories. Of cool rooms, warm breezes. Slatted sunlight through shutters and bittersweet spices that caught in his throat like the drifting candle-smoke.

He shut his eyes. 'Don't go.'

Warm lips pressed to his brow. 'I have to, love. My order needs me.'

Those very words had been said last time, almost twenty years ago when the desert war ended and he was recalled to Dremen, whilst she had to stay at the hospital with the remaining wounded. Only now she was the one leaving, and he was the one who could not follow. He held her tight, cursing the gap in their ages that had made an old man of him when she was still in the last ripe flush of womanhood. Cursed the wasted opportunities, the decisions taken that had changed the course of both their lives.

'I would have married you, you know.'

Her hand stroked his hair. 'I know.'

'I would have given up the Order, everything, to be your husband.'

'You couldn't, love. You had a calling, a task to complete. It would have been a far greater sin to give that up.'

Pain clenched his chest. 'I could have been a father to her.'

'And instead you have been a father to every boy who's passed through the Motherhouse's doors.' Another kiss, on his mouth this time. He tasted salt and wine. 'How many hundreds of lives have you helped to shape, Ansel? What is one life measured against that?'

'Nothing.' His eyes burned. 'Everything.' He had to swallow the sudden lump in his throat before he could ask, 'Does she know?'

'I only told her that her father was a Knight, nothing more. But I wouldn't be surprised if she's worked it out for herself.'

Ansel looked up, no longer even trying to hide the tears. 'Please stay a little longer. Just a day or two. We have so much to say.'

Easing out of his embrace, she caught his hands in hers and squeezed them, careful of his twisted fingers. 'Good night, Preceptor. Thank you for supper.'

'Good night, Superior.' His hands fell back into his lap, empty again.

The door to his private rooms closed behind her and with the snick of the latch, Ansel's heart broke. For her, for himself, for the war about to resume in the desert that would take so many lives.

Across the room on the vast tapestry, Endirion's diamond helm glittered in the last rays of the sun, fading with the day, like Ansel's hopes for his Order. He'd thought he could restore it to its ideals, clean and upright and true, as their vows had ever been, but all he could see was endings.

29

STONE

As the mountain road swung around the last ridge, the keep came into view. Square and forbidding, throwing its wall across the valley like a sentry's arm held out in interdiction. Each time Duncan saw it, it made him vaguely uncomfortable. His ancestors tapping him on the shoulder with their spears, no doubt, reminding him that the great pile of stone was a symbol of the sundering of his people. Generations ago, now, but still. Events of that nature left a scar on a nation's soul.

He looked back over his shoulder to where the Banfaíth rode at the head of her people. Probably the first of his estranged kinsmen to ride into Arennor since the Breaking. His mouth twisted. The Empire referred to that time as the Founding and celebrated what was built, whereas the clans, in their hearts, mourned what was lost. Maybe that line of ragged people signified the start of some healing.

'Go on,' he said to his second, riding next to him. 'I'll ride in with the Banfaíth.'

The clansman nodded acknowledgement and urged his horse ahead. Duncan turned his own mount and trotted back down the line until he was level with Teia's slab-shouldered dun. She looked drained by the journey, he thought, her face pale and pinched with pain.

'Banfaíth,' he greeted her, falling his horse in beside hers. 'We are almost at the keep. You'll be able to rest there.'

'Thank you,' she said. 'How did you know my back was hurting?'

Duncan coughed, embarrassed at having been caught paying attention. 'I have, uh, married sisters,' he said, and concentrated on the road ahead until they rounded the bend and the keep came into view. He pointed. 'There it is.'

Teia looked up and gasped, halting her horse in the middle of the road. Duncan reined up and looked back at her as she stared at the keep with a mixture of fear and awe.

'This is your fortress?' Behind her the rest of her people shuffled to a stop as well, whispering anxiously amongst themselves. Any words were lost in the thunder of the meltwater-swollen river.

'Not mine, Banfaíth, but yes – this is Saardost Keep.'

'And all your war band go inside this . . . keep?' She pronounced the alien word awkwardly. Her gaze traced the outline of the towers, the flapping banners, and she shuddered. 'Stone shouldn't be raised so high.'

Frowning, Duncan wondered whether he'd misheard. 'Banfaíth?'

'Lord Aedon raised the mountains up to keep the sky above and the earth below, and gave men and beasts all the space between,' she said. It was the same creation story he'd heard since the cradle. 'Men shouldn't try to imitate what the Eldest wrought.'

'But Aedon gave us stone, and the wits to make tools to work it. Why would He be displeased that men made use of His gifts?' He smiled, to show he was only teasing. 'It's perfectly safe, I assure you.'

The Nimrothi girl didn't respond to his humour, regarding the keep with deep distrust. 'So you say.'

'Would it help if I explained how it was built?' He was hazy on

328

the details, but he'd been to Fleet many times and seen the river-rock foundations of the merchants' houses there. He guessed the construction of a fortress wasn't much different, except for the scale.

'No.' Sounds of hammering and sawing from inside said repairs were still ongoing. A saw shrieked and she winced. 'So much noise.'

'Saardost has stood empty for hundreds of years,' said Duncan, by way of an apology. 'All that was not made of stone was carried away by time.'

The Banfaíth gave him a sideways look. 'And yet you tell me it's perfectly safe?'

Well, she had him there. Time to change the subject.

'This is where the Warlord holds his command,' he said, and pointed at the green banners that flew from each tower, the highest topped with the white bull of the Durannadh. 'See? His personal standard. If you would meet with him, you must go inside.'

She didn't look any less dubious.

'I will walk in with you, Banfaíth, and no harm will come to you,' he assured her. 'You have my word.'

'You cannot protect me when the war band reaches us,' she said. Violet-blue eyes regarded him calmly. 'I know what the future holds, Captain. I will not hide behind walls when the time comes to face it.'

She eyed the fortress's gates again and her mouth set into a resolute line. 'Well, if it must be done, I will ride in with my people to show them there is nothing to fear.'

With a shake of the reins she urged her gelding into motion and rode back to join Baer, the rest of the Lost Ones clustering after her like ducklings after their mother.

Duncan watched her go and had to remind himself again that she was no older than his youngest sister. Her composure stole his breath away. Little more than a child, and she was Banfaíth to a band of Maenardh who had followed her through the mountains for no more compelling reason than that she made them feel safe.

'Astonishing,' he murmured.

'Captain?'

Duncan realised he'd spoken aloud and faced forward to find his second was back beside him, brow furrowed in concern.

'The line stopped – is aught amiss?'

'It's nothing,' he said. 'Ride on and make the identification.'

Talking to himself now! He shook his head. If he didn't know better, he'd suspect the Banfaíth had worked a charm on him to addle his wits.

The first of the ride crested the bridge across the river that zigzagged through the valley and a bugle sounded from the fortress. To a rattle of chains and creak of windlasses, the tarred gates inched open. Beyond, a double row of green-clad pikemen shielded the busy cobbled bailey. In the centre, arms folded, stood a lanky figure Duncan knew only too well.

'Welcome, brother!' Sor called. 'What kept you?'

'Oh, you know,' Duncan shouted back. 'The landscape's so pretty here I lose all track of time.'

He urged his horse to a trot to cover the remaining distance from the bridge to the keep. Sor caught his reins as he halted and as soon as Duncan's boots hit the weedy cobbles his older brother grabbed him into a rough embrace.

'It's good to see you.'

'It's good to be seen,' Duncan said, stepping back to arm's length. 'I see our cousin's here.'

'Indeed he is – rode in yesterday with a gaggle of *gaeden* at his heels.'

'*Gaeden?*' Duncan echoed, surprised. 'Up here? Is this because of the Speakers with the war band?'

His brother shrugged. 'All Aradhrim told me was that they were to meet the Gatekeeper here. A Leahn and two Astolans, one of them some kind of high-born lady, though she says she's

330

just a physician.' He eyed the ragged folk trailing behind the incoming ride. 'I see you've picked up some strays of your own.'

Duncan followed his gaze. 'They're Maenardh, exiles from the Nimrothi clans,' he said, and a grin tugged at his lips. 'Sor, a sixteen-year-old girl led them through the mountains.' He pointed past the arriving clansmen. 'That's her, with the fur cloak and the staff. She's their Banfaíth, if you can believe it. Sixteen!'

His brother's eyebrows rose. 'Nimrothi?' he repeated. 'The people we're about to go to war with, and you brought them *here*? Slaine's stones! How do you know one of them isn't a spy?'

Duncan rolled his eyes. 'I'm not stupid, Sor. They're just trying to escape the trouble that's coming.'

Sor snorted. 'And you've deduced this on the strength of your, oh, two years' experience as a ride-captain?'

'Look at the state of them! They're no danger to anything but some hot food. She,' Duncan jabbed a finger towards Teia, 'came to warn us about the war band and her Speaker's intentions to loose the Hunt.'

That gave Sor pause. He thumbed his lip thoughtfully. 'You're sure that's her real motive? The Nimrothi have no love for us – why would she risk the mountains in winter for people her kind swore blood feud on?'

'She's got the foretelling,' Duncan said. 'She sees destruction for all of us if the Hunt rides free, and she thinks coming south to the Empire is the best chance of stopping it.' His brother shot him a sceptical look. 'I believe her, Sor. There's something about her, the way she looks at you, like she's seeing into your soul. When you meet her, you'll understand.'

Sor grunted. 'Doesn't mean there isn't still a scout hiding in her party.'

Mention of scouts reminded Duncan of something he'd almost forgotten, too bewitched by the enigma that was the Lost Ones' Banfaíth – and the young girl who occasionally peeped out from behind her eyes.

'Actually, it wouldn't matter if there was.' He dug in his pocket for the travelling charm he'd taken from his slain kinsman and held it out. 'They already know we're here.'

Sor took the little piece of carved bone and turned it over on his palm as Duncan described how he and his men had found the dead Morennadh. 'Where?' he asked at last.

'Two days east of King's Gate on the north side of the mountains. Kael said the Nimrothi were heading this way.'

His brother swore softly. 'Well, it's a direction.' He bounced the charm in his hand, then tucked it away in his pocket. 'I'll pass the word around the other captains to be vigilant.'

The last of the ride clattered in, leaving only the Nimrothi outside. Baer and the girl were in heated conversation, her hands spread imploringly and him shaking his grizzled head. The chief-in-exile pointed up at the fortress, leaning forward to say something emphatic. Then one by one the Maenardh peeled off the road onto the river meadow with their ponies and their bundles, well away from the walls that perturbed Baer so, and only the girl came up the last slope beneath the frowning gatehouse towers.

Sor leaned towards Duncan's ear. 'Careful, little brother. Your eyes are about to fall out of your head.'

Duncan elbowed him in the ribs. 'Give over.'

'You should see yourself – you're all but drooling.'

'I am not!' His ears, however, were starting to burn.

'She's pretty, mind. Give her a bath and— Slaine's stones, she's in pup!'

'Keep your voice down,' Duncan hissed. 'She's got no wedding tattoo and she's never mentioned a promised man, so I suspect she had no say in the getting of that child. Now not another word!'

Teia reined up at the sight of the row of pikemen and sat her horse uncertainly as the rest of the Arennorians milled around her, shouting greetings to friends. Duncan motioned to the sergeant in charge of the gate guard to dismiss his troop and led Sor towards her through the crowd of men and horses.

'Welcome to Saardost Keep,' he said, reaching up to help her dismount. She hesitated at first, then leaned on his shoulder and let him lift her down. Mother and baby together weighed less than his saddlebags. 'I'd be happier if Baer had brought the others inside – there's plenty of shelter.'

Kneading her back to ease it, the girl shook her head. 'I tried, but he prefers to make camp out there. He doesn't trust this place.' A rare smile flickered across her lips. 'Between the Empire's walls and your clansmen, I think he'll sleep with one eye open tonight.'

The smile made her pretty, instead of just thin and cold and pale. Duncan found himself wanting to touch her cheek and warm it with his hand.

'I'll make sure some provisions are sent out so your people can make a hot meal,' he said. 'This is my brother Sor, clan chief to the Morennadh.'

To his relief, Sor said nothing untoward, greeting her formally. 'Be welcome here, Banfaíth.'

'My name is Teia,' she said. A small frown creased her brow, puckering the savage scar that ran into her hairline. 'So you are not the battle chief I am to meet here? The Warlord?'

'No,' Sor said, 'but he is here.'

Teia drew herself up and stood proud as any queen despite her dirt and darns, the weariness that dragged at her features and smudged her eyes with shadows.

'Then take me to him. I have news that will not wait.'

Duncan caught Sor's look when it flickered his way and held up his hand to forestall any more questions. 'Where is he?'

'In the hall. He's been inspecting the outer defences.' Sor began to frown. 'You're absolutely sure about this?'

'She's ridden a long way to meet him,' Duncan said, 'and I gave her my word.' With his other hand he gestured towards the body of the keep. 'Banfaíth?'

The strange stone passages reminded Teia of the caves. After so long under the sky again they pressed down over her, without air, without light but what was afforded by the torches wedged into rusted iron rings on the walls, or the narrow slits that overlooked the churned slush in the yard outside. All she smelled was smoke and stone, new-cut wood and unwashed men. And her unwashed self, to her shame.

A fine sight to present to their battle chief – stinking of horse and worse!

Still, it was too late to worry about that now. With no clean clothes to change into, a wash would have made little difference even if she'd taken the time, although it might have made her feel a fraction more confident about what lay ahead. She eyed the gloomy passage in front of her, leading her deeper into the keep, and her throat dried.

It was unnatural, so much stone piled up so high with only the ingenuity of men long dead to support it. Unnatural, and not a little unnerving. She stole a glance at the tall young Arennorian walking beside her. He didn't appear perturbed by it, but she supposed he was accustomed to the strange structure. Perhaps he even lived in one like it, though if he did she couldn't imagine how he slept well at night. She'd be too afraid that it would all tumble down and crush her even to close her eyes.

Duncan was not at all what she'd been expecting. All the stories named the Arennorians faithless: cravens who had sacrificed their honour when they broke spears before the Empire. Yet on the trail they had shared their food and let the weakest of her people ride their spare horses. Hardly the actions of cowards and traitors. She darted another glance at him. Hardly the actions of sworn enemies.

He caught her look. 'Banfaíth? Am I walking too fast?'

Quickly she faced forwards again, flustered. 'No, not at all.'

In fact he had matched his pace to hers and never let his long strides overtake her as she waddled along behind her monstrous belly, puffing like a foaling mare. The man was a continuing source of surprises. 'Your people are not quite what I expected to find,' she ventured.

'How so?'

'I expected you to hate us. Instead you've been kind.' There. It was said. She dared another look and saw a little frown crease his brows.

'Our peoples were cousins once. Why would we hate our own kin?'

'My ancestors swore blood feud on yours. My people maintain it to this day, bitter as ever.'

'I can't imagine a hatred hard enough to last a thousand years.' He gestured at one of the window slits as they passed. Edges that must once have been square and sharp were now sculpted into curves by wind and weather. 'Even stone erodes in that time.'

One more corner brought them to a tall, pointed arch blocked with rough-cut wood so new it was still weeping resin from the knots. Flanking it stood a pair of warriors dressed in the same green as the banners she had seen flying from the watchtowers. Each was armed like the men outside, with a weapon that resembled a long, heavy spear with a second, crescent-shaped blade below the head, backed by a wicked-looking point. The men appeared to know Duncan, for one nodded companionably as the other rapped on the rough wood.

'Enter,' called a voice from the other side.

The warrior lifted a handle set into the wood and the makeshift door swung inwards. Beyond lay a larger space, puddled with daylight from openings high up in the wall. Stone blocks shaped into round columns supported the roof, reminding her of the great fangs of rock that decorated the deeper caves. Knowing they had not grown from the bones of the mountains but had been made by the hand of man gave her a chill. She shuddered and kept her eyes fixed firmly straight ahead as she followed Duncan inside.

It was a hall, she realised, like in the old stories. A fire smouldered in a recessed hearth at the base of the far wall; similar recesses on the side walls contained wood and kindling not yet lit. In front of the fire stood a long table with an assortment of stools scattered about, and at its head, a tall man in buckskins sipped from a horn cup as he studied something spread out before him. Muddy slush puddled around his boots and dripped from a cloak flung carelessly across the end of the table.

At the sound of footsteps the man looked up. Crag-cat eyes fixed on Teia and in the space of three strides she knew she'd been weighed, measured and reckoned up to the last half-ounce, like a bale of furs.

He must be their battle chief, the one Duncan had called Aradhrim. The Warlord. Well, she had faced down the Speaker of the Crainnh; a crag-cat would not make her quail now. She gripped her staff firmly and lifted her chin, then with her steps as confident as she could make them, walked towards the table.

'Be welcome, Banfaíth.' He drew out a stool for her and Duncan shed his cloak, folding it onto the seat to make a cushion of sorts. 'Please, sit. You must be tired after your journey.'

'You are too kind.' Teia wished she didn't sound so out of breath. Gingerly she eased herself down, one hand cradling her unborn child's weight. Blessed Macha, her back was aching something fierce from the ride.

The Warlord poured another cup from the gently steaming jug on the table and handed it to her. 'I can't offer you much in the way of comfort, but this should warm you at least.'

Spices tickled her nose and she peered into the cup. The liquid in it was as red and hot as freshly drawn blood.

'It's mulled wine,' said Duncan, seeing her hesitate. 'I shouldn't think a little will harm your child.' At a nod from Aradhrim, he poured for himself and took a seat on the opposite side of the table.

Teia studied the stuff dubiously. It certainly looked like wine, though she didn't recognise the other word he'd used to describe it. She hazarded a sip. Thinner on the tongue than mead; not as harsh as *uisca*. Out of the corner of her eye she saw Duncan drinking with every sign of enjoyment, so tried a larger mouthful and found that when she swallowed, it lit a comforting glow inside.

'It's good, thank you.'

Slowly, sensation began to return to fingers and toes that had been cold for so long she had forgotten what it was like to feel them – though mostly that sensation was pain at first. Even the icy dread in her stomach began to thaw, reminding her how empty it was. She'd have to be careful; too much wine without food to cushion it might make her ill.

'I developed a taste for it in Elethrain,' Aradhrim said as he topped up his own cup. 'They drink a lot of it in winter there, to keep the cold out. To tell the truth, it's about all the army wine-ration is fit for.'

Now she could see what was spread on the table. Drawings, many of them, and each one on a sheet bigger than all the parchment she'd ever seen put together. On the topmost sheet she recognised the lake at the moot-ground, where the Speakers had cast their viewing of the forts. How strange that the Empire could waste so much paper making drawings that showed the shape of the world when they had only to look up to see it.

Shoving the sheets to one side, the Warlord hitched his backside onto the edge of the table.

'Very well,' he said. 'From what Duncan's messenger said you've travelled a long way to snag my ear, and now you have it. Speak.'

This was what she had come for, the moment that made all the harsh white leagues worthwhile: an audience with the Empire. It should have given her some sense of achievement, triumph even, but all she felt was tired. Tired down to her bones. Where should she begin? Where could she? Did it even matter, now that the iron men were gone and all would come to dust and ashes?

'Banfaíth?' he asked softly. 'What do you see?'

'Darkness. Death.' She gulped some wine to combat the sudden dryness in her throat. 'The Raven is coming.'

His expression didn't change, confirming that this was not news to him. 'Do you know when?'

'No, but She is closer than She has ever been.'

The crag-cat eyes narrowed a little. 'You have seen Her?'

Teia nodded. 'Many times, in my dreams. At the Gathering, when Drwyn was raised chief of the Crainnh, I witnessed the summoning of Her shade and I heard Her speak.'

That bloody-taloned voice scraped around inside her head again, filling her thoughts with the rustle of black feathers. She flinched from the memory.

'You are certain of what you saw?' the Warlord pressed. 'It was not an illusion or a trick designed to impress?'

'I saw what I saw.'

'I do not mean to disparage you, Banfaíth, but it has been a thousand years since your Speakers have had the strength to rend the Veil, and you are . . . inexperienced in the ways of power.'

Teia caught the hesitation in his words. He had tried to phrase it kindly, but still. The implication was clear.

'I am young, Lord of Arennor,' she said firmly, 'but I am not blind. I saw the shade of Maegern appear in the fire. I heard Her promise to ride with the war band if the Speakers could free Her. I know my gift is untrained and my understanding of what I see is . . . imperfect. Sometimes it only becomes clear afterwards. Some of my earliest visions still make no sense, but the ones that do have been true telling. This.' She touched the scar on her brow, then fingered her fur robe. 'And this.'

'So the Hunt will ride.' Aradhrim muttered something under his breath that Teia didn't quite catch – a curse, perhaps – and ex-changed a glance with his kinsman. 'If only Theodegrance were here now, eh?'

'Theode—' The strange syllables tangled her tongue. 'He is your Emperor?' A nod. 'Drwyn's war band doesn't worry him?'

The pause before the Warlord spoke said he was choosing his words with some care. 'He believes it is a threat,' he said, 'but he can only act on what can be proved to the satisfaction of the imperial Council, and my word alone is not enough for them. Without the Council's assent, the Emperor's power is limited.'

In this at least the Empire was not so different from her own people. Amongst the Nimrothi, all the clans had to agree before there could be a Chief of Chiefs, and only then could he act for all of them. But if the Emperor's advisers could not agree . . . Prescience fluttered at the corners of Teia's mind.

'How many men do you have to meet Drwyn in battle?' she asked.

'It won't come to that, Banfaíth,' said Duncan. 'We'll choke him in the passes without any need for weight of numbers. These old Suvaeon keeps can be held with a hundred men apiece.'

She set her cup down and pressed her hand flat on the table beside it. Her other hand tightened on her staff, knuckles whiten-ing. Now the darkness was closing in, blacker than a carrion-bird's eye. Smoke was acrid and dry in her throat; the plains were aflame, their bright flowers shrivelling into ash. And she knew, as surely as she had known that Isaak had a son, that what she saw was Arennor's defeat.

'Drwyn has the war bands of all seventeen clans waiting on his command,' she said, staring unseeing at the table before her. 'Even without the Hunt he has more than forty thousand spears, led by battle-tried captains, and seventeen Speakers to aid him. How many men do you have, my lord?' Silence. *'How many?'*

'One legion,' Aradhrim said abruptly.

Teia stared. A legion? Was that many or few?

339

He met her gaze level-eyed, expressionless. 'Nine hundred men, to defend three passes through the mountains. A thousand more on the road up from the south, if the Emperor doesn't countermand my orders and hold them at Mesarild.'

Two thousand warriors – fewer, in fact. It couldn't possibly be enough.

Duncan thrust himself to his feet. 'You'll have every spear in Arennor, too, if it comes to it. If I have to lead them myself!'

That brought a ghost of a smile to the Warlord's lips.

'Bravely spoken, cousin, but don't be too quick to promise the Empire what Arennor herself may have need of before we're done.' He fingered a heavily carved ring on his left hand. 'I need to make a report to the imperial Council. Insist on more men, though it may already be too late for that.'

'You must send for the Knights, my lord,' Teia said. Aradhrim drew breath to interrupt but she hurried on. 'Without them, you will not survive this war. Not against the Hunt. Only the iron men have the power to cage the Raven.'

His expression grew bleak. 'Once, they did,' he said. 'When their captain, Corlainn Fellbane, took the starseed from Gwlach's Speaker and used it to undo what she had done. But not any more.'

No. Surely that wasn't possible. 'The stone is lost?'

He nodded. 'Since Corlainn died, and all record of its whereabouts is lost with it.'

'But they defeated us! They drove us into exile! How could that great—' A sharp twinge through her lower back threw her thoughts into momentary confusion. 'How could so great a power be *lost*?'

Aradhrim spread his arms. 'It was long ago, and times have changed. The Knights will not be our saviours in this battle.'

The hollowing out of her hopes stung at her eyes. Dust and ashes. The plains devastated. *Lord Aedon protect us all from Ytha's folly.*

Duncan leaned on the table, frowning as if thinking through a riddle.

'Banfaíth,' he said. 'Do you remember when you told me how the Speakers bargained with Maegern, She said they had not a fraction of a fraction of the power of the ones who sealed Her away?'

'That's right. Seventeen Speakers and a blood sacrifice and they could only summon Her shade.' Teia wasn't sure where Duncan was leading. 'Why? I don't understand what—'

'So how does Ytha plan to free the Hunt?'

Of course. She had forgotten, in everything that had happened. Not all hope was lost, and it lifted her voice, carried it over the discomfort in her lower back.

'Maegern knew the location of the key to Her prison. She said that which it locked, it could also unlock. She sent her Hounds to guide Ytha to it.' The two clansmen exchanged a look, bright with renewed enthusiasm. 'The key is the starseed?' she asked, and Duncan showed his teeth.

'And the starseed is the key, yes. It has to be.' His hand smacked down on the tabletop. 'If we can find it first, we can stop Drwyn and Ytha in their tracks.'

'Unless we're already too late,' Aradhrim grunted. 'Does she have it yet?'

Teia shook her head. 'If she has, I saw no sign. She'd have boasted of it at the Scattering, for sure.'

'Do you know where it is?'

At that she could only shrug. 'All I can remember is that it's in a place She called a city. A city of seven towers, guarded by seven warriors.'

'Slaine's stones, that could be anywhere!' Duncan's shoulders slumped, his elation turning quickly to frustration. 'Trust an Elder God to speak in riddles.'

It was Teia's turn to frown. 'You don't know it? I thought—' She broke off; she hadn't thought anything at all, just assumed that the Empire would know, since Gwlach's defeat was a part of their history.

'Don't despair, cousin,' said Aradhrim. 'It's more information than we had yesterday.'

Clapping his kinsman's shoulder as he passed, the Warlord came around to Teia's side of the table and began spreading out the drawings again. As well as the one with the lake she had recognised there were others, with the great knobby spine of the an-Archen across the top, marked with lines that wound and turned like rivers, and strings of symbols she didn't understand.

'I cannot imagine the Knights would have taken it far, certainly not any farther than Dremen,' the Warlord muttered, running his gaze over the symbols. 'If we can puzzle out the city's name . . .' He looked up at his cousin. 'There are some *gaeden* here, who came with me looking for the Gatekeeper – maybe they can help. Send someone to fetch them, will you?'

With a nod, Duncan headed for the door. Before he'd reached it, distant shouting penetrated the thick stone walls. Running feet clattered in the passage outside, then the door opened to admit a grim-faced sentry. After exchanging a few hurried words with him, Duncan turned to the Warlord.

'You'd better come,' he said. 'This is something you should see.'

30

DEAD MEN

∾

Up on the walk atop the curtain wall, Gair swung his longsword instinctively and tried to make sense of his dreams from the night before. Whether it was down to Sorchal's snores or simply the fact that it was the first night in weeks he'd spent under a roof, he hadn't slept well, and what rest he'd managed had been fractured with strange images.

He'd seen the angel from the thorn maze, but this time he'd been the one wielding the flaming sword. Savin's face, too, swimming in and out of focus as if seen through smoke, though he tried not to dwell too much on that one. There'd been other images as well, some that lingered, others that were quickly – and mercifully – forgotten. Finding his way through them to some kind of understanding was next to impossible – or perhaps there was no meaning to find. Perhaps his mind was still restoring order to itself after the reiving, and what he was seeing were bright, brittle fragments of something larger, trying once more to form a whole.

And somewhere in the middle of it was what Masen had told him about Danilar.

Steel rang on steel and his blade locked with Sorchal's. A twist of the wiry Elethrainian's shoulder shrugged him off, then he brought his own sword around to press flat against Gair's arm.

'Point,' he said, green eyes dancing. 'And it's only taken me all morning to win it.'

Gair stepped back and saluted him. 'Sorry. My head's somewhere else today.'

'I'll take a point off you however I can get one – they're rare enough!' said Sorchal with a rueful laugh.

Plucking his shirt away from his sweaty back, Gair managed a smile, then set his feet in the first position.

'We're going again?' Sorchal asked.

'Unless you have somewhere you'd rather be.'

'I'm in a remote fortress in northern Arennor in the company of over three hundred men, with no unattached girls within a week's ride in any direction.' The Elethrainian tossed his borrowed longsword from hand to hand. 'Where could I possibly rather be?'

'If you're that lonely, there's several women in Duncan's ride,' Gair said.

'Have you seen the size of the knives they carry? I'd prefer to stay lonely and keep my tripes on the inside. Guard.'

Parrying Sorchal's first strokes, Gair turned aside an attempted thrust and forced him into a back-step.

The Gatekeeper's face had been a picture when Gair had told him who Danilar was. Jaw hanging like he'd been gut-punched, expression veering from shock to incomprehension and finally disbelief. All Masen had known was that Alderan's brother lived in Dremen. Not where, not his occupation, nothing but his name.

Gair could scarcely comprehend what Danilar had risked to intercede for him. The trust and respect of Preceptor Ansel, his standing as the cure of souls in the Suvaeon, all put in jeopardy for the sake of one sinner, and his brother's love. Was that why Alderan hadn't told him, even when he'd asked, because so much had been at risk?

You kept too many secrets, old man, even from your friends.

Quick steps advanced and retreated. Steel rang on steel and breath burned in his lungs. From the corner of his eye, he saw two soldiers watching from the tower doorway, and coins changing hands. Sorchal blocked him, but Gair surged forwards, dipping his shoulder and forcing his hands up to break clear of Sorchal's blade, and the dance resumed.

He'd missed working the forms. There'd been no time on the road up from the Havens, especially once he'd fallen in with the Warlord and his hard-riding clansmen. Finally he had an outlet for some of the aggression swilling around in his blood, and a sparring partner he trusted to have the skill to withstand it without him having to pull his blows too much. And watching Ailric shadow Tanith's every move, biting his tongue each time the Astolan found an excuse to stand too close to her, no matter how often she shied out of his reach, had surely made his sword-hand itch.

Blades sparked and sang on the cool air, flashing the noon sunlight back at their wielders. They'd attracted a few more spectators, judging by the amount of green Gair glimpsed in the corners of his vision. The glint in Sorchal's eye said he had noticed them, too, and his ripostes and parries acquired extra flourish. The Elethrainian would do anything for an audience. Gair just redoubled his concentration and tried to ignore them.

Tanith had taken to keeping as close company with Magda as the ride-captain's duties allowed, for only the scar-faced clans-woman appeared able to give Ailric the least pause. Certainly nothing Tanith herself said or did made any difference. Maybe it was the long-bladed dagger that never seemed far from Magda's hand that warded him off; anything that could quell Sorchal's wandering eye would certainly make another man think twice.

Feet scraped and blades rang. Parry and counter, ground taken and yielded in turn. In a flurry of quick blows, Gair took the next point by jarring his opponent's hand so hard the Elethrainian's fingers numbed and he had to shake life back into them before he could continue. Back and forth along the curtain wall the dance went as Gair searched for a little calm, but came no nearer to finding it.

'Horsemen in the pass!'

The cry went up from the daughter keep at the far end of the wall and was repeated at the nearest bastion. Green uniforms boiled from the watchtowers, dispersing the spectators who had been lounging nearby. At once Gair put up his sword, followed by Sorchal, and they pressed themselves against the parapet out of the way of the running soldiers.

'Range?' A stocky sergeant pulled a small spyglass from his belt and trained it up the twisting valley, searching for the painted marker stones set out along the line of the ancient road to measure distance from the walls.

'Eight hundred!'

The sergeant grunted, and Gair knew what he was thinking. Eight hundred yards was far beyond the range of the soldiers' bows, whatever the elevation. It was too far for even a 160-pound-draw Leahn longbow with the Master of Arms' bull-like shoulders behind it.

'Identification?'

'Unknown. Six hundred!'

Gair squinted into the wind for the target. There, rounding the last steep ridge. Three horses came into view, kicking up sparkling ice crystals from the windrows of snow that crusted the old stones. He pointed, and Sorchal shaded his eyes against the brightness of sun on snow as he peered over the wall.

'Three horses,' he said. 'But only one rider.'

'You're sure?' Gair asked.

'I'm sure.' The Elethrainian turned away, his face grim. 'Dead men.'

'Five hundred – and slowing.' The soldier's voice cracked. 'Imperial.'

Two riderless horses, their green saddle-cloths flapping, galloped towards the keep. Slung over their backs were bundles of bloody rags in the shapes of men. Still well out of bowshot, the Nimrothi horseman pulled his mount into a rear, brandishing a spear over his head, shouting something that the wind tore to shreds before it reached Gair's ears. Then he wheeled away and pounded out of sight. A few bowstrings twanged as soldiers sent arrows after him when they saw what burdens the horses carried.

'Don't waste your arrows,' barked the sergeant, snapping his spyglass shut. 'Open the gates and bring our boys home.'

With some force, Sorchal thrust his sword back into its scabbard. 'Sometimes I hate being right.'

Picking up his own scabbard from where he had propped it against the parapet, Gair watched as the lathered horses were caught and led through gate in the curtain wall. Dried blood streaked their flanks and their rolling eyes were ringed white with fear. On their backs, their former riders were barely recognisable as men.

The watching soldiers fell silent as the grim procession passed under the gatehouse into the bailey. Even their officers stared with them, their duties temporarily put aside.

Aradhrim was waiting on the steps of the keep when the gates were winched closed behind the terrified animals. He gave a crisp order and the horses were led over to him. Gently he lifted each man's head to study the face.

'He can't recognise them, surely,' said Sorchal. 'Not out of three hundred.'

'I wouldn't be surprised if he does. He's the kind of man to know the name of every soldier under his command.' Gair sheathed his sword and hung the baldric over his shoulder. 'But I think he wants to make sure he remembers their faces now.'

In the bailey, the Warlord stepped back, heedless of the blood on his hands.

'Take them to the infirmary. Ask Lady Tanith to examine them, then see that they are bathed and given a fitting burial.' His voice was clear, cold, his feelings buried deep. 'Sor, you and Commander Brandt join me in the hall with the Guardians in an hour. As soon as our remaining northern patrols return, seal the gates.'

Then he turned and strode back inside.

⊘⊘

Teia followed the sounds of commotion, steadying herself against the wall of the passageway. Walking eased the ache in her back a little, but every so often a slow pulse of pain all through her abdomen made her pause to catch her breath. Sweat broke on her top lip and between her breasts, and her stomach surged uneasily. Perhaps that mulled wine had not been such a good idea.

Soldiers passed her at a trot, war-harness creaking, and spilled outside. Voices barked back and forth. Two tall silhouettes stood to one side of the open door, watching the activity in the yard. A mighty boom shook the air, followed by a clatter of chains, then there was no sound at all. No one spoke. No one moved.

Another pain. Teia clung to the wall and shut her eyes. Oh, dear Macha she was going to throw up. Tighter, tighter the invisible fist squeezed her belly, but she took deep breaths and slowly the pain began to ebb.

At the entrance, the taller of the two silhouettes took a step forward and said something. Though she didn't understand the words, she recognised the Warlord's voice, so the other man must be Duncan.

She shuffled closer. 'Duncan? What's happening?'

He turned to face her, his expression unreadable with the noon sun behind him. Two horses stood in the yard, laden with dripping bundles. Another step and she saw that the drips were the colour of blushberry juice in the melting slush and the bundles were staring back at her with ruined, eyeless faces.

'Macha's ears!'

Quickly Duncan put himself between her and the horses' dreadful burden. His arms swept around her, tucking her face into his shoulder.

348

'Don't look,' he urged. He stroked her hair over and over. 'Please, don't look.'

The void yawned and she spiralled down into it, buffeted by dark wings. Image after image flashed through her head, twisting and tumbling like leaves in the wind of her fall. Flickering lamp-light. A bloody blade. A woman's face, contorted, screaming – her own face, barely recognisable, lank hair clinging to the sweat and the tears. Moaning, she screwed her eyes shut but could not block out the foretelling.

'There now, it's all right,' soothed Duncan, rocking her in his arms. 'It's all right, Teia. I've got you.'

Another pain, sharper now. Warm wetness between her legs, spreading, soaking into her clothes. Her knees buckled.

'Neve,' she managed, knotting her fingers in Duncan's jerkin. 'Where's Neve?'

'Banfaíth? What's wrong?'

'I need Neve. My daughter.' Her gaze darted around the frozen faces, the unfamiliar green coats of the strangers surrounding her. Sudden panic fluttered in her chest. 'My daughter's coming.'

၄ဝ၁

Commander Brandt leaned his fists on the table, blocky face jutting into the banners of dusty sunlight that hung from the hall's high windows.

'The gates are sealed.' Every word was bitten off as if by the jaws of a trap.

Sor shook his head. 'Not while my men are still out there.'

Closing the hall doors quietly behind him, Gair slipped into the only vacant seat at the table, next to the lanky clansman Duncan. Across the maps and scattered cups, Masen nodded a greeting, his battered old shoe of a face lined even deeper with weariness than it had been yesterday.

'If they're not back by now, they're not coming back,' Brandt growled.

'I don't agree.'

'War is sacrifice, Clansman. In the life of a soldier, there is no room for sentiment.'

Sor threw up his hands. 'This has nothing to do with sentiment! Those scouts might have vital information regarding the war band's whereabouts. We are fumbling in the dark without it, and if you can't see that then I thank Slaine I'll never have to serve under your command!'

At the head of the table, the Warlord shifted in his seat. 'Easy, Sor. Our foes are out there, not in this room. How overdue are your men?'

'Three days.' Arms folded, the Morennadh Clansman prowled back and forth at the far end of the table. 'They went out a week ago and there's been no sign since.'

Uneasy glances skittered from man to man. No one said anything out loud, but the spectres of the two dead soldiers were so palpable they might as well have been sitting at the table.

'Then it's likely they've run into trouble,' Aradhrim said.

'I've been trying to tell him that, my lord,' interjected Brandt. 'He wants to send yet more men out to look for them!'

'They're my kin, Aradhrim,' Sor said. 'Morennadh, the four of them, from my own ride.'

The commander's heavy features tightened into a scowl.

'Sentimental foolishness. This was a job for professional soldiers who know what they're about, Clansman, not amateurs.'

Sor rounded on him. 'Amateurs? My clansmen are better suited to this kind of work than any of yours. They know their enemy.'

'Three hundred generations ago, maybe,' the commander grunted. 'Now? I don't think so.'

Sor shook his head. 'Trust me, they're unlikely to have changed much in any way that matters.'

'They still hate us as hard as they ever did,' Duncan put in. 'That hasn't changed, so Te— the Banfaíth told me.'

Brandt stabbed a thick forefinger at the table. 'The Sixth's pathfinders are the finest in the imperial army. They can secure this pass as well as any man and they should have been allowed to do so.'

'And Morennadh rangers were scouting the an-Archen before your grandfather's grandfather soiled his first swaddling,' Sor muttered, almost but not quite under his breath.

The crash of Aradhrim's fist on the tabletop rattled the empty cups on the tray.

'Slaine's stones, *enough!*' he barked. 'Settle your differences in the yard with knives if you have to, but not in here. Right now our only concern should be the forty thousand spears that might be coming through that pass!'

Green eyes flicked their gaze around the table like a whip.

'Now, I don't care for this any more than the rest of you, but Sor, your men will have to make their own way back here if they can. If they can't, I must consider them lost.'

Gair sat forward. 'I can look for them.'

'Excuse me?' The commander gaped and Aradhrim looked up.

'I can scout up the pass for you, my lord.'

'Didn't you hear what the Warlord just said? It's not safe to send riders—'

Aradhrim held up his hand and Brandt fell silent. 'No one here doubts your courage,' the Warlord said, 'but it is out of the question. I won't throw more good men to the wolves.'

'I don't mean to go on foot. I can scout unobserved. That Nimrothi rider we saw wasn't carrying much in the way of supplies, so we know the war band's close. A day's march away, if they're following the old road, maybe two. I can be there and back within a day.'

Now he had the Lord of the Plains' attention. Eyes fixed on him, Aradhrim straightened up and folded his arms. 'Go on.'

He hadn't wanted to reveal it like this, in front of other people, but there was no alternative. He didn't like the idea of leaving

Sor's men to face the same fate as the two legionaries, and if the war band was close, they needed to know where.

And I have to be sure I can fly.

'I'm *gaeden*, like Masen, but I have other abilities, too.'

The garrison commander rolled his eyes. 'Do they include the ability to render yourself invisible?'

'Almost. I can shape-shift.'

'Poppycock. There's no such thing as magi—'

He fell silent as Masen leaned across the table and opened his hand to call a glim into being above it. 'You were saying, Commander?' he said.

Brandt stared at the yellowish globe with his mouth hanging open. 'Good Goddess,' he managed. One hand came up, wavered somewhere between the sign of blessing and reaching out, fell again. 'Good Goddess.'

At the head of the table, Aradhrim was unmoved. 'I have heard tell of this, from Maera,' he said thoughtfully. 'We have legends of men who could take the form of other creatures. Skin-walkers. I had always thought they were no more than stories to hurry wayward children to bed.'

'It's not a common talent,' Gair said, 'but it's real.'

With a heroic effort, the commander gathered himself. 'It's an abomination!'

'It's a tool the Warlord can use,' Gair fired back.

'When a nail needs driving, eh?' Aradhrim gave him a thin smile. 'It would be helpful to know what Drwyn's about, or at least when he begins his advance. Even the best of soldiers grows careless when held on his guard for too long.' Rubbing his chin, he glanced up at the high windows. 'How quickly can you be ready?'

'I'm ready now.'

'There's half a day's good light left. Make the most of it.'

31

NIGHTFALL

⨯

Walking out onto the parapet, Gair's skin contracted into goose-flesh and he almost wished he'd gone back to his quarters for his jerkin. Despite the bright skies, the sunshine, a chill breeze gusted and swirled out of the north, a constant reminder that although all but the deepest snow had melted and the tiny plants that made this rocky place their home were rushing into bloom to make the most of the short mountain summer, Saardost Keep was many miles into the high an-Archen.

Eyes closed, he turned his face into the sun and filled his lungs with the glass-clear air. He'd missed this, even more than he'd missed his sword-work. Something in him cried out for rock and space and high places, where only an eagle's cry pierced the stillness.

Almost like home.

For the first time in longer than he could remember, a yearning for Leah plunged its dart into his chest.

Except I can't go back. He opened his eyes again. *It's not my home any more.*

Out in the middle of the wall, equidistant from the keep and its daughter tower, Ailric lounged with his rump against the parapet. Arms folded, he watched Gair walking the wall with feline disdain.

'Ailric,' Gair said, keeping his tone neutral. What the hell did he want?

'Leahn.' The reply was equally cool. 'At last we have a chance to talk.'

Gair raised his eyebrows. He wasn't sure they had anything to talk about. 'Can we be quick? I've got things to do.'

'Oh?'

'There's four clan rangers missing in the pass, and I'm flying out to look for them.' It was petty, he knew, but he couldn't resist adding, 'It's the least I can do.'

'Always the hero, eh?' The Astolan made a show of brushing lint from his sleeve. Even in a much-worn, sporadically washed shirt and riding leathers he managed to look as elegant as if he was clad head-to-toe in court silks. 'You humans. So eager to impress with your gifts.'

Gair bit down on the first words that sprang to mind. 'I'm not trying to impress anyone.'

'Really?' A trace of a smile played around Ailric's perfectly sculpted mouth. 'Have you never seen the paradise-bird dance to woo a mate? Strutting and posturing, flourishing his fine golden feathers to dazzle her. You human men are no different.'

Paradise-bird? A mate? 'I haven't the first idea what you're talking about.'

The smile vanished. 'I am not blind. I have seen the way she follows you with her eyes.'

Surely he didn't mean— *'Tanith?* That's absurd.'

Shaking his head, Gair turned to face north. Whatever Ailric thought he had seen, he'd clearly made up his own mind about what it signified and Gair was in no mood to try to persuade him otherwise. He doubted it would do any good.

The fire-eagle's lonesome melody skirled, beckoning him. Restless music plucked at his nerves, urging him to return to his true home on the wind. He was holding the Song on the very edge of shifting when Ailric's hand closed on his arm and dragged him back.

'She was mine before she knew you.' The words came swift and venomous, like an adder's bite. 'She was mine until you came to Arennor.'

'Was she? She told me she broke it off with you years ago.' Gair pulled his arm free. 'I don't know what you think you've seen, but Tanith is my friend. That's all.'

Flame-coloured eyes flared. 'You will not have her, Leahn!'

'I'm not trying to.'

'Then why does she not come to me? We promised ourselves to each other before she went to the Isles. Now it appears she cares more for you humans than she does for her own people. Than she does for me!'

Before his temper burned away his control, Gair flung the Song aside. 'Saints and angels, will you listen to yourself? If she won't come to you, it's nothing to do with me. Tanith's not your property, Ailric. She makes her own choices and a gentleman should respect them!'

'A gentleman such as you, perhaps?' the Astolan sneered. 'A failed Knight, outcast even amongst his own people. A nameless, landless exile.'

Oh, that stung. More than it had any right to, considering it was only the plain truth. Gair's fists twitched to bunch in Ailric's fancy shirt front, but somehow he kept them still at his sides.

'I may be all of those things,' he rasped, 'but you can be sure I will never treat a woman as a chattel. If she doesn't want you, be a man about it and let her go.'

Then he walked away, whilst he still had a rein on the anger surging through him. The Song beckoned again and he shut it from his mind. He didn't dare open himself to that power, not at that moment, or he would be unable to fend off the beast when it roared. With his temper raging, who knew what he might become?

'She will never be yours, human,' Ailric called after him. 'I will make her my bride and rule Astolar with her at my side.'

Gair rounded on him, but the Astolan was already striding back towards the keep. He ground his teeth against the urge to go after him. Nobleman Ailric might be, but that did not give him any right to a lady's affections – certainly not against her wishes. And such jealousy! Where had that sprung from? Neither he nor Tanith had done anything to prompt it.

No. He would not be provoked. Nor would he shift before he was ready, before he was calm. Deep breaths slowed his pulse, honed his focus. Better. The hot rush of fury became the stillness he sought in the practice yard, only instead of a sword in his hands he held the music of the songs of the earth.

He let the power fill him slowly. One by one his muscles changed, re-formed onto bones that arched into new shapes. His breastbone deepened, his fingers stretched, sweetly painful. Hair became feathers, and then the fire-eagle flew.

❧

'So we still don't know where they'll strike.'

Aradhrim pinched his brows, as if his head ached. Masen wasn't the least surprised. They'd been squinting at maps for hours, since the war council broke up; all sorts of maps. Military charts, crisp and flat from the adjutant's map-case, and ragged old parchments that he had unearthed from the bottom of his own packs, ringed by forgotten bottles and faded into near-illegibility. They differed in minor details, older names for rivers and settlements, thriving towns on one marked as ruins on the other, but neither gave any clue where the city of seven towers stood, or had stood. Or even if it had ever existed at all.

'We need older maps, I think,' he said, rubbing his chin. His palm made a sandpapery sound, reminding him that he hadn't shaved that day. Or the day before, come to that.

'I could send a courier south to the university at Mesarild, but I

356

think we might all be dead men by the time an answer comes back.'

Masen looked up. 'You don't think the garrisons will hold?'

'Oh, they'll hold to the last man – beyond the last man, if Commander Brandt has anything to do with it. He has the Sixth so well drilled that if he gave the order, the dead themselves would stand to attention.'

The Warlord levered himself away from the table and stretched his back.

'No, what worries me is the Hunt. If we cannot stop the Speakers claiming the starseed and summoning Her, I am afraid we might be caught with the Nimrothi clans on one side and the Raven on the other.'

And between them, Arennor would burn. 'Not a pretty picture.'

'You are sure nothing sparks a memory?'

'Sure as I can be. Gair would be the one to ask when he gets back – I'd imagine he knows the histories of the Founding Wars up, down and inside out.'

'But you tell me the Church has distorted those histories.'

Masen scrubbed his fingers through his hair. He needed a bath, deep and hot. Some days he felt as if he still had damp in his bones from his journey through Syfria's floods, and couldn't get warm.

'As best as I can tell, they changed the why and the how, but I don't know that they altered overmuch of the where. Caer Ducain is still Caer Ducain and River Run is still River Run. Those remain facts, whatever was fabricated around them.'

Staring at the maps, Aradhrim grunted. 'It could be any city in the Empire.'

'We can rule out a few that weren't founded when the clans were defeated.' Masen pulled the largest chart towards him and tapped it in time with his thoughts. 'Most of Belistha wasn't settled. Dremenir ran out fifty miles north of the Awen, even Yelda wasn't much more than a market town, compared to its size today. Cities

357

rose and fell in the space of a hundred years when the Empire was new.'

He spread his hands, let them fall. 'I'll send to the other *gaeden*, see if they remember something I don't, but even with this new information from the Banfaíth we have no more choices than we had before. We're just going to have to dig in and wait.'

'Until we see which way the fox jumps, yes.' Hands on hips, Aradhrim sucked his teeth. 'Slaine's stones. Waiting irks me, Masen. I'd rather be hunting than hunted.'

Now wasn't that the truth? 'I know how that feels. If Alderan was here . . .' He stopped.

'Alderan?'

'The leader of the Guardians. An old friend. Gair told me he was killed in Gimrael.'

Even after a few days to digest the news, it sounded wrong. Impossible. The idea of Alderan being dead left an ugly crack right across the bowl of Masen's world that could never be mended.

He'd been eighteen, nineteen at the most when he'd first met the Guardian. Possessed of not much more than the clothes on his back, with a quick tongue and quicker fists that had more than once landed him in the town gaol, until a conversation with a stranger through the rusted bars had set his feet on a new path and forged a friendship that had lasted thirty-three years.

Now his friend was gone and it fell to Masen, who had never had to take responsibility for anyone but himself, to hold the remaining Guardians together in the days to come.

Which would be a whole lot easier if I knew what the hell I was supposed to be doing. You were always the one who could think on his feet, Alderan. We never planned for this!

'My heart grieves for your loss,' said the Warlord. 'Who leads your Order now?'

Masen leaned back in his chair. 'Me, it appears. Until the Council of Masters elects someone more suitable, anyway. Barin, perhaps, or Godril. I'll just have to play the cards I'm dealt until then.'

He glanced over the charts spread before him one more time, but there was nothing new to see. He'd done what he could, argued to send powerful *gaeden* to the other fortresses as soon as word had reached the Isles that the Warlord feared an assault. All that was left to do was pray Goddess they had arrived in time.

'Very well.' The Warlord sighed. 'We've done all we can do here. Let's hope Gair brings us some good news, eh?'

ↁↃ

Cross-legged in the soughing grass of a mountain meadow, painted orange with the last of the day's light, Ytha waited for moonrise.

The war band had made good time across the thawing plains. Even the rivers, dark and deep with snowmelt, had slowed them only a little and the breezes had blown the rain away as quickly as it arrived. Now they were camped high in the winding pass, close but not too close to the stone fort that crouched over the valley like a crag-cat over a herd.

Gone were the crows on the walls. The yawning arches were stopped up and green banners flew from the high towers. Smells of pitch and smoke and new wood thickened the air and the shouts and curses of men sounded where before there had been only silence. The Empire was waiting.

Ytha watched them in her bronze basin, the antlike figures marching to and fro. Insects, scrambling about their towers of spit and sand until a careless foot crushed them.

A smile twitched at her lips. A pretty thought, that; it pleased her to imagine her boots striding across the Empire, and men running from her wrath like greenback beetles. The smile became gleeful. Yes. A pretty, pretty thought.

She let her scrying go and the water in the basin shimmered and cleared once more. Let the Empire wait. Their doom would taste all the finer if left to stew a bit.

Closing her eyes, she spread her arms and opened herself to her magic. It rose up singing, stealing out from the corners of her soul to touch every part of her with tingling, throbbing power. Out, out into the air, down into the earth, reaching, seeking the secret rivers in the land, the pathways in the air that only the Talent knew.

Sun burned on her back. Animals walked on her skin. In her bones was time and in her breath was the sky. And she felt the slow climb of the dawn moon beneath her eastern flank as she felt the turning of the age.

Trinity begins.

∽

Treetop after treetop lashed the fire-eagle's breast and snow stung his eyes. Branches snatched at his wings, tore pale golden feathers from them that spiralled away into the dark. And still the beast roared.

I can't fight this.

Every breath rasped raw night air through his lungs. Every wing-beat tore at the muscles of his chest and back as he fought for height, fought for distance. Under the pitiless stars, across a landscape of rock and pine he flew on, trying to outrun the monstrous entity that was stalking him through his own mind.

Another roar. Closer now. Hot on the back of his neck. The air tasted briefly of char; was it his imagination? He couldn't tell and didn't dare spare the time to think on it. The beast was closer, that was all he knew.

He flew on, reaching through the pain in his shoulders for one more stroke, a few more precious yards. Across the back of his neck, the faint line of the scar throbbed with the memory of a desperate flight between the Five Sisters.

I can't fight this!

There. Ramparts, glimpsed through the overlapping trees. The keep, at last. Gair spread his wings wide and let his fire-eagle shape slip down the wind into the open air, following the path of the old road along the valley bottom. His face and chest stung from the lash of the trees, even through his feathers. His heart pounded against his ribs and every muscle burned. Jagged notes shrieked through the eagle's Song, but somehow he held on to it, refused to let go. Somehow he kept its bright melody fixed in his mind and flew on.

Yellow light spilled from the watchtower windows. Silhouettes moved; dark shapes on the walls. Soldiers watching the pass, blowing on their hands to warm them as they waited to take their turn around the brazier in the tower.

Out on the middle of the curtain wall, a figure held up one arm. Familiar colours touched his mind.

I was starting to get worried, Sorchal said. *Did you find them?*
No sign.

Fiery talons scored his brain and the fire-eagle screamed. The beast reached for him again but he clung to the eagle's shape. Oh, sweet saints, it hurt.

Half a mile, less; just a few minutes more. He could hold the shape that long, surely. Distantly he heard the sullen snap of the banners, a snatch of laughter. It wasn't enough. That other Song was still pulling at him, dragging at his will.

Fire. Fury.
No!

Another wing-beat, another yard gained. Ignore the pain and hold that high, piercing melody clearly. Hold it in his heart, in every bone and sinew, every feather. Another wing-beat. Closer, closer, but the heat of the beast's breath was already lifting his feathers, scorching his tail as its jaws opened beneath him, ready to swallow him whole—

Releasing the eagle's shape, Gair hurled himself toward his human one and fell through the air. He barely cleared the parapet, almost overshot the wall-walk altogether. Sorchal's outstretched arm steadied him and he clung to it to keep from overbalancing into the bailey below.

In the light of the two moons, the Elethrainian's normally swarthy face was pallid as a ghost's. 'Are you all right?'

Gair nodded, straightening up. The unfamiliar musculature of human legs crumpled underneath him and he sprawled on the cobbled walkway. Fabric tore across his back.

'You don't look all right.'

'I'm fine.' Sweet saints, it was cold. It bit deep into his body and he shivered. Something was wrong. 'There's no s-sign of Sor's men but I saw fires in the pass. H-hundreds of them.'

'The war band?'

'It's got to be. Tell Aradhrim. I—'

Goddess, his teeth were chattering. Every muscle shuddered and shook; he was shivering so hard he thought his bones would wrench apart. 'Cloak. Please.'

Sorchal bit his lip. 'I'll fetch Tanith.'

'No. She c-can't heal this. It's the reiving.'

Something was wrong with him. This shape felt wrong. Muscle, bone, skin, it was all different, it wasn't how he remembered it. He groped over his shoulder and found the tear in his shirt. *No.*

'Gair, something's wrong. Maybe she can help.'

'No!' His voice cracked. 'Just give me your damn cloak!'

He had to get away. Wool draped awkwardly across his shoulders, he staggered to his feet, clutching the merlons of the parapet for support. He had to get out of sight. Sorchal offered an arm and he dashed it away.

'Leave me alone.'

Any second now the sentries at the next bastion would see and point. Oh, Goddess! He pulled himself along the wall, stumbling, unable to balance in that strange shape.

'Just leave me alone!'

32

SMALL HOURS

ɔ⊙

It came in waves. A tightening of the deep muscles inside Teia, a heavy downward pressure as insistent as the urge to open her bowels. Harder and harder, then it eased again, fell away and let her relax for a few breaths before the next time.

'There now,' Neve murmured, rubbing Teia's back in slow circles as the contraction passed. 'That wasn't so bad.'

'Bad enough,' Teia panted. 'How long will this last? The pains have been coming for hours.'

'The first one always takes its time. Could be a while yet.'

'I'm tired, Neve.'

'I know, sweetling. You just have to ride it out.'

Teia shifted on the thick pallet where she knelt in front of the older woman. The pain would get worse before it was over, she knew that. She'd seen it with Lenna and with her sister two years ago. She was in Macha's hands now.

A brazier in the corner warmed the little room made of wood and canvas partitions, and there were clean cloths and water ready to bathe the baby when she arrived. More comfort than Lenna had had for Aren's birth, out in the forest. The fire-haired woman with the lilting voice, Tanith, had brought herbs and oil to soften Teia's skin, and pinned up her hair for her when she began to sweat, but there was only so much the healer could do. Labour was a woman's hardest work and hers alone. It could not be shared.

The door behind Neve opened and the healer slipped back into the room, accompanied by the Arennorian girl who spoke tongues they could both understand. She smiled as she knelt beside the pallet, and it lit up those strangely coloured eyes of hers.

Another wave of pain rocked Teia forward. She held on to Neve's shoulders, panting, until it peaked and passed. Her belly felt different afterwards; there was something hard down in the cradle of her pelvis.

'She's coming down.'

Neve slipped a hand between her legs. 'I can't feel the crown yet.'

'I can feel her.' Teia caught her breath. 'She's started to move.'

'May I examine you?' the healer asked through the clan girl.

Teia nodded and sat back on her heels. Cool hands were laid either side of her distended belly, pressing gently. Then like a cold draught through the warm room, the tingling rush of power raised the hairs on her arms.

'You have the Talent!' she exclaimed.

'I do.' Tanith's hands moved slowly, sending pulses of warmth and light through Teia's awareness. In her mind she saw colours, the pale hues of the healer over the richer, more vibrant tones she knew belonged to her daughter.

'Are you a Speaker?'

'Not as you understand it, no.' The tingling warmth intensified as the healer palpated Teia's abdomen. Her brow creased thoughtfully. 'Your daughter has a strong talent, but your son has no gift that I can detect.'

'What? I don't—' She bit her lip as the pain began to build again. 'My son?'

Tanith nodded, sitting back. 'Didn't you know? You're carrying twins.'

Teia's thoughts raced. How was that possible? Surely she would have felt two lives inside her, sensed them somehow? Then the contraction rolled through her and left her gasping. Neve soothed her, mopping her face with a damp cloth.

'There now, lass,' she murmured. 'There now.'

'The Speaker,' Teia managed. 'Why couldn't Ytha see there were two, and you can?'

'Perhaps you didn't want her to see,' the healer said. 'Were you afraid of what might happen?'

Teia nodded. 'But I didn't do anything – I don't know how!'

'When we first come into our gift, we often do things without really knowing how. I have a friend who learned to change shape like that.' The healer helped Teia return to her kneeling position.

Neve kissed her on the cheek and smiled. 'You are twice blessed, praise Macha.'

Her thoughts were still tumbling, struggling to grasp this new information. 'But it can't be. There was only one— Neve, you only heard one heart!'

'Sometimes it happens that way,' said Tanith. 'If one twin is larger and stronger than the other, it muffles the second heartbeat unless you listen with a trumpet.' She paused, then curled her fingers around Teia's. 'I'm sorry to tell you this, but your daughter is very small.'

Teia stared. 'I saw her aura. She's so strong!'

'Her gift, I think, is all that is sustaining her.' The healer squeezed her hand. 'I will do everything I can, I promise.'

No. Her daughter would live. Those glorious colours, so strong, so bright— She must live! The slow clench of a new contraction began and Teia moaned. Neve rubbed her back, whispering soothing words, but she didn't hear, didn't feel. All she felt was the child inside her pushing his way out to the air.

A son. Drwyn's heir, just as he'd always believed. A chill slithered down Teia's spine, turning her sweat to ice-rime. It

365

couldn't be. *I'm birthing a daughter!* She clung to Neve's shoulders, panting, until the pain passed.

Gentle fingers stroked her hair from her forehead. 'All will be well, Teia,' the healer said, her eyes warm. 'Don't be afraid.'

'I'm not.' Teia gritted her teeth as the next wave came. *I want my daughter!*

ᘓᘐᘐ

Aradhrim's adjutant was with him when Tanith entered the hall, shuffling papers and pens by the light of a couple of storm lanterns. Beside the embers of the fire, Duncan drowsed in a chair, an empty *uisca*-cup drooping from his fingers. Beyond the circle of lamplight, thick shadows pooled in the corners. This far into the mountains, even in the middle of the year, night came down with the suddenness of a falling shutter.

The Warlord looked up as she approached the table. 'How is our guest?'

'Malnourished, exhausted and in labour.'

'That's succinct,' he said, with a flash of his teeth.

'Her friend Neve is sitting with her for now, but I think Teia has a long night ahead of her.'

'It's her first?'

Tanith nodded. 'And she's very young.'

The adjutant cleared his throat delicately, nudging another sheet of paper under the Warlord's pen. He signed it, then looked back at Tanith.

'How young, would you say?'

'Sixteen summers at most. Ill-used, too, probably by whoever got the child on her. There are signs of old injuries under her skin, not visible to the eye. A broken rib. Bite marks.'

'Human?'

She nodded, and Aradhrim clicked his tongue.

'The more I come to know of these people, the less I like their being my kin, no matter how distant.'

Another discreet *ahem*. This time the adjutant proffered a stick of imperial green sealing wax and a lighted taper.

Muttering, Aradhrim wrenched off his signet and threw it across the table at him. 'You do it, man. I'll sign the rest later.' He got to his feet and stretched, knuckling his back. 'Is the infirmary to your satisfaction?'

'Under the circumstances, it's quite good,' Tanith said. Compared to Chapterhouse's scrubbed tiles and groaning dispensary shelves it was utterly primitive, but serviceable. Familiarising herself with it had given her some hours away from Ailric, too. 'Your surgeon and his orderlies are well supplied and we have adequate space. It will still be difficult to prevent sepsis, but as field hospitals go, we could have much worse to work with.'

Aradhrim gave her a mirthless smile. 'Then I shall endeavour not to send you too many patients once battle begins.'

'Will it be soon, do you think?'

'With recalling the patrols, I am blind for the moment, but I think yes, it will be soon. When Gair flew out, he saw what appeared to be the war band camped further up the pass.' He pinched his brows. 'When the last of Sor's riders report in, I will know more – if they ever do report in, that is.'

Gair had shape-shifted? Dear spirits. Tanith swallowed nervously, her head full of memories of him falling.

'If?'

'They are overdue. Three days, Sor tells me. Gair saw no sign of them, so they are either in hiding, or have been taken.'

There was no need for him to put words around his fears, not after what had been borne back into the keep that afternoon. And so she came to the news that had brought her to the hall in the first place; news that for all her training and experience she hardly knew how to break.

'The men you asked me to examine,' she said. 'Your scouts. As you suspected, their injuries were consistent with a prolonged period of torture and their end was neither merciful nor quick.'

The words stuck in her throat like dry bread. 'They were choked to death with each other's genital organs.'

The adjutant gasped and blessed himself. The Warlord simply looked away, the only outward sign of distress a muscle flexing in his jaw. Somehow that was more affecting than the army surgeon's red-faced revulsion when her forceps had brought into the light the objects that had been forced into each man's throat.

Silence fell, broken only by the soft sputter of the adjutant's taper as it dripped wax onto the table. The fussy little man sat with the seal-ring forgotten in his other hand, eyes wide with horror in his ashen face.

Arms folded, Aradhrim frowned at the floor. His hands clenched on his biceps hard enough to whiten his knuckles.

'Can you see to it that they are buried as their mothers would want to remember them?' he asked. 'Whole?'

'It's been done.'

She'd closed those wounds herself, with silk thread and careful stitches, and not let the army physician near. Kellin was competent enough, for a field surgeon, but repairing the indignity done to those soldiers was no work for a man's hands.

Gently, she added, 'I have to go back to Teia, my lord. You should try to get some sleep. It's close to Low bell.'

He did not appear to hear her.

'Drwyn shows his contempt for the Empire. I will not have my men mocked in such a fashion.' Each word was clipped, precise. Abruptly he swung around, snatched up his pen and signed the remaining papers in front of his stricken adjutant, then raised his voice. 'Duncan. *Duncan!*'

The young clansman jolted awake, the *uisca*-cup clattering onto the floor. He scrubbed his hands over his face. 'My lord?'

'Find me some riders to take these dispatches south. It's time Theodegrance knew exactly what we are facing here.'

☙❧

The low-vaulted infirmary was quiet, the few patients sleeping despite the smell of fresh whitewash that still lingered in the air. Tanith walked along the rows of beds with a shuttered lantern, the huddled shapes of her charges anonymous beneath grey army blankets and swaying shadows.

When the clans came through the pass, this peaceful space would quickly be overwhelmed, but for now she had only minor injuries to tend: gashes and broken bones from logging accidents; a young man with blisters from the march that had gone septic and proved resistant to Kellin's store of medicaments. A Healing had set him on the mend, though it would still take time for new flesh to grow.

At the far end of the ward, canvas screens partitioned off some space for patients who required isolation. Only one of the small cubicles was occupied, the glow of a lamp still visible through the screen, though it was well into the small hours.

Teia's labour had been hard, as Tanith had predicted; it had ended only an hour ago as the third moon set, and at the last, it had taken a scalpel to bring her son into the world. Tanith had kept the blade concealed in her hand for as long as she could, until it became obvious that the girl's tender flesh would tear unless she acted. After that, it had been mercifully quick. There had barely been time for Teia to feel the sting of the steel and recognise it for what it was before she had a son in her arms, red-faced and squalling, and felt no more pain at all.

But one child was all she had. Her daughter had arrived in a bloody rush with the afterbirth, already blue and soon cold. Even the briefest examination had shown that the child was unlikely to live long, and nowhere under the sun would such life that re-mained have been anything but suffering. Neve met her eye and quickly, silently, shook her head.

Tanith shivered despite the warmth provided by the charcoal braziers set at intervals down the long room. The Nimrothi woman had been right, but it still cut at her to let a life go. No matter how many stillbirths she attended, it never grew any easier. Feeling the last warmth flee from the flesh under her hands. Carrying a tiny corpse to the cold room to await burial. Knowing that she'd spared a soul untold suffering was small comfort.

The only real mercy was that Teia had not seen it and would never be haunted by the twisted spine and unfinished limbs. When her heart had been set on a daughter, a healthy son had done nothing but deepen her disappointment. Perhaps it was better that she did not know the truth of what she had lost.

Spirits keep you, Teia. May sleep bring you some peace.

Tanith turned and walked back up the ward. If only she could find some portion of peace for herself. Her control of her emotions frayed a little further with every day and left her open-hearted, impetuous; the cool physician she had always dreamed she would be was all but gone. When she returned to Astolar, her father would scarcely recognise her.

And then there was Ailric. She could only hide in the infirmary for so long, then she'd have to confront him again. Oh, spirits, how had her life come to be such a mess?

She should go to her quarters and sleep, perhaps meditate a little. Too much tragedy and not enough rest; no wonder she felt so wrung out. And with the trinity so close now . . . It would change everything. There was no way she could know how, not even whether the change would be for better or worse, and it was all superstitious nonsense anyway that she should not give a moment's credence to, but nonetheless she felt change coming as surely as she would feel the edge of a precipice beneath her feet.

At the entrance to the ward she stopped to exchange a word or two with the duty orderly at his station before she left. The door opened and she looked up. Leaning in from the corridor was Sorchal, his usually mobile mouth fixed in an anxious twist.

'I looked for you earlier but you were in with the Nimrothi girl. Can you come?'

'Of course. What's happened?'

'It's Gair.' His gaze slipped to the seated orderly for no more than a beat. 'Please, just come.'

Oh, dear spirits watch over him.

Collecting her scrip on the way, she followed Sorchal out into the corridor, closing the door behind her. She raised the lantern. 'Tell me.'

'It's something to do with the Song,' he said. 'I don't know what exactly – I've even less of a gift for Healing than anything else. He won't let me into the room and I didn't know what else to do.'

Some consequence of the reiving; it had to be. First the fire, then the failed shape-shift down on the plains. Her heart lurched at the memory. She started along the corridor, fear quickening her steps, and Sorchal strode after her.

'Tell me everything,' she said. 'Everything that happened.'

'He was scouting the pass, flying. When he came back, when he landed, something went wrong. He's been in our quarters since then. I wanted to send for you straight away but he told me not to.'

Stubborn, stubborn. How like a man – how like a Leahn.

Past the great hall they hurried, sidestepping the soldiers yawning their way to the refectory after coming off watch. Up a winding tower stair, where the strike of shoe on stone beat time with the rapid tattoo of her heart. By the time they reached the moon-slatted corridor that led past her own room, the dread tightening her throat was all but choking her – and every hair on her arms was standing up.

Sorchal stopped before they were halfway along the passage.

'You know me, Tanith. I can barely fill a teacup with my gift unless it's to do with sensing Gates, but if I go down there . . .' He swallowed, raked a hand back over his hair. 'It makes my nerves crawl just standing outside the door.'

She summoned the Song and reached ahead. What she felt was

not the gentle tug at her senses of another *gaeden*'s working but a blow, forceful enough to knock the breath from her lungs. Whatever Gair was doing, its power reached out from that small room, through the air around her and the stone under her feet, and clawed at her colours like a drowning animal.

'Leave it to me,' she said.

'I'll wait, in case you need me.'

She touched his arm in thanks, and tried not think about why she might need his help. 'You've done the right thing, Sorchal. I'll be fine.'

She started towards the furthest of the rough wooden doors and within two strides knew exactly what he had meant. Her arms were prickling so intensely she wanted to scratch them raw, as if she'd blundered into stinging nettles.

Dear Goddess in heaven, if You can hear a stranger, look kindly on Gair now.

'What's wrong?' Sorchal asked from several paces behind her.

'I'm not sure. There's a massive weaving, but it's tangled somehow.'

'Can you help him?'

'I can try.' *If he'll let me.* Looking back over her shoulder, she dragged a smile out of her doubts. 'He'll be fine, I'm sure of it.'

She walked the last few steps and laid one hand flat on the door's coarsely sawn planks. Every hair on her arms and scalp stood to attention. Gently, she tapped on the wood.

'Leave me alone.' Gair's voice, but ragged and torn.

She tapped again.

'Damn it, Sorchal! I told you to go!'

Something crashed against the door from the inside and rattled the latch in its keeper.

'Gair?' No answer. 'May I come in?'

From inside the room came the sound of a pallet dragging on the floor under someone's weight, but he didn't speak. She glanced back at Sorchal, who shrugged, helpless.

Lifting the latch, she eased the door open. An object scraped across the floor behind it. When she held her lantern out into the darkened room she saw a man's boot, presumably the missile flung at the door in answer to her knock. Squeezing inside, she held the lantern higher.

A shape in the far corner flinched away from the light. 'Don't come any closer.'

Spirits, the power he held! Not wielding it, nothing so disciplined as that; he gripped it by the scruff as if it was rabid and about to bite. The barely contained violence of it made her own Song shriek in alarm.

'What's wrong?' she asked softly.

'I mean it, Tanith! Don't come any closer.'

Dark fingers swept through the air and swirled her hair around her face. What was happening to him? She raised the lantern shutter to let out more light. For a second she glimpsed wild eyes and golden feathers, then something disturbed the air with enough force to blow out the flame.

'Please. Leave me alone.' The strain was evident in his voice. Exhaustion, frustration, despair. No wonder Sorchal had come looking for her.

The darkness in the room was not quite absolute. Moonlight picked out the window-slits and part of one wall. As her eyes grew accustomed to it, the shadows gave up their secrets. A torn shirt on the floor. A tangle of blankets in the corner. Bare feet, a bowed head, and eagle wings swept around him like a cloak.

Spirits keep him and guard him from harm.

Tanith set the useless lantern down and moved towards Gair but he shrank back. Hunted eyes flashed her way. Startlingly large, then human again.

'It's not safe.'

'I'm not afraid.'

'You should be.'

Heart thumping, she knelt down beside him. When she reached

373

out a hand to touch him, the wings shivered. Feathers bristled erect up his neck, across his chest. He was caught between two shapes, unable to take either of them fully.

'Oh, Gair,' she whispered.

'I can barely control it, Tanith. I don't want to hurt you.'

'You won't.'

As soon as she laid her hand on his back, he shuddered. More feathers whispered over her hand, but underneath she felt feverishly hot skin, muscles twisted hawser-tight. She stroked his back, trying not to think of gentling a fractious hunting bird, but it was difficult not to when she saw a fire-eagle's wings blurring into a man's neck and head and neither was completely solid to Song-augmented eyes.

'Everything will be all right, you'll see.'

'I can't change back.' Despairing. He pressed his face to his knees and tightened his wings around them. His toes gripped the pallet and for a few seconds his bare feet turned scaly, tipped with black talons. 'I get halfway and there's something waiting for me. I daren't let go.'

'Shh. Don't try to. Just stay with me for a while.' *Let me help.*

I can't.

Let me in. I can help you.

It's not safe.

With the merest thread of power she touched his mind, but he closed her out with a shield as subtle and impermeable as glass. Controlled or not, in a trial of strength with him she was sure to lose, and it might even make the situation worse. The breadth, the depth of his gift was unlike anything she had ever encountered, even amongst her own people. If he closed his mind to her, it would remain closed.

Well, that was not strictly true. She bit her lip. There were techniques available to her to force her way in, with the help of certain drugs to subjugate his will. The necessary ingredients were in her scrip; with a little honey and nutmeg to disguise the taste, he wouldn't even know it was anything more than a warm milk posset to help him sleep. He trusted her enough that he'd drink it. But the idea was abhorrent, even as a last resort. She couldn't stomach the dishonesty.

'Tanith, please.' His voice cracked. 'I can feel the Song in you. It . . . pulls at me.'

She let her power go. As it drained back into quiescence, her impressions of him became less clear, as if seen through a smeary lens, and he was merely a shape in the shadows once more. She kept stroking his back, feeling it change from feathers to skin again.

'Can you tell me what happened?' If she could persuade him to talk, maybe she would learn something that might let her help him. Maybe having to concentrate on speech would even help pull him towards his human form. 'What did you see?'

'I was looking for Sor's men. For the war band. When I lost the light, I tried to change into an owl, but I couldn't. It was waiting for me.'

'What was?'

'I don't know what it is, but it's always waiting. Some kind of beast.' His wings shuddered again. Feathers whispered on the floor around him. 'When I try to change shapes I can feel it reach out for me. Begin to change me. The Song is trying to change me, and once it starts I'm not sure I can stop it. It's so hard to resist . . .'

Was this what had happened back on the plains, when she'd seen him tumble through shape after shape? When she'd felt her heart plummet in her breast as he'd plummeted into the grass and *oh spirits I thought I'd lost you lost you before I'd ever held you touched you loved you.*

'It's all right, Gair. I'm here.'

The words were meaningless, the soothing nonsense a parent would use with a child afraid of the night's monsters, but it was also the oldest medicine of all: the sound of another voice in the darkness.

Carefully Tanith felt around the silver clasp at his nape until she found the catch and clicked it open. His hair fell loose, pine needles pattering onto the blanket. She snapped the *zirin* closed again and tucked it into her pocket for safe keeping, then slowly combed her fingers through his hair. It was sweat-damp and tangled with bits of twig; she imagined a panicked bird crashing through the trees as it fled the beast inside, and her heart ached.

'I don't know how to fight it. I'm not sure I can any more.'

'You're safe here, Gair,' she murmured. 'Shush, now. I'll keep you safe.'

Little by little, she eased out the snarls and debris in his hair. As she worked she hummed a melody her mother used to sing whilst she combed Tanith's own hair, years ago when she was small. She'd long forgotten the words but the music came readily enough, and when she reached the end she picked up the next section of hair and started again.

Slowly, some of the tension drained out of Gair's body. The shadow of feathers across his chest became the pale gleam of skin and his head began to droop. 'I'm so tired,' he mumbled.

'I know. Rest now, try to get some sleep.' Sleep would let his natural shape reassert itself, when he finally released his hold on the Song – if she could help him to see it.

'Can't sleep. Too many dreams.'

'I'll keep you safe, I promise.' *Come to me, my brave one. Let me Heal you.*

Blindly he reached out for her. She opened her arms, pulled him close and felt the great eagle wings fold around them both. Squeezing her eyes shut against a sudden sting, she cradled his head into her neck.

For all the time that had passed, his pain had not lessened. Hearing it in his voice twisted the knife of her own guilt inside her. She could have spared him, if only she'd been quicker. If she'd fought harder, longer. Unshed tears burned in her eyes. *If, if, if.*

'I'm scared, Tanith. Scared of what I've become.'

'Shh. It's all right.' She pressed her lips to his brow. 'I'm here. I'll always be here with you.'

If, if, if, and none of it mattered, because he was still as much Aysha's now as he had ever been when she was alive.

His body sagged. Moments later his head lolled and she found herself supporting his weight as sleep finally claimed him. Soft as a breath, the eagle wings shimmered into nothingness, replaced by human limbs. She eased him down onto the pallet, stretching out beside him with her arm folded under her head as a pillow. With her other hand she pulled the blankets up around his shoulders. In the space of a few breaths he was deeply asleep.

Rest, that was what he needed. Without dreams, without memories; it would give him time for more of the reiving to heal. He'd had little enough of it lately, with Gimrael and Alderan and the accident he refused to speak of that had left his arm burning like a coal. Now a battle loomed over them that would require all his strength. She could only wonder how he had anything at all left to give.

Very carefully, Tanith reached out a finger and lifted a stray strand of hair back from his eyes.

Sleep, Gair. I'll wake you if you're needed. For now, just sleep.

She should go, leave him to his rest. But spirits keep her, she didn't want to. She almost didn't dare put words around what she wanted, because she was weak enough to dream it might happen. Those dreams, like Gair's, could bring only pain. A few minutes couldn't hurt, though. Just a few minutes to make sure he was all right, then she would go.

Her eyes drifted closed.

33

DAWN

〇✕〇

There. The first moon, the one that rose with the dawn, edging out from behind the high peaks like a Nordman longship breasting the White Sea. Only a quarter full, less than a quarter, but no matter. The trinity had begun. On that day, all three moons would ride the sky together and all that she had planned would come to pass.

Ytha opened her eyes again. The world was so much clearer, seen through her magic. Every colour was more vivid, every scent sweeter. Nothing was too far away to touch, no detail too small to see. If she reached out a hand, she could prick her finger on the twin tines of Tir Malroth; if she bent her eye upon it, she could count the grains of pollen on a bee's haunch between two beats of its wings.

I am Macha, the Mother in the Land. I am Aedon, Father of the Skies. All is in me and I am in all.

She saw the other Speakers as jewels amongst the stars and gathered them up in her hands. *It begins*, she said to them. *Be ready.*

Hoofbeats on the turf behind her. Loud, thrumming in her bones like thunder through the hills. With a sigh, she let the magic go and all colour drained out of the day. In the blink between one moment and the next, the mountains receded, the sun dimmed and all that was so remarkable in the world was hidden once more behind a veil. She looked over her shoulder.

Drwyn was dressed in his best plaid, the white spear cradled in one hand as the other reined his warhorse towards the crest of the hill where she sat. No armour, no shield across his back, though he had his father's short-sword on his hip. Cocksure. Arrogant as ever Drw had been, maybe more. He would have to learn.

'The spear will not protect you from every blow, Drwyn. You may still take a hurt that will kill you if not swiftly tended.'

'I will not hide behind armour, woman. My men will see me like this and take heart.' He thumped his chest, half-bared by his unlaced shirt.

'And the enemy's archers will see you like that and take aim!'

Lips thinned, she turned her gaze back to the pass. By the Eldest, he tried her patience now. Since the other chiefs had sworn their allegiance, his arrogance – his wilfulness! – had grown beyond all measure.

'Have a care, my chief. Who will lead your people to victory if you fall?'

Silence. No sound at all but the wind through the grass, the restless chewing of the horse at his bit. If she opened herself to her magic again, she was sure she would hear the turning of his thoughts. First anger at being upbraided, then resentment. Then finally, if he had paid heed to all she had tried to teach him, a grudging acknowledgement that perhaps she made a valid point. He would look down at his hands, or away over the land, jaw working on words he burned to say but didn't dare. And then . . .

'There is some merit in what you say, Speaker,' he said.

At last.

'It is wise to be cautious in these lands, since they are strange to us.' She kept her tone even, neutral. No need to raise his hackles further. 'When we have taken the measure of our foes, there will be time enough for grand gestures.'

'Indeed.' The horse shifted behind her, saddle harness creaking. *Uncomfortable, Drwyn? Is your pride so very difficult to swallow?*

'I see the first moon is up. How soon can we advance?'

'Soon,' she said. Sinking into the music of her power, she listened to the land around her and saw the slow climb of the silver moon. 'Two hours to the wandering moon. The trinity will be complete by dusk.'

'Dusk? I cannot order my men to attack in the dark!'

'Patience, Drwyn.' Ytha held up her hand. 'I only said the trinity would be complete. I did not say that would be when we sound the advance.'

Now she turned and smiled over her shoulder at him. The smile of a hunting cat. He began to chuckle.

'Tell your captains we ride under the second moon and the trinity will shine on our victory.'

The chuckle became a laugh that shook the birds from the grasses, twittering in alarm. Further up the pass, the trumpet sounded that marked the start of the Empire's day. Ytha darted a glance at the distant fortress, its banners curling in the morning sun. Eldest willing, she would make it their last.

∞

Tanith eased the door to Gair's room closed behind her. The day had barely begun; the dusty stone corridors were still pooled in shadow, the windows on the mountain-facing side of the fortress mere grey rectangles. It would be another two hours or more before the sunlight that had roused her would reach over the walls to the far side. For now only the sentries were awake, and there was no one to see her creeping back to her room from a man's bed.

Spirits, the foolishness of it. She'd only intended to stay for a little while, just long enough to see Gair safely asleep, but as she lay beside him exhaustion had crept up on her like a thief and robbed her of several hours. She'd not stirred until the first fingers of dawn touched her eyes.

Now she felt grubby and crumpled from sleeping in her clothes, her neck had a kink in it that no amount of rubbing would ease, and all she could think about was waking up with Gair's arm over her waist.

Tanith's steps faltered and she shut her eyes. Spirits keep her. His arm over her waist and his face close enough to hers that they shared each breath. Close enough to kiss. Opening her eyes again she hurried on, back to her own room. Quick strides distanced her from him and from what might have been, but she couldn't outrun her thoughts. They remained in the room at the far end of the corridor from her own, in his arms, kissing him awake and watching his eyes light with a smile.

Worse than foolishness: it was a dream, nothing more. She was not the woman he wanted to kiss. Even if she was, it didn't change the fact that he was her patient, and a human. Not for her, in so many ways, and he never could be. She had to accept that. Dwelling on hopeless fantasies would only hurt her. But oh, she felt his arm around her still, as if his touch had seared into her skin.

The one mean window in her quarters was already bright with the new day, sunlight slicing across the dimness of the cell like a sword. She closed the door behind her, weaving a simple ward to secure the latch and give her a modicum of privacy whilst she washed and changed her shirt. Not that any of her clothes were truly clean any more after so long travelling, with only river water to launder them in and campfires to dry them. Even here in the fortress, the best she could hope for to clean herself with was a bucket and washcloth.

Tanith eyed the bucket on the floor as she undressed, letting her crumpled clothes fall on her unslept-in blankets. Oh, for one of Chapterhouse's deep tiled baths that she could soak in up to her ears!

'If wishes were crowns,' she muttered, and called a thread of the Song to warm the water.

Something metal chimed on the floor as she kicked out of her leathers and she cast around for it. There, gleaming silver in the early light: Gair's *zirin*. She'd fled his room in such haste she'd forgotten it was still in her pocket. She picked it up, turning it to trace the inscription between the intricate knotwork borders. He would miss it when he woke, but the thought of facing him to give it back made her stomach flutter. That silver band symbolised secrets shared in the dark; to drag them unwilling out into the light would be like breaking open the nest of something blind and helpless.

I'm scared, Tanith.

Carefully, she set the *zirin* on the window ledge and laid her mother's ring next to it. Later. She'd take it to him later, when she'd bathed and changed, and try to catch him alone. Yes. Quickly she pinned up her hair and began to wash. Goosebumps chased the flannel over her limbs as her wet skin chilled but she soaped and rubbed briskly. The sooner she finished, the sooner she could be dry and warm again.

'You are even more beautiful by daylight,' said Ailric's voice behind her.

Heart leaping, she dropped the flannel and fumbled for her towel to cover herself. It was far too small; she felt more naked with it than without as she whirled to face him.

He was leaning casually against the door-frame, his other hand on the latch. Amused eyes flickered over her from wet shoulders to bare feet.

'What are you doing in here? Get out!'

'Am I not welcome?' he asked, stepping towards her. The door swung closed behind him with a brief tingle as her ward was restored.

'No, you are not.' Her voice trembled, no matter how she willed it to be firm. 'I put a ward on the door for a reason, Ailric.'

'Ah, love, I have always known how to slip through your defences.' He was closer now, close enough for her to smell *uisca* on every word. She backed away.

'I want you to leave.'

'But I very much want to stay.'

Two more steps. Two steps too close. Her bare bottom met the cold stone wall and she flinched.

'Did I startle you?' he murmured. His hands pressed to the wall either side of her face. 'Please forgive me.'

'You're drunk.'

He smiled lazily and leaned in towards her. 'I have found a taste for this *uisca*, I think.'

'Get out.'

Tanith turned her head away from the smell of stale spirits. He *was* drunk – must have been drinking all night. Not too drunk to know what he was doing, though, just drunk enough not to care. She swallowed, her heart fluttering like a moth, bruising its wings on the bars of her ribs.

'I looked for you last night.'

One hand trailed up her arm from the wrist, fingertips sliding easily through the sudsy water that still clung to her skin. Fresh goosebumps darted after them.

'I was at the infirmary until late. I had patients— Ailric, *please*! I'm trying to bathe.'

Now his smile widened, fiery eyes heated as they roamed over her. 'So I see.'

For an instant she remembered the boy he had been, the one who had thrown pebbles at her window at midnight and dived off Belaleithne Falls just to prove he could, and wondered what had happened to him. How he'd become this man she hardly recognised, now standing so close to her that with each breath he took his chest brushed against her hands, where she held the wholly inadequate towel to her breasts.

'I went to the infirmary, but I could not find you.'

'A patient needed me,' she said, hitching the towel higher and realising too late how little of her thighs it now covered.

'A patient not in the infirmary.'

'Yes.'

The moth was fluttering faster now. Why did he look so much taller, so much stronger? His fingers stroked down her arm and a feather of the Song stroked directly across her nerve endings. Her mouth dried.

No. Don't do this to me. Don't touch me like that. Please, go!

'So you were with *him*.' His face was very close now, lips trailing over her cheek. 'You went to a human.'

'I— Don't.' His lips grazed her neck, drifted out to her shoulder. His Song strummed over hers and left her singing. 'I told you, I was with a patient.'

'All night?'

'I fell asleep. It'd been a long day, for both of us.' She was gabbling. Thoughts careered around her head, too panicked to find their way into words.

'A long day,' he said slowly against her skin, 'and a long night. I can smell him on you, Tanith. You reek of him.'

The insinuation that she might have forgotten her ethics as a Healer outraged her enough to fire her courage.

'How dare you? It's none of your business!' She pushed at him, trying to lever him away from her. Her wet hand left dark shapes on his shirt. 'Gair is a patient of mine. He needed something to help him sleep.'

'And you were that something, yes?'

'No!' Why did he make her feel so threatened, so defensive? She had done nothing wrong – oh, spirits! – why was she justifying herself to him? 'Get out. Now.'

In an instant he had seized her wrists and pinned them to the wall above her head. The towel fell at her feet. He buried his face in her neck, kissing, nipping, breathing her in.

'Do not lie to me. I can smell the lust on you. I can taste it.'

Shifting his grip so that one hand held her wrists cruelly tight, Ailric lifted the necklace of glass flowers at her throat with the other. He sneered. 'Is this how he won you, with trinkets?'

A jerk of his hand snapped the fine silver chain and flung the necklace across the room. Glass broke and angry tears spilled from Tanith's eyes.

'That was a gift from—'

'It is a bauble. A gaudy nothing. That is all you are to him. He cares nothing for you – I have the words from his own mouth. Why do you waste yourself on him when I could give you so much more?' The back of his fingers stroked down her cheek, his eyes searing into hers. 'So much more, love. Status. The skills to rule. True-blood daughters to grace your House, instead of mongrels.'

A kiss crushed her lips, his tongue probing her mouth. Cool fingers pushed between her thighs, seeking, caressing. Tanith's mind reeled as she twisted away from him. After the cruel things he'd said, did he really think she would give herself to him like this, in fear? His weight bore down on her, heavy on her chest; she writhed under him but it only made him chuckle, deep in his throat.

Panic clutched her. Lungs burning, unable to draw a full breath, she bit his lip as hard as she could. She tasted blood and Ailric pulled his head back, a smear of scarlet at the corner of his mouth. Kicking out, she struggled to free her hands from his grip but he pinned them again, slamming her wrists against the stone wall. She yelped.

'Such fire,' he whispered and laughed softly. Scarlet teeth gleamed, like those of an animal at the kill. Booted feet kicked her ankles apart. 'You are mine, Tanith, and you always will be.'

ᘒᕽᘓ

Campfires glittered in the shadows of the pass like a field of stars. Too many to count, too far away for Gair to even guess at the numbers of men surrounding them. The Nimrothi had arrived under cover of darkness and been revealed by the dawn. It was too late.

Fire after fire swam larger in the spyglass lens and drifted away again as Gair turned, but he didn't see them. All he saw was shadow and flames and the beast, roaring again, filling his head with ashes. For a moment panic closed his throat, but he swallowed it down, forced himself to breathe. Concentrated on filling and emptying his lungs again and again to keep it at bay.

He barely remembered the journey back up the pass in the fading light. He recalled only fragments of it: crashing through the treetops, the turpentine smell of pine-sap on the frosty air as he struggled for control of the beast. For control of the fear. But he remembered Sorchal's face, moon-white with shock when he saw what had returned. He shut his eyes, the glass drooping.

If he tried to change shapes again, it would consume him. There could be no standing against it, no defence. The beast was already inside him. In quiet moments, he felt it turn over, coiling restlessly in the back of his mind. All it would take to free it was to reach deeply into the Song.

He forced his eyes open once more, compelled himself to refocus the glass, but the fires were already fading as the light strengthened and the dawn's golden line edged down the western mountains. There was nothing more to see. Breath steaming in the morning chill, he handed the spyglass back to Sorchal.

'How many?' the Elethrainian asked.

'I can't tell. More than I can count from here, that's for sure.'

Holding the glass to his eye, Sorchal sighed. 'Wonderful. Another siege. I hate sieges.'

Gair eased the baldric on his shoulder. The longsword's scabbard was dragging at his hair where it hung loose down his back. His *zirin* had come undone somehow and was missing. Maybe he'd lost it out in the pass; certainly there'd been no sign of it on his pallet or anywhere on the floor in the small chamber when he woke. He'd become so accustomed to its cool weight on the back of his neck that its absence unsettled him. He kept reaching for it, and each time his fingers closed on the space where it should have been, the loss wrenched at him a little more.

'Could you see any more sign of the rangers?' Sorchal asked, scanning the old road.

'No. If they're still in the valley, I think they've been taken. If they're out on the plain, they're past our help now.'

'Poor bastards. Do you think Savin's out there, too?'

'I doubt it. If he got that close to a battle he might soil one of his precious silk shirts. Besides, we don't even know he's got a hand in this, although it wouldn't surprise me.' Chess pieces on a board, moved about by unseen hands . . . It would certainly suit him. Gair looked away up the valley again. 'I'm sorry, Sorchal. About yesterday.'

'It's all right, I bunked down in the guardhouse. No harm done.' The Elethrainian shrugged and closed the glass. 'Was Tanith able to help?'

Gair didn't know. Perhaps she had done something, Healed him after he'd fallen asleep, for all she'd told him that the reiving's scars were beyond her skill. All he knew for certain was that he'd slept, deeply, thoroughly, for the first time since— For the first time in too long. He'd even dreamed, not of darkness and loss but of a warm, light place filled with music that felt both strange and utterly familiar at the same time.

'Some. Thanks for deciding to take no notice of me.'

Sorchal bounced the spyglass in his hand and shrugged. 'I had to do something to try to get my bed back. I know how much you would have missed my snoring.'

Help me!

The desperate hail tore into Gair's head, the sender's familiar colours of rose and jade shuddering with fear.

Tanith! He loped along the wall towards the tower, already searching the keep for her colours. When she didn't answer, he broke into a run.

Sorchal shouted after him. 'Gair? What is it?'

'It's Tanith. I have to go.'

In the tower he flung himself down the stairs with her colours fixed in his mind; only the tight spiral prevented him from taking them two at a time. She was in her room. Flashes of pain quickened his pace. Running feet sounded behind him and followed him across the churned, slushy bailey and into the keep proper. Wet boots skidding on the stone flags, he raced up the stairs to the sleeping quarters on the floor above the soldiers' barracks.

Tanith's room was at the end, the door closed. A ward prickled over his senses when he reached for the latch, but he didn't dare waste time trying to unpick it. Leaning back, he drove his heel into the wood and the door flew inwards in a shower of splinters. Ailric had her pinned against the wall, holding her golden arms above her head and his body forcing her thighs apart.

The white-blond man glared back over his shoulder. Blood stained his teeth. 'This does not concern you, Leahn.'

'I beg to differ.' Steel hissed into Gair's hand as he strode into the room. 'Let her go or so help me I'll spit you where you stand.'

'In front of the lady?' Ailric snickered, but he released Tanith's hands and stepped back. She dropped to the floor, shuddering. 'And this is what you pant after like a brach in heat? This . . . *primitive* is what you choose over one of your own kind? You are a disgrace to your House and I will make sure your father knows it.'

Gair seized Ailric's shoulder and flung him against the wall by the door, well away from Tanith. Away from him and his blade as well. 'I warned you to have a care for her,' he growled. 'Get out of here.'

Fury tasted sour in his mouth. He had to keep every muscle in his arm locked tight or the sword would run red. One wrong word from Ailric, one more glimpse of Tanith huddled on the floor, would be all it took.

Out of the corner of his eye he saw Sorchal skid to a halt at the door, a pair of knives drawn and ready. The Elethrainian took in the tableau before him and his lips thinned.

Ailric levered himself away from the wall, dabbing at his bloody mouth with his wrist. His eyes burned.

'Once more the hero. Enjoy your pet while you can, Tanith. It will not be long before night falls on his world.'

Throwing one last scornful glance at her, he stalked out.

34

BESIEGED

၁၀

Such an insult could only be answered with steel. The sword in Gair's hand pulled at him to answer it, whispering, hungering, and for a heartbeat he was tempted to let it lead. It would be so easy, but no. Not this time. Slowly, he sheathed the blade. Uncurled his fingers from the hilt and stepped back from the precipice.

Out in the corridor, Sorchal tucked his knives back into his belt, careful not to look at Tanith crouched naked by the wall.

'I'll watch him,' he said, and loped away.

Unslinging his baldric, Gair knelt at her side. 'Are you all right?'

Her eyes were fixed on something only she could see. Tears shone but didn't fall. He took off his cloak and gently draped the thick wool around her. Her eyes closed convulsively and she gulped a breath. The gulp became a sob and Gair gathered her against his chest.

'It's all right,' he murmured, even though it wasn't and nothing he could say would make it so. 'It's all right, he's gone.'

She burrowed under his arm and clung to him as if he was the only rock in a world of storms. If she was weeping, though, she didn't make a sound.

'I never expected this from him,' she said at last, into his shirt. 'I was so surprised I couldn't even reach for the Song.'

'I understand.'

'He was crushing me – I couldn't breathe. I bit him.'

'I saw. That was quick thinking.'

'I didn't know what to do. He wouldn't listen to me.'

'I don't think he's listened to a word you've said in quite some time.' She stayed silent and he kissed the crown of her head. 'There's no reasoning with him, Tanith. I tried and he wouldn't hear me, either.'

'He never used to be like that, when he was younger. When he used to play the lute and sing to me and cared nothing for politics or power.' She faltered. 'Oh, spirits!'

Her body shook. Gair wrapped her more closely in his arms. How slender she was; so lightly boned, like a deer. A beautiful, tawny hind, and that arrogant *bhakkan* had lifted his hand against her. The cloak slipped, baring her golden shoulder, and as he folded it more securely around her he saw an angry welt at the base of her neck.

Somehow he kept his tone gentle. 'What happened?'

'He changed when he took on some of his House's estates. He got to like the authority. A little too much.'

'I meant just now.'

'I know what you meant.'

He waited, needing to know, not wanting to ask. *Damn you, Ailric! Damn you to whatever hell awaits your kind!*

'No,' she said. 'He didn't. He . . . touched me, that's all.'

'I see.' Relief that Ailric hadn't raped her warred with the fear that he'd been about to when he was interrupted. 'Did he hurt you?'

'Not really.' Tanith extended her hands, showing him her skinned knuckles, the bruises blooming on her delicate wrists.

'What happened to your neck?'

She fingered the mark. 'My necklace, from my students. He thought it was a gift from another man. From you, actually.' Her gaze hunted amongst the pieces on the floor by the far wall then fell, defeated. 'It's broken now.'

'Maybe it can be mended.'

'Maybe.' She shivered. 'I'm cold.'

'Then let's get you up off this floor.'

Gair steadied her as they stood. His cloak swamped her, pooling on the stone floor, and spirals of coppery hair hung about her face, come loose from its pins. For the first time in the year and more he'd known her, her Astolan poise was shattered and she looked vulnerable.

'Shall I send for Magda, or . . .'

She leaned into his shoulder. 'No. I'd rather not have people talking.'

That was understandable. Talk would find its way to Ailric eventually, and it would only provoke him. 'Is there anything else I can do?'

'You've done more than enough.'

'I think it was your turn to be helped.' He dropped a kiss onto her forehead, then stooped to pick up his sword. 'I'll wait outside whilst you get dressed.'

Tanith closed the damaged door after him and dragged something across the floor behind it to wedge it shut in the absence of a latch. Gair settled his longsword across his back and paced the corridor with his arms folded to keep from reaching for the hilt. With every step, his anger burned a little brighter. Ailric had the gall to sneer at humans, to call him a primitive, but he'd never press his attentions on a woman like that. Not on any woman, high-born or low.

After a minute or two, Sorchal's colours touched his. *He's on the east ramparts, sulking like a thunderhead. Is Tanith all right?*

She says so, but she's badly shaken. I swear, if he so much as looks crosswise at her . . .

I'll be there to hold your coat. No fear. A careful pause. *Did he force her?*

392

If he had, he'd be a gelding by now.

Ouch. Remind me not to get on your bad side.

Can you keep an eye on him for me? I don't trust him.

Of course. A pause. *I don't suppose there's any truth in what he was frothing about her and you?*

Sorchal!

I was only asking. She is beautiful and I have a reputation to maintain, after all.

A reputation as a milk-hound of the very basest kind, you mean.

Reputations like that don't fall from heaven with the rain, you know. I've worked hard for it. It's my duty to ensure its upkeep to the best of my ability.

Sometimes, Sorchal's irreverence drove Gair to distraction. *Blood and stones, can't you be serious about anything?*

I try to avoid seriousness if at all possible.

Behind Gair, the door creaked. He turned. Dressed in her leathers, with her hair loose and his cloak folded over her arm, Tanith looked calm, if a little pale.

'Feeling better?' he asked.

'Better. Thanks to you.'

'I can't say it was my pleasure, but I was glad to help. You know I'll always come if you need me. Any time.'

'My knight-protector?' she teased, and he made a face. She held out his cloak for him to take. 'When you kicked in the door like that, you looked so fierce I almost felt sorry for Ailric.'

'Don't feel too tender-hearted. I'm not sure I'm done with him yet.'

The new bruises darkening her wrist were not quite covered by the sleeve of her leathers. Gair frowned. *Definitely not done.*

'I don't like you being alone down here. What if he comes back? This room's right at the end of the corridor and I broke the latch on your door.'

'I'll be fine.'

'I know it's not proper for a lady, but you could share with me and Sorchal can take this room,' he said, but Tanith shook her head.

'I won't run from him, Gair. Besides, if I did that it would only make him think he was right, that I'm yours.'

He snorted. 'I don't really care what he thinks.'

'But it's no reason to antagonise him.'

How could she be so reasonable? He'd seen the fear in her eyes, the marks on her skin.

She laid a hand on his arm. 'If I asked you, would you leave him be?'

Either his thoughts were written on his face, or she knew him too well. 'Why?'

'Because threatening him won't change his mind. You'll only harden his opinion.'

'He had no right to treat you like that, Tanith. No matter what he thinks.'

A smile tugged at the corners of her mouth. 'So very, very fierce.' As he began to protest, she added, 'I'll be fine, really. One of the carpenter's mates can fix the latch and I promise from now on I'll ward it with something Ailric doesn't know how to unpick.'

She was the composed, assured Healer again. Of the windflower girl who had trembled in his arms not half an hour previously, there was no sign.

He blew out a long breath. 'You're set on this, aren't you?' Tanith nodded. 'I'm not happy about it, but all right.'

'The White Court will deal with him when I return to Astolar. Queen Emelia will not forgive this, I assure you, and I will press for the fullest censure under the law.'

Gair, who at that moment would have preferred something more immediate and preferably permanent, said nothing. Tanith gave him a look that said she knew exactly what he was thinking.

'I won't let him use his grandmother's status as First Ascendant to escape the consequences of what he did here,' she said firmly. 'His father's wealth won't save him, either.'

His lips quirked; he couldn't help it. 'Now who's being fierce?'

She dug something from her pocket and held it out to him. 'Here. This is yours.'

In the palm of her hand was his *zirin*.

'Where did you find that? I was sure I'd lost it.'

'My fault,' she said, with a little moue. 'Your hair was full of pine needles last night, and I thought you'd be more comfortable without it. I forgot I had it in my pocket.'

He turned the *zirin* over in his hand. Perhaps that dream hadn't been a dream at all. The gentle fingers combing through his hair, the lilting lullaby voice, singing him down into the first unbroken sleep he'd had since the funeral, it had all been real.

Chest tight with emotion, he pulled Tanith into a close embrace. 'Thank you.'

It wasn't enough, but he hadn't any more words. The *zirin* and a book of al-Dinn's poetry were all that remained of Aysha, and of his heart. Eyes shut against the threat of tears, he pressed his face into Tanith's hair and closed his fist tightly around the silver band.

✑

Something jolted Teia out of her doze. Not her bladder, nor any sound from the crib at the foot of her bed, but every hair on her arms had prickled upright.

She sat up, blinking in the dim light. Nothing had changed in her small room, with its two walls of batten-and-canvas screens, two of rendered stone. Washstand, bed, crib. Her staff propped in the corner, and Neve's shadowy figure drowsing on a stool against the wall. Someone snoring gently out in the ward. There was nothing new.

Teia rubbed her arms through the man's shirt she'd been given for a night-shift. It must have been a dream. Perhaps one with a hint of foretelling that she couldn't remember now that she was awake.

Some light would help. Reaching out to the lamp on the crate that did duty as a table, she fumbled for the screw that would turn up the wick.

The shadowy figure stood up and leaned forward.

'Here, let me help,' said a man's voice.

'Duncan?' Teia's hand flew to the gaping neck of her shirt and bunched it closed. 'What are you doing here? Where's Neve?'

'She was dead on her feet, so I sent her to get some sleep.' The lamp brightened, pushing the shadows back from his sun-browned face and quick blue eyes. 'I'm sorry, I didn't mean to startle you. Is that enough light?'

'Yes. Yes, thank you.' She fumbled to refasten her shirt, suddenly embarrassed with him so near.

He gestured towards the door. 'I can go, if you want some privacy.'

'It's all right. I just wasn't expecting to see you.' Macha, she was all thumbs and couldn't grasp the buttons. Heat bloomed in her cheeks. 'Why are you here, Duncan?'

'I wanted to make sure you'd come to no harm, after yesterday.'

Yesterday? Oh, of course, those poor soldiers. 'I'm fine.'

'Good. That's good. I was worried that the shock had brought on your labour. Lady Tanith said it was just your time, but, well . . .' His hands rubbed together restlessly, as if he didn't quite know what to do with them. 'I wanted to be sure.'

'That was very kind of you.' Finally she managed to persuade a button through its hole and started on the next one.

'I also thought you should know that the clans have moved into the pass.'

Her hands froze as a cold, cold weight descended on her heart. She looked up. 'When?'

'Some time after sunset. We saw them at first light.'

It had begun. Ytha would be out there, Drwyn, too. There was nothing more she could do, no more warnings she could give.

Robbed of their strength, her hands fell back into her lap. 'So I failed.'

Duncan dropped to one knee next to her bed and took her hand in his. Earnest eyes searched her face. 'Never say that. You achieved something extraordinary, worthy of a bard's song. Bringing those people through the mountains. Bringing new life out of the snows.'

She had to look away as tears began to burn. 'I brought only death.'

'But your daughter—'

'My daughter was stillborn.'

Silence. Then the hand that held hers was covered by another. Strong hands, warm on her cold fingers. 'I didn't know. I'm sorry.' A dry click as he swallowed. 'Then . . . ?'

He was looking at the crib. She knew it, could feel it as if his gaze rested on the back of her neck. 'A boy. A twin I never knew I carried.'

Teia waited for the pity, the mindless platitudes that would follow. The well-meaning assurances that would never, could never, bridge the gulf inside her.

'My heart grieves for your loss, Banfaíth.'

'Why?'

'Why?' he echoed, confused.

'Why should you grieve? You don't know me. You didn't know my daughter.' Hating the way her voice thickened with grief, Teia snatched her hands out of his grasp and tucked them under her arms, folded across the hollow place inside her where her daughter had died. 'Please leave me alone.'

More silence, then a shift in the air, soft creaks of leather as he stood up.

'Of course. Forgive me for intruding.'

Scalding tears spilled onto Teia's cheeks. She didn't dare look around and see pity on his face – couldn't bear it, and screwed her eyes shut against it.

Footsteps sounded, only two or three strides to the door. The latch squeaked, then came a pause that lasted for ever before he spoke. 'You're right, Banfaíth. I don't really know you. But if I may, I would very much like to. And your son.'

He closed the door carefully behind him and she was left alone with her loss.

ᢒᢙ

Along the walk atop the curtain wall, green-uniformed archers marched into position, gear jingling. Every button gleamed, every scrap of leather oiled and buffed to a shine. On each man's back was a full quiver and the regiment's boys scuttled amongst the men with sheaves of fresh arrows. Down in the bailey, squads of pikemen were making ready.

Standing next to the Warlord out of the way of the pounding boots and the red-faced sergeants with their shrill whistles, Masen watched and shook his head. Toy soldiers, dressed up for parade. The Empire had been at peace for so long, not one of them had speared anything that wasn't stuffed with straw. They'd never lost their footing in an enemy's blood, never felt that chill when their weapon snagged on a corpse's ribs as another sword came at them from the side.

He glanced at the tall clansman beside him. *But he knows, I'd wager. He knows that a battlefield is a roaring, stinking swamp of shit and mud and horse piss and broken gear. Broken men. And if you're lucky, a quick end. That's all.*

Further along the wall stood Commander Brandt's blocky figure. Feet squared, free hand tucked in the small of his back between his polished belt and impeccable uniform tunic, he surveyed the valley below through a shiny brass spyglass.

Masen's lip curled and he turned away, looking over the wall at the road that ran northwards into the valley.

Praise Goddess someone here does know.

Five women, robed in snow-fox furs, stood in a line across the old road. They faced the fortress with their staffs held upright before them, the air above their heads faintly luminescent, as if the morning sun glanced off a soap-bubble. At their backs were horse-soldiers, in ranks so deep the rearmost were barely visible. Braids and manes stirred in the crisp breeze. Banners snapped over their heads and sunlight glinted on spears. Here and there a horse snorted, but not a single human voice broke the silence. The air thrummed with power.

'Utter folly.' Commander Brandt harrumphed and snapped his spyglass closed. 'Cavalry attacking fixed fortifications? The Sixth will cut them to pieces without leaving the walls. They're not even out of bowshot!'

'They don't have to come any closer than this,' Masen said, with tired patience. 'They have all the weapons they need right there .'

'Those women? Preposterous.'

'I imagine Preceptor Malthus thought much the same thing before he sent out his Knights against similar women.'

'What are you talking about, man?'

'Perhaps you should reread your history books, Commander. I'm talking about the last time an army squared up to a Nimrothi war band.'

Brand snorted. 'Archers, put a volley into them. Let's see how well they stand up to a few broad-head arrows.'

Bowstrings snapped and a flight of arrows hissed into the air.

Masen sighed. 'You're wasting your time. They're shielded.'

'Everyone knows iron is sovereign against magic.'

How much knowledge had been forgotten. How potent the myths and superstitions that had sprung up in its place had grown.

'Tell that to the Knights whose heads were crushed inside their iron helms, whose bodies broiled as their iron-plate armour was heated cherry-red around them.' He cocked his hands on his hips. 'Forget everything you think you know about magic, Commander. It's nonsense. Iron doesn't do a damn thing. Witches don't fly through the night on yarrow-stalks and if you put out a saucer of milk for the feylings to come and darn your socks, all you'll attract is your neighbour's cat!'

Brandt blinked. Overhead the arrows had reached the apex of their flight and begun their plunge towards the five unarmed and unarmoured women standing on the road. Five feet above their heads, the arrows shattered. Broken shafts slithered down the curve of the shield and pattered onto the road like rain.

Song shivering, Masen stabbed a finger towards them.

'See? Do you believe in magic now?'

'I—' The garrison commander swallowed, discomfited.

Beside him, Aradhrim stirred. 'The Gatekeeper's point is well made, Brandt. The Nimrothi Speakers are just as skilled as Arennor's own. It would be a mistake to underestimate them.'

Then it came, a deep thrumming pressure in Masen's head as the Song was drawn up in a mighty gulp.

☙

As if a cold draught had blown over him, every hair on Gair's head lifted away from its root. He straightened, opening his eyes.

Tanith's embrace tightened and she looked up. 'What was that?'

Familiar tingling climbed his arms, up to his scalp. Prickling, tugging at his will. It was the Song, but it danced with no colours that he knew. 'I'm not sure, but it's huge.'

Anxious shadows darkened her gaze as she released him. 'The clans?'

'It must be.'

He led the way to the tower stairs. As the weaving intensified his pace quickened, until he took the last few steps two at a time and strode out into the morning sun with Tanith close behind.

Atop the curtain wall, archers were in position, arrows nocked ready to take aim. Looking over the wall he saw the smeared colours of a shield above the north road.

'Spirits, can you feel it?' Tanith asked, rubbing her arms through her leathers.

'I'd have to be dead not to.'

The weaving was enormous. Beyond just the shield he could see, it clenched the very air around him, made his skin feel a size too small to contain his flesh.

'Do you have any idea what they're doing?'

'No, but I don't think we're going to like it.' Gair reached for the Song, but the only weave visible to him was the shield. Whatever else the Speakers might be doing remained hidden. Next to him, he sensed Tanith reaching out.

They're strong, she said. *At least three of them have starseed rings.*

You can see that? Your eyesight's better than mine.

The stone gives a crystalline quality to their weaving. There's something else at work, too, but it's very subtle. I can't quite tell what it is.

Masen might know more.

Gair set off along the wall towards where the Gatekeeper stood with the Warlord and the blocky garrison commander. Before he'd taken two steps the keep's stones began to vibrate beneath his feet.

Earth-Song. It had to be. Now the archers felt it, too, exchanging worried glances, steadying themselves against the parapet. He peered over the wall, his own Song humming in response. Water shook from the trees to either side of the ancient road through the pass. Melting snow shivered and slipped. Even the air quivered. Further along the wall, soldiers shouted and pointed in alarm.

Gair took Tanith's hand. 'Stay close to me.'

She hurried after him to join the others. Masen's scowl and the beet-red suffusion of Brandt's bulldog features said they'd clashed again, over the Speakers, most likely. The garrison commander pressed a hand to the crenellated wall as the trembling underfoot increased.

'Good Goddess, what is that? A landslide?'

'Earth-Song,' said Gair.

'And what is . . . earth-Song?'

'It's what you use to make landslides happen,' interjected Masen sourly, 'which you could have worked out for yourself if you'd paid attention to a word I said, instead of dismissing it all as *poppycock*!'

The commander bristled. 'I don't have to stand here and be insulted—'

Abruptly, Tanith pointed down the valley. 'Look!'

The valley slopes were visibly shuddering. Trees swayed and sheets of slushy mud slithered down towards the road, leaving raw brown scars in the earth.

The resonances in the Song were almost painful. Every deep, ringing chord echoed through Gair's body, made him feel as if he was about to be crushed flat by the weight of the Speakers' weaving. It pressed down, down until he thought it would drive him to his knees, and Tanith clung desperately to his arm. Then something shifted.

Further down the valley, five massive boulders heaved into the air and the crushing weight of the working eased. Ears ringing, Gair stared. They were huge – hunks of rock the size of haystacks, of houses, pieces of mountain too large ever to be described by so small a word as *boulder*.

Brandt's bulldog jaw dropped open. 'Holy Goddess and all Her angels.'

Clods of earth and slush pattering down over the heads of the Speakers, they formed up into a rough chevron and, with the ponderous implacability of merchantmen under full sail, bore down on the keep.

Realisation struck Gair like a blow. 'They're aiming for the walls!'

He reached into the Song. It surged up to his will, its music rushing in his ears. There were too many lives at stake to spare an ounce of concentration for what might happen if the beast roared; he threw it all into weaving a shield. Flinging out his arms, he spread it down over the wall and as far along it as he could reach in both directions. It wasn't a sophisticated weaving; he only had time for brute strength to resist impact. He hoped it would be enough.

Around him whistles shrilled and orders were bellowed. Brandt cupped his hands to his mouth and yelled, 'Brace the gates!'

The enormous boulders accelerated. Nothing that heavy should move that fast. Something so massive shouldn't even be in the air at all, and the closest one was only a hundred yards away. Gair gritted his teeth. If the beast came, so be it.

'Oh, they're good,' Masen muttered and began working a weaving of his own. Earth-Song groaned around him like thunder, shuddering through his colours at the periphery of Gair's aware-ness. Sweat beaded on his forehead.

I can't break it. It's too big.

Seventy yards. Gair reached deeper into the Song. Maybe if he and Masen worked in concert they could crack it between them. Saints and angels, the thing was monstrous. Its sheer bulk pressed down on the air as the weaving supporting it pressed on his brain, its Song rolling over him as if to crush the breath from his lungs. Fifty yards. Running out of time.

If we can't smash it, can we steer it away from us? he asked.

We can try. To the west?

West.

Air-Song was needed now. Light as a breath at first, its power built quickly and Gair sent it against the leading stone. Forty yards; the stone's shadow swept across the melting snow, swing-ing towards the keep like a giant's fist. Soldiers swore; one of them started to pray in a quavering voice; a couple more broke and ran. At once Brandt's voice bellowed out, bawling at them to stand or he'd gut them himself.

Thirty yards. The air-Song screamed like storm winds, but the stone's course did not alter. Gair felt the sawing dissonance begin, the first lick of fear, and ruthlessly smashed it down. There simply was no time. Deeper into the Song he plunged. Nerves and muscles strained as if he were attempting to lever the rock away with main force. Tanith's colours joined the weave, adding her strength to theirs as Masen too redoubled his efforts. Head pounding *holy Goddess it hurts*. Twenty-five yards. Twenty. Gair screwed shut his eyes and braced his feet.

It's veering! There was a note of hope in Masen's thoughts.

Another push. Fifteen yards. Then ten. Gair gathered up every shred of power he had summoned.

Reinforce the shield!

Impact.

35

THE STAND

℘ℴ

Even though Gair had readied himself for it, the percussion still staggered him. Earth and dust bloomed in the air. Deadly splinters of stone flew overhead, whirring like partridges, and punched clean through the watchtowers' banners and clattered off the body of the keep itself into the bailey.

His shield groaned under the onslaught. Every bone, every shred of his muscle screamed, but the joyful music of the Song never faltered and the wall's ancient stones held. With a colossal shrug, he pushed back with all the force at his command.

After the shock of impact, the renewed pressure was enough to break the rock into several pieces. With hammers of air, Gair drove them back up the valley towards the other four approaching boulders. If the Nimrothi could use earth and air for a mangonel, so could he. The first fragment struck the nearest boulder squarely and it fractured along a natural fault. A shove with air-Song sent one half ploughing into the forested western slopes of the pass, filling the air with the crack and swish of falling trees and the smell of pitch-pine. The other reeled into the next nearest boulder and knocked it off course; before the Speakers could react, a final push from Masen sent it careering into a third. Both boomed apart.

Stone shards clattered off Gair's shield across the keep's curtain wall and tumbled harmlessly onto the earth, but the last boulder was looming ever closer and he had no missiles left to hurl at it. There was only one thing he could do.

'Ware below!' he yelled.

Soldiers took up the cry, green-uniformed figures running for cover in the lee of the parapet. From the corner of his eye he saw Tanith duck, then the boulder's shadow reached him and there was no more time. Gathering all the Song he held into a fist, he punched upwards as hard as he could into the belly of the rock.

Will met stone like a smith's hammer on forge-fresh steel, showering hot sparks into Gair's brain. He gasped. The boulder cracked with a thunderclap that shook the air then blew apart into a deadly rain.

Masen and Tanith dropped their weavings and flung the Song into a hasty shield overhead, but they were a fraction too late to stop all the debris. The Warlord reeled, clutching his forearm. A running soldier dropped in his tracks, the bloody hole torn through his throat pumping scarlet across his comrades' boots. Down in the bailey, stone shards shattered on the cobbles like dropped teacups, then the shield snapped into place.

Archers, crouched with their arms over their heads, cursed in disbelief at the broken stone that bounced and slid across the empty air above them. Fear-frozen faces melted into stunned gapes of relief as they looked for friends and found them safe. Thunderous noise became a booming, dust-choked silence broken only by the sobbing of the wounded and the fusillade of the last few fragments onto the cobbles.

Dissonance lanced through the Song in Gair's mind like crow-calls through a choir. Slowly he relaxed his grip, letting the potent music quieten, the wrong notes dissipate. He had survived the first barrage. Nothing had reached for him through the Song. Wiping a hand across his face, he peered over the parapet at the wall below.

Where fragments of rock had struck when the last boulder shattered, the limestone had spalled, the newly exposed surfaces bright and clean amongst the lichen of the old, but the blocks were intact. The gates had held, too, though what he could see of the timbers was gouged as if they'd held off a demented axeman. Jagged rocks littered the old road, and the scrub and grass to either side of it; if the boulders had struck the wall in one piece, the ancient defences would not have fared so well.

Nonetheless, like a Knight in the lists, Saardost had withstood the first course. Time to collect a fresh lance.

From behind the Speakers came a new rumbling. It rolled down the valley like the waves past Drumcarrick Head, the drumming of thousands of spear-butts on shields, pierced with whooping war cries, until the air itself trembled.

Breathless after his exertions, Masen showed his teeth. 'I think they enjoyed that.'

Gair grunted, watching the five women ranged across the road. Only the stirring of their furs and hair in the restless wind indicated that they weren't carved from stone themselves. They'd made their opening move. Now he had to puzzle out their next gambit.

'Goddess rot you, is that the best you can do? A few rocks?' Stone dust frosting his brushlike dark hair, Brandt shook his fist towards the cheering Nimrothi. 'Is that all you damned witches have to throw against us?'

'This is only the beginning,' said Aradhrim. 'Something to take the measure of us.'

Blood dripped freely from his left arm, despite his other hand clamped tightly above the wound. Tanith used her belt-knife to slit open his torn sleeve and examined the injury.

'Aye, well, they've learned we have teeth,' said Masen. 'I think next time we can expect them to serve us something with a mite more gristle.'

'But you held them off!' Brandt exclaimed.

'Barely,' said Gair. He was starting to sweat as the sun warmed the thin mountain air; he took off his cloak and slung it between two merlons, out of the way. 'Do you play chess, Commander?'

'A little, as a boy, but I fail to see the relevance—'

'You don't send your queen into the field in the first few moves. You send pawns, to force your opponent to commit his pieces. You harry his flanks with your lector, eat away at his defences. Then, when he is weakened and his king is exposed, your knights close in for the kill.'

'Attrition,' said Aradhrim. A Healing made him shiver and he nodded his thanks to Tanith. 'Those five women represent less than a third of the clans' full strength, Brandt. Imagine what they could do if they brought up eight of them, or ten. The odds are not in our favour.'

'I will help,' said Tanith, tucking her knife away. 'And Ailric, too.'

Masen chuckled. 'Bless your heart, lass, but you're the only Healer we have. There's bloody work ahead – we might need you to stitch us back together. We'll take Ailric if he's willing, though.'

Gair shot her a look. *Are you sure?*

'I'll ask him.' *Don't worry.*

He won't risk himself to save humans.

No, but I think he'd help to save himself. It's worth a try.

You'd speak to him, even after what he did? Tanith, please—

This is more important than me, Gair, she said gently. *What other choice do we have?*

With that, her colours drew away from him, and reached out for the Astolan.

He let her go. She was right. There *was* no other choice, whether he liked it or not. If Ailric could be persuaded to help, Gair would just have to swallow his animosity towards the fellow and keep it down. *But it doesn't mean I have to like the taste.*

Tanith touched his arm to catch his attention. 'Ailric's guarding his colours. I can't find them.'

'Sorchal's watching him. Ask him where he is.'

Her expression grew distant, then creased into a frown. 'I can't find Sorchal either. Wait, there's something—' Mounting horror dragged at her features, draining them of colour. 'He's hurt!'

Masen frowned. 'Ailric?'

'No, Sorchal. Down in the stables – he's barely conscious. I have to go!' Tanith hurried away, copper hair flying. Gair sent out a thought of his own, hunting for his friend's colours, and found only a smear, like smudged paint. Not dead, but not responding either, and reluctantly he let them go. There was nothing he could do from the battlements; it would be up to Tanith to tend him.

Brandt motioned to the nearest soldiers. 'You two, assist the lady.'

Shouldering their bows, they loped after her. Gair watched them catch up in the rock-strewn bailey, then precede her into the stables. He folded his arms to contain his anxiety. *Not another friend. Please, not Sorchal, too.*

'This is my fault,' he muttered. 'I should never have let Ailric out of my sight, damn him.'

'Sounds like I've missed something,' said Masen, but Gair barely heard him. All he could hear was his own heart, thudding loudly, painfully, in his chest.

Goddess help me, I keep getting my friends killed.

৩৩

The Speakers had come.

Teia lifted her hands from her ears as the last echoes of stone smashing on stone rolled away. Dust clouded the air. Fragments of whitewashed render dotted her blankets, her arms, and her magic buzzed within her like a broken hive in response to so much of the power being wielded nearby. Footsteps hurried past her little hutch of a room. Voices spoke crisply, calmly; the voices of skilled men doing what they had been trained to do. Faint in the distance, she heard the cries of wounded and felt sickened.

The Speakers had come and there were no iron men to stand

against them. No Knights, only a few hundred lightly armed soldiers and stone walls that already trembled at the powers ranged against them. They could not stand for long – already men were dying. Everything she had tried to do had been in vain.

Pulling her knees up to her chest, or as close as she could manage with her still-swollen womb distending her belly, she wrapped her arms around them and hid her face. All had come to ruin. Her parents, her sisters, doomed with the rest of her people – even her Lost Ones – by Ytha's arrogance. Her daughter gone, too, dead before she ever drew a breath.

Oh, Macha, I can't bear this. I thought I was doing the right thing, but all that's come of it is disaster. I don't know what to do any more. Help me, please!

But the Mother didn't answer. Bitter tears boiled through her lashes onto her cheeks. *Tell me what to do! Macha! Please!*

Only silence met her plea, a silence broken at last by a snuffling cough from the crib at the foot of her bed. Teia lifted her head. The cough became a cry, a thin, petulant sound. She winced and folded her arms over her head again to blot it out, but the crying grew louder.

'Stop it.'

Now it grew to a full-throated wail.

'Stop it!' A hot, hard bubble of emotion swelled in Teia's chest. Rising up, crushing her lungs into breathlessness. She bunched her fists and drove them into the mattress under her. 'Just stop it stop it stop it—'

The infant shrieked and Teia screamed back. *'Stop it!'*

Hinges squeaked as the door swung open behind her. Quick feet crunched over pieces of fallen plaster.

'There now, there now, it's all right. Come to me.'

It was Duncan's voice saying those soothing words, his hands rustling the blankets as he picked the child up. The crying stopped but Teia sobbed all the harder, with exhaustion and a dozen sour emotions she couldn't disentangle. That he was there to witness it only threw her further into the storm.

Weight settled on the foot of her bed and she flinched away, hiding the shame that burned in her face behind her arms.

'Go away.' Her voice was thick with tears.

'No,' he said calmly.

She dragged the back of one hand across her eyes as more tears welled. 'Please, Duncan. Just go.'

'I can't do that, Banfaíth.'

'Why not?'

'Because you need a friend.'

'Neve's my friend.'

'Neve's had no sleep worth a light for the last two days.'

True enough. Neve had been tireless; she deserved her rest. Teia pressed her face into her knees. Slowly her tears drained away and with them her strength. She leaned against the wall and let it hold her up.

'Why are you here, Duncan?'

'I was bringing a wounded man to the infirmary and I heard you cry out.'

She winced. Screaming at a baby; she had every right to feel ashamed. By the Eldest, her eyes were heavy. Heavy and sore and her weeping had so stuffed up her nose she couldn't breathe properly.

'This little one's hungry, I think.'

'I'm tired.'

'I know you are. Why don't you feed your son, then both of you can get some rest?'

She squinted at him through her disordered hair. Duncan sat on the edge of the bed, quite at ease with an infant cradled on his arm and suckling busily at the tip of his smallest finger.

'You've done that before.'

'Sor has three children,' he said, smiling down at the boy. 'My oldest sister has two more. I was an uncle by the time I was eight years old.' The smile flicked her way. 'I've probably changed more swaddling than you have.'

And that was true, too. Feeling suddenly foolish huddled against the wall like a little girl afraid of a scolding, she hitched herself up on her pillows.

'I don't think I'm ready to be a mother,' she said, and pushed her hair back from her face. Plaster fragments showered from it onto her shirt.

'Is any woman, the first time?' he asked. Wisdom and understanding from a man were the last things she had expected, and her ears began to burn. 'Ready?'

She sniffed, nodded. Carefully, Duncan laid the infant in her arms. Teia looked down at the red-faced, fist-waving bundle that had replaced her daughter. A stranger, with lightning-struck black hair and a querulous frown. The chief's son that she had known she would bear before ever she caught for a child.

Her hand hesitated on the buttons of her shirt, then firmly, resolutely, opened them one by one. It wasn't the boy's fault. He was Drwyn's get, yes, but he was also hers, and she would have the raising of him. He would not grow up in his father's image. She eased out her breast, and with only a little encouragement the tiny mouth latched on and began to suckle. Fresh tears rushed to Teia's eyes.

I will make him mine.

'There now, that's better, eh?' Duncan stroked the infant's head. Bending down, he grazed her forehead with a kiss. 'Banfaíth.'

He turned to leave, and she said, 'My name is Teia.'

∽

High overhead, pale against the blue sky, rode two moons. The dawn moon, barely a quarter full, was well past its zenith; the second, the wandering moon, sat between two peaks like a skull on a cairn and leered at her.

Watching them through the open tent flap, Ytha sighed. Still some hours to go before the trinity was complete and, as yet, the Empire's fortress was far from falling. The walls remained stubbornly strong, despite everything her Speakers had hurled against them. She turned to look down the valley. Shields gleamed over the stone, pearly as an oyster shell wedged in the neck of the pass. Beyond them, dimly, the shapes of men moved back and forth atop the walls.

Someone down there had the Talent – perhaps several someones. The faithless had brought their Speakers, maybe; they had stabbed their brothers in the past, they would do so again. A sneer tugged at her lip. House-dogs who had sacrificed their liberty for a warm fireside and a chain around their necks, barking at their master's command. Fools.

Still, it was a complication she could have done without. Their resistance was slowing the war band's advance, and she could not let that happen. It was time to tighten the noose.

'They are better defended than I had hoped,' she said. She kept her back to Drwyn so that he would not see the way her mouth twisted at the taste of the words.

The Chief of Chiefs grunted and slurped his ale. A sticky, gristly sound became a sharp snap as he wrenched another limb from the roasted fowl in his plate.

Ytha's eyes twitched closed. That was another good reason for keeping her back turned: she didn't have to watch him eat. Listening to it was bad enough. Seeing him chew, tongue pushing a wad of half-masticated meat and bread from one side of his mouth to the other, would have robbed her of any appetite for her own noon meal.

She opened her eyes again and fixed them on a point out beyond the smoke and stink of the camp. 'Apart from that minor difficulty, our plan proceeds as it should.'

Bone clattered onto plate behind her. 'The walls will break?'

'Eventually.'

'Before night falls?' A monstrous belch. 'You promised me the trinity moon would shine over our victory.'

'And so they shall, my chief.'

'The men become restless with all this waiting. Their spears are thirsty.'

She turned. Sprawled across a pile of cushions, Drwyn had half his hand in his mouth, picking something from between his teeth with a fingernail. Whatever it was it was obviously edible; he sucked it from his finger then wiped his greasy hands carelessly on his trews. Ytha suppressed a shudder.

'The men must learn to be patient.' *Just as you did, you oaf.* 'Great victories are not won in a matter of hours. Nothing of true value is ever obtained without a price.'

'My father used to say that. I think he got all his saws from you.'

She smiled thinly. 'I have been Speaker of the Crainnh for a very long time. I would be surprised if some of my wisdom had not rubbed off on him.'

Drwyn grinned into his ale cup then drained it in two swallows. Another eructation followed, of even greater volume than the last. The sour smell of beer rolled past Ytha's face.

'A shame his table manners did not rub off on you,' she said tartly, resisting the urge to wave the stench away. 'Be ready to ride within the hour. Now that the Empire's defenders are fully engaged, it is time we pressed them a little harder.'

'You mean to breach the walls?'

'My chief, I mean to bring them down around their ears.'

She smiled and Drwyn began to laugh.

36

THE SONG IN
THE STONE

಄

From the door to the keep's stables, Tanith was confronted by row after row of muscular rumps and swishing tails. It was a fusty, ill-lit place, roughly partitioned with unseasoned timber between the stone pillars supporting the roof. The air was thick with the odour of dung, pierced by the sharper reek of urine in the glistening channel that bisected the cobbled floor.

The two soldiers with her took down the lanterns that hung to either side of the door and began searching the stalls, one on each side. Tanith started down the centre, careful to keep her feet clear of the stream of waste. She could still sense Sorchal's colours, but they were worryingly weak. There was no time to lose.

A thought brought a glim into being at her shoulder as she passed out of the lamplight. It threw the horses' silhouettes across the walls, fantastically distorted. In the corner of her eye, ears stretched into horns, long equine heads became dragons rearing from the shadows. She shivered and pressed on.

Behind her, she heard the soldiers clapping hands on hides and muttering to the horses to get over as they moved from stall to stall. If Ailric had taken his mount, then the place to look first was surely the empty stalls at the far end. She quickened her pace, boots scuffing through the litter of wood-shavings from the animals' bedding, heart rapping on her ribs.

Beyond Aradhrim's big bay was a glossy black back and high-crested neck she recognised as belonging to Gair's *sulqa*, Shahe. Her own brown mare occupied the stall on the far side, looking around with a wisp of hay trailing from her mouth. Tanith gave her a pat as she passed. The next few stalls stood empty, freshly littered and with hay-nets hung ready, all the way to the far wall. No sign of Sorchal, and no sign of Ailric's horse, either.

Fear for Sorchal quivering in her breast, Tanith sought his colours again. Faint, but very close. He was somewhere in this space, no doubt about it. Up in the loft, perhaps? She glanced up at the crude post and rails that fenced the edge of the loft, the pillowy mounds of wood-shavings behind it, and her heart sank. He could suffocate amongst that before they found him.

On the other side, one of the soldiers raised his arm. 'My lady, over here!'

Oh, spirits, thank you!

She hurried across, the other trooper following with his lantern held high. Sorchal was sprawled on the floor of a recently used stall like a child's abandoned toy. Kneeling in the litter, the soldier turned him over. His eyes were closed, his mouth slack, and wood-shavings stained an ominous red clung to the side of his face.

'Had the wits knocked out of him, I think,' the soldier said, wiping the shavings away.

Tanith dropped to her knees beside him and laid her hand on Sorchal's brow. Drawing delicately on the Song, she sent her awareness into him. Dark, turbid colour surrounded her with a thick heat, like summer in Syfria. With her other hand, she felt carefully over his skull. Amongst the sticky blood matting his hair to his scalp she found a spongy area at the right temple. When she touched it, shards of pain stabbed into her awareness. Quickly she thumbed back Sorchal's eyelids. His right pupil was dilated and did not shrink when she willed her glim closer.

'His skull is fractured and he's bleeding beneath it,' she said. Cool, precise words; though her breath trembled in her lungs her fingers did not, carefully probing, assessing. 'I need a litter to take him to the infirmary, as quick as you can.'

The two soldiers left at the double. Heedless of the blood on her hands, Tanith stripped off her jacket and folded it under Sorchal's head to keep it as stable as possible whilst she delved him for other injuries. There was nothing more serious than bruises, spirits keep him, but the pressure on his brain from the bleeding meant she'd have to trephinate to relieve it.

She pursed her lips. Had Ailric done this? Struck Sorchal when he tried to prevent him leaving? She could hardly credit him with the capacity to do violence; he had never shown a sign of it, in all the years she had known him. But then he had never threatened her or used his strength against her, either, until that morning. How could she judge what Ailric was or was not capable of doing after that?

Gathering her Song, she placed her hands either side of Sorchal's head and dipped back into his flesh. Life still beat within him; slowly, greatly weakened, but alive nonetheless. If she could stop the bleeding, the pressure on his brain would get no worse, but time could still kill him. Head injuries such as his required prompt attention and she had no idea how long he'd been lying there in the stable's filth.

'Don't give up, Sorchal,' she murmured, though she knew he would not hear her, and added a silent prayer that the soldiers would return with a litter quickly. Then she reached out with her Healer's senses and searched for the source of the blood that was gradually crushing his brain from within.

Sorchal's alive, barely, she sent to Gair. *Ailric's gone.*

☙❧

'Ailric's gone?' Masen repeated, his face creased into a puzzled frown. 'Why?'

Gair shook his head. 'It's not my place to tell.'

Tanith hadn't asked him to keep the assault in confidence, but she hadn't wanted talk about it, either. It should be her choice whether to speak of what had happened between her and the man she'd once loved.

The frown deepened. 'Gair, you're not the easiest man to read but I can see there's more to this. What's happened?'

Gair hesitated, then excused himself to the Warlord and the commander and motioned the Gatekeeper a little way further along the wall to explain. He kept it brief, but from the way Masen's eyebrows rose he could guess at the conclusions forming in the other man's head.

'Please tell me she wasn't hurt!'

'Only bruises, but if she hadn't sent for help it might have got much worse. I had to draw steel on him before he let her go.'

'He hit her?'

'It was mostly verbal, but . . .' Gair left the sentence unfinished rather than reveal what was not his to tell. 'Ailric doesn't care for humans and he thinks Tanith cares for them too much.' Never mind the other things he'd said.

'I see.' Now Masen's comfortably battered face resembled less an old shoe than a bunched fist, knotted and scarred. 'I've known Tanith since she was a little bit of a girl, this tall.' He gestured vaguely at waist height. 'I knew her mother. I had a high opinion of Astolans until now.'

'That one's had my teeth on edge since the moment I met him.'

'Alderan said your instincts were sound. It looks like you were right.' The Gatekeeper sighed. 'And now the bastard's run rather than stand with us.'

'There was only a small chance that he would help, so we're no worse off without him.'

Casting a glance towards the massed clan war band, still waiting behind their Speakers, Masen grunted. 'Could have been a whole lot better.'

'We have to play the hand we're dealt. It's all we can do.'

'I know, lad, I know.' He sighed. 'Can't say I like it though.'

They turned and walked back to the others.

Grim-faced, Aradhrim stared over the wall into the valley. 'I do not care much for these odds,' he said, rubbing absently at the dried blood crusting his arm around the red-brown seam of a fresh scab. 'There must be some way we can shorten them. Is Tanith's kinsman able to help?'

'He's run.' Masen folded his arms across his chest with a finality that precluded any further questions. The Warlord looked from him to Gair and back again, green eyes puzzled.

'It's just the two of us, my lord,' Gair said. 'We'll do what we can.'

'Can you send for more *gaeden*?' Aradhrim asked.

'The nearest battle-trained Guardians are at King's Gate. Even if they could leave the pass undefended, they'd need at least a week to get here.'

'Could you hold until then?'

'With two of us?' Masen shook his head. 'We'll be lucky to last seven or eight hours, my lord, never mind seven or eight days.'

'There is a way we could tip the balance in our favour.' Brandt stuck out his jaw pugnaciously. 'We ride out against them. The Sixth has eighty light cavalry – that should be more than adequate to deal with five women.'

Gair had read enough histories of the Founding Wars to know that against five well-shielded Speakers, Brandt's eighty light cavalry would stand no chance at all.

'Huh,' Masen snorted. 'And swords and spears will be more effective against their shield than arrows were, will they?'

Above his high collar, Brandt's meaty jowls reddened. 'I resent your tone, sir.'

'And I—' With a visible effort, the Gatekeeper bit back whatever he'd been about to say. 'I think sending cavalry out would be a mistake. They'd be overwhelmed in minutes.'

'Don't you Guardians have some way of breaking down that shield?'

'If only it was that simple,' Gair said, as mildly as he could given the implicit insult in Brandt's words – or maybe it was only ignorance; he was hard-pressed to choose. Whichever it was, it touched off Masen's temper like a taper to a firework.

'By all the saints!' He rolled his eyes. 'This isn't a storybook, Brandt! There's no spell to recite and – poof! – obstacles disappear in a puff of purple smoke. *We Guardians*,' he said, with heavy emphasis, 'can either try to break the Speakers' shield or we can defend the keep against a further attack. Which would you prefer?'

'Gentlemen.' Aradhrim raised a hand. That one word was enough to silence the two men, though they continued to bristle and glower at each other like two tomcats in a locked room. 'The war band has the advantage of numbers,' he went on. 'We have the advantage of the keep. The only way this fortress will fall is if they force their way inside. I think it is safe to assume that the Speakers will continue to attack the walls and gates in order to effect a breach, so that is where we must defend ourselves.' He treated both men to a stern eye. 'Not against each other.'

'The Sixth will give a good account of themselves, my lord,' said Brandt stoutly. 'Have no fear of that.'

All the courage in the world wouldn't save the Sixth if the Nimrothi broke through the walls, Gair knew, and only he and Masen stood in the way of it. Maybe Tanith, too, if she could be spared from the infirmary. He glanced in the direction of the stables, wondering how Sorchal was faring, then dragged his attention back to the valley below. He couldn't allow himself to dwell on anything else now, no matter how much concern for his friends plucked at him. There was precious little time; he had to think of a way in which the Speakers' attacks could be stopped before it ran out altogether.

Behind the silent Speakers, secure beneath the iridescent haze of their shield, the war band waited. Here and there the sun glinted on some jewelled adornment or polished bit of gear. Their horses' manes lifted on the brisk mountain breeze; apart from a tossed head or a stamped foot, nothing else moved in the valley. Not even birds.

And then there was a quiver in the air. Barely perceptible, it would have been lost in the wind if not for the accompanying nettle-sting buzz across the back of Gair's mind.

'It's starting,' he said.

'I feel it.' Masen scrubbed his hands up and down his arms. 'Saints, it's building fast. Better get ready.'

Gair studied the five women. Nothing betrayed their intent, not a movement, not a sound, but the weight of their working settled over his senses like a storm cloud. All that was left unknown was where the lightning would strike.

Carefully, he let the Song rise up. It was turbulent in response to whatever the Speakers were weaving and foamed like white water in a narrow gorge. His nerves tingled. He'd held off the dissonance last time, let go before it broke his control, but he couldn't be sure he'd be able to do it again. The more Speakers there were, the longer their attack lasted, the more the risk grew.

No. He had to stay focused on the present, on what was happening now. Letting himself be distracted by what might happen would only weaken him.

The gates were the fortress's most vulnerable point. The curtain wall had straddled the pass for a thousand and some years, withstanding whatever wind and weather could bring to bear, but the gates were only newly made, and from unseasoned timber at that. Surely the Speakers would strike there to force the first chink in Saardost's armour.

It was the logical move to make. The proudest Knight could be brought down with a stiletto blade: at the armpit, the back of the knee. Into the throat behind the gorget. There were a dozen ways; more than a dozen, if you knew where to strike.

Faintly, a vibration trembled the stone beneath his feet. It paused, then came again, and he knew. 'They're going to attack the stones,' he said.

'So we shield the walls, like before,' said Masen, reaching for the Song.

'That's not what I meant. They're going to attack the foundations of the wall itself.'

'You sound very sure,' Aradhrim said, giving him an appraising look.

'I spent a long time studying the history of the Suvaeon, my lord. Battle plans, tactics, the whole business of warcraft.' The words came quickly now, spilling out as the certainty crystallised in his mind. 'Gwlach's war band came at the Knights like a wolf pack. No fixed divisions, no orderly lines of battle, and until the Knights learned to adapt, they were slaughtered. In those days, their armour was iron plate; it took two squires to arm a Knight for battle and a heavy destrier to carry him onto the field. If you brought down that horse he was all but helpless.'

'Like a beetle on its back.' Realisation lit up the Warlord's eyes. 'I see where your thoughts are leading. We are like those Knights, in that our strongest defence, the walls, is also our greatest weakness.'

'But Saardost's built on bedrock!' Brandt interjected. 'To destroy the foundations, they'd have to bring down the mountain.'

'I would not put it past them, Commander,' Aradhrim said. 'They have five potent Speakers there, and more than enough nerve to try it.'

'Damned sorcery.' The garrison commander harrumphed and tugged at his collar. 'A civilised enemy would use siege engines – at least I could spike them with fire-arrows!'

Gair pinched his brows. The weight of the weaving had grown

oppressive. Every moment that passed ground it down a little harder, squeezed more spiky, staccato notes from the Song inside him.

He was right, he was convinced of it. The Nimrothi had no experience of siege warfare, no aptitude for the construction of engines and battering rams. They made war on the run. Encircle, hamstring, then once their prey was helpless, overwhelm it. Unless the Speakers could be stopped, it would be over in minutes.

Now the weaving had taken on a sound all its own. A thin, discordant whine at the edge of hearing that made Gair want to shake his head, like a horse tormented by flies. The Song swelled inside him in response, and an idea formed in his mind.

Reaching out, he laid his hands on the nearest merlon and sent his awareness into it. Limestone, close-grained and dense. Not as obdurate as granite but it was harder to work than sandstone, and it was *old*. Old as the world, its origins hidden deeper in the past than the minds of men could go. This would not be easy.

The vibration had intensified, too. Even the soldiers were feeling it, looking anxiously around them. From somewhere beneath his feet came the faint, gritty creak of rock under immense stress.

'Gair?' Masen touched his arm. 'Look.'

Below in the valley, the Speakers had raised their staffs high.

Blood and stones.

'Get everyone down off the walls!' Gair exclaimed, and thrust his awareness into the fabric of the keep. Sergeants blew their whistles and men began to run, but already the Speakers' staffs were descending.

'It's too late,' said Masen. 'Grab on to something and pray!'

❧

The floor was trembling. Specks of broken plaster strewn across it quivered, then began to dance as the trembling intensified.

Teia sat up in bed, all drowsiness gone. Her skin prickled where

423

the hairs lifted under her clothing; the air fair hummed with power.

Macha preserve her, what on earth—

Even her bed began to judder, its joints and hinges squeaking as if under enormous stress. On the crate next to her, the lamp's glass chimney rattled against its brass body, and the whole thing slowly wandered towards the edge. She put out a hand to stop it and felt the vibrations travel up through her fingers, her arm, along the bones and into the music inside her.

Then the earth bucked and the chimney-glass tumbled over her restraining hand to shatter on the stone floor.

 infinity

The heels of the staffs met the road and the earth heaved. Trees thrashed and birds boiled into the air, chattering in alarm. The keep shook violently, tumbling men from their feet. Masen hit the worn cobbles hard and swore at a burst of pain in his left knee.

As the noise rolled away, the shuddering in the stone underfoot diminished. Ears ringing, wincing at the pain that accompanied putting any weight on his leg, he pulled himself up on the wall and looked across at Gair. The Leahn was still standing, his hands spread on the merlon before him, but his eyes were focused inwards on something only he could see. The only sign of any reaction to the impact was the faint frown that creased his brow, gleaming with a little sweat in spite of the breeze.

Reaching out a hand towards him brought the hair on Masen's arm bristling to attention. When he touched the Song for himself, he saw the bluish sparks that wept from the stone under the Leahn's hands and writhed around his boots. The scope of the weaving almost made him dizzy.

'Holy saints, you're working hard,' he muttered.

Another concussion through the keep almost threw Masen from his feet again. He grabbed the wall to steady himself, barking his other knee in the process, but again Gair didn't move. In some way, he had become one with the stone beneath his feet. Masen tried to study what he was doing, follow the tracery of earth-Song block by block out through the fabric of the wall, but could make no sense of it and let his power go. Whatever Gair was working, he couldn't see a way to help.

Somewhere off to the left, stone cracked. Hunched against the parapet, careful of his bruised knee, Masen looked in the direction of the sound. Broken masonry fell lazily away from the base of one of the bartizan towers on the keep's shoulder and tumbled through the air. In a puff of dust and old mortar, two more small blocks followed it. Another, louder crack, and the upper two-thirds of the structure slumped outwards.

'Clear the yard!' he shouted, at almost the same instant as Brandt.

Slowly, stone grating on stone, the tower leaned away from the wall and toppled into space. Whistles shrilled orders and boots pounded, but the massive weight of masonry plunged into its own well of silence until it crashed through an outbuilding in a welter of noise and splintered timber.

☙❧

The blocks for Saardost's great curtain wall had been cut so long ago that the music was almost gone, diminished to the merest shimmer in Gair's mind. Deep, dark and cool, starred with the whorls of ancient sea-creatures like a midnight sky.

Would it hear him if he called? Could it, after so long asleep? There was only one way to find out. With the music in him swelling to his will, he sought the Song in the stone.

Down, sinking through block after block. Lichen prickled over his skin. Tiny insects scuttled in the minute gaps between the stones; spiders waved their palps and stared eight-eyed as he moved through their webbed crevices. Deeper still, past the statues carved into the bastions that flanked the north gate, their feet chilled by the snow, until finally he touched the mountain itself.

Wake.

'Come—'

Masen's voice came from far away, took an age to articulate a single syllable.

He started to turn his head. *It's all right, Masen.*

Slowly, so slowly, he opened his arms and embraced the mountain's Song with his own. *Wake*, he breathed.

'—back—'

So still, yet every fibre of his being was wrenched up and to one side by the memory of the seismic convulsion that had raised the an-Archen from the rolling plain. It twisted him, contorted him, left him groaning with the monstrous pressures of the shifting earth.

'—you're—'

Fault-lines scored him like scars. Rivers carved ever-deeper channels through his flesh and hidden waters sounded in his caves like lifeblood through the chambers of his heart.

Hear me and wake.

'—not—'

No sound. Or rather, no sound he could hear, but he could feel it. It vibrated through the stone around him, a single note so deep and ancient that its first striking had been the birth-cry of the earth itself, and so long-lived that its last echo lay millennia ahead. How could he channel that music? How could he slow himself enough to even hear it?

'—breathing—'

But he was, he had to be: his lungs weren't burning, his head didn't pound. He must be breathing. *I'm fine.*

Grip on his shoulder. Squeezing, like a tree root around a pebble. Slowly. Wind blew over him. Clouds billowed across the sky, brought rain, blew away again.

And still the mountain sang to him.

ॐ

Masen threw the empty canteen back to the soldier he'd borrowed it from. Flinging its contents into the Leahn's face hadn't even made him blink. He stood with his hands spread on the weathered stone before him, water dripping from his nose and chin and his wet shirt snapping in the breeze. His grey eyes focused on a place deep inside himself. Tugging at his arm hadn't budged him. He was as immovable as one of the stone Knights who flanked the gates.

'Damn it, Gair!' *Tell me you can hear me.*

'What's happened?' the Warlord asked, turning away from his conversation with Brandt.

'He's lost in the Song, somehow. I can't reach him.' Masen dashed a hand over his face. 'I'm not even sure what he's doing.'

Green eyes flicked briefly towards the Speakers. 'Have they attacked him? Is he in danger?'

'I don't know.'

The quiver in the air had become almost audible again, a suggestion of far-away thunder, but when Masen touched the stone of the keep's wall he couldn't feel anything yet. It would come, though. The gathering immensity of the Speakers' working stung his awareness like thistles, made him want to scratch right through his scalp. It drowned out any sense of what Gair might be doing. The Leahn's weaving was huge, but as subtle as a breeze in comparison to the Speakers, who clenched the air in the valley like a storm about to break.

He peered again into the Leahn's face. 'At least, I don't think he's in any danger, beyond not taking a breath in five minutes.' *Come back, Gair. Tell me what's happening.*

The Leahn's colours shifted, infinitesimally slowly.

Can you hear me? Silence. *For the love of the saints, tell me you can hear me! Gair! I need you!*

Silence still, as empty and ringing as the mountain sky.

Muttering in frustration, Masen reached up and pressed two fingers under Gair's jaw. He felt no pulse but the flesh was firm, with no sign of the doughy slackness of death – quite apart from the fact that the lad was still standing on his feet.

Blood and stones, what was he doing? Then, with appalling certainty, Masen knew. 'You're calling the mountain,' he breathed. 'You stupid son of a—'

'Gatekeeper?'

'He's calling to the mountain itself, to its Song. He must be trying to bind the keep's stones to their foundations to help them resist the Speakers' attack.'

The Warlord frowned. 'Is that even possible? I've never heard tell of it, not even in old stories.'

'I'll ask him when he comes back.' *If he comes back.*

'Will it work?'

Masen raked his hands through his hair to the back of his neck and sighed gustily. 'Damned if I know,' he said, 'but if anyone can make it work, he can. It's the bravest, stubbornest, most *Leahn* thing I think I've ever seen.'

∞

Louder now. Ringing, chiming through the webs of quartz around him. Making the frozen seashells resonate like a tray of wine glasses in a thunderstorm. Like tiny bells, bright and clear.

Hear me.

And there it was. The Song in the stone surrounded him, permeated him. He felt it in the minerals in his bones, in the swirling currents of his blood. He was a part of it and the mountain was a part of him. When he flexed his shoulders, the rock groaned.

Hear me and remember.

37

RESOLVE

❦

All five Speakers looked up, their gazes focused on the ramparts where Masen and the others stood. They knew. They must be feeling Gair's working now, too, as surely as he could. Their conjoined will throbbed through the air, a sudden force gathering. Together, they raised their whitewood staffs and drove them down against the ground.

Earth heaved. A small landslip on the valley side showered rocks and soil across the remaining slush, sent stones bouncing onto the road. Trees slumped into the arms of their fellows and underfoot, the keep shuddered again. Loosened by previous impacts, blocks of heavy ashlar tumbled from the hole torn in the fortress's side by the falling bartizan and detonated like fireworks on the bailey cobbles.

From the west side of the fortress came more sounds of falling masonry, punctuated by a shrill scream, abruptly cut off. Masen flinched. Only the most abject terror could make a man's voice break that way.

Aradhrim strode past him with Brandt on his heels, calling for reports of damage and casualties. Then Masen felt it. Where his hands rested on the coping atop one of the merlons, heat flushed through the stone. Further along the wall, a soldier snatched his hands back and swore.

'It's hot!' the legionary exclaimed, rubbing his fingers together in disbelief. The nearest archers looked around them uneasily. Several shifted their feet as if expecting their boots to burst into flame.

'Don't worry, it won't burn you.' Masen raised his voice enough to carry, keeping it cheerful. The soldiers didn't appear convinced. He spat on the nearest merlon, and only when the spit failed to sizzle did the men begin to relax.

Again the Speakers raised their staffs and drove them into the ground. Again the earth convulsed, tree roots snapping, rocks cracking apart like walnut shells before the wave of power struck the keep's foundations with a thunderous boom.

The impact staggered every man along the great curtain wall and showered them with gobs of mud thrown up from the base of the walls. Human cries of alarm mingled with frantic whinnying from the stables. Across the bailey, the support posts on a lumber stack swayed and toppled, sending logs rolling across the cobbles. Brandt strode about barking orders to his sergeants, and soldiers scampered to do his bidding.

Masen looked back at Gair. The Leahn's frown had deepened and perspiration ran freely down his neck. Where his hands pressed the limestone, his knuckles had whitened. He was working harder still, but the keep's walls were holding as a result.

'Whatever you're doing,' he said, 'it looks like it's having an effect.'

A bugle blared a challenge from the south gate tower and he turned, wincing at the pain in his stiffening knee. Faintly, another trumpet blew answering blasts, two short, two long.

Aradhrim, returning along the wall, shaded his eyes against the noon sun and squinted across the bailey. 'That's an imperial signal,' he said, his tone brightening.

'Reinforcements?' Masen asked.

A uniformed figure appeared from the gatehouse and set off across the bailey at a run, dodging obstacles and working parties like a coursing-hound after a hare. As soon as the soldier was close enough to hear him the Warlord shouted down from the wall. 'What's the report?'

'Column approaching, sir,' the man yelled back. 'Identifying as the Ninth.'

Masen raised an eyebrow. 'You were expecting them to be held at Mesarild, as I recall.'

'I was sure they would be, but apparently Ysen has as little patience for damn-fool orders as I do.'

'I can't imagine the Emperor will be too happy with him – or you.'

'The Emperor's not here.' Green eyes flashing, Aradhrim bared his teeth. 'Quite frankly, Gatekeeper, at the minute, he can go whistle.'

ळ्

With fire and air, focused by her will, Tanith began to shave Sorchal's head. The stink of burning hair tickled at her nose, but in less than a minute it was done, his scalp bared in a neat arc from ear to midline, faster and closer than a barber could have managed with a razor. The army surgeon standing next to her said nothing, simply steadied her tray of instruments against the trembling transmitted through the floor. Kellin had seen her at work enough already not to be surprised by her gifts any more.

She selected a scalpel from the tray and quickly incised through skin and muscle to the pale bone beneath. As the flesh was retracted by the surgeon, the spidering fracture lines were revealed. What-ever the weapon, its impact had had the same effect on Sorchal's skull as a sharp rap on a boiled egg, but no shards of bone appeared to have been driven inwards far enough to penetrate the brain capsule. Good. Once she'd eased the pressure underneath, it would respond well to Healing.

Relieved, she discarded the bloody scalpel. 'Trephine, please.'

The instrument placed in her hand was still warm from being boiled. Carefully, she measured the distance above and behind the orbital process of Sorchal's skull with the last joint of her index finger and set the toothed head of the trephine in place. Then she held her breath.

Precision now was the key. Location, pressure, speed; everything mattered. Too fast or too heavy-handed and she risked penetrating the membrane that enclosed the brain, or worse, the precious matter itself. Too slow, and Sorchal would die. Closing her hand firmly around the brass T-piece, she began to turn it.

Steel teeth scraped and then bit, pinkish bone-fragments foaming up around them. The vibration coming through the floor worsened. Her discarded scalpel chattered against the tray it lay in; the tray itself started edging closer to the end of the table, but she couldn't spare any attention for it. Another turn, another rasp of steel on bone. She took a deep, careful breath. Kellin's big hands remained steady on the hooked retractors, but she heard him swallow, the click of his throat betraying his nervousness. Another turn. Then the whole world lurched.

Tanith snatched her hand away from the gleaming trephine as earth-Song boomed through her, echoing in every hollow space inside with the force of a thousand thunder-claps. The concussion flung her sideways over Sorchal's waist and she bruised her hip on the edge of the surgery table. His head lolled; one of the retractors slipped free as Kellin swayed on braced legs. Behind him, the door slipped its latch with a click and swung open, letting in the cries from the main ward outside.

At last the reverberations faded. The tray of instruments down by the patient's feet, teetering on the edge of the table, finally clattered onto the floor, shockingly loud in the sudden silence. Wincing, Tanith straightened up.

'You're all right?' Kellin asked. His big, blunt face was pale, one hand still holding a retractor in place, the other extended well away from his body where it couldn't damage the patient or touch anything unclean.

Tanith rubbed her sore hip with her elbow, careful to keep her hands elevated. 'Yes, I think so.'

'What was that?'

'The Speakers are attacking again.' She took another deep breath and huffed a tendril of hair out of her eyes. 'Let's get this done before they bring the roof down.'

∽

Shoes. That was the first thing to find. The last concussion had cracked the plaster in several places and left the floor resembling the Muiragh Mhor with all the dust and fragments, never mind the broken glass. Teia hitched herself along the bed away from it, then picked her way carefully through the plaster to her saddlebags, propped in the corner, and found her boots standing next to them. They didn't smell the best, but they were all she had.

Now, clothes. Her trews were gone, most likely pushed into a fire with a very long stick, and good riddance. The shirt she wore covered her decently enough to mid-thigh – though Ana would have disagreed – but it was too thin and alarmingly draughty around her nethers. She needed something more substantial.

She cast around the small room. Over by the washstand there was another folding stool with a pile of what looked like clothes on top. It turned out to be a couple more shirts and some trews made of the same green stuff as the soldiers' uniforms.

She held them against herself. Cut for a man, they'd fit her still-thick waist well enough but were far too long in the leg; she'd break her neck tripping over them. They'd have to be rolled up, but at least they were clean and warm.

Another concussion shook the floor and Teia steadied herself against the washstand. The discharge of so much power so close crawled over her skin and she shuddered. Inside, her own power

433

seethed like a pot on the boil. The baby grizzled unhappily and she shushed him, brushing fallen plaster off his bedding.

There was so much magic in the air around her that when she called a little fire to warm the water in the pitcher, bluish sparks crawled around her fingers. *So much power,* she thought, *and I brought it down on them. It's my fault.*

Quickly she stripped off her makeshift nightgown and washed, careful of her still-tender flesh. Tanith had Healed her after the birth, so the cut that had freed her son no longer stung, but muscle and membrane had endured much. She touched herself gingerly, then hurried on with her wash. There was no time to dwell on what was past, either.

Once the sweat and self-pity had been sluiced away, she dressed in her borrowed clothes and looked down at herself. Rolled-up trews flopped over her boots, held up by the size of her belly, with the oversized shirt belted around her middle over the top.

If she could have made a halter of some sort she would have felt more comfortable. With every step she took, her milk-heavy breasts swayed ponderously under the shirt. She dug her sealskin jerkin from her pack and put it on, but could only do up the lowest buttons. The rest simply wouldn't reach the holes, no matter how she hitched and squeezed. No doubt she looked ridiculous, but it would have to do.

In the crib, the baby slept once more, lulled by his full belly. She touched his cheek. So soft. Even his hayrick of dark hair was soft, unlike his father's. A pang of something sharp and fiery lanced through her.

I bore him a son, Dada, but I don't think he'd wed me now.

With a blanket from the bed carefully tented over the crib to keep falling plaster away from the child's face, he would be safe enough. She was reluctant to leave him, but didn't dare take him where she was going. At least here he was safe, with people nearby who would hear if he cried. Quietly, Teia eased up the latch and let herself out of her room.

Turning the trephine grew more difficult as the teeth engaged the denser bone that comprised the lower table of the skull. The muscles in Tanith's hand and forearm ached and tension dewed her forehead with perspiration. With every rotation, steel squeaked on bone and shot straight across her nerves. The humming resonance in her Song had diminished, but she kept half her mind alert for it building again. One more concussion like the last might be too much for Sorchal to survive.

Another turn, another squeak. The slightest change in resistance, and with a sticky sound blood began to well around the instrument. Purplish, venous, thick. A quarter-turn more and she could withdraw the trephine altogether, a neatly excised disc of bone held securely in its crown. More blood followed it, soaking into the thick swab that Kellin held ready.

'Neat,' he grunted. 'As neat a job as I ever saw. I half-expected you to magic it away.'

'I can't do that. Healing stopped the bleeding but it can't make all the blood that was already pooling disappear.'

She cast around for somewhere to put the trephine now that her soiled-instrument tray was on the floor and caught sight of a figure passing the surgery door. It had a tangle of brown hair and was dressed in ill-fitting clothes.

'Hold this,' she said to the surgeon. 'Let the blood drain, then we can close him up. I'll only be a moment.'

Quickly rinsing her hands in a basin, she hurried out into the ward, drying them on a towel. The figure was almost at the door.

'Teia?' Tanith called.

The Nimrothi girl gasped at being noticed and looked back over her shoulder. Shadows haunted her pale, pretty face, but couldn't hide her resolve. There was no sign of her child with her. Tanith spread her hands in a shrug to indicate a question, hoping it would be understood. With a helpless spread of her own hands, Teia nodded towards the door. She had to go.

Pressing her palms together, Tanith held her hands to her cheek and closed her eyes to mime sleep. So soon after giving birth, after that dreadful journey, the girl needed rest. When she opened her eyes again, Teia was shaking her head. No. Nodding again to the door, the Nimrothi girl laid her hand on the latch. She was determined.

For that, Tanith had no answer. Had she been in Teia's position, no doubt she would have acted no differently. She remembered hot words in a cool council chamber, the shocked and angry faces of the Ten when she'd defied them.

No, I would act no differently at all.

She folded her hands and nodded. Teia shot one last anxious look back towards the cubicle where she'd left her son.

'I will take care of him. May your gods go with you, Banfaíth,' Tanith said, though she knew she wouldn't be understood, and watched Teia slip out.

☯

Teia barely remembered the passage outside the infirmary. Half-seen through a haze of pain and exhaustion the afternoon before, it could have been any one of the passages Duncan had led her through after she arrived. They were all stone, all similar; only the number and shape of the doors varied.

She looked left, then right. Left, the corridor ended in a small door. To the right it led a short distance to an archway through which she glimpsed steps, lit by a single torch, curving up into the gloom.

Up. That was a sign, sure as elk-spoor in the earth. Up was the way to go; back into the air, where she could see the Speakers and the mess she had made instead of merely feeling it in the roiling magic inside her. If she could see them she could fix this, somehow. No more men would have to die. Not the Empire's people, not her people; none of them.

Ytha had to be stopped, no matter what it cost her. And it was her responsibility to do it.

Teia reached the steps and began to climb. The stair wound in a tight spiral, its gloom relieved only by slits in the curved outer wall once every rotation and torches at the entrance of each arched passage leading away into the keep. It had been built to accommodate the long strides of men; each step was made even more of a stretch by her aching muscles. By the third rotation her legs were trembling fit to fold under her and she had to stop to catch her breath.

Macha's mercy, she could hardly stand. She should have brought her staff to lean on. Reaching out, she steadied herself against the wall. The stone was warm, almost hot, and the hum of her magic inside her increased in pitch. She snatched her hand away again, rubbing her thumb and fingers together. How strange. Even in high summer the sun could not have warmed the stone that much. It should still have felt cool, not like the flank of a horse. Her fingers slowed. Not as if it was alive. Hesitantly, she laid her hand on the wall again and pressed her palm down flat.

Magic chimed, filling her mind with shimmering colours. They spread out around her, above her, vast as the starry fields of the sky at night, and oh, Macha, the *music*! It called to her, so clear and pure it drove her close to weeping. Teia's mouth fell open in astonishment. Then she heard the voice that threaded through it. A man's voice, rhythmic and oddly compelling. The words he used were unfamiliar, but when he spoke, the earth itself answered him.

☙❧

Remember.

The mountain's Song surrounded him, its single silent note ringing endlessly in his mind. It throbbed through every fibre of his being, from the tips of his fingers down to the marrow of his bones.

Once you were one. One stone. One strength. Remember that strength. Remember your Song.

Music struck up from the bedrock. Through the limestone blocks, up through his arms, into the place where his own Song lived, and burst into light.

Gair fell to his knees. It was vast, so vast it was scarcely comprehensible, and it was inside him. All thought was frozen. For one heartstopping second he was the spine of the world, before the weight, the sheer immensity of the Song he embraced overwhelmed him. And in the instant before his consciousness winked out, the beast's eyes opened.

ॐ

The Ninth Legion marched into Saardost Keep in good order, four men abreast. Their green uniforms were barrack-fresh, their boots spit-shined with barely a sign of dust from the road. Their officers, sitting their glossy horses in a knot by the keep's entrance, were immaculate.

'They don't look as if they just marched straight from Yelda,' Masen said.

'They don't even look as if they just marched from Fleet,' the Warlord mused. 'I must ask Ysen what his secret is.'

Clapping the Gatekeeper on the shoulder as he passed, he strode to the tower stair. A minute later he was loping across the bailey to greet the officer in charge.

A sleek-haired desertman dismounted from a lively chestnut horse with its quarters cross-combed into a striking chequerboard pattern. Masen grunted. Another toy soldier, no doubt, all bees-wax polish and no substance. He was too far away to hear what the fellow said as he stripped off his gloves to clasp hands with the Warlord, but he saw the formal clasp become squeezed shoulders and warm smiles. Old friends, then. Still no guarantee that he was any sort of a soldier.

Turning away, he looked at Gair. His shoulders had slumped as if he was having a hard time keeping them squared. Masen frowned. The lad's eyes were closed, too. Without warning, Gair's knees folded and Masen hobbled to catch him before he measured his length on the wall-walk.

'All right, I've got you, lad.' Wincing and cursing, he lowered Gair's dead weight to the cobbles, propped his shoulders against the parapet and hunkered next to him. His head drooped, eyelids fluttering, his breath coming in harsh gasps between slack lips. 'Can you hear me?'

Sibilance. Was that the start of a word?

Masen snapped his fingers in the direction of the nearest archer. 'I need some water, quickly now.'

A canteen was pushed into his hand. He flicked out the cork with his thumb and held the neck of the bottle to Gair's mouth, steadying his head with his other hand. The first mouthful spilled over the Leahn's chin, but then he tried to swallow and managed to get a little down his throat.

'Better?' Masen asked.

Unfocused eyes opened, blinked a time or two. Slowly, awareness returned from wherever it had been. Masen gave him some more water.

'You had me worried there.'

'It's huge,' Gair managed thickly.

'What is? What the hell happened?'

'The Song. I did it, Masen.'

'Did what? Saints, don't make me shake it out of you!'

Gair groped for the canteen and raised it to his lips. He drank deeply, savouring each mouthful as if it was the finest wine, then wiped his mouth with the back of his hand.

'I woke the mountain.'

Holy Mother Goddess and all Her angels. He'd actually

managed it. Despite the pain in his knee, Masen sat back on his heels in disbelief.

'The stones were quarried here, and they remember when they were part of it. It's deep and it's old and the Song is almost gone, but they remember. If the Speakers want to come through these walls they'll have to shake down the mountain itself to do it, at least for a while.'

'How long?'

'I'm not sure. Long enough to end this, anyway.'

Closing his eyes, Gair let his head fall back against the wall. Though the desert sun had browned his face, it did not entirely hide the sleepless shadows, the weariness that blurred the hard lines of his features.

'You need some rest, Gair. You're about ready to drop.'

'It's not over yet.'

'But you said—'

'I've strengthened the keep, but it won't stand for ever. The stones will go back to sleep eventually. We have to stop the Speakers before that happens.'

'So what are you proposing?'

Gair opened his eyes. 'We ride out.'

Slack-jawed, Masen stared at him. 'That's insane.'

'Brandt was right, in a way – I just didn't see it.' Gair hitched himself up and leaned his elbows on his bent knees. 'We have to meet them head-on. If we try to wait them out, they'll batter us into pieces. We can't last much longer, not just the two of us against that many. Especially not me.'

'You've been pushing yourself too hard. All that way up from Gimrael, then today – I told you, you need some rest.'

'It's not that.' The Leahn rubbed his hands over his face, blew out a long breath. 'I can't control the Song.'

Surely Masen had misheard. 'I don't understand. You just woke a bloody *mountain* with the Song and now you're telling me you can't control it?'

'Exactly.' Grey eyes met his with disarming honesty. 'Ever since the reiving, there's been something wrong with my gift. Lately, it's got worse. I can't always complete shape-shifts, and when I draw deeply on the Song it doesn't always obey me. If it slips away from me, people get hurt. Innocent people.'

Gair drank some more, rolling the water around his mouth before he swallowed, almost as if he was washing away the taste of the words. 'We have to end this now, whilst I still can.'

'Can't Tanith help you?'

'She was the one who told me the reiving couldn't be Healed, that I had to let it heal itself in its own time.' The Leahn smiled suddenly, sadly. 'It looks like that time's run out.'

'There must be something we can do. I can call up other *gaeden* to reinforce us. Barin and Eavin are at King's Gate, they could—'

Gair shook his head. 'They're too far away. We'd never last until they got here and you know it. We've already talked this out, Masen.'

'I know, I know.' Masen scrubbed his unshaven chin, hunting for something – anything – else to suggest and coming up dry. 'So what are you saying? We're done for?'

'Not yet. There's one move left on the board.'

'Which is?' He was almost afraid to hear the answer.

'Something a friend taught me, something you can do when all the other options have been taken away from you.' Gair pushed the cork back into the canteen and held it out. 'It's called a queen sacrifice.'

A chess move. In the right circumstances, it assured a win, or at least brought about the tactical or positional advantage from which a win could be played out. It also meant surrendering the most powerful piece on the board.

'You cannot expect me to let you do that. It's madness!'

'If that's what it takes to end this, it's a price worth paying. We can wait for them to crush us slowly, or we can take the initiative. Attack, instead of defend. It'll save more lives in the long run.'

Much as it pained Masen to admit it, the Leahn had a point. 'How?'

'We turn their weaving back on them. If we can call enough earth-Song just before they strike, make a shield of it in the earth, their weaving should rebound on them like a hammer off an anvil.'

'And I suppose you'll be the one to ride out there to do it?' Masen retorted.

'We've not got many other *gaeden* to choose from.'

He stuck out his chin. 'I could do it. I'm a fair hand with earth-Song. You could tell me what to do.'

'No, I can't.' Gair met Masen's gaze steadily. 'You're leading the Order now, Masen. Alderan told me I should help you – it was pretty much the last thing he said to me. This is the best way for me to do that. With you here, if it all goes to hell there'll still be someone on hand with enough reliable ability to cover the retreat.'

'Don't start talking like that – I don't want to hear it!'

'We have to be realistic, Masen. There's a good chance it won't work.' Stiffly, Gair got to his feet and glanced down at himself. 'Why is my shirt wet?'

'I threw a canteen of water over you.'

'I thought it was raining. Why?'

'To try to make you start breathing again.'

'I never stopped. I just slowed it right down.' A trace of amusement quirked the corners of Gair's mouth. 'Haven't you noticed how slowly mountains breathe?'

Masen pushed himself upright with a wince and tossed the canteen back to the archer to whom it belonged.

'You know, I've changed my mind,' he said. 'It's not your plan that's insane. It's you.'

38

QALEN AL JINN

പ്രൈ

'*Sayyar* Gair?'

The Gimraeli-accented voice was familiar enough to catch Gair's attention and he turned. Striding towards him, his hand outstretched in greeting, was a smiling desertman in immaculately cut imperial green, with the Warlord and the blocky figure of Brandt following along behind.

'The sun smiles on us both today, I think,' Ysen said.

Gair returned the man's clasp. 'I see you've survived – so far, anyway.'

'Does your decision still stand?'

'It does, I'm afraid.'

Aradhrim looked curiously from Gair to Ysen and back again.

'When we met outside Yelda, he wanted to buy my horse,' Gair explained.

Ysen beamed. 'And you would not sell her to me, but we parted as friends nonetheless.'

'You might not feel the same way when I ask if I can borrow your cavalry,' Gair said.

'You have thought of a plan?' Aradhrim asked.

'I think I can stop the Speakers, but I'm going to need some help to get close enough.'

'To do what?'

'Masen told you what I did to strengthen the walls?' The Warlord nodded. 'I can do something similar to the bedrock in front of the Speakers and turn their own power against them.' If it worked. No. It *had* to work; it was the only move left to end the game.

Puzzled, Ysen tipped his head to one side. 'Power? Forgive me, I have not understood.'

Masen jerked his head northwards in the direction of the five Speakers. 'What they're using against us. We're going to fight fire with fire – or rather Gair is.' He folded his arms, his glowering face more boot-like than ever. 'One last throw of the dice.'

The desertman's expression hardened, his black eyes unreadable as they fixed on Gair. 'Sorcery. Devils' work.'

'We call it the Song,' Gair said. 'It's the only weapon we have that can bring this siege to an end, and we need to end it quickly.'

'The Song.' Ysen repeated it slowly, savouring the phrase as if it tasted strange and he wasn't yet sure he liked it. 'When I was a boy, I saw a woman who made fire burn blue and white. My father told me afterwards that salts of copper and lead can change the colour of a flame, but he could never explain how she made it dance around her head. That was the Song?'

'Probably, yes.' Gair paused. 'If you want no part of it, *sayyar*, I will understand.'

Ysen nodded thoughtfully, lips pursed, then folded his hands behind his back and squared his shoulders. 'I have a full platoon of light cavalry, one hundred men.'

'Are they well rested? It'll be a hard charge into the pass.'

'We camped last night barely two miles from here.'

That was good news. If Gair was honest with himself, it was better than he could have hoped for, especially given Ysen's obvious reservations. He looked over at Brandt. 'And you said your legion has sixty or so, Commander?'

Frowning, Brandt gave a curt nod. 'Eighty, all told, but I thought the idea of riding out had been discounted.'

'At the time, it wasn't the right move.' Now it was the only one with any chance of removing the Speakers from the field. Gair turned back to the Warlord. 'How many men in Duncan's ride, my lord? Magda's, too, if you can spare them.'

'With Sor's as well, close to a hundred.' Aradhrim clicked his tongue against his teeth. 'It's risky. If you engage their warriors hand to hand, you'll be overrun.'

'If all goes well, I'll only need a few minutes.'

Shading his eyes with his hand, Ysen studied the rock-strewn pass.

'Narrow,' he mused, 'and the terrain is not good for horses. In such a place, only a few hundred at a time can bring spears to bear, no matter how many the enemy has.'

'And it only takes one spear through the guts to kill you,' Masen muttered sourly, not quite under his breath.

'It's the only way,' Gair said. 'This has to be done, and the sooner the better.' He didn't elaborate on the reasons why. As long as Masen knew, that was enough – except the Gatekeeper did not look convinced, turning away with a snort.

Brandt drew breath to speak but before he could open his mouth, Gair appealed to Aradhrim. 'We've run out of other options, my lord. I've shored up the walls for now, but the Speakers outnumber us. Whatever we do, eventually they'll pound the keep into dust.'

He watched the clansman consider it. If he had the Warlord's agreement, the Commander's objections wouldn't matter. Actually, none of it mattered – there was no other choice. Darin had shown him that, all those months ago. Sometimes you had to gamble everything you had.

Aradhrim glanced at Ysen, eyebrows raised in a question. The desertman nodded. 'It is feasible.'

The Warlord clapped his hands together. 'Then so be it. Brandt, assemble the men.'

Finally, the garrison commander boiled over. 'This is madness,' he snapped. 'You'll get my men slaughtered, Guardian!'

'It's no worse than you suggested,' Gair said mildly.

'That was before I saw their foul sorceries at work.' The Commander stabbed a finger towards the Speakers. Some of his bulldog pugnacity had leaked away, replaced by horror. 'You cannot ask me to expose my men to such . . . deviltry!'

Given the choice, Gair wouldn't have asked anyone to ride out with him, but choice was a luxury he did not have. 'So ask for volunteers, then. No man rides unless he's willing.'

Neck reddening above his tight uniform collar, Brandt bristled. 'My lord, I must protest!' he spluttered.

Aradhrim laid a hand on his arm. 'The decision's made, Brandt,' he said. 'Form up the horse and get Sor to roust his clansmen. Ysen was a cavalry captain – he can lead, since the Ninth is providing the bulk of the men. And that's final.'

Masen pushed past the commander to Gair's side.

'I'll go with you.'

'And then who's going to shield the keep if we fail? Sorchal has no talent for it. Tanith, maybe?' Gair shook his head. 'No, Masen. You're the Guardian of the Veil now. You're too important to risk.'

Thunder-faced, Masen cocked his hands on his hips. 'And what about you? You think *you're* not important? You're the strongest talent we've had in decades!'

'Then I think that makes me the best man for the job, don't you?' Gair tried to keep his tone light, but Masen shook his head in disgust.

'They say the Goddess watches over madmen,' he said. 'I pray She's watching over you.' Then he turned and limped away.

'*Qalen al jinn.*' Ysen chuckled. 'Dragon-hearted indeed. I knew I liked you, Gair. Now I understand why.' He bowed. 'You have my sword, *sayyar*, as God has my soul.'

℘

The great wall was dotted with men in green. Archers with bows on their shoulders, sentries atop the towers where banners snapped in the fresh breeze bustling down from the north. Teia watched them from the safety of the tower arch, where she could not see what lay beyond the wall, and wondered how their souls did not freeze in terror.

In the mountains, great heights did not perturb her. The mountains were Aedon's work, perfect and unchanging; they would hold her up for as long as she chose to walk upon them. She could stand at the mouth of the Crainnh's winter caves naked to the wind and never fear that she would fall. But this place called Saardost had been built by the hand of man, and surely only the Eldest could have the power to raise stone so high and keep it there.

Macha's ears, her heart was racing so fast it made her dizzy. The bright sky skewed and wavered before her eyes; she shut them tight, but even the ruddy dimness behind her eyelids throbbed with her pulse. Sweat broke on the palms of her hands where they gripped the carved stone arch and her clothes prickled on her overheated skin.

I can't do this! Panic beat its wings in her ears. *I can't!*

But she had to. She had taken the task upon herself, because there was no one else to take it.

Teia opened her eyes again, focused on the irregularly shaped stones underfoot. Perhaps if she didn't look up, and stayed close to the inner wall, where the drop into the wide yard was merely daunting, she wouldn't be aware of the great void of the pass on the far side. Perhaps.

Nauseated by fear, she took a step out into the sunshine. Then another, and moved beyond the shelter of the fortress onto the great wall itself. A gust of wind snatched at her and she stopped, stifling a whimper. Another step, then two more in a rush and she was shuddering against the massive stones of the inner wall.

Oh, by the Eldest, who had she tried to fool? No matter what she did, she could sense the open valley sucking at her like the black maw of her prescience. Eyes screwed shut again, she pressed her forehead to the rough, cold stone. She would not look; she didn't dare, no matter how the void called to her.

Someone touched her arm, said words she didn't understand. Looking up through her windblown hair, Teia saw a soldier stooping to meet her gaze. Sour breath, battered nose, but kindly brown eyes. He spoke again and she scrambled away from him, realising only too late that she was moving further out onto the wall. Shrugging, the soldier called something after her and went back to his post.

The wind was stronger out there, tugging at her clothes. She clung to the stones and wished for Duncan, with his strong arm to lean on. But Duncan had duties of his own, elsewhere in the fortress; she couldn't expect him to hold her safe every time the wind blew. Teia dashed the back of her hand across her eyes. She had to do this herself. Step by step, hand over hand on the stones, she edged out along the wall.

At the first bastion, she stopped to marshal her courage. Her heart still pounded, her breath still came in short gasps, but when she stole a glance over her shoulder and saw how far she had come, it strengthened her. Almost a third of the way. One more bastion and she would be almost to the midpoint of the pass.

Holding tight to the stones, she dared a glance ahead. The next stretch of wall was horribly exposed. More wind, more men in green who glanced her way, idly curious. Whistles and shouts from down in the yard, torn by the fitful breeze. Clattering hooves, men laughing. Cheerful insults in the rolling Arennorian tongue that was so like her own. It could have been Teir joking with his men in the war band; she started to look, then had to snatch her gaze back to the stone between her hands when the drop yawned dizzyingly beneath her. No. Don't look down, or she'd fall for sure. *Oh, Macha!*

Swallowing hard, she crept away from the bastion and the soldiers' stares. She kept her eyes on the cobbles, just far enough ahead that she wouldn't blunder into anyone. Fitful gusts of wind kept pushing her hair across her face; she lifted a hand to hold it back and saw how far still remained to go, the wall narrowing alarmingly in her sight. The open pass to her left tugged at her eye.

Don't look. Dread shoved its fist up into her throat and made every breath a wheeze. She snatched her gaze down again. *Don't look.*

Tiny steps, like an infant tottering at its mother's side. Tiny steps, with her tongue cleaving stickily to the roof of her mouth and her heart thumping like a smith's hammer, but she made them, one after another, and moved further away from the shelter of the fortress.

Out in the middle of the wall, a group of men stood with the Warlord. Some were in green, with swords on their hips and gold and silver winking from their coats. Two other men, dressed in everyday clothes, appeared by their posture to be arguing. The one facing her was dark and sturdy, the other toweringly tall, with sand-coloured hair swept into a horse-tail and a long-hilted sword slung across his back. She didn't recognise either of them, but when she looked at them the magic stirred inside her. Did they have the Talent, then? Was it one of their voices she'd heard in the stone?

It still bewildered her that men could be gifted in the ways of Speakers. Everything she had been taught connected those powers to the feminine, to tides and moons and blood. But with her own ears she had heard the sound of a man singing through the stones to the mountain beneath this ancient place. She had felt his power resonate with her own. What other explanation could there be but that what she had been taught was not the whole truth?

Shaking his head as if he'd lost the debate, the brown-haired man limped away. The taller fellow glanced after him; the way his straight, level brows shaded his eyes gave him the look of a hawk – no, more stern, with that long nose: an eagle. Prescience yawned, filling her mind with the dusty rustle of feathers. Not raven plumes this time, but bright eagle feathers in russet and gold, and great sweeping wings wreathed the face she now recognised from the blood scrying.

Staggered by the sudden clarity of the image, she stumbled over her own feet and landed hard on her hands and knees. The wings in her head beat once, twice, and surrounded her with the sounds of battle. Screaming horses, the clash of steel on steel. A thunderous sky loured overhead, underlit with sullen lightning, as weapons swung and blood flew.

The sandy-haired man sat astride a black horse, his sword above his head as he urged men forward into the baying jaws of war. Blood streaked his face and leather coat, and cords stood out in his neck as he roared defiance at an unseen foe. Then he spurred his mount on and the battle swallowed him. With a peal of thunder, the storm broke and her vision turned to darkness.

∞

Two soldiers shambled into the infirmary, carrying a third man slung between them on a blanket. Masonry dust crusted his torn and bloodied uniform and his hands were balled into fists.

'Bring him through here,' said Tanith, gesturing into the screened-off surgery area. 'What happened?'

'He was hit when the bartizan came down,' said the older of the two. 'Had to dig him out. This'll hurt, son,' he added to the wounded man, and they heaved him up onto the scrubbed table. He screamed a curse; the right leg of his uniform trousers was a bloody mess, the limb itself flopping sideways, rotating around what was clearly an ugly break mid-thigh.

Kellin, the army surgeon, soaping his forearms and hands in a basin of hot water, caught Tanith's eye as the legionaries trooped out. He raised his brows and glanced towards the gleaming steel boiler, grumbling over its bellyful of instruments. Tanith shook her head. Amputation shouldn't be necessary, but if it was, she'd use a gentler tool than a saw.

She bent over the injured man. He was breathing fast, but strong. His uniform was well bloodied but she saw no bright arterial pulsing, and when asked his name he answered lucidly.

'Beck. Tomas Beck, third platoon.'

He had blue eyes, fearful and shadowed with pain – blue as those of the man she'd saved and lost beyond the runestones, she realised, with a sudden twist of sorrow.

'All is well, Tomas. I'm going to do something about the pain first, to make you comfortable, then I'll see to your leg.'

He grabbed her arm. Fresh sweat cut trails through the dirt on his face.

'Please, don't take it off,' he whispered fiercely. His eyes rolled from her to the surgeon across the room, lifting instruments from the boiler with tongs and laying them out on a tray. Steel glittered and steamed. 'Promise me!'

'I'll do what I can.'

His grip tightened, dusty fingers digging into her golden skin. 'Don't take my leg!'

'Shush now, Tomas.' She smiled and laid her other hand across his forehead. 'Shh.'

The Song came willingly and spilled into him through her touch. His eyes widened in surprise, then drifted closed. The grip on her arm eased and his hand dropped onto the table as limp as a boned fish.

With the assistance of the surgeon and a pair of shears, she stripped Beck of his clothes and boots. He was cut and battered from head to foot, but his right thigh was a mess. Skin abraded raw in places, bruises already blooming. The degree of swelling and deformity said the broken thigh bone was badly displaced, but by some small miracle it hadn't pierced the skin. That made infection less of a worry, though there was still a risk the bone wouldn't take, no matter what she did.

Gathering the Song again, she plunged her senses into the torn muscle, seeking the bone fragments and visualising their positions in the patterns of pain she saw in her mind.

'I can save this,' she murmured, then to the surgeon, 'Take his foot and straighten the ankle.'

He did as she asked, meaty hands surprisingly gentle. She laid her own hands either side of Beck's thigh, aligning them carefully, mapping the normal positions of muscle and bone in her mind.

'Now pull slowly. Straight and steady – I need some traction on the limb to realign the fracture.'

Under her hands she felt the bone shift. Beck groaned, but didn't stir. Good; the last thing she needed was the patient to start thrashing with the pain. A little more. The jagged edges of the fracture grated together, sending arpeggios of hurt shrieking through the Song.

'Almost there.'

She tightened her grip, fingers digging into Beck's flesh to immobilise the upper end of the bone as the lower retreated. Fresh blood leaked from his various cuts at the hard handling, trickling around her fingers, but the hideously distorted shape of his thigh had begun to straighten.

'Hard work,' grunted the surgeon. She glanced at him; his face was flushed, brow furrowed in concentration.

'The last part's the hardest,' she said. 'Just a little more.'

And then it was done. The bruised muscle yielded enough to let her seat the faces of the fracture together, and she wrapped them immediately in the warmth of her power. 'That's it.'

Concentrating, she reached deep into the patient's own Song, smoothing out the pain, soothing the clangour of ravaged nerves and coaxing the Healing to begin. Several minor cuts were bleeding freely now, reopened by the traction and her manipulation of the broken bone, but that was a small thing, easily dealt with. What was important was that the limb had been saved. With rest and care her patient would walk, ride, even dance again.

The surgeon approached from the foot of the table and peered at Beck's bloody thigh, already darkening with bruises, but straight.

'Good work,' he said, with an approving nod. Then he caught sight of something over her shoulder at the door. 'Someone to see you, I think.'

She looked around. Waiting in the doorway was Masen, favouring his left leg, with his trousers sporting a bloody rip and his face like thunder.

'One moment,' she told him, crossing the room to rinse the blood from her fingers. To the surgeon, she said, 'Once that leg's immobilised, he can be moved to the ward. I'll check on him later.'

Drying her hands, she went to the door. 'Now don't tell me you fell off the wall.'

Masen flashed her a tight grimace. 'Nothing so dramatic, I'm afraid. I bashed my knee in the last attack.'

'Come in and I'll take care of it.'

She steered him to a camp stool by the wall and he sat down, wincing as he straightened his injured leg out in front of him. Tanith knelt down and tore the rip in his pants leg wider. His knee was ruddy-purple and already puffy, oozing blood from a ragged scrape. Above it, an old scar disappeared up his thigh, twisting through the dense black hairs like a road through a forest. Carefully, she felt around the swelling, her Song probing the tissues underneath.

'Nothing appears to be broken,' she murmured as she worked, 'but I bet it hurts.'

'Some,' said Masen through gritted teeth.

His knee had been subjected to a lateral, twisting force; there was a tear to the rearmost ligament. She could Heal it, but he'd need to keep his weight off it for several days to avoid destabilising the joint.

'You're like a daughter to me, you know that, don't you?'

She smiled, still focused on her work. 'Of course I do. You've been welcome at the White Court all my life – you used to bring me presents when I was small.'

'What I've got to bring you now's not much of a gift.'

She looked up. Masen's face was lined with pain, but not the kind that came from physical harm. This was soul-pain, which neither drugs nor Healing could touch. She saw it in his eyes, beyond the reflection of her own suddenly pale face.

A cold knot formed in the pit of her stomach. 'What's happened?'

He took a deep breath. 'Gair means to take on the Speakers face to face.'

Dear spirits, no.

Gently, Masen took her hands in his. 'The Warlord's assembling a small force to clear a path for him. They ride out within the hour.' He paused. 'Did he tell you? That he can't control the Song any more?'

'Some of it.' Her mind filled with images of Gair tumbling through a dozen shapes, unable to hold any of them for more than a moment. Of great wings and a bowed head. *I'm scared.*

The weaving she had begun for Masen's knee slipped away.

'The reiving . . . it scarred him in ways I couldn't Heal.' *And in ways he won't even let me try to.* Her vision blurred.

'He told me what he's planning. I tried to talk him out of it, to let me go instead, but he wouldn't have it. And he's right, damn it.' Masen's voice caught, snagged on the barbs of an uncomfortable truth. 'This is the only way, and he's the only one of us who's strong enough to make it work, but it's going to take everything he's got.'

'Everything?' she echoed, horrified at what that might mean. Masen looked pained.

'Maybe.'

'Tell me the truth, Masen!'

His shoulders lifted. 'I honestly don't know. It all depends whether he can hold on to the Song long enough, but he sounded resigned to the possibility that he might not come through it.'

Tanith looked down at her hands, smeared with scarlet from the Gatekeeper's injury, but all she could see was other blood, pools of it, staining Chapterhouse's milky stone, from wounds she'd been unable to do anything to staunch.

'The beast,' she murmured. Tears thickened her throat, threatened to close it up altogether. She swallowed them down but they rose again, burning at the back of her eyes. 'That's what he calls it, what he's afraid he's going to become when he finally loses his grip.'

Masen pulled her into a bear-like hug, engulfing her in warmth and comfort. 'I'm sorry, lass, but I thought you should be told.'

So he knew, had read her feelings as if they were written on her face. 'Is it so obvious?'

'Only to those of us who know you.' He kissed her cheek. 'He's a good lad, from what I've seen. You could do a lot worse.'

She bit her lip. Assuming Gair survived. Assuming the effort of working the Song didn't break his mind completely. No. She couldn't accept that, wouldn't; he was too strong. He could hold on, defeat the beast one more time. Couldn't he?

'My father would never approve.'

'Meh, fathers never think any man is good enough for their daughters.' Masen patted her back, then eased her away to arm's length. 'Go on,' he said. 'This knee of mine will keep.'

Dread and fear and hope all roiled together inside her like soup on the boil. Her heart hammered so fast that all she wanted to do was run, as fast as she could. She pushed herself to her feet.

'Are you sure?'

'I'm sure.' He winked. 'Love shouldn't be kept waiting at the door. There's no knowing if it'll call again.'

39

INTO BATTLE

༄

Shahe stood quietly as Gair checked her harness, ensuring all her buckles were secure and nothing pinched or rubbed that might make her shy at a crucial moment. A bronze-rimmed bullhide shield borrowed from one of Duncan's men hung from her saddle, and Brandt's armourer had found him a gambeson in the garrison's stores that just about fitted, though he suspected the seams would chafe him raw under his arms before he was done. At the cost of a little freedom of movement, the thick layers of horsehair, wool and silk wadded beneath the leather would provide him with some protection, even against arrows, but Shahe would have nothing to defend her except her speed.

'So best be fast, eh?' he murmured to her. Dark eyes gazed back at him, fringed with the sweep-the-desert lashes so characteristic of *sulqa*, and he stroked her face. 'I'll try not to get you killed.'

It was surely foolish to be sentimental over a horse, but he couldn't help it. Shahe had become more than just a mount to carry him over the miles; truth told, she'd been more than that from the moment he'd laid eyes on her in the stable-yard at N'ril's house in Zhiman-dar. She butted his chest and he smiled, patting her neck. He would be sorry to let her go.

A dull concussion struck the Song inside him through the buzz of the Speakers' weaving. Someone shouted a warning down from the wall, repeated by the sentries at each watchtower, and Gair spread his feet ready for the impact. When it came the cobbles shuddered underfoot, making Shahe dance, but no more masonry fell, not even from the damaged bartizan. The Song he'd woken in the stone was holding, for now. How long it would continue to do so was another question entirely.

Around him the bailey was filling with horsemen. The number of volunteers had been higher than he'd expected; he'd thought to get maybe one in three, but nearly all of the clansmen had turned out, along with a good half of the imperial cavalry, judging by the forest of green-pennoned spears. Some two hundred men and their animals, thickening the air with the smells of sweat and horse.

On one side of the yard, the clansmen sat their mounts easily, round shields on their arms and short spears ready. Compared to the crisp lines of the imperial horse across the yard from them they looked undisciplined, but their jokes and banter did not disguise the steady-eyed assurance with which they handled themselves. They were every bit as ready, every bit as determined as the serving soldiers. Every bit as prepared to die if Slaine called their name.

And if the Goddess calls mine?

Gair's hand slowed on Shahe's satiny hide, then stopped. He was a liability now, a danger to those around him. The brigands on the road north had taught him that. Each time he touched the Song the beast's claws sank a little deeper into him, dragged him a little closer to its jaws, and it was more difficult to fight free. Tanith had been there for him when he'd been caught between shapes. Only unconsciousness had saved him when he called to the mountain. He'd not be that lucky again.

No, there was only one path left to walk, whatever Maera had said. He understood the choices now. The beast would have him regardless; the only question was when. Either he lived in fear of it for however long remained to him, or he made a stand now, whilst he still could, and maybe it would make a difference to this battle.

The mare lifted her head, ears pricked at something behind him. Checks complete, Gair gave her one last pat and turned around.

Tanith was standing in the keep doorway, her hands gripping the edges of the frame on either side of her as if she'd been arrested in flight. Her face was pale, and at once he feared the worst.

'Tanith?' He dropped the reins and hurried up the steps to where she stood. 'Is everything all right? How's Sorchal?'

'He's sleeping,' she said. 'I had to bore a hole in his skull to relieve the bleeding, but he'll mend. I'll know more when he wakes up.'

Wisps of copper hair blew around her face on the fitful breeze and she lifted a hand to push them back. Her fingers were trembling. Gair's relief about Sorchal's condition faded.

'What's wrong? Has Ailric said something?'

'I haven't heard a word from him.' As if realising they'd betrayed her, she tucked her hands away beneath folded arms. 'I'm tired, that's all.'

A quick smile, there and gone, not really convincing, and she didn't hold his eye. Something *was* wrong, and badly so.

Gair touched her arm, felt the tremor in her muscles through her shirt. 'You're shivering. Please, what's the matter?'

She looked past him, gaze roving restlessly over the assembled cavalry. 'So few,' she murmured. 'Masen told me what you're going to do. Is there really no other way?'

'Not that I can see. The Speakers are the real threat, not the war band. If I can't go through their shield, maybe I can go under it and use their own gifts against them.' He searched for a way to explain, to make her understand. 'I have to do this, Tanith. I won't shy from a fight if I can help turn it the right way. I can't.'

'You never have. Not at Chapterhouse, not in Gimrael. It's the way you're made.'

459

Alderan had said much the same thing, back in the Daughter-house infirmary, when he'd told him he was a Knight in his heart as true as any who'd stood vigil for his spurs. Gair had never considered it in such terms; it was simply the right thing to do. To have the capacity to bring about an end to this battle was to have the responsibility to see it done. There was no more and no less to it than that.

'I'll be careful,' he said.

A single tear spilled over her lashes, raced down her cheek. 'I'm not sure you know how to be careful any more.'

'That's not true.' Not knowing what else to do to comfort her, he folded her into his arms. 'Please, don't cry.'

He stroked her hair, the copper curls coiling around his fingers like something alive. They smelled of the wildwood, and growing things, a world away from stone and steel and war.

'I will be careful,' he said again. 'I promise.'

'And what if the beast wakes? What then, Gair?' Her voice was muffled in his gambeson, thick with more tears.

He'd been trying not to think of that. 'If it happens, it happens. Stopping the Speakers is more important.'

'No matter what it costs?'

Oh, Goddess. 'Sometimes the price is worth paying.' He kissed the crown of her head, an uncomfortable weight pressing on his lungs. 'You know what's at stake here. There's no Corlainn Fellbane to throw a wall of iron in front of the clans this time.'

'There's only you.' She fingered the lacing of his gambeson. 'And you haven't even got any proper armour.'

'The legion only have mail shirts, and there wasn't a spare one that would fit me. This was the best the Sixth's armourer could do.'

Gently, he lifted her chin and wiped the tear-trail from her cheek with his thumb. 'I'm not a hero like Corlainn, Tanith. I'm not even a Knight, but if I can make a difference in this battle, then I have to do this. No matter what it costs.'

She tried to smile. 'To hear Alderan tell it, Fellbane was just a man doing what had to be done, too. I think you have more in common with him than you realise.'

A slow clench through the Song said the Speakers were drawing in their power again. There was no more time.

'It's starting.' He hesitated, reluctant to give farewell a shape by putting words around it and making it real. 'I don't know how much longer the walls will hold.'

'Then you should go.'

Lifting herself on her toes, she kissed his cheek. Someone cheered, and several clansmen drummed their spear-butts on their shields. She ducked her head, cheeks suddenly rosy.

'For luck,' she said and backed out of his arms, towards the door. For a second she hesitated on the threshold and looked over her shoulder, luminously beautiful, tears still shining in her eyes.

Come back to me, she whispered.

I'll try. It was all he could say.

Then she was gone, closing the door behind her, leaving Gair alone on the steps with only a breath of her wildflower scent to take with him.

Coming back wasn't his first consideration. It couldn't be – if he was to have any chance of defeating the Speakers, he had to commit to his task absolutely, with no thought for what might come after. Nonetheless he couldn't shake the thought that if somehow he did survive, he'd need Tanith more than ever.

He descended the steps to where he'd left Shahe and mounted up. Familiar figures were waiting by the gates: Duncan, saying something to Magda that made the ride-captain flash her broken-toothed smile, and Ysen, with his immaculate uniform tunic still buttoned to the neck, but now the officer's sash around his waist had a *qatan* thrust through it. Behind them, a tense-faced winch party had their hands ready on the bars of the windlass that would open the way into the valley.

He nudged Shahe over to join them. The rest of the horsemen

followed, the clansmen in a group, the cavalry in neat ranks, their horses leading off on the same foot and even stepping together, by the sound of their hooves on the cobbles. It wouldn't last. Once the gates opened, there would be no time for parade-ground discipline, only quick feet and swift spears.

Ysen nodded companionably as Gair fell in beside him.

'One of us at least has a reason to return, yes?' he said, inspecting his well-buffed fingernails.

So Ysen had seen Tanith's kiss – probably half the men in the bailey had, if the reaction of the clansmen had been anything to go by. His ears warmed. 'She's just my friend, wishing me luck.'

The desertman's dark eyes twinkled. 'To have such friends, you are truly blessed.'

Gair unshipped his borrowed shield from behind the saddle and concentrated on fitting his hand and arm through the straps.

'More than you know, *sayyar*. I owe her my life.'

'Then if that was her bloodprice, it is one I would gladly pay!' Ysen laughed.

There was no bloodprice Gair could imagine that would pay Tanith what he owed her. It was more than just his life, it was his mind, his precious memories of Aysha that Savin had violated. He rubbed the back of his neck, feeling for the faint line of the scar that was all that remained of his injuries from the Five Sisters. Without Tanith's care, he would have lost everything.

Another tremor struck, shuddering the keep's ancient stones. Earth-Song resonated through the restless roil of his own gift and made his skin prickle. A few horses startled as thrown soil pattered down around them, the odd pebble bouncing off a raised shield. Ears snapped back, Shahe jinked unhappily and he settled her with a few low words, then reached over his shoulder to loosen the longsword in its scabbard to ensure a clean draw. It was time.

He took a deep breath, blew it out. The last air trembled as it left his lungs and he tasted a sourness in his mouth like he'd just thrown up, or was about to. No matter how many times he swallowed, it wouldn't go away. And still the Song churned, picking out that skittery, jittery melody again, the one he'd heard in the square in El Maqqam. The one that capered like flames through dry wood.

Pulse thudding so hard in his head it made his eyeballs throb, he nodded to the sergeant in charge of the gate party.

'All right.' To his surprise, his voice was steady. 'Let's see this done.'

Chains clattering, the windlass took the strain and the great tarred gates began to groan open.

Ysen's *qatan* flashed silver as he raised it to the salute, levelled above his head in the desert way.

'May God shelter us in His hand, *sayyar*.' He grinned fiercely. 'Or speed us on our way!'

The gates boomed against their posts. Gair urged Shahe forward, and let the dance begin.

ତ୨

'Banfaíth?'

Stone felt gritty under her cheek, cool for all the warmth of the sun on the other side of her face. Teia opened her eyes. She saw a pair of boots, creased at the ankles as their owner hunkered down beside her.

'Let me help you.'

She recognised the Warlord's voice, the glittering bulk of the ring on the hand he held out to her. For a moment she wondered what she was doing on the ground.

'Are you all right?'

'I think so.' Slowly she dragged one arm under her and pushed herself up onto her knees. Macha's ears, her hands stung something fierce. She turned them over and saw the heels were scraped raw, pinpricked with tiny beads of blood. 'Ow.'

With his hand under her arm, the Warlord helped her to her feet. 'You are not hurt anywhere else?'

She squinted at his face. The day was too bright and the pounding in her head made it impossible to think clearly. 'No, I'm all right. I think. What happened?'

'I was about to ask you that. One of the men shouted, I turned around and there you were in a faint.'

The Warlord steered her a step or two to where she could lean against the parapet. He peered into her face, and she was reminded how intent his gaze could be. 'Was it a foretelling?'

She nodded. 'I saw him, the tall man. I recognised him.'

'Gair?'

The name meant nothing to her. 'I don't know his name, only his face. I've seen it before, in a blood scrying.' She looked around but the man was gone. 'He will bring the storm.'

The Warlord frowned. 'Banfaíth, what did you see?'

'He has a part to play in a great battle. As a leader of men, many men.' Images swirled in the storm clouds of her memory, each one sharp and shining as shards of metal, stabbing into her flesh. 'They will follow him to their deaths.'

In-drawn breath hissed. 'Are they victorious?'

'I didn't see that much. Only a battle, a storm.' *Oh, Macha!*

Her head boomed with darkness and flame, blood and death. Abandoned war-gear rusting on a sodden plain, the sky black with ravens. Bodies of men and horses and things that were neither, all bloated and stinking.

Her stomach churned, saliva filling her mouth. Moaning, she thrust her head between two of the wall's great stone teeth and vomited. Only bile, brown and bitter, but her belly heaved over and over as if it sought to empty itself of every morsel she had ever swallowed.

At last, the cramping ceased. Weakly, she pushed herself upright and opened her eyes. The vast expanse of the valley below swooped around her and she had to quickly shut her eyes again and cling to the stones until she was sure she wasn't about to pitch over them. Gradually, the frantic beating of her heart slowed.

Never before had the sight of a face triggered a vision so powerful. The number of times her foretellings had shown her a face she recognised at all, save for Maegern, could be counted on the fingers of one hand. Though the images were gone now, their impact continued to ripple through her thoughts like a stone thrown into a pool. That nightmarish battle was significant in ways she had yet to fathom.

Someone laid an arm across her shoulders and gently turned her away from the wall. Only when she was sure her back was to the pass did she dare to open her eyes again. The Warlord offered her a leather bottle.

'Here. Some water will help.'

She rinsed her mouth, spat, rinsed and spat again, but could still taste bile in her throat. Like the visions she had seen, it would not be easily washed away.

From below and to her right came the clatter of hooves on hard ground. Three or four horses at first, then perhaps a dozen, then so many that it was impossible even to estimate their number. War cries echoed from the walls of the pass to add to the noise, clan names and catcalls of the sort that wouldn't have been out of place amongst the Crainnh war band.

Stomach griping uneasily, Teia listened to them ride out, not daring to watch. Would this be the battle she had seen? A sideways glance showed the sky bright and clear, only two moons aloft. No storm clouds, no lightnings, but magic hummed at the edge of her hearing.

'What's happening?' she asked.

'Gair has a plan to bring down the Speakers' shield,' said Aradhrim. 'He said he could turn their own weaving against them. I confess I am unsure quite how, but the Guardians are gifted with powers I cannot begin to comprehend.'

'Guardians?'

'Guardians of the Veil,' he said. 'Men and women with the Talent, who dedicate themselves to ensuring the Veil between worlds remains intact. Gair is one. So is his friend Masen, and Lady Tanith. They continue the work begun by the Knights who defeated Gwlach.'

Confused, she frowned. 'But Duncan said there were no Knights in Arennor.'

'The Knights of the Church of Eador parted ways with the Guardians long ago. The Gatekeeper tells me they have been at odds ever since.' The Warlord smiled wryly. 'Much like our two peoples, eh?' He squinted up the valley over her shoulder. 'And here they come,' he murmured.

Mouth suddenly dry, Teia gulped some more water. She didn't have to look to imagine the war band beginning their charge; it played out in her mind more vividly than her eyes could ever have shown it to her. Was her father with them, despite his lameness? She hoped not, but at the same time she knew Drwyn was so hungry for victory that he would not spare a single spear.

Clammy fingers of prescience danced down her spine again. The Hunt would ride. Arennor would fall. She had seen it all a hundred times, more, acted out before her like a shadow-play at the fireside, only not with puppets made from twigs and feathers on her father's fingers, but with men. Flesh that rent and blood that spilled, and Maegern was not the keeper of the dead in a raven's-wing cloak but a stalking horror that froze the marrow in her bones.

True telling, all of it. Since she'd left her clan, too many visions had come to pass for her to have any doubt that she possessed the gift of foretelling. Knowing that they were not mere nightmares or fever-dreams but a promised future that she would one day have to live through made them all the more chilling.

Magic. The air was rank with it now. Crawling over her skin, singing along her nerves like spirit voices. The Speakers' magic, the voice in the stone, all twisting together and pulling at her.

'This is not his battle,' she said.

The Warlord frowned, puzzled. 'Banfaíth?'

'These are my people. If I don't stop them, the Hunt will ride. I have seen it.' Teia touched her power, felt it well up into her will and knew what she had to do. 'This is not his battle to fight, not this time. It's mine.'

40

TRINITY

೧⅏

Shyly, peeping around the eastern flank of the mountain like a child around its mother's skirts, the third moon rose. At last, the trinity was complete. Yeha reached down to the massive shoulders of the Hounds standing to either side of her and scratched their thick ruffs.

'Soon, my pets,' she crooned. 'Soon you will eat your fill.'

Then she spoke to the minds of the other Speakers facing the fortress. *Begin.*

Summoning her magic, she raised her staff. Through the binding she felt the others do the same, and felt the sweat on each palm, the flutter in each belly, as if it was her own. Firethorn burned where she had drawn the sigils on them and they on each other, doubled and redoubled by each link in the binding and each beat of their hearts. Magnificent. She was giddy with it, exultant. Drunk in a way that *uisca* could never make her.

Under her feet a wave of power reared up through the earth and she focused her will towards the high stone walls that closed the pass against her. They would not close it for much longer.

Bring them down.

As one with her, the Speakers drove their staffs into the earth.

Closing the doors behind her had taken almost all of Tanith's strength. She wasn't sure she had any left for the walk back to the infirmary. Only her fingers knotted through the cold iron ring of the door handle were keeping her upright.

Gair was riding out to battle, and he didn't expect to return.

He hadn't admitted the danger, but she'd heard it; not so much in what he had said as in what he hadn't, in the spaces between the words that her imagination had filled up with darkness and dread. No, all he'd said as he stood there in the bailey, ready to ride out with nothing but a clansman's hide shield and a padded jack for protection, was that he'd be careful.

An incredulous laugh bubbled up inside her. Careful? A Leahn? One part stones to two parts stubborn, the lot of them, and more honour than sense besides. He didn't know the meaning of the word *careful*, not when it applied to himself and, spirits keep her, she loved him for it. That he accepted the task ahead of him with such grace only made her love him all the more.

Touching her mouth, she remembered the warmth of his skin and the prickle of a two-day beard against her lips. That had been a mistake. Sweet, but a mistake nonetheless. She knew he was not for her. She'd steeled herself to it, so why couldn't she maintain that resolve? An unguarded look was enough to start her dreaming; a breath of his scent left her undone. One kiss, even a chaste and sisterly one, had sharpened her longing to a razor's edge, and it was cutting her to shreds.

Her fingers began to tremble. 'Come back to me,' she whispered against them, and screwed her eyes shut.

For a long, long moment she teetered on the brink of weeping. Emotion boiled, rushing through her like white water, threatening to sweep her away. Then she forced herself to draw a deep breath, let it out slowly. It was shaky, but she repeated it and the next one was steadier. That was better. Another breath and she could stand up straight and tug her shirt down neatly. The thought of losing Gair still hurt so much she wanted to scream, but she was mastering it, pushing it down beneath what remained of her professional detachment.

Better. She dried her eyes and tidied her hair with hands that only shook a little bit. She was a Master Healer, and she had a sickbay to run. She had to check on Sorchal, on Teia's baby and on Beck, the legionary with the broken leg. Kellin and his orderlies were depending on her – especially now, with more casualties likely. She could not afford to let herself be overwhelmed by emotion or she would be no use to any of them.

Chin up, she forced herself to start walking down the stone-flagged passage back to the infirmary. Gair was doing what had to be done; she could do no less.

⌾

The pull of the Speakers' weaving was compelling, but Teia knew how to resist it now. It would not drag her in helplessly the way the summoning had, like a fish on a line. Now she could watch and listen, could even admire their skill, without being overpowered by it.

Five Speakers floated in the blackness before her mind's eye. Five knots of shifting colour in the void, bright as flowers after rain, dancing and shimmering on the wind of their working. It should have been a simple matter to reach out to them and try one more time to reason away Ytha's madness.

Except the Speaker of the Crainnh was not there.

Teia's eyes flew open, the image in her mind unravelling. She hadn't expected this. Ytha had held Drwyn's reins since long before his father died; this was her plan, every twist and turn and wrinkle of it, from conception to birth. She wouldn't trust anyone else to see it through.

Closing her eyes again, Teia reached further north, well beyond the assembled war band. There were other colours there, fainter than the five Speakers under the shield, but none she recognised. Ytha was nowhere in the valley.

So where was she?

She needed a viewing to confirm it. Though Teia trusted her magic, she'd trusted her own two eyes for longer. The Speakers were too far away to see clearly, but there was one knot of colour amongst them that she recognised. She'd seen it at the Gathering and many times before that; their clans had adjacent ranges.

Quickly she dug her bronze basin out of the pouch on her belt and filled it from the water bottle still clutched in her other hand, then set the bottle down. Holding the bowl before her, she summoned a thread of her power to the water. The reflection shimmered, stilled. Bird's-egg sky, looming mountain, snow. Now to focus into the valley.

There. A woman as lean and leathery as Eirdubh, the clan chief she served. She stood in the centre of the line, the other women fanned out on either side of her. Only one of the other four looked at all familiar – the White Lake Clan, maybe. The rest must have come from more distant ranges. She'd almost certainly seen them before, but taken no more note of them than the snow-fox and whitewood that signified their status. It never did to draw a Speaker's attention down on you – especially not when you were desperate to hide your own gift.

Foolishness. What was she now if not a Speaker herself? Banfaíth, no less. She could look any one of them in the eye and not falter. The image trembling in the basin made a liar of her, but she stiffened her arms and steadied it. She had to see, because she could not afford to fail.

Beneath the translucent rainbow of their shield, the five women gripped their staffs. Outside, the battle raged. Horses rearing; spears gleaming. Silver flashed and scarlet drops rained across her vision, dappling the shield. More horsemen closed in, the war band by their plaids, and ran hard against a knot of green uniforms with their long spears levelled. In the centre of the ring was the sand-haired man on the black horse.

Off to one side, she heard running footsteps, then urgent words in the tongue the flame-haired Healer spoke, not the one she shared with the Arennorians. The Warlord said something and the footsteps pattered away again. He caught her elbow, pulling her to face him, and the bowl fell from her hands. It rang as it bounced off the stones, splashing her legs with water.

'Did you know?'

His voice was clipped, furious. A muscle worked in his jaw like the pulse of something ugly. For the first time, his crag-cat glare unnerved her and she flinched from it.

'Did I know what? I don't understand.'

'Did you know that Drwyn has divided his forces!'

Still reeling from what she'd seen in her viewing, she struggled to make sense of the Warlord's words. 'What? No! Macha as my witness, I told you all I knew.'

'The Gatekeeper has received word from the other *gaeden*. King's Gate is under attack.'

King's Gate? She knew the name, though it took her a moment to recall where she had heard it. Of course – the fortress below the Haunted Mountain, where Duncan had wanted to take her. Abruptly, all became clear.

'Then that's where Ytha is,' she said.

The Warlord frowned. 'Is she not here?'

'No, and I couldn't understand why I couldn't find her, but now it makes sense.' It made perfect, horrible sense. 'Drwyn will want to lead the war band out of the mountains, and she'll be with him.'

'You are sure of this?'

'Sure as the sun rises in the east,' Teia said. 'She made him the Chief of Chiefs; she won't let him out of her sight.' Misdirection, distraction; they had always been Ytha's weapons, and she was as deft with them as the pedlars were at the fair, cozening coppers from the unwary with three cups and a bean.

'So there are good men out there dying for nothing.' Aradhrim spat a curse. 'Gair means to throw the Speakers' power back at them through the earth. Can you do anything to help him?'

She'd felt a little of the stormbringer's power, in the walls of the fortress, and it more than matched her own. But she knew the Speakers, and the pattern of Ytha's mind in particular, in a way that he never could. And this was her battle.

'We can help each other. If I work to distract the Speakers, he may have a better chance of success. Then I can finish it.'

His brow puckered. 'Five Speakers? Are you sure?'

'I'm sure. This is my responsibility.'

'Then whatever you can do, do it quickly. The men with him will not survive long against the war band.'

Teia wrapped herself in her magic and sought the still eye at its heart. If she knew Ytha at all, she knew one thing: she guarded her power jealously. She would never have sent Speakers away to act for her unless she had a rein of some kind on them – a binding, most likely, so they could not act without her knowledge. So if Teia was to distract them, she would have to distract Ytha.

As she reached into the power, she reflected that if she had not insisted on meeting the Warlord, she would have been at King's Gate now, facing Ytha in person. Though her belly hollowed at the thought, a small part of her wished for one more chance to pit herself against the Speaker of the Crainnh on equal terms.

Ytha was the strongest Talent in all the Broken Land but she could be bested. Teia had done it. If she could have done it again, with so many other Speakers there to see it, maybe she could have smashed Ytha's plans and stopped this war before it began. But it was too late to fret over ifs and maybes. All that mattered now was the five women in the valley below.

She wove the dazzling strands of power together, shaping and sharpening them to suit her intent. She had never tried to work a weaving at this distance before; there was no knowing even whether it would work, but she had to try. Too much was at stake for her not to.

Slowly at first, the knife took shape in her mind. Gleaming, precise, she honed it on the whetstone of her will to an edge so fine that it could cut the soul from a body and neither would notice the severing. Ytha had taught her this, though it was never a lesson she had intended her to learn. But Teia *had* learned it, and learned it well. Now she was ready to prove it.

Pulse quickening, she reached out to the five whorls of colour in the darkness. A faint, misty halo enveloped them, made them glow like the moon behind thin clouds. Was that the binding? She'd witnessed a binding once before, when the plague had come. Just a child then, she hadn't understood the magic at work, but she'd felt it pluck at something deep inside her mind, a rough and ragged fingernail picking at her thoughts as if seeking a way into the power within.

This ends here, she threw into the void.

The darkness shimmered around her, then filled with a vast, glacial contempt shot through with colours as cold and remote as Finndail's Banner.

You cannot command us, child. Ytha's voice was chill as the breath of winter. *We are bound, my sisters and I. We will see this done, and you will not prevent it.*

Maegern will turn on you, Ytha. I have seen it. You know I have the gift of foretelling.

Mocking laughter curled back to her. *The gift of imagination, perhaps.*

You will doom us all!

You no longer have a place in the clans, exile. Run back to the Lost Ones where you belong. I am done with you.

The sense of Ytha's presence was gone, cut off as if by the closing of a door. Teia reached out for it to make one last attempt to reason with her, but found nothing. Either she was too far away to see the colours of Ytha's aura or the Speaker of the Crainnh had hidden herself. Teia was alone in the void once more, save for the minds of the five Speakers in the valley below. She expected them to disappear, too, and follow Ytha into the dark, but they didn't. Interesting. Perhaps they did not have the skill to do as she had done and cut themselves off from communication. Hope brightened in Teia's breast. Perhaps she could do more than merely distract them.

Listen to me.

No response.

You know what Ytha intends. You were there at the summoning, you heard Maegern speak. She called you little women, as if you were nothing of consequence. Do you really believe that someone who treats you with such scorn will do anything other than toss you aside when you are of no further use?

Still no response, no reaction but the measured pulse of their conjoined wills.

Please! Hear me!

The Eldest are beyond our knowing, exile. We do not question Them.

The voice was unfamiliar, harsh and dry; a Speaker's voice. Teia would find no sympathetic hearing there. In the end, as she had long suspected, resolution would come only at the edge of a blade.

So be it. If a thing was to be done, it was best done quickly, as Drw used to say.

Then I am sorry for you all, she said.

Around her the void sucked at her will as the Speakers began drawing in their power for another assault on the fortress. Teia flung up a wall of her own magic and hardened it, so that their weaving slid away from her as easily as water under a coracle. Secure behind her lambent wall, she readied her knife and waited for the stormbringer's strike.

41

WAR BAND

⚂

Mud and slush flew up from Shahe's hooves and spattered her belly as Gair squeezed her up to a canter. Behind him, steel horse-shoes clattered over the weed-crusted stones of the road as the rest of the horsemen poured from the keep's gates. When each rank hit their stride the noise increased exponentially, reflected and amplified by the walls of the pass into a rolling thunder that all but deafened him.

Ahead, only a few hundred yards away, the Speakers waited beneath the pearly dome of their shield. Already the war band beyond them were stirring, horns blaring commands and men jerking at reins. He didn't have much time. He had to reach those women before the Nimrothi warriors reached him or his plan would fail.

The first group of clansmen drew level with him on either side, baying like demons. One of them was Palgrim, teeth bared, brandishing his spear above his head.

The Song clenched its fist. As one, the Speakers raised their staffs and drove them down to the ground. The earth bucked, throwing Shahe sideways into the horse next to her. It went down whinnying in a welter of limbs and curses from its unseated rider. The *sulqa* stumbled and almost fell; Gair had to grab the saddle horn to stay astride whilst she collected herself and surged back to her feet.

By then the clansmen to either side had swept past, spears high; ears back, Shahe charged after them, her stride lengthening, stretching into a gallop. She wanted to lead. Bent low over her neck, the exhilaration of the chase taking hold, Gair gave the mare her head.

The Speakers were closer now, close enough for him to see their starseed rings winking in the sunlight and the fixed expressions they wore under the lines painted on their faces. Their combined grip on the Song crawled over his brain like insects. Beyond them, distorted by the shield, the war band thundered forward.

In a few strides, Shahe had gained on the charging clansmen. In a few more, she was drawing level, neck outstretched, mane flying. With every bunch of her muscles, each stretch of her long legs that brought Gair closer to his target, the music of the dance skirled louder. His heart raced with it, sweat blooming beneath the thick gambeson and trickling down the furrow of his spine. His mouth still tasted sour, his throat was dry and there was a fair chance he was running to his death, but all he wanted to do was laugh.

The same bubbling recklessness had infected him in El Maqqam. Was it madness, or another, more subtle aspect of the beast? Either way, it had him in its grip. It twisted up his innards into a hard knot of anticipation, stretched his lips back from his teeth, and inside him, the music danced like water drops on a smoking skillet.

Only a hundred yards separated him from the Speakers now. It would be close, possibly too close to call, but he'd committed himself. It was too late to turn back. He reached into the Song, seeking the complex, subtle melodies he needed. Seventy yards, and the war band had closed enough that he could pick out individual figures through the distortions of the shield. Sixty yards. Teeth gleamed in bearded faces. Wild eyes shone, on men and horses, and spear-points glittered in the sun. He was cutting it fine.

As Shahe surged into the lead over Palgrim's clansmen, the first Nimrothi warriors pounded into view. They broke around the Speakers and flowed back together like a river around a rock, less than a spear-throw ahead. At Gair's back was the gear-creaking, defiance-roaring, hoof-drumming cacophony of the imperial charge. He snatched out his sword in readiness. Galloping beside him, Palgrim struck the blade with his spear and made it sing.

'A flask of *uisca* for first blood,' he yelled, and laughed. Then the Nimrothi were upon them.

Horses barged Shahe from all sides. A spear thrust towards Gair; he slammed it aside with his shield and chopped the long-sword down hard. The blade took the warrior across the shoulder, where it met his neck, and bit deep. Blood from a slashed artery fountained into the air, pattering across Gair's shield like rain. He jerked the blade free and the man slumped, eyes already glazing as his horse's momentum carried him past.

Gair kicked Shahe on, trying to find a way through to the Speakers, but she was soon hemmed in again by jabbing weapons and jostling horses. He laid about him with the sword, landing blows wherever he could make one tell. Against shields, onto backs and necks; there was no time to face his foes honourably or finish them clean. There was barely time to register the meaty thuds, the howls of rage and pain that clawed at his ears, or the shrill cries of wounded, terrified animals. The world's compass was reduced to the reach of his arm and the blade at its end. He had no attention to spare for anything beyond it.

A few more clansmen had pushed into the mix alongside him, shoving, hacking, forcing the braided Nimrothi back with the ferocity of their charge. It couldn't last long, but for a few seconds, before the enemy's weight of numbers began to tell, they held the whip-hand. They had to press on, and quickly, before that advantage was lost.

'Empire!' he roared. 'Forward!'

Voices picked up the cry and several figures in the press raised weapons in acknowledgement. He gave Shahe his heels and she leapt ahead.

Horses and men surged like flotsam on the sea. Bruising blows fell onto him, onto his shield, and then something clipped the side of his head hard enough to ring his skull. For half a heartbeat the world was silent, stark white, then the battle crashed back into his senses in stink and thunder, in too-bright sun and swirling, muddy colours, out of which came a lunging spear.

Gair only just leaned out of the way in time. Twisting, he brought his longsword down on the blurry shape wielding the spear, the blade making a dull sound as it hit the Nimrothi's shield. He swung again, once, twice, desperate crashing blows to disable the warrior before the next spear-thrust could find his own belly. The third blow sheared down through the thick hide shield and into the meat of the man's forearm. Shield hanging uselessly, the Nimrothi tried to turn his horse to escape Gair's sword only for a spear-point to burst through his leather tunic from the other side.

Something thumped into Gair's right ribs and flung him onto Shahe's neck. Another spear, its head fouled in the thick padding of his gambeson, pressing and pricking at his skin as the hand holding it tried to wrench it free or drive it in. To his right, Gair saw blood-spattered furs, yellow teeth bared in a snarl, and hacked awkwardly for them with his sword. The spear-head twisted, drawing a hot gouge across his ribs. He cursed at the sudden pain, the burst of wetness across his skin, hacked again, then the pressure was gone.

Ears back, Shahe kicked at something behind her, then began to rear and plunge, unsettled by the other horses around her. All Gair could do was press his sword-arm to his injured side and hold on as she lashed out. The seething mass of horsemen parted briefly, affording him a glimpse of the Speakers' shield. Closer than before, maybe half a chain at the most, with only a few Nimrothi warriors between it and him. He squeezed his calves firmly into Shahe's sides, urging her into motion.

In the same instant, a Nimrothi wheeled his mount for the same slushy patch of road. He saw Gair and his spear came up in his left hand, the wrong side for Gair to shield himself. And then the man charged.

One second drew out, held, and observation crowded into it. Gair saw the Nimrothi's arm draw back. He felt Shahe's quarters bunch and surge as she reached into her next stride. Saw his own sword-arm rising up to knock the spear away, too slow, too late, the sunlight glittering along the spear-head's edge as it thrust for his chest to finish what the other warrior had attempted.

He reached for the Song, but Shahe was even quicker. Teeth bared, she snaked her head towards the Nimrothi horse and it shied. Not far, no more than half a step, but it was enough for the spear to miss its mark. The longsword completed its arc and bit into the man's chest with a sound like an axe into a tree-stump, whipped through and up trailing a banner of scarlet from the severed arm. Gair's side burned with the effort, fresh blood soaking his shirt. Another stride and Shahe was past.

Only a few yards now separated him from the edge of the Speakers' shield. A sea of men and horses eddied around him, yelling, snorting, shrieking. Out of the corner of his eye, he glimpsed a green arm and a flashing curved blade. It struck like a serpent, swift and precise, and where it bit men fell. Ysen. The desertman nodded to him.

'A fine day's sport, eh?' he shouted, even as he lunged and took a Nimrothi clean through the throat. The man fell back gurgling and was lost in the press.

Riderless horses reared and whinnied, terrified by the noise, the stench of blood and worse. Gair slapped one out of his way, urging Shahe on. The Speakers were close, but he had to get closer yet to be sure what he'd planned would work.

Another Nimrothi charged towards him, shield gone but a spear in each hand. Gair blocked the first with his shield high and lunged hard underneath, but only managed to wound the man. The second spear opened a burning slash across his thigh. The Nimrothi pulled back for another blow; teeth clenched against the pain in his side, Gair drove the longsword up under the clansman's breastbone. He grunted, dropped his spears and clutched at the blade, as if he could somehow stop its journey through stomach and lung and furs into the air behind him. Then he sighed as the blood welled from his mouth and his hands dropped. Gair tightened his grip on the hilt against the sagging weight, until the corpse slid off and disappeared under the plunging hooves of its former mount.

The current of battle had shifted, and for the space of a breath or two there was no one to fight. Long enough for Gair to acknowledge the fire in his thigh, his side; the dull thudding in his head. Panting, he looked around for the Speakers. Somehow Shahe had been turned about and instead of them being ahead of him, they were behind and to his right. He reined her around and caught sight of the handful of Nimrothi remaining between him and his target. At their head was a husky, pale-haired fellow on a gleaming bay horse, with a heavy-looking short-sword on his hip and fur trimming his plaid cloak. Gold winked around his throat as he waved a half-spear above his head and bellowed at the men Gair had fought through. A leader of some kind, then, and he was in the way.

Flexing his grip on the blood-slick hilt, Gair brought the longsword up. Pain flared across his ribs but it was bearable, as was the ache in his shield-arm from the blows he had taken. Strangely, the most discomfort came from the itch of drying blood around his eye and down his neck that begged to be scratched. He glanced back and saw Ysen a few yards away, carving through the

Nimrothi line at the head of a dozen clansmen and maybe twice that many imperials.

It was time to dance.

He gave Shahe his heels again. One stride, two. The Nimrothi chief and his men didn't turn, intent on the knot of imperial cavalry who had broken through with the clansmen and were beginning to spread out. Three more strides and one of them finally noticed the black horse charging from their right and yelled a warning, arm raised to point. By then Shahe was in behind them. Whipping the longsword up, Gair laid open the pointing warrior's back from hip to opposite armpit, then brought the blade crashing down on his companion's unprotected skull. As the *sulqa* surged into her next stride the man fell away, his brains opened to the sky.

Ysen's detachment were moving to encircle the Nimrothi. The white-blond man wheeled his horse, weapon in hand, to rally his remaining warriors. Spear-points flashed, hooves pounded and men fell. Two charging imperial cavalrymen burst into the group; one took a shield-boss to the face that struck him senseless, but the other couched and drove his lance deep into the chest of the chief's bay. It went down squealing, pitching its rider onto the stony ground. The last two Nimrothi closed on Gair, but before they could reach him they were engaged by a pair of whooping clansmen.

A panicked horse fled the fighting, eyes rolling as it tried to outrun the bloody, moaning ruin of a legionary on its back, and blundered across Shahe's path. She reared, shying away. Gair rode it out, soothing her with his voice, and steered her back towards the Speakers. A handful of yards separated him from them, and there was the white-blond man again, rolling back onto his feet. Shouting something Gair didn't understand, pointing with his spear in a way that required no translation.

Come, it said. *Try again.*

Shahe was still restive, dancing and chewing her bit as the battle swayed around her. Gair let his gaze slip to the nearest Speaker. She was little more than a girl, licking her lips nervously, eyes over-wide and hunted, fingers clasping and unclasping on the staff held upright before her. Little time remained. It couldn't be long before they struck again and he had to be ready when they did.

Snarling, the chief shifted his grip on the spear and cocked back his arm to throw. So be it. Gair had to reach the Speakers and the burly blond was standing in his path. A word launched Shahe forward, then the warrior was swallowed up in a mêlée as Duncan appeared, his mount hurdling the dead bay horse with Ysen and several others close behind. Spears flashed and men screamed.

Slowly, a space was opening around Gair. A space of churned slush, mud and blood. Dead men, fallen weapons, slowly widening as more and more of Saardost's soldiers battled through.

'Do what you must, *sayyar* – we will buy you the time,' Ysen shouted. Reining his horse in a tight circle, he flourished his scarlet blade above his head. '*Qalen al jinn!*'

All around Gair clansmen and cavalry fought, eddying back and forth as each gained and lost ground, but he had a few feet of clear space, room enough to work. And there, mere feet away now, were the soap-bubble colours of the Speakers' shield. Underneath, five women raised their staffs.

Quickly, he dismounted. Pain shot through his wounded leg when he put weight on it, almost sending him to the ground. The Song boiled still, its melodies snarled, bursts of brilliant music tangled with buzzing dissonance. He had only one chance to do this. Only one chance to make it work and throw the Speakers' weaving back at them, then the beast would have him.

Opening himself to the music in all its beautiful, terrible glory, he reversed his grip on his sword and drove its bloody point down towards the stones of the road with the weight of the Song behind it.

Checkmate.

Steel struck stone and threw Gair to his knees. Hands clasped tight around the hilt, he leaned on the sword and without any sound but a faint chime, like the ring of struck crystal, the blade slid through the pitted paving into the earth beneath.

Iron, carbon, stone. All one in the Song, all forged in the same fire. He sent his call down towards the bedrock as he had through the stones of the fortress, and the mountain answered with a pulse of power up into his hands that flung his head back, dragged a cry from his throat as it surged into his own Song and amplified it ten thousandfold.

Winds blew in the high valleys when he breathed, and rivers ran with the rush of his blood. What he'd touched through the fortress walls was only a fraction of this. The songs of the earth resonated through his entire substance, pealing like thunder, like a carillon from the Sacristy bells.

He spread his arms wide and his will surged out into a shield. Dissonance yowled but the earth-Song drowned it out, ringing and multiplying until every particle of him thrummed in sympathy with its music. Holy Goddess, it was magnificent. Even the pain felt like a joy so immense he feared his heart would burst with it.

Gair opened his eyes. Under the pearly dome of their shield, the Speakers' whitewood staffs were raised high. This time he was ready. Infinitesimally slowly yet at the same time fast as a lightning strike, they brought them down and five fingers of force stabbed the earth. He felt them as violent blows against his flesh, the percussive forces rolling towards him like a wave up the shore. Pressure built ahead of it, making the bedrock groan. Minute fissures cracked, split, and stone sheared with the strain as the earth around him trembled and began to shift. Gair turned his hands palms uppermost and the shield turned with them, became a breakwater ahead of a storm tide. He gritted his teeth in anticipation of the impact, and waited. This was his chance and he had no choice but to take it.

The Speakers' weaving smashed into his shield with hideous force. Gair groaned, heard the stone squeal around him, and thrust upwards to brace it. The Song roared. Jagged notes lashed his mind – too much! He had called too much and it was burning him up. Every nerve a shriek, every fibre of him incandescent, he flung his arms out and howled. Muscles trembled. Fingers spread, curled into claws with the pain that scarified him. From the heart of the music, the beast reached out and sank its talons into him.

42

VICTORY

෨෮

The Speakers raised their staffs, and the sand-haired man plunged his sword into the earth.

It sliced through Teia's senses as if it had pierced her own flesh, a bolt of brilliant, blinding will. She recognised the colours of it, could almost hear his voice again in the thrum of her magic. The stormbringer *was* the one who had called through the fortress walls. She hadn't heard him speak but she knew it was his voice she'd heard in the music, his call she'd sensed when she touched the tower stones. He was calling again, this time to the very bones of the earth.

She felt rather than heard the earth's answer – a note so low and resonant it made the power surrounding her quake as it spread out, steadily intensifying. Beyond the lambent wall of her magic, the Speakers' colours blurred. Were they sensing it, too? They had to be, surely, wondering what it was and where it had come from, which meant they were no longer paying any attention to *her*.

I am strong. She whispered it to herself, over and over, and firmed her grip on the blade. If a binding could be made with the power, surely it could be unmade, too. *I am strong – and I am stronger than you, Ytha.*

Five whitewood staffs slammed down, and Teia slashed her knife through the first knot of colour.

ᏋᏇᎶ

The severing of the bond lashed across Ytha's mind like an open hand across her face, across the faces of sixteen other women simultaneously, and she felt every blow. First their stunned incomprehension, then the stinging, burning pain that followed it, amplified until the clangour of it filled her head and left no room for thought.

She staggered, and in the glorious constellation of her sisters, one of the stars grew dim.

'No . . .'

Impossible. A binding held to the grave, unless dissolved by the one who forged it. It could not be cut – what had that wretched girl done? Snatching up her magic, she sought Teia's mind.

You cannot do this!

'Ytha? Is something amiss?'

I can and I will, the girl replied. *This must stop, Ytha.*

A second star flared and faded as another Speaker's weaving was sliced apart. This time the pain drove Ytha to her knees, her hands clutched to her head. Firethorn boiled beneath her skin.

NO!

'Ytha.' A touch on her shoulder, someone shaking her. She lashed out, fingers clawed. Hard hands caught her arms and fended her off. 'Easy, woman! What's happened?'

Her concentration broke and finally the voice registered. Drwyn.

'Teia!' she spat. 'It seems she survived the snows after all.'

His frown became a gawping, foolish grin. 'She did? Can you tell if she's whelped?'

Ytha snatched her arms out of his grasp. 'We have more pressing concerns than her brat – she's trying to break the binding!'

Fool of a man, daring to lay his hands on a Speaker! She reached for her magic to hurl him across the tent for his presumption but found only confusion. The music was turned to shrieks filled with jagged shapes of colour and light. Every time she reached for it, it cut at her like shards of glass.

She kneaded her temples and winced. 'Oh, you little *bitch*.'

Voices clamoured for her attention. Swirling colours, flickering on the edge of panic. Pleading, demanding, warning, sobbing. She gritted her teeth.

'Can she do that? I thought—'

'She's cutting through the other Speakers' gifts. They have no power but the binding stays intact, and we still feel each other's pain. If she cuts them all she will cripple us.' *Curse you! Curse you to the ninth hell!*

If you won't stop this, then I must stop you, before you doom all our people. Please. It's in your hands, Ytha. I don't want to hurt anyone but if you give me no choice, I will.

'She wants to see us fail,' Ytha growled. Sitting back on her heels, she fixed him with a glare. 'You should have let me destroy her when we had the chance.'

Drwyn grunted. 'Did my son survive?'

The man was worse than a fool; he was an imbecile. 'Macha's ears, have you heard a word I said? That traitorous bitch is fighting for the Empire against us!'

Delicate as the kiss of a razor's edge on skin, Teia brought her will to bear again, and Ytha howled.

NO!

❧

As each knot of colour flared and dimmed, the halo around it dissolved like smoke. Something brushed over Teia's senses, cobweb-soft, and was gone.

So now Ytha knew her intent, and the extent of her resolve. She raised the knife again and a furious shriek clawed at her.

NO!

I warned you, Ytha. I will do it, if you give me no choice.

By the Eldest, I will see you dead for this!

A stroke of the knife silenced her. Again Teia felt that rush as of a hunter's arrow hissing past her cheek before it vanished into the void around her. This time the colours faded further, a flower dying before her eyes.

Foul curses echoed in the silence of her mind, in the hollow endless instant between the double beat of her heart, between one breath and the next. The two remaining tangles of colour flared painfully bright as some distant working began, an attempt to thwart her, perhaps. She severed the two with a single stroke and they shrivelled into ashen greys on the edge of her blade.

∞

Leaning on her staff, Ytha pushed herself to her feet. Her chest burned, the firethorn twitching and writhing through her flesh like snakes beneath her skin. Burning hotter by far was her rage.

That jumped-up chit! Defying a Speaker to her face, threatening them – using her powers against them! How *dare* she?

Ytha's fist tightened around her staff, grinding the bones of her hand together until they creaked. The aged whitewood bit into her palm and the discomfort steadied her, gave her something to focus on beyond the pain that crashed and reeled through her mind like a tundra-rat in a cage. No Speaker would stand for her power to be challenged – not in such a fashion, and not by an exile. It was not to be borne.

She reached out into the void. *Sisters.*

At once the clamour returned, voices keening, their distress communicated to her through the bond. Ytha closed her ears to the silence of the five she could no longer hear. There would be time to mourn them later. For now, grief was a luxury she could not afford.

Sisters, hear me.

—hurts—

—where is she?—

—Ailsa? Ailsa, answer me—

—hurtshurtshurts—

—Macha save me, I can't see—

They were bewildered, adrift in their own pain. Only a firm hand would jolt them out of it.

Stop snivelling!

Silence, hot and ringing with affront, and faintly, the sound of someone sobbing. Then—

Ytha? What's happened? Where's Ailsa?

—I can't see!—

Quiet! You are Speakers, counsellors to chieftains, not witless girls – act like it! We have work to do here, in case you have all forgotten. The silence thickened, stiffened by her scorn. Good. By the Eldest, she'd see this done.

What would you have us do, Ytha? The words were spoken as if through clenched teeth.

I gave you a plan. We will see it through. She flexed her fingers on her staff, imagined smashing it into the ground. No half-trained girl would best her this time. She would make certain of it. *Bring the walls down.*

But—

Bring them down! Every wall, every tower; leave not one stone standing atop another! By the gods, I will have my victory today, or may Maegern Herself strike me dead! I will finish this, and I will take back what is ours. In the privacy of her own mind, she added: *And that hell-spawned bitch will not stop me.*

ᥫᩚ

Pain.

Fire in his veins instead of blood. Living flame instead of skin, muscle, bone. Sparks for nerves, as quick as thought.

Such pain. It darted and fluttered over Gair like fire over paper.

Caressed him, lapped at him, loved him even as its touch blackened his skin and shrivelled it to ash. The first breath of wind would fray him apart, scatter him like smoke, and the man he was would be gone. Only the beast inside him would remain.

He had no strength left to fight it. Every ounce of his will was bent on the shield he had woven to divert the Speakers' assault, on containing the stupendous forces rushing through him. He felt the beast crouched behind his eyes, all scales and cinders. Felt its fiery talons driven deep into his mind, heard the growl in its throat as it reared up. He wanted to scream but had no strength even for that. He was done.

The growl intensified, reverberating through Gair's skull. Reverberated through the stone underneath him, deepening until it shook his bones. His shield trembled. Somewhere on the edge of hearing he heard shouting, animals screaming, and was dimly aware of a change in the texture of the storm around him. Then with a gritty, rasping sound, the earth bucked.

ᗧᗤ

Scant seconds after the Speakers' staffs struck the earth, their shield had vanished like a soap-bubble in a draught. Two of the women dropped to the ground, limp as poleaxed cattle. A third staggered, clutching at her head, mouth stretched wide in a silent scream.

Teia watched with a sick hollowness in the pit of her stomach. This was her doing. She had done this: with firm intent and the sharp edge of her will, she had cut the Talent from them as casually as if she were cutting flowers for her hair.

Oh, Macha forgive me.

She flung the knife away and the weaving dissolved back into the gyre around her as if it had never been. But she could still feel the hilt in her hand, sweat-slick and hard as bone. Bile rose up in her throat, filling her mouth with saliva.

Beneath her feet, the cobbled walk quaked. She'd not been able to halt whatever working the Speakers had begun; it was up to the man she'd dubbed the stormbringer to deflect that now, but she'd bought him time in which to work and freedom from interference. She hoped it was enough.

The juddering underfoot intensified. Teia staggered, arms flung out for balance, and fell against the wall, bruising her elbows on the massive stone blocks. A new reverberation raced through the song of her magic. It wasn't so much a sound as the foreshadowing of it, a low, slow resonance through the deepest part of her that loosened her bowels.

'What is that?' she asked as the Warlord reached out to help her back upright. Macha's ears, she was going to soil herself. 'Can't you feel it?'

'Feel what, the shaking?'

'No, the sound.' She pressed one arm across her belly and clenched her nether muscles as tight as she could as the sound throbbed on. 'It's making me feel ill.'

The Warlord looked puzzled. 'I can't hear anything, Banfáith.'

So it was in her gift, then, not in the air. Reaching into her magic, she tried to throw up a shield against it, but every weaving she attempted vibrated at the same pitch and only increased the awful pressure in her belly. Fragments of stone started to dance around her feet, rattling and pattering amongst the cobbles like knucklebones in a cup. And still the sound-that-was-not-a-sound grew, not louder but more intense, more ominous. Even the air in her lungs hummed with it, and like a cloud of shrieking black birds bursting up from cover, prescience swarmed into her mind once more.

In the hottest summers, wind-storms came that scoured the plains. Storms that tore away tents and scorched the earth bare, leaving nothing but a few shreds of grass that crumbled like tinder and the bleaching bones of animals that had not fled fast enough. The clans called them Maegern's Breath, and made the sign that warded against Her eye to avoid drawing them down. Every child was taught the signs – the featherlike clouds high overhead, the dusty veil over the sun – and knew when to run back home.

A storm was coming now. She saw it in the dancing dust along the wall-walk, felt it in the uneasy shifting of the soldiers, like horses about to bolt. It was coming, and it was time to run or die. Distantly, down in the valley, the tenor of the sounds of battle changed.

Teia clutched at the Warlord's arm. 'Something's coming. We have to get down off the wall.'

'Why? What's happening?'

'I'm not sure, but he's at the heart of it. What he's weaving . . .' She rubbed at her temple. The sandy-haired man's sword glittered in her mind like a starseed splinter, and around it the pressure built, straining against her magic. Between that and the clamour of prescience, her head would surely explode. 'Macha, it hurts!'

From behind her came the hiss of wind through trees, though not a breath stirred against her skin, then the shuddering, grinding groan of rock subjected to terrible stress. Beneath her feet, the quaking intensified.

'If you want your men to live, my lord,' she said, 'order them down, now. There's no more time!'

୭ଓ

It was beautiful, the way a flower opening was beautiful. One moment the fortress was a bud, hard and unyielding, then in the next the sepals flew back and the petals blossomed silently across the sky in stone and dust and broken bodies, scattering like pollen on the wind. Magnificent.

Ytha smiled. The smile widened, became an exultant, full-throated laugh. *Yes!* Triumph surged through her in a wave, from the soles of her feet and the tips of her fingers to the roots of her hair, lifted her, squeezed her, rushed out on the gale of her voice and left her shuddering, more fulfilled than she had ever felt astride a man. Even the noise, when it came, was glorious. Like thunder, like the drum of spears on shields. She spread her arms and closed her eyes, gathering it to her bosom as if it was the most precious child, and it was *hers*.

This was what she had worked so long towards, and it was within her reach at last. She wanted to sing, to dance and clap with delight, but instead she folded her hands neatly together on the shaft of her whitewood staff and wrapped herself in the composure that befitted her station, though inside she was glowing fiercely as a coal.

'Do you see what I have wrought, my chief?'

'I see it.' Holding up one hand to shield his eyes from the dust billowing towards him, Drwyn shot her a grin. 'How could I not?'

She showed her teeth. There was no containing her glee now; before the convulsing earth had stilled, she started down into the pass, the two Hounds loping along at her side. Drwyn scrambled after her, but she was in no mood to wait for him. Not now. The fortress was hers for the taking, and with it the gateway to the south was opened.

With clubs of air she smacked aside the obstacles before her, the uprooted trees, the cracked and tumbled blocks, clearing her path until she came to the foot of a great scree of rubble leading up into the thick pall of dust that shrouded the remains of the fortress.

The defenders rallied enough to send a flight of arrows in her direction, but a gesture cast a shield above her head and the missiles pattered into fragments. Barbs and broken fletchings showered down and were crushed by her boots.

Pathetic insects. Mere green-backed beetles, scrabbling and scurrying over their broken nest, still trying to sting her even as she ground them beneath her feet. A few more arrows flew and met the same fate as the first, then a lone spearman charged down the slope towards her, his face bloody. A twitch of her fingers snapped his spine and he fell, his spear clattering away across the shattered stones. It was so easy. With the weight of the binding behind her, even weakened as it was, she had only to think a thing and it was done. Such strength, such power. It was glorious.

Another flight of arrows hissed overhead, more disciplined this time, but just as fruitless. Two more spearmen appeared, their green tunics caked in dust and blood, and scrambled over the broken wall, yelling defiance.

It was only fair to allow the Hounds to share in the victory. Ytha gestured ahead at the charging spearmen. 'Go, my pets.'

The great beasts surged forward and the soldiers' defiance became gurgling screams.

Strident shouts rang out from up ahead. A leader of some kind was rallying his men to hold the breach. Useless. He might as well attempt to hold back an avalanche in the mountains or a river in flood. At Ytha's side, Drwyn laughed and raised his horn to his lips. Three long blasts called up his men, the war band roaring as they charged. On foot, spears ready, they surged up to the breach like the sea onto a pebbled shore and poured through the broken walls. Green beetles fell back and were drowned in the flood.

Ytha laughed. Victory, under a trinity moon, as she had promised. The first victory, which opened the way to the south and the rich lands of the faithless. She would make those craven whoresons curse the names of their forefathers who broke spears and swore fealty to the Empire. She would make them beg her for release from this life and then feed them to the Hunt for sport.

Exhilaration lightening her steps, she climbed the shattered wall to a wider place from which she could look down on the slaughter below. Drwyn's warriors outnumbered the defenders scores to one, and still more scrambled over the fallen stones, eager for their own chance to participate. Yet the greenbacks were not done. They had formed a tight knot behind interlocked shields, a knot that bristled with spears like a prickleback's spines. Step by step they retreated towards the southern walls, not panicking, and the rise and fall of their weapons left clansmen on the ground in their wake. If one of their own fell, they closed up their shields and did not miss a step.

So one man at least in the beetle-nest still had his wits about him. No way to tell from here who he was, even with magic sharpening her eyes. The badges and symbols on their coats meant nothing to her, though she guessed that the more shiny bits, the higher the man's standing. Yet the longer she watched, the more it appeared that the man who commanded was the one who wore no sign of rank at all. He stood in the heart of the knot in his shirtsleeves and where he looked, white fire turned men into screaming torches.

Each working sent a tremor through Ytha's power and she halted, staring. The man had the Talent. By Aedon's swinging balls, that was impossible – the iron men had quit the mountains long ago! But the resonance humming across her mind confirmed it for the truth: at least one of them remained, and he had no small gift.

Remained, or had returned? Quickly, she reached out with her senses towards the eastern fortress – where there was one there would surely be others, like rats in the grain stores – but the distance was too great, and curse the girl, Teia had broken her bond to the Speakers there. She was blind, but no matter. If there were any iron men to the east, they were too far away to be a threat to her plans, and with the bound power of a dozen women to call upon, the one in front of her was no more than a nuisance.

Besides, despite the man's efforts, the defenders were dwindling. Slain greenbacks littered the bloody stones all the way to the southern gates. No more than a score of warriors remained around the white-shirted man, and they were hard-pressed by the war band.

Did they actually think escape was possible?

Laughing, Ytha summoned all the magic of the remaining bonded Speakers to her will.

43

THE FALL

❦

Staying busy would keep Tanith sane. With her hands full and her mind bent on wielding the Song, she would have no attention to spare for anything but the patients in her care. They were her responsibility. If she surrendered to her emotions now she'd be no use to the wounded when they most needed her clear head and steady hands. Failing them would betray her sacred oaths as a Healer, and that she would not do.

There would be time later to deal with the shock of Ailric's actions, the sick dread of what might be happening out beyond the fortress walls. When the battle was over and the wounds were staunched, then she could falter, but not now. For now she would keep herself busy doing what she could for others, until she had the time to weep.

She rolled up her sleeves and opened the infirmary door with her mask of professionalism pasted in place. The surgeon, Kellin, gave her a nod but the orderlies didn't even look up from their tasks, scrubbing down the table and measuring out medicines. This was the only world she could be concerned with until the waiting was over.

Masen had moved his stool down the ward to beside Sorchal's bed, and she bustled over to him.

'You shouldn't be putting any weight on that leg,' she scolded.

'Oh, hush, lass.' He winked at her. 'One of the orderlies strapped it up for me. It's fine.'

'Yes, well, it will be when I've started it Healing – assuming you haven't done any more damage to it in the meantime.' Tanith knelt beside him and laid her hands either side of his knee, the Song already humming.

'Sorchal's colour's picked up a bit,' the Gatekeeper said as she worked. 'Still out cold, though.'

'He will be for a while yet.' Tanith had her eyes closed the better to concentrate on the colours and music swirling through her. 'He should be up and about in a couple of days.'

'And how are you faring, eh?' he asked gently, voice pitched low.

She opened her eyes but couldn't make herself look up. 'I'm fine.'

'You sure?'

The Song drained away, its work done. Finally she forced herself to meet Masen's concerned gaze. 'It's hard,' she said. 'I can't let myself think about it or I'll fall to pieces.'

'I wish I had something to say that would make it easier to bear,' he said, laying his hand over hers. 'Did you tell him how you feel?'

'I couldn't.' The words had been on her lips and ready to fly, but she'd held them back. They would only have distracted him, maybe confused him, at a time when he needed all his concentration. And besides . . . Her shoulders lifted helplessly, tears threatening. 'He's still in love with Aysha.'

Masen clicked his tongue sympathetically. 'Give him time,' he said. 'He's not completely dense – he'll see what's in front of him eventually.'

Tanith felt Gair's arms around her, his cheek under her lips. 'And what if there's no time left for either of us?' She blinked her eyes clear, looked away down the ward to master herself.

'Ah, lass,' Masen sighed. 'That's a question only the Goddess Herself can answer.' He squeezed her fingers and then stood up, gingerly testing his weight on his heavily strapped knee. 'That's sound enough now for me to get back to the wall,' he said, and kissed her on the cheek. 'Keep your head up. You never know what might happen under a trinity moon.'

Tanith watched him limp to the door and felt the clutching hands of despair tugging her down. It was going to take more than the alignment of the moons to bring Gair safely back to her. It was going to take every ounce of courage he possessed, and every scrap of luck he could make for himself. She pushed those thoughts away before what strength she had crumbled completely. She had to focus on her duties now. Nothing else could be allowed to matter.

She did her rounds of the infirmary. Teia's baby was sound asleep in his crib, and the soldier with the blistered feet would be able to return to light duties in a day or so. In the opposite bed, Beck, the legionary with the broken leg, was splinted and sleeping off her Healing, quite oblivious to the rumbles and groans of the fortress's ancient stonework. The few other patients she gave quick smiles and words of encouragement as she moved back down the ward to Sorchal.

A bandage swathed his head, hiding the bald side of his scalp and leaving the rest of his dark hair sticking up in tufts and swirls. She thumbed back his eyelids and flicked a tiny glim from side to side to make sure his pupils responded appropriately. The right one was still a little sluggish, but much improved. Laying her hand lightly on the bandage, she traced the fracture lines in his skull with the Song. Already knitting, and she could hear the faint, whispery music of new bone forming at the trephination site. Good.

She sighed, relieved. 'You'll be back on your feet tomorrow, I think,' she said, more for her own benefit than his, since Sorchal wouldn't hear it. He'd had a lucky escape. Lucky he hadn't been hit harder, and that the soldiers found him quickly. Lucky there'd been a reason to go looking for him in the first place. Tanith twitched the blanket straight and patted his shoulder. The outcome could have been much worse for him.

She was turning to her next task when she felt the brush of familiar colours. Bitter green, cool blue. Ailric's colours.

A pretty show, but a waste of time. They will all die here.

Frozen in place, Tanith couldn't respond, couldn't even breathe. Her head was filled with memories: stale *uisca*, her wrists slamming against stone. The coppery taste of blood in her mouth.

You should leave, he said. *Before it is too late.*

Finally, she found the will to speak. *No. These people need me.*

Then you will die with them.

Her temper ignited. *Then so be it! At least I'm not running away.*

Ailric gave an indelicate snort. *Someone has to save your family's honour, since you care so little for it. You are better than these peasants, Tanith. You deserve better. I could have given it to you.*

The man's arrogance was breathtaking. *I want nothing from you!*

Then I hope your pet was worth what you have thrown away, Ailric sneered. *Be thankful your father is not here to see the betrayal of your House.*

Tanith gasped. *What are you going to tell him?*

He didn't answer.

Ailric? Ailric!

But her words fell into the void unanswered. Tanith reached out as far as she could, south into the pass, and found no trace of his colours. Wherever he had been, Ailric was gone now – heading back to Astolar, and her father.

Oh, spirits.

Shocked, she slumped back against the wall next to Sorchal's bed and covered her face with her hands. What was Ailric going to say to her father – or the Court, come to that? His grandmother Morwenna could be a powerful ally or just as easily a deadly enemy. Tanith pressed her fingers into her eyes, trying to squeeze out the images that thronged for her attention. No. There was no time for this. She had patients to attend to and there would be many more before the day was done. What came after, she would deal with when it came.

Levering herself way from the wall, she felt a low, grinding vibration shake the infirmary floor as the Speakers sent another wave of earth-Song against the keep. Tanith steadied herself against the wall again to ride out the impact, but it never came. Instead the vibration grew deeper, stronger, shook her own Song until it rang in sympathy. Across the ward the door slipped its latch once more. Something metallic clattered to the floor in the surgery, and slowly, an unoccupied bed began juddering its way across the flagstones.

This was wrong. Panic touched a cold finger to Tanith's heart. She dipped into her power, felt the great clanging chords of earth-Song booming and rolling underneath her feet. Dust drifted down from the vaulted roof. Followed by flakes of render, then chunks of mortar. The stone blocks of the wall quivered under her hands.

'Kellin!' she shouted. The surgeon stuck his head around the door of the surgery cubicle. 'We've got to get the patients out, right now!'

Somewhere overhead, stone cracked.

∞

The earth convulsed. Trees fell and the ground slipped as a bowel-loosening concussion shook the valley. Great slabs of rock shuddered away from the mountain slopes and began to slide, scouring swathes from the forest as easily as a boy stripping grass-seeds from a stem between his finger and thumb. The Speakers' shield had vanished, two of the women sprawled senseless on the ground, then the other three were tossed into a heap of fur robes and frightened cries. With a sound so immense, so deafening that it had no sound at all, the valley bottom tore across like a sheet of paper between two giant hands.

Terrified horses screamed and plunged. Cavalrymen and Nimrothi warriors sawed at reins to bring them under control and
failed. Kicking, twisting, horse after horse tumbled with their
riders into the maw of the earth in a shower of slush and stone
and mud. Other, luckier animals scrambled to safety. And the
noise went on and on.

Thrown backwards by the violence of the earth's paroxysm,
Gair clung to the old road's cobbles and waited for them to stop
shaking beneath him. Hearing returned only slowly; his ears
were so brutalized by the cacophony that at first he could not
even hear the Song inside him. Then the ringing silence began to
break. A cavalry sergeant, steadying his men. Incredulous laughter
from several voices, one of them a woman's. Magda, maybe? He
couldn't be sure.

Holy Goddess, he hurt. Never mind his flayed-feeling skin, the
wounds that marked him, every muscle, every bone felt as if it had
been torn loose from its moorings and flung back together. His
left arm ached where his borrowed shield had slammed into the
ground and split; he shook himself free of the straps and, joints
twanging in protest, levered himself into a sitting position.

In front of him gaped a chasm some sixty yards wide. It had
broken the backs of the mountains to either side, left them
slumped like victims of a mortal wound. Ridges ended in precipitous cliffs. Slopes that had once been thickly treed were ripped
bare, bleeding muddy water amidst the stumps and scars. Everywhere Gair looked he saw signs that some savage had taken an axe
to the Goddess's handiwork.

He looked down at his hands. *And that savage was me.*

For a moment he'd called on the earth itself, used its power
to turn the Speakers' weaving back against them, and somehow
turned it loose instead. Every shattered tree, every fractured rock
screamed out with the enormity of what he'd done, and he had to
look away. Except there was nowhere he could turn his eyes that
didn't show him more of the devastation he had wrought.

Wild-eyed horses shied at every groan and shudder of the earth. Wounded ones struggled to rise on broken legs and hamstrung hocks. Survivors, standing numbly with weapons hanging at their sides, or dragging themselves across the ground as if they could haul themselves away from their pain. And all around them the dead, in green uniforms, in buckskins, in fur and leather, staring up at three moons in a sky they could no longer see.

Goddess forgive me.

Something bumped his shoulder. When he reached up to fend it off, a whiskery muzzle pushed into his hand and lipped at his fingers. He looked up. Shahe stood beside him, ears flicking anxiously, and Gair patted her neck. She at least had survived.

Holding on to the stirrup, he hauled himself to his feet. A throb of pain through his injured thigh almost pitched him straight down again and he had to steady himself on the saddle. The wound was an ugly line of clots and dirt but the bleeding had stopped, more or less; it wouldn't kill him any time soon. Gingerly, he tested his weight on the leg. As long as he was careful how he moved, he could walk on it.

Out of the corner of his eye he saw the Speakers on the far side of the chasm, and turned to look. Their impressive furs were soiled, their whitewood staffs in flinders around them. The youngest was sobbing in the arms of a grey-haired woman with a bloody gash on her forehead, who regarded him over the girl's shoulder with flat, expressionless eyes. Two of the others lay in awkward abandon: struck senseless or dead, he had no way to tell. The fifth stared into space, a thread of drool from her mouth fraying like spider-silk on the wind.

The grey-haired Speaker stared at him stonily. Then she sneered something and spat on the ground. A curse, no doubt; the words had the rhythm of something foul. Gair turned away. It was no less than he deserved. That he'd done what he'd set out to do, and stopped the war band advancing through the valley, was small consolation.

He felt the war band's stares on him from across the chasm. Apart from the odd snort of a horse, the muttered complaints of the violated earth, they made no sound, but they watched him, and their loathing prickled over him like stinging ants on his skin. Angrily he snatched up Shahe's reins and led her over to his longsword, still upright in the broken ground like a grave-marker.

Duncan's clansmen wheeled their horses around him as they moved to take the surviving Nimrothi on this side of the chasm under guard. Several threw nods in his direction or touched spear to shield-rim as they passed. Magda was with them, and heeled her rangy dun out of the pack towards him. Horse and rider were streaked with blood, some of it the ride-captain's own, judging by the rips in her buckskins. A dripping half-spear in her fist told its own story.

'Northman,' she said.

Gair acknowledged her with a weary gesture. Saints, he was exhausted. Even the Song sounded muted, spent.

'Tell me,' she went on, her tone oddly flat, 'was that supposed to happen?' She pointed her spear south, towards Saardost Keep.

When Gair followed her gesture, the shock of what he saw almost felled him. Saardost's gates were gone, the great curtain wall breached. The hulking keep itself was missing at least two more towers. Shattered masonry, limestone blocks the size of hay-bales, littered the road under a pall of pale dust. Even from that distance he could hear the cries of the wounded as if the fortress itself sobbed in pain.

Behind him, one of the Nimrothi women began to laugh, harsh as the cackling of crows.

⁊ⳤ

Steadying herself against the broken wall, Ytha opened herself to her power, searching for the weaving behind the tremor that had rolled through the earth. She found nothing. Not in this place, not as far out as her senses could reach, but it was a puzzle that would have to wait to be solved.

Below her, the remaining defenders had reached the gates and begun to open them. The creaking and clanking of the mechanism was audible even over the clash of weapons. It required the turning of two great wheels; they had barely enough men to work them and maintain their defences, but the white-shirted man fought hard for them. He threw the war band back again and again with walls of air, launched fire at them, and Ytha felt each weaving as a jolt through her power.

Tiresome little bug. Time to squash it like any other pest.

She summoned her magic, spread her fingers out in the direction of his chest. He looked up, as if he'd sensed her will being brought to bear. Behind him the gates had opened enough to allow the remaining defenders to flee, but it was much too late, and there were too few of them to make a difference. The war band closed in and the man in the ragged shirt simply stood, watching her watch him. At the last moment he flung up his hand and the encircling warriors ran into a shield that tumbled half of them to the ground.

Irked out of all patience, Ytha closed her fist. The man staggered, one hand pressed to his chest, but managed a few more steps towards the narrow gap between the gates. This time, she twisted his heart in her grip. He fell to one knee, doubled over the pain she wrought in his chest, but hands reached through the gap to help him.

More bugs. Always scrambling, scurrying, bees around a broken hive. Time to smash them once and for all. Then a voice spoke in her thoughts. It was ragged and strained, reaching out to her from a great distance.

Sister.

Ytha recognised the voice and paused in her weaving. Eirdubh's Speaker was the only one of the five she'd sent to the eastern pass who had the strength to reach across that great distance. *Yes?*

The pass is closed to us. They have torn the earth and we cannot cross.

Perhaps that had been the source of the tremor. *Iron men?*

I saw only one. He carried a sword, but he had none of the marks that the old tales describe.

A lack of marks meant nothing after what she had already seen in the ruined fortress below. If the iron men now chose not to identify themselves so clearly, it only made them harder to pick out, not harder to kill.

I felt severings. How many have we lost?

Four. I had some warning and was able to escape the worst of it, but . . . I am wounded. The Speaker's voice trembled, with exhaustion or despair Ytha could not discern. *We lost some few score warriors also. Those that escaped the pit have been captured by the Empire.*

Four Speakers was more than Ytha would have liked to lose, but every victory had its price. *Are our sisters alive?*

One for sure, and one struck mute. The other two cannot be roused.

Oh, she would make Teia pay for that. Pay and pay and pay, until she begged for death – her and her faithless allies! *Very well. You have done enough. We have our victory.*

Closing her mind to the other woman, Ytha turned her attention back to the yard below. The clash of arms was dwindling, drowned out by cheers. Drumming their spears on their shields, the war band roared their triumph into the sky, at the three moons that shone down on them just as she had promised. Victory was hers.

Smiling, she looked around her at the broken stones, the bloodied corpses. *And this is just the beginning.*

The man in the white shirt was gone, his few warriors with him. Ytha paid him no further mind. He would be dead in a day, maybe two, depending on his strength. One less iron man to stand between her and her goal. As for the others, out in the east with that wretch of a girl, they were too far away to do her harm.

Gory to the ears, the two Hounds loped through the crowd

towards her, leaping from stone to stone until they stood at her side.

'And so the south falls,' she said, then laughed again as the Hounds reared up and licked her face with their bloody tongues.

44

A PROMISE MADE

The walls should not have fallen.

Gair stared at them in disbelief. He'd strengthened them when he woke the mountain; they should not have fallen. But fallen they had: Saardost's great curtain wall gaped like the mouth of a man with his teeth punched in. The gatehouse's east tower was gone entirely, the westernmost no more than a shattered stub. Fully a third of the wall's width had been reduced to a scree of rubble, from which the splintered timbers of the gates protruded like broken bones from a wound.

'Mother have mercy.'

Dust caught in his throat; his voice didn't sound like his own. It was the voice of a stranger, the stranger who had ripped the earth apart and with the same blow torn down those massive fortifications without a thought to what he was doing.

Saints and angels, what have I become?

Duncan, who'd been issuing orders to his surviving men concerning the Nimrothi captives, looked around and his eyes flew wide. 'Slaine's stones! Did the Speakers do that?'

'No.' *I did. Oh, Holy Eador, I did!*

For the first time in years, since long before the Motherhouse, Gair wanted to pray. To fall on his knees and ask forgiveness for what he had done, out of the very best intentions. And then he remembered. 'Aradhrim and Masen were on the wall.'

A touch on the Song showed him Masen's colours, throbbing sickly, but when he hailed there was no answer. Alive then, but hurt, perhaps unconscious, or otherwise unable to answer. He had no way to tell what had happened to the Warlord. Tanith's colours were silent.

She was probably busy with the wounded – dear Goddess, all the wounded he'd sent her! – and had no time to spare for him. Or maybe she'd realised what he'd done and been appalled by it. She was a Healer; preserving lives was her calling, and he'd just squandered so many . . .

He snatched up Shahe's reins and mounted. Pain shot through his thigh; he clung to the saddle horn until the waves of dizziness passed and he could urge her on. The road's cobbles were tossed about, leaving leg-breaking holes scattered amongst the slush and mud and scrubby weeds, so he didn't dare urge the mare up to anything more than a fast walk. Just as well, when each misstep or stumble sent a fresh jolt of pain through him; he had to let her pick her own way back to the keep, whilst the dread and the guilt hammered at him with every beat of his heart.

As he neared the keep, shattered masonry made the already treacherous footing downright dangerous. Shahe stumbled more frequently but didn't go down, threading through the rubble until it became impossible to find safe places to put her feet. He had to leave her then and scramble up to the keep on foot, his thigh alight with pain.

I did this. The voice in Gair's mind refused to be silenced. *I brought the wall down.*

All he'd meant to do was deflect the Speakers' weaving and turn it back on them, but he hadn't thought it through. He'd drawn too much power, without considering what would happen when those immense forces collided. His recklessness had torn the mountain open, rent the earth. No fortress could have withstood that. He stared helplessly at the blasted limestone that surrounded him, dotted with dusty patches of green, unmoving and twisted into impossible shapes, and wanted to weep.

At the remains of the gate, a nightmare greeted him. What had once been the bailey was now a wasteland of splintered stone and collapsed outbuildings, strewn with the shapes of the fallen. Survivors stood stunned and bleeding, or hauled at broken masonry with their bare hands in search of comrades trapped underneath. Panicked horses screamed and kicked in what had once been the stables, its outer wall now slumped at a drunken angle, incredibly whole, but so spidered with cracks it could not remain that way for long.

This is my fault.

With so much rubble, so much damaged masonry a sneeze away from falling and adding to the carnage, it was impossible to know where to start. Clambering down into the bailey, Gair made for the nearest soldier. He had to grab the man's arm to get his attention, and even then the infantryman stared uncomprehending when asked where the Gatekeeper was.

'The Gatekeeper,' Gair repeated. 'Or the Warlord – what about him? They were on the wall together.'

The man shrugged and waved an arm vaguely in the direction of the keep. Seeing blood running from the infantryman's ears, Gair let him go. No wonder the fellow couldn't hear.

He cast around the ruined bailey. More soldiers were emerging from the dust clouds, and from the keep itself. One of them had one hand tucked between the buttons of his uniform tunic as a makeshift sling, whilst the other held a thick field dressing to his head. When he barked orders at the milling legionaries, gesturing impatiently with the bloody cloth to make his point, Gair realised the man was Brandt.

'Commander!' he shouted. Brandt turned. Dried blood clumped his hair and streaked his face as if painted on. Gair limped towards him, his own wound burning with every step. 'Commander, have you seen Masen, or the Warlord?'

'Aradhrim's over there.' Brandt nodded to where a shirtless Lord of the Plains sat amidst the fallen stonework whilst an orderly secured a bandage around his chest. 'I haven't seen the other *gaeden* since before you rode out.'

Then the garrison commander was gone, shouting, cajoling, seemingly everywhere at once. Wherever he went, order followed, as if a firm, familiar voice issuing instructions was all the soldiers needed to begin moving with some purpose.

By the time Gair reached the Warlord, the orderly had tied off the bandage and hurried away to his next patient. Carefully, Aradhrim got to his feet.

'You're looking the worse for it,' he said, shrugging back into the remains of his buckskin shirt. 'Did you bring any of my men back with you?'

'About half of them, I think. Have you seen the Gatekeeper?'

'He went down to the infirmary,' he said. As Gair turned to go, the Warlord seized his arm. 'Gair, wait. You shouldn't go down there.'

Dread clamped its fist in Gair's chest. There was another reason why Tanith might not have answered him. 'Why? What's happened?'

'Part of the rear wall and roof of the infirmary has collapsed. I understand Lady Tanith was still inside at the time.' The clansman's grip on his arm tightened. 'There are men working to free the injured and they say they've heard her voice, but the remainder of the roof is unstable. There may be another collapse at any moment.' Cat-green eyes held his steadily. 'They are working as fast as they can but time is running out. I thought you should know.'

Not Tanith, too. Oh, Goddess in glory.

'Have they found Masen or Sorchal?'

'I am waiting on another report. Slaine's stones, it grieves me to be the bearer of such news.'

Gair felt cold, so cold, despite the warmth of the sun. 'You haven't given me any news yet, my lord.'

'Gair—'

'No! I won't believe they're dead until I see it for myself.' He tugged his arm and the Warlord released him. 'I need to— I have to help them.'

Limping, hurrying despite the pain, he climbed the steps to the keep's doors, hanging drunkenly ajar. Where only a couple of hours ago, Tanith had kissed him for luck. The irony was bitter as bile. She'd brought him luck for sure, and with it he'd doomed everyone else.

Afraid of what he might find, he ducked inside the keep and reached for her colours again.

ॐ

Duncan rode slowly along the line of disarmed, kneeling warriors. His blood was still singing from the fight, so much so he hardly felt the gash in his arm that he'd bound up with the remains of his shirtsleeve, but the rest of his senses were alive with the adrenalin thundering through him.

Those same senses told him he was being stared at by one of the captives, a white-blond man whose eyes burned as Duncan approached. When he was close enough, he could see the gold torc of a clan chief around the man's neck, almost hidden by torn and bloody plaid. A tattoo of an ice-bear blued his left cheek, the same as most but not all of the men who had been captured with him.

Duncan met his stare and the man's lip curled in disdain. No quiet acceptance of defeat for that one. Nothing but contempt and defiance. Duncan's blood roared. Well, that Ice-Bear was about to have the arrogant sneer wiped from his face, and by Slaine Himself, he would enjoy doing it.

He swung his horse around and rode back to the head of the line, where Magda was waiting with several of her ride, all with shortbows drawn, just in case. He dismounted and handed her the reins.

'I'll take his surrender,' he said.

The scarred woman frowned. 'You won't wait for my chief, or for Sor?'

'Aradhrim has enough to chew on for now, and I've stood for my brother before.'

Her eyes narrowed. 'It is not the custom, Captain. A chief demands a chief.'

'No, it's not the custom, and I don't care,' Duncan said roughly. 'This needs to be done, and done quickly. I took his spear – I'll make him break it.'

Turning his back on Magda's disapproving stare, he walked back down the line to face the Nimrothi chief.

'Do you lead here?' he asked.

'No.' The Nimrothi bit off the word.

'But these are your men, these Feathain.'

'Yes.'

'So who commands here?' No answer. He gestured along the line. 'I see Ice-Bears, three Stone Crows, a White Lake man. I know I killed a pair of Eagles. Four clans, but I see only one chief. Do you have the authority to treat with me on their behalf, as well as on behalf of the Feathain?'

The chief sneered. 'Who are you, boy?'

So be it, then. 'My name is Duncan. My brother is Clansman to the Morennadh, I am cousin to the Lord of the Plains and I suggest you don't call me *boy* again unless you want an arrow in your throat.' Without any prompting, Magda's bowmen put a little more tension on their strings and their bows creaked. 'Now, do you have the authority to treat with me?'

Blue eyes in a sun-browned face spat malice. 'Yes.'

Reaching around to the small of his back, Duncan tugged a

513

decorated half-spear out of his belt. Strips of white fur fluttered in the restless wind as he held it out to the kneeling chief. 'Break it.'

The Nimrothi bared his teeth. 'Never!'

'You were captured in battle, Feathain. I took this spear from you. Your honour is mine. Swear to me and I will let you live.'

On the far side of the rift in the valley floor, deep in the pack of watching Nimrothi, someone put a horn to their lips and blew a long, mournful blast. Duncan looked up as the blast was repeated. In groups of a few dozen at a time, as space opened up around them, the war band wheeled their horses and rode away. A solitary figure emerged from the press of men on horseback. A woman, dressed in a stained snow-fox mantle, her iron-coloured hair blowing about her blood-streaked face. She walked up to the lip of the chasm and stared across the unbridgeable gap at her captured kinsmen, then raised one hand high above her head. The horns blew a final blast, then she too turned and walked away.

Still on his knees in the bloody mud, the Feathain chieftain chuckled. 'The other fortress has fallen, faithless,' he mocked. 'The way south is open. Arennor will be ours again.'

'Not whilst I have breath in my body!'

Temper ignited, Duncan struck the man across the face with the butt of his own clan spear. He sprawled in the muck, scarlet leaking from his mouth.

'It's too late.' The Nimrothi spat blood onto the ground and propped himself on one arm. 'The Hunt will ride, and with it we will take back what was ours. Then *you*, boy, will kneel before *me*.'

❧

Green uniforms filled the corridor outside the keep's hall. Some carried litters bearing wounded men, others bore their injured comrades slung between them in their bare hands. The air stank of rock dust and blood. Everywhere men sobbed and sweated or lay ominously still, the light of life already fading from their eyes.

Pushing through the crowd, Gair searched for a glimpse of

coppery hair. Tanith took her role as a Healer seriously; she would not be far from her patients, even if she had been injured herself. But every face he scanned that wasn't hers or Masen's increased his anxiety; reaching for her colours and finding nothing but a smear left his heart drumming on his ribs as if he'd just run a ten-mile foot-race.

At the doors to the hall, a harassed junior officer with a single gold stripe on his sleeve and a bandage over one eye was directing the flow of wounded inside. He took one look at Gair approaching and flapped his hand in dismissal.

'Walking wounded back outside,' he snapped, then waved to two soldiers carrying a third with shattered bone protruding from his thigh. 'Bring him in, there's space on the right, at the back. The surgeon will be with you shortly. Next!'

Gair stood aside to let the injured trooper be carried through, then snatched the corporal's arm. 'Where is Lady Tanith?'

'I sent you outside— Let go of me, we've men dying here!'

'I'm not here for me. Where's Tanith? Have you seen her?'

'Who? No, she's not here. They're still evacuating the infirm-ary, try there.'

Gair let the fellow pull away and limped on, his wound throb-bing with every beat of his heart. He dodged and darted his way through the press of wounded as best he could until he reached a joining passage and some space to get his bearings.

With the air so dust-clouded, all the passages looked unfamiliar. Left or right? Instinct said right. A pair of soldiers jogging past carrying an empty litter turned the same way and made the decision for him. He broke into a semblance of a run after them.

The infirmary's arched door was skewed to one side, the adjacent wall bulging out into the passageway as if someone had pushed their thumb into a model castle whilst the clay was still soft. Great gaps had opened up in its masonry. Broken stone and chunks of mortar littered the flags underfoot, which were as heaved about as the cobbles of the old north road. A couple of torches had been wedged into cracks in the ashlar, and by their wholly inadequate light two soldiers were easing a blanket-wrapped body through the doorway.

Gair flung half a dozen glims into the air over their heads, flooding the passage with blue-white light. The men flinched but their faces were too numb to show any more fear.

'Who've you got?" he asked. 'Have you found Tanith yet?'

One of the soldiers shook his head, the other shrugged and they bent back to their work. Close to, Gair saw that much of the doorway was choked with rubble, some of which had spewed into the corridor leaving only a narrow gap into almost total darkness beyond.

Shadows shifted, brightening suddenly.

'That's the last one,' said a muffled voice.

An arm appeared from the hole, holding a lantern. The soldiers laid down their burden carefully and one of them took the lamp. A pair of dusty boots appeared, followed by legs in trousers torn and caked with dirt, which were followed in turn, accompanied by much grunting and swearing, by the body and finally the head of none other than the Gatekeeper.

'Masen!' Gair exclaimed, hurrying to help him up from the rubble. 'Thank the Goddess you're alive.'

'The Goddess had nothing to do with it.' Masen raked his fingers back and forth through his hair, dislodging a considerable quantity of mortar flakes. 'Tanith did, and a whole hell of a lot of dumb luck.'

'She's alive? Where is she?'

There was barely a flicker of Masen's eyes towards the blanket-shrouded body, but it told Gair everything. His belly hollowed painfully.

Goddess, no.

He pushed past the soldiers, dropped to his knees beside the body. Sticky wetness across his thigh said the wound had begun bleeding again but the pain felt distant, almost as if it belonged to someone else. Hands shaking, he turned back the blanket. Copper hair covered her face, gleaming in the stark light of his glims. Carefully, he pushed it aside. Her eyes were closed and her breaths came tight and shallow. A little blood crusted at the corner of her mouth.

'Tell me,' he said. 'Tell me what happened.'

'Half the ceiling fell in when the wall came down. By the time I got here, Tanith and the surgeon had evacuated the patients, but she went back for Teia's baby. I tried to stop her, but she insisted she'd be quicker.' Masen shrugged helplessly. 'She passed the child to me, but she was still inside when the rest collapsed.'

Gair was no longer listening. He'd already guessed much of what had happened from the scuffs and scrapes on Tanith's leathers. He brushed her cheek with the back of his fingers. 'Can you hear me?'

Masen's hand came down on his shoulder, squeezed. 'She's as good as gone, son.'

'She's still breathing.'

'I had to lift the stones off her with the Song.' The grip on his shoulder didn't relent. 'I'm sorry, Gair, but you'd best say your farewells now.'

'No!' Gair shrugged him off. 'She's still breathing – that means there's still a chance.'

Plunging into the Song, he sent his awareness into her body and reeled at what he found. Incredible pain, dark and jagged. Sickly purple flares of crushed flesh, the red heat of blood pooling between her organs. Tears burning the backs of his eyes, Gair bowed his head. Tanith had minutes left to live, if that.

The two soldiers with the litter he'd overtaken further down the corridor came trotting up. 'Get out,' he snarled at them. 'Leave her in peace, damn you!'

Confused, they fell back a pace, looking from him to Masen and back. Gair ignored them, smoothing Tanith's disordered hair away from her face. A distant part of him was aware of Masen ushering

all four soldiers down the passageway with murmurs about helping the other wounded, but all he heard clearly was his own pulse
hammering in his ears and wished it was hers.

'Tanith, stay with me now. I need you to be strong.' He had to
be able to help her, somehow – take the pain away, at least. He
began gathering the Song again.

'Gair, you can't Heal this,' Masen said softly. 'Goddess knows
you've got the strength, but I'm not sure even Tanith has the skill.
Please, son. Let her go.'

'I won't.' He swallowed hard, blinked back the tears. 'I can't.' *I
won't let another woman die because I was too late.*

A tiny furrow appeared between Tanith's brows and her eyelids
fluttered. Her head turned to one side, lips stretching wide in a
soundless cry as pain returned with consciousness.

Quickly, Gair touched her colours, tried to smooth out the
spikes of hurt. Slowly, her respiration grew easier.

'Easy there. Don't try to move.'

She opened her eyes. Their beautiful river-gold was dark now,
dulled.

'I was afraid . . . you wouldn't come back.' One hand groped
out from under the blanket and he took it, curling his fingers
around hers.

'Tell me how to help you. There must be something I can do.'

'There is.' She swallowed; when next she spoke her voice was
fainter. 'Touch the Song.'

'You'll show me how to Heal you?'

'No. You can't Heal me, but you can keep me alive.'

'How? I don't understand.' Though he fought against it, his
voice cracked.

'No time. Touch the Song. I need your strength.'

Without hesitation he opened his mind to the music and let it
flood into him, as much as he could hold. 'I'm ready.'

Her eyes drifted closed. Spring-dawn colours caressed his,

bright and fragile as butterfly wings. *When this is done, take me home to Astolar.*

Oh, saints, did she mean when she was dead? *Don't talk like that.*

You're not listening. I'm going to fold the Veil. It should give you enough time. She broke off, face contorted in a grimace. Her fingers clutched at his. *Just take me to my father. He'll know what to do.*

I will.

Promise me?

I swear it.

A trace of a smile curved her lips. *Thank you.*

She reached into him, into the surging power he held, and twisted the world to silver-white.

The pain bent Gair's back like a bow. Every muscle spasmed, tearing a cry from his throat. A scintillating chord sounded through his Song then exploded outwards in a firework of music that sent its million sharp notes through every fibre of him. Then it was gone and he was left displaced in his own skin as if he had been wrenched violently sideways without moving an inch. Gasping, he fell back against the passage wall.

'Are you all right, lad?' asked Masen.

He opened his eyes. His glims had gone out but the Gatekeeper had called a few of his own to supplement the meagre torchlight. Beside him lay a rumpled blanket, but there was no sign of the woman who had been wrapped in it. Tanith was gone.

Struck stupid, Gair looked up and down the corridor for her. 'What happened? Where is she?'

'I don't know. One minute you were both there, then there was a bright light and a sound in the Song like I've never heard before. When I could see again, she was gone.'

Masen stooped and picked up the blanket, and something pale rolled from its folds. It resembled a smooth white pebble, oval in shape and as long as the last joint of a man's thumb. Gair picked it up. The instant his fingers touched it, colours flickered through his mind: pale rose and jade, like a spring dawn. Tanith's colours. Surely it couldn't be her?

Close to, the object had a soft radiance, more like pearl than stone. As he turned it this way and that, a faint iridescence shimmered over its surface.

'I think she's here,' he said slowly.

Masen held out his hand. 'May I?'

Gair passed it to him. Almost at once a prickle over his senses said the Gatekeeper had called the Song. Masen turned the object over in his palm, summoning his glims over to see it more clearly.

'I think you're right,' he said at last. 'She's woven a retreat of some kind. I can't see into it but it feels very much like the Veil.' He returned the pearl to Gair. 'Astolar exists in a wrinkle between this world and the Hidden Kingdom. It's how they can close their borders at will and why time flows differently there. Bregorin's the same, more or less.'

'She said she was going to fold the Veil. She asked me to touch the Song, then reached through me to do what she needed to do.' Gair looked down at the pearly thing nestled in his palm, trying to wrap his mind around what Tanith had done.

Masen scratched his stubbled chin. 'Well, that'd be one way to buy some time. There's stories about Gatekeepers who've folded the Veil, but I've never seen it done before this. It's extraordinary.' He cocked his head on one side. 'So what now? Did your crazy plan work?'

'More or less.' Gair closed his hand around the pearl and pushed himself to his feet. His thigh was on fire, the sodden fabric of his trousers clinging stickily to him.

'It was a waste of time, in the end.' Masen shook out the blanket, began folding it, then suddenly hurled it at the opposite wall with a curse. 'King's Gate has fallen.'

Mind still whirling with what had happened, what he had to do now, Gair thought he'd misheard. 'What?'

'All this –' Masen flung up his hands '– it was a feint. A

diversion. The bulk of their war band was never even here.' He aimed a kick at a piece of rubble and sent it careening down the passage. 'What a waste. What a bloody useless, *donkey-swiving* waste!'

Words wouldn't come. Gair's voice was stuck in his throat, his tongue immobile. He couldn't even swear. Everything they'd fought for, everything they'd lost, was for nothing.

'How?' he managed.

'Barin told me,' Masen said shortly. 'Just as these walls came down here, the war band poured into King's Gate. Most of the garrison's dead, but he and Eavin saved those they could. Eavin was badly hurt in the retreat.' He rubbed his eyes, face twisted up as if he wanted to spit, then he shook his head. 'He's good, that chief of theirs. Timed it to perfection. I'd be impressed if I didn't want to wring the bastard's neck.'

A Nimrothi war band was loose on the plains of Arennor, with a Speaker at their head who was bound and determined to loose the Wild Hunt. And Savin, out there somewhere, laughing at them all. Gair's fist tightened around the pearly retreat Tanith had woven for herself. Warmth pulsed through his hand, like the beat of a living heart, and was gone.

Startled, he turned the pearl over and over between his fingers, but the pulse did not come again. Was Tanith aware of him, wherever she was? Was she sleeping? Only the thickness of a thought separated them, and yet she'd never felt further away, not even when he was in the desert and she was in Astolar.

Can you hear me? he flung out into the void, but she did not answer. Staring at the pearl, he fancied he saw a flicker of her colours, but it was so brief he could not be sure whether his tired eyes were playing tricks on him.

'I have to take her to Astolar,' he said.

'Now?' Masen's brows shot up incredulously. 'You'll have the war band on your tail the whole way! And what about King's Gate?'

'You said the fortress is lost. What good could I possibly do there?' Gair closed his hand around the pearl to keep it safe. Tanith was still alive and he had to keep her that way. 'If I can reach the Great Forest, I can travel the wildwood. Tanith gave me the name of the guide she found.'

Conversations around a campfire filled his memory. Telling tales of their journeys as the night winds snatched sparks from the embers, each a moment in time that could never be recaptured, burning brighter than a fire-fly and then gone.

Masen was shaking his head. 'Don't do this, Gair, I'm begging you. Until we can muster more *gaeden* in the north, you're our strongest weapon against the Speakers.'

'I gave her my word.'

The Gatekeeper spread his hands. 'We need you.'

'I'm a liability and you know it!' Gair laughed bitterly and swept out his arm to encompass the tumbled stone, the ruined infirmary. 'Look at it. I did this! What do you think will happen next time I try to wield the Song? How many men do you think I'll kill then?'

Masen winced and Gair lowered his voice. 'I promised her, Masen. I promised her that if she ever needed me for anything, I'd do it.'

'What about Savin, the starseed? I love Tanith like my own daughter, but please! The future of the Veil is at stake – she wouldn't want you to put her ahead of that!'

The pain, the dragging weight of exhaustion became too much for Gair's temper to bear.

'Don't lecture me, Masen! I don't know what else to do. I don't know where the starseed is. I don't know where Savin is. How am I supposed to find them? I've been running all this time chasing shadows and I'm no further forward than I was when I left the Isles.'

'Gair—'

'I've lost everything in this life that ever mattered to me. Do you understand? I lost my home when I was ten years old. I lost

Aysha, I lost Darin and Alderan, and I can never get them back. All I know how to do, all I *can* do, is this.' He held up the retreat, gleaming in the glim-light like the most precious jewel. 'I have to take her home. She's all I've got left.'

45

FAREWELLS

⚭

Baer was drinking tea outside the women's tent below the walls of Saardost when Duncan found him. His woman, Neve, folded her arms over her shawl and regarded him with narrowed eyes as he approached, but the Banfaíth, seated on a stool by the fire, gave him a smile. Someone, at least, looked happy to see him. He hoped the man himself would be a little more reasonable.

'Good morning, Banfaíth, Neve,' Duncan greeted them. Neve said nothing but her mouth tightened, as if she didn't trust him to be sincere. 'Chief Baer.'

The grizzled man snorted. 'Thank you, Captain, but I'm no chief.'

'The Warlord thinks otherwise,' Duncan said. 'He's sent me to beg a moment of your time – he needs your help.'

That made the man's tea-bowl halt halfway to his mouth. 'I thought the battle was won.'

Out of the corner of his eye, Duncan saw Teia's expression flicker with pain. Aradhrim had told him what she'd done, turned her powers against her own people in defence of the fortress. He could hardly even guess how difficult that must have been for her, but now it looked as if it had hurt her more than he could have imagined, and his heart ached for her.

'It is,' he said, 'but we find ourselves with a few-score prisoners from the war band that you could help us with, if you're willing.' *And there's something I want to ask you, too.*

'Up there?' Baer looked from Duncan to the fortress walls and back again. 'No. Especially not after the Speakers did their work.'

Duncan tried again. 'The Warlord asked for you specifically.'

'And I still say no. I told you, stone ain't meant to be raised so high.'

Eyeing the walls, Duncan could understand the Nimrothi's reluctance to enter the fortress. Seen at a distance, from the Lost Ones' camp on the river meadow, the damage didn't look so bad, as long as he ignored the broken-tooth stumps of the keep's upper watchtowers, and pretended he couldn't see the slew of rubble that had once been the curtain wall across the north road, where working parties with pry bars and *gaeden* assistance were already attempting to clear a route through the fallen masonry so that a couple of hundred horses could be brought back from the far side. Safe and secure it was not.

'Baer, we need you,' he said at last. 'We've got some eighty-odd prisoners to deal with – mostly Feathain, but there's half a dozen clans represented in all. We don't know their allegiances, how best to get information from them that might be helpful in understanding their Chief of Chief's intentions.'

Baer laughed. 'And you think they'll talk to me? A Lost One? You're dreaming, lad.'

'If they're not your clan, why should they even know?'

The grizzled man's hand went to the clan tattoo on his cheek. 'No Iron Elk?'

Duncan shook his head. 'Not that I saw. Feathain, Crainnh, three or four others. None of them has the same mark as you.'

Baer rubbed at the elk's head thoughtfully, considering. From what Duncan had seen on the journey through the hills from Tir Malroth, Baer was a natural leader of men, a chief in all but name, as Teia had described him, and like most chiefs, he had his pride. He'd not go begging for favours from anyone and charity would make him uncomfortable, but if he could be persuaded that fostering a good relationship with the Lord of the Plains was in his people's best interests, he wouldn't let pride stand in the way of practicality.

'You'd be a great help,' Duncan said.

Baer grunted. 'You'll not get me inside yon pile of rock, though.'

'You don't have to. The hall's been taken over as an infirmary, so Aradhrim's command post is out in the yard.'

ℝ+

Of course, 'command post' was describing it generously. The map-strewn table was made of carpenter's trestles and unfinished planks, and its only shelter from the elements was a piece of canvas strung from ropes anchored to the remains of a smashed outbuilding. At one end sat Aradhrim with a sheaf of papers, attended by his adjutant, who had somehow managed to remain immaculately neat despite the devastation around him. By contrast the Lord of the Plains was dressed in the same torn and bloodstained buckskins he had worn yesterday, and the shadows around his eyes and stubble on his cheeks said he'd most likely been working all night.

He looked up as Duncan approached and gave him a companionable nod, then stood.

'Chief Baer, be welcome here.'

'Chief Aradhrim,' Baer replied, with a cautious nod. For a moment the two of them eyed each other like a pair of bull elk trying to work out who was straying onto whose range, then Aradhrim stuck out his hand.

'The Banfaíth speaks highly of you,' he said.

After the merest hesitation, Baer accepted the clasp. 'And she of you. I understand from your captain here that you've some prisoners from the war band.'

'I have indeed. If you will grant me your indulgence for a few minutes more to finish this report –' he gestured with the papers in his hand '– there's a Feathain chieftain amongst them I would like you to speak with. All he'll give me is braggery and bravado.'

Baer barked a laugh. 'That's about what I'd expect from an Ice-Bear.'

Aradhrim's smile was thin-lipped. 'Entertaining as it is, it is less than helpful when the Wild Hunt is about to be turned loose on my lands.'

'I'll do what I can.'

'Then you have my gratitude. If you will excuse me?'

As the Warlord went back to his work, Duncan led Baer to the far end of the table where there was a jug of water and cups on a tray, and some stools on which to sit. This was his chance.

'Since we have a few minutes,' he said, sitting down, 'there's something I'd like to discuss with you.'

Baer made himself comfortable. 'I'm listening.'

Duncan took a deep breath, then reached for a cup from the tray and set it down on the table between them. He filled it with water from the jug, praying he wouldn't spill it and make a fool of himself.

The older man took in the single cup and his eyes narrowed. 'Do your people still follow the old ways, then?'

'Some do.'

'And this?' Baer gestured at the cup.

Suddenly Duncan's palms were damp and sticky and he desperately wanted to wipe them on his trews, but somehow managed to keep his hands flat on the table. 'I thought it would be respectful.'

Baer gave him a long look, then carefully lifted the brimming beaker and sipped. He set it down again equidistant between the two of them. 'Speak.'

My turn. Duncan took a deep breath and reached for the cup.

He barely moistened his lips, not knowing how long he might have to make the water last.

'Teia,' he said.

The older man's brows twitched up a fraction. 'She's not my daughter, nor my ward.'

'I know, but her father's far away and you are her chief, in every sense that matters. I'm not seeking a price,' Duncan added hastily, seeing the Nimrothi's expression harden.

At that, Baer showed his teeth. 'Just as well, because any man who tries to buy a Banfaíth's hand is liable to wish he hadn't.' He sat up straight and folded his arms. 'So what *are* you seeking, Captain?'

'Only your blessing to approach her. Nothing more.'

Baer eyed him levelly. ''Tis a strange time to be asking.'

One throw of the bones was all Duncan had. 'I can't think of a better one.' He fingered the bandage on his arm. 'Slaine's stones, after yesterday, I wasn't sure I'd get another chance, and that's the gods' own truth.'

'Good answer.' Baer picked up the cup and raised it to his lips. 'I'm still listening.'

☙❦☙

Gair pushed open the broken-latched door to what had been Tanith's room and stepped into the gloom beyond. Splinters of stone crunched under his boots, dust dancing in the fingers of light poking through the crack in the outer wall. It was almost wide enough to admit his hand, twin to the one that had sheared across his own room, floor and wall, when the earth shrugged. Saardost had taken a mortal wound.

He squashed that thought down hard. He couldn't afford to dwell on it or the guilt would swallow him, and he had things to do. Quickly summoning a glim to supplement the patchy daylight, he set about collecting Tanith's possessions.

Her blankets were neatly folded, saddlebags nearby with a shirt laid on top, perhaps to remind her to put it away later. Everything was coated in a layer of pale dust as if she'd been gone for weeks. It made her absence feel disturbingly permanent.

Trying not to think about how permanent that might actually be, he shook the stone fragments off her shirt and folded it into her bag, then cast around for any personal items. There was an ivory comb on the window ledge, with a strand of tawny hair still caught in it, and couple of long agate-headed pins, so he tucked those in the bag, too. On the floor below the window he found a plump acorn still in its cup – presumably a memento from her travels in the wildwood. It reminded him of the horse chestnuts and eagle feathers and pebbles with holes in them that he'd collected as a boy, and he almost smiled. Such a human thing for her to have kept. His throat thickened. Such a painful reminder of how little he knew about her.

Then, careful of his bandaged thigh, he knelt down next to the undamaged wall where the broken necklace lay and willed his glim closer. Fragments of glass glittered under its light. One by one he collected them – dabbing up the smallest shards with a moistened fingertip – and deposited them carefully on a sheet of paper he'd begged from the Warlord's adjutant, then laid the chain with its remaining flowers on top.

A shout from outside in the yard made him look towards the door. With the glim down low he could see his footprints in the dust, and another, fainter set that his overlapped. They were barely visible, but by moving the glim around he could just about make them out. Man-sized, and the stride length was almost the same as his own, so whoever the man was he was better than averagely tall.

Ailric. The bastard had been in Tanith's room again. After the Speakers started their assault, or there'd be no dust to hold his boot prints, but before the heavier fall triggered by the quaking earth that had all but obscured them. Anger rekindled inside him, and his hand went instinctively to the pearly retreat in his pocket.

What had Ailric wanted? Gair looked around the little hutch of a room once more, even though he knew it was pointless. He hadn't known what effects Tanith had brought with her, so there was no way he could identify if something was missing, but he looked anyway, because he owed it to her to at least try.

But there was nothing more to see, and nothing of Tanith's remained. He folded up the paper around the pieces of her necklace and eased himself to his feet, thigh throbbing. Then he picked up her saddlebags, collected his own from where they waited in the corridor outside and limped away down the listing passageway. He had one more task to complete, and then it would be time to go. This place held too many ghosts.

ళ౧

She'd left the caves with little enough; now Teia was leaving Saardost with even less. Provisions, some clothing from the army stores and rags for swaddling the baby slung across her chest, that was all. Everything she'd brought with her from north of the mountains was buried beneath the collapsed roof of the infirmary.

It shouldn't have stung so much, but it did. They were only things, after all, and things weren't as important as people – or so Ana used to say. If only the people that were most important to her weren't so far away that she'd had only those few bits and pieces to remind herself of them.

Teia's fingers faltered on the saddlebag she was fastening. *I miss you so much, Mama.*

She blinked the tears away before they overwhelmed her. Now was not the time to be grieving for what she had lost; not unless she could find a way to take that grief and turn it into something useful, like a weapon. She would need all her strength, all her weapons, to survive the next few days.

Eldest, she was tired. Even though she'd slept for twelve hours, between tending to her son, she felt as weary now as she had when she'd laid down her head the night before. With so much of the fortress damaged, she'd had to sleep amongst the Lost Ones, back in the women's tent once more. The few Maenardh women had clucked and fussed over the baby, offering all manner of well-meant – and occasionally contradictory – advice, but all she'd wanted was for them to leave her alone to rest.

Not one of them had the least inkling of what she'd seen, what she'd endured. The clutching terror of the foretelling that had all but paralysed her, until the Warlord had hustled her down the steps from the wall. The sound that shook the sky, ground lurching, stone tumbling; the choking dust that filled the air and the shrilling cacophony where the music of her magic should have been, howling through her like a storm. She shuddered at the memories, eyes flinching shut.

Only Neve had come close to understanding. Baer's woman had seen her settled with a warm blanket and a bowl of tea, and shooed the others back to their tasks as if they were chickens. Dear Neve. Tears threatened again, and Teia dashed them away with the back of her hand. There was no time for that any more. Every hour's delay meant another hour in which Ytha drew closer to finding the starseed.

'You shouldn't be riding this soon,' Neve said, emerging from the women's tent and coming to stand at Finn's head. The big dun curled his lip at her half-heartedly, then went back to chewing his bit. 'It's scarce a day and a half since you gave birth, girl.'

'I don't have a choice.' Teia fed the strap through the last buckle and pulled it tight.

'Not even for your babe's sake?'

She looked down at her son, snug in his blanket sling, and touched his silky head. By Aedon's grace, he'd escaped the devastation in the infirmary; a man she vaguely recognised had brought him to her, wriggling and demanding to be fed, none the worse for his adventures.

'We'll be fine, Neve.'

The other woman grunted. 'The afterblood's still coming, isn't it? Your bones are still cradle-soft. Should scarce even be walking about, much less in the saddle.'

'The healer—'

'That healer's never borne a child of her own. Not with those little breasts – flat-dugged as a maiden hound, I'd bet! What can she know?'

'She told me she'd apprenticed to a Master Healer for five years,' Teia said. 'The afterblood's not so bad I can't deal with it. I have to do this, Neve.'

The older woman frowned and looked away, mouth pulling into a thin, tight line. 'That child needs a name,' she said at last.

'I'm not sure what to call him,' she said.

'It's traditional to take something from his father's name.'

Teia curled her arm protectively around the child. 'I don't want anything to do with his father.'

'Aye, well.' Looking down at her shawl, Neve picked away a bit of fluff. 'Could always name him after your da, then. Make a new tradition, since we're making a new life down here.'

Teir would burst with pride at the thought of a grandson named after him. Teia imagined her father lifting him up, the baby's tiny fists grabbing for the dangling ends of his moustaches and Teir laughing and laughing, until tears came again and she had to put the image away for another time, when it wouldn't matter so much if her heart shattered.

Neve ducked back into the tent and returned with a grey army blanket, neatly folded. 'You should take an extra one. Nights are still plenty cold, for all we're out of the snow. Don't want the little one to catch a chill.'

'Thank you.' Teia busied herself rolling it and tying it behind the saddle, until she was sure her eyes were dry again.

'You have all you need?' Neve asked gruffly.

'I think so.' Teia mustered something of a smile. 'The Warlord's arranged for me to have all the supplies I want.'

Lips pursed, Neve made a non-committal sound. 'Powerful friends you have now, Banfaíth.'

Teia winced. 'Don't call me that. Please. My name is Teia.'

The older woman said nothing, refusing to meet Teia's eye until she took Neve's hands in hers and squeezed them.

'Please, Neve. Use my name. We're friends now, aren't we?' She ducked a little to peer up at the other woman's face. 'Please?'

Neve's lips twitched. 'As you wish, Banfaíth.' The twitch became the beginnings of a smile, creasing up her dark eyes. 'Teia.'

They hugged, careful of the infant between them, and Neve kissed Teia's cheeks.

'Best get on now,' she said, a little gruffly. 'Many miles to go.' Straightening up, she hesitated, as if she had more to say, then she tugged her shawl tight across her bosom and disappeared back into the tent.

So much for farewells. Baer was up at the keep somewhere, helping with the prisoners and still coming to terms with being addressed as a clan chief by the Warlord. Teia had said her goodbyes to him earlier. Last night Lenna had cried, and Isaak, bless him, had offered to ride with her as escort, though she could see in his eyes it tore him apart to have to choose between his Banfaíth and his bairn. He hadn't been able to entirely hide his relief when she'd turned him down.

No, this was her task and no one else's. She cast one last glance at the closed tent flap, then walked to Finn's shoulder. As she prepared to mount, she saw Duncan riding down the road from the keep at the head of a double line of clansmen, each with a round shield on his back and a spear to hand. The men pulled up at the edge of the Maenardh camp and Duncan alone rode up to where Teia waited.

'Neve still doesn't trust me, I see,' he said as he reached her, and swung down from the saddle.

'I don't think Neve trusts anyone south of the mountains,' she said. 'She'll come around. Eventually.'

533

'Aye, when I'm grey, perhaps!' He gave her a long look, a thoughtful one, right into her face. 'I can't change your mind on this, can I?' he asked softly.

She shook her head, too weary to have to explain herself again, but he didn't argue, just lifted a bundle of fur down from behind his saddle. 'Then you'll need this.'

He snapped the string binding the bundle and silvery fur tumbled down to his boots. Teia gaped at it, then at him, and he smiled.

'It was awful dusty when I found it, but a good shaking took care of that. Your staff was broken, though.'

She touched the thick fur, pushed her fingers into the pile. Ytha might not consider her an equal, but she would go accoutred as one nonetheless. The bearing, the appearance of power, was almost as important to a Speaker as the gift of magic itself.

'Thank you,' she said. 'Thank you very much, Duncan.'

He gave her a little bow, in the fashion of the southerners, and held the garment out for her to put on. 'Your mantle, Banfaíth.'

'Stop calling me that!' she chided, but turned her back to let him drape the cloak across her shoulders. He fussed with it until it was just so, then eased her hair out from underneath the fur. As he did so his fingers brushed her neck and sent a shiver chasing over her skin.

'There.' Duncan stepped back as she turned around. 'You look the part again.'

Teia gathered up Finn's reins. 'You don't have to do this, you know.'

'I'm afraid I do. You didn't think the Warlord would let you ride out to face Ytha alone, did you? Or Baer, come to that? After you told him your plans, he was all set to steal a horse and come with us.'

Baer? 'I don't want to put anyone in harm's way. This is my mess – I should be the one to clean it up.'

'Doesn't mean you can't have a little help,' he said, and flashed her that easy smile again. 'Besides, Aradhrim's going back to Fleet, and the Gatekeeper's headed west to rejoin the other *gaeden* from King's Gate, so we'd be on the road anyway. Might as well ride together.' Linking his hands, he offered them to help her mount. 'Banfaíth?'

She let him boost her into the saddle and settled herself as comfortably as she could so soon after giving birth. Despite the copper-haired woman using her gift to speed her recovery, this journey would be hard.

If it's worth having, it's worth fighting for, Teisha, her father had said once. What would he make of his youngest daughter now, riding out to war?

☙☙

Gair was stowing the last of his supplies in Shahe's packs when he felt someone's eyes on him. He'd hoped to be away before now; he had little time and a great many miles to cover, so many in fact that even the few minutes required to check over the *sulqa's* feet and legs and see that she was fit for the road felt like an indulgence, for all that he knew it insured against the loss of precious hours later should she cast a shoe somewhere on the journey. The last thing he wanted now was more interruptions.

He fastened the final buckle and tucked the tail of the strap through its keeper, then paused, half-turned. Masen was leaning on the wall by the gate, keeping the weight off his newly Healed knee. His boot of a face was crumpled and weary.

'Planning on slipping out without saying goodbye?' he asked sourly.

That stung – and not least because it was the truth. Gair hadn't wanted to argue it out again; he just wanted to go, get away from Saardost and its ghosts as soon as he could.

'I looked for you but you were meeting with the Warlord. I didn't want to intrude.'

'Gair—' Masen began, then stopped and shook his head. 'Don't do this. Please.'

'There's nothing else I can do here except more damage.' He turned back to his horse, checking over the rest of her harness one more time so he wouldn't have to face the Gatekeeper's disappointment. Selfish? Probably. Cowardly? He was already so mortified by what he'd done in the pass that he wanted to leave it far behind him as quickly as possible. But he owed Masen an explanation. 'Tanith needs my help.'

'We all do, lad,' said the other man, and then he sighed. 'Is she safe?'

Gair's hand went to his breastbone and the shape of the Song-woven retreat under his shirt. Sacrificing one of his last few oakmarks for its silver, with fire and air he'd woven a web of wire around the pearl with a loop at the top so it could be threaded onto a thong. Wearing it around his neck was the safest way to carry it; he didn't dare take the chance that it might fall out of his pocket, and after it had pulsed that one time he wanted to keep it close, so that he would know if it happened again. So that he'd know Tanith was still alive.

'She's safe.' Shahe lipped at his hand and he scratched her chin. 'I have to do this, Masen. She's important.'

The Gatekeeper said nothing, merely looked away across the rubble-strewn yard. Unspoken words hung in the air between them. *Is she more important than Arennor? More important than the Veil itself?* Gair fiddled with Shahe's forelock as the answers churned through his head. Wasn't Astolar just as important? Wasn't a life and a kingdom saved far better than condemning untold hundreds more to death?

I am a monster.

Heat burned in his cheeks and he ducked his head to hide it. Memories flickered like coals in a draught: scaly coils hissing as they rubbed together, eyes that seared right through him and knew him more intimately than he knew himself. All his rage. All his capacity for violence. His stomach lurched. Part of him had enjoyed the destruction he had wrought. It had revelled in the deep thrum of the earth's Song, roared exultantly as it was unleashed. That part of him wanted to dive back into the fire and feel its caress again. Something close to panic fluttered in his throat.

Now I am lost in a place of darkness, O Mother, I am fallen from Thy path.

He made himself look down at his left hand, at the witchmark branded into his palm. Parts of it were pale as wax now, others still as red and angry as the day the farrier had pressed the iron to his skin. His fist closed convulsively and he shuddered. He had fallen so very much further since then.

'Day's a-wasting, Gair.' Masen's voice pulled him out of his thoughts.

Gair nodded. He couldn't pretend he had more preparations to make; it was time to go. He made himself walk over to the Gatekeeper and offer his hand. After the merest hesitation, Masen accepted the clasp, but without a great deal of warmth. He was probably glad to see the back of him, Gair supposed. After all that had happened, the Gatekeeper was entitled to some rancour.

'So what will you do?' he asked. 'Go up to King's Gate?'

'Aye.' Masen released his hand and folded his arms. 'Barin and I will do what we can to harass the war band until Maera mobilises her Speakers and we can get more *gaeden* support from the Isles. I'll strip Chapterhouse to the bone if I have to.'

'And the Warlord?'

'As soon as he's able, he's moving his headquarters back to Fleet. Saardost's safe for the time being, and so's the Fall now that the Nimrothi have made their move. What happens next is up to them, but we'll be a step behind all the way unless we figure out where the starseed is.'

'I wish there was something more I could tell you, but the stone barely warrants a mention in the official histories.'

The texts Gair had studied at the Motherhouse had been more

concerned with the punishment of Corlainn's sin than with what he had actually done to warrant the censure. He suspected that the First Knight was only mentioned at all in order to be castigated with every word.

Masen waved his words away. 'We'll find some older maps and see what we can see,' he said. 'You'd best get gone. There's more than a few miles to Astolar.'

Gair gave another nod. 'When he wakes up, tell Sorchal I'm sorry.'

Then he swung up onto Shahe's back and steered her through the fallen masonry to the gatehouse. Its mighty arch was cracked and leaning, the gates crookedly ajar, the windlass broken. A few soldiers glanced up from their work as he passed, but their gazes were blank, only idly curious. They didn't know who he was, or what he'd done, and for that he was grateful. That knowledge was already hard enough to bear.

46

SEVEN TOWERS

ᘛᘚ

From the highest remaining bastion of the fortress, Ytha looked down the valley at the road emerging from the dawn shadows, winding through the pass. There in the distance were the towers, their ancient stones gleaming in the early light.

A day or two's respite from the long journey had been welcome, and the men had surely earned a celebration after their victory, but it was time to be moving again. She felt it in her bones, and it gave her no more stomach for delay. At last she was going home, to the lands of her ancestors. At last she could set right the wrong that had driven her people into a thousand years of exile north of the Archen Mountains, cut off from their sacred places. At long, long last.

Unable to keep the smile from her lips, she laced her fingers together and pushed her arms high above her head to stretch out her spine. It popped and cracked like *duga*-nuts left too close to the fire and she winced. Too much *uisca* last night had sent her into too deep a sleep and knotted her muscles like poorly spun wool. She thought about the warrior she'd left snoring in his furs and the smile became a grin. Too much of him as well, perhaps; her *cuinh* was still tingling. For a moment she toyed with the idea of taking him for one last ride, then finished her stretch and put him from her mind. He'd scratched her itch well enough for now. It was time to concentrate on the south, and the starseed waiting for her.

Down in the valley, the day was brightening. The morning breeze brought the sounds of men stirring in the camp below the fortress walls and the tang of smoke from cook-fires. No doubt there'd be a few sore heads after the celebrations, but that was just too bad. She'd cautioned Drwyn against allowing the war band too much carousing, but men would be men, and wise words were too often lost on them.

Ytha grimaced. Well, let them sweat the *uisca* out on the journey; it might teach them to moderate themselves. Like children, they needed to burn their fingers to learn to fear the fire.

Claws rattled on stone behind her and she turned. One of the Hounds trotted up the steps from below and out into the sunshine. Its thick yellow-grey fur was splotched and smeared with blood and its sagging belly said it had eaten well. It watched her, swiping its long tongue around its muzzle, then made a throaty sound somewhere between a bark and a cough.

She held out her hand, clicking her fingers. 'Come here, my pet.'

The Hound continued to stare but made no move towards her. Frowning, Ytha snapped her fingers again, but the beast dropped its rump to the stones and yawned.

Intolerable. She drew herself up, folding her snow-fox mantle around her. 'I said—'

The Hound's jaws stretched even wider. Its ears turned back into its fur, its tongue curling delicately between its teeth. Its yellow, disturbingly serrated teeth, which progressed to fangs as long as her smallest finger and as sharp as knives. Ytha could not drag her eyes away. With a sound like a bone breaking, the jaws clacked back together, and she started.

Foolish woman, she chided herself. *It's naught but a dog.* A dog with a gape wide enough to swallow her head, but a dog nonetheless.

'Maegern sent you to me—'

The beast coughed again, in the pointed manner of a man who had been interrupted whilst speaking, and pricked its ears. Unblinking orange eyes fixed on her face. And it waited.

Ytha had outstared warriors before. Met the eye of grief-crazed fathers, faced down the rage of chiefs, but holding the gaze of Maegern's hunting Hound was enough to break sweat on the palms of her hands. Carefully, she closed her mouth and let the rest of the words she'd been about to say die on her tongue. Sometimes there was more wisdom in silence.

Swallowing her pride scratched her throat like cockleburrs, but she did it, lowered her eyes and thanked the Eldest that there was no one present to witness it.

Stiff-backed, she walked to the stone steps that led down into the tower. The Hound's stare followed her every stride of the way, searing her spine until the stairs' spiral finally blocked it. Only then did she let herself exhale a slow, shaky breath.

They are not coursing-dogs, Ytha. They will not come when you call and go where you bid them. To her chagrin she heard the words in Teia's voice and ground her teeth. Damn that girl! Why couldn't she simply have died in the snows?

Claws clicked behind her, then the Hound pushed past her skirts and trotted ahead down the stairs, its great plumy tail waving. It did not spare her so much as a backward glance.

Out in the yard, the sprawled and broken corpses of the defenders still lay where they had fallen. The clans' own dead had been taken beyond the walls the night before and given a chief's burial, with fire, since there was so much wood to hand. Those souls lost to secure their homeland would have seats of high honour in the Hall of Heroes, and Maegern Herself would raise a cup to Her glorious dead.

To Ytha's surprise, she found Drwyn at the foot of the tower, seated on a pile of broken stone with three or four of his chosen men, all with mugs in their fists and variously slack and bleary expressions.

'A good morning to you, Speaker,' he called, taking a slender pipe from between his teeth and saluting her with it. Fragrant blue smoke curled around his words. 'Care to try some? It's sweeter than *bilcha*-root – I took it off one of the greenbacks.' Pursing his lips, he blew a thin plume of smoke up above his head and laughed.

She ground her teeth. What she had at first mistaken for alertness was in fact inebriation. He was as drunk as his men and, from the number of flasks and barrels around their feet, they'd been drinking more or less continuously since the fortress fell, two days ago.

'Assemble the men,' she snapped. 'We need to move.' Ahead of her, the Hound was already at the half-open gates, where it stopped to scent the air. The other one poked its head around the gate from outside, ears pricked alertly.

'Already?' Drwyn complained. 'It's barely sun-up.'

'It's time.' The Hounds looked back at her, panting. Those orange eyes were all too knowing, all too aware. Then the beasts turned and loped out through the gates. 'We did not come all this way to lie abed, Drwyn!'

He sighed, looking wistfully at his unfinished pipe. 'As you wish, Speaker – though it will take an hour or more to break camp, with half the war band still with their heads in the slops bucket—'

'I don't care!' Ytha rounded on him, her earlier good mood now thoroughly shredded. 'Get them up and on their horses – if their bellies are tender they can puke from the saddle!'

Drwyn pushed himself to his feet and came towards her. Close to, he stank of *uisca* and stale beer. By Aedon's holy *daigh*, he was the *chief*, not a child – why did she have to explain everything to him?

'The starseed is within our grasp,' she hissed. 'Or have you forgotten why we left the Broken Land in the first place? We did not come here for pipe-fodder!'

'No need to shout, woman, I'm right here,' Drwyn grumbled, and drained the last of his ale. 'Rouse the men, Harl.'

'But my chief—'

'You heard the Speaker.' Swinging on his heel, Drwyn hurled the empty mug at the blond warrior. 'If she says we ride, we ride.'

ᴔ

It took what felt like an eternity to get the men moving. Moaning and clutching their heads, they dragged their feet at the simplest tasks, as if they had no concept of what was at stake. Even snapping and snarling at them had no noticeable effect. By the Eldest, if she hadn't been the Speaker to the Chief of Chiefs she'd have saddled her own damned horse and had it ready twice as quickly. But at last it was done, Drwyn and the other chiefs and their chosen men at least. Leaving the rest of the war band in various stages of wakefulness and under stern instruction to follow as soon as they could get a leg across a horse, Ytha rode out after the Hounds.

The beasts were waiting for her at the first bend in the trail, ears pricked and tongues lolling. As soon as they judged they were close enough to have been seen and their direction marked, they set off again. So eager was she to reach her destination, Ytha was sorely tempted to urge her horse up to a trot after them, but exhausting her mount now would serve little purpose when she had no way of knowing how long the road ahead would be. But oh, it was difficult to rein herself in each time those thickly furred tails disappeared from sight around the next bend – especially when rounding that same bend brought the towers rising up from the trees ahead back into view again. Like children at play they slipped in and out of sight as the road wound down from the heights of the pass, and every time they reappeared they were closer, clearer, and her magic tingled in anticipation.

Of the few survivors who'd escaped when the fortress fell there was no sign, bar some scuffled tracks in the dirt. She paid them no mind; all she had time for now was her victory and the prize that awaited her. The excitement built with every mile, rising in her chest, pulling at the corners of her mouth until her cheeks ached with suppressing the grin that threatened to break out at any moment. Gods, she'd waited so long for this!

'What awaits us in that place?' Drwyn asked as the morning wore on and the day warmed. He was squinting against the brightness of the sky, fortifying himself with frequent sips from a flask.

'Seven warriors, so the Raven tells it. Beyond that?' She shrugged. 'Does it matter? Our prize is within our grasp now.' Eyeing the flask as it made another trip to his mouth, she pursed her lips. 'Water will clear your head faster than more spirits, you know.'

He merely grunted and downed another mouthful. Ytha rolled her eyes and kicked her horse on. The man never had a thought for anything but his appetites. Not for the first time, she wondered how so canny a chief as Drw could have sired that lump of a son. Grimacing, she urged the horse to a canter to run off some of her irritation. The road was wide and firm despite the lingering slush and runnels of meltwater that sparkled over it; she could let the animal stretch its legs a while.

The Hounds were waiting at the next bend. Their mouths stretched wide when they saw her, and with cheerful yips they fell in on either side, effortlessly matching pace with her mount. It was almost tempting to try for a gallop, purely to see if they could keep up. But her horse was starting to blow, weary after the long journey through the mountains and in need of some good pasture, so she slowed him to a walk and idled the rest of the way south and east from the shattered fortress, until the light began to fail and the party was obliged to make a scratch camp beneath the trees.

Soon after first light, Ytha was back in the saddle, eager to resume the journey, and on the trail again before the others were even fully awake, too impatient to wait for them. The towers were markedly closer today, rising out of the valleys ahead like a stand of spears. She bared her teeth, unable to contain her fierce glee. Yes. All her years of planning and waiting, of moulding a chief behind whom a people would rally, were coming to fruition, and she would not be denied. The grin grew wider and she tipped back her head, savouring the warmth of the sun on her face, then looked around at the landscape as it emerged from the morning shadows.

So these were her people's ancient lands. They were not so different from those she had left behind: the same dense blanket of pine and larch clothed the slopes, threaded with bright streams, and the haze of the plains in the distance looked much the same as the view from the Crainnh's winter quarters when the thaw began, but there were differences, subtle ones. A familiar flower with a broader leaf or a longer stem. A spotted bird with an altered cadence to its song. Even the air was softer, she fancied, with less of the chill tang of winter to it – or maybe that was just the sunshine warming her mood. Either way, she had a feeling she would enjoy her new home very much indeed.

Paws pattered on the stony trail behind her and the two Hounds trotted past to disappear around the next bend. They were as impatient as her, it appeared – and eager to rejoin the Hunt. Excitement building, Ytha urged her horse after them.

Bend after swooping bend, the trail wound through the many-folded skirts of the mountains. Each turn brought the towers closer, sharpening in the sun, then the fifth bend abruptly opened up the vista. The tangled ridges fell back and Ytha jerked her mount to a stop in sheer amazement. She stared at the slumped and tumbled walls, at the forest of towers within, and her mouth fell open. It was painfully ugly, an abomination of piled stone that thrust up like the fingers of a giant clutching for the heavens, but it was also shockingly beautiful, bathed in the afternoon sun, with its great arched entrance open in welcome.

The Raven had been as good as Her word. Her Hounds had led the way to the city just as She had promised; Ytha had no reason to think they would not lead her to the stone itself. Then the starseed would be hers, and with it the power to lead her people to their rightful home.

You should have trusted me, Drw.

She began to laugh. The Hounds exchanged a look and plopped their rumps down on the road, tongues lolling, and Ytha roared until her ribs ached.

From up the road behind her came the drumming of hooves. Drwyn and his chosen men burst around the bend with weapons readied and then reined up in confusion because there was no danger, nothing but their Speaker and the city laid out before them. Several made signs of warding and sat their horses uneasily, but Drwyn urged his tall black through the group to Ytha's side.

Fighting to subdue the waves of mirth, she extended her hand with a flourish. 'My chief, I give you the city of seven towers.'

Drwyn shaded his eyes and peered at the piles of stone. 'There must be a hundred of them. Are you sure this is the right place?'

One of the Hounds made a gruff sound much like a snort of derision. Of course it was the right place. Ytha refrained from rolling her eyes and pointed.

'Look.'

In the centre of the city, just visible between the intact towers and the broken stubs of their less fortunate brethren, was a ring of seven identical shapes, evenly spaced like petals on a flower.

'Then the Raven spoke truly,' he breathed.

'Was Her word ever in any doubt?'

Drwyn flashed her a wolfish grin. In the valley below them, a crow took flight from one of the ruined towers, cawing loudly. Two more followed it. Squinting, Drwyn tracked them across the valley and then returned to studying the city.

'It looks deserted,' he said. 'No smoke.'

No sound, either. Nothing but birds and water and the restless hiss of the wind through the pine forest around them. Bushes and small trees grew in cracks in the walls. Moss carpeted the scree of fallen blocks nearest the road as if whatever structure it had once been had collapsed generations ago. Ytha scanned the outlines of the buildings, looking for movement, and found none. Summoning her magic, she reached out, but the only lives she could feel were small and fast: insects, birds, rodents.

Abandoned, she thought. Like the forts had been – until recently, anyway – but the greenbacks had given themselves away with their trumpets and their hammers. If anyone was waiting for them in Maegern's city, they were silent as the stones.

'Ask the other chiefs and their Speakers to join us,' she said. 'All should witness this.'

'All the chiefs in one place?' Drwyn frowned and clicked his tongue against his teeth. 'I cannot say I like this idea, Ytha. What if the Empire is waiting for us here, too?'

'Have no fear, my chief.' She gathered up her horse's reins. 'This city is long abandoned. I think perhaps the Empire has forgotten it exists.'

'And what of the warriors the Raven warned us about?'

'Gone to dust, I expect, like everyone else. Only wild things live here now.'

She started her horse walking. At once the Hounds jumped to their feet and set off down the trail towards the city. After a moment, Drwyn followed, his chosen men and the other chiefs and their Speakers, who by now had caught them up, falling in behind. Led by the Hounds, Ytha rode under the weathered stone arch in the outer wall into a wide area that had once been covered with flat slabs of stone, their interlocking pattern now obscured by the tussocks of tough mountain grass that had sprouted between them.

As she had suspected, the southerners' city was soulless. Even the trees and plants that grew amongst the stones had a sickly, stunted look, as if only stubbornness kept them there. All else was grey and cold and hard and dead: empty holes gaping in the walls like the eye sockets of skulls, yawning like mouths onto a darkness within. Hooves rang loud on stone and the walls threw the sound back as if it was not welcome after so long in silence.

She ignored the uneasy mutters of the men riding behind her and smiled to herself.

Your time is over, usurpers. The horse-lords have come and we will make these lands ours again!

Ahead of her, the Hounds trotted along side by side, their claws clicking on the square stones underfoot. From time to time, one or the other would glance back to make sure she was following, but they never broke their stride, never faltered, and every turn brought their destination a little closer. Sometimes the seven towers disappeared behind a taller structure then reappeared a little to the left or the right as the Hounds plotted their route through the long stony canyons towards them, and every time Ytha saw them again her heart leapt.

This was the day when all the long years of waiting and scheming would prove worthwhile. On this day she would finally lead her people home, at the head of the Wild Hunt itself. The excitement was almost too much to contain. She looked across at Drwyn riding next to her, to bask in his gratitude, but all she saw was anxiety. He peered about at the gaping maws of the surrounding structures as if expecting wild animals to launch themselves at him, flinched every time some covey of birds, startled by the approaching horses, burst for the air. Her lips thinned. Even more of a dullard than she'd feared. Insufficient imagination to conceive of the glories to come, but just enough to people the shadows with monsters, like a child.

'The city is dead,' she said quietly, so the other chiefs and their men wouldn't hear. If the Chief of Chiefs looked weak, it damaged her position as his Speaker. 'No one has lived here in generations.'

His hunted eyes flicked from doorway to doorway, and his hand kept straying to the hilt of the sword on his belt. 'Dead things leave ghosts.'

'And shades make you nervous, my chief?'

'Who knows what could be waiting for us?' he muttered. 'The Empire may be craftier than we thought.'

'I told you, nothing lives here. All that awaits us is a victory greater than the clans have seen since Gwlach's time, so do not forget it!'

She faced forward again, determined not to let his skittishness dent her triumphant mood. By the Eldest, she would have her victory, with him or without.

The echoing stone canyon ended a little way ahead. The two Hounds trotted out of the shadows between the looming walls into warm sunlight and stopped, their plumy tails waving. Beyond them, a bowshot's length away, reared a cliff-like wall carved and ornamented with stone figures, flushed rosy by the settling sun. Up and up it rose, its highest reaches silhouetted against the sky. The Hounds looked back over their shoulders, long tongues lolling.

Yes.

Ytha straightened in her saddle, firming her grip on the white-wood staff resting upright on the toe of her boot. 'We appear to have arrived at our destination.'

Without waiting for her chief or the Speakers behind her, she urged her horse out of the canyon towards the vast structure.

Its walls spread wide, further than her gaze could encompass without turning her head. In the centre, tiered steps broad and deep enough to ride up led to a many-arched entrance black as a cave mouth, flanked by towering figures three times and more the height of a man. Time and weather had blurred their features but they were robed like iron men of old, holding long swords upright before them, pointed shields resting at their sides. Above them, row after row of smaller openings, all empty as the ones she'd seen in the canyons but for a few birds, white as motes in the walls' blind eyes. She tipped her head back and squinted against the sun. And at the highest point, seven towers thrusting up around a domed construct resembling a tent, which gleamed in the afternoon light.

That men had dared to lift their dwellings so high astonished her. But of course the southerners had dared. They were godless, so in love with their own cleverness they no longer looked up at the sky and pondered who put it there. No wonder their city had fallen into ruin. When gods chose to visit their vengeance on men, a lack of belief offered scant protection. Still, the impudence – the arrogance! – of these southerners, to challenge Aedon so, left her breathless. Breathless with excitement, too, that far outweighed any trepidation she might have felt at being confronted by so vast a creation.

Hooves rang sharply on the stones behind her. In moments, Drwyn's black warhorse was falling into step beside her bay, the Chief of Chiefs straight-backed in the saddle, his face carefully impassive.

'I cannot let you enter alone, my Speaker,' he said, loudly and firmly enough to be heard by the rest of the party.

Ytha hid a smile. She could smell the sweat on him, feel the apprehension rolling off him in waves. But she inclined her head graciously, also for the benefit of the others. 'My chief.'

Ahead, the Hounds bounded up the steps and disappeared into the shadows inside the structure. The horses baulked at first, but with encouragement began to clop up the pitted stone slabs. Rust stains spilled down from the highest steps like old blood, as if the doorway had been the scene of a desperate defence. Drwyn swallowed and gripped the hilt of his father's sword more tightly as they approached the top. Even Ytha felt a flutter of fear: the blackness within was fathomless. With the sun already sinking behind the mountains, no light penetrated beyond the arches, though she could hear the rattle of the Hounds' claws from somewhere inside.

'A little light, I think,' she murmured.

A touch of her magic conjured half a dozen pale spheres and sent them inside. Shadows moved with the globes, surging forward and falling back in a ghostly dance as the orbs revealed more of the interior. Flat slabs of stone on the floor, rows of columns and more arches, all spattered and crusted with bird-droppings and so begrimed by the ages that only the dullest glimmer remained of what must once have been a high shine.

One of the Hounds trotted out of the shifting dark and gave an impatient cough. It echoed oddly inside the structure, and somewhere far overhead, wings whirred.

Ytha reined up and dismounted, looking around at the strange place. Its roof rose high on stone ribs that met in geometric patterns, every notch and crevice of which was jammed with birds' nests. The dry air smelled acrid, stale, laden with the dust of feathers that caught in the throat and edged with the faint aroma of things long dead. As she turned in a slow circle to follow her lights as they roamed the space, tiny bones crunched under her boots.

Once, this place must have appeared grand, with the coloured stone of walls and floor all polished, maybe rich furnishings scattered about. Here and there amongst the heaped bird-lime she made out shapes that might once have been objects of wood or cloth but were now so collapsed and rotten they were as grey as the cobwebs that covered them.

Drwyn left his horse at the entrance and walked to join her, his posture tense and his gaze darting about. Sweat gleamed on his brow and in the hollow of his throat. The emerald eyes of the wolf-heads on his torc glittered as he swallowed nervously.

'This place disturbs me,' he said.

The Hound coughed again. Its orange eyes glowed in the half-light as if afire, clearly impatient.

'Courage, Drwyn,' Ytha sang. 'Power is almost within our grasp.' She gestured to the Hound. 'Lead on, my pet.'

It glared at her and snapped its jaws shut with a loud click. Briefly, Ytha wondered if it was the same beast that had defied her at the fortress, but there was too much excitement bubbling in her chest for her to care. She could almost feel the presence of the starseed: there was a resonance in the magic she had spun to make the orbs, a chiming note that bounced and echoed through the music the way she felt one of her sister Speakers working the Talent through a ring.

With a snort, the Hound turned and trotted away into the corner. Ytha sent a couple of globes after it to light the way and followed, with Drwyn close by her side. The beast led them through another grand arch into a part of the structure where the darkness crowded more thickly. It reminded her of some of the deep tunnels in the winter caves, where the very density of the silence was oppressive.

Beside her she heard Drwyn swallowing again and spun a couple more lights overhead to supplement the others. They revealed warped and cracked wood on the walls, glistening with curls of peeling lacquer. The stone underfoot had kept some of its lustre, dark red marbled with white, like a fine cut of meat. Flat floor became another flight of steps, ten or more, then a corner, then another ascent. Two more turns, two more ascents, and another arch, smaller this time, disgorged into an open space. There the Hound stopped. Across the space, another pair of orange eyes glowed, presumably belonging to its twin.

The ringing in Ytha's magic intensified, became a thrumming in her ears, in the very core of her soul. Her power leapt joyfully inside her, a hound pup eager to play. Excellent; her treasure was close. Soon it would be revealed. Pulse quickening, she gathered together all the twists of power that made her lights and released them above her head.

Monstrous figures loomed out of the dark. Glaring helms, sharp blades. Shadows leapt and danced around them. Drwyn gasped and fumbled for his sword as Ytha snatched for her magic and readied air and lightning to hurl. But no weapons clashed, no voices roared a challenge. As the glowing orbs drifted higher into the ceiling vault, their radiance pushed the shadows back to the corners of the room and revealed seven kneeling figures arranged around a short, broad pillar. All were carved from the same pale, smooth stone.

Feeling slightly foolish, Ytha let her power go. In all her excitement to find the starseed, the shapes of warriors looming out of the dark had caught her off guard. Now her heart was hammering and her nerves were prickling in anticipation of another scare. Blowing out a long breath, she leaned on her staff and waited for her pulse to steady. Beside her, Drwyn straightened from his fighting crouch and lowered his sword.

'The seven warriors, I suppose,' he said in disgust, slamming the blade back into its scabbard. Squinting at the nearest figure, he rapped his knuckles on its helm and dust bloomed in the air. 'Not much fight in them, eh?'

He laughed at his own joke, a little too loudly. The dense, dry air soaked it up and threw echoes back at odd intervals, so that it sounded like someone else in the room was laughing at them. A puzzled frown creased his brows and he looked around uncertainly, as if trying to work out where the laughter had originated. It no longer sounded anything like his.

Ytha looked around, too, eyes probing the shadowy corners, mind reaching out through her power. No signs of living beings, apart from a few rodents and skittering, many-legged things – and the chiefs and their Speakers making their way up the steps and into the vast hall below.

'Peace, Drwyn,' she said. 'We are alone.'

The chiming was stronger. It resonated in the starseed chip in her ring, strange colours refracting through her. Bluish sparks sputtered around her hand, trickled down her staff to the dusty floor. So much potential, humming there just out of her reach. Like the strength of the binding, only keener, somehow, more pure. She began to smile.

'The stone is here.'

'It is?' Drwyn forgot his unease, excitement lifting his voice. 'Where?'

'Very near,' she said. 'In this room, I am sure of it.' She turned slowly in place, gaze scanning the kneeling stone warriors, searching for buckles, adornments, clasps or brooches. Nothing stood out as the starseed. Not even any ornamented sword pommels or diadems on helms. Nothing.

From below came the sound of footsteps on stone. Many footsteps. Murmuring voices, the words distorted by echoes, and the prickling sense of the Talent. The other Speakers were coming. She had to find the stone, and quickly – she didn't dare risk that one of the others might find it first.

Her eye kept drifting back to the pedestal at the centre of the ring of statues. They all faced it, and their posture, kneeling on one knee with their naked swords upright in front of them, suggested obeisance. Reverence, even. Had the southerners worshipped something there, perhaps the starseed itself? Her heart skipped. Had they even known what it was?

But the drawn swords, the shields to hand, also suggested readiness. Ytha crossed the mouse-tracked dust to stand beside the pedestal and looked at each of the iron men in turn. None had their heads bowed. They faced the pedestal as if their unseen eyes were fixed on it, and they had weapons in their fists. Warriors, anticipating danger.

Except without the Talent and the will to wield it, the stone itself was naught but a bauble, no more dangerous than a glass bead on a saddle-charm. But in the hands of any one of those women now climbing the stairs, it threatened everything she had worked and waited for.

Macha's ears, where is it?

The voices were growing louder. The darkness within the arched entrance to the chamber brightened as light leaked around the corners from the stairs below, the weavings rippling and tickling through Ytha's awareness of her own power. Blast them, she was running out of time! Closing her eyes, she sifted through the swirling music in her mind for the crystalline shimmer of the starseed.

'The chiefs are coming. Have you found it?' Drwyn again.

She quietened him with a gesture, her thoughts reaching out.

'Ytha!'

Gods, couldn't the man let her *think*?

Music surrounded her. She was adrift in it, in the murmurations of the cut stone, almost silent after so many years, in the bright and skittering melodies of the tiny creatures that had colonised this dead place.

The music eddied. Something clear and cold caught her up—

Silence where there should have been song.

Silence, and it was waiting.

Barely aware of the footsteps behind her, deaf to the voices questioning, urging, Ytha balled her fist, raised it high. She called her power and heard the other women gasp as magic roared into them through the binding. Then she brought her fist down.

Stone shattered. Dust billowed in the air. Fragments careened off the statues, tearing holes in artfully carved cloth, gouging their cold flesh, and rebounded from the walls. Ytha ducked and turned her head aside to spare her eyes. Around her, men and women yelped as they were bruised by whirring stone shards. She felt some of the blows dimly on her body, either impacts on her own flesh or reflected through the binding, but the pain was transient, immaterial. All that mattered was her reward.

When the waves of noise diminished, to be replaced by coughing and moaning, and the last splinters of stone had clattered to rest, she straightened up. Under the force of her blow, the pedestal's capping stone had fractured into several pieces. With air she heaved the first one aside, disturbing the others, and they slid away to smash on the floor. In the well in the top of the pedestal, amongst the dust and broken stone, something glittered.

At last.

Ytha reached out her hand and closed it around the starseed.

She'd expected the stone to feel cold, or hot, or make her flesh creep. It did none of those things. In fact, it did nothing at all but sit in her hand, not much larger than a goose egg and as inert as a river pebble. She was unable to help feeling a twinge of disappointment.

She lifted the stone up to eye level and gently blew off the dust. The surface beneath was as brilliantly reflective as the little looking-glass Drwyn's mother had treasured, showing her own face peering back at her. A perfect reflection of her own face, with none of the eye-watering distortions that a curved surface usually produced. Her hand, her fingers, were mirrored in the stone as if in water, even though her mind insisted that was impossible. She looked more closely. The detail was remarkable: she could see every line and pore in her skin, every eyelash, and in the starseed's reflection of her pupil was another starseed, another eye, another starseed—

She snatched her gaze from the stone before the reflections of reflections sucked her wits away, and found herself facing Drwyn. He was staring at the stone hungrily. Crowded around him were half a dozen other chiefs and their Speakers, some rapt, some sceptical.

'Is that it?' he asked.

The resonance in her gift said that what she held was a starseed of immense potential, but there was only one way to be sure. Reaching through the stone, Ytha touched her magic.

Firethorn blazed on her skin as the power hit her and all the others still bound to her. A silent concussion shook the walls, the floor, stone grating on stone, dust dancing into strange, beguiling patterns. One of the younger Speakers collapsed, her eyes rolling back until they showed only the whites. Even the chiefs were shaken as the floor trembled.

Gods above, it was everything Ytha had dreamed and more. She stared at the stone, no longer afraid. With this, she could *be* a god and no one would challenge her. With this, she would *rule*.

'Yes,' she breathed.

A sigh rippled through the crowd.

'We will be free.'

'We can go home.'

'Wake the Raven, sister!'

She heard their voices, but the words drifted over her and floated away like leaves on the wind. There was only the power now. It gave the oceans their rise and fall, it was the axle on which the seasons turned, and it was hers to command.

A hand grasped her wrist. A hard hand, and harder eyes behind it, in a Speaker's face. 'Wake the Raven, so we can go home!'

Ytha dismissed the interruption, went back to staring at her prize and the graceful spiral of reflection upon reflection spinning away into the dark behind the pupil of her eye.

'Do it, or I will!'

Scrabbling fingers, clawing at her treasure. Ytha's hand spasmed closed around the starseed and she pushed a thought at the woman – she couldn't recall her name, but that didn't matter – who had tried to take it from her. With a startled shriek, the Speaker flew backwards across the room and collided with the far wall. A meaty thud silenced her and she tumbled limply into the dust.

The others recoiled, but that was as it should be. She would not tolerate dissent, not from any of them. Letting her staff clatter to the floor, she wrapped both hands around the starseed and made her way to the arch that led outside.

Down the stairs, barely aware of the hesitant footsteps following her, the mutterings. Her mind was singing with possibilities, with patterns and colours and thoughts that flickered fast as summer lightning. Through the echoing hall, out into the glorious, fiery evening with the three moons aloft in the crimson sky, and she thrust the starseed up above her head so that the waiting people could see it, and how it shone.

The crowd surged towards her on a wave of speculation. She smiled. This time she did not require a sacrifice to summon the Raven; she had all the power she needed. In a clear, strong voice, she began to declaim the summoning. Ancient syllables rolled from her tongue and dropped into the growing stillness around her. The silence in which her voice was the only sound spread out, encompassing the crowd, flowing around them like water, rising up against the walls of the structures that surrounded them, building, surging out into the city.

The evening held its breath.

A shimmer appeared in the air at the foot of the steps. It flickered, steadied, became a sooty smear. Awed, the crowd fell back, their circle widening the larger and darker the smear grew. The blackness at its heart writhed.

Yes. The Goddess would come and their pact would be fulfilled. Aid for aid, as they had each promised. Yes!

Exhilaration surged through Ytha's body as she chanted the final words, the starseed humming between her hands. The bruise on the air convulsed, then was wrenched apart with a sound like the bite of a blade into flesh. From the teeming void stepped a figure. Tall, armour-clad, all spikes and ragged cloak. In one fist it held an iron spear, cold and dull, its only adornment a tangle of bone and feather charms behind the head. The figure's free hand reached up and tugged off its horned helm, and a mane of braided black hair tumbled free.

The Raven's face was pale and coldly handsome, one half painted the colour of old blood. Bone charms gleamed in Her hair, some augmented with blackened bronze and what might have been teeth, most animal, some definitely human. She looked Ytha up and down.

We meet again, summoner. Her teeth shone bright and sharp as steel in a mouth that resembled the red slash of a wound.

Ytha brought the starseed down and held it before her, its song diminished to a crystalline murmur. This was what she had waited for, for so many years. She hid her exultation and bowed deeply. 'My Goddess, be welcome.'

The goddess looked around Her, gaze raking hungrily over the ruined city, the mountains that ringed it. *It is good to breathe the air again,* She said. *You have done well, little women.*

Two bone-yellow shapes bolted past Ytha and hurled themselves at the Goddess's legs. Yipping and bouncing up on their hind limbs, they pushed their heads against Her, for all the world like pups at play.

Ah, my pets. The Raven tucked Her helm beneath her spear-arm and fussed the Hounds in turn. *Are you ready to hunt?*

They howled with delight.

She rapped the butt of Her spear on the stones with a clang like the dashing of all the world's hope. Further figures appeared in the darkness behind Her, stepped into the light, stretching and shaking off the stiffness in their limbs. Hounds poured out of the rent in the air: a dozen at first, two dozen, then more than Ytha could count, milling around the dark warriors emerging to stand with their captain. Some of the hunters carried bows as tall as they were, or barbed spears decorated with feathers and clattering charms. Some wore axes slung across their backs. All bore a round shield painted with a bloody sigil, and they all looked hungry as winter wolves.

Fear and excitement thrilled down Ytha's spine. These warriors would tear through the Empire in a flood. Rip open its soft belly and leave its entrails smoking at its feet. With them she would have her victory.

Steely teeth bared, Maegern watched Her Hunt assemble. At Her side the two Hounds threw back their heads and gave voice, followed a scant second later by the rest of the pack until the air itself shook with raw, unearthly howls. Ytha's heart leapt. Next to her, Drwyn thrust his ancestors' sword aloft and lent his own whoop to the cacophony. Soon all the chiefs and their chosen men were hollering their war cries, and even Ytha could not suppress a shout of triumph. Finally, she was leading her people home.

Her black eyes shining, the Goddess began to laugh. *Then we shall hunt!*

EPILOGUE

❧

Alderan dreamed of fire and darkness.

Orange sparks fountained into the sky. Glowing fragments drifted on the air, scorching clothes and skin alike when they landed on him. A swirl of desert robes. Running. Stumbling. Pieces of paper fluttering away into the night like pale birds. Then the cool gloom of the chapel, where the air smelled of incense and old books, and the stained-glass saints blazed with the fires outside. Martial saints, Agostin and Benet and Simeon the Just with his sword aflame, and on the other side of the nave, Nerissa and Tamas and Margret the Merciful, barely visible in the dark. No mercy to be found on this night.

He woke with a start, eyes flying wide, the bitter tang of burning paper catching in his throat. It took a breath or two to fade and be replaced by the smell of sweet herbs and sun-baked stone. Around him, insects hummed in the somnolent heat. At the far end of the garden the fountain tinkled, and beyond the walls of the courtyard the city droned on. Aside from the occasional bray of a mule or a ringing shout, nothing stood out to eyes or ears or nose as the cause of his sudden wakefulness.

Nonetheless he listened a while, sifting through the sounds around him until he was certain there was no threat. These were troubled times in Gimrael, and every day they grew more dangerous. It was no place to be caught off guard.

His mouth quirked irritably. And there he was, drowsing in the middle of the day like an old man! Careless, careless. He had to stay focused, or someone with silent feet and a quick blade would open his throat for him, and that would be that.

Shifting in his seat, he eased his splinted leg down off the stool it had been resting on and wriggled his toes to restore circulation. He'd be glad when that wretched contraption could come off – after six weeks of it, his leg was itching fiercely. But it was his own stupid fault; what did he expect, hurrying down the badly lit stairs to the crypt with his arms full? Fortunately the books had softened his landing and all he'd broken was his ankle, but in the absence of a *gaeden* Healer it was having to mend the old-fashioned way, which only made the whole process more frustrating.

The book he'd been reading began sliding off his lap and he lunged to catch it. By now his hands had healed enough that he could hold a book without pain, but the tender flesh where the burns had been was still new enough that he needed to be careful, however impatient it made him.

Above his head, the vine leaves fluttered, sending spangles of sunlight dancing across the faded script, and it took his eyes a moment to focus on the words again. Ah, yes; it was a journal, of sorts, the entries intermittent and the author no great man of letters. No wonder he had nodded off whilst reading. But tempting as it was to put it aside, he had to finish it. He could not afford to discard any of the books simply because it was tedious – not when they had been bought with such pain.

He flexed his fingers, eyeing the pattern of scars from the burns over the backs of his hands, up his forearms. All things considered, he was lucky to have escaped as lightly as he had. The outcome could have been so much worse.

No more brooding. He'd spent long enough lying abed with a damp cloth over his eyes and nothing to do but fret, so he wouldn't waste more time with it now. Smoothing the pages, he resumed reading, but when he turned the leaf, the journal entry ended with some mundane domestic minutiae and the subsequent page was blank. Not so, however, the one that followed. It was packed with small, neat script, and it was also upside down.

Despite the desert heat, a chill settled on his limbs. Could it really be that simple? That someone had found a partly filled notebook and, in need of somewhere to write, had flipped it over and used the blank pages for themselves?

Alderan closed the book, turned it end over end and studied it anew. The plain leather binding was scuffed and well worn, the book itself not much longer than a man's hand from heel to fingertips. Quite unremarkable, in other words, yet already his palms were tingling, anticipation trembling in the pit of his stomach.

Could it really be?

He opened the cover, turned the flyleaf and began to read.

My thoughts are so tumbled I find it hard to organise them into coherent words, to structure sentences in such a way that whoever reads them will know the true meaning, will receive my clear intent. For days I have been unable to add to this journal, so pressed by circumstance at first and then later, when my book was mislaid and I had no new volume to fill. Now that I again have the means and a few hours' leisure, I find myself unsure where to begin to set down the events I have witnessed.

So let me commence with that which is most significant, and follow my pen wherever it may lead. I do not know how long remains to me, so I dare not waste time in reflection that might yet be needed for truth.

It is done.

We have taken a forlorn hope and wrung from it a victory, but at a cost so great my mind flinches from accepting it, and my heart quails to set down its details. But the truth must be told. What has been done here should not go unacknowledged, though there are those who will not wish to hear it spoken aloud. Nevertheless I say it freely, and in full knowledge of the fate to which it will doubtless condemn me: I, Malthus, Preceptor

563

of the Suvaeon Order, asked my First Knight to surrender his soul to damnation for the sake of us all.

Unable to help himself, Alderan closed his eyes. It was Malthus's journal that he held in his hands – or part of it, at least. Perhaps the most important part. After all these years, he would know the truth of those painful, bloody days at the end of the Founding Wars. No longer would he merely suspect, deduce, extrapolate from the few facts he had; he would *know*.

Taking a deep breath to steady the anxious flutter in his belly, he opened his eyes again and turned the page.

As we sit here and nurse our hurts, which are many and grievous, I wish I remained as sure in my faith as Fellbane. He has a tranquillity to his demeanour now that I find . . . almost beatific. When I am troubled in my mind and cannot rest, I find my feet carrying me to the highest of the seven towers and an hour in conversation with him grants me a degree of ease I cannot find in prayer alone. Truly, he walks in the Goddess's grace now, or so my heart tells me – yet by the laws and customs of our Order he is bound for the stake in Traitor's Court.

Dremen feels so far away today, in both time and distance. As I look out upon the mountains from the fabled towers of Milanthor, I find myself not wanting to return. I invent tasks for myself to postpone the hour, but now that the garrisons at the keeps have been relieved and the remainder of the Knights who rode out with me have assembled here, I know I cannot delay much longer. This has been a brief respite between the clangour of war and the heavy responsibility of the days ahead, but it cannot last for ever, however great the victory we have won. All our actions have consequences, and now is the time to face them.

Strangely, the First Knight appears to be the only one at peace with what is to come.

Alderan let the book fall closed in his lap. Milanthor. Dear Goddess, how had he never seen it? It was so obvious now: at the time of the founding it was the largest city north of Fleet; it would have been the ideal mustering point for an army on the move from Caer Ducain. Somewhere to reprovision before pushing on to the rout at Brindling Fall, and then after, to regroup, ready for the long march back to the Holy City.

Which the starseed had never reached.

Which meant, in all probability, it was still there, in the ruins. Waiting for someone to pick it up.

'Oh, holy hell,' Alderan exclaimed. He fumbled for the crutch propped against the wall beside him to lever himself out of his chair. 'Tierce!' he bellowed. 'I need to borrow a horse. *Tierce!*'

☙

It wasn't much of a tree. Stunted by the weather and warted with galls, it stooped over the stream like an old man gazing at his reflection in the water, but it was an oak and that was all that mattered.

Warmth pulsed against Gair's chest. He pressed his hand over the shape of the pearl beneath his shirt and once more glimpsed the subtle colours he sometimes saw when he touched it. Twelve times he'd felt that pulse, in the days since he'd left Saardost. Only twelve, and each time he feared they were growing further apart.

Stay with me, Tanith, he breathed. *Stay strong.*

He had no idea if she could hear him, but he talked to her regardless. Told her stories from his childhood, even sang to her – badly – anything to make the time pass, and to keep his mind off the burning pain in his thigh. Even though he'd cleaned and dressed it as best he could before he left Saardost Keep, the heat and the swelling told him the wound was infected. It needed a Healer's touch now, and the only Healer within a hundred leagues of him was locked inside the Song, dying of her own injuries. Such bitter irony. It was almost enough to make him laugh.

He dismounted carefully, but still the pain of bearing his own weight on that leg was enough to make the world spin crazily around him, and he had to hang on to Shahe until it passed. That was getting worse, too – and the sweats were more frequent, especially at night – but he had no choice but to press on, as hard as he dared.

Almost eight days, now, south like an arrow from dawn until the summer-late dusk. Shahe was as strong and willing as ever, but like him, she was at her limit and needed a week's rest in rich pasture to rekindle the spark in her eye.

When he felt steadier, he stripped off her saddle and packs and removed her bridle. Then he rubbed her down with handfuls of dry grass, though his muscles ached and the creeping infection in his thigh made every step agony. She had carried him this far; she deserved his first attention. After it was done, he poured out the last of the oats he'd traded for at a farm in the Marches and gave her a pat.

'Good girl.' She snorted, lipping at the grain on the ground. 'I'm sorry for everything I've put you through.'

The *sulqa* flipped her ears and continued eating. She couldn't understand him any more than he could understand her, beyond what he could read from the set of her ears and such, but he felt better for saying it. He hoped that counted for something.

He looked around him. Sunshine and shadow danced over the grass with the breeze, then fell still again. There was nothing to see or sense that said this place, hidden in the slow roll of northern Elethrain, was in any way special apart from the tree. Oaks were portals, Tanith had said. Gateways between worlds, between time and timelessness, between thought and memory, that only the forestals knew how to unlock.

Anxiety plucked at Gair's back. This tree was not part of Elethrain's Great Forest, but he was not sure Tanith could wait the extra hundred miles he had to ride to reach it. Since he was ten years old, everything he had cared about had been taken from him. His home. His friends. Aysha. If there was even a chance that he could spare Tanith the same fate, he was prepared to take it.

'Owyn!' he called out. 'Can you hear me?'

The oak leaves whispered together, children sharing secrets

behind their hands. Touching the Song, he sent out a hail wrapped in his colours, as far as he could broadcast it.

Owyn! That too went unanswered, swallowed by the vastness of the land around him. 'Forestal! Can you hear me? Please, I need your help.'

Shahe snorted again and shook her mane at some insect that was bothering her, then continued nosing through the grass. Apart from her, nothing stirred as far as Gair's sight could reach.

'Tanith spoke kindly of you, Owyn. She's in trouble and I'm trying to take her home. She hasn't got much time.' Twelve pulses of warmth. Twelve heartbeats. He didn't know how many she had left.

Feeling eyes on him he swung around, but it was only a bird that flew away as soon as he moved. The grass whispered, the stream chuckled over its stones and ran on.

'Is there anybody there?'

ACKNOWLEDGEMENTS

Once again I am indebted to the team at Gollancz who look after me so well, notably my publicist Jon Weir and my editor, Gillian Redfearn. An honourable mention must also go to my agent, Ian Drury, who continues to earn himself bottles of gin on a regular basis. I just hope it's not me who makes him need to drink it.

I also want to thank Douglas Reeman, a.k.a. Alexander Kent, who was the first person outside my family to encourage me to keep at this writing thing. I don't think my 15 year old self ever imagined I'd end up here, but I have a sneaky feeling that Douglas was expecting it.

Much love as always goes to my parents and brother, and most especially my long-suffering husband, Rob. Keep the tea coming, love – I think I'm going to need it.